高等院校文科教材

美国文学选读

SELECTED READINGS IN AMERICAN LITERATURE

下册

李宜燮　常耀信　主编

南开大学出版社

天　津

图书在版编目(CIP)数据

美国文学选读. 下 / 李宜燮，常耀信主编. —天津：南开大学出版社，1991. 8(2014. 8 重印)

高等院校文科教材

ISBN 978-7-310-00396-9

Ⅰ. 美… Ⅱ. ①李…②常… Ⅲ. 文学史—美国—高等学校—教材 Ⅳ. I712. 09

中国版本图书馆 CIP 数据核字(2000)第 22912 号

南开大学出版社出版发行

出版人：孙克强

地址：天津市南开区卫津路 94 号　　邮政编码：300071

营销部电话：(022)23508339　23500755

营销部传真：(022)23508542　　邮购部电话：(022)23502200

*

天津市蓟县宏图印务有限公司印刷

全国各地新华书店经销

*

1991 年 8 月第 1 版　　2014 年 8 月第 18 次印刷

880×1230 毫米　32 开本　26.875 印张　2 插页　1049 千字

定价：38.00 元

如遇图书印装质量问题，请与本社营销部联系调换，电话：(022)23507125

前　言

美国文学是世界文学的重要组成部分。它对英国文学既有继承，又有创新。初期的美国文学曾有明显的模仿英国文学的痕迹，但从19世纪中期开始，美国文学便异军突起，屹立于世界文学之林。它具有浓厚的民族气息和自己独特的风格，宛如世界文学园圃的一朵奇葩，散发出沁人心脾的幽香。近来年，我国对美国文学的介绍和研究日益重视，不少大专院校已开设美国文学课程。

《美国文学选读》是根据国家教委教材编写计划而编写的教科书。全书共分2册：上册从17世纪至第一次世界大战前；下册从第一次世界大战迄今。它的对象是大专院校英文系本科高年级学生和社会上有相当英语基础的美国文学爱好者。

本书在编选作家及作品的过程中一直恪守重点突出的原则。每位作家项下都有作者介绍、作品介绍、原文和注释四部分。作者介绍力求简短明了；作品介绍力求画龙点睛；原文的选择力求有代表性；注释力求深入浅出。所附评语尽量利用国内外评论界数十年来的研究成果，尤其重视介绍美国文学评论界近些年来的研究状况，但决不断章取义，不拘一人之见，不守一家之说。对所选作品采取谨慎的态度，以它对当代及后世的影响作为衡量准则。

本书由南开大学外文系英美文学研究室负责规划和选材。李宜燮、常耀信任主编。参加编写的有（以姓氏笔划为序）：马振铃、王蕴茹、刘士聪、谷启楠、李前程、吴伏生、徐齐平、高冬山、常耀信。

《美国文学选读》（下册）脱稿之后，国家教委高校外语专业教材编委会英语编审组根据1989年教材审稿计划，邀请社科院董衡巽研究员任主审，北京大学英语系陶洁教授、天津师范大学外语系王占梅教授参加审稿，审稿会对书稿提出了宝贵意见，谨在此表示衷心感谢。

尽管我们尽了最大的努力，但由于水平有限，一定会有不妥和错误之处。我们诚恳地希望同行专家和广大读者不吝指正。

编　者

1988年11月

CONTENTS

EDWIN ARLINGTON ROBINSON

〔作者介绍〕

埃德温·阿灵顿·罗宾逊（Edwin Arlington Robinson，1869～1935），美国诗人，生于新英格兰的传统家庭，在缅因州的加丁纳镇长大。曾在哈佛大学读书两年，后因家道没落而辍学。1897 年后住在纽约，当过地铁建筑监工，并利用业余时间写诗，生活贫困，善饮。后西奥多·罗斯福总统赏识他的才华，于 1905 年帮他在纽约海关谋到一个挂名领薪的闲差，使他能有更多时间来写诗。1901 年后专事诗歌创作。

1896 年罗宾逊自费出版第 1 部诗集《急流与昨夜》（*The Torrent and the Night Before*）。第 1 部为他赢得诗誉的是 1910 年发表的《河下游的城镇》（*The Town Down the River*），其中有名篇《米尼弗·契维》（"Miniver Cheevy"）。1916 年发表《天边人影》（*The Man Against the Sky*）后，他的成就获得了广泛的承认，并确立了在美国诗坛的地位。他和弗罗斯特（Robert Frost）、桑德堡（Carl Sandburg）、马斯特斯（Edgar Lee Masters）等著名诗人一起促进了本世纪第 2 个 10 年内的诗坛复兴。在 20 年代罗宾逊曾被视为当时最伟大的美国诗人。他于 1922 年、1925 年和 1928 年 3 次获得普利策诗歌奖。

罗宾逊的诗歌创作大体可以分作两个阶段。1916 年前，他以描绘新英格兰风土为内容的、形象鲜明、乡土气息浓郁的诗歌而著称。他那虚构的"蒂尔伯里镇"人物肖像诗尤其令人喜爱，如《理查德·科里》（"Richard Cory"）、《弗罗德先生的酒会》（"Mr. Flood's Party"）等。诗人把现实主义和浪漫主义相结合，刻画出一幅幅动人的失意者的"心理肖像"。他的诗谑而不虐，把嘲讽与怜悯熔于一炉。罗宾逊的诗以写人为主，写景很少。在谈到自己的第一部诗集时，他曾说："全书中没有一只红颈知更鸟。"在第 2 阶段他对亚瑟王传奇产生了浓厚兴趣，重述梅林（Merlin）、兰斯洛特（Lancelot）和特里斯特拉姆（Tristram）的故事，并借题发挥，发表关于西方衰落的长篇哲理性议论。诗风时而庄重有力，时而冗长隐涩。一般说来，当代批评界对他的第 1 阶段的作品更感兴趣。

罗宾逊反对物质主义，对现代生活的庸俗与徒劳进行了尖刻批评。他关心人际关系、心灵的创伤与孤独，以及人的意志与非人的命运之间永存的矛盾。他象同代英国作家哈代一样，怀念浪漫的豪勇的过去，留恋它的信仰和传统。罗宾逊的诗歌情调阴沉而富于讽刺性。他擅长运用传统韵律来表达具有现代意味的“悲剧观”。他的诗格律工整，用字贴切，立意清新，为美国诗歌增添了一种严峻、诚恳、精确的文风。他的短诗尤其受到读者的青睐。

罗宾逊对现代文明的认识不如叶芝、T. S. 艾略特和庞德等大师们那样深刻，在技巧方面缺乏他们的勇敢精神，在思想和感情方面也不具备他们的广度和深度。尽管如此，作为一位声誉崇高的诗人，他的诗风是别具一格的。

Richard Cory

〔作品介绍〕

本诗发表于1896年，是罗宾逊最著名的几首人物肖像短诗之一。它从科里邻居的角度刻画这位富翁的形象。罗宾逊的多数诗作都描写失败这一主题：事业上的失败、一个社会或阶层的失败、生与死博斗的失败等。物质主义的胜利使他感到痛心，使他认识到感情和美的满足何等重要。理查德·科里和罗宾逊所塑造的其他人物形象如克拉弗林、弗拉蒙德与克莱格等同属于失败者的类型。他们高贵的出身和修养使他们更易于感受到生活的创伤，生活中美好的事物反而成为致命的东西。

短诗表现出罗宾逊对描写现代文明造成的人的“心理谜”（psychological enigma）的强烈兴趣。

Richard Cory

Whenever Richard Cory went down town,
We people on the pavement looked at him:
He was a gentleman from sole to crown,[1]
Clean favored,[2] and imperially slim.

And he was always quietly arrayed,[3]

And he was always human when he talked;
But still he fluttered pulses[4] when he said
"Good-morning," and he glittered when he walked.

And he was rich—yes, richer than a king—
And admirably schooled in every grace:
In fine, we thought that he was everything
To make us wish that we were in his place.

So on we worked, and waited for the light,
And went without the meat, and cursed the bread;
And Richard Cory, one calm summer night,
Went home and put a bullet through his head.

〔注释〕

1. from sole to crown：从头到脚，浑身上下。
2. clean favored：长相眉清目秀。
3. quietly arrayed：穿着素静。
4. fluttered pulses：指他向人道早安时，人们感到受宠若惊，脉搏激烈地跳动。

Miniver Cheevy

〔作品介绍〕

本诗发表于诗集《河下游的城镇》(*The Town Down the River*, 1907)。在这首人物肖像诗中，作者忠于生活的本来面目，真实地再现了城镇中破落青年充满怨恨的心灵。生活是复杂的，人的感情也是复杂的。诗中的青年契维正是如此。

米尼弗·契维生活在19世纪后半叶拜金主义猖獗的美国，他一方面贪恋金钱和物质，另一方面又向往古人的高尚精神。他是在浑浑噩噩中尚有独清独醒特点的美国人的典型。契维抱怨自己生不逢时，在苦酒中寻求慰藉。他前途未卜，走的似乎是一条通向失败的黑暗道路，但他具备一种"绝望中的勇气"：他虽以酒浇愁，却仍在"思索"着寻找出路。他的生活无疑是失意的，但那又似乎是一种让人尊重和惋惜的失意。罗宾逊力求在诗中表达这种失意的神秘性。《米尼弗·契维》的情调在诗人的《弗拉蒙德》(“Flammonde”)、《信条》(“Credo”)以及《天边人影》等诗中均有所反映。这首诗标志着诗人对亚瑟王的故事等中世纪题材开始发生兴趣。

Miniver Cheevy

Miniver Cheevy, child of scorn,[1]
Grew lean while he assailed the seasons;[2]
He wept that he was ever born,
And he had reasons.

Miniver loved the days of old
When swords were bright and steeds were prancing;
The vision of a warrior bold[3]
Would set him dancing.

Miniver sighed for what was not,[4]
And dreamed, and rested from his labors;
He dreamed of Thebes and Camelot,
And Priam's neighbors.[5]

Miniver mourned the ripe renown
That made so many a name so fragrant;
He mourned Romance, now on the town,
And Art, a vagrant.[6]

Miniver loved the Medici,[7]
Albeit he had never seen one;
He would have sinned incessantly
Could he have been one.

Miniver cursed the commonplace
And eyed a khaki suit[8] with loathing;
He missed the medieval grace

Of iron clothing.[9]

Miniver scorned the gold he sought,
But sore annoyed was he without it;
Miniver thought, and thought, and thought,
And thought about it.

Miniver Cheevy, born too late,
Scratched his head and kept on thinking;
Miniver coughed, and called it fate,
And kept on drinking.

〔注释〕

1. child of scorn：双关语，既是嘲讽者，又是嘲讽的对象。

2. assailed the seasons：步履维艰，度日如年。

3. a warrior bold＝a bold warrior.

4. what was not＝what did not exist.

5. Thebes…Priam's neighbors：（他梦见）中世纪传奇故事发生的地点古埃及及古希腊的底比斯城（Thebes）、位于威尔士的亚瑟王都城卡米洛特（Camelot）、小亚细亚的古国特洛伊（其国王为普赖姆［Priam］）以及与特洛伊交战达10年之久的邻国希腊诸邦。

6. He mourned Romance, now on the town, /And Art, a vagrant.：这两行哀叹文学艺术不被重视，日趋没落。

7. the Medici：有钱有势的麦第奇家族，自15至16世纪统治文艺复兴时期的佛罗伦萨城，以残忍和邪恶著称。该家族成员中有银行家、政治家、文学艺术家的恩主等，曾有3位教皇来自该家族。

8. khaki suit：指现代军装。

9. iron clothing：指古代盔甲。

Mr. Flood's Party

〔作品介绍〕

本诗载于1920年发表的诗集《三个酒馆》(*The Three Taverns*)。这是诗人的又一幅小城人物肖像画。罗宾逊喜欢描绘某些老人的形象。他们身体虽然羸弱，但精神却坚韧不拔，体现出人与时间之变化的内在关系。弗拉德便是这样一位老人。他的酒会只有他自己在场，独饮独白，自破自立，因为他的同龄人都早入鬼簿，而年轻一代对他又极其冷漠。在某种意义上，老人孤零零的形象反映出新英格兰乡村普遍存在的孤苦与失落感。弗拉德虽举目无亲，但绝不是顾影自怜。全诗充溢着一种幽默感和人情味，使人感到这位经历了世态炎凉的老人在评述悠悠万世的人生的永恒变迁。

本诗在情调上颇似中国唐代诗人李白的《月下独酌》。

Mr. Flood's Party

Old Eben Flood, climbing alone one night
Over the hill between the town below
And the forsaken upland hermitage
That held as much as he should ever know
On earth again of home, paused warily.
The road was his with not a native near;
And Eben, having leisure, said aloud,
For no man else in Tilbury Town[1] to hear:

"Well, Mr. Flood,[2] we have the harvest moon
Again, and we may not have many more;
The bird is on the wing, the poet says,[3]
And you and I have said it here before.
Drink to the bird." He raised up to the light[4]
The jug that he had gone so far to fill,
And answered huskily: "Well, Mr. Flood,
Since you propose it, I believe I will."

Alone, as if enduring to the end
A valiant armor of scarred hopes outworn,
He stood there in the middle of the road
Like Roland's ghost winding a silent horn.[5]
Below him, in the town among the trees,
Where friends of other days had honored him,
A phantom salutation of the dead

Rang thinly till old Eben's eyes were dim.[6]

Then, as a mother lays her sleeping child
Down tenderly, fearing it may awake,
He set the jug down slowly at his feet
With trembling care, knowing that most things break;[7]
And only when assured that on firm earth
It stood, as the uncertain lives of men
Assuredly did not, he paced away,
And with his hand extended paused again:

"Well, Mr. Folld, we have not met like this
In a long time; and many a change has come
To both of us, I fear, since last it was
We had a drop together. Welcome home!"
Convivially returning with himself,
Again he raised the jug up to the light;
And with an acquiescent quaver said:
"Well, Mr. Flood, if you insist, I might.

"Only a very little, Mr. Flood—
For auld lang syne.[8] No more, sir; that will do."
So, for the time, apparently it did,
And Eben evidently thought so too;
For soon amid the silver loneliness
Of night he lifted up his voice and sang,
Secure, with only two moons[9] listening,
Until the whole harmonious landscape rang—

"For auld lang syne." The weary throat gave out,
The last word wavered, and the song was done.
He raised again the jug regretfully
And shook his head, and was again alone.
There was not much that was ahead of him,
And there was nothing in the town below—
Where strangers would have shut the many doors
That many friends had opened long ago.[10]

〔注释〕

1. Tilbury Town：蒂尔伯里镇，其原型为诗人的故乡加丁纳镇(Gardiner)。罗宾森早期的诗常以此镇为背景。

2. Well，Mr. Flood：诗人自言自语，自问自答。

3. The bird is on the wing，the poet says：the poet 指 12 世纪波斯著名数学家、天文学家和诗人莪默·伽亚姆（Omar Khayyam）。他写了几百首四行体诗(Rubaiyat，郭沫若译本称为《鲁拜集》)。1857 年英国诗人爱德华·菲茨杰拉德（Edward Fitzgerald，1809～1883）把它们译成英文，从此伽亚姆的诗歌风靡世界各国，对 19 世纪后半叶的诗风产生巨大影响。"The Bird is on the Wing"引自《鲁拜集》的第 7 首，全文如下：

Come，fill the cup，and in the fire of Spring
Your Winter-garment of Repentance fling：
The Bird of Time has but a little way
To flutter—and the Bird is on the Wing.

来呀，请来浮此一觞，
在春阳之中脱去忏悔的冬裳：
"时鸟"是飞不多时的—
鸟已在振翮翱翔。

（郭沫若译）

此句引言旨在加强上句中关于秋月的话。

4. the light＝the moon.

5. Like Roland's ghost winding a silent horn：法国中世纪英雄史诗《罗兰之歌》(*Chanson de Roland*) 中查理大帝的外甥罗兰，受叛徒加奈隆出卖，回师途中在山谷遭敌人重兵伏击，全军覆没。罗兰与敌人战斗到最后一口气，在临死前才吹起微弱的求援号角，但为时已晚。在新英格兰的背景下提到罗兰的亡魂，上下文似不协调。埃本和罗兰之间相似之处甚少。诗人或许旨在说明他们都在进行着注定要失败的斗争而最后又终于战败倒下这一共同点。这也在一定程度上反映出诗人对中世纪的迷恋。

6. old Eben's eyes were dim：老埃本泪水盈眶。

7. knowing…break：老人感伤自己将不久于人世。

8. For auld lang syne＝For the days of long ago. 这是苏格兰诗人罗伯特·彭斯（Robert Burns，1759～1796）的著名诗句，歌颂友谊地久天长。

9. two moons：指月晕现象，这是风暴即将来临的征兆。

10. Where strangers…long ago.：最后两行是老人埃本对世风日下、人情淡薄的哀叹。

WILLA CATHER

〔作者介绍〕

威拉·凯瑟（Willa Cather，1873～1947），美国小说家、短篇小说家、诗人。她生于弗吉尼亚州，9 岁时随家移居内布拉斯加州，在西部大草原乡镇里长大。1895 年从内布拉斯加大学毕业，对音乐和文学（尤其是亨利·詹姆斯的作品）极感兴趣。后来到匹兹堡一家报社工作，开始文学创作。1900 年，她开始发表短篇小说和诗歌，1903 年发表诗集《四月的黄昏》（*April Twilight*）。在那些年月里，她的主要思想是披露西部小城镇文化的落后和思想的狭窄，这表现在她的最著名的短篇故事《雕刻家的葬礼》（"The Sculptor's Funeral"）、《华格纳音乐会》（"A Wagner Matinée"）等作品中。1906 年她移居纽约，在《麦克卢尔杂志》（*McClure's Magazine*）工作，后任总编（1908～1911）。在此期间，她结识了著名乡土文学作家萨拉·奥恩·朱厄特（Sarah Orne Jewett），并听从其劝告，辞去总编职务，悉心从事文学创作，陆续发表了《亚历山大的桥》（*Alexander's Bridge*，1912）、《啊，拓荒者！》（*O Pioneers*！1913）、《我的安东妮亚》（*My Antonia*，1918）、《百灵鸟之歌》（*The Song of the Lark*，1915）、《我们自已人》（*One of Ours*，1922）、《迷途的女人》（*A Lost Lady*，1923）、《教授的住宅》（*The Professor's House*，1925）及《大主教之死》（*Death Comes For the Archbishop*，1927）等作品。凯瑟还发表了 4 部短篇小说集和几部中长篇小说。

总的说来，凯瑟的价值观是属于传统性的。她曾说过，在 1922 年前后，世界已一分为二。她似乎生活在两个世界之间，拒绝接受现代生活，力图逃避到过去的日子去。她的主要作品都是她生活中这种矛盾心情的写照。对她来说，昔日的西部乡镇在精神上总是比堕落的城市高尚得多，它是衡量现代生活中道德与伦理的尺度。西部移民朴素、高洁，他们的生活虽然尚存原始的味道，但有意义、有目的、有秩序。《我的安东妮亚》里的安东妮亚是一个典型的西部乡村女人。她和生活在城里的吉姆·伯登形成显明对比，一个是朴素、率直，爱的真诚、活的实在，另一个是生活枯燥和不安。吉姆就像寻觅失去的乐园一样回西部去看她。在吉姆对往事的回忆中有一种动人的怀旧情感，一种感人肺腑的哀叹：过去的简朴生活已经一去不复返了。“在人的生活里，”吉姆回忆大学期间读过的一本书上说，“最美好的日子消逝得最快”。《百灵鸟之歌》实际暗含着对文化发达的东部的批评。女歌手虽然在东部有更理想的发展机会，但她总是思绪不宁，怀念曾经关怀她长大的大草原上的人们。在这部小说里，作者是用西部的理想标准衡量东部的非理想生活的。《迷途的女人》中的老福雷斯特上尉在内战中打过仗，在草原上筑过铁路，是西部拓荒者的典型形象，勇敢、侠义、谦虚、仁爱。然而，现代生活节节进逼，传统价值观愈来愈难维持，生活正以惊人的速度堕落成低级的物质主义。以艾维·彼得斯为代表的现代人正在建立令开拓者瞠目的充满小城气息和商业化标准的新价值观。《教授的住宅》这一部被视为作者代表作的长篇小说，充分地反映出凯瑟摈弃现代生活、逃回到传统的过去的坚决态度。圣彼得教授用写书得到的奖金建起一座现代设备齐全的新房子，这所房子虽然舒适，但他认为却很乏味，他还是喜欢他曾在其中写出获奖的书的旧房子，那所虽然简陋然而却纯洁、动人、令人遐思的旧房子。凯瑟在这部小说的前言中说，现代生活令人感到窒息。

凯瑟本人和这位教授一样，在后期作品中逃逸到历史的过去中去。《大主教之死》及《盘石上的阴影》(*Shadows on the Rock*, 1931) 两部作品都再现了理想的过去，前者描述19世纪中叶在新墨西哥建立教区的故事，后者颂扬18世纪魁北克人以不屈不挠的精神建立新国家的事迹。凯瑟认为，以传统武装起的开拓者一定能在新的土地上建立起身心健康的新生活。凯瑟自始至终坚持传统、坚持理想，她的作品是她这种态度的最有力的佐证。她曾被说成是“心际忐忑不安的上个世纪的幸存者”，这是有道理的。

凯瑟的文笔清新抒展，遣词用字相当考究。她描述人或事时笔墨浓淡有致，颇具一种抒情散文的特点。

Neighbour Rosicky

〔**作品介绍**〕

《邻居罗西基》(“Neighbour Rosicky”)是反映威拉·凯瑟思想的一篇著名短篇小说，最初发表于1930年。它主要通过回忆和追述的手法，勾勒出老罗西基朴素、充实的一生的故事。老罗西基是捷克后裔，曾在城市里工作和生活过，但后来深感城市对人的窒息，终于回到了乡下。在那里，他结婚、生子、耕种土地，夫妇同心，父母子女和谐地生活在自己的田园上。他们不求发家，只求人自然、健康地发展，他们保持了在城市和乡村某些家庭里业已消失了的人的基本品质——爱、同情、诚朴、尊严。老罗西基一家是理想的人，他们的生活是理想的生活，老罗西基的人格和生活是人的理想的典型。小说文字优美，性格刻划清晰、感人，描写和追述巧妙相间，产生一种感人的艺术效果。美中不足之处在于对城市的缺憾描写比较空洞，城乡对比不鲜明，从而在一定程度上影响了小说主题的充分发挥。

Neighbour Rosicky

I

When Doctor Burleigh told neighbour Rosicky he had a bad heart, Rosicky protested.

"So? No, I guess my heart was always pretty good. I got a little asthma, maybe. Just a awful short breath when I was pitchin' hay last summer, dat's all."

"Well now, Rosicky, if you know more about it than I do, what did you come to me for? It's your heart that makes you short of breath, I tell you. You're sixty-five years old, and you've always worked hard, and your heart's tired. You've got to be careful from now on, and you can't do heavy work any more. You've got five boys at home to do it for you."

The old farmer looked up at the Doctor with a gleam of amusement in his queer triangular-shaped eyes. His eyes were large and lively, but the lids were caught up in the middle in a curious way, so that they formed a triangle. He did not look like a sick man. His brown face was creased but not wrinkled, he had a ruddy colour in his smooth-shaven cheeks and in his lips, under his long brown moustache. His hair was thin and ragged around his ears, but very little grey. His forehead, naturally high and crossed by deep parallel lines, now ran all the way up to his pointed crown. Rosicky's face had the habit of looking interested, —suggested a contented disposition and a reflective quality that was gay rather than grave. This gave him a certain detachment, the easy manner of an onlooker and observer.

"Well, I guess you ain't got no pills fur a bad heart, Doctor Ed.

I guess the only thing is fur me to git a new one."

Doctor Burleigh swung round in his desk-chair and frowned at the old farmer. "I think if I were you I'd take a little care of the old one, Rosicky."

Rosicky shrugged. "Maybe I don't know how. I expect you mean fur me not to drink my coffee no more."

"I wouldn't, in your place. But you'll do as you choose about that. I've never yet been able to separate a Bohemian from his coffee or his pipe. I've quit trying. But the sure thing is you've got to cut out farm work. You can feed the stock and do chores about the barn, but you can't do anything in the fields that makes you short of breath."

"How about shelling corn?"

"Of course not!"

Rosicky considered with puckered brows.

"I can't make my heart go no longer'n it wants to, can I, Doctor Ed?"

"I think it's good for five or six years yet, maybe more, if you'll take the strain off it. Sit around the house and help Mary. If I had a good wife like yours, I'd want to stay around the house."

His patient chuckled. "It ain't no place fur a man. I don't like no old man hanging round the kitchen too much. An'my wife, she's a awful hard worker her own self."

"That's it; you can help her a little. My Lord, Rosicky, you are one of the few men I know who has a family he can get some comfort out of; happy dispositions, never quarrel among themselves, and they treat you right. I want to see you live a few years and enjoy them."

"Oh, they're good kids, all right," Rosicky assented.

The Doctor wrote him a prescription and asked him how his oldest son, Rudolph, who had married in the spring, was getting on. Rudolph had struck out for himself, on rented land. "And how's Polly? I was afraid Mary mightn't like an American daughter-in-law, but it seems to be working out all right."

"Yes, she's a fine girl. Dat widder[1] woman bring her daughters up very nice. Polly got lots of spunk, an'she got some style, too. Da's nice, for young folks to have some style." Rosicky inclined his head gallantly. His voice and his twinkly smile were an affectionate compliment to his daughter-in-law.

"It looks like a storm, and you'd better be getting home before it comes. In town in the car?" Doctor Burleigh rose.

"No, I'm in de wagon. When you got five boys, you ain't got much chance to ride round in de Ford. [2] I ain't much for cars, noway."

"Well, it's a good road out to your place; but I don't want you bumping around in a wagon much. And never again on a hay-rake, remember!"

Rosicky placed the Doctor's fee delicately behind the desk-telephone, looking the other way, as if this were an absent-minded gesture. He put on his plush cap and his corduroy jacket with a sheepskin collar, and went out.

The Doctor picked up his stethoscope and frowned at it as if he were seriously annoyed with the instrument. He wished it had been telling tales about some other man's heart, some old man who didn't look the Doctor in the eye so knowingly, or hold out such a warm brown hand when he said good-bye. Doctor Burleigh had been a poor boy in the country before he went away to medical school; he had known Rosicky almost ever since he could remember, and he had a deep affection for Mrs. Rosicky.

Only last winter he had had such a good breakfast at Rosicky's, and that when he needed it. [3] He had been out all night on a long, hard confinement case at Tom Marshall's,—a big rich farm where there was plenty of stock and plenty of feed and a great deal of expensive farm machinery of the newest model, and no comfort whatever. The woman had too many children and too much work, and she was no manager. When the baby was born at last, and handed over to the assisting neighbour woman, and the mother was properly attended to, Burleigh refused any breakfast in that slovenly house, and drove his buggy—the snow was too deep for a car—eight miles to Anton Rosicky's place. He didn't know another farm-house where a man could get such a warm welcome, and such good strong coffee with rich cream. No wonder the old chap didn't want to give up his coffee!

He had driven in just when the boys had come back from the barn and were washing up for breakfast. The long table, covered with a bright oilcloth, was set out with dishes waiting for them, and the warm kitchen was full of the smell of coffee and hot biscuit and sausage. Five big handsome boys, running from twenty to twelve, all with what

Burleigh called natural good manners,—they hadn't a bit of the painful self-consciousness he himself had to struggle with when he was a lad. One ran to put his horse away, another helped him off with his fur coat and hung it up, and Josephine, the youngest child and the only daughter, quickly set another place under her mother's direction.

With Mary, to feed creatures was the natural expression of affection,—her chickens, the calves, her big hungry boys. It was a rare pleasure to feed a young man whom she seldom saw and of whom she was as proud as if he belonged to her. Some country housekeepers would have stopped to spread a white cloth over the oilcloth, to change the thick cups and plates for their best china, and the wooden-handled knives for plated ones. But not Mary.

"You must take us as you find us, Doctor Ed. I'd be glad to put out my good things for you if you was expected, but I'm glad to get you any way at all."

He knew she was glad,—she threw back her head and spoke out as if she were announcing him to the whole prairie. Rosicky hadn't said anything at all; he merely smiled his twinkling smile, put some more coal on the fire, and went into his own room to pour the Doctor a little drink in a medicine glass. When they were all seated, he watched his wife's face from his end of the table and spoke to her in Czech. Then, with the instinct of politeness which seldom failed him, he turned to the Doctor and said shyly: "I was just tellin' her not to ask you no questions about Mrs. Marshall till you eat some breakfast. My wife, she's terrible fur to ask questions."[4]

The boys laughed, and so did Mary. She watched the Doctor devour her biscuit and sausage, too much excited to eat anything herself. She drank her coffee and sat taking in everything about her visitor. She had known him when he was a poor country boy, and was boastfully proud of his success, always saying: "What do people go to Omaha for, to see a doctor, when we got the best one in the State right here?" If Mary liked people at all, she felt physical pleasure in the sight of them, personal exultation in any good fortune that came to them. Burleigh didn't know many women like that, but he knew she was like that.

When his hunger was satisfied, he did, of course, have to tell them about Mrs. Marshall and he noticed what a friendly interest the boys took in the matter.

Rudolph, the oldest one (he was still living at home then), said: "The last time I was over there, she was lifting them big heavy milkcans, and I knew she oughtn't to be doing it."

"Yes, Rudolph told me about that when he come home, and I said it wasn't right," Mary put in warmly. "It was all right for me to do them things up to the last, for I was terrible strong, but that woman's weakly. And do you think she'll be able to nurse it, Ed?" She sometimes forgot to give him the title she was so proud of. "And to think of your being up all night and then not able to get a decent breakfast! I don't know what's the matter with such people."

"Why, Mother," said one of the boys, "if Doctor Ed had got breakfast there, we wouldn't have him here. So you ought to be glad."

"He knows I'm glad to have him, John, any time. But I'm sorry for that poor woman, how bad she'll feel the Doctor had to go away in the cold without his breakfast."

"I wish I'd been in practice when these were getting born." The doctor looked down the row of close-clipped heads. "I missed some good breakfasts by not being."

The boys began to laugh at their mother because she flushed so red, but she stood her ground and threw up her head. "I don't care, you wouldn't have got away from this house without breakfast. No doctor ever did. I'd have had something ready fixed that Anton could warm up for you."

The boys laughed harder than ever, and exclaimed at her: "I'll bet you would!" "She would, that!"

"Father, did you get breakfast for the doctor when we were born?"

"Yes, and he used to bring me my breakfast, too, mighty nice. I was always awful hungry!" Mary admitted with a guilty laugh.

While the boys were getting the Doctor's horse, he went to the window to examine the house plants. "What do you do to your geraniums to keep them blooming all winter, Mary? I never pass this house that from the road I don't see your windows full of flowers."

She snapped off a dark red one, and a ruffled new green leaf, and put them in his buttonhole. "There, that looks better. You look too solemn for a young man, Ed. Why don't you git married? I'm worried about you. Settin' at breakfast, I looked at you real hard, and I seen you've got some grey hairs already."

"Oh, yes! They're coming. Maybe they'd come faster if I married."

"Don't talk so. You'll ruin your health eating at the hotel. I could send your wife a nice loaf of nut bread, if you only had one. I don't like to see a young man getting grey. I'll tell you something, Ed; you make some strong black tea and keep it handy in a bowl, and every morning just brush it into your hair, an' it'll keep the grey from showin' much. That's the way I do!"

Sometimes the Doctor heard the gossipers in the drug-store wondering why Rosicky didn't get on faster. He was industrious, and so were his boys, but they were rather free and easy, weren't pushers, and they didn't always show good judgment. They were comfortable, they were out of debt, but they didn't get much ahead. Maybe, Doctor Burleigh reflected, people as generous and warm-hearted and affectionate as the Rosickys never got ahead much; maybe you couldn't enjoy your life and put it into the bank, too.

II

When Rosicky left Doctor Burleigh's office he went into the farm-implement store to light his pipe and put on his glasses and read over the list Mary had given him. Then he went into the general merchandise place next door and stood about until the pretty girl with the plucked eyebrows, who always waited on him, was free. Those eyebrows, two thin India-ink strokes, amused him, because he remembered how they used to be. Rosicky always prolonged his shopping by a little joking; the girl knew the old fellow admired her, and she liked to chaff with him.

"Seems to me about every other week you buy ticking, Mr. Rosicky, and always the best quality," she remarked as she measured off the heavy bolt with red stripes.

"You see, my wife is always makin' goose-fedder[5] pillows, an'de thin stuff don't hold in dem little down-fedders."

"You must have lots of pillows at your house."

"Sure. She makes quilts of dem, too. We sleeps easy. Now she's makin' a fedder quilt for my son's wife. You know Polly, that married my Rudolph. How much my bill, Miss Pearl?"

"Eight eighty-five."

"Chust[6] make it nine, and put in some candy fur de women."

"As usual. I never did see a man buy so much candy for his wife. First thing you know, she'll be getting too fat."

"I'd like dat. I ain't much fur all dem slim women like what de style is now."

"That's one for me, I suppose, Mr. Bohunk!" Pearl sniffed and elevated her India-ink strokes.

When Rosicky went out to his wagon, it was beginning to snow,—the first snow of the season, and he was glad to see it. He rattled out of town and along the highway through a wonderfully rich stretch of country, the finest farms in the county. He admired this High Prairie, as it was called, and always liked to drive through it. His own place lay in a rougher territory, where there was some clay in the soil and it was not so productive. When he bought his land, he hadn't the money to buy on High Prairie; so he told his boys, when they grumbled, that if their land hadn't some clay in it, they wouldn't own it at all. All the same, he enjoyed looking at these fine farms, as he enjoyed looking at a prize bull.

After he had gone eight miles, he came to the graveyard, which lay just at the edge of his own hay-land. There he stopped his horses and sat still on his wagon seat, looking about at the snowfall. Over yonder on the hill he could see his own house, crouching low, with the clump of orchard behind and the windmill before, and all down the gentle hill-slope the rows of pale gold cornstalks stood out against the white field. The snow was falling over the cornfield and the pasture and the hay-land, steadily, with very little wind,—a nice dry snow. The graveyard had only a light wire fence about it and was all overgrown with long red grass. The fine snow, settling into this red grass and upon the few little evergreens and the headstones, looked very pretty.

It was a nice graveyard, Rosicky reflected, sort of snug and home-like, not cramped or mournful,—a big sweep all round it. A man could lie down in the long grass and see the complete arch of the sky over him, hear the wagons go by; in summer the mowing-machine rattled right up to the wire fence. And it was so near home. Over there across the cornstalks his own roof and windmill looked so good to him that he promised himself to mind the Doctor and take care of himself. He was awful fond of his place, he admitted. He wasn't anxious to leave it. And it was a comfort to think that he would never have to go farther than the edge of his own hayfield. The snow, falling over his barnyard and the graveyard, seemed to draw things together like. And they were all old neighbours in the graveyard, most of them friends; there was nothing to feel awkward or embarrassed about. Embarrassment was the most disagreeable feeling Rosicky knew. He didn't often have it,—only with certain people whom he didn't understand at all.

Well, it was a nice snowstorm; a fine sight to see the snow falling so quietly and graciously over so much open country. On his cap and shoulders, on the horses' backs and manes, light, delicate, mysterious it fell; and with it a dry cool fragrance was released into the air. It meant rest for vegetation and men and beasts, for the ground itself; a season of long nights for sleep, leisurely breakfasts, peace by the fire. This and much more went through Rosicky's mind, but he merely told himself that winter was coming, clucked to his horses, and drove on.

When he reached home, John, the youngest boy, ran out to put away his team for him, and he met Mary coming up from the outside cellar with her apron full of carrots. They went into the house together. On the table, covered with oilcloth figured with clusters of blue grapes, a place was set, and he smelled hot coffee-cake of some kind. Anton never lunched in town; he thought that extravagant, and anyhow he didn't like the food. So Mary always had something ready for him when he got home.

After he was settled in his chair, stirring his coffee in a big cup, Mary took out of the oven a pan of *kolache* stuffed with apricots, examined them anxiously to see whether they had got too dry, put them beside his plate, and then sat down opposite him.

Rosicky asked her in Czech if she wasn't going to have any coffee.

She replied in English, as being somehow the right language for transacting business: "Now what did Doctor Ed say, Anton? You tell me just what."

"He said I was to tell you some compliments, but I forgot 'em." Rosicky's eyes twinkled.

"About you, I mean. What did he say about your asthma?"

"He says I ain't got no asthma." Rosicky took one of the little rolls in his broad brown fingers. The thickened nail of his right thumb told the story of his past.

"Well, what is the matter? And don't try to put me off."

"He don't say nothing much, only I'm a little older, and my heart ain't so good like it used to be."

Mary started and brushed her hair back from her temples with both hands as if she were a little out of her mind. From the way she glared, she might have been in a rage with him.

"He says there's something the matter with your heart? Doctor Ed says so?"

"Now don't yell at me like I was a hog in de garden, Mary. You know I always did like to hear a woman talk soft. He didn't say anything de matter wid my heart, only it ain't so young like it used to be, an'he tell me not to pitch hay or run de corn-sheller."

Mary wanted to jump up, but she sat still. She admired the way he never under any circumstances raised his voice or spoke roughly. He was city-bred, and she was country-bred; she often said she wanted her boys to have their papa's nice ways.

"You never have no pain there, do you? It's your breathing and your stomach that's been wrong. I wouldn't believe nobody but Doctor Ed about it. I guess I'll go see him myself. Didn't he give you no advice?"

"Chust to take it easy like, an' stay round de house dis winter. I guess you got some carpenter work for me to do. I kin make some new shelves for you, and I want dis long time to build a closet in de boys' room and make dem two little fellers keep dere clo'es hung up."

Rosicky drank his coffee from time to time, while he considered. His moustache was of the soft long variety and came down over his mouth like the teeth of a buggy-rake over a bundle of hay. Each time he put down his cup, he ran his blue handkerchief over his lips. When he took a drink of water, he managed very neatly with the back of his hand.

Mary sat watching him intently, trying to find any change in his face. It is hard to see anyone who has become like your own body to you. Yes, his hair had got thin, and his high forehead had deep lines running from left to right. But his neck, always clean shaved except in the busiest seasons, was not loose or baggy. It was burned a dark reddish brown, and there were deep creases in it, but it looked firm and full of blood. His cheeks had a good colour. On either side of his mouth there was a half-moon down the length of his cheek, not wrinkles, but two lines that had come there from his habitual expression. He was shorter and broader than when she married him; his back had grown broad and curved, a good deal like the shell of an old turtle, and his arms and legs were short.

He was fifteen years older than Mary, but she had hardly ever thought about it before. He was her man, and the kind of man she liked. She was rough, and he was gentle,—city-bred, as she always said. They had been shipmates on a rough voyage and had stood by each other in trying times. Life had gone well with them because, at bottom, they had the same ideas about life. They agreed, without discussion, as to what was most important and what was secondary. They didn't often exchange opinions, even in Czech,—it was as if they had thought the same thought together. A good deal had to be sacrificed and thrown overboard in a hard life like theirs, and they had never disagreed as to the things that could go. It had been a hard life, and a soft life, too. There wasn't anything brutal in the short, broad-backed man with the three-cornered eyes and the forehead that went on to the top of his skull. He was a city man, a gentle man, and though he had married a rough farm girl, he had never touched her without gentleness.

They had been at one accord not to hurry through life, not to be always skimping and saving. They saw their neighbours buy more land and feed more stock than they did, without discontent. Once when the creamery agent came to the Rosickys to persuade them to sell him their cream, he told them how much money the Fasslers, their nearest neighbours, had made on their cream last year.

"Yes," said Mary, "and look at them Fassler children! Pale, pinched little things, they look like skimmed milk. I'd rather put some colour into my children's faces than put money into the bank."

The agent shrugged and turned to Anton.

"I guess we'll do like she says," said Rosicky.

III

Mary very soon got into town to see Doctor Ed, and then she had a talk with her boys and set a guard over Rosicky. Even John, the youngest, had his father on his mind. If Rosicky went to throw hay down from the loft, one of the boys ran up the ladder and took the fork from him. He sometimes complained that though he was getting to be an old man, he wasn't an old woman yet.

That winter he stayed in the house in the afternoons and carpentered, or sat in the chair between the window full of plants and the wooden bench where the two pails of drinking-water stood. This spot was called "Father's corner," though it was not a corner at all. He had a shelf there, where he kept his Bohemian[8] papers and his pipes and tobacco, and his shears and needles and thread and tailor's thimble. Having been a tailor in his youth, he couldn't bear to see a woman patching at his clothes, or at the boys'. He liked tailoring, and always patched all the overalls and jackets and work shirts. Occasionally he made over a pair of pants one of the older boys had outgrown, for the little fellow.

While he sewed, he let his mind run back over his life. He had a good deal to remember, really; life in three countries. The only part of his youth he didn't like to remember was the two years he had spent in London, in Cheapside, working for a German tailor who was wretchedly poor. Those days, when he was nearly always hungry, when his clothes were dropping off him for dirt, and the sound of a strange language kept him in continual bewilderment, had left a sore spot in his mind that wouldn't bear touching.

He was twenty when he landed at Castle Garden in New York, and he had a protector who got him work in a tailor shop in Vesey Street, down near the Washington Market. He looked upon the part of his life as very happy. He became a good workman, he was industrious, and his wages were increased from time to time. He minded his own business and envied nobody's good fortune. He went to night school and learned to read English. He often did overtime work and was well paid for it, but somehow he never saved anything. He couldn't refuse a loan to a friend, and he was self-indulgent. He liked a good dinner, and a little went for beer, a little for tobacco; a good deal went to the girls. He often stood through an opera on Saturday nights; he could get standing-room for a dollar. Those were the great days of opera in New York, and it gave a fellow something to think about for the rest of the week. Rosicky had a quick ear, and a childish love of all the stage splendour; the scenery, the costumes, the ballet. He usually went with a chum, and after the performance they had beer and maybe some oysters somewhere. It was a fine life; for the first five years or so it satisfied him completely. He was never hungry or cold or dirty, and everything amused him: a fire, a dog fight, a parade, a storm, a ferry ride. He thought New York the finest, richest, friendliest city in the world.

Moreover, he had what he called a happy home life. Very near the tailor shop was a small furniture-factory, where an old Austrian, Loeffler, employed a few skilled men and made unusual furniture, most of it to order, for the rich German housewives up-town. The top floor of Loeffler's five-storey factory was a loft, where he kept his choice lumber and stored the odd pieces of furniture left on his hands. One of the young workmen he employed was a Czech, and he and Rosicky became fast friends. They persuaded Loeffler to let them have a sleeping-room in one corner of the loft. They bought good beds and bedding and had their pick of the furniture kept up there. The loft was low-pitched, but light and airy, full of windows, and good-smelling by reason of the fine lumber put up there to season. Old Loeffler used to go down to the docks and buy wood from South America and the East from the sea captains. The young men were as foolish about their house as a bridal pair. Zichec, the young cabinet-maker, devised every sort of convenience, and Rosicky kept their clothes in order. At night and on Sundays, when the quiver of machinery underneath was still, it was the quietest place in the world, and on summer nights all the sea winds blew in. Zichec often practised on his flute in the evening. They were both fond of music and went to the opera together. Rosicky thought he wanted to live like that for ever.

But as the years passed, all alike, he began to get a little restless. When spring came round, he would begin to feel fretted, and he got to drinking. He was likely to drink too much of a Saturday night. On Sunday he was languid and heavy, getting over his spree. On Monday he plunged into work again. So he never had time to figure out what ailed him, though he knew something did. When the grass turned green in Park Place, and the lilac hedge at the back of Trinity churchyard put out its blossoms, he was tormented by a longing to run away. That was why he drank too much; to get a temporary illusion of freedom and wide horizons.

Rosicky, the old Rosicky, could remember as if it were yesterday the day when the young Rosicky found out what was the matter with him. It was on a Fourth of July afternoon, and he was sitting in Park Place in the sun. The lower part of New York was empty. Wall Street,

Liberty Street, Broadway, all empty. So much stone and asphalt with nothing going on, so many empty windows. The emptiness was intense, like the stillness in a great factory when the machinery stops and the belts and bands cease running. It was too great a change, it took all the strength out of one. Those blank buildings, without the stream of life pouring through them, were like empty jails. It struck young Rosicky that this was the trouble with big cities; they built you in from the earth itself, cemented you away from any contact with the ground. You lived in an unnatural world, like the fish in an aquarium, who were probably much more comfortable than they ever were in the sea.

On that very day he began to think seriously about the articles he had read in the Bohemian papers, describing prosperous Czech farming communities in the West. He believed he would like to go out there as a farm hand; it was hardly possible that he could ever have land of his own. His people had always been workmen; his father and grandfather had worked in shops. His mother's parents had lived in the country, but they rented their farm and had a hard time to get along. Nobody in his family had ever owned any land,—that belonged to a different station of life altogether. Anton's mother died when he was little, and he was sent into the country to her parents. He stayed with them until he was twelve, and formed those ties with the earth and the farm animals and growing things which are never made at all unless they are made early. After his grandfather died, he went back to live with his father and stepmother, but she was very hard on him, and his father helped him to get passage to London.

After that Fourth of July day in Park Place, the desire to return to the country never left him. To work on another man's farm would be all he asked; to see the sun rise and set and to plant things and watch them grow. He was a very simple man. He was like a tree that has not many roots, but one tap-root that goes down deep. He subscribed for a Bohemian paper printed in Chicago, then for one printed in Omaha. His mind got farther and farther west. He began to save a little money to buy his liberty. When he was thirty-five, there was a great meeting in New York of Bohemian athletic societies, and Rosicky left the tailor shop and went home with the Omaha delegates to try his fortune in another part of the world.

IV

Perhaps the fact that his own youth was well over before he began to have a family was one reason why Rosicky was so fond of his boys. He had almost a grandfather's indulgence for them. He had never had to worry about any of them—except, just now, a little about Rudolph.

On Saturday night the boys always piled into the Ford, took little Josephine, and went to town to the moving-picture show. One Saturday morning they were talking at the breakfast table about starting early that evening, so that they would have an hour or so to see the Christmas things in the stores before the show began. Rosicky looked down the table.

"I hope you boys ain't disappointed, but I want you to let me have de car tonight. Maybe some of you can go in with de neighbours."

Their faces fell. They worked hard all week, and they were still like children. A new jack-knife or a box of candy pleased the older ones as much as the little fellow.

"If you and Mother are going to town," Frank said, "maybe you could take a couple of us along with you, anyway."

"No, I want to take de car down to Rudolph's, and let him an' Polly go in to de show. She don't git into town enough, an' I'm afraid she's gettin' lonesome, an' he can't afford no car yet."

That settled it. The boys were a good deal dashed. Their father took another piece of apple-cake and went on: "Maybe next Saturday night de two little fellers can go along wid dem."

"Oh, is Rudolph going to have the car every Saturday night?" Rosicky did not reply at once; then he began to speak seriously: "Listen, boys; Polly ain't lookin' so good. I don't like to see nobody lookin' sad. It comes hard fur a town girl to be a farmer's wife. I don't want no trouble to start in Rudolph's family. When it starts, it ain't so easy to stop. An American girl don't git used to our ways all at once. I like to tell Polly she and Rudolph can have the car every Saturday night till after New Year's, if it's all right with you boys."

"Sure it's all right, Papa," Mary cut in. "And it's good you thought about that. Town girls is used to more than country girls. I lay awake nights, scared she'll make Rudolph discontented with the farm."

The boys put as good a face on it as they could. They surely looked forward to their Saturday nights in town. That evening Rosicky drove the car the half-mile down to Rudolph's new, bare little house.

Polly was in a short-sleeved gingham dress, clearing away the supper dishes. She was a trim, slim little thing, with blue eyes and shingled yellow hair, and her eyebrows were reduced to a mere brush-stroke, like Miss Pearl's.

"Good evening, Mr. Rosicky. Rudolph's at the barn, I guess." She never called him father, or Mary mother. She was sensitive about having married a foreigner. She never in the world would have done it if Rudolph hadn't been such a handsome, persuasive fellow and such a gallant lover. He had graduated in her class in the high school in town, and their friendship began in the ninth grade.

Rosicky went in, though he wasn't exactly asked. "My boys ain't goin' to town tonight, an' I brought de car over fur you two to go in to de picture show."

Polly, carrying dishes to the sink, looked over her shoulder at him. "Thank you. But I'm late with my work tonight, and pretty tired. Maybe Rudolph would like to go in with you."

"Oh, I don't go to de shows! I'm too old-fashioned. You won't feel so tired after you ride in de air a ways. It's a nice clear night, an' it ain't cold. You go an' fix yourself up, Polly, an' I'll wash de dishes an' leave everything nice fur you."

Polly blushed and tossed her bob. "I couldn't let you do that, Mr. Rosicky. I wouldn't think of it."

Rosicky said nothing. He found a bib apron on a nail behind the kitchen door. He slipped it over his head and then took Polly by her two elbows and pushed her gently toward the door of her own room. "I washed up de kitchen many times for my wife, when de babies was sick or somethin'. You go an' make yourself look nice. I like you to look prettier'n any of dem town girls when you go in. De young folks must have some fun, an' I'm goin' to look out fur you, Polly."

That kind, reassuring grip on her elbows, the old man's funny bright eyes, madé Polly want to drop her head on his shoulder for a second. She restrained herself, but she lingered in his grasp at the door of her room, murmuring tearfully: "You always lived in the city when you were young, didn't you? Don't you ever get lonesome out here?"

As she turned round to him, her hand fell naturally into his, and he stood holding it and smiling into her face with his peculiar, knowing, indulgent smile without a shadow of reproach in it. "Dem big cities is all right fur de rich, but dey is terrible hard fur de poor."

"I don't know. Sometimes I think I'd like to take a chance. You lived in New York, didn't you?"

"An' London. Da's bigger still. I learned my trade dere. Here's Rudolph comin', you better hurry."

"Will you tell me about London some time?"

"Maybe. Only I ain't no talker, Polly. Run an' dress yourself up."

The bedroom door closed behind her, and Rudolph came in from the outside, looking anxious. He had seen the car and was sorry any of his family should come just then. Supper hadn't been a very pleasant occasion. Halting in the doorway, he saw his father in a kitchen apron, carrying dishes to the sink. He flushed crimson and something flashed in his eye. Rosicky held up a warning finger.

"I brought de car over fur you an' Polly to go to de picture show, an' I made her let me finish here so you won't be late. You go put on a clean shirt, quick!"

"But don't the boys want the car, Father?"

"Not tonight dey don't." Rosicky fumbled under his apron and found his pants pocket. He took out a silver dollar and said in a hurried whisper: "You go an' buy dat girl some ice cream an' candy tonight, like you was courtin'. She's awful good friends wid me."

Rudolph was very short of cash, but he took the money as if it hurt him. There had been a crop failure all over the country. He had more than once been sorry he'd married this year.

In a few minutes the young people came out, looking clean and a little stiff. Rosicky hurried them off, and then he took his own time with the dishes. He scoured the pots and pans and put away the milk and swept the kitchen. He put some coal in the stove and shut off the draughts, so the place would be warm for them when they got home late at night. Then he sat down and had a pipe and listened to the clock tick.

Generally speaking, marrying an American girl was certainly a risk. A Czech should marry a Czech. It was lucky that Polly was the daughter of a poor widow woman; Rudolph was proud, and if she had a prosperous family to throw up at him, they could never make it go.

Polly was one of four sisters, and they all worked; one was book-keeper in the bank, one taught music, and Polly and her younger sister had been clerks, like Miss Pearl. All four of them were musical, had pretty voices, and sang in the Methodist choir, which the eldest sister directed.

Polly missed the sociability of a store position. She missed the choir, and the company of her sisters. She didn't dislike housework, but she disliked so much of it. Rosicky was a little anxious about this pair. He was afraid Polly would grow so discontented that Rudy would quit the farm and take a factory job in Omaha. He had worked for a winter up there, two years ago, to get money to marry on. He had done very well, and they would always take him back at the stockyards. But to Rosicky that meant the end of everything for his son. To be a landless man was to be a wage-earner, a slave, all your life; to have nothing, to be nothing.

Rosicky thought he would come over and do a little carpentering for Polly after the New Year. He guessed she needed jollying. Rudolph was a serious sort of chap, serious in love and serious about his work.

Rosicky shook out his pipe and walked home across the fields. Ahead of him the lamplight shone from his kitchen windows. Suppose he were still in a tailor shop on Vesey Street, with a bunch of pale, narrow-chested sons working on machines, all coming home tired and sullen to eat supper in a kitchen that was a parlour also; with another crowded, angry family quarrelling just across the dumbwaiter shaft, and squeaking pulleys at the windows where dirty washings hung on dirty lines above a court full of old brooms and mops and ash-cans . . .

He stopped by the windmill to look up at the frosty winter stars and draw a long breath before he went inside. That kitchen with the shining windows was dear to him; but the sleeping fields and bright stars and the noble darkness were dearer still.

V

On the day before Christmas the weather set in very cold; no snow, but a bitter, biting wind that whistled and sang over the flat land and lashed one's face like fine wires. There was baking going on in the Rosicky kitchen all day, and Rosicky sat inside, making over a coat that Albert had outgrown into an overcoat for John. Mary had a big red geranium in bloom for Christmas, and a row of Jerusalem cherry trees, full of berries. It was the first year she had ever grown these; Doctor Ed brought her the seeds from Omaha when he went to some medical convention. They reminded Rosicky of plants he had seen in England; and all afternoon, as he stitched, he sat thinking about those two years in London, which his mind usually shrank from even after all this while.

He was a lad of eighteen when he dropped down into London, with no money and no connexions except the address of a cousin who was supposed to be working at a confectioner's. When he went to the pastry shop, however, he found that the cousin had gone to America. Anton tramped the streets for several days, sleeping in doorways and on the Embankment, until he was in utter despair. He knew no English, and the sound of the strange language all about him confused him. By chance he met a poor German tailor who had learned his trade in Vienna, and could speak a little Czech. This tailor, Lifschnitz, kept a repair shop in a Cheapside basement, underneath a cobbler. He didn't much need an apprentice, but he was sorry for the boy and took him in for no wages but his keep and what he could pick up. The pickings were supposed to be coppers given you when you took work home to a customer. But most of the customers called for their clothes themselves, and the coppers that came Anton's way were very few. He had, however, a place to sleep. The tailor's family lived upstairs in three rooms; a kitchen, a bedroom, where Lifschnitz and his wife and five children slept, and a living-room. Two corners of this living-room were curtained off for lodgers; in one Rosicky slept on an old horsehair sofa, with a feather quilt to wrap himself in. The other corner was rented to a wretched, dirty boy, who was studying the violin. He actually practised there. Rosicky was dirty, too. There was no way to be anything else. Mrs. Lifschnitz got the water she cooked and washed with from a pump in a brick court, four flights down. There were bugs in the place, and multitudes of fleas, though the poor woman did the best she could. Rosicky knew she often went empty to give another potato or a spoonful of dripping to the two hungry, sad-eyed boys who lodged with her. He used to think he would never get out of there, never get a clean shirt on his back again. What would he do, he wondered, when his clothes actually dropped to pieces and the worn cloth wouldn't hold patches any longer?

It was still early when the old farmer put aside his sewing and his recollections. The sky had been a dark grey all day, with not a gleam of sun, and the light failed at four o'clock. He went to shave and change his shirt while the turkey was roasting. Rudolph and Polly were coming over for supper.

After supper they sat around in the kitchen, and the younger boys were saying how sorry they were it hadn't snowed. Everybody was sorry. They wanted a deep snow that would lie long and keep the wheat warm, and leave the ground soaked when it melted.

"Yes, sir!" Rudolph broke out fiercely; "if we have another dry year like last year, there's going to be hard times in this country."

Rosicky filled his pipe. "You boys don't know what hard times is. You don't owe nobody, you got plenty to eat an' keep warm, an' plenty water to keep clean. When you got them, you can't have it very hard."

Rudolph frowned, opened and shut his big right hand, and dropped it clenched upon his knee. "I've got to have a good deal more than that, Father, or I'll quit this farming gamble. I can always make good wages railroading, or at the packing house, and be sure of my money."

"Maybe so," his father answered dryly.

Mary, who had just come in from the pantry and was wiping her hands on the roller towel, thought Rudy and his father were getting too serious. She brought her darning-basket and set down in the middle of the group.

"I ain't much afraid of hard times, Rudy," she said heartily. "We've had a plenty, but we've always come through. Your father wouldn't never take nothing very hard, not even hard times. I got a mind to tell you a story on him. Maybe you boys can't hardly remember the year we had that terrible hot wind, that burned everything up on the Fourth of July? All the corn an' the gardens. An' that was in the days when we didn't have alfalfa yet,—I guess it wasn't invented.

"Well, that very day your father was out cultivatin' corn, and I was here in the kitchen makin' plum preserves. We had bushels of plums that year. I noticed it was terrible hot, but it's always hot in the kitchen when you're preservin', an' I was too busy with my plums to mind. Anton come in from the field about three o'clock, an' I asked him what was the matter.

" 'Nothin',' he says, 'but it's pretty hot, an' I think I won't work no more today.' He stood round for a few minutes, an' then he says: 'Ain't you near through? I want you should git up a nice supper for us tonight. It's Fourth of July.'

"I told him to git along, that I was right in the middle of preservin', but the plums would taste good on hot biscuit. 'I'm goin' to have fried chicken, too,' he says, and he went off an' killed a couple. You three oldest boys was little fellers, playin' round outside, real hot an' sweaty, an' your father took you to the horse tank down by the windmill an' took off your clothes an' put you in. Them two box-elder trees was little then, but they made shade over the tank. Then he took off all his own clothes, an' got in with you. While he was playin' in the water with you, the Methodist preacher drove into our place to say how all the neighbours was goin' to meet at the schoolhouse that night, to pray for rain. He drove right to the windmill, of course, and there was your father and you three with no clothes on. I was in the kitchen door, an' I had to laugh, for the preacher acted like he ain't never seen a naked man before. He surely was embarrassed, an' your father couldn't git to his clothes; they was all hangin' up on the windmill to let the sweat dry out of' em. So he laid in the tank where he was, an' put one of you boys on top of him to cover him up a little, an' talked to the preacher.

"When you got through playin' in the water, he put clean clothes on you and a clean shirt on himself, an' by that time I'd begun to get supper. He says: 'It's too hot in here to eat comfortable. Let's have a picnic in the orchard. We'll eat our supper behind the mulberry hedge, under them linden trees.'

"So he carried our supper down, an' a bottle of my wild-grape wine, an' everything tasted good, I can tell you. The wind got cooler as the sun was goin' down, and it turned out pleasant, only I noticed how the leaves was curled up on the linden trees. That made me think, an' I asked your father if that hot wind all day hadn't been terrible hard on the gardens an' the corn.

" 'Corn,' he says, 'there ain't no corn.'

" 'What you talkin' about?' I said. 'Ain't we got forty acres?'

" 'We ain't got an ear,' he says, 'nor nobody else ain't got none. All the corn in this country was cooked by three o'clock today, like you'd roasted it in an oven.'

"'You mean you won't get no crop at all?' I asked him. I couldn't believe it, after he'd worked so hard.

"'No crop this year,' he says. "That's why we're havin' a picnic. We might as well enjoy what we got.'

"An' that's how your father behaved, when all the neighbours was so discouraged they couldn't look you in the face. An' we enjoyed ourselves that year, poor as we was, an' our neighbours wasn't a bit better off for bein' miserable. Some of 'em grieved till they got poor digestions and couldn't relish what they did have."

The younger boys said they thought their father had the best of it. But Rudolph was thinking that, all the same, the neighbours had managed to get ahead more, in the fifteen years since that time. There must be something wrong about his father's way of doing things. He wished he knew what was going on in the back of Polly's mind. He knew she liked his father, but he knew, too, that she was afraid of something. When his mother sent over coffee-cake or prune tarts or a loaf of fresh bread, Polly seemed to regard them with a certain suspicion. When she observed to him that his brothers had nice manners, her tone implied that it was remarkable they should have. With his mother she was stiff and on her guard. Mary's hearty frankness and gusts of good humour irritated her. Polly was afraid of being unusual or conspicuous in any way, of being "ordinary," as she said!

When Mary had finished her story, Rosicky laid aside his pipe.

"You boys like me to tell you about some of dem hard times I been through in London?" Warmly encouraged, he sat rubbing his forehead along the deep creases. It was bothersome to tell a long story in English (he nearly always talked to the boys in Czech), but he wanted Polly to hear this one.

"Well, you know about dat tailor shop I worked in in London? I had one Christmas dere I ain't never forgot. Times was awful bad before Christmas; de boss ain't got much work, an' have it awful hard to pay his rent. It ain't so much fun, bein' poor in a big city like London, I'll say! All de windows is full of good t'ings to eat, an' all de pushcarts in de streets is full, an' you smell' em all de time, an' you ain't got no money,—not a damn bit. I didn't mind de cold so much, though I didn't have no overcoat, chust a short jacket I'd outgrowed so it wouldn't meet on me, an' my hands was chapped raw. But I always had a good appetite, like you all know, an' de sight of dem pork pies in de windows was awful fur me!

"Day before Christmas was terrible foggy dat year, an' dat fog gits into your bones and makes you all damp like. Mrs. Lifschnitz didn't give us nothin' but a little bread an' drippin' for supper, because she was savin' to try for to give us a good dinner on Christmas Day. After supper de boss say I can go an' enjoy myself, so I went into de streets to listen to de Christmas singers. Dey sing old songs an' make very nice music, an' I run round after dem a good ways, till I got awful hungry. I t'ink maybe if I go home, I can sleep till morning an' forgit my belly.

"I went into my corner real quiet, and roll up in my fedder quilt. But I ain't got my head down, till I smell somet'ing good. Seem like it git stronger an' stronger, an' I can't git to sleep noway. I can't understand dat smell. Dere was a gas light in a hall across de court, dat always shine in at my window a little. I got up an' look round. I got a little wooden box in my corner fur a stool, 'cause I ain't got no chair. I picks up dat box, and under it dere is a roast goose on a platter! I can't believe my eyes. I carry it to de window where de light comes in, an' touch it and smell it to find out, an' den I taste it to be sure. I say, I will eat chust one little bite of dat goose, so I can go to sleep, and tomorrow I won't eat none at all. But I tell you, boys, when I stop, one half of dat goose was gone!"

The narrator bowed his head, and the boys shouted. But little Josephine slipped behind his chair and kissed him on the neck beneath his ear.

"Poor little Papa, I don't want him to be hungry!"

"Da's long ago, child. I ain't never been hungry since I had your mudder to cook fur me."

"Go on and tell us the rest, please," said Polly.

"Well, when I come to realize what I done, of course, I felt terrible. I felt better in de stomach, but very bad in de heart. I set on my bed wid dat platter on my knees, an' it all come to me; how hard dat poor woman save to buy dat goose, and how she get some neighbour to cook it dat got more fire, an' how she put it in my corner to keep it away from dem hungry children. Dey was a old carpet hung up to shut my corner off, an' de children wasn't allowed to go in dere. An' I know she put it in my corner because she trust me more'n she did de violin boy. I can't stand it to face her after I spoil de Christmas. So I put on my shoes and go out into de city. I tell myself I better throw myself in de river; but I guess I ain't dat kind of a boy.

"It was after twelve o'clock, an' terrible cold, an' I start out to walk about London all night. I walk along de river awhile, but dey was lots of drunks all along; men, and women too. I chust move along to keep away from de police. I git onto de Strand, an' den over to New Oxford Street, where dere was a big German restaurant on de ground floor, wid big windows all fixed up fine, an' I could see de people havin' parties inside. While I was lookin' in, two men and two ladies come out, laughin' and talkin' and feelin' happy about all dey been eatin' and drinkin', and dey was speakin' Czech,—not like de Austrians, but like de home folks talk it.

"I guess I went crazy, an' I done what I ain't never done before nor since. I went right up to dem gay people an' begun to beg dem: 'Fellow-countrymen, for God's sake give me money enough to buy a goose!'

"Dey laugh, of course, but de ladies speak awful kind to me, an' dey take me back into de restaurant and give me hot coffee and cakes, an' make me tell all about how I happened to come to London, an' what I was doin' dere. Dey take my name and where I work down on paper, an' both of dem ladies give me ten shillings.

"De big market at Covent Garden ain't very far away, an' by dat time it was open. I go dere an' buy a big goose an' some pork pies, an' potatoes and onions, an' cakes an' oranges fur de children,—all I could carry! When I git home, everybody is still asleep. I pile all I bought on de kitchen table, an' go in an' lay down on my bed, an' I ain't waken up till I hear dat woman scream when she come out into her kitchen. My goodness, but she was surprise! She laugh an' cry at de same time, an' hug me and waken all de children. She ain't stop fur no breakfast; she git de Christmas dinner ready dat morning, and we all sit down an' eat all we can hold. I ain't never seen dat violin boy have all he can hold before.

"Two three days after dat, de two men come to hunt me up, an' dey ask my boss, and he give me a good report an' tell dem I was a steady boy all right. One of dem Bohemians was very smart an' run a

Bohemian newspaper in New York, an' de odder was a rich man, in de importing business, an' dey been travelling togedder. Dey told me how t'ings was easier in New York, an' offered to pay my passage when dey was goin' home soon on a boat. My boss say to me: 'You go. You ain't got no chance here, an' I like to see you git ahead, fur you always been a good boy to my woman, and fur dat fine Christmas dinner you give us all.' An' da's how I got to New York."

That night when Rudolph and Polly, arm in arm, were running home across the fields with the bitter wind at their backs, his heart leaped for joy when she said she thought they might have his family come over for supper on New Year's Eve. "Let's get up a nice supper, and not let your mother help at all; make her be company for once."

"That would be lovely of you, Polly," he said humbly. He was a very simple, modest boy, and he, too, felt vaguely that Polly and her sisters were more experienced and worldly than his people.

VI

The winter turned out badly for farmers. It was bitterly cold, and after the first light snows before Christmas there was no snow at all,—and no rain. March was as bitter as February. On those days when the wind fairly punished the country, Rosicky sat by his window. In the fall he and the boys had put in a big wheat planting, and now the seed had frozen in the ground. All that land would have to be ploughed up and planted over again, planted in corn. It had happened before, but he was younger then, and he never worried about what had to be. He was sure of himself and of Mary; he knew they could bear what they had to bear, that they would always pull through somehow. But he was not so sure about the young ones, and he felt troubled because Rudolph and Polly were having such a hard start.

Sitting beside his flowering window while the panes rattled and the wind blew in under the door, Rosicky gave himself to reflection as he had not done since those Sundays in the loft of the furniture-factory in New York, long ago. Then he was trying to find what he wanted in life for himself; now he was trying to find what he wanted for his boys, and why it was he so hungered to feel sure they would be here, working this very land, after he was gone.

They would have to work hard on the farm, and probably they

would never do much more than make a living. But if he could think of them as staying here on the land, he wouldn't have to fear any great unkindness for them. Hardships, certainly; it was a hardship to have the wheat freeze in the ground when seed was so high; and to have to sell your stock because you had no feed. But there would be other years when everything came along right, and you caught up. And what you had was your own. You didn't have to choose between bosses and strikers, and go wrong either way. You didn't have to do with dishonest and cruel people. They were the only things in his experience he had found terrifying and horrible; the look in the eyes of a dishonest and crafty man, of a scheming and rapacious woman.

In the country, if you had a mean neighbour, you could keep off his land and make him keep off yours. But in the city, all the foulness and misery and brutality of your neighbours was part of your life. The worst things he had come upon in his journey through the world were human,—depraved and poisonous specimens of man. To this day he could recall certain terrible faces in the London streets. There were mean people everywhere, to be sure, even in their own country town here. But they weren't tempered, hardened, sharpened, like the treacherous people in cities who live by grinding or cheating or poisoning their fellow-men. He had helped to bury two of his fellow-workmen in the tailoring trade, and he was distrustful of the organized industries that see one out of the world[10] in big cities. Here, if you were sick, you had Doctor Ed to look after you; and if you died, fat Mr. Haycock, the kindest man in the world, buried you.

It seemed to Rosicky that for good, honest boys like his, the worst they could do on the farm was better than the best they would be likely to do in the city. If he'd had a mean boy, now, one who was crooked and sharp and tried to put anything over on his brothers, then town would be the place for him. But he had no such boy. As for Rudolph, the discontented one, he would give the shirt off his back to anyone who touched his heart. What Rosicky really hoped for his boys was that they could get through the world without ever knowing much about the cruelty of human beings. "Their mother and me ain't prepared them for that," he sometimes said to himself.

These thoughts brought him back to a grateful consideration of his own case. What an escape he had had, to be sure! He, too, in his time, had had to take money for repair work from the hand of a hungry child who let it go so wistfully; because it was money due his boss. And now, in all these years, he had never had to take a cent from anyone in bitter need,—never had to look at the face of a woman become like a wolf's from struggle and famine. When he thought of these things, Rosicky would put on his cap and jacket and slip down to the barn and give his work-horses a little extra oats, letting them eat it out of his hand in their slobbery fashion. It was his way of expressing what he felt, and made him chuckle with pleasure.

The spring came warm, with blue skies,—but dry, dry as a bone. The boys began ploughing up the wheat-fields to plant them over in corn. Rosicky would stand at the fence corner and watch them, and the earth was so dry it blew up in clouds of brown dust that hid the horses and the sulky plough and the driver. It was a bad outlook.

The big alfalfa-field that lay between the home place and Rudolph's came up green, but Rosicky was worried because during that open windy winter a great many Russian thistle plants had blown in there and lodged. He kept asking the boys to rake them out; he was afraid their seed would root and "take the alfalfa." Rudolph said that was nonsense. The boys were working so hard planting corn, their father felt he couldn't insist about the thistles, but he set great store by that big alfalfa field. It was a feed you could depend on,—and there was some deeper reason, vague, but strong. The peculiar green of that clover woke early memories in old Rosicky, went back to something in his childhood in the old world. When he was a little boy, he had played in fields of that strong blue-green colour.

One morning, when Rudolph had gone to town in the car, leaving a workteam idle in his barn, Rosicky went over to his son's place, put the horses to the buggy-rake, and set about quietly raking up those thistles. He behaved with guilty caution, and rather enjoyed stealing a march on Doctor Ed, who was just then taking his first vacation in seven years of practice and was attending a clinic in Chicago. Rosicky got the thistles raked up, but did not stop to burn them. That would take some time, and his breath was pretty short, so he thought he had better get the horses back to the barn.

He got them into the barn and to their stalls, but the pain had come on so sharp in his chest that he didn't try to take the harness off. He started for the house, bending lower with every step. The cramp in his chest was shutting him up like a jack-knife. When he reached the windmill, he swayed and caught at the ladder. He saw Polly coming down the hill, running with the swiftness of a slim greyhound. In a flash she had her shoulder under his armpit.

"Lean on me, Father, hard! Don't be afraid. We can get to the house all right."

Somehow they did, though Rosicky became blind with pain; he could keep on his legs, but he couldn't steer his course. The next thing he was conscious of was lying on Polly's bed, and Polly bending over him wringing out bath towels in hot water and putting them on his chest. She stopped only to throw coal into the stove, and she kept the tea-kettle and the black pot going. She put these hot applications on him for nearly an hour, she told him afterwards, and all that time he was drawn up stiff and blue, with the sweat pouring off him.

As the pain gradually loosed its grip, the stiffness went out of his jaws, the black circles round his eyes disappeared, and a little of his natural colour came back. When his daughter-in-law buttoned his shirt over his chest at last, he sighed.

"Da's fine, de way I feel now, Polly. It was a awful bad spell, an' I was so sorry it all come on you like it did."

Polly was flushed and excited. "Is the pain really gone? Can I leave you long enough to telephone over to your place?"

Rosicky's eyelids fluttered. "Don't telephone, Polly. It ain't no use to scare my wife. It's nice and quiet here, an' if I ain't too much trouble to you, just let me lay still till I feel like myself. I ain't got no pain now. It's nice here."

Polly bent over him and wiped the moisture from his face. "Oh, I'm so glad it's over!" she broke out impulsively. "It just broke my heart to see you suffer so, Father."

Rosicky motioned her to sit down on the chair where the teakettle had been, and looked up at her with that lively affectionate gleam in his eyes. "You was awful good to me, I won't never forgit dat. I hate it to be sick on you like dis. Down at de barn I say to myself, dat young girl ain't had much experience in sickness, I don't want to scare her, an' maybe she's got a baby comin' or somet'ing."

Polly took his hand. He was looking at her so intently and affectionately and confidingly; his eyes seemed to caress her face, to regard it with pleasure. She frowned with her funny streaks of eyebrows, and then smiled back at him.

"I guess maybe there is something of that kind going to happen. But I haven't told anyone yet, not my mother or Rudolph. You'll be the first to know."

His hand pressed hers. She noticed that it was warm again. The twinkle in his yellow-brown eyes seemed to come nearer.

"I like mighty well to see dat little child, Polly," was all he said. Then he closed his eyes and lay half-smiling. But Polly sat still, thinking hard. She had a sudden feeling that nobody in the world, not her mother, not Rudolph, or anyone, really loved her as much as old Rosicky did. It perplexed her. She sat frowning and trying to puzzle it out. It was as if Rosicky had a special gift for loving people, something that was like an ear for music or an eye for colour. It was quiet, unobtrusive; it was merely there. You saw it in his eyes,—perhaps that was why they were merry. You felt it in his hands, too. After he dropped off to sleep, she sat holding his warm, broad, flexible brown hand. She had never seen another in the least like it. She wondered if it wasn't a kind of gypsy hand, it was so alive and quick and light in its communications,—very strange in a farmer. Nearly all the farmers she knew had huge lumps of fists, like mauls, or they were knotty and bony and uncomfortable-looking, with stiff fingers. But Rosicky's was like quicksilver, flexible, muscular, about the colour of a pale cigar, with deep, deep creases across the palm. It wasn't nervous, it wasn't stupid lump; it was a warm brown human hand, with some cleverness in it, a great deal of generosity, and something else which Polly could only call "gypsy-like,"—something nimble and lively and sure, in the way that animals are.

Polly remembered that hour long afterwards; it had been like an awakening to her. It seemed to her that she had never learned so much about life from anything as from old Rosicky's hand. It brought her to herself; it communicated some direct and untranslatable message.

When she heard Rudolph coming in the car, she ran out to meet him.

"Oh, Rudy, your father's been awful sick! He raked up those thistles he's been worrying about, and afterwards he could hardly get to the house. He suffered so I was afraid he was going to die."

Rudolph jumped to the ground. "Where is he now?"

"On the bed. He's asleep. I was terribly scared, because, you know, I'm so fond of your father." She slipped her arm through his and they went into the house. That afternoon they took Rosicky home and put him to bed, though he protested that he was quite well again.

The next morning he got up and dressed and sat down to breakfast with his family. He told Mary that his coffee tasted better than usual to him, and he warned the boys not to bear any tales to Doctor Ed when he got home. After breakfast he sat down by his window to do some patching and asked Mary to thread several needles for him before she went to feed her chickens,—her eyes were better than his, and her hands steadier. He lit his pipe and took up John's overalls. Mary had been watching him anxiously all morning, and as she went out of the door with her bucket of scraps, she saw that he was smiling. He was thinking, indeed, about Polly, and how he might never have known what a tender heart she had if he hadn't got sick over there. Girls nowadays didn't wear their heart on their sleeve. But now he knew Polly would make a fine woman after the foolishness wore off. Either a woman had that sweetness at her heart or she hadn't. You couldn't always tell by the look of them; but if they had that, everything came out right in the end.

After he had taken a few stitches, the cramp began in his chest, like yesterday. He put his pipe cautiously down on the window-sill and bent over to ease the pull. No use,—he had better try to get to his bed if he could. He rose and groped his way across the familiar floor, which was rising and falling like the deck of a ship. At the door he fell. When Mary came in, she found him lying there, and the moment she touched him she knew that he was gone.

Doctor Ed was away when Rosicky died, and for the first few weeks after he got home he was hard driven. Every day he said to himself that he must get out to see that family that had lost their father. One soft, warm moonlight night in early summer he started for the farm. His mind was on other things, and not until his road ran by the graveyard did he realize that Rosicky wasn't over there on the hill where the red lamplight shone, but here, in the moonlight. He stopped his car, shut off the engine, and sat there for a while.

A sudden hush had fallen on his soul. Everything here seemed strangely moving and significant, though signifying what, he did not know. Close by the wire fence stood Rosicky's mowing-machine, where one of the boys had been cutting hay that afternoon; his own work-horses had been going up and down there. The new-cut hay perfumed all the night air. The moonlight silvered the long, billowy grass that grew over the graves and hid the fence; the few little evergreens stood out black in it, like shadows in a pool. The sky was very blue and soft, the stars rather faint because the moon was full.

For the first time it struck Doctor Ed that this was really a beautiful graveyard. He thought of city cemeteries; acres of shrubbery and heavy stone, so arranged and lonely and unlike anything in the living world. Cities of the dead, indeed; cities of the forgotten, of the "put away." But this was open and free, this little square of long grass which the wind for ever stirred. Nothing but the sky overhead, and the many-coloured fields running on until they met that sky. The horses worked here in summer; the neighbours passed on their way to town; and over yonder, in the cornfield, Rosicky's own cattle would be eating fodder as winter came on. Nothing could be more undeathlike than this place; nothing could be more right for a man who had helped to do the work of great cities and had always longed for the open country and had got to it at last. Rosicky's life seemed to him complete and beautiful.

〔注释〕

1. Dat widder＝that widow：指罗西基的大儿媳 Polly 的母亲。

2. de Ford＝the Ford：福特牌汽车。

3. and that when he needed it：that 指上面整个句子。

4. She's terrible fur to ask questions：fur＝for，罗西基为捷克后裔，说英语不合乎语法，如此句中"fur"应略去。

5. goose-fedder＝goose-feather.

6. chust＝just.

7. clo'es＝clothes.

8. Bohemian papers：波希米亚文的报纸。

9. mudder＝mother.

10. the organized industries that see one out of the world：指城市里负责葬埋事宜的行业部门。to see one out of the world：打发死者离开人世。

AMY LOWELL

〔作者介绍〕

艾米·洛威尔（Amy Lowell，1874～1925），美国诗人、批评家。她出生于波士顿的名门世家，是19世纪著名作家詹姆斯·罗素·洛威尔（James Russell Lowell，1818～1891）的旁系后代。艾米·洛威尔对20世纪英美诗歌的主要贡献在于：他和庞德是意象派运动（1909～1917）的主要倡导者与组织者。庞德离去后，她成为该运动的领导人。她性格倔强，我行我素，其独断作风与庞德并无二致。虽然在她的主持下意象派的范围比以前更为广泛，创作题材也更为多样，但不少批评家认为，她的“统治”实际上标志着意象派诗歌的衰落。她把意象派早期的创作三原则扩充为6条，虽然其中并无新意，但使先前的原则变得更具体与明确，就连对她颇有偏见的庞德也承认这一点。洛威尔的6条原则是：1. 运用日常语言作诗，用字要绝对精确，不可带有任何不确切和多余的修饰成份. 2. 创造新的节奏来表达新的意绪；在诗歌中，新的节奏即意味着新的思想。3. 主题选择的绝对自由。4. 表现一个意象，反对空泛。5. 诗歌要紧凑、明晰，切忌模糊与游移。6. 集中、提炼是诗歌的本质。

洛威尔也是一位出色的批评家。她所著的两卷本《约翰·济慈传》（*John Keats*，1925）被认为是研究济慈的经典著作之一。她的主要作品还有诗集《彩色玻璃大厦》（*A Dome of Many Coloured Glass*，1912）、《剑刃与罂粟花籽》（*Sword Blades and Poppy Seed*，1914）、《男人、女人和幽灵》（*Men, Women and Ghosts*，1916）、《浮世图》（*Pictures of the Floating World*，1919）和《传奇》（*Legends*，1921）等。她对中国古诗兴趣浓厚，并作过翻译与介绍。

Patterns

〔作品介绍〕

这首诗的背景虽为18世纪，它所表现的却是20世纪文学的一个重要主题：即社会的异化及其对人性的摧残。

诗中的女主人公是一位被这种异化现象剥夺了身心自由的贵族女子。她的堂皇居处、华丽衣着，都成了非人性的模式（pattern）的象征。人类的物质文明非但没有为人性的自由发展提供更广阔的天地，反而成为一种异己的力量，处处限制着人的行动乃至思维，并最终把人推向毁灭；而这种毁灭又正是由人类智慧所精心设计的各种模式（patterns），如诗中的服饰、建筑、战争等，来实现的。这便是现代人类所面临的悲剧。

此诗的形式是戏剧独白（dramatic monologue）。这种形式的特点往往是通过一个主人公的言行举止，将读者直接带入一个特定情境之中，而导致这种情境的原因则常常在诗的字里行间，或甚至在结尾处方被揭示出来。在本诗的开首处，读者突然面对的是一位郁郁寡欢的贵族女人于烂漫春色中徘徊在规划整齐的花园里；她在想象中与情人幽会。只是在诗的第5节，我们才了解到她郁闷的原因；最后一节是女主人公对自己今后孤寂、沉闷的生活的想象，和对各种摧残人性的“模式”的不满。在这种安排中，现在、过去、将来3个时间向度交织在一起，由女主人公的主导心境揉合起来，密而不乱，从而收到增加诗中感情的复杂与强度、寓多样与统一的效果。全诗怨而不怒，意在言外。

Patterns

I walk down the garden paths,
And all the daffodils
Are blowing,[1] and the bright blue squills.
I walk down the patterned garden paths
In my stiff, brocaded gown.
With my powdered hair and jewelled fan,
I too am a rare

Pattern. As I wander down
The garden paths.

My dress is richly figured,
And the train
Makes a pink and silver stain
On the gravel, and the thrift
Of the borders.
Just a plate of current fashion,
Tripping by in high-heeled, ribboned shoes.
Not a softness anywhere about me,
Only whale-bone and brocade.
And I sink on a seat in the shade
Of a lime tree. For my passion
Wars against the stiff brocade.
The daffodils and squills
Flutter in the breeze
As they please.
And I weep;
For the lime tree is in blossom
And one small flower has dropped upon my bosom.

And the plashing of waterdrops
In the marble fountain
Comes down the garden paths.
The dripping never stops.
Underneath my stiffened gown
Is the softness of a woman bathing in a marble basin,
A basin in the midst of hedges grown
So thick, she cannot see her lover hiding,
But she guesses he is near,
And the sliding of the water
Seems the stroking of a dear
Hand upon her.
What is Summer in a fine brocaded gown!
I should like to see it lying in a heap upon the ground,
All the pink and silver crumpled up on the ground.

I would be the pink and silver as I ran along the paths,
And he would stumble after
Bewildered by my laughter.
I should see the sun flashing from his sword hilt and the
  buckles on his shoes.
I would choose
To lead him in a maze along the patterned paths,
A bright and laughing maze for my heavy-booted lover,
Till he caught me in the shade,
And the buttons of his waistcoat bruised my body as he
  clasped me,
Aching, melting, unafraid,
With the shadows of the leaves and the sundrops,
And the plopping of the waterdrops,
All about us in the open afternoon—
I am very like[2] to swoon
With the weight of this brocade,
For the sun sifts through the shade.

Underneath the fallen blossom
In my bosom,
Is a letter I have hid.
It was brought to me this morning by a rider from the Duke.
"Madam, we regret to inform you that Lord Hartwell
Died in action Thursday se'n-night."[3]
As I read it in the white, morning sunlight,
The letters squirmed like snakes.
"Any answer, Madam," said my footman.
"No," I told him.
"See that the messenger takes some refreshment.
No, no answer."
And I walked into the garden,
Up and down the patterned paths,
In my stiff, correct brocade.
The blue and yellow flowers stood up proudly in the sun
Each one.
I stood upright too,

Held rigid to the pattern
By the stiffness of my gown.
Up and down I walked,
Up and down.

In a month he would have been my husband.
In a month, here, underneath this lime,
We would have broke the pattern;
He for me, and I for him,
He as Colonel, I as Lady,
On this shady seat.
He had a whim
That sunlight carried blessing.
And I answered, "It shall be as you have said."
Now he is dead.

In Summer and in Winter I shall walk
Up and down
The patterned garden paths
In my stiff, brocaded gown.
The squills and daffodils
Will give place to pillared roses, and to asters, and to snow.
I shall go
Up and down,
In my gown.
Gorgeously arrayed,
Boned and stayed.
And the softness of my body will be guarded from embrace
By each button, hook, and lace.
For the man who should loose me is dead,
Fighting with the Duke in Flanders,
In a pattern called a war.
Christ! What are patterns for?

〔注释〕

1. blowing：blooming，开放。
1. like：即 likely。
3. se'n：即 seven。

ROBERT FROST

〔作者介绍〕

罗伯特·弗罗斯特（Robert Frost，1874～1963），美国著名诗人，生于旧金山一个教师家庭，在美国西部度过童年。他11岁时父亲去世，全家返回祖籍新英格兰祖父家。弗罗斯特由母亲抚养成人。他母亲是苏格兰人，其朴实的性格和虔诚的宗教信仰对弗罗斯特的个性和文学事业有很大影响。弗罗斯特自小喜爱读诗和写诗，在中学时代就显露出诗才。1892年中学毕业后，他进入达特第斯学院，但因感到学校生活索然无味，7星期后就退了学，开始一面工作一面写诗。这期间他游历过南部，当过教员，做过新闻工作，并与高中时学业上的“劲敌”埃莉诺·怀特结婚。1894年，他在《独立》杂志（*Independent*）11月号首次发表题为《我的蝴蝶》（“My Butterfly”）的诗作。1897年弗罗斯特进入哈佛大学，对拉丁文、希腊文和哲学极感兴趣，但两年后因肺病中途辍学。在这以后的12年里，他在写诗的同时，以教书和经营祖父留给他的农场勉强维持一家人的生活。

1912年他卖掉农场，举家离开新罕布什尔，去英国专事诗歌创作。在伦敦他很快出版了第1部诗集《少年的意志》（*A Boy's Will*），同时结识了一些英国乔治王朝时期的诗人，其中包括年轻的意象派诗人。著名诗人和评论家埃兹拉·庞德（Ezra Pound）当时也在伦敦，十分赞赏弗罗斯特的诗才，曾在美国芝加哥的《诗刊》杂志（*Poetry: A Magazine of Verse*）上评介弗罗斯特的《少年的意志》，并努力帮助他出版诗作。1914年弗罗斯特在伦敦发表第2本诗集《波士顿以北》（*North of Boston*），首先在英国赢得诗誉。英国评论界的热情赞扬引起美国出版界的重视，开始向他约稿。至1915年弗罗斯特举家返回美国时，他的两本诗集已在美国出版，受到读者欢迎。此后，他继续务农和教书，同时又陆续发表《山间》（*Mountain Interval*，1916）、《新罕布什尔》（*New Hampshire*，1923）、《向西流去的小溪》（*West-Running Brook*，1928）、《又一片牧场》（*A Further Range*，1936）、《见证树》（*A Witness Tree*，1942）、《尖塔丛》(*Steeple Bush*, 1947)、《假慈悲》(*A Masque of Mercy*, 1947)、《诗选》(*Collected Poems*, 1939)、《诗歌全集》(*Complete Poems*, 1949)、《林间空地》(*In the Clearing*, 1962) 等诗集。

随着这些著作的出版，弗罗斯特的声誉日增，先后被哈佛等几十所大学聘为教授或客座诗人。他应邀到全国各地朗诵自己的诗作；4次获得普利策诗歌奖。1950年在他75岁生日时，美国参议院通过决议向他祝寿，尊称他为美国民族诗人，这在美国历史上还是第一次。1961年他应邀出席约翰·肯尼迪总统的就职典礼，在仪式上朗诵他的诗作《全心全意的奉献》(“The Gift Outright”)。

弗罗斯特的一生象新英格兰的农民一样朴实无华；他的诗多以田园生活为题材，生活气息浓郁，形象鲜明活泼，表现了新英格兰乡村的道德风尚。他喜欢写景、写事、写人，让读者自己去咀嚼和琢磨。他的一些诗具有神秘色彩和宗教意义；有的象征性很强，富于哲理，有较深的含义。他曾说，“我喜欢举隅法——以部分代全体的比喻方式”。他从整体上运用这种修辞方法，不把含义点明，内容寄寓遥深。他认为诗应“以欢乐开始，以智慧终结”，他自己的诗正是这样的。在诗的创作手法上，弗罗斯特与20世纪多数诗人不同，没有进行诗歌新形式的试验和改革，而是“旧瓶装新酒”，多用传统的四行诗体的各种变体及无韵体；语言通俗，善用普通人的口语抒发感情，描写日常生活的事件与情景。某些诗中洋溢着轻快的气氛，让人百诵不厌。

弗罗斯特有“新英格兰诗人”之称。虽然他颇受古典作家如维吉尔(Virgil, 70～19 B. C.)，以及美国作家爱默生 (Ralph Waldo Emerson, 1803～1882)、梭罗 (Henry David Thoreau, 1817～1862)，迪金森 (Emily Dickinson, 1830～1886) 等的影响，但是诗人所接受的文化遗产和生活环境是铸造他的诗风的决定性因素。波士顿以北多岩石的农场，绿叶萋萋的树林，古老的殖民地时代的建筑，扬基人耐人寻味的石头围墙，以及那里居民的粗犷、感情危机、耕耘生活的艰辛等等，都成为诗人作品取之不尽的素材。自第1部诗集问世，他便似已决定，自己的作品中应有“家乡”，即新英格兰；他似已决心使自己的艺术扎根于他曾亲手耕种过的土地。他的前两部诗集表明，当他全面认识和理解了新英格兰时，弗罗斯特便发现了他的灵感的源泉。他的诗把他家乡的风貌和人民的特征一览无遗地展现在读者面前。谁也没有弗罗斯特对家乡的静林幽谷及屋宇良田所具有的那种亲切的感情和敏锐的反应。林中樫鸟在歌唱，高空雄鹰在盘旋，紫茎山莓遍地丛生，新熟的苹果散出幽香，晚秋草地湿润葱郁，隆冬白雪覆盖山林等等，这一切都在他的诗歌里有所表现。新英格兰乡间生活的各个侧面，弗罗斯特的笔都点到了。人们不禁感到，平凡的日常见闻也颇具令人陶醉的诗意，可成为诗人思想驰骋的“催化剂”。

然而，弗罗斯特并未隐遁乡里，沉湎于描绘它的美丽山川和旖旎景色。他知道如何将其变形，使其成为可以用象征手法表达人生真谛及充满神秘色彩的世界。他企图在新英格兰这一地区内寻觅现代美国业已失去的鲜明色调、激情和纯真，使他的近原始的故乡成为检验和评论现代文明城市的标准。弗罗斯特的杰出贡献之一正在于，他通过诗歌把乡村和城市、地方和世界、人和自然等因素并列、对比与揉合起来，令人通过一地、一时、一人、一物而领悟到人世间的普遍真理。

弗罗斯特的诗虽多保持传统的形式和格律，气氛虽然轻快，语言虽然貌似简明，但它象海明威（Ernest Hemingway）的小说一样，具有一种“骗人的朴素”。弗罗斯特认识到生活的复杂性。在他的笔下，生活既悲惨又快活，既有美也有丑，杂乱之中又寓有统一。他力求避免简单化和极端化，善于透过现实中的现象深入浅出地说明深刻的哲理。

弗罗斯特终生孜孜不倦地献身于艺术，88岁时发表了他最后的一首诗。他不愧为美国最受人们喜爱的一位杰出诗人。

Stoping by Woods on a Snowy Evening

〔作品介绍〕

《雪夜停在林边》（“Stopping by Woods on a Snowy Evening”）于1923年发表在诗集《新罕布什尔》（*New Hampshire*）上。这是弗罗斯特最闻名的诗作之一。弗罗斯特曾谈到此诗的创作过程，大意是：某天晚饭后他拟写一首长素体诗（blank verse），他通宵搜索枯肠，竟一字无成。忽然晨光显在窗上。他立起身，来到窗前向外张望，就在这时，《雪夜》诗突然涌现在脑际。他回转桌边，提笔录下。这《雪夜》诗可能就是他长诗的胚芽，但弗罗斯特不留残稿，因而后人便无从得知其底细了。

依据《牛津美国文学手册》（*The Oxford Companion to American Literature*）编者的意见，这首独白诗的讲话人是诗人自己。在一雪夜诗人到郊区林边欣赏静谧诱人的雪景。马在诗中人格化了，它对主人无故停步迷惑不解。这时一个念头忽然闪现在诗人的心田：如果在这黑暗的雪夜中长眠，那是多美啊！但是他想到人生的路途还很长，他不能死，因为诗人对人类是负有使命的。

这首诗的基本韵律是抑扬格四音步，运用连锁抱韵（interlocking enclosed rhyme），即每诗节的1、2、4行押韵，第3行的尾音成为下一节的韵脚，使诗节与诗节之间的声音与意义珠联璧合。只有最后一节4行全押韵，给人以完整和谐的感觉。

Stopping by Woods on a Snowy Evening

Whose woods these are I think I know.
His house is in the village, though;
He will not see me stopping here
To watch his woods fill up with snow.[1]

My little horse must think it queer
To stop without a farmhouse near[2]
Between the woods and frozen lake
The darkest evening of the year.[3]

He gives his harness bells a shake
To ask if there is some mistake.
The only other sound's the sweep
Of easy wind and downy flake.[4]

The woods are lovely, dark and deep,
But I have promises to keep,[5]
And miles to go before I sleep,
And miles to go before I sleep.[6]

〔注释〕

1. Whose woods…with snow：诗人认识树林的主人，也知道他住在林外的村镇里。林主和村镇在诗里代表一种力量，诗人虽然暂时离开，但最后还要同到村镇和熟悉的人接触。这样第1诗节不仅确立起人与林的关系，而且表明了个人与整体的关系。

2. My little…near：马提出主人为什么停在林边的问题。马习惯于从事有目的的行动。它认为主人的行为反常这一点，说明叙事人的行动并无明确目的。叙事人想象马在提问，于是开始探讨自己的动机。

3. The darkest…year：黑暗的雪夜除写实外，亦可能象征人有时在瞬间会感到渴求最后安息的愿望（death wish）。

4. He gives…flake：至第3诗节末，诗内已出现3种力量同时左右着雪夜骑者的心理——他同林主的世界的关系，他同马的动物世界的关系，以及他同大自然的关系。风仍在吹，雪仍在飘，不管骑者心里想的是什么，这都和大自然无关。大自然的活动是不以人的意志为转移的。骑者感到黑夜在向他发出最后的呼唤：走进树林，让毛茸茸的白雪覆盖起来，是多么容易，又多么美呀。

5. The woods…keep.：然而第4节诗又引进第4种力量。这种力量的名称很多：社会责任、个人承诺或使命、或者人不能凭感悟行事等等。骑者感到自己应做出抉择。"The woods are lovely, dark and deep"句表明叙事人依然在流连忘返，但转折词"but"又把他带回到现实中来。

6. And miles…sleep.：末尾这两句的重复耐人咀嚼。前句无疑是写实，叙事人感到睡前尚有一段长的路程要走；重复句令人突然感到句子的象征意义。"miles to go"有"人生之路还很漫长"之意，而"before I sleep"似同"我最后安息前"相近。许多读者曾向弗罗斯特问及后两句的内涵，诗人总是避而不答。伟大的诗篇总有多种蕴含，供读者推敲。

Mending Wall

〔作品介绍〕

本诗1914年发表在《波士顿以北》(*North of Boston*)诗集里。

在弗罗斯特描写新英格兰风光的文学作品中，常出现的一个细节是主人竭力维修和保护的石围墙，《补墙》(*Mending Wall*)写的就是春天人们修墙的情景。诗中的"我"(即叙事人)思想不落俗套，讲话饶有风趣；他的邻居似为抱残守缺、因袭旧套的人，把父辈的思想和言论奉若天经地义。叙事人开首谈到，自然如何在不知不觉中和墙作对，颇有所感。之后他说到他和邻居一年一度相逢共同补墙的事。邻居合作筑墙以便把两家隔开，可是石墙实际上并没有什么用途。在两人的对话中，叙事人诙谐地向对方指明这一局面的荒诞性质。然而邻居却不加思索，态度温和地对他重复先人的格言："墙高出睦邻"。本诗似在写实，又像一则寓言，探究传统与自然的关系，阐述传统如何逆自然而行，把人甚至民族与国家分割开。本诗把人的尴尬处境描写得很清楚：一方面，墙高能出睦邻，另一方面又存在着把墙推倒的因素；墙不可无，而它又把友爱拒之门外。这恰是西方现代文明社会的窘境所在。

这首诗的基本韵律是抑扬格五音步的无韵体，文字通俗，妙语纷呈。

Mending Wall

Something there is that doesn't love a wall,
That sends the frozen-ground-swell under it
And spills the upper boulders in the sun,
And makes gaps even two can pass abreast.
The work of hunters is another thing:
I have come after them and made repair
Where they have left not one stone on a stone,
But they would have the rabbit out of hiding,
To please the yelping dogs. The gaps I mean,
No one has seen them made or heard them made,
But at spring mending-time we find them there.
I let my neighbor know beyond the hill;
And on a day we meet to walk the line
And set the wall between us once again.
We keep the wall between us as we go. [1]
To each the boulders that have fallen to each. [2]
And some are loaves and some so nearly balls
We have to use a spell to make them balance:
"Stay where you are until our backs are turned!"
We wear our fingers rough with handling them.
Oh, just another kind of outdoor game,
One on a side. It comes to little more:
There where it is we do not need the wall:
He is all pine and I am apple orchard. [3]
My apple trees will never get across
And eat the cones under his pines, I tell him.
He only says, "Good fences make good neighbors."
Spring is the mischief in me, and I wonder
If I could put a notion in his head:
"*Why* do they make good neighbors? Isn't it
Where there are cows? But here there are no cows. [4]
Before I built a wall I'd ask to know

What I was walling in or walling out,
And to whom I was like[5] to give offense.
Something there is that doesn't love a wall,
That wants it down." I could say "Elves" to him,[6]
But it's not elves exactly, and I'd rather
He said it for himself. I see him there,
Bringing a stone grasped firmly by the top
In each hand, like an old-stone savage armed.[7]
He moves in darkness[8] as it seems to me,
Not of woods only and the shade of trees.
He will not go behind his father's saying,[9]
And he likes having thought of it so well
He says again, "Good fences make good neighbors."

〔注释〕

1. We keep…go：我们走着，中间始终隔一堵墙。这句话表现了生活中人际关系的现实。

2. To each…to each：落到谁那边的石头，就由谁去料理。

3. He is all pine…orchard：邻居种的是松树，叙事人种的是苹果树。

4. Why do they…no cows：此两句的意思是说，只有养牛的人家才需要围墙，而我们这里并没有牛啊！

5. like＝likely.

6. I could say "Elves" to him：叙事人本来可以告诉邻居，是妖精作怪推倒了墙。

7. like an old-stone savage armed：像旧石器时代的野人一样手持武器。

8. He moves in darkness：愚昧无知，尚未受到启蒙。

9. He will…saying：他信守父辈教诲。

The Road Not Taken

〔作品介绍〕

本诗1916年发表在《山间》(*Mountain Interval*)，写于1915年2月诗人全家离伦敦回美国前夕。其时诗人已先在英国获得承认，这是他一生事业的重要转折点。而同时他的挚友爱德华·托马斯(Edward Thomas, 1818～1917)却被卷进第一次世界大战的旋涡，生死未卜。此时此刻，诗人深感择路的重要，不由得回忆起4年前在美国新罕布什尔树林中的一次难忘的经历，感慨之余写成此诗。叙事人在林中选择道路，象征世人多数都会在生活的十字路口作出抉择。从某种意义上说，生活本身就是选择，选择得好，生活就有意义。诗人不步前人后尘，选择的是一条人不常走的路。也许这就是此诗留给读者的启示吧。

The Road Not Taken

Two roads diverged in a yellow wood,
And sorry I could not travel both
And be one traveler, long I stood
And looked down one as far as I could
To where it bent in the undergrowth;

Then took the other, as just as fair,
And having perhaps the better claim,
Because it was grassy and wanted wear;
Though as for that, the passing there
Had worn them really about the same,

And both that morning equally lay
In leaves no step had trodden black.
Oh, I kept the first for another day!
Yet knowing how way leads on to way,

I doubted if I should ever come back.

I shall be telling this with a sigh
Somewhere ages and ages hence:
Two roads diverged in a wood, and I—
I took the one less traveled by,
And that has made all the difference.

Design

〔作品介绍〕

本诗 1923 年发表于《新罕布什尔》上，写于 1922 年。诗人通过蜘蛛捕蛾这一细微的自然现象，表现对控制世界的神秘力量的恐惧，具有一种命定论的意味。

Design

I found a dimpled spider, fat and white,
On a white heal-all, holding up a moth
Like a white piece of rigid satin cloth—
Assorted characters of death and blight
Mixed ready to begin the morning right,
Like the ingredients of a witches' broth—[1]
A snow-drop spider, a flower like a froth,
And dead wings carried like a paper kite.

What had that flower to do with being white,
The wayside blue and innocent heal-all?
What brought the kindred spider to that height,
Then steered the white moth thither in the night?
What but design of darkness to appall? —

If design govern in a thing so small.

〔注释〕

1. Like…broth：此处借用莎士比亚悲剧《麦克白斯》中使麦克白斯上当的女巫用各种毒虫做汤的典故。参见《麦克白斯》第4幕第1场。

After Apple-Picking

〔作品介绍〕

本诗于1914年发表在《波士顿以北》。

这是一首较典型的描写新英格兰田园风光的农事抒情诗。华兹华斯(William Wordsworth，1770～1850) 说："诗是强烈感情的自然流露。它起源于在平静中回忆起来的情感。"诗人在旅居英国伦敦期间写的这首诗，是对新英格兰的田园生活的美好回忆。丰收带来欢乐，诗人陶醉在苹果那醉人的馥郁芬芳之中，同时也没有忘记劳动的辛苦。诗人借用浪漫主义手法抒发对农场生活的热爱留恋之情。诗中着力描写了劳动之后的梦境：硕大鲜美的苹果，及其果枝、果花、褐斑。诗中暗示，叙事人将永生难忘这愉快的劳动场面，即使在以后的"长眠"中也会梦见。弗罗斯特有在半夜到田里干活的习惯，曾被邻里称为"怪人"，因此诗中劳动与瞌睡常常交织在一起.

After Apple-Picking

My long two-pointed ladder's sticking through a tree
Toward heaven still,
And there's a barrel that I didn't fill
Beside it, and there may be two or three
Apples I didn't pick upon some bough.
But I am done with apple-picking now.
Essence of winter sleep is on the night,
The scent of apples: I am drowsing off.
I cannot rub the strangeness from my sight

I got from looking through a pane of glass
I skimmed this morning from the drinking trough
And held against the world of hoary grass.
It melted, and I let it fall and break.
But I was well
Upon my way to sleep before it fell,
And I could tell
What form my dreaming was about to take.
Magnified apples appear and disappear,
Stem end and blossom end,
And every fleck of russet showing clear.
My instep arch not only keeps the ache,
It keeps the pressure of a ladder-round.
I feel the ladder sway as the boughs bend
And I keep hearing from the cellar bin
The rumbling sound
Of load on load of apples coming in.
For I have had too much
Of apple-picking: I am overtired
Of the great harvest I myself desired.
There were ten thousand thousand fruit to touch,
Cherish in hand, lift down, and not let fall.
For all
That struck the earth,
No matter if not bruised or spiked with stubble,
Went surely to the cider-apple heap
As of no worth.
One can see what will trouble
This sleep of mine, whatever sleep it is.
Were he not gone,
The woodchuck could say whether it's like his
Long sleep, as I describe its coming on,
Or just some human sleep.

SHERWOOD ANDERSON

〔作者介绍〕

舍伍德·安德森（Sherwood Anderson，1876～1941），美国小说家，出生于俄亥俄州的坎登镇。幼年时家境贫寒，中学没有毕业，便辍学回家。在美国——西班牙战争时期，他去古巴服役约1年。回国后，入威顿堡学院学习了1年左右。

安德森是一位熟悉生活、社会经历丰富的作家，曾从事广告编写，担任公司经理，开办油漆工厂，后来移居乡间。他曾是两家报纸的出版人。

安德森于1916年发表第1部作品，题为《饶舌的麦克逊的儿子》（*Windy McPherson's Son*）。小说一开始，以他自己的童年生活为模型，讨论父子之间的关系，继而描述对于家庭与工作的追求。总的说来，它不是一部成功的作品。他于1919年出版的《小城畸人》（*Winesburg, Ohio*）最受读者欢迎，小说确立了他在美国文学史中的地位。

安德森擅长于短篇小说的创作，先后出版了几本短篇小说集，其中《鸡蛋的胜利及其他》（*The Triumph of the Egg and Other Stories*，1921）与《林中之死及其他》（*Death in the Woods and Other Stories*，1933）最负盛名。他的传记性小说《讲故事人的故事》（*A Story-Teller's Story*，1924）也一直为人们所喜爱。

安德森颇受弗洛伊德心理分析理论的影响，注重刻划人物的心理活动，善于捕捉人们在瞬间迸发出来的强烈情绪，揭示他们内心深处的激情；在艺术风格上形成了他自己的特色。

他是继马克·吐温之后又一位运用口头语言进行创作的作家，语言流畅自然，简洁有力，颇受同时代的女作家格特鲁特·斯泰因（Gertrude Stein，1874～1946）的影响。斯泰因在文学创作的语言技巧方面，强调句子与句子之间某些用词的重复，好象电影胶卷上每一幅画面的重复之间所呈现的状况，当一系列的画面快速地通过放映机镜头时，便形成了活动的情景。他希望通过语言的重复，在读者心中产生形象的现实感。安德森认为斯泰因恢复了语言的活力，并把它应用到自己的作品中以表达强烈的感情。

在美国文学史上，安德森是一位产生过重大影响的作家。威廉·福克纳（William Faulkner，1887～1962）在1956年春同《巴黎评论》的记者谈话时指出，安德森是“我们这一代美国作家之父，体现着美国创作的传统，这一传统将由我们后人继承下去。”

Winesburg, Ohio

〔作品介绍〕

《小城畸人》（*Winesburg, Ohio*）是美国小说中的一部经典作品，由20多篇小说组成，每篇之间在情节上没有直接联系，每一短篇的注意中心集中在一个人物生活中的某一方面或某一时刻，着重表现他（她）在生活中由于追求、失败和痛苦所引起的心理状态变化的一个特征，小说把这些人物汇集在一起，成为一组心理畸形人群的集锦。

《小城畸人》的故事发生在美国中西部的一个小城市，据考证，它可能是作者幼年时生活过的克拉德；故事由一位名叫乔治·威拉德的新闻记者一段一段地叙述，这位记者是以年轻时期的作者本人为模型而塑造的。

安德森于1915年在芝加哥开始创作《小城畸人》。当时，他所读过的两本书对他影响极大，一本是埃德加·李·马斯特思（Edgar Lee Masters）的《匙河诗集》（*Spoon River Anthology*，1915），另一本是斯泰因的《三个人的生平》（*Three Lives*，1909）。前者启发他创作一部发掘人物内心世界的作品；后者引导他运用生动、朴素、接近口语韵律的语言。

《小城畸人》是作者内心情感迸发的结晶。他在一篇回忆该书创作情景的文章中写道，当时他处境十分困难，生活窘困，租借了一间简陋的房子安身。一天下午，天下起大雪，他身体不适，又有人告诉他说，他将被解雇，下班后，他回到了寒冷的房间，孤身一人，百感交集。他打开电灯，“一挥而就，写下了短篇《双手》”。《双手》是构成《小城畸人》的一篇故事。这段回忆说明了艺术创作与灵感的关系。

《小城畸人》的意义在于它表现了人们在社会经济发展过程中所发生的思想变化和心理反应。安德森认为，人们在生活中寻求真理，有的人忠于爱情，追求忠贞；有的人信仰神明。但是，某一方面的真理往往不能适应复杂的、庞大的社会生活实际，从而使追求某一方面真理的人们遭受挫折。生活中的失败使人们感到困惑，变得怪癖，成为“心理畸人”。作者对本书的最初题名是《畸人集》。

Winesburg, Ohio

PAPER PILLS

He was an old man with a white beard and huge nose and hands. Long before the time during which we will know him, he was a doctor and drove a jaded white horse[1] from house to house through the streets of Winesburg. Later he married a girl who had money. She had been left a large fertile farm when her father died. The girl was quiet, tall, and dark, and to many people she seemed very beautiful. Everyone in Winesburg wondered why she married the doctor. Within a year after the marriage she died.

The knuckles of the doctor's hands were extraordinarily large. When the hands were closed they looked like clusters of unpainted wooden balls as large as walnuts fastened together by steel rods. He smoked a cob pipe[2] and after his wife's death sat all day in his empty office close by a window that was covered with cobwebs. He never opened the window. Once on a hot day in August he tried but found it stuck fast and after that he forgot all about it.

Winesburg had forgotten the old man, but in Doctor Reefy there were the seeds of something very fine. Alone in his musty office in the Heffner Block above the Paris Dry Goods Company's store, he worked ceaselessly, building up something that he himself destroyed. Little pyramids of truth he erected and after erecting knocked them down again that he might have the truths to erect other pyramids.

Doctor Reefy was a tall man who had worn one suit of clothes for ten years. It was frayed at the sleeves and little holes had appeared at the knees and elbows. In the office he wore also a linen duster with huge pockets into which he continually stuffed scraps of paper. After some weeks the scraps of paper became little hard round balls, and when the pockets were filled he dumped them out upon the floor. For ten years he had but one friend, another old man named John Spaniard who owned a tree nursery. Sometimes, in a playful mood, old Doctor Reefy took from his pockets a handful of the paper balls and threw them at the nursery man. "That is to confound you, you blithering old sentimentalist," he cried, shaking with laughter.

The story of Doctor Reefy and his courtship of the tall dark girl who became his wife and left her money to him is a very curious story. It is delicious, like the twisted little apples that grow in the orchards of Winesburg. In the fall one walks in the orchards and the ground is hard with frost underfoot. The apples have been taken from the trees by the pickers. They have been put in barrels and shipped to the cities where they will be eaten in apartments that are filled with books, magazines, furniture, and people. On the trees are only a few gnarled apples that the pickers have rejected. They look like the knuckles of Doctor Reefy's hands. One nibbles at them and they are delicious. Into a little round place at the side of the apple has been gathered all of its sweetness. One runs from tree to tree over the frosted ground picking the gnarled, twisted apples and filling his pockets with them. Only the few know the sweetness of the twisted apples.

The girl and Doctor Reefy began their courtship on a summer afternoon. He was forty-five then and already he had begun the practice of filling his pockets with the scraps of paper that became hard balls and were thrown away. The habit had been formed as he sat in his buggy behind the jaded grey horse and went slowly along country roads. On the papers were written thoughts, ends of thoughts, beginnings of thoughts.

One by one the mind of Doctor Reefy had made the thoughts. Out of many of them he formed a truth that arose gigantic in his mind. The truth clouded the world. It became terrible and then faded away and the little thoughts began again.

The tall dark girl came to see Doctor Reefy because she was in the family way[3] and had become frightened. She was in that condition because of a series of circumstances also curious.

The death of her father and mother and the rich acres of land that had come down to her had set a train of suitors on her heels. For two years she saw suitors almost every evening. Except two they were all alike. They talked to her of passion and there was a strained eager quality in their voices and in their eyes when they looked at her. The two who were different were much unlike each other. One of them, a slender young man with white hands, the son of a jeweler in Winesburg, talked continually of virginity. When he was with her he was never off the subject. The other, a black-haired boy with large ears, said nothing at all but always managed to get her into the darkness, where he began to kiss her.

For a time the tall dark girl thought she would marry the jeweler's son. For hours she sat in silence listening as he talked to her and then she began to be afraid of something. Beneath his talk of virginity she began to think there was a lust greater than in all the others. At times it seemed to her that as he talked he was holding her body in his hands. She imagined him turning it slowly about in the white hands and staring at it. At night she dreamed that he had bitten into her body and that his jaws were dripping. She had the dream three times, then she became in the family way to the one who said nothing at all but who in the moment of his passion actually did bite her shoulder so that for days the marks of his teeth showed.

After the tall dark girl came to know Doctor Reefy it seemed to her that she never wanted to leave him again. She went into his office one morning and without her saying anything he seemed to know what had happened to her.

In the office of the doctor there was a woman, the wife of the man who kept the bookstore in Winesburg. Like all old-fashioned country practitioners, Doctor Reefy pulled teeth, and the woman who waited held a handkerchief to her teeth and groaned. Her husband was with her and when the tooth was taken out they both screamed and blood ran down on the woman's white dress. The tall dark girl did not pay any attention. When the woman and the man had gone the doctor smiled. "I will take you driving into the country with me," he said.

For several weeks the tall dark girl and the doctor were together almost every day. The condition that had brought her to him passed in an illness, but she was like one who has discovered the sweetness of the twisted apples, she could not get her mind fixed again upon the round perfect fruit that is eaten in the city apartments. In the fall after the beginning of her acquaintanceship with him she married Doctor Reefy and in the following spring she died. During the winter he read to her all of the odds and ends of thoughts he had scribbled on the bits of paper. After he had read them he laughed and stuffed them away in his pockets to become round hard balls.

MOTHER

Elizabeth Willard, the mother of George Willard, was tall and gaunt and her face was marked with smallpox scars. Although she was but forty-five, some obscure disease had taken the fire out of her figure. Listlessly she went about the disorderly old hotel looking at the faded wall-paper and the ragged carpets and when she was able to be about, doing the work of a chambermaid among beds soiled by the slumbers of fat traveling men. Her husband, Tom Willard, a slender, graceful man with square shoulders, a quick military step, and a black mustache trained to turn sharply up at the ends, tried to put the wife out of his mind. The presence of the tall ghostly figure, moving slowly through the halls, he took as a reproach to himself. When he thought of her he grew angry and swore. The hotel was unprofitable and forever on the edge of failure and he wished himself out of it. He thought of the old house and the woman who lived there with him as things defeated and done for. The hotel in which he had begun life so hopefully was now a mere ghost of what a hotel should be. [1] As he went spruce and business-like through the streets of Winesburg, he sometimes stopped and turned quickly about as though fearing that the spirit of the hotel and of the woman would follow him even into the streets. "Damn such a life, damn it!" he sputtered aimlessly.

Tom Willard had a passion for village politics and for years had been the leading Democrat in a strongly Republican community. [2] Some day, he told himself, the tide of things political will turn in my favor and the years of ineffectual service count big in the bestowal of rewards. [3] He dreamed of going to Congress and even of becoming governor. Once when a younger member of the party arose at a political conference and began to boast of his faithful service, Tom Willard grew white with fury. "Shut up, you," he roared, glaring about. "What do you know of service? What are you but a boy? Look at what I've done here! I was a Democrat here in Winesburg when it was a crime to be a Democrat. In the old days they fairly hunted us with guns."

Between Elizabeth and her one son George there was a deep unexpressed bond of sympathy, based on a girlhood dream that had long ago died. In the son's presence she was timid and reserved, but sometimes while he hurried about town intent upon his duties as a reporter, she went into his room and closing the door knelt by a little desk, made of a kitchen table, that sat near a window. In the room by the desk she went through a ceremony that was half a prayer, half a demand, addressed to the skies. In the boyish figure she yearned to see something half forgotten that had once been a part of herself re-created. The prayer concerned that. "Even though I die, I will in some way keep defeat from you," she cried, and so deep was her determination that her whole body shook. Her eyes glowed and she clenched her fists. "If I am dead and see him becoming a meaningless drab figure like myself, I will come back," she declared. "I ask God now to give me that privilege. I demand it. I will pay for it. God may beat me with his fists. I will take any blow that may befall if but this my boy be allowed to express something for us both." Pausing uncertainly, the woman stared about the boy's room. "And do not let him become smart and successful either," she added vaguely.

The communion between George Willard and his mother was outwardly a formal thing without meaning. When she was ill and sat by the window in her room he sometimes went in the evening to make her a visit. They sat by a window that looked over the roof of a small frame building[4] into Main Street. By turning their heads they could see through another window, along an alleyway that ran behind the Main Street stores and into the back door of Abner Groff's bakery. Sometimes as they sat thus a picture of village life presented itself to them. At the back door of his shop appeared Abner Groff with a stick or an empty milk bottle in his hand. For a long time there was a feud between the baker and a grey cat that belonged to Sylvester West, the druggist. The boy and his mother saw the cat creep into the door of the bakery and presently emerge followed by the baker, who swore and waved his arms about. The baker's eyes were small and red and his black hair and beard were filled with flour dust. Sometimes he was so angry that, although the cat had disappeared, he hurled sticks, bits of broken glass, and even some of the tools of his trade about. Once he broke a window at the back of Sinning's Hardware Store. In the alley the grey cat crouched behind barrels filled with torn paper and broken bottles above which flew a black swarm of flies. Once when she was alone, and after watching a prolonged and ineffectual outburst on the part of the baker, Elizabeth Willard put her head down on her long white hands and wept. After that she did not look along the alleyway any more, but tried to forget the contest between the bearded man and the cat. It seemed like a rehearsal of her own life, terrible in its vividness.

In the evening when the son sat in the room with his mother, the silence made them both feel awkward. Darkness came on and the evening train came in at the station. In the street below feet tramped up and down upon a board sidewalk. In the station yard, after the evening train had gone, there was a heavy silence. Perhaps Skinner Leason, the express agent, moved a truck the length of the station platform. Over on Main Street sounded a man's voice, laughing. The door of the express office banged. George Willard arose and crossing the room fumbled for the doorknob. Sometimes he knocked against a chair, making it scrape along the floor. By the window sat the sick woman, perfectly still, listless. Her long hands, white and bloodless, could be seen drooping over the ends of the arms of the chair. "I think you had better be out among the boys. You are too much indoors," she said, striving to relieve the embarrassment of the departure. "I thought I would take a walk," replied George Willard, who felt awkward and confused.

One evening in July, when the transient guests who made the New Willard House their temporary home had become scarce, and the hallways, lighted only by kerosene lamps turned low, were plunged in gloom, Elizabeth Willard had an adventure. She had been ill in bed for several days and her son had not come to visit her. She was alarmed. The feeble blaze of life that remained in her body was blown into a flame by her anxiety and she crept out of bed, dressed and hurried along the hallway toward her son's room, shaking with exaggerated fears. As she went along she steadied herself with her hand, slipped along the papered walls of the hall and breathed with difficulty. The air whistled through her teeth. As she hurried forward she thought how foolish she was. "He is concerned with boyish affairs," she told herself. "Perhaps he has now begun to walk about in the evening with girls."

Elizabeth Willard had a dread of being seen by guests in the hotel that had once belonged to her father and the ownership of which still stood recorded in her name in the county courthouse. The hotel was continually losing patronage because of its shabbiness and she thought of herself as also shabby. Her own room was in an obscure corner and when she felt able to work she voluntarily worked among the beds, preferring the labor that could be done when the guests were abroad seeking trade among the merchants of Winesburg.

By the door of her son's room the mother knelt upon the floor and listened for some sound from within. When she heard the boy moving about and talking in low tones a smile came to her lips. George Willard had a habit of talking aloud to himself and to hear him doing so had always given his mother a peculiar pleasure. The habit in him, she felt, strengthened the secret bond that existed between them. A thousand times she had whispered to herself of the matter. "He is groping about, trying to find himself," she thought. "He is not a dull clod, all words and smartness. Within him there is a secret something that is striving to grow. It is the thing I let be killed in myself."

In the darkness in the hallway by the door the sick woman arose and started again toward her own room. She was afraid that the door would open and the boy come upon her. When she had reached a safe distance and was about to turn a corner into a second hallway she stopped and bracing herself with her hands waited, thinking to shake off a trembling fit of weakness that had come upon her. The presence of the boy in the room had made her happy. In her bed, during the long hours alone, the little fears that had visited her had become giants. Now they were all gone. "When I get back to my room I shall sleep," she murmured gratefully.

But Elizabeth Willard was not to return to her bed and to sleep. As she stood trembling in the darkness the door of her son's room opened and the boy's father, Tom Willard, stepped out. In the light that streamed out at the door he stood with the knob in his hand and talked. What he said infuriated the woman.

Tom Willard was ambitious for his son. He had always thought of himself as a successful man, although nothing he had ever done had turned out successfully. However, when he was out of sight of the New Willard House and had no fear of coming upon his wife, he swaggered and began to dramatize himself as one of the chief men of the town. He wanted his son to succeed. He it was who had secured for the boy the position on the *Winesburg Eagle*.[5] Now, with a ring of earnestness in his voice, he was advising concerning some course of conduct. "I tell you what, George, you've got to wake up," he said sharply. "Will Henderson has spoken to me three times concerning the matter. He says you go along for hours not hearing when you are spoken to and acting like a gawky girl. What ails you?" Tom Willard laughed good-naturedly. "Well, I guess you'll get over it," he said. "I told Will that. You're not a fool and you're not a woman. You're Tom Willard's son and you'll wake up. I'm not afraid. What you say clears things up. If being a newspaper man had put the notion of becoming a writer into your mind that's all right. Only I guess you'll have to wake up to do that too, eh?"

Tom Willard went briskly along the hallway and down a flight of stairs to the office. The woman in the darkness could hear him laughing and talking with a guest who was striving to wear away a dull evening by dozing in a chair by the office door. She returned to the door of her son's room. The weakness had passed from her body as by a miracle and she stepped boldly along. A thousand ideas raced through her head. When she heard the scraping of a chair and the sound of a pen scratching upon paper, she again turned and went back along the hallway to her own room.

A definite determination had come into the mind of the defeated wife of the Winesburg hotel keeper. The determination was the result of long years of quiet and rather ineffectual thinking. "Now," she told herself, "I will act. There is something threatening my boy and I will ward it off." The fact that the conversation between Tom Willard and his son had been rather quiet and natural, as though an understanding existed between them, maddened her. Although for years she had hated her husband, her hatred had always before been a quite impersonal thing. He had been merely a part of something else that she hated. Now, and by the few words at the door, he had become the thing personified. In the darkness of her own room she clenched her fists and glared about. Going to a cloth bag that hung on a nail by the wall she took out a long pair of sewing scissors and held them in her hand like a dagger. "I will stab him," she said aloud. "He has chosen to be the voice of evil and I will kill him. When I have killed him something will snap within myself and I will die also. It will be a release for all of us."

In her girlhood and before her marriage with Tom Willard, Elizabeth had borne a somewhat shaky reputation in Winesburg. For years she had been what is called "stage-struck"[6] and had paraded through the streets with traveling men guests at her father's hotel, wearing loud clothes and urging them to tell her of life in the cities out of which they had come. Once she startled the town by putting on men's clothes and riding a bicycle down Main Street.

In her own mind the tall dark girl had been in those days much confused. A great restlessness was in her and it expressed itself in two ways. First there was an uneasy desire for change, for some big definite movement to her life. It was this feeling that had turned her mind to the stage. She dreamed of joining some company and wandering over the world, seeing always new faces and giving something out of herself to all people. Sometimes at night she was quite beside herself with the thought, but when she tried to talk of the matter to the members of the theatrical companies that came to Winesburg and stopped at her father's hotel, she got nowhere. They did not seem to know what she meant, or if she did get something of her passion expressed, they only laughed. "It's not like that," they said. "It's as dull and uninteresting as this here. Nothing comes of it."

With the traveling men when she walked about with them, and later with Tom Willard, it was quite different. Always they seemed to understand and sympathize with her. On the side streets of the village, in the darkness under the trees, they took hold of her hand and she thought that something unexpressed in herself came forth and became a part of an unexpressed something in them.

And then there was the second expression of her restlessness. When that came she felt for a time released and happy. She did not blame the men who walked with her and later she did not blame Tom Willard. It was always the same, beginning with kisses and ending, after strange wild emotions, with peace and then sobbing repentance. When she sobbed she put her hand upon the face of the man and had always the same thought. Even though he were large and bearded she thought he had become suddenly a little boy. She wondered why he did not sob also.

In her room, tucked away in a corner of the old Willard House, Elizabeth Willard lighted a lamp and put it on a dressing table that stood by the door. A thought had come into her mind and she went to a closet and brought out a small square box and set it on the table. The box contained material for make-up and had been left with other things by a theatrical company that had once been stranded in Winesburg. Elizabeth Willard had decided that she would be beautiful. Her hair was still black and there was a great mass of it braided and coiled about her head. The scene that was to take place in the office below began to grow in her mind. No ghostly worn-out figure should confront Tom Willard, but something quite unexpected and startling. Tall and with dusky cheeks and hair that fell in a mass from her shoulders, a figure should come striding down the stairway before the startled loungers in the hotel office. The figure would be silent—it would be swift and terrible. As a tigress whose cub had been threatened would she appear, coming out of the shadows, stealing noiselessly along and holding the long wicked scissors in her hand.

With a little broken sob in her throat, Elizabeth Willard blew out the light that stood upon the table and stood weak and trembling in the darkness. The strength that had been as a miracle in her body left and she half reeled across the floor, clutching at the back of the chair in which she had spent so many long days staring out over the tin roofs into the main street of Winesburg. In the hallway there was the sound of footsteps and George Willard came in at the door. Sitting in a chair beside his mother he began to talk. "I'm going to get out of here," he said. "I don't know where I shall go or what I shall do but I am going away."

The woman in the chair waited and trembled. An impulse came to her. "I suppose you had better wake up," she said. "You think that? You will go to the city and make money, eh? It will be better for you, you think, to be a business man, to be brisk and smart and alive?" She waited and trembled.

The son shook his head. "I suppose I can't make you understand, but oh, I wish I could," he said earnestly. "I can't even talk to father about it. I don't try. There isn't any use. I don't know what I shall do. I just want to go away and look at people and think."

Silence fell upon the room where the boy and woman sat together. Again, as on the other evenings, they were embarrassed. After a time the boy tried again to talk. "I suppose it won't be for a year or two but I've been thinking about it," he said, rising and going toward the door. "Something father said makes it sure that I shall have to go away." He fumbled with the door knob. In the room the silence became unbearable to the woman. She wanted to cry out with joy because of the words that had come from the lips of her son, but the expression of joy had become impossible to her. "I think you had better go out among the boys. You are too much indoors," she said. "I thought I would go for a little walk," replied the son stepping awkwardly out of the room and closing the door.

〔注释〕

Paper Pills

1. a jaded white horse：一匹疲惫不堪的白马。
2. a cob pipe：烟斗，它用来装烟叶的碗状容器，系用玉米的棒子芯制成。
3. in the family way：怀孕了。

Mother

1. a mere ghost of what a hotel should be：哪里还象一家旅馆应该有的样子。
2. the leading Democrat in a strongly Republican community：在共和党势力强大的居民区中一位主要的民主党人。
3. the years of ineffectual service count big in the bestowal of rewards：几年来不见成效的工作，却是以后奖赏中的重要依据。
4. a small frame building：一个小型的木结构建筑。
5. *Winesburg Eagle*：当地一家报纸名称。
6. stage-struck：痴心地爱慕演员或希望从事戏剧演出事业。

CARL SANDBURG

〔作者介绍〕

卡尔·桑德堡（Carl Sandburg，1878～1967），美国现代诗人及传记作家。他出身于贫寒的瑞典移民家庭，未受过正规教育，一生做过流动工人、勤杂工、士兵、记者和市长秘书等工作。卑微的身世与丰富的阅历为他的创作生涯提供了丰富的经验与素材。作为一位社会主义者和民主战士，桑德堡创作的目的是"为朴素的人民写朴素的诗"。他生活的最崇高理想是成为"人民的声音"，以诗来表达普通人的思想、感情和愿望。他一生同民众保持着密切联系，热情讴歌他们，受到他们的爱戴与欢迎，是二、三十年代最受读者喜爱的诗人之一。

桑德堡早在大学期间便开始写诗，出版过名为《心醉神迷》（*In Reckless Ecstasy*，1940）的诗集。1916 年他的《芝加哥诗集》（*Chicago Poems*）由一全国闻名的霍尔特，莱因哈特及温斯顿出版公司（Holt，Rinehart and Winston，Inc.）出版，桑德堡便从此而扬名。他早期和意象派新诗运动颇有联系，在其影响下写过诸如《雾》（"Fog"）、《失落——》（"Lost——"）以及《港口》（"The Harbour"）等著名意象诗。他的一些长诗也表现出意象诗的影响。桑德堡对民歌也极感兴趣，20 年代他在旅行中注意收集牛仔、流浪汉和黑人的歌曲，并登台演唱。这些歌曲后来被他收集在《美国歌集》（*The American Songbag*，1927）中。桑德堡还写了 6 卷《林肯传》，1 部自传和 1 部历史小说。

桑德堡的诗歌和惠特曼的诗歌颇多相似之处。他和惠特曼一样包罗"一切"。他也看到了现实生活中的丑恶现象，读一下他的《港口》便可得知：这里到处是罪恶和失意，拥挤丑陋的茅屋，出卖肉体的娼妓，恣意杀人的枪手等令人目不忍睹的现实。他的一些诗作表现出他对穷苦人民的同情。在另外一些诗如《清冷的墓》（"Cool Tombs"）中，他的情绪是低沉沮丧的。然而桑德堡的写作目的在于给人民带来希望。在同代人中，应该说他最了解人民大众的重要性。人民是创造者，他们终有一天会成为自己命运的主人。桑德堡的诗作《我是人民群众》（“I Am the People，the Mob”）及《人民，是的》(*The People*, *Yes*) 充分表现出他的这种信念。因此，桑德堡是乐观主义者。他洞察美国未来的状况。他对美国工业机械文明的态度也有别于其他人。钢与机器虽然给人带来痛苦，但这些既是人民生产的，就最终会为改善人的境遇服务。

桑德堡的创作和现代诗歌的发展息息相通。他运用自由体写诗，作品中充满着活力充沛的口语和俚语。他的文笔有时粗犷豪放，有时又绮丽多姿。他对美国文学中口语风格的发展做出了卓越的贡献。

桑德堡的作品曾获得美国诗歌奖（1919，1920）和普利策奖（1950）。他的其他作品还有《剥玉米机》(*Cornhuskers*，1918)、《烟与钢》(*Smoke and Steel*，1920)、《早安，美国》(*Good Morning*，*America*，1928) 和《诗集》(*Collected Poems*，1951) 等。

这里选注的是《芝加哥》、《雾》及《港口》3首诗。

Chicago

〔作品介绍〕

《芝加哥》（“Chicago”）是桑德堡的成名作。1914年它出现在《诗刊》(*Poetry*) 中时曾引起激烈的争论。它那不平常的节奏、造词及艺术形象似乎有意同传统诗歌决裂，诗歌的结构也很随便。桑德堡喜欢芝加哥，这座城市新鲜、粗犷，充满希望，它无视过去，而憧憬未来。如果芝加哥象征目前和未来，那么桑德堡则是歌颂那些时代的诗人。

诗的开首5行描绘该城的状貌，以第5行为总结，表明城市的威力。6至8行写出该城市的阴暗面，以第9行为转机，开始为它的缺陷做辩护。19至23行辩词趋向高潮，说明它的力量克服了前面诗行中所描绘的苦楚与肮脏，最后一行重复开首几行的描绘，令人感到芝加哥的骄傲，听到它的笑声。

在这首诗中，惠特曼的影响是显而易见的：火一般的激情和节奏、平行结构及长句等。这首诗具有一种独特的美，正如评论家所说：“它是张牙舞爪的美，是被豺狼盘踞着长满雏菊花的美。”

Chicago

Hog Butcher for the World,

Tool Maker, Stacker of Wheat,
Player with Railroads and the Nation's Freight Handler;
Stormy, husky, brawling,
City of the Big Shoulders:[1]
They tell me you are wicked and I believe them, for I have seen your painted women under the gas lamps luring the farm boys.
And they tell me you are crooked and I answer: Yes, it is true I have seen the gunman kill and go free to kill again.
And they tell me you are brutal and my reply is: On the faces of woman and children I have seen the marks of wanton hunger.
And having answered so I turn once more to those who sneer at this my city, and I give them back the sneer and say to them:
Come and show me another city with lifted head singing so proud to be alive and coarse and strong and cunning.
Flinging magnetic curses amid the toil of piling job on job, here is a tall bold slugger set vivid against the little soft cities;[2]
Fierce as a dog with tongue lapping for action, cunning as a savage pitted against the wilderness,
Bareheaded,
Shoveling,
Wrecking,
Plannin g,
Building, breaking, rebuilding,
Under the smoke, dust all over his mouth, laughing with white teeth,
Under the terrible burden of destiny laughing as a young man laughs,
Laughing even as an ignorant fighter laughs who has never lost a battle,
Bragging and laughing that under his wrist is the pulse, and under his ribs the heart of the people,
Laughing!
Laughing the stormy, husky, brawling laughter of Youth, halfnaked, sweating, proud to be Hog Butcher, Tool Maker, Stacker of Wheat, Player with railroads and Freight Handler to the Nation.

〔注释〕

1. city of the Big Shoulders：指芝加哥是宽肩膀的，身强力壮的劳动者的城市，因为他们创造了社会财富。

2. 将芝加哥比喻为棒球比赛中的猛击手（slugger），以示其他城市的无足轻重。

Fog

〔作品介绍〕

这是一首典型的意象派小诗。它将雾描写为一只潜行的小猫，雾的运动也恰似猫的匍行，它的消逝也如猫一样，来无影，去无踪。

Fog

The fog comes
on little cat feet.

It sits looking
over harbor and city
on silent haunches[1]
and then moves on.

〔注释〕

1. on silent haunches：默默地蹲着。

The Harbor

〔作品介绍〕

《港口》（“The Harbor”）一诗描写的也是芝加哥市。桑德堡说过，“诗源于心境。我并非每日都以一种情绪描写同一题材。”《港口》和《芝加哥》对同一城市的描写就迥然不同。这里出现在读者面前的不是一座快活和充满希望的城市，而是肮脏和丑陋的景象。桑德堡看到的是饥饿和贫穷。在诗中城墙的限面和大自然的开阔形成对比，丑恶的、令人失望的城市和美好的、未经破坏的大自然相互映衬，从侧面表达出诗人的怅惘和忧愤。

The Harbor

Passing through huddled and ugly walls
By doorways where women
Looked from their hunger-deep eyes,
Haunted with shadows of hunger-hands,
Out from the huddled and ugly walls,
I came sudden, at the city's edge,
On a blue burst of lake,
Long lake waves breaking under the sun
On a spray-flung of shore;
And a fluttering storm of gulls,
Masses of great gray wings
And flying white bellies
Veering and wheeling free in the open.

WALLACE STEVENS

〔作者介绍〕

华莱士·史蒂文斯(Wallace Stevens, 1879～1955),美国著名诗人。他出生于宾夕法尼亚州一个律师家庭,中学毕业后曾在哈佛学习3年,后辍学,到纽约法学院学习法律。1904年起当了几年律师,但很不得意。1908年在一家证券公司的纽约办事处任职,几年后到康涅狄格州哈特福特保险公司工作,最后升任该公司董事长。早在哈佛大学期间,史蒂文斯的诗作便在《哈佛月刊》(*Harvard Advocate*)上发表,后来他虽忙于从商,但从未停止过写诗。他在两个貌似矛盾的领域——保险业和诗歌创作——中都取得了成功。他一向认为,诗人应在现实和想象两个领域内生活,努力在它们之间架设桥梁。他一生热衷于探讨和表现这两个领域的关系。这是理解他的诗歌的关键所在。

史蒂文斯同艾略特(T. S. Eliot)和庞德(Ezra Pound)一样,最关心的问题是在这个道德沦丧、信仰动摇、孤独苦闷的现代世界中,艺术家的使命与艺术的价值究竟何在?支撑西方世界千余年的基督教传统价值及道德规范既已被摧毁殆尽,人们的精神空虚及信仰危机何以补偿?对于这些问题,诗人们的回答是不约而同的:现实中失去的秩序与信念可在艺术中重现,艺术家应象过去的教士乃至上帝那样,在这个迷惘的世界中为人们指明方向,作他们的精神向导。用史蒂文斯的话讲,诗人的职责在于"在人们的现实生活中肩负起自己的使命,并努力为他们和他本人创作出他们在这种生活中所需要的诗歌。"史蒂文斯的诗反复探讨想象力的作用。他认为诗人要从污秽的现实里发现美、快乐、意义和目的。在他看来,具有想象力的诗人是英雄般的诗人,诗歌是现代生活中的一种重要启示,它启示人们看到英雄主义,看到现代人正视现代生活的虚无性质,并赋予生活以秩序和意义,给人以勇气和力量。

在艺术上,史蒂文斯有自己的特色与追求。他有意识地与当时诗坛的各种运动保持适当的距离,他的诗歌所表现的中心主题是艺术(想象)与现实的关系。他认为艺术应稳固地根植于目前的现实生活中;艺术作为一种创造,只有以现实为基础方具有客观的真实价值,“梨的形象并不/依从观察者的愿望。”另一方面,现实生活的混乱和无意义也可通过艺术得到克服。史蒂文斯的这种探讨集中体现在诸如《关于高度虚构的笔记》(*Notes toward a Supreme Fiction*, 1942)等作品中。他极重视语言,并深挖语言的表现功能。他的诗风简洁,流畅自如,常常借用绘画与音乐的表现技巧,意象鲜明,内涵朦胧。他还故意不使用韵脚,以便读者对字面效果的欣赏与理解不受韵律流动的干扰。史蒂文斯和济慈一样,注意从感官角度描绘世界,他的诗有声有色,充满各种独特的意象。以颜色为例,蓝色在他的诗中为天的颜色,常代表想象、愿望;绿色代表大自然的生命活力;红色代表生命力和生殖力,等。在诸感官中,他最重视视觉,他的诗中充溢着各种视觉意象。只是到了后期,史蒂文斯的诗风才变得越来越富于沉思味道,令人感到费解。总的来说,史蒂文斯是美国诗歌史上对诗歌艺术追求最执着、成就也最大的伟大诗人之一。他对美国诗歌创作影响很大,当代诗人西奥多·罗特克(Theodore Roethke, 1908～1963)曾在一首诗中说,“噢弟兄们,他是我们的父亲!”这表明了年轻一代对他的景仰。

史蒂文斯应当说是一位“晚熟”的诗人。1923年他的第1部诗集《风琴》(*Harmonium*)出版时,诗人已经44岁了。他的主要作品有:《关于秩序的思想》(*The Idea of Orders*, 1935),《携蓝色吉他的人》(*The Man with the Blue Guitar*, 1937),《一个世界的某些部分》(*Parts of a World*, 1942),《转入夏季》(*Transport to Summer*, 1947),《秋天的晨曦》(*The Auroras of Autumn*, 1950),《诗集》(*Collected Poems*, 1945),《遗作集》(*Opus Posthumous*, 1957),以及文集《必不可少的安琪儿》(*The Necessary Angel*, 1951)等。

Anecdote of the Jar

〔作品介绍〕

《坛子的故事》(“Anecdote of the Jar”)所表现的可能是艺术的功能及其与现实的关系。坛子可能是艺术和想象力的象征;田纳西州的荒野是自然界的象征。当坛子站立在荒野上时,一个奇迹出现了:本来混乱无章的荒野(the slovenly wilderness)变得秩序井然。换言之,坛子为荒野带来形式、秩序和意义。诗人可能在说,人所见到的秩序是他自己造就的,他所生活的世界大多也是自己造就的。另一方面诗人又似乎在说,坛子作为人造的“艺术品”又与其周围的一切有所不同,它所以能发挥任何作用,又是因为有周围世界的存在,即四周的自然界对它有限制作用。

Anecdote of the Jar[1]

I placed a jar in Tennessee,[2]
And round it was, upon a hill.
It made the slovenly wilderness
Surround that hill.

The wilderness rose up to it,
And sprawled around, no longer wild.
The jar was round upon the ground
And tall and of a port in air.

It took dominion everywhere.
The jar was gray and bare.
It did not give of bird or bush,
Like nothing else in Tennessee.

〔注释〕

1. the Jar：坛子，一种陶器；在所有民族的文化史上，陶器和瓷器是人类艺术创造力的最佳体现。

2. I…Tennessee："I"可能指艺术的精神；Tennessee：田纳西州；诗人之所以提到这个州，可能是因为本世纪初在田纳西州突然出现了一批天才的作家和艺术家，如在1922年至1925年间活跃在该州纳什维尔市的"流亡派诗人"(the Fugitives)。从美学角度看，这些艺术家把艺术带到"艺术荒原"田纳西州，使其面貌被崇高的人类理解所改变。

The Idea of Order at Key West

〔作品介绍〕

《在基韦斯特的秩序的思考》("The Idea of Order at Key West")一诗表现

了艺术家通过想象赋予无形、流动不定的现实以秩序和形式，从而创造了一个新世界的艺术创作过程。诗中在海边歌唱的女孩可能代表进行艺术创造的诗人或任何人。该诗表明，人所了解的——真正了解的——唯一世界是他通过艺术想象所见到和理解的那个现实，其余一切都是流动不定、没有形式和意义的。诗的第1节描写一个女孩在咆哮的大海边唱歌。第2节讲女孩所唱的虽然是大海声音的再现或重复，但是大海的声音经过她（艺术家）的歌喉，便已脱离其自然的形体而成为艺术品（it was she and not the sea we heard）。第3节指出，之所以如此，是因为她是歌（艺术品）的创造者，而大海（自然界）仅是她的创造汲取素材、得以进行的场合而已。第4节说的是：产生于艺术与自然相互作用的艺术品，高于单纯的大海的声音或“她”和“我们”的声音。第5节是对诗人艺术观的直接陈述：艺术家被赋予了造物主的地位；对艺术家来讲，只有艺术所创造的世界才是真实的。第六节将艺术创造力比做夜间海上的灯光（方向与秩序的赋予者）。全诗以对创造秩序的艺术欲望（Blessed rage for order）之赞叹而结束。

The Idea of Order at Key West[1]

She sang beyond the genius of the sea.
The water never formed to mind or voice,
Like a body wholly body, fluttering
Its empty sleeves; and yet its mimic motion
Made constant cry, caused constantly a cry,
That was not ours although we understood,
Inhuman, of the veritable ocean.

The sea was not a mask. No more was she.
The song and water were not medleyed sound
Even if what she sang was what she heard,
Since what she sang was uttered word by word.
It may be that in all her phrases stirred
The grinding water and the gasping wind;
But it was she and not the sea we heard.

For she was the maker of the song she sang.
The ever-hooded, tragic-gestured sea

Was merely a place by which she walked to sing.
Whose spirit is this? we said, because we knew
It was the spirit that we sought and knew
That we should ask this often as she sang.

If it was only the dark voice of the sea
That rose, or even colored by many waves;
If it was only the outer voice of sky
And cloud, of the sunken coral water-walled,
However clear, it would have been deep air,
The heaving speech of air, a summer sound
Repeated in a summer without end
And sound alone. But it was more than that,
More even than her voice, and ours, among
The meaningless plungings of water and the wind,
Theatrical distances, bronze shadows heaped
On high horizons, mountainous atmospheres
Of sky and sea.

It was her voice that made
The sky acutest at its vanishing.
She measured to the hour its solitude.
She was the single artificer of the world
In which she sang. And when she sang, the sea,
Whatever self it had, became the self
That was her song, for she was the maker. Then we,
As we beheld her striding there alone,
Knew that there never was a world for her
Except the one she sang and, singing, made.

Ramon Fernandez,[2] tell me, if you know,
Why, when the singing ended and we turned
Toward the town, tell why the glassy lights,
The lights in the fishing boats at anchor there,
As the night descended, tilting in the air,
Mastered the night and portioned out the sea,
Fixing emblazoned zones and fiery poles,
Arranging, deepening, enchanting night.

Oh! Blessed rage for order, pale Ramon,
The maker's rage to order words of the sea,
Words of the fragrant portals, dimly-starred,
And of ourselves and of our origins,
In ghostlier demarcations, keener sounds.

〔注释〕

1. Key West：在美国佛罗里达州，是大西洋中的一个岛屿。

2. Ramon Fermandez (1894～1944)：法国批评家、随笔作家。史蒂文斯称此名系他所杜撰，与前者本人无关。

The Emperor of Ice-Cream

〔作品介绍〕

《冰淇淋王》(“The Emperor of Ice-Cream”)是一首挽歌。一个女人死了，挽歌颇具讽刺意味地要人“庆祝”。诗的第一节说，让生命的力量或上帝(the muscular roller of big cigars)继续激起人的激情吧；让风流少妇们穿着平常穿的艳丽服装闲荡吧；让少年们送来用旧报纸裹着的花束吧：诗人通常歌颂的一些价值在这里都呈现出琐碎和微不足道的状貌。诗里又说，至少这一次让人们认为具有变动能力的想象力停止活动，让我们看一看我们亲眼见到的悲惨事实吧。世上除了想象力——或曰头脑的冰淇淋，或曰冰淇淋王，或那位并非存在的“肌肉发达”的神——世上除了它如此天真而任意强加的秩序外，再没有别的秩序可言：这大概是第1节最后两行的含意。第2节直接表达见到死者时的惊恐心情。女人躺在那里，浑身冰冷，一动不动，绣有扇形尾巴鸽子图案的被单也没能盖住她那僵硬的脚。诗人似在说，无论艺术或是虔诚都不能欺骗人了。

史蒂文斯在谈到这首诗时曾说：“这（首诗）穿着故意做得寻常的衣服，然而在我看来却包含着诗歌的某种基本的艳丽。”诗中寻常的成份无疑是那些普通的人或物；诗的艳丽之处可能是诗行的声音，特别是压头韵的第3行和诗节结尾的重复句。

The Emperor of Ice-Cream

Call the roller of big cigars,
The muscular one, and bid him whip
In kitchen cups concupiscent curds.
Let the wenches dawdle in such dress
As they are used to wear, and let the boys
Bring flowers in last month's newspapers.
Let be be finale of seem. [1]
The only emperor is the emperor of ice-cream.

Take from the dresser of deal, [2]
Lacking the three glass knobs, that sheet
On which she embroidered fantails[3] once
And spread it so as to cover her face.
If her horny feet protrude, they come
To show how cold she is, and dumb.
Let the lamp affix its beam.
The only emperor is the emperor of ice-cream.

〔注释〕

1. Let be be finale of seem：让现实结束幻象吧。此句似为全诗的点睛之笔，表明诗人的立场：接受现实，接受女人已死去的现实。

2. dresser of deal：松木梳妆台。

3. fantails：一种尾巴展开时呈扇形的鸽子的专名。诗人自已解释此字时曾说："The word fantails does not mean fans, but fantail pigeons."

Sunday Morning

〔作品介绍〕

《星期天的早晨》(“Sunday Morning”)描绘一个女人在星期天早餐时刻沉思的景状。它写出她的见、闻、感觉和思绪，也夹杂诗人对她这些体验的评论；两者又常常相混合，产生一种微妙的艺术效果。在这首诗中，基督教的信念和态度与异教的观点和态度形成鲜明对比；异教的观点和态度是以对生活的深刻体验为基础的，其中也不乏对太阳和大自然的崇拜。诗主张人在生活许可的范围内尽量愉快地实现自我的价值，其语气不免有些悲伤的成份。对于死，诗的态度既凄伤，又冷静。这种复杂的感情使全诗具有一种独特的悲壮意味。这首诗表达了人与环境、与今世、与自己都要和谐无争的愿望，描绘了人为实现这种愿望而应体验的人与自然的协调、人与自然环境的相互依赖，以及通过对绝对价值的理解而应得到的对永恒的信念。

诗的第1节说“她”在安息日的早晨坐在阳光铺地的院中用早餐，在大自然的宁静和丰饶中，想到了死，想到了在巴勒斯坦遇难的耶稣。第2节说到她面对气象万千的自然界和自己的现实生活与情感，开始怀疑神圣和永恒是否只存在于黑暗和梦幻之中，进而认识到神圣性就存在于美丽的自然界和她的自身之中，这个现实世界是衡量她的心灵的尺寸。第3节谈“她”的思绪转移到古代神话中的主神宙斯，他虽为天神，但从未斩断尘缘；进而想到人神合一、人神不分世界的情状。第4节中“她”提出“除此尘世，天堂何在”的想法；诗人似发议论说，任何福地乐土都不如阳春的新绿那样永世长存。第5节谈到“她”虽然对尘世已感到满足，但仍渴望永恒的快乐，诗人似发议论说，死是美的发端，因为有了死才有更新可言。第6节似“她”的意识流，又似诗人的评论，惊叹天堂竟酷似人间。第7节更似诗人的评论，提出一种世俗的“宗教”，指出“人间乃天堂”之说。最后一节中“她”听到一个声音，意识到耶稣原来和人一样也是要死的，意识到尽管她渴求永恒的快乐，但她必须接受死的事实；诗人——或“她”——在谈到黄昏到来之时似乎很悲伤，然而他们又看到鸽子落地时的确有一种感人的高尚姿态。

这首诗之所以为后人称道，是因为史蒂文斯将上述思想用异常简明的语言与鲜明的意象表现出来，使全诗形淡而味浓，意深而不玄，并无他后期诗歌那种艰深难解之嫌。

Sunday Morning[1]

I

Complacencies of the peignoir, and late
Coffee and oranges in a sunny chair,
And the green freedom of a cockatoo
Upon a rug mingle to dissipate
The holy hush of ancient sacrifice.[2]
She dreams a little, and she feels the dark
Encroachment of that old catastrophe,[3]
As a calm darkens among water-lights.
The pungent oranges and bright, green wings
Seem things in some procession of the dead,
Winding across wide water, without sound.
The day is like wide water, without sound,
Stilled for the passing of her dreaming feet
Over the seas, to silent Palestine,
Dominion of the blood and sepulchre.[4]

II

Why should she give her bounty[5] to the dead?
What is divinity if it can come
Only in silent shadows and in dreams?
Shall she not find in comforts of the sun,
In pungent fruit and bright, green wings, or else
In any balm or beauty of the earth,
Things to be cherished like the thought of heaven?
Divinity must live within herself:
Passions of rain, or moods in falling snow;
Grievings in loneliness, or unsubdued
Elations when the forest blooms; gusty
Emotions on wet roads on autumn nights;
All pleasures and all pains, remembering

The bough of summer and the winter branch.
These are the measures destined for her soul.[6]

Ⅲ

Jove[7] in the clouds had his inhuman birth.
No mother suckled him, no sweet land gave
Large-mannered motions to his mythy mind
He moved among us, as a muttering king,
Magnificent, would move among his hinds,
Until our blood, commingling, virginal,
With heaven, brought such requital to desire
The very hinds discerned it, in a star.
Shall our blood fail? Or shall it come to be
The blood of paradise? And shall the earth
Seem all of paradise that we shall know?
The sky will be much friendlier then than now,
A part of labor and a part of pain,
And next in glory to enduring love,
Not this dividing and indifferent blue.

Ⅳ

She says, "I am content when wakened birds,
Before they fly, test the reality
Of misty fields, by their sweet questionings;
But when the birds are gone, and their warm fields
Return no more, where, then, is paradise?"
There is not any haunt of prophecy,
Nor any old chimera of the grave,[8]
Neither the golden underground, nor isle
Melodious, where spirits gat them home,[9]
Nor visionary south, nor cloudy palm
Remote on heaven's hill, that has endured
As April's green endures; or will endure
Like her remembrance of awakened birds,
Or her desire for June and evening, tipped
By the consummation of the swallow's wings.

V

She says, "But in contentment I still feel
The need of some imperishable bliss."
Death is the mother of beauty; hence from her,[10]
Alone, shall come fulfilment to our dreams
And our desires. Although she strews the leaves
Of sure obliteration on our paths,
The path sick sorrow took, the many paths
Where triumph rang its brassy phrase, or love
Whispered a little out of tenderness,
She makes the willow shiver in the sun
For maidens who were wont to sit and gaze
Upon the grass, relinquished to their feet.
She causes boys to pile new plums and pears
On disregarded plate.[11] The maidens taste
And stray impassioned in the littering leaves.

VI

Is there no change of death in paradise?
Does ripe fruit never fall? Or do the boughs
Hang always heavy in that perfect sky,
Unchanging, yet so like our perishing earth,[12]
With rivers like our own that seek for seas
They never find, the same receding shores
That never touch with inarticulate pang?
Why set the pear upon those river-banks
Or spice the shores with odors of the plum?
Alas, that they should wear our colors there,
The silken weavings of our afternoons,
And pick the strings of our insipid lutes!
Death is the mother of beauty, mystical,
Within whose burning bosom we devise
Our earthly mothers waiting, sleeplessly.

Ⅶ

Supple and turbulent, a ring of men
Shall chant in orgy on a summer morn
Their boisterous devotion to the sun,
Not as a god, but as a god might be,[13]
Naked among them, like a savage source.
Their chant shall be a chant of paradise,
Out of their blood, returning to the sky;
And in their chant shall enter, voice by voice,
The windy lake wherein their lord delights,
The trees, like serafin, and echoing hills,
That choir among themselves long afterward.[14]
They shall know well the heavenly fellowship
Of men that perish and of summer morn.
And whence they came and whither they shall go
The dew upon their feet shall manifest.

Ⅷ

She hears, upon that water without sound,
A voice that cries, "The tomb in Palestine
Is not the porch of spirits lingering.
It is the grave of Jesus, where he lay."[15]
We live in an old chaos of the sun,[16]
Or old dependency of day and night,[17]
Or island solitude, unsponsored, free,
Of that wide water,[18] inescapable.
Deer walk upon our mountains, and the quail
Whistle about us their spontaneous cries;
Sweet berries ripen in the wilderness;
And, in the isolation of the sky,
At evening, casual flocks of pigeons make
Ambiguous undulations as they sink,
Downward to darkness, on extended wings.

〔注释〕

1. 此诗最初发表于《诗刊》(*Poetry*)杂志(1915年),当时的编辑哈莉特

·门罗（Harriet Monroe）只刊印了其中5节；根据史蒂文斯的意见，当时的顺序是Ⅰ，Ⅷ，Ⅳ，Ⅴ，Ⅶ。后来此诗重印时，史蒂文斯恢复了原诗的格式。

2. ancient sacrifice：指耶稣遇难。

3. that old catastrophe：指死。

4. the blood and sepulchre：指耶稣的死和他的墓。

5. bounty：大自然的施舍。

6. the measures…for her soul：衡量她灵魂的尺寸；意她的神圣性和大自然、和今世分不开。

7. Jove：即古希腊神话中的主神宙斯。宙斯虽为天神，但他并未断尘缘，常和凡尘女子相爱，生出半人半神的英雄。

8. old chimera of the grave：对死后能进天堂的古老信念和幻想。

9. Neither…home：此处指福地乐土。the golden underground：可能指希腊神话中的 Elysium（死后所去的乐土），isle melodious：可能指 islands of the blest（海外福地）。

10. her：指 Death；本节下文中的“she”皆指 Death.

11. disregarded plate：久置不用的盘子。这个意象暗示死是一种解脱，又是一种更新的力量。前人不用的东西，后人又用上了。

12. Unchanging，yet so like our perishing earth：不变，可又这么象我们的不永恒的尘世。这里说天堂不变可又酷似人间。

13. Not as a god，but as a god might be：本节提出一种尘世的、和基督教成对比的“宗教”，这种宗教似有似无，实乃尘世生活本身。

14. And in their…afterward：指天人不分，天人合一。

15. It is the grave of Jesus，where he lay：言耶稣亦如凡人死后被埋葬。

16. in an old chaos of the sun：太古鸿蒙之时，远在基督教、甚至希腊神话产生之前。

17. old dependency of day and night：日夜相接不分。

18. that wide water：喻无边无际、无限制的生活。

WILLIAM CARLOS WILLIAMS

〔作者介绍〕

威廉·卡洛斯·威廉斯（William Carlos Williams，1883～1963），美国著名诗人。他出生在新泽西州的拉瑟福德区，就读于宾夕法尼亚州大学医科，后来赴德国学习儿科1年，回国后在故乡行医，直至1951年退休。威廉斯一生很少离开美国。20年代他曾两度赴欧作短期旅行，遇到了当时欧洲文坛的名作家叶芝、乔伊斯、瓦雷里等。在宾州大学学习期间，他曾结识埃兹拉·庞德，受到他的很大影响。1909年，他自费出版第1部诗集——《诗》（*Poems*），但没有引起世人的注意。1913年出版《气质》（*The Tempers*），初次显示出他的诗歌的特点。1923年，他的诗集《春天及一切》（*Spring and All*）问世后，威廉斯已成为美国诗坛的一位主要诗人。威廉斯一直保持着与欧美主要作家和画家的联系，从他们那里汲取自己所需要的艺术营养。他的《一篇中篇小说及其他散文作品》（*A Novelette and Other Prose*，1921～1931）反映出立体画派的影响；他的《柯拉在地狱中》（*Kora in Hell*，1920）体现出超现实主义的印记；此外，还有意象派诗歌的影响等。

1926年，威廉斯获《日轨》（*Dial*）奖，1950年获全国图书奖，1952年和诗人麦克勒什共获伯灵根奖，同年被任命为国会图书馆诗歌顾问，但后因被指责有左倾思想而未能到任。50年代初先后出版了他的《早期诗集》（*Collected Earlier Poems*）、《晚期诗集》（*Collected Later Poems*），短诗《沙漠音乐》（"The Desert Music"）和《爱的旅程》（"Journey to Love"）。1962年他的诗集《布鲁格尔的名画》（*Pictures from Breughel*）问世。威廉斯的最著名的诗作应推《红色手推车》（"The Red Wheelbarrow"），他迄今仍有"红色手推车诗人"之称。他的压卷作是长诗《佩特森》（*Paterson*），共5卷，自1946年首卷问世至1958年第5卷付梓，先后费时达10余年；1960年底拟写第6卷，未能如愿，便于1963年卒世。威廉斯还是一位小说家，写过《白骡》（*White Mule*）等三部曲；他还是一位剧作家，他的剧作收集在《爱情的梦及其他剧作》（*Many Loves and*

Other Plays，1961)。他的散文作品《美国性格》(*In the American Grain*，1925)，通过叙述拓荒者和作家的生平及作品，指出美国人特有的性格，美国人及美国作家所特有的文化和地理环境，强调了“本土”的重要性。威廉斯还写了《自传》(*Autobiography*，1951)，出版了《散文选》(*Selected Essays*，1954)及《书信选》(*Selected Letters*，1957)等著作。

威廉斯对文学创作有自己的独立见解。他对诗歌的性质、诗人的作用，以及诗歌创作，有着鲜明的、与T. S. 艾略特很不相同的观点。他之所以进行诗歌创作是因为他想写诗；他不认为自己必须得到当时诗坛的巨擘如艾略特、庞德及叶芝等人的承认才行。现代诗歌的明显特征之一是诗论的多元化。艾略特和威廉斯各代表着一种极端倾向。事实上，威廉斯一生都是反艾略特的，他花了许多时间抨击艾略特。他和艾略特的对抗至少从后者《荒原》(*The Waste Land*)一诗的发表时就开始了。他认为这是对美国自由诗歌的一种反动。威廉斯极不赞同庞德—艾略特式的“国际的”、旁征博引的、文人味十足的诗歌。他主张美国诗歌必须根植于美国本土，着眼于美国本土，这是美国诗歌创作灵感和素材的源泉；同时诗人的灵感和想象力必须根植于现实世界中。现实世界是一切艺术的基础。威廉斯认为，诗歌只有表现出乡土的状貌才能具有普遍的意义。他一生都致力于在乡土环境中寻觅艺术的原动力和基本原则，致力于通过诗歌再现美国的生活、美国的灵魂和美国的音乐。细细品味他的长诗《佩特森》和其它短诗，即可了解到他的这种苦心。

威廉斯坚决主张诗歌必须使用普通人的语言及这种活语言的韵律来表现日常生活，诗歌必须剥去一切虚饰，剔除一切哲理的、形而上学的议论，不可使之在诗歌中占有任何位置。威廉斯一生所写的最重要的一行诗应推《佩特森》第1卷里的“思想仅寓于事物中”(No ideas but in things)。他主张，写诗要用具体的事物来表达，诗人要通过具体事物进行艺术构思。诗人不应以玄妙为本，而应该象医生医治病人一样从具体和特殊出发，在特殊性中发现普遍性，发现现实世界与精神世界的关系，古和今的关系，用自己独特的方法表达富有创见的思想。对威廉斯来说，现实生活是诗人创作的起点和终点。经过诗人仔细观察和充分理解的具有各种细节和节奏的生活，其本身便是地道的诗歌。诗人如能忠于现实，坚持客观地反映现实，那么，他不用雕琢刻画，不用引经据典，生活的浑金璞玉自有其瑞彩仙气放射出来，诗的生命就会永葆青春。威廉斯认为，诗歌创作如果不是从生活、从现实世界，而是从书本和过去寻觅灵感，那么它就失去了自身存在的目的和意义。他坚信，如果自己背离对生活的信念，他便一定会绝望。而他一生的确总是着眼于他的祖国的。

威廉斯一生孜孜不倦地进行着自由体诗、“重音诗”(accentual verse)技巧方面的尝试。他认为，诗歌不应仿效《荒原》那样运用英诗传统的抑扬格，而应该运用实际语言的节奏，一种随重音而变化的节奏。他的努力取得了出色的成果：他创造了一种可以包罗各种情感、吸收各种经验的通俗文体。他成功地把诗歌变成生活里的语言。正如美国当代诗人罗伯特·洛厄尔(Robert Lowell) 1962 年所说的，除威廉斯外，没有任何其他的人看到了美国或听到了它的音乐。

公众对威廉斯的承认是在他创作生涯的后期。在很长的时间里，他仿佛生活在艾略特和庞德的阴影中。《荒原》出版后，威廉斯曾担心美国诗歌会改变方向，会从着眼于现实世界转变到在形而上学的基础上建立信念，会从形式的尝试折回到对诗律习俗的沿袭上去。事实证明，他的担心是不无根据的。艾略特的影响直到 60 年代才开始减弱，威廉斯诗歌才有机会发挥它的作用。综观美国当代诗坛，威廉斯的影响最广泛最深远。所有的主要流派，包括自白诗、黑山派、纽约派等，都承认他们受到了威廉斯的理论和实践的影响。他的声音已成为美国现当代诗歌史上的一个强音。

The Red Wheelbarrow

〔**作品介绍**〕

《红色手推车》(“The Red Wheelbarrow”)是威廉斯最著名的一首短诗，它充分体现了诗人的诗歌创作理论。威廉斯一生主张写实，反对抽象的逻辑周密的论述，认为客观事物本身就寓有诗意。一辆红轮子手推车，轮子刚在雨中滤过，一片晶亮中透出光艳照人的红色，又和站立在旁边咕咕啄土的一群小鸡的白色交相辉映，这在威廉斯看来是最美好不过的诗了。诗中几个简单的字如“手推车”、“水”、“鸡”等，被放在各行的关键位置上，一下子具有了一种在其他情况下它们所没有的意义。小诗以其特有的静物写生的特征感染着读者的想象力，使人们意识到，认识和体味存在于日常现实生活中的这种美，对生活和诗歌创作都是极重要的。这大概是本诗第 1 行的内涵所在。

The Red Wheelbarrow

so much depends
upon

a red wheel

barrow

glazed with rain
water

beside the white
chickens.

Spring and All

〔作品介绍〕

《春天及一切》（“Spring and All”）几乎通篇写观察和知觉。它旨在捕捉冬天即将离去然而又仍在徘徊、春天即将到来然而又仍在踌躇的那一瞬间。诗中没有描述早春的闲话和俗套，每行都充满感染读者视觉的活生生的意象，令人真切地意识到冬春交替时美妙的自然景象。本诗以其感人的视觉印象而著称，被认为是威廉斯在诗歌创作中把握客观性的醒目的例证。

Spring and All

By the road to the contagious hospital
under the surge of the bluc
mottled clouds driven from the
northeast—a cold wind. Beyond, the
waste of broad, muddy fields
brown with dried weeds, standing and fallen

patches of standing water
the scattering of all trees

All along the road the reddish
purplish, forked, upstanding, twiggy

stuff of bushes and small trees
with dead, brown leaves under them
leafless vines—

Lifeless in appearance, sluggish
dazed spring approaches—

They enter the new world naked,
cold, uncertain of all
save that they enter. All about them
the cold, familiar wind—

Now the grass, tomorrow
the stiff curl of wildcarrot leaf
One by one objects are defined—
It quickens: clarity, outline of leaf

But now the stark dignity of
entrance—Still, the profound change
has come upon them: rooted, they
grip down and begin to awaken

〔注释〕

1. 第1～8行：第1诗节描写诗的背景是在去传染病医院的路上，寒风、枯草、东倒西歪的树木，一派死气沉沉的景象。

2. 第9～19行：第2、3、4等诗节为过渡诗节，描写从死气沉沉到万物复苏的景状，二者并立，在没有生气的外表下面，在一片灰蒙蒙的景色中，业已出现了红色、紫色，灌木丛已吐出嫩枝幼叶。春天正从冬眠中醒来。

3. 第20～23行：生的景象已出现，春天开始迈步。

4. 第24～27行：最后一诗节表明整个自然周期的循环已开始。最后两行表现出诗人惊人敏锐的观察力。

Paterson

〔作品介绍〕

《佩特森》(*Paterson*)是威廉斯的代表作，共5卷，第1卷于1946年问世。当时威廉斯已在诗苑内笔耕近40载，他做为美国现代主要诗人的地位已稳定，他的诗作已开始对美国当代诗歌的发展进程发挥举足轻重的影响。最初，他计划写4卷：第1卷介绍“本土的自然特点”，第2卷描绘现代风景，第3卷寻求一种使之发出声音的语言，第4卷写瀑布下的河流及由此忆起的往事。第2、3、4卷分别于1948、1949和1951年出版之后，他发现自己叙述的乃是一个漫长的没有结尾的故事；同时他又希望在自己的心目中保留一个完整的佩特森的形象。于是又写了第5卷做为结尾，于1958年出版。然而，这仍不是结尾。1960年底和1961年初，威廉斯又开始计划写第6卷，并且逐步写了几页札记和草稿。但是他未能完成该卷，便于1963年去世了。

《佩特森》体现了威廉斯的美学观点。他通过写这首长诗，希冀寻觅一种可以体现他周围的可知世界的意象。他曾说：“我在故土自己生活的细节中居住得愈久，我便愈发现，需要把这些孤立的观察和体验汇总到一起，以获得‘深刻性’。”《佩特森》第2卷内有一行著名的诗：“我为什么要从这个地方搬走？/我是在这里降生的。”这一行诗明确表现出诗人对故土的无比深情和眷恋。他对早期田园般的佩特森的描绘，表现出他对故土的强烈热爱。他望见了河谷中的农田，望见了人民简朴的田园式生活，他们身穿家织衣服，自己饲养禽畜，室内是铺沙的地板，粗糙的家具，他们的生活虽有些原始，但却安静、快活。威廉斯在这里，在他的家乡——新泽西的佩特森，发现了艺术和诗歌的源泉。

《佩特森》在技巧上是革新的。它从容不迫地时而运用诗歌，时而运用散文，时而巧妙自然地加进自白、对话和书信，以其清新、飘逸的风格忠实地再现出生活自身恬静的节奏。长诗以极其灵活的形式包括了它所表现的诸多主题。威廉斯一生不断进行的自由体和重音诗（accentual verse）的尝试在长诗中开花结果了。他通过运用丰富的想象力，运用亲耳听到的语言，成功地把自己熟悉的周围环境和外貌，提高到具备新内涵的精神高度和境界。

这里选注的是长诗第1卷第1章。

Paterson

THE DELINEAMENTS OF THE GIANTS

I

Paterson lies in the valley under the Passaic Falls[1]
its spent waters forming the outline of his[2] back. He
lies on his right side, head near the thunder
of the waters filling his dreams! Eternally asleep,
his dreams walk about the city where he persists
incognito. Butterflies settle on his stone ear.
Immortal he neither moves nor rouses and is seldom
seen, though he breathes and the subtleties of his
        machinations
drawing their substance from the noise of the pouring
        river
animate a thousand automatons. Who because they
neither know their sources nor the sills of their
disappointments walk outside their bodies aimlessly
        for the most part,
locked and forgot in their desires—unroused.

    —Say it, no ideas but in things—
    nothing but the blank faces of the houses
    and cylindrical trees
    bent, forked by preconception and accident[3]—
    split, furrowed, creased, mottled, stained—
    secret—into the body of the light!

From above, higher than the spires, higher
even than the office towers, from oozy fields
abandoned to grey beds of dead grass,
black sumac, withered weed-stalks,

mud and thickets cluttered with dead leaves—
the river comes pouring in above the city
and crashes from the edge of the gorge
in a recoil of spray and rainbow mists—

(What common language to unravel?
• • combed into straight lines
from that rafter of a rock's
lip.)

A man like a city and a woman like a flower
—who are in love. Two women. Three women.
Innumerable women, each like a flower.

But
only one man—like a city.

In regard to the poems I left with you; will you be so kind as to return them to me at my new address? And without bothering to comment upon them if you should find that embarrassing—for it was the human situation and not the literary one that motivated my phone call and visit.

Besides, I know myself to be more the woman than the poet; and to concern myself less with the publishers of poetry than with•••living•••

But they set up an investigation•••and my doors are bolted forever (I hope forever) against all public welfare workers, professional dogooders and the like. [4]

Jostled as are the waters approaching
the brink, his thoughts
interlace, repel and cut under
rise rock-thwarted and turn aside
but forever strain forward—or strike
an eddy and whirl, marked by a
leaf or curdy spume, seeming
to forget
Retake later the advance and

are replaced by succeeding hordes
pushing forward—they coalesce now
glass-smooth with their swiftness,
quiet or seem to quiet as at the close
they leap to the conclusion and
fall, fall in air! as if
floating, relieved of their weight,
split apart, ribbons; dazed, drunk
with the catastrophe of the descent
floating unsupported
to hit the rocks: to a thunder,
as if lightning had struck

All lightness lost, weight regained in
the repulse, a fury of
escape driving them to rebound
upon those coming after—
keeping nevertheless to the stream, they
retake their course, the air full
of the tumult and of spray
connotative of the equal air, coeval,
filling the void[5]

And there, against him, stretches the low mountain.
The Park's her[6] head, carved, above the Falls, by the quiet
river; Colored crystals the secret of those rocks;
farms and ponds, laurel and the temperate wild cactus,
yellow flowered • • facing him,[7] his
arm supporting her, by the *Valley of the Rocks*, asleep.
Pearls at her ankles, her monstrous hair
spangled with apple-blossoms is scattered about into
the back country, waking their dreams—where the deer run
and the wood-duck nests protecting his gallant plumage.

In February 1857, David Hower, a poor shoemaker with a large family, out of work and money, collected a lot of mussels from Notch Brook near the City of Paterson. He found in eating them many hard substances. At first he threw them away but at last submitted some of them to a jeweler who gave him twenty-five to thirty dollars for the lot. Later he found others. One pearl of fine lustre was sold to Tiffany[8] for $900 and later to the Empress Eugenie[9] for $2,000 to be known thenceforth as the "Queen Pearl," the finest of its sort in the world today.

News of this sale created such excitement that search for the pearls was started throughout the country. The Unios (mussels) at Notch Brook and elsewhere were gathered by the millions and destroyed often with little or no result. A large round pearl, weighing 400 grains which would have been the finest pearl of modern times, was ruined by boiling open the shell.

Twice a month Paterson receives
communications from the Pope and Jacques
Barzun[10]
(Isocrates). His works
have been done into French
and Portuguese. And clerks in the post-
office ungum rare stamps from
his packages and steal them for their
childrens' albums

Say it! No ideas but in things. Mr.
Paterson has gone away
to rest and write. Inside the bus one sees
his thoughts sitting and standing. His
thoughts alight and scatter—

Who are these people (how complex
the mathematic) among whom I see myself
in the regularly ordered plateglass of
his thoughts, glimmering before shoes and bicycles?
They walk incommunicado, the
equation is beyond solution, yet
its sense is clear—that they may live
his thought is listed in the Telephone
Directory—

And derivatively, for the Great Falls,
PISS-AGH![11] the giant lets fly! good *Muncie*, too

They craved the miraculous!

A gentleman of the Revolutionary Army, after describing the Falls, thus describes another natural curiosity then existing in the community: In the afternoon we were invited to visit another curiosity in the neighborhood. This is a monster in human form, he is twenty-seven years of age, his face from the upper part of his forehead to the end of his chin, measures *twenty-seven inches*, and around the upper part of his head is twenty-one inches: his eyes and nose are remarkably large and prominent, chin long and pointed. His features are coarse, irregular and disgusting, his voice rough and sonorous. His body is twenty-seven inches in length, his limbs are small and much deformed, and he has the use of one hand only. He has never been able to sit up, as he cannot support the enormous weight of his head; but he is constantly in a large cradle, with his head supported in pillows. He is visited by great numbers of people, and is peculiarly fond of the company of clergymen, always inquiring for them among his visitors, and taking great pleasure in receiving religious instruction. General Washington made him a visit, and asked "whether he was a Whig or a Tory." He replied that he had never taken an active part on either side.

A wonder! A wonder!

From the ten houses Hamilton[12] saw when he looked (at the falls!) and kept his counsel, by the middle of the century—the mills had drawn a heterogeneous population. There were in 1870, native born 20,711, which would of course include children of foreign parents; foreign 12,868 of whom 237 were French, 1,420 German, 3,343 English—(Mr. Lambert who later built the Castle among them), 5,124 Irish, 879 Scotch, 1,360 Hollanders and 170 Swiss—

Around the falling waters the Furies hurl!
Violence gathers, spins in their heads summoning
them:

The twaalft,[13] or striped bass was also abundant, and even sturgeon, of a huge bigness, were frequently caught: —On Sunday, August 31, 1817, one seven feet six inches long, and weighing 126 pounds, was captured a short distance below the Falls basin. He was pelted with stones by boys until he was exhausted, whereupon one of them, John Winters, waded into the water and clambered on the back of the huge fish, while another seized him by the throat and gills, and brought him ashore. The *Bergen Express and Paterson Advertiser* of Wednesday, September 3, 1817, devoted half a column to an account of the incident, under the heading, "The Monster Taken."

They begin!

The perfections[14] are sharpened

The flower spreads its colored petals
wide in the sun
But the tongue of the bee
misses them
They sink back into the loam
crying out
—you may call it a cry
that creeps over them, a shiver
as they wilt and disappear:
Marriage[15] come to have a shuddering
implication

Crying out

or take a lesser satisfaction:
a few go
to the Coast without gain—
The language is missing them
they die also
incommunicado.[16]

The language, the language
fails them
They do not know the words
or have not
the courage to use them
—girls from
families that have decayed and
taken to the hills: no words.
They may look at the torrent in
their minds
and it is foreign to them.

They turn their backs
and grow faint—but recover!
Life is sweet

they say: the language!
—the language
is divorced from their minds,
the language· ·the language!

If there was not beauty, there was a strangeness and a bold association of wild and cultured life grew up together in the Ramapos:[17] two phases.

In the hills, where the brown trout slithered among the shallow stones, Ringwood—where the old Ryerson farm had been—among its velvet lawns, was ringed with forest trees, the butternut, and the elm, the white oak, the chestnut and the beech, the birches, the tupelo, the sweet-gum, the wild cherry and the hackleberry with its red tumbling fruit.

While in the forest clustered the ironworkers' cabins, the charcoal burners, the lime kiln workers—hidden from lovely Ringwood—where General Washington, gracing any poem, up from Pompton for rest after the traitors' hangings could be at ease—and the links were made for the great chain across the Hudson at West Point.[18]

Violence[19] broke out in Tennessee, a massacre by the Indians, hangings and exile—standing there on the scaffold waiting, sixty of them. The Tuscaroras,[20] forced to leave their country, were invited by the Six Nations[21] to join them in Upper New York. The bucks went on ahead but some of the women and the stragglers got no further than the valley-cleft near Suffern. They took to the mountains there where they were joined by Hessian deserters from the British Army, a number of albinos among them, escaped negro slaves and a lot of women and their brats released in New York City after the British had been forced to leave. They had them in a pen there—picked up in Liverpool and elsewhere by a man named Jackson under contract with the British Government to provide women for the soldiers in America.

The mixture ran in the woods and took the general name, Jackson's Whites. (There had been some blacks also, mixed in, some West Indian negresses, a shipload, to replace the whites lost when their ship, one of six coming from England, had foundered in a storm at sea. He had to make it up somehow and that was the quickest and cheapest way.)

New Barbadoes Neck, the region was called.

Cromwell, in the middle of the seventeenth century, shipped some thousands of Irish women and children to the Barbadoes to be sold as slaves. Forced by their owners to mate with the others these unfortunates were succeeded by a few generations of Irish-speaking negroes and mulattoes. And it is commonly asserted to this day the natives of Barbadoes speak with an Irish brogue.

I remember
a *Geographic*[22] picture, the 9 women

of some African chief semi-naked
astraddle a log, an official log to
be presumed, heads left:

Foremost
froze the young and latest,
erect, a proud queen, conscious of her power,
mud-caked, her monumental hair
slanted above the brows—violently frowning.

Behind her, packed tight up
in a descending scale of freshness
stiffened the others

and then . .
the last, the first wife,
present! supporting all the rest growing
up from her—whose careworn eyes
serious, menacing—but unabashed; breasts
sagging from hard use . .
Whereas the uppointed breasts
of that other, tense, charged with
pressures unrelieved.
and the rekindling they bespoke
was evident.

Not that the lightnings
do not stab at the mystery of a man
from both ends—and the middle, no matter
how much a chief he may be, rather the more
because of it, to destroy him at home

. . Womanlike, a vague smile,
unattached, floating like a pigeon
after a long flight to his cote.

Mrs. Sarah Cumming, consort of the Rev. Hopper Cumming, of Newark, was a daughter of the late Mr. John Emmons, of Portland, in the district of Maine. . . . She had been married about two months, and was blessed with a flattering prospect of no common share of Temporal felicity and usefulness in the sphere which Providence had assigned her; but oh, how uncertain is the continuance of every earthly joy.

On Saturday, the 20th of June, 1812, the Rev. Cumming rode with his wife to Paterson, in order to supply, by presbyterial appointment, a destitute congregation in that place, on the following day. . . . On Monday morning, he went with his beloved companion to show her the falls of the passaic, and the surrounding beautiful, wild and romantic scenery, —little expecting the solemn event to ensue.

Having ascended the flight of stairs (the Hundred Steps) Mr. and Mrs. Cumming walked over the solid ledge to the vicinity of the cataract, charmed with the wonderful prospect, and making various remarks upon the stupendous works of nature around them. At length they took their station on the brow of the solid rock, which overhangs the basin, six or eight rods from the falling water, where thousands have stood before, and where there is a fine view of the sublime curiosities of the place. When they had enjoyed the luxury of the scene for a considerable length of time, Mr. Cumming said, "My dear, I believe it is time for us to set our face homeward"; and at the same moment, turned round in order to lead the way. He instantly heard the voice of distress, looked back and his wife was gone!

Mr. Cumming's sensations on the distressing occasion may, in some measure, be conceived, but they cannot be described. He was on the borders of distraction, and, scarcely knowing what he did, would have plunged into the abyss, had it not been kindly ordered in providence that a young man should be near, who instantly flew to him, like a guardian angel, and held him from a step which his reason, at the time, could not have prevented. This young man led him from the precipice, and conducted him to the ground below the stairs. Mr. Cumming forced himself out of the hands of his protector, and ran with violence, in order to leap into the fatal flood. His young friend, however, caught him once more. . . . Immediate search was made, and diligently continued throughout the day, for the body of Mrs. Cumming; but to no purpose. On the following morning, her mortal part was found in a depth of 42 feet, and, the same day, was conveyed to Newark.

A false language. A true. A false language pouring—a
language (misunderstood) pouring (misinterpreted) without
dignity, without minister, crashing upon a stone ear. At least
it settled it for her. Patch[23] too, as a matter of fact. He
became a national hero in '28, '29 and toured the country
diving from cliffs and masts, rocks and brodges—to prove his
thesis: Some things can be done as well as others.

THE GRRRREAT HISTORY of that

old time Jersey Patriot

N. F. PATERSON!

(N for Noah; F for Faitoute; P for short)
"Jersey Lightning" to the boys.

So far everything had gone smoothly. The pulley and ropes were securely fastened on each side of the chasm, and everything made in readiness to pull the clumsy bridge into position. It was a wooden structure boarded up on both sides, and a roof. It was about two o'clock in the afternoon and a large crowd had gathered—a large crowd for that time, as the town only numbered about four thousand—to watch the bridge placed in position.

That day was a great day for old Paterson. It being Saturday, the mills were shut down, so to give the people a chance to celebrate. Among those who came in for a good part of the celebration was Sam Patch, then a resident in Paterson, who was a boss over cotton spinners in one of the mills. He was my boss, and many a time he gave me a cuff over the ears.

Well, this day the constables were on the look for Patch, because they thought he would be on a spree and cause trouble. Patch had declared so frequently that he would jump from the rocks that he was placed under arrest at various times. He had previously been locked up in the basement under the bank with a bad case of delirium tremens, but on the day the bridge was pulled across the chasm he was let out. Some thought he was crazy. They were not far wrong.

But the happiest man in the town that day was Timothy B. Crane, who had charge of the bridge. Tim Crane was a hotel keeper and kept a tavern on the Manchester side of the Falls. His place was a great resort for circus men. Such famous circus men of the long ago as Dan Rice and James Cooke, the great bareback rider, visited him.

Tim Crane built the bridge because his rival, Fyfield, who kept the tavern on the other side of the falls, was getting the benefit of the "Jacob's Ladder," as it was sometimes called—the "hundred steps," a long, rustic, winding stairs in the gorge leading to the opposite side of the river—it making his place more easy to get to. . . . Crane was a very robust man over six feet tall. He wore side whiskers. He was well known to the other citizens as a man of much energy and no little ability. In his manner he resembled the large, rugged stature of Sam Patch.

When the word was given to haul the bridge across the chasm, the crowd rent the air with cheers. But they had only pulled it half way over when one of the rolling pins slid from the ropes into the water below.

While all were expecting to see the big, clumsy bridge topple over and land in the chasm, as quick as a flash a form leaped out from the highest point and struck with a splash in the dark water below, swam to the wooden pin and brought it ashore. This was the starting point of Sam Patch's career as a famous jumper. I saw that, said the old man with satisfaction, and I don't believe there is another person in the town today who was an eye-witness of that scene. These were the words that Sam Patch said: "Now, old Tim Crane thinks he has done something great; but I can beat him." As he spoke he jumped.

There's no mistake in Sam Patch!

The water pouring still
from the edge of the rocks, filling
his ears with its sound, hard to interpret.
A wonder!

After this start he toured the West, his only companions a fox and a bear which he picked up in his travels.

He jumped from a rocky ledge at Goat Island into the Niagara River. Then he announced that before returning to the Jerseys he was going to show the West one final marvel. He would leap 125 feet from the falls of the Genesee River[24] on November 13, 1829. Excursions came from great distances in the United States and even from Canada to see the wonder.

A platform was built at the edge of the falls. He went to great trouble to ascertain the depth of the water below. He even successfully performed one practice leap.

On the day the crowds were gathered on all sides. He appeared and made a short speech as he was wont to do. A speech! What could he say that he must leap so desperately to complete it? And plunged toward the stream below. But instead of descending with a plummet-like fall his body wavered in the air—Speech had failed him. He was confused. The word had been drained of its meaning. There's no mistake in Sam Patch. He struck the water on his side and disappeared.

A great silence followed as the crowd stood spellbound.

Not until the following spring was the body found frozen in an ice-cake.

He threw his pet bear once from the cliff overlooking the Niagara rapids and rescued it after, down stream.

〔注释〕

1. the Passaic Falls：巴塞克河的瀑布。巴塞克河（the Passaic）位于新泽西州西北部。

2. his：指佩特森市。在长诗中，佩特森不仅是一座城市，也是一个人，一个团体的人。

3. preconception and accident：指自然的力量。

4. In regard to…and the like：这一段散文文字似乎是诗人写给出版社编辑的信。文中似表露出诗人对自己诗作所受的冷待和社会上右翼小报攻击的不满情绪。

5. Jostled as are…/…/filling the void：似在写河水奔流之状，又似写人的思潮在澎湃，两者交融，充分体现出诗人的“思想仅寓于事物中”的美学主张。

6. her：指上面的“the low mountain”。

7. him：指佩特森。

8. Tiffany：蒂凡尼（Charles Lewis Tiffany，1812～1902），美国珠宝商。

9. Empress Eugenie：法国王后，拿破伦三世之妻（1853～1871）。

10. Jacques Barzum：雅克·巴曾（1907～），美国教师、历史学家、作家，主张大学生应接受广泛的文科教育后再专业化。著作颇丰。有“艾索克拉底”（公元前436～338），雅典演说家）之称。

11. PISS-AGH：拟声字，指瀑布的声音。

12. Hamilton：汉密尔顿（Alexander Hamilton，1755～1804），华盛顿总统时代的财政部长。年轻时曾在新泽西州的伊丽莎白敦预科学校进修一年。

13. twaalft：即鲈鱼（striped bass）的方言名称。

14. The perfections：指花朵。

15. Marriage：指花瓣与泥土的结合。

16. they die also/incommunicado：以花之默默凋零喻人之不能表达自已。在《佩特森》这首长诗中，诗人常因自己发现了表达乡土特色的诗歌语言而自喜。

17. the Ramapos：阿巴拉契亚山脉的一段，位于新泽西州北部、纽约州南部。

18. General Washington…the Hudson at West Point：指1780年美国军官本尼迪克特·阿诺德（Benedict Arnold，1741～1801）叛变事件。阿诺德为得到位于哈德孙河西岸的西点军事区的指挥权，同英军私通，后事发，他的英国联络人约翰·安德烈少校被俘，以奸细罪被处死；阿诺德则逃到一只英国船上。这样，美军的行动才免受损失。

19. Violence：可能指美国印第安人移居法案（1830年通过）公布后，政府用武力迫使印第安人迁居而引起的包括佛罗里达州和田纳西州在内的东南部地区的动乱；一些州的印第安人曾武装反对迁居。

20. the Tuscaroras：图斯卡罗拉人，印第安人的一支，曾住在与田纳西州接壤的北卡罗来纳州，最繁盛时有5600人，现只剩下几百人，居住在纽约州和毗邻的加拿大各地。

21．the Six Nations：六族，为住在纽约州的五族（the Five Nations）印第安人和图斯卡罗拉族的合称；五族是莫霍克人（Mohawks）、奥内达人（Oneidas）、奥农达加人（Onondagas）、塞内卡人（Senecas）以及卡尤加人（Cayugas）。

22．*Geographic*：为 *National Geographic* 杂志的简称。

23．Patch：指 Sam Patch，关于他的事迹，见下文。

24． the Genesee River：杰纳西河，位于纽约州西部，向北流入安大略湖。

EZRA POUND

〔**作者介绍**〕

埃兹拉·庞德（Ezra Pound，1885～1972），美国著名诗人，生于爱达荷州海利市，在宾夕法尼亚州长大。他在哈密尔顿学院和宾州大学读书，主修罗曼司语言，饱读古典文学。在宾州大学学习期间，他结识了两位年轻诗人——威廉·卡洛斯·威廉斯和希尔达·杜利特尔（Hilda Doolittle）。他熟读英国诗人罗塞蒂（Dante Gabriel Rossetti，1828～1882）和史文朋（Algernon Charles Swinburne，1837～1909）的诗作，对勃朗宁（Robert Browning，1812～1889）钦仰备至，对惠特曼的重要性也开始有所认识；后来惠特曼的诗歌对他的文学创作产生了全面而持久的影响。

1908 年庞德到达欧洲，在威尼斯发表第一部诗集《灯光熄灭之时》（*A Lume Spento*）。之后，他回到伦敦，决心革新英诗，逐渐成为文学界活动的中心人物。他和 T. E. 休姆（T. E. Hulme，1883～1917）一起，发起意象新诗运动（Imagism），和理查德·奥尔丁顿（Richard Aldington，1892～1962）、希尔达·杜利特尔等人一起于 1912 年提出意象派诗歌创作三原则：(1) 直接描绘主观的或客观的“事物”；(2) 决不使用无助于表达的任何词语；(3) 关于节奏，依附于音乐性词语的顺序、而不是依照节拍的顺序进行写作。第 1 条旨在反对 19 世纪“丁尼生式”诗歌中抽象的道德训诫与浮华之风，反对任何解释和说明，主张用鲜明的意象，直接表达诗人的感受与体验。第 2 条主张言简意赅，剔除与意象无关的任何多余的成分。第 3 条说明，在韵律上，诗歌创作要突破英诗传统格律——五步抑扬格——的限制，追求一种更灵活的自由体；诗的音乐美在于句中字与字之间的错落起伏，而不是行与行之间的重复押韵。庞德在自己的创作中认真运用这些原则，他的《在地铁站里》（“In a Station of the Metro”）已成为意象诗的经典作品。在他的指导下，意象新诗运动，在英美诗歌史上谱写了重要的一章。

1914 年后，他又和画家温德姆·刘易斯（Windham Lewis，1882～1957）

一起发起“漩涡主义”(Vorticism)运动，主张创作以一种意象为中心的感染力强的诗歌。“漩涡主义”对庞德的长篇诗作《诗章》(*The Cantos*) 产生了深刻影响。在伦敦期间，庞德做为芝加哥小型杂志《诗歌》(*Poetry*) 驻欧洲的记者，竭力奖掖诗坛新秀，罗伯特·弗罗斯特、T·S·艾略特及玛丽安·门罗等诗人的脱颖而出，都和他的提携与赞助有关。他还影响过本世纪初便已功成名就的爱尔兰诗人叶芝(William Butler Yeats，1865～1939)。说庞德是本世纪前20年英美诗歌革新和复兴的主导力量，并不过分。在这期间，他发表了诗作《人物》(*Personae*，1909)、《狂喜》(*Exultations*，1909)、《向塞克斯特斯·普罗波蒂斯致敬》(*Homage to Sextus Propertius*，1917) 及《休·塞尔温·莫伯利》(*Hugh Selwyn Mauberley*，1920) 和译著《华夏》(*Cathay*，1915) 等。《华夏》是庞德所译的中国古诗集。

约在1915年，庞德开始创作他的鸿篇巨制《诗章》，1921年到巴黎后，继续这部长诗的写作。他同客居巴黎的美国作家格特鲁德·斯泰因等有所交往，对海明威等年轻作家不吝指导。1924年移居意大利的拉巴洛，悉心研究和创作，《诗章》的写作出现长足进展。30年代初，他愈益相信墨索里尼代表着建设性的鼓舞人心的力量可以消除贫苦、疾病和流血。第二次世界大战期间，他在罗马电台多次发表亲法西斯、反犹太种族的演说，战后被捕，以判国罪被押回美国受审判，不料经过医院检查，被宣布为精神失常，在华盛顿的圣伊丽莎白精神病院长住12年之久。其间他在比萨牢笼里书写的《比萨诗章》(*the Pisan Cantos*) 于1948年获柏林根诗歌奖，使文学界为之哗然。后来，经过诸如弗罗斯特、艾略特及海明威等著名文豪的多方努力，庞德终于在1958年获释回意大利。《诗章》经过他长达半个世纪的惨淡经营，数目已达100余篇。庞德回首几十年的荣枯得丧，承认自已一生的失败，行将就木之前很有一种“风高花闲满地黄”的凄凉之感。1972年，他在威尼斯病逝，享年87岁。

庞德是英美现代诗坛一位巨匠。他谙熟古今，善于旁搜博采，撷取各国文明之长以为已用。他的诗作突出地体现出古希腊、古意大利、古英诗以及法国中世纪普罗旺斯诗歌传统的影响。庞德还是中国古代文明的歌颂者，对孔子的思想非常崇拜；他似乎从中国文明中看到了现代西方所急需的理智和理想。庞德对中国文化的认识始于1913年，当时他结识了美国著名东方学者厄内斯特·凡诺洛萨(Ernest Fenollosa，1853～1908)的遗孀，后者把丈夫的东方文化研究手稿交付他收藏。其后几十年内，庞德不断研究中国文学与诗歌，探索孔子哲学的真谛。象形表意的汉字和充满意象的中国古代诗歌对庞德的诗歌创作产生了深刻影响，孔子哲学的基本思想成为贯穿《诗章》的主导精神。庞德认真翻译过《四书》和《诗经》，对在西方传播孔学起过一定作用；然而由于他的诗人性格和不很懂中文两种原因，他的译文错讹遗漏之处甚多。

庞德一生著作甚多。除诗作外，还有不少散文作品，如《罗曼司精神》(*The Spirit of Romance*，1910)、《要革新》(*Make It New*，1934)、《阅读入门》(*ABC of Reading*，1934)、《文化指南》(*Guide to Kulchur*，1938)、《影响：论愚昧和美国文明的衰落》(*Impact*：*Essays on Ignorance and the Decline of American Civilization*，1960)及由诗人艾略特编辑的《埃兹拉·庞德的文学论文集》(*The Literary Essays of Ezra Pound*，1954)等。

A Pact

〔作品介绍〕

《协约》("A Pact")一诗表明了庞德对惠特曼较全面的理解和评价。惠特曼对生活所采取的积极和乐观态度，在本世纪曾引起包括庞德在内的许多诗人的不满。然而，他在革新美国诗歌形式和内容方面所做的贡献，及在这些方面对包括庞德在内的后代诗人的影响，是毋容置疑的。庞德对惠特曼的认识经历了一个从厌恶到承认的过程。

A Pact

I make a pact with you, Walt Whitman—
I have detested you long enough.
I come to you as a grown child
Who has had a pig-headed father;[1]
I am old enough now to make friends.
It was you that broke the new wood,[2]
Now is a time for carving.[3]
We have one sap and one root—
Let there be commerce between us.

〔注释〕

1. a pig-headed father：指惠特曼。
2. broke the new wood：劈开新木；指创新。
3. carving：雕琢；指进一步创新。

In a Station of the Metro

〔作品介绍〕

《在地铁站里》(“In a Station of the Metro”)是意象主义诗歌的一首上乘佳作。1913年的某天，诗人从巴黎的协约车站走出潮湿幽暗的地铁。他在忽明忽暗的熙攘的人群里，看到了几个美丽的面孔，几个女人和儿童的美丽面孔。这一场景给他留下极为深刻的印象。他开始搜索枯肠，几经努力，曾写成130余行的诗，终因不如意而销毁。一年之后，他才写下了两行充满内在活力的日本俳句式的诗。

在这首诗中，诗人运用的意象是“阴湿的树枝上面的几片花瓣”。他用阴湿的树枝比喻潮湿幽暗的地铁，用鲜艳的花瓣形容人的美丽脸庞，从而捕捉住事物的形象，几笔便勾勒出两幅气氛融洽的画面，写出了比兴恰切的精妙诗句。

In a Station of the Metro

The apparition of these faces in the crowd;
Petals on a wet, black bough.

The River-Merchant's Wife: A Letter

〔作品介绍〕

《船商的妻子：一封信》(“The River-Merchant's Wife: A Letter”)是庞德根据美国东方文化学者厄内斯特·凡诺洛萨的研究手稿所译的李白《长干行》一诗，后收入庞德编译的诗集《华夏》中。

这首译诗，如庞德所译的其他中国古诗一样，有不少欠贴切之处，读时应注意。

The River-Merchant's Wife: A Letter

While my hair was still cut straight across my forehead
I played about the front gate, pulling flowers.
You came by on bamboo stilts, playing horse,
You walked about my seat, playing with blue plums.
And we went on living in the village of Chokan:
Two small people, without dislike or suspicion.

At fourteen I married My Lord you.
I never laughed, being bashful.
Lowering my head, I looked at the wall.
Called to, a thousand times, I never looked back.

At fifteen I stopped scowling,
I desired my dust to be mingled with yours
Forever and forever and forever.
Why should I climb the look out?

At sixteen you departed,
You went into far Ku-to-yen, by the river of swirling eddies,
And you have been gone five months.
The monkeys make sorrowful noise overhead.

You dragged your feet when you went out.
By the gate now, the moss is grown, the different mosses,
Too deep to clear them away!
The leaves fall early this autumn, in wind.
The paired butterflies are already yellow with August
Over the grass in the West garden;

They hurt me. I grow older.
If you are coming down through the narrows of the
    river Kiang,
Please let me know beforehand,
And I will come out to meet you
                As far as Cho-fu-Sa.

By Rihaku[1]

〔注释〕

1. Rihaku：李白的日文名。

Hugh Selwyn Mauberley

〔作品介绍〕

《休·塞尔温·莫伯利》(*Hugh Selwyn Mauberley*)被认为是庞德的最优秀的作品。它写的是艺术的商业化和贬值，艺术家的失望和失败，以及诗人本人的思想。这首诗里不少成份说明，它具有明显的自传性质。它痛苦地记录了诗人从拒绝写“利于社会”的诗（如他在《向塞克斯特斯·普罗波蒂斯致敬》一诗中所表明的那样）到最后懂得唯美主义在现代世界上行不通这样一个转变过程。全诗共由两部分组成：第1部分共有13首诗，第2部分包括5首诗。第1部分第1首诗写诗人对自己的自我流放和象征性死亡的思考；第2、3首写艺术和现代文明的堕落；第4、5首哀叹价值的衰颓，第一次世界大战的残酷；此后的7首诗回顾了19世纪80年代以来西方的文学历史状况，说明了艺术家的离异和降格；在最后一首诗中，诗人重申对美的信念和对艺术的献身精神。总的说来，第1部分描绘了诗人在一个冷漠世界中的不断追求。

第2部分依然写诗人的追求，但层次有所不同。诗人在追求，希冀找到他的真正的家——他的伊大卡（Ithaca）和彭妮洛佩（Penelope），然而最后他却发现，他的“真正的彭妮洛佩”是福楼拜（Flaubert）的真正艺术，即现代世界上的真正古典主义；而这种美是脆弱的，不为人所欣赏的。诗人感到失望，将视线转向内心世界，孤独感于是油然而生。他开始怀疑艺术的作用，认识到自己的艺术的不完善之处。他不相信自己会离开艺术世界；又觉得世界既不能理解和欣赏他，他也不可能为之效力。

该诗淋漓尽致地勾勒了艺术家在现代世界里的困境。

这里选注的是该诗第1部分第1首。

Hugh Selwyn Mauberley

(LIFE AND CONTACTS)

I

E. P. ODE POUR L'ELECTION DE SON SEPULCHRE[1]

For three years, out of key with his time,
He strove to resuscitate the dead art
Of poetry; to maintain "the sublime"
In the old sense. Wrong from the start[2]—

No, hardly, but seeing he had been born
In a half savage country,[3] out of date;
Bent resolutely on wringing lilies from the acorn;
Capaneus;[4] trout for factitious bait;

'Ἴδμεν γάρ τοι πάνθ', ὅσ' ἐνὶ Τροίῃ[5]
Caught in the unstopped ear;[6]
Giving the rocks small lee-way
The chopped seas held him, therefore, that year.

His true Penelope was Flaubert,[7]
He fished by obstinate isles;
Observed the elegance of Circe's[8] hair
Rather than the mottoes on sun-dials.

Unaffected by "the march of events,"
He passed from men's memory in *l'an trentiesme*
De son eage;[9] the case presents
No adjunct to the Muses' diadem.

〔注释〕

1. E. P. …Sepulchre：法文，英文为“E. P. (Ezra Pound) Ode on the Choice of His Tomb”。此句引自法国诗人龙沙（Pierre de Ronsard，1524～1585）的挽歌“De l'élection de son sépulchre”。

2. For three…start：写庞德本世纪初到欧洲痛切地感到艺术的衰落，有必要革新艺术，特别是诗歌，使之担负起它应起到的责任。

3. a half savage country：指美国。美国作家自19世纪的欧文、霍桑开始，一直有人认为美国和欧洲相比较在文化上是贫瘠的，是不利于文学创作的。

4. Capaneus：希腊神话中攻打底比斯国的七英雄之一，后因反抗主神宙斯被雷击死。

5. 希腊文，英文为“For we know everything that is in Troy”，引自荷马史诗《奥德赛》第12章第189行。

6. Caught…ear：指古希腊英雄奥德修斯在特洛伊战争结束后回国途中遇到一群海妖——塞壬(the Sirens)，她们的美妙歌声曾把许多航海者引向死亡。奥德修斯听了锡西（Circe）的劝告，事前让人把自己绑到船杆上，把水手的耳朵用蜡堵住，从而既听到了塞壬的歌声，又使船平安驶离险滩。

7. His true…Flaubert：Penelope，彭妮洛佩，奥德修斯的妻子；Flaubert：福楼拜（Gustave Flaubert，1821～1880），法国小说家。

8. Circe：锡西，奥德修斯回国途中遇到的女巫，曾把他的同伴变成猪。

9. L'an trentiesme/De son eage：法文，英文为“the thirtieth year of his life”，引自法国诗人维雍(Francois Villon，1431～1463?)的《遗嘱》(“Le Testament”)一诗。

Cantos

〔作品介绍〕

庞德的著述颇多，他的代表作应推长近千页的《诗章》(*Cantos*)。《诗章》由120章组成。这首耗费了诗人大半生的长诗是庞德“1915年后的思想日记”。它记录了诗人在长达半个世纪时间内的经历和见地。恰如交响乐的乐章一样，它可分成不同诗组。前6章确定诗中讲话人的身份为奥德修斯—庞德；第7章似为过渡章。第8至11章为《文艺复兴章》，14至16章为《地狱章》，把西方现代社会比做腐败、肮脏的地府。第13章援引孔子关于“秩序”的论述，使前面诸章内的污浊空气一扫而光，让读者抬首望到天堂般的光辉与安谧气氛（16～17章）。此后10余章总结、强调已谈到的主题，为后面阐述诸如约翰·亚当斯等美国开国元老的社会经济原则（30～41章、62～71章或亚当斯章）埋下伏笔。这些章是一组现代资本主义经济活动的特写境头。第49章引用中国古典诗歌与古代舜王时的《卿云歌》，第52章为《礼记》的意译，而53～61章则是著名的《中国章》，简述自古至清代乾隆帝时的中国历史，都表现出诗人渴求天下大治的愿望。《比萨章》（74～84章）与《石钻章》（85～95章）把读者首次带入现当代生活，是诗人在极度痛苦、经历了深思熟虑之后的基本态度的总结。《列王章》（96～109章）及《草稿与片断》（110～120章）在对现代西方精神"荒原"的巨画作进一步描绘之后结束长诗。

《诗章》在不少方面体现出现代诗的共同特点。面对以混乱和支离破碎为特点的现代生活的挑战，现代诗人在其诗作中都表现出一种寻求秩序和意义的强烈愿望。《诗章》同艾略特的《荒原》（*The Waste Land*）、哈特·克兰（Hart Crane）的《桥》（*The Bridge*）等诗一样，具有史诗般的长度，由许多在形式上并无联系，但内容却统一的独立部分组成，每部分都表现某种凌乱的经历、事件或情景，其效果宛如交响乐一般。"寻求"的主题在各部分反复出现，给混乱带来秩序，使支离破碎状态呈现为新的整体。《诗章》又和不少其他现代诗作一样，借用过去和传统来烘托和加强"寻求"的气氛。因此，这首由120章组成的长诗便产生了如艾略特在其《荒原》第5章内所说的"这些片断我用来支持我的残垣断壁"、以及他所说的现代作家应当"通过古今对比给当代生活无能和混乱的巨幅全景以形式和意义"的艺术效果。

《诗章》是美国现代诗歌的巨著，不乏优美的抒情笔墨和铿然有力的辩辞。庞德善取多种文化之长，将其熔为一炉，说《诗章》是由多种成份熔铸锤炼而成是有道理的。通篇用典，多种语言的出现，在增加诗的韵味和创设诗的意境的同时，也自然增加了理解该诗的难度。所以，庞德的这首长诗即便是英美学者也多望而却步，敬而远之，时至今日，也无人敢说全无疑难之处了。

这里选注的是该诗第4章。

Cantos

Ⅳ

Palace in smoky light,
Troy but a heap of smouldering boundary stones,
ANAXIFORMINGES! Aurunculeia!
Hear me. Cadmus of Golden Prows!

The silver mirrors catch the bright stones and flare,
Dawn, to our waking, drifts in the green cool light;
Dew-haze blurs, in the grass, pale ankles moving.
Beat, beat, whirr, thud, in the soft turf
        under the apple trees,
Choros nympharum, goat-foot, with the pale foot alternate;
Crescent of blue-shot waters, green-gold in the shallows,
A black cock crows in the sea-foam;

And by the curved, carved foot of the couch,
        claw-foot and lion head, an old man seated
Speaking in the low drone... :
            Ityn!
Et ter flebiliter, Ityn, Ityn!
And she went toward the window and cast her down,
            'All the while, the while, swallows crying:
Ityn!
            'It is Cabestan's heart in the dish.'
            'It is Cabestan's heart in the dish?
            'No other taste shall change this.'
And she went toward the window,
                the slim white stone bar
Making a double arch;
Firm even fingers held to the firm pale stone;
Swung for a moment,
                and the wind out of Rhodez
Caught in the full of her sleeve.
        ... the swallows crying:
'Tis. 'Tis. Ytis!
        Actæon...
                and a valley,
The valley is thick with leaves, with leaves, the trees,
The sunlight glitters, glitters a-top,
Like a fish-scale roof,
                Like the church roof in Poictiers
If it were gold.
                Beneath it, beneath it

Not a ray, not a slivver, not a spare disc of sunlight
Flaking the black, soft water;
Bathing the body of nymphs, of nymphs, and Diana,
Nymphs, white-gathered about her, and the air, air,
Shaking, air alight with the goddess,
        fanning their hair in the dark,
Lifting, lifting and waffing:
Ivory dipping in silver,
        Shadow'd, o'ershadow'd
Ivory dipping in silver,
Not a splotch, not a lost shatter of sunlight.
Then Actæon: Vidal,
Vidal. It is old Vidal speaking,
        stumbling along in the wood,
Not a patch, not a lost shimmer of sunlight,
        the pale hair of the goddess.

The dogs leap on Actæon,
        'Hither, hither, Actæon,'
Spotted stag of the wood;
Gold, gold, a sheaf of hair,
        Thick like a wheat swath,
Blaze, blaze in the sun,
        The dogs leap on Actæon.
Stumbling, stumbling along in the wood,
Muttering, muttering Ovid:
        'Pergusa... pool... pool... Gargaphia,
'Pool... pool of Salmacis.'
        The empty armour shakes as the cygnet moves.

Thus the light rains, thus pours, *e lo soleils plovil*
The liquid and rushing crystal
        beneath the knees of the gods.
Ply over ply, thin glitter of water;
Brook film bearing white petals.
The pines at Takasago
        grow with the pines of Isé!

The water whirls up the bright pale sand in the spring's mouth
'Behold the Tree of the Visages!'
Forked branch-tips, flaming as if with lotus.
        Ply over ply
The shallow eddying fluid,
        beneath the knees of the gods.

Torches melt in the glare
        set flame of the corner cook-stall,
Blue agate casing the sky (as at Gourdon that time)
        the sputter of resin,
Saffron sandal so petals the narrow foot: Hymenæus Io!
        Hymen, Io Hymenæe! Aurunculeia!
A scarlet flower is cast on the blanch-white stone.

        And So-Gioku, saying:
'This wind, sire, is the king's wind,
        This wind is wind of the palace,
Shaking imperial water-jets.'
        And Ran-ti, opening his collar:
'This wind roars in the earth's bag,
        it lays the water with rushes;
No wind is the king's wind.
        Let every cow keep her calf.'
'This wind is held in gauze curtains...'
        'No wind is the king's...'

The camel drivers sit in the turn of the stairs,
        Look down on Ecbatan of plotted streets,
'Danaë! Danaë!
        What wind is the king's?'
Smoke hangs on the stream,
The peach-trees shed bright leaves in the water,
Sound drifts in the evening haze,
        The barge scrapes at the ford,
Gilt rafters above black water,
        Three steps in an open field,

Gray stone-posts leading...

Père Henri Jacques would speak with the Sennin, on Rokku,
Mount Rokku between the rock and the cedars,
Polhonac,
As Gyges on Thracian platter set the feast,
Cabestan, Terreus,
        It is Cabestan's heart in the dish,
Vidal, or Ecbatan, upon the gilded tower in Ecbatan
Lay the god's bride, lay ever, waiting the golden rain.
By Garonne. 'Saave!'
The Garonne is thick like paint,
Procession, — 'Et sa'ave, sa'ave, sa'are Regina!' —
Moves like a worm, in the crowd.
Adige, thin film of images,
Across the Adige, by Stefano, Madonna in hortulo,
As Cavalcanti had seen her.
        The Centaur's heel plants in the earth loam.
And we sit here...
        there in the arena...

〔注释〕

Canto Ⅳ

第1～2行：描述特洛伊城陷落后全城一片火海的景象。据希腊传说，古代希腊和位于小亚细亚的特洛伊国交战达10年，最后希腊人巧施木马计，里应外合攻破特洛伊城，杀其王，灭其国，把王后及王室成员掳做奴隶。庞德显然是以古罗马诗人维吉尔（Virgil）的史诗《伊尼德》（*Aeneid*）第2章第417～420行为本章第1～2行的底本的。维吉尔的诗说：

> The Palace of Deiphobus ascends/In smoky flame, and catches on his frierds/Ucalegon burns next: seas are bright/with splendeur, not their own, and shine with Trojan light.
>
> （狄弗布斯宫翻腾起浓烟滚滚的火焰，点燃起它的朋友，/乌卡勒宫接着起火：海面通明，/不是由于自身的光辉，/而是借助于特洛伊的火光。）

第2行颇有T. S. 艾略特的《荒原》一诗第1章第22行内“一堆支离破碎的形象”的意味。

第3行："Anaxiforminges"为古希腊诗人品达（Pindar，522～443B. C.）第2首奥林匹克颂的序诗的音译。品达的原文是：

Hymns that are Lords of the lyre,
What god, what here, what man
　　　　　　shall we sing of?

（琴的主人呀，颂歌，
我们要歌颂
哪一位天神、英雄或勇士？）

"Aurunculeia"即 Vinia Aurunculeia（维尼娅·奥伦库莱娅），是古罗马诗人卡塔拉斯（Catullus，84～54B. C.?）的新婚曲中幸福新娘的名字。因此，本诗第3行可意译为：

琴的主人呀，我们要歌颂什么？
女人！

Canto Ⅳ 的主题是女人与爱情对生活和命运的影响。忠贞、幸福的奥伦库莱娅和本诗中谈及的其他女人形成鲜明对比。

第4行：这是女神雅典娜对卡德摩斯讲话。据希腊神话，古底比斯城的建造者卡德摩斯应雅典娜之召乘金船前来，奉命把守卫底比斯国迪尔西泉的巨龙杀死，把龙牙播入地中，其后一批武士破土而出，要斩杀他。雅典娜指点他把一宝石扔入武士们中间，引起众武士相互残杀，后来仅剩五名，他们帮助卡德摩斯建起底比斯城。古罗马诗人奥维德（Ovid，48 B. C. ～17 A. D.）在其《变形记》（*Metamorphoses*）中讲了这段故事，本行说的是女神突然命令卡德摩斯前来的一节。庞德在《诗章》里把卡德摩斯描绘成一名英雄水手，是后文里奥德修斯及迦太基将领汉诺的先驱。本行同第2行形成对比：卡德摩斯遵照神示获得成功，特洛伊城则因悖逆天启而被夷为平地。

第1～4行诗概括了第4章的基本内容，堪称为点睛之笔。

第5～12行：在第4章内共有3个自然抒情片断，即"晨曲"（第5～12行）、"午曲"（第68～80行）及"夜曲"（第103～109行）。诗人以独特的形象和绚丽的词藻，细腻地描绘了不同时间内光的变化，并为全章中多种典故提供了巧妙的支架。

第5行：拂晓清亮的月光俯照在光滑的石面上，石面仿佛是一面面银光闪闪的明镜熠熠生辉。

第6～9行：晨光清冷，透过绿草叶上模糊的露珠看到白晰的脚腕在苹果树下柔软的草地上"啪嗒、啪嗒"地移动。这是讲话人清晨醒来时，躺着透过青草露珠所见到的景象。4个拟声字突然表现出生命脉搏的跳动。apple trees 为爱神维纳斯的圣树。

第10行：choros nympharum 意"仙女之舞"；goat foot 指酒神狄俄尼索斯的狂欢伙伴——好色的人身羊足的森林之神；pale foot 指月亮女神的贞洁、美丽的侍女。色鬼和淑女的混舞给人一种不祥之感。

第11行：月牙状的碎波细浪在晨曦中如翠绿上镀了一层金光；crescent 似暗指新月状或镰刀形的剑，希腊神话中克洛诺斯（Kronus）便是手持此剑阉割其父尤冉诺斯（Uranus）的。不祥之感遂递增。

第12行：一只黑色公鸡的啼鸣声透过岸边细浪的窃窃细语而传入读者的耳中；a black cock，双关语，明显的性形象；sea foam 暗指爱神维纳斯，据希腊神话，这位女神由海里出生，是“放荡不羁的欲望”的象征。

“晨曲”由熹微的“天光”写起，以暗示爱情和欲望的凶恶的一面结束，镰形剑和维纳斯为后面对不贞之爱及非分之想所引起的暴力、兽行及死亡的描写埋下伏笔。

第13～32行：这20行诗的连贯意象是燕子的悲叫声。庞德的典故主要来自古罗马抒情诗人贺拉斯（Horace，约65～8 B.C.）的诗作。

第13～15行：写吊唁者——一个老者坐在床边悼念，亲人老泪横流、暗然神伤的景状。老者指古雅典王潘底庸（Pandion）。据希腊神话，雅典被包围，色雷斯王提列欧斯（Tereus）前来救援，雅典王遂将长女普洛克尼（Procne）嫁之以示谢意。普洛克尼生一子名伊提拉斯（Itylus），后因思乡求丈夫去雅典接妹妹菲洛米拉（Philomela）前来小住。回来路上提列欧斯慕妻妹之貌，欲火中烧，将她奸污后割其舌，囚于林中，以防败露。菲洛米拉把苦难经历绣入一块织锦，托人送给姐姐。普洛克尼大怒，救出妹妹，杀掉儿子，以其肉做筵席献给提列欧斯。提列欧斯发现事败，持剑追杀两姐妹。万分危急之际，天神把普洛克尼变做燕子，菲洛米拉变做夜莺，把提列欧斯变成凶鹰。潘底庸顿时失去两女及外孙3位亲人。英美许多著名诗人都以这个故事为题材写过不朽的诗篇，如柯勒律治、阿诺德、史文朋和 T. S. 艾略特便是适例。史文朋的《伊提拉斯》（“Itylus”）一诗开首处的“燕子呀，我的姐姐，啊，燕子姐姐！”一句很可能是庞德这几行诗的灵感来源。

claw-foot and lion head：指床上雕刻的吐火女怪（Chimera）形状的装饰物；据希腊神话，这是一个具有狮头、羊身和龙尾的神妖。an old man：指潘底庸。

第16～17行：Ityn＝Itylus：Et ter flebiliter，Ityn，Ityn，引自贺拉斯《春光颂》，意“三行泪下”，一说老国王既哭外孙伊提拉斯，又哀悼二女的变形；一说为变做燕子的普洛克尼为自己失去妹妹、儿子和丈夫而悲伤不已。

第18～32行：据普罗旺斯传说，雷蒙（Raymond de Chateau Roussillon）出于嫉恨，杀死妻子索洛蒙达夫人（Soremonda）的情夫、吟游歌手卡贝斯坦（Guillem da Cabestan），雷蒙以其心做菜“奉献”给妻子，索洛蒙达发现后誓不再食，旋即跳楼自尽。

第18行：she 指索洛蒙达；她在跳楼。

第19～20行：点出了普洛克尼和雷蒙两者禽兽般罪行的基本相似之处。

第21～22行：透露出自杀的女人的身份。

第23行：索洛蒙达夫人得知吃掉情人的心后，以一种悲剧女主人公的傲岸宣称此后再也不吃任何食物，使洋洋自得的丈夫惊诧不已。

第24～30行：这是索洛蒙达跳楼的慢镜头。诗人以摄影机般的精确记录身体下降的景况。在一瞬间，时间似乎停滞不前（第28行），索洛蒙达双袖充满罗德兹城（Rodez）的风，宛如两臂生翼，在气流中消失。这好比电影的画外音，形象虽然已从银幕上消逝，然而余声却未断，于是我们看到：

第31～32行：再次强调雷蒙与普洛克尼行为之间的酷似。第32行可做两种解释："'Tis. 'Tis. Ytis!"可被视为燕子呼唤"Itylus"之声。亦可能是对第22行中索洛蒙达所提问题的肯定答复。

庞德曾对普罗旺斯诗歌极感兴趣，多次遨游该地，极其熟悉那里燕子环绕城堡及高塔飞翔的情景，这应当是这段伊提拉斯—卡贝斯坦文字的背景吧。弥漫在这两个食人肉故事里的悲剧气氛，反映出诗人的坚定信念：生活中的任何暴力行为，人际间或国际间的任何暴力，都是应当取缔的。

第33～68行：描述亚克提庸（Actaeon）之死。据希腊神话，青年猎手亚克提庸不意闯入月亮女神黛安娜（Diana）的圣地，望见赤身的女神和侍女们在池中沐浴。女神震怒，将年轻猎手变做金鹿，使他被自己的猎犬咬死。

第34行：a valley 指加尔加菲亚谷地（Gargaphia）亚克提庸的死难之地。

第35行：奥维德《变形记》中一行诗的直译文。茂密的树叶的遮盖表明此处为秘密、安静、神圣的地方。

第37～39行：浓密的树叶笼罩着下面的女神浴塘，宛如圣希莱尔教堂的屋顶一般。the church... in Poictiers：指法国中西部波瓦提尔斯城内圣希莱尔教堂（the Church of St. Hilaire），Poictiers 应拼为 Poitiers。诗中提到教堂，以烘托该处的神圣性。第39行指树叶呈一片金色，为下文（第60行）埋下伏笔：阳光倘能把树叶变做金色，金鹿的颜色便更令人目眩了。

第40～52行：诗人概述奥维德关于青年猎手和沐浴的月神及其侍女们偶然相遇的故事。

第41行：slivver＝sliver.

第48行：暗喻白晰的身躯坠入清亮的水中。

第49行：以树荫渲染神秘的气氛。

第52行：无辜的青年猎手突然出现，见到裸体的窈窕月神及少女们，一时呆若木鸡，目光盯在女神的闪闪发光的浅发上（第56行），不知所措。月神疑其存心不良，因而怒不可遏，对他进行了下面提到的骇人听闻的惩罚。

第53～54行：Vidal，即传说中性格怪僻的吟游诗人 Peire Vidal。他自愿变做一只狼，以和教名意为"母狼"的情妇（Loba of Penautier）相配。第54行及后面的第64行皆写 Vidal 变形后在森林中趔趄向前的情状。Vidal 的故事映衬年轻猎手的厄运，两者都在林中受到猎手的追杀。关于亚克提庸的神话故事的另一种讲法是，青年猎手为取悦于女神而自愿披上鹿皮；这种说法同 Vidal

的自愿变形则完全如出一辙，有异曲同工之妙。

第56行：月神的本色为银白色，故称其发为浅发或银发。

第57行：青年猎手被变做光彩照人的长颈鹿（第59行）后，他自己的猎犬便向他扑来。

第60行：据传说，鹿本为月神所喜爱的动物，银白色为其保护色，免受追猎之苦。月神动怒，便把青年猎手变做金色鹿，从她的庇护范围中赶出。

第62行：鹿在骄阳的照耀下闪烁出致命的金光，招引起猎犬狂热的捕杀本能，它们在无知中呼叫自己的主人前来相助（第58行）。猎鹿颇有“淘金热”的蕴涵，为庞德在《诗章》里多次尖刻抨击的“高利贷”埋下伏笔。

第63行：亚克提庸之死。

恰如索洛蒙达跳入空中的一瞬间时间犹有片刻停顿一般，猎犬在炎炎烈日下追捕金鹿的景象颇有古瓮漆画的美妙。

第64～67行：注意力再度集中在 Vidal 身上（第64行），他要求变形的迫切愿望被奥维德在喃喃自语中（第65行）提到的几处具有丰富联想意味的地方客观化了（第66-67行）：“Pergusa... pool.... pool”指希腊神话里冥王后波塞逢涅被冥王掳入地府去的波古沙（Pergusa）湖；Gargaphia，如上所说是亚克提庸罹难之地；“Pool... pool of Salmacis”系希腊神话中神女萨尔玛西斯（Salmacis）与赫玛夫洛戴特斯（Hermaphroditus）二体合一成双性人的地方。3个故事皆似 Vidal 的爱情悲剧。

第68行：本行根据奥维德《变形记》第12章第143～145行写成；奥维德描写希腊名将阿基里斯（Achilles）在特洛伊战争中同海神之子、小天鹅希格诺斯（Cygnus）进行决战的情形。本行诗内阿基里斯的胄甲和希格诺斯的同步动作再次表明庞德认为暴力是无济无事的：阿基里斯杀死希格诺斯后激怒海神，自己终于死于海神的谋划。

第69～81行：舞曲，歌颂东方的忠贞及美德；通过一系列精巧的形象对光进行了细腻的描绘。

第69行：“e lo soleils plovil”意为“the raining sun”，取自12世纪普罗旺斯诗人丹尼尔（Arnaut Daniel）的诗句“tro lai on lo soleils plovil”（庞德的英文译文为“To where the rain falls from the sun”）。丹尼尔的这一隐喻后来在庞德的《石钻章》（“Rock-Drin”）及《列王章》（“Thrones”）里也出现过。

第70行：透明的潺潺流水。

第71行：the gods 指月神及其侍女们。

第72行：ply over ply 形容微波荡漾。

第73～74行：歌颂忠贞的美德。the pines at Takasago：在日本的高山市有两株著名的松树，据说里面住着一对永远相爱的夫妻的精灵；夫妻相互忠贞不渝的这一佳话，酷似希腊神话里鲍西斯（Baucis）与菲洛蒙（Philemon）生前相依为命、死后变做并立的橡树的故事。the Pines at Isé：在日本的另一圣地伊势市的松林里有两处神宫，是日本皇帝朝圣之地。据日本传说，两处的松树相互间可能有神秘的联系，故有“grow with”之说。

第77行：庞德仍在谈论日本文化。他在论述日本传统的“能剧”（noh plays）时说，舞台的背景上画有3株松树，代表天、地、人，象征人的一株位于天、地之间；在演剧过程中，当提到其中某棵松树时，演员便向它望去，故有“Behold the Tree of Visages”之说。

第78行：树好象被金色光环所围绕。这儿的“金色”与前面的“骄阳”和“金鹿”遥相呼应。

舞曲结构工整，“the liquid and rushing crystal”、“the shallow eddying fluid”以及重复出现的“ply over ply”把一系列鲜明的形象置列在匀称的结构中，突出了一个“光”字，艺术效果妙不可言。

第82～88行：新婚曲，为奥伦库莱娅新婚之夜而作。庞德在这里以古罗马诗人卡特拉斯的新婚曲为张本，以明快的语言和意象，渲染静谧、和谐、夫妻相亲相爱的气氛，进一步加强第74～75行所阐述的主题。

第82～83行：描写送婚及贺喜的队伍。第82行：新婚之夜，青年男女手持火把列队行至新房外唱新婚颂歌，移动的火炬与自身耀眼的光融为一体。第83行：set flame：一定形状的火焰；the corner cook-stall：意婚礼为居民的集体节日，故设炉灶摆宴招待众人。

第84行：夜空如宝石一般坚实，状似一座天篷，确保婚礼不受干扰，就像月神的神圣与贞操需要教堂屋顶的树叶层予以保护一样。这种“玛瑙环绕的天空”，不是诗人凭空臆想的，而是他在普罗旺斯的一个城市古尔敦逗留时亲眼见过的。

第85行：贺喜的人群愈来愈近，火把上树脂噼啪的燃烧声都可听到了。sputter 是拟声字。

第86～88行：诗人的彩笔转而描写贺喜队伍的中心——新娘。恰如“晨曲”中的舞蹈只用舞者的脚来表示一样，新娘的容貌读者可从其秀丽的新鞋所陪衬的小巧的脚揣测出来。Hymen：即司婚姻之神，这时他把新娘领到新郎面前（第87行）。据希腊传说，Hymen 是把新娘当做祭献品献给新郎的。这一“祭献”概念在第88行内体现出来：红花被丢落在白石上。给人一种遭受抛弃的感觉，但因有天神的承认、人类的祝贺，婚礼又在东方神圣气氛（第74—75行）的余波中进行，因此一对新人的幸福已肯定无疑。

第89～99行：为庞德对中国古代楚国作家宋玉的《风赋》的引伸。《风赋》题宋玉作，后人疑为伪托。该篇记录宋玉和楚襄王之间的一次谈话。宋玉借题发挥，把风分作“雄风”和“雌风”，向楚王婉转地指出百姓的疾苦，暗含讽刺楚王骄奢的生活之意。

第89行：So-Gioku，宋玉名字的日文拼法。庞德1913年曾从已故的美国日本研究学者凡诺洛萨的夫人处接收这凡诺洛萨的文稿，其中包括一些凡诺洛萨生前在日本学者的帮助下所译汉诗的日文稿，《风赋》极可能是其中一首，故宋玉之名以日文出现。宋玉的生卒年不详，关于他的生平，后人只知他是屈原的弟子，曾在楚襄王朝内任职，官位不高。《风赋》开首说："楚襄王游于兰台之宫。宋玉、景差侍。有风飒然而至。王乃披襟而当之，曰：'快哉此风！寡人所与庶人共者邪？'"于是宋玉对曰：

第90行："此独大王之风耳……"

第91～92行：是庞德引伸《风赋》第3段内关于"王风"（或"雄风"）的叙述而写成。

第93行：Ran-ti，本为"兰台之宫"的日文拼法，庞德误写成楚王之名。opening his collar 当为该赋开首处"王乃披襟而当之"中"披襟"一词的改写和意译。

第94行：《风赋》第3段内"盛怒于土囊之后"的译文，"盛怒"句原系宋玉所讲。

第95行：原赋内并无此句，似为赋的第4段内对"雌风"的某些叙述的概括。

第96行：似对原赋内楚王的"夫风者，天地之气，溥畅而至。不择贵贱高下而加焉"一语的改写和引伸，但是原文的精神在这里有所变动。《风赋》内楚王在向宋玉请教；这里国王听宋玉谈风，心里烦燥，似在回驳宋玉，说风将河水弄脏，并无益处，风无王风和"庶人之风"之分。

第97行：国王语带嘲讽之意，风并非牛犊，国王也不是母牛，风并非为王所生。

第98行：似为原赋第3段内"跻于罗帷"一语的改写，"跻于罗帷"句及本行皆系宋玉所言。

第99行：重复第96行，有承上启下的作用。据希腊神话，风乃为主神宙斯所驱使，因而为下面一段内达那厄的故事埋下伏笔。

第100～101行，游牧人瞻仰雄伟的埃克巴坦城而肃然起敬的景状。Ecbatan：古大米底亚国（Media Magna）的都城。plotted streets：据古希腊史学家赫罗多得斯（Heroditus，约454～425 B. C.）的记载，埃克巴坦城宏大威严，设计精美，由7层同心圆墙组成，城堞由外向内逐步升高，外5层墙分别涂成白、黑、红、蓝、橙五色，第6层墙外镀白银，第7层外镀黄金，金库和王室设在最里层。诗人描绘游牧人望见该城的华美，都想攀登更高一层的文明阶梯。the turn of the stairs：表示精神升华的意象；现代诗人T. S. 艾略特在其《圣灰节》（"Ash Wednesday"）中也曾利用同种意象表示相似的含义（如"at the first turning of the second stair"等句）。埃克巴坦是庞德心目中的理想之城，它在《比萨章》（Pisan Cantos）诗人瞥见天国之光时又出现过。

第102～103行：据希腊神话达那厄为古阿格斯国王之女，天神之主宙斯慕其貌，变作天光将其包围，使她受孕，国王动怒，待她分娩后，把母子置入木盒内，放入海里随波荡漾。宙斯助以顺风（第103行），使母子脱险。第103行似为《风赋》第2段内“今子独以为寡人之风，岂有说乎？”一句的改写。

第104～110行：夜曲；如果在“晨曲”里水色呈朦胧状，在“午曲”中水光透澈明亮，那么在“夜曲”中，夜幕徐徐降下，水望去则一片灰暗。光如秋叶一般落下、逝去（第105行），只有黄昏的雾霭笼罩在水面上（第104行），然而我们听到驳船入港停泊的声音（第108），灰暗的水面上金黄色的船在暮色中仍然依稀可辨（第109行），在傍晚的朦胧中，声音在空中飘荡（第106行）。夜幕下河面上“漂流的金黄色”暗喻黑夜或死亡的即将来临。透过暮色，我们看到旷野里有3个台阶，灰色石柱向前引伸而去（第110行～111行），至于伸向何处，诗人未讲，但《诗章》第16章似又谈到这点：

The grey stone post's,
　　and the stair of grey stone,
the passage clean-squared in granite
　　descending
and I through this, and into the earth.

（灰色的石柱，
　　灰色的石阶，
整齐的方块花岗石路：
　　往下倾斜
而我也顺着，到土里去。

第111～112行：Père Henri Jacques：据庞德1922年7月8日的信，提到他是法国一位耶稣会神父。Sennin 是中文“仙人”的日文译音，庞德在同一封信中说，“仙人是中国的自然精灵或空气之神。”Rokku，同第112行内的 Mount Rokku，即六空山。庞德可能见过这位法国耶稣会神父或阅读过他的事迹，使他感触颇深的是这位神父对这些东方仙人们的崇敬：他和他们交谈，感情交融。这种圣礼为下文渲染了气氛。

第113～118行：以爱情的高尚和神圣同变态和暴力为主题的总结性对比。

第113行：Polhonac，指中世纪闻名的法国波里亚克家族的一名成员 Viscount Heracle Ⅲ of Polignac。他对妻子和吟游诗人吉尤姆（Guillaume de St Didier）间的私通一事漠然置之，甚至对妻子唱起吉尤姆创作的关于他们通奸的歌，以示鼓励。

第114行：Gyges，杰吉斯，传说中的武士和国王。他原为小亚细亚古国利底亚王坎多拉斯（Candaulus）所宠信的侍卫，在国王的纵恿下与王后私通，后来弑君而自立为王，娶王后，同亚述国交战，建立新王朝。the feast on Thracian platter：承上启下，把杰吉斯和伊提拉斯两个故事巧妙地连接起来。Thracian 在古诗中是各种暴力的同义词。

第117～118行：对达那厄传说的进一步补充。Vidal or Ecbatan：两者的并列象征感情由粗野的肉欲向神圣的爱升华。the god's bride 一指达那厄，墙面镶金的埃克巴坦塔是达那厄怀孕的理想之地；一指圣母玛利亚，两者在诗人的心目中显然合二为一了。

第119～125行：对圣母的两种截然不同的态度：亵渎的与纯洁态度对比。

第119行：Garonne（加伦河）位于法国西南部，此行写在河岸上正在举行一项宗教仪式；Saave，同第121行中的"Sa'ave"，人群高呼着的一句庸俗化的祷词，郑重的原文应为"Salve Regina"，意为"圣母万福"，译做"圣母晚福"，以示人群的心不在焉、喊声走调之状。

第120行：Garonne 河水混浊，故曰"thick like paint"。

第121行：procession 指宗教仪式中的人群队伍；Et：法文，意"and"；Sa'ave Regina＝Salve Regina.

第122行：明喻"Like a worn"的内涵为，人群的粗野兽性是无法改变的。

第123行：Adige（阿的治河）位于意大利北部，注入亚得里亚海；河水清澈如镜，各种形影倒映其中，和混浊污秽的 Garonne 河形成鲜明对比。关于此河的传说颇多，为崇拜圣母提供了纯洁和高尚的气氛。只有在这种河的岸边，人方可悟到爱情的最高含义。

第124～125行：Stefano，即 Stefano da Verona（约1375～1451），意大利画家，善画圣母像。他的圣母像恰如意大利诗人卡瓦尔坎迪（Guido Cavalcanti，c. 1250～1300）在圣米歇尔（San Michele）处见到的圣母像一样，令人洞见爱情与天光和圣灵的一致性。卡瓦尔坎迪是庞德喜爱的诗人之一，他在一首十四行诗里曾写道：

My Lady's face is it they worship there
At San Michele in orto

庞德的"in hortulo"（拉丁语）由卡瓦尔坎迪的"in orto"（意大利语）演化而来，读来声音谐美。

第126～128行：最后3行所表现的思想和 Canto Ⅳ 的主题似无明显联系；它是关于全部《诗章》的创作方法及指导思想的文字。

第126行：the Centaur，希腊神话中的马身人面怪。庞德在其《严肃的艺术家》（"The Serious Artist"）一文中说："诗歌象马身人面怪。思维、用字、表达的机能必须和充满活力的、感觉的、富于音乐感的机能一起动作、跳跃……"。这里的人马怪形象似乎表明诗人的这种认识，即诗人的同其本性密切相关的感情，归根结底是深深扎根于肥沃的土地的。

第127～128行：这两行诗是在1921年后、很可能在庞德写完 Canto Ⅻ 之后，才添在 Canto Ⅳ 末尾的。Canto Ⅻ 的开首4行诗为：

And we sit here
Under the wall

Arena romana, Diocletian's, les gradins
　quarante-trois rangés en calcaire
而我们坐在这儿
　戴克里先的
罗马斗技场的，墙根下，四十三蹬
　石灰石台阶。）

显然，罗马皇帝戴克里先（Diocletian，245～313）的宏伟的斗技场（Arena romana）在庞德看来乃是堕落的一种象征。但是，Canto Ⅳ结尾出现的片断（And we sit here…/there in the arena…）却似另有一番意味：诗人似在以介绍者、旅伴或导游的身份和读者对话，代词"we"和第6行中的"our"遥相呼应，旨在诱导读者共享诗人真实的或想像的经历。诗人在介绍了欲望的残酷、爱情的高尚、理想之城的宏伟之后，把读者引向和谐静谧的境界，邀他们共赏精神的圣洁之美：庞德认为，艺术家的作用之一是充当"大千世界——事、人及感情的永恒的旁观者"（Canto Ⅶ）。

SINCLAIR LEWIS

〔作者介绍〕

辛克莱·刘易斯（Sinclair Lewis，1885～1951），美国小说家，出生在明尼苏达州的一个乡镇里，幼年丧母，父亲是一位医生。1908年，他毕业于耶鲁大学，后来在纽约、衣阿华、加利福尼亚等地从事编辑与新闻报道工作。自1914年发表题为《我们的雷恩先生》（*Our Mr. Wrenn*）小说起，他一生共创作小说22部，其中最著名的是《巴比特》（*Babbit*，1922）、《大街》（*Main Street*，1920）《阿罗史密斯》（*Arrowsmith*，1925）和《这不可能在这里发生》（*It Can't Happen Here*，1935）。

刘易斯的小说多以美国中西部的中、小城镇为背景，以中产阶级成员为描写对象。他用犀利的讽刺笔锋勾划出一个个粗线条的漫画式人物，对本世纪初美国社会的风气进行了入木三分的剖析，故有"社会问题小说家"之称。事实上，他受美国进步作家阿普顿·辛克莱（Upton Sinclair，1878～1968）的影响，对社会主义颇感兴趣。刘易斯从批判现实主义角度出发进行创作，是当时出现在中西部的"来自乡村的叛逆"思潮的代表作家。他的作品结束了在此之前的文学传统：即把乡村生活描绘得完美无缺，把中产阶级描写成慈祥、善良的化身。他的名著《大街》所描绘的是一幅沉闷、单调、闭塞的小市镇画面，刻划的是一个个平庸保守，趋附时势，毫无热情与生气的市民画像。小说对乡村生活和中产阶级的猛烈抨击，颇有振聋发聩的社会作用，在美国文学界曾引起一场异常激烈的争论。"大街"一词也从此获得了新的内涵，表示小城镇市民沾沾自喜、沉缅于对物质享受的单纯追求。《阿罗史密斯》以发生在医学界的事件为素材，着重反映美国社会生活中狭隘、尔虞我诈及拜金主义的不良倾向。《埃尔默·甘特利》（*Elmer Gantry*，1927）描述美国宗教信仰的严重危机，而《多滋沃思》（*Dodsworth*，1929）又对中西部居民那种怡然自得、目光如豆的精神状态进行了无情的嘲讽。《这不可能在这里发生》认为，民主若不健全，暴力和偏见若不予以抑制，美国便可能出现法西斯主义。

刘易斯的小说情节大多按照一种逃避——追求——妥协的模式展开。主要人物往往不满现实，竭力逃避现实，追求理想生活，最终无奈而与社会妥协。刘易斯虽然致力于揭露中产阶级的短处，但是他也讴歌人们的优秀品质，如自助、勤恳、理智、谦恭，常常把它们体现在正面人物身上。这一点是他之所以受到他所抨击的社会热烈称颂的原因之一。

刘易斯的小说创作在本世纪第 2 个 10 年（1910～1918）期间渐趋成熟。这是严肃的美国文学家重新认识“真实的美国”的时期。刘易斯笔下的美国，尽管缺陷很多，但同时也存在着希望，现实与理想之间的张力为他的作品提供了感人的力量，提高了美国自身以及外部世界对于美国文明的认识。他所塑造的某些典型人物栩栩如生，独立于他们所属的小说世界之外，成为某一特定历史时期的美国生活中的一个概念。刘易斯目光敏锐，讽刺尖刻，作品不以情节取胜，而是通过夸张的手法达到漫画的效果。他蜚声欧美文坛近 20 年，是第一位获得诺贝尔文学奖（1930）的美国作家。诚然，也应指出，他的作品着重描绘表面和具体的事物，忽略对人物内心世界的挖掘，对人生缺乏悲剧观认识，这使他和同代（如德莱塞）与后代（如海明威等）作家之间产生了一种距离。这是他生前不受他们尊重的原因；刘易斯去世前也曾说过，他对年轻一代作家的影响很小。但是，总的说来，他在美国文学史上做为一名主要作家的地位是不容怀疑的。

Babbit

〔作品介绍〕

《巴比特》(*Babbit*) 是刘易斯的佳作之一，1922 年出版，轰动当时美国文坛，使作者名噪一时。

小说共 34 章，原拟描述主人公乔治·巴比特在 24 小时内的生活情景。这一写作计划依然体现在前 7 章的内容中。其余 27 章则向读者介绍美国中产阶级社会的价值观念，论述诸如政治、社交、娱乐、工会、宗教、阶级结构、劳资关系、家庭与婚姻等社会生活的各个侧面。全书似无连贯的情节，而是通过主人公的活动把不同的事件和场合联结在一起。巴比特是中西部一个中等城市里一位事业兴隆的地产经纪人，对于中产阶级的传统观念和行为准则表示不满，进而反抗，后来终于退却、妥协，返回到旧的生活道路上。巴比特所经历的 3 个阶段体现在小说的 3 个不同的故事中：因杀妻而入狱的故事；巴比特竭力寻求同情；良民协会的压力及其妻子的紧急手术。

《巴比特》是美国文学中第一部描写美国商业界“二道贩子”生活的小说。第一次世界大战以后，为权力、金钱和地位而奋斗的工厂主、金融家、企业主已不复是美国商业社会的典型人物。既趋附厂主又取悦于顾客、固守陈规、嘲弄新奇事物的“小商人”成为生活中引人瞩目的阶层。这些人注重公众关系，忽略人际感情，是非人格化的美国机械文明的必然产物。《巴比特》一反描写商业界巨头的传统，第一次把笔锋指向市侩阶层。刘易斯不是从中心人物、事件或思想着手，而是仔细地选择中产阶级的一个阶层，一种职业或一个问题，以社会学家的研究方法进行追踪、记录、分析。这使他能以点睛之笔把美国社会的风貌逼真地描绘出来。因此，巴比特这个主人公的名字便以“粗俗的市侩”的含义而进入现代英语词汇中。《巴比特》与刘易斯的其他作品一样，对外部世界的描写纤细翔实，表现出作者惊人的观察力和记忆力。然而有时也过于繁冗，使人厌烦。

这里选注的是该书第1章，叙述巴比特在清晨时的生活细节。

Babbitt

CHAPTER Ⅰ

The towers of Zenith[1] aspired above the morning mist; austere towers of steel and cement and limestone, sturdy as cliffs and delicate as sil ver rods. They were neither citadels nor churches, but frankly and beautifully office-buildings.

The mist took pity on the fretted structures of earlier generations: the Post Office with its shingle-tortured mansard,[2] the red brick minarets of hulking old houses, factories with stingy and sooted windows, wooden tenements colored like mud. The city was full of such grotesqueries, but the clean towers were thrusting them from the business center, and on the farther hills were shining new houses, homes they seemed—for laughter and tranquillity.

Over a concrete bridge fled a limousine of long sleek hood and noiseless engine. These people in evening clothes were returning from an all-night rehearsal of a Little Theater play, an artistic adventure considerably illuminated by champagne. Below the bridge curved a railroad, a maze of green and crimson lights. The New York Flyer.[3] boomed past, and twenty lines of polished steel leaped into the glare.[4]

In one of the skyscrapers the wires of the Associated Press were closing down. The telegraph operators wearily raised their celluloid eye-shades after a night of talking with Paris and Peking. Through the building crawled the scrubwomen, yawning, their old shoes slapping. The dawn mist spun away. Cues of men with lunch-boxes clumped toward the immensity of new factories, sheets of glass and hollow tile, glittering shops where five thousand men worked beneath one roof, pouring out the honest wares that would be sold up the Euphrates[5] and across the veldt.[6] The whistles rolled out in greeting a chorus cheerful as the April dawn; the song of labor in a city built—it seemed—for giants.

II

There was nothing of the giant in the aspect of the man who was beginning to awaken on the sleeping-porch[7] of a Dutch Colonial house in that residential district of Zenith known as Floral Heights.

His name was George F. Babbitt. He was forty-six years old now, in April, 1920, and he made nothing in particular, neither butter nor shoes nor poetry, but he was nimble in the calling of selling houses for more than people could afford to pay.

His large head was pink, his brown hair thin and dry. His face was babyish in slumber, despite his wrinkles and the red spectacle-dents on the slopes of his nose. He was not fat but he was exceedingly well fed; his cheeks were pads, and the unroughened hand which lay helpless upon the khakicolored blanket was slightly puffy. He seemed prosperous, extremely married[8] and unromantic; and altogether unromantic appeared this sleeping-porch, which looked on one sizable elm, two respectable grass-plots, a cement driveway, and a corrugated iron garage. Yet Babbitt was again dreaming of the fairy child, a dream more romantic than scarlet pagodas by a silver sea.[9]

For years the fairy child had come to him. Where others saw but Georgie Babbitt, she discerned gallant youth. She waited for him, in the darkness beyond mysterious groves. When at last he could slip away from the crowded house he darted to her. His wife, his clamoring friends, sought to follow, but he escaped, the girl fleet beside him, and they crouched together on a shadowy hillside. She was so slim, so white, so eager! She cried that he was gay and valiant, that she would wait for him, that they would sail—[10]

Rumble and bang of the milk-truck.

Babbitt moaned, turned over, struggled back toward his dream. He could see only her face now, beyond misty waters. The furnace-man slammed the basement door. A dog barked in the next yard. As Babbitt sank blissfully into a dim warm tide, the paper-carrier[11] went by whistling, and the rolled-up *Advocate*[12] thumped the front door. Babbitt roused, his stomach constricted with alarm. As he relaxed, he was pierced by the familiar and irritating rattle of some one cranking a Ford:[13] snap-ah-ah, snap-ah-ah, snap-ah-ah.[14] Himself a pious motorist, Babbitt cranked with the unseen driver, with him waited through taut hours for the roar of the starting engine, with him agonized as the roar ceased and again began the infernal patient snap-ah-ah—a round, flat sound, a shivering coldmorning sound, a sound infuriating and inescapable. Not till the rising voice of the motor told him that the Ford was moving was he released from the panting tension. He glanced once at his favorite tree, elm twigs against the gold patina of sky, and fumbled for sleep as for a drug. He who had been a boy very credulous of life was no longer greatly interested in the possible and improbable adven tures of each new day.

He escaped from reality till the alarm-clock rang, at seven-twenty.

Ⅲ

It was the best of nationally advertised and quantitatively produced alarm-clocks, with all modern attachments, including cathedral chime, intermittent alarm, and a phosphorescent dial. Babbitt was proud of being awakened by such a rich device. Socially it was almost as creditable as buying expensive cord tires.[15]

He sulkily admitted now that there was no more escape, but he lay and detested the grind of the real estate business, and disliked his family, and disliked himself for disliking them. The evening before, he had played poker at Vergil Gunch's till midnight, and after such holidays he was irritable before breakfast. It may have been the tremendous home-brewed beer of the prohibition-era[16] and the cigars to which that beer enticed him; it may have been resentment of return from this fine, bold man-world to a restricted region of wives and stenographers, and of suggestions not to smoke so much.

From the bedroom beside the sleeping-porch, his wife's detestably cheerful "Time to get up, Georgie boy," and the itchy sound, the brisk and scratchy sound, of combing hairs out of a stiff brush.

He grunted; he dragged his thick legs, in faded baby-blue pajamas, from under the khaki blanket; he sat on the edge of the cot, running his fingers through his wild hair, while his plump feet mechanically felt for his slippers. He looked regretfully at the blanket—forever a suggestion to him of freedom and heroism. He had bought it for a camping trip which had never come off. It symbolized gorgeous loafing, gorgeous cursing, virile flannel shirts. [17]

He creaked to his feet, groaning at the waves of pain which passed behind his eyeballs. Though he waited for their scorching recurrence, he looked blurrily out at the yard. It delighted him, as always; it was the neat yard of a successful business man of Zenith, that is , it was perfection, and made him also perfect. He regarded the corrugated iron garage. For the three-hundred-and-sixty-fifth time in a year he reflected, "No class to that tin shack. [18] Have to build me a frame garage. But by golly it's the only thing on the place that isn't up-to-date!" While he stared he thought of a community garage for his acreage development, Glen Oriole. He stopped puffing and jiggling. His arms were akimbo. His petulant, sleepswollen facc was set in harder lines. He suddenly seemed capable, an official, a man to contrive, to direct, to get things done.

On the vigor of his idea he was carried down the hard, clean, unused-looking hall into the bathroom.

Though the house was not large it had, like all houses on Floral Heights, an altogether royal bathroom of porcelain and glazed tile and metal sleek as silver. The towel-rack was a rod of clear glass set in nickel. The tub was long enough for a Prussian Guard, [19] and above the set bowl was a sensational exhibit of tooth-brush holder, shaving-brush holder, soap-dish, sponge-dish, and medicine-cabinet, so glittering and so ingenious that they resembled an electrical instrument-board. But the Babbitt whose god was Modern Appliances was not pleased. The air of the bathroom was thick with the smell of a heathen toothpaste. "Verona been at it again! 'Stead of sticking to Lilidol, [20] like I've re-peat-ed-ly asked her, she's gone and gotten some confounded stinkum stuff that makes you sick!" [21]

The bath-mat was wrinkled and the floor was wet. (His daughter

Verona eccentrically took baths in the morning, now and then.) He slipped on the mat, and slid against the tub. He said "Damn!" Furiously he snatched up his tube of shaving-cream, furiously he lathered, with a belligerent slapping of the unctuous brush, furiously he raked his plump cheeks with a safety-razor. It pulled. The blade was dull. He said, "Damn—oh—oh—damn it!"

He hunted through the medicine-cabinet for a packet of new razor-blades (reflecting, as invariably, "Be cheaper to buy one of these dinguses and strop your own blades,") and when he discovered the packet, behind the round box of bicarbonate of soda, he thought ill of his wife for putting it there and very well of himself for not saying "Damn." But he did say it, immediately afterward, when with wet and soap-slippery fingers he tried to remove the horrible little envelope and crisp clinging oiled paper from the new blade.

Then there was the problem, oft-pondered, never solved, of what to do with the old blade, which might imperil the fingers of his young. As usual, he tossed it on top of the medicine-cabinet, with a mental note that some day he must remove the fifty or sixty other blades that were also temporarily, piled up there. He finished his shaving in a growing testiness increased by his spinning headache and by the emptiness in his stomach. When he was done, his round face smooth and streamy and his eyes stinging from soapy water, he reached for a towel. The family towels were wet, wet and clammy and vile, all of them wet, he found, as he blindly snatched them—his own face-towel, his wife's, Verona's, Ted's, Tinka's, and the lone bath-towel with the huge welt of initial. Then George F Babbitt did a dismaying thing. He wiped his face on the guest towel! It was a pansy-embroidered trifle which always hung there to indicate that the Babbitts were in the best Floral Heights society. No one had ever used it. No guest had ever dared to. Guests secretively took a corner of the nearest regular towel.

He was raging, "By golly, here they go and use up all the towels, every doggone one of 'em, and they use 'em and get 'em all wet and sopping, and never put out a dry one for me—of course, I'm the goat! [22]—and then I want one and— I'm the only person in the doggone house that's got the slightest doggone bit of consideration for other people and thoughtfulness and consider there may be others that may want to use the doggone bathroom after me and consider—"

He was pitching the chill abominations[23] into the bath-tub, pleased by the vindictiveness of that desolate flapping sound; and in the midst his wife serenely trotted in, observed serenely, "Why Georgie dear, what are you doing? Are you going to wash out the towels? Why, you needn't wash out the towels. Oh, Georgie, you didn't go and use the guesttowel, did you?"

It is not recorded that he was able to anwer.

For the first time in weeks he was sufficiently roused by his wife to look at her.

IV

Myra Babbitt—Mrs. George F. Babbitt—was definitely mature. She had creases from the corners of her mouth to the bottom of her chin, and her Plump neck bagged. But the thing that marked her as having passed the line was that she no longer had reticences before her husband, and no longer worried about not having reticences. She was in a petticoat now, and corsets which bulged, and unaware of being seen in bulgy corsets. She had become so dully habituated to married life that in her full matronliness she was as sexless as an anemic nun. She was a good woman, a kind woman, a diligent woman, but no one, save perhaps Tinka her ten-year-old, was at all interested in her or entirely aware that she was alive.

After a rather thorough discussion of all the domestic and social aspects of towels she apologized to Babbitt for his having an alcoholic headache; and he recovered enough to endure the search for a B. V. D.[24] undershirt which had, he pointed out, malevolently been concealed among his clean pajamas.

He was fairly amiable in the conference on the brown suit.

"What do you think, Myra?" He pawed at the clothes hunched on a chair in their bedroom, while she moved about mysteriously adjusting and patting her petticoat and, to his jaundiced eye, never seeming to get on with her dressing. "How about it? Shall I wear the brown suit another day?"

"Well, it looks awfully nice on you."

"I know, but gosh, it needs pressing."

"That's so. Perhaps it does."

"It certainly could stand being pressed, all right."

"Yes, perhaps it wouldn't hurt it to be pressed."

"But gee, the coat doesn't need pressing. No sense in having the whole darn suit pressed, when the coat doesn't need it."

"That's so."

"But the pants certainly need it, all right. Look at them—look at those wrinkles—the pants certainly do need pressing."

"That's so. Oh, Georgie, why couldn't you wear the brown coat with the blue trousers we were wondering what we'd do with them?"

"Good Lord! Did you ever in all my life know me to wear the coat of one suit and the pants of another? What do you think I am? A busted bookkeeper?"

"Well, why don't you put on the dark gray suit to-day, and stop in at the tailor and leave the brown trousers?"

"Well, they certainly need—Now where the devil is that gray suit? Oh, yes, here we are."

He was able to get through the other crises of dressing with comparative resoluteness and calm.

His first adornment was the sleeveless dimity B. V. D. undershirt, in which he resembled a small boy humorlessly wearing a cheesecloth tabard at a civic pageant. He never put on B. V. D.'s without thanking the God of Progress[25] that he didn't wear tight, long, old-fashioned undergarments, like his father-in-law and partner, Henry Thompson. His second embellishment was combing and slicking back his hair. It gave him a tremendous forehead, arching up two inches beyond the former hair-line. But most wonder-working of all was the donning of his spectacles.

There is character in spectacles—the pretentious tortoiseshell, the meek pince-nez of the school teacher, the twisted silver-framed glasses of the old villager. Babbitt's spectacles had huge, circular, frameless lenses of the very best glass; the ear-pieces were thin bars of gold. In them he was the modern business man; one who gave orders to clerks and drove a car and played occasional golf and was scholarly in regard to Salesmanship. His head suddenly appeared not babyish but weighty, and you noted his heavy, blunt nose, his straight mouth and thick, long upper lip, his chin overfleshy but strong; with respect you beheld him put on the rest of his uniform as a Solid Citizen.[26]

The gray suit was well cut, well made, and completely undistinguished. It was a standard suit. White piping[27] on the V of the vest added a flavor of law and learning. His shoes were black laced boots, good boots, honest boots, standard boots, extraordinarily uninteresting boots. The only frivolity was in his purple knitted scarf. With considerable comment on the matter to Mrs. Babbitt (who, acrobatically fastening the back of her blouse to her skirt with a safety-pin, did not hear a word he said), he chose between the purple scarf and a tapestry effect with stringless brown harps among blown palms, and into it he thrust a snake-head pin with opal eyes.

A sensational event was changing from the brown suit to the gray the contents of his pockets. He was earnest about these objects. They were of eternal importance, like baseball or the Republican Party.[28] They included a fountain pen and a silver pencil (always lacking a supply of new leads) which belonged in the righthand upper vest pocket. Without them he would have felt naked. On his watch-chain were a gold penknife, silver cigar-cutter, seven keys (the use of two of which he had forgotten), and incidentally a good watch. Depending from the chain was a large, yellowish elk's-tooth—proclamation of his membership in the Brotherly and Protective Order of Elks.[29] Most significant of all was his loose-leaf pocket note-book, that modern and efficient note-book which contained the addresses of people whom he had forgotten, prudent memoranda of postal money-orders which had reached their destinations months ago, stamps which had lost their mucilage, clippings of verses by T. Cholmondeley Frink[30] and of the newspaper editorials from which Babbitt got his opinions and his polysyllables, notes to be sure and do things which he did not intend to do, and one curious inscription— D. S. S. D. M. Y. P. D. F.[31]

But he had no cigarette-case. No one had ever happened to give him one, so he hadn't the habit and people who carried cigarette-cases he regarded as effeminate.

Last, he stuck in his lapel the Boosters' Club button. With the conciseness of great art the button displayed two words: "Boosters—Pep!" It made Babbitt feel loyal and important. It associated him with Good Fellows, with men who were nice and human, and important in business circles. It was his V. C., his Legion of Honor ribbon, his Phi Beta Kappa key.[32]

With the subtleties of dressing ran other complex worries. "I feel kind of punk[33] this morning," he said. "I think I had too much dinner last evening. You oughtn't to serve those heavy banana fritters."

"But you asked me to have some."

"I know, but—I tell you, when a fellow gets past forty he has to look after his digestion. There's a lot of fellows that don't take proper care of themselves. I tell you at forty a man's a fool or his doctor—I mean, his own doctor. Folks don't give enough attention to this matter of dieting. Now I think—Course[34] a man ought to have a good meal after the day's work, but it would be a good thing for both of us if we took lighter lunches."

"But Georgie, here at home I always do have a light lunch."

"Mean to imply I make a hog of myself, eating down-town? Yes, sure! You'd have a swell time if you had to eat the truck[35] that new steward hands out to us at the Athletic Club! But I certainly do feel out of sorts, this morning. Funny, got a pain down here on the left side—but no, that wouldn' be appendicitis, would it? Last night, when I was driving over to Verg Gunch's, I felt a pain in my stomach, too. Right here it was—kind of a sharp shooting pain. I—where'd that dime go to? Why don't you serve more prunes at breakfast? Of course I eat an apple every evening—an apple a day keeps the doctor away—but still, you ought to have more prunes, and not all these fancy doodads."

"The last time I had prunes you didn't eat them."

"Well, I didn't feel like eating 'em, I suppose. Matter of fact, I think I did eat some of 'em. Anyway—I tell you it's mighty important to—I was saying to Verg Gunch, just last evening, most people don't take sufficient care of their diges—"

"Shall we have the Gunches for our dinner, next week?"

"Why sure; you bet."

"Now see here, George: I want you to put on your nice dinner-jacket that evening."

"Rats![36] The rest of 'em won't want to dress."

"Of course they will. You remember when you didn't dress for the Littlefields' supper-party, and all the rest did, and how embarrassed you were."

"Embarrassed, hell! I wasn't embarrassed. Everybody knows I can put on as expensive a Tux.[37] as anybody else, and I should worry if I don't happen to have it on sometimes. All a darn nuisance, anyway. All right for a woman, that stays around the house all the time, but when a fellow's worked like the dickens all day ,he doesn't want to go and hustle his head off getting into the soup-and-fish[38] for a lot of folks that he's seen in just reg'lar ordinary clothes that same day."

"You Know you enjow being seen in one. The other evening you admitted you were glad I'd insisted on your dressing. You said you felt a lot better for it. And oh, Georgie, I do wish you wouldn't say 'Tux.' It's 'dinner-jacket.'"

"Rats, what's the odds?"

"Well, it's what all the nice folks say. Suppose Lucile McKelvey heard you calling it a 'Tux.'"

"Well, that's all right now! Lucile McKelvey can't pull anything on me! Her folks are common as mud, even if her husband and her dad are millionaires! I suppose you're trying to rub in *your* exalted social position! Well, let me tell you that your revered paternal ancestor, Henry T., doesn't even call it a 'Tux.'! He calls it a 'bobtail jacket for a ringtail monkey,' and you couldn't get him into one unless you chloroformed him!"

"Now don't be horrid, George."

"Well, I don't want to be horrid, but Lord! you're getting as fussy as Verona. Ever since she got out of college she's been too rambunctious to live with—doesn't know what she wants—well, I know what she wants! —all she wants is to marry a millionaire, and live in Europe, and hold some preacher's hand, and simultaneously at the same time stay right here in Zenith and be some blooming kind of a socialist agitator or boss charity-worker or some damn thing! Lord, and Ted is just as bad! He wants to go to college, and he doesn't want to go to college. Only one of the three that knows her own mind is Tinka. Simply can't understand how I ever came to have a pair of shillyshallying children[39] like Rone and Ted. I may not be any Rockefeller or James J. Shakespeare,[40] but I certainly do know my own mind, and I do keep right on plugging along[41] in the office and—Do you know the latest? Far as I can figure out, Ted's new bee is he'd like to be a movie actor and—And here I've told him a hundred times, if he'll go to college and law-school and make good, I'll set him up in business and—Verona just exactly as bad. Doesn't know what she wants. Well, well, come on! Aren't you ready yet? The girl rang the bell three minutes ago."

V

Before he followed his wife, Babbitt stood at the westernmost window of their room. This residential settlement, Floral Heights, was on a rise; and though the center of the city was three miles away—Zenith had between three and four hundred thousand inhabitants now—he could see the top of the Second National Tower, an Indiana limestone building of thirty-five stories.

Its shining walls rose against April sky to a simple cornice like a streak of white fire. Integrity was in the tower, and decision. It bore its strength lightly as a tall soldier. As Babbitt stared, the nervousness was soothed from his face, his slack chin lifted in reverence. All he articulated was "That's one lovely sight!" but he was inspired by the rhythm of the city; his love of it renewed. He beheld the tower as a temple-spire of the religion of business, a faith passionate, exalted, surpassing common men; and as he clumped down to breakfast he whistled the ballad "Oh, by gee, by gosh, by jingo"[42] as though it were a hymn melancholy and noble.

〔注释〕

1. Zenith：虚构的城市名，据说以中西部的辛辛那提市（Cincinnati）为模拟依据。

2. its shingle-tortured mansard：被木瓦板压得变了形的屋顶。

3. The New York Flyer：纽约特快列车。

4. twenty lines of polished steel leaped into glare：20条亮晶晶的钢轨在灯光下闪耀。

5. the Euphrates：亚洲西南部的幼发拉底河，从土耳其的东部流经叙利亚与伊拉克，同底格里斯河相汇合。

6. the veldt：非洲南部的草原。

7. the sleeping porch：四周按装玻璃，可作为卧室的门廊。

8. extremely married：一副十足的已婚者的神态。

9. a silver sea：参阅莎士比亚《理查二世》（*Richard* Ⅱ）的第2幕第1场：This happy breed of men, this little world/This precious stone set in the silver sea。这一个镶嵌在银色的海水之中的宝石。

10. that they would sail：这一段表述巴比特的心理矛盾，他不满足于常规的生活方式，充满着梦幻般的憧憬与希望，要求从现实生活中解脱出来，却又承受着环境的压力。

11. the paper carrier：分送报纸的人。

12. *Advocate*：《倡导者》报。

13. a Ford：一辆福特牌汽车。

14. snap—ah—ah：（拟声词）汽车喇叭声。

15. Socially it was almost as creditable as buying expensive cord tires：从社会意义来讲，这如同购买了一套价格昂贵的钢丝圈汽车轮胎一样体面。以前，人们用棉线作汽车轮胎的衬里，后来改用钢丝或尼龙丝。

16. the prohibition-era：美国禁酒年代（1920～1933）。

17. It symbolized gorgeous loafing, gorgeous cursing, virile flannel shirts：它是游手好闲、骂骂咧咧、精力充沛的纨绔子弟的生活象征。

18. No class to that tin shack：这种白铁皮小屋没有一点气派。

19. a Prussian Guard：一名普鲁士卫兵，一般都是彪形大汉。

20. Lilidol：一种牙膏的商标，这里指这种牙膏；'Stead of 即 Instead of。

21. she's gone and gotten some confound stinkum stuff that makes you sick!：她却搞来了一些讨厌的、臭气熏天的破烂货，真叫人恶心。stinkum 即 stinking。

22. I'm the goat：我却成了替罪羊。

23. the chill abominations：讨厌的、又湿又冷的东西，指毛巾。

24. B. V. D.：男子内衣的商标。

25. God of Progress：19 世纪末、20 世纪初，美国经济有了长足的发展，人民的物质生活也得到极大改善。但是与此同时，各种社会弊端大量出现，引起了人们的普遍关注，先进人士提出了许多改革的主张与立法。

26. a Solid Citizen：一位有财产与社会地位的公民。

27. white piping：白色的镶边条子。

28. like baseball or the Republican Party：把共和党与棒球并列，意在讽刺。

29. the Brotherly and Protective Order of Elks：一个慈善组织，它的名称是：Benevolent and Protective Order of Elks。

30. T. Cholmondeley Frink：查无记载，可能指一位用诗歌的形式撰写新闻广告的人。

31. D. S. S. D. M. Y. P. D. F.：巴比特的记事符号，连成一串，无具体意义。

32. V. C., his Legions of Honour ribbon his Phi Beta Kappa key：V. C. 即 Victoria Cross，维多利亚勋章，创于 1856 年，颁发给海陆空军作战勇敢的战士；Legion of Honour，法国的功勋组织，会员都是对法国有特殊功勋的人；1802 年由拿破仑创立；Phi Beta Kappa，美国全国性大学生荣誉组织，吸收成绩优秀的学生为成员，成立于 1776 年。

33. kind of punk：有几分不舒服。

34. Course：即 of course。

35. the truck：乱七八糟的东西，这里指食物。

36. Rats：感叹词，表示失望，厌恶。

37. Tux：又叫 Tuxedo，美式晚礼服。

38. the soup-and-fish：正式的男子晚礼服。

39. shilly-shallying children：变化多端，没有主见的孩子们。

40. any Rockeffeller or James J. Shakespeare：某个大富翁或大文豪。James J. Shakespeare 指 William Shakespeare，说话人把他的教名搞错了。

41. plugging along：坚持不懈地努力工作。

42. by gee，by gosh，by jingo：感叹词，语气委婉的咒语，连续出现，意在强调。

HILDA DOOLITTLE（H. D.）

〔作者介绍〕

希尔达·杜利特尔（Hilda Doolittle，1886～1961），美国诗人，意象派(Imagism)的主要代表人之一。其父曾担任过位于宾夕法尼亚大学内的天文台的主任，H. D. 就是在这里与当时正在该校就读的著名作家庞德相识并相爱的。尽管他们后来分道扬镳，但他们之间的友谊对她的创作生涯产生了深远的影响；是庞德把她介绍给伦敦文学界的知名人士，并修改和推荐了她的诗作。庞德曾说过，意象派新诗运动最初就以出版 H. D. 的诗作为目的而发起的。H. D. 终生沿用庞德为她设计的这一笔名。

H. D. 的诗作典型地体现出意象派诗歌创作原则。她的诗多短小精悍，具有一个主导的意象，用字以简代繁，以直接、具体、生动地再现自己的感观为准则。她的诗明朗、洗炼，极少空洞的阐述或逻辑推理，总是通过客观事物的形象，作用于读者的感官，充分发挥读者的想象力，从而取得提示(suggest）的效果。H. D. 刻意追求灵活的、充分表现瞬间感受与体验的艺术形式，反对传统的五步抑扬格的束博，崇尚自由体。她注意声韵效果。这是意象派主帅之一的庞德极其推崇她的诗作的主要原因。

H. D. 在诗歌创作中善于将个人的经验与历史的沉思融为一体，充实客观意象的容量与内涵。这在其长诗《不倒的墙》（*The Walls Do Not Fall*，1944）、《向天使的献礼》（*Tribute to Angels*，1945）和《枝干开花》（*The Flowering of the Rod*，1946）中表现得尤为明显。H. D. 把这三首诗合为一集，称《三部曲》(*Trilogy*)。她的诗常运用古典意象（classical images），她想象中的希腊乃是一个完善的梦想的世界。她诗作如《海门》（*Hymen*，1921）《赫里奥多拉及其他》（*Heliodora and Other Poems*，1924），《诗集》（*Collected Poems*，1925，1940）等都是醒目的例子。她的诗集还有《海伦在埃及》（*Helen in Egypt*，1961）等。H. D. 还从事小说创作。她的长篇小说有《赫迪拉斯》（*Hedylus*，1928）及《叫我活着》（*Bid Me to Live*，1960）等。

H. D. 在美国文学史上素以意象诗人闻名；但从 60 年代起，美国当代诗人如罗伯特·邓肯（Robert Duncan 1919～）等，开始注意她诗作中抒情的特点，他们认为有必要对这位女诗人进行再评价。这是值得注意的。

Oread

〔作品介绍〕

这是庞德最欣赏的一首意象诗。

由于强调对瞬间经验的感性捕捉，意象派诗歌多以短小见长；也由于诗人剔除了诗中所有的解说成份，甚至必要的关联词，意象派诗歌往往表现出很大的歧义性：读者所面对的，只是一个或数个客观意象，而对其中的象征意义，不同的读者则难免有不同的理解与联想。这便要求读者在阅读中充分调动自己的创造性思维及想象力，尽可能设身处地地去体会诗中的意境与情感，然后再将这些感性的体验归结为理性的认识。要求读者的积极参与（participation），正是现代诗歌的基本特征之一。

H. D. 诗中的意象大多取自自然中两个对立的侧面，如本诗中的山峰与海洋。对于这些对立，可作多种理解，如历史与现实，贫瘠与丰收，欢乐与哀伤等等，这些都不很重要；诗人如何将上述思想通过意象生动地表现出来，才是诗的意义之所在。

Oread[1]

Whirl up, sea —
whirl your pointed pines,[2]
splash your great pines
on our rocks,
hurl your green over us,
cover us with your pools of fir.[3]

〔注释〕

1. Oread：山林女神。诗人此处以古希腊神话中的女神为标题，借以在时间上赋予本诗以永恒的意义：诗人把此刻的感受与上古仙人的经历放在同一框架中进行审视，形成一种苍茫的历史感。

2. your pointed pines：在山林女神（或诗人）看来，翻起的波浪宛若尖顶的松树。

3. your pools of firs：拍击在山岩的浪花成了一塘塘冷杉。诗人的这种感受可谓独特。

Heat

〔作品介绍〕

《热》（"Heat"）突出了热与风两种自然现象的对立。诗的主题，似乎是自然界及人类周而复始的运动的发展过程。在这一过程中，一种自然力量只在某一时期起某种作用，正如炎热的作用在于为自然带来足够的热量，为丰收作好准备。但它在完成了使命之后，必将为其他自然力所代替，此乃自然法则。故诗人请求风将热驱散。

Heat[1]

O wind, rend open the heat,
cut apart the heat,
rend it to tatters.[2]

Fruit cannot drop
through this thick air—
fruit cannot fall into heat
that presses up and blunts
the points of pears[3]
and rounds the grapes.

Cut the heat—
plough through it,
turning it on either side
of your path.

〔注释〕

1. 此诗原为另一首诗《花园》（“Garden”，1925）的第2部分。
2. rend it to tatters：将炎热撕成碎片。这一节为诗人对风的请求。
3. points of pears：梨的斑点。

EUGENE O'NEILL

〔作者介绍〕

尤金·奥尼尔（Eugene O'Neill，1888～1953），美国著名剧作家。他的一生充满了不幸的遭遇，颇具悲剧色彩。他出生在纽约市一家旅馆内。父亲詹姆斯·奥尼尔（James O'Neill）是当时美国著名的演员，常在美国做巡回演出，童年时的奥尼尔经常随行。他于1906年就读于普林斯顿大学，但一年后被校方开除。之后他开始了漫长的、但对其创作有重大影响的漂泊生涯。他从事过多种职业，饱尝生活的艰辛，熟知社会底层的生活。他在纽约当过秘书，1909年赴洪都拉斯，以期淘金致富。在那里他染上了疟疾，被迫回国，协助管理他父亲的剧团。不久他便不满于这种生活，南渡阿根廷，在那里供职一段时间。以后他又赴南非、中美洲等地，归国后在往返于纽约和英国海港的船上谋生。他还演过戏，当过记者，并曾因酗酒过度、精神沮丧而险些自杀。1912年，即他24岁那年，他因患肺结核不得不疗养治疗。在被迫休息的半年中，他阅读了诸如易卜生（Henrik Ibsen，1828～1906）和斯特林堡（August Strindberg，1849～1912）等大师的剧作，开始进行严肃的思考，决定进行戏剧创作，以戏剧形式表现自己的人生观。从此，他潜心创作，1913至1914年间写过8部独幕剧和2部长剧。1914年至1915年在哈佛大学贝克教授（G. B. Baker）的戏剧写作班学习，并在艺术家集中的纽约市格林尼治村度过一冬。他对美国戏剧界的模仿风气和商业气息深恶痛绝，于1916年参加非商业性的普罗文斯敦剧社的创作和演出活动。该剧社上演了他的许多独幕剧。他还曾参与管理格林尼治村剧场。

二、三十年代是奥尼尔戏剧创作的鼎盛期。1920年，他的一部以美国农民家庭生活悲剧为题材的《天边外》（*Beyond the Horizon*）上演了。该剧的上演标志着美国严肃戏剧的开端，并使他首次获普利策奖。同年，他还创作了《琼斯皇》（*Emperor Jones*）和《克里斯·克里斯托夫逊》（*Chris Christopherson*）。他于1922年将后者改写为《安娜·克里斯蒂》（*Anna Christie*），该剧使他再获普利策奖。以后他接连创作了《毛猿》(*The Hairy Ape*, 1922年上演)、《榆树下的欲望》(*Desire under the Elms*, 1924)、《大神布朗》(*The Great God Brown*, 1926)、《拉散路笑了》(*Lazarus Laughed*, 1927)、《悲悼》(*Mourning Becomes Electra*, 1931)、《啊,荒野》(*Ah, Wilderness!*, 1933)。从1934年起他长期患病,沉默了很长时间,直到1946年《卖冰的人来了》(*The Iceman Cometh*)上演。他这时的生活并不如意,所受的打击很多。最后,他在一家旅馆内孤独地去世。他的另一名作《进入黑夜的漫长旅程》(*Long Day's Journey into Night*)在他逝世后于1956年出版并上演。

奥尼尔对美国戏剧的发展有划时代的影响。在19世纪,虽有几位剧作家的潜心创作、惨淡经营,但美国剧坛的成就不大,美国戏剧远远不能同美国小说和诗歌相题并论。当时的剧作家和演员多刻意追求浪漫的情节和华丽的布景,直到1916年普罗文斯敦剧社上演奥尼尔的独幕剧《东航加迪夫》(*Bound East for Cardiff*)以后,在美国剧作家——首先是奥尼尔——的努力下,美国戏剧才逐步取得了不比小说和诗歌逊色的成绩,并赢得了国际性的声誉。

奥尼尔是一位严肃的戏剧家,他的剧作可以说是美国严肃戏剧、实验戏剧之滥觞。他才华横溢,擅长写作悲剧。《啊,荒野》是他剧作中唯一的一部喜剧。他性格郁悒,个人生活不如意,长期颠沛流离,因而他的人生观比较阴郁,作品中忧郁、压抑、悲观的成分较多。他是探索人的复杂心理的大师。他的写作题材相当广泛;他关心社会问题,也为现代社会的冷酷、残暴和现代人没有归宿的境地所困扰。奥尼尔是一位敏感的艺术家。他感觉到他的时代的"毫不协调、支离破碎、没有信仰的节奏",努力发掘人的欲望及失意的根源。关于现代人无能为力的悲剧意识贯穿在他一生所有作品中。《毛猿》里的司炉"扬克"为寻找"归宿",竟绝望地到动物园和毛猿"认亲",而毛猿却报之以无情的打击。全剧由始至终迷漫着一种绝望的悲剧气氛:在这个冷漠孤寂的世界中,人原无归宿可言。《卖冰的人来了》所描写的乃是一些失意者的心境。这些人虽然来自不同的社会阶层,但却有一个共同特点:当他们在河畔酒店会面时,他们都已学会依靠幻想来得到慰藉。他们畏惧现实生活,总是回首往事,或对未来夸夸其谈。虽然未来总是未来,他们却似乎从幻想中汲取到生活下去的勇气。他们知道,幻想一但破灭,他们便会随之堕入漫长的黑夜中去。奥尼尔的悲观思想在这出剧里被表现得淋漓尽致。他的其他作品如《琼斯皇》、《榆树下的欲望》、《安娜·克里斯蒂》及《悲悼》等,都深刻地表现了他的人生观。

奥尼尔一生坚持不懈地革新戏剧艺术。他把戏剧从19世纪的传统束缚中解放出来,使之在现实生活中扎根、成长。他首次把现实主义乃至自然主义的传统手法运用于美国戏剧的创作中,他的艺术风格以多种多样和精深圆熟而著称。他博览群书,深谙欧洲戏剧传统,且深受古希腊悲剧、易卜生、斯特林堡、表现主义作家、尼采(Nietzsche, 1844～1900)和弗洛伊德(Sigmund

Freud，1856～1939）的影响，如《悲悼》一剧是在现代舞台上表现古希腊悲剧观和运用古希腊悲剧表现技巧的尝试；在《奇异的插曲》中有许多精神分析和意识流技巧的印记。他的表现手法和技巧有现实主义、浪漫主义、神秘主义、表现主义、象征主义等等；如《安娜·克里斯蒂》以现实主义为主要特征，《大神布朗》以象征主义取胜，《琼斯皇》是表现主义的杰作，而《毛猿》更兼有象征主义、表现主义和现实主义 3 种特点。奥尼尔还特别重视背景和道具的作用。

奥尼尔一生 4 次获普利策奖（1920，1922，1928，1957），并于 1936 年获诺贝尔文学奖。

Long Day's Journey into Night

〔作品介绍〕

该剧是奥尼尔自传性的作品，开始创作于 1940 年，在他逝世后出版并上演，被一些批评家称为“美国最好的悲剧”。

该剧描写了蒂龙一家的悲剧经历。父亲詹姆斯·蒂龙是一位著名演员，信仰爱尔兰天主教。蒂龙夫人玛丽曾就读于一所天主教修道院，梦想当一名修女或钢琴家。她与詹姆斯一见钟情，但同他结婚后，由于社会上对演员这一职业存有偏见，她的朋友多离她而去。蒂龙在全国巡回演出，她则随他同行。她先后生下杰米、尤金（夭折）、埃德蒙三子。埃德蒙出生后，蒂龙夫人由于长期精神郁闷，加上一个庸医用吗啡治疗她的病痛，逐渐染上了吸毒的恶习。

该剧描写了 1912 年 8 月某日蒂龙一家发生的事。该剧开始时，杰米 33 岁，无业，在百老汇街区游荡，出语辛辣刻薄。埃德蒙则是一个有着病态心理的知识分子，羸弱多病，正患肺结核。蒂龙夫人刚刚从疗养院出来，但因为对埃德蒙的担心而再次开始吸毒。从早晨开始，剧中人一直在吵架，互相指责。蒂龙夫人指责丈夫没有给她一个真正的家，指责孩子们让她担惊受怕。孩子们指责父亲吝啬，而父亲指责他们令他失望。大家都指责蒂龙夫人吸毒。父母、孩子们都有自己的理由。但不幸的根源到底是什么？奥尼尔始终为这一问题所困扰。蒂龙夫人只是要求大家理解她。午夜降临，希望让位于绝望：蒂龙夫人完全处在毒品的控制之下；埃德蒙因肺结核需要疗养，生存希望不大；蒂龙先生心力交瘁，老态龙钟；杰米更加愤世嫉俗。黑夜取代了白天。

本剧是以奥尼尔一家的遭际为蓝本的；埃德蒙的原型可能是奥尼尔本

人。他在这出剧中倾注了对自己家庭全部的爱、怨和理解。它表现了他对人生的悲观认识，以及他对人类悲剧处境的深切同情。它表现的不仅是一个家庭的悲剧，而且是现代人孤独无助、无所皈依的困境。同时，本剧的艺术特色值得称道之处颇多。奥尼尔在这部剧中大量运用了象征手法，如白日象征希望，雾象征忧虑、困扰，黑夜象征绝望。他善于利用外在景物反映人物的心态，能在极短的篇幅内表现深刻的意蕴。他的舞台设计别具一格，人物对话耐人寻味。

这里选注的是第 2 幕第 2 场。

Long Day's Journey into Night

ACT 2，SCENE Ⅱ

SCENE *The same, about a half hour later.*[1] *The tray with the bottle of whiskey has been removed from the table. The family are returning from lunch as the curtain rises. Mary is the first to enter from the back parlor. Her husband follows. He is not with her as he was in the similar entrance after breakfast at the opening of Act One. He avoids touching her or looking at her. There is condemnation in his face, mingled now with the beginning of an old weary, helpless resignation.*[2] *Jamie and Edmund follow their father. Jamie's face is hard with defensive cynicism. Edmund tries to copy this defense but without success. He plainly shows he is heartsick as well as physically ill.*

Mary is terribly nervous again, as if the strain of sitting through lunch with them had been too much for her. Yet at the same time, in contrast to this, her expression shows more of that strange aloofness which seems to stand apart from her nerves and the anxieties which harry them.

She is talking as she enters—a stream of words that issues casually, in a routine of family conversation, from her mouth. She appears indifferent to the fact that their thoughts are not on what she is saying any more than her own are. As she talks, she comes to the left of the table and stands, facing front, one hand fumbling with the bosom of her dress, the other playing over the table top. Tyrone lights a cigar and goes to the screen door, staring out. Jamie fills a pipe from a jar on top of the bookcase at rear. He lights it as he goes to look out the window at right. Edmund sits in a chair by the table, turned half away from his mother so he does not have to watch her.

MARY

It's no use finding fault with Bridget. [3] She doesn't listen. I can't threaten her, or she'd threaten she'd leave. And she does do her best at times. It's too bad they seem to be just the times you're sure to be late, James. Well, there's this consolation: it's difficult to tell from her cooking whether she's doing her best or her worst.

She gives a little laugh of detached amusement—indifferently.

Never mind. The summer will soon be over, thank goodness. Your season will open again and we can go back to second-rate hotels and trains. I hate them, too, but at least I don't expect them to be like a home, [4] and there's no housekeeping to worry about. It's unreasonable to expect Bridget or Cathleen to act as if this was a home. They know it isn't as well as we know it. It never has been and it never will be.

TYRONE

Bitterly without turning around.

No, it never can be now. But it was once, before you—[5]

MARY

Her face instantly set in blank denial.

Before I what?

There is a dead silence. She goes on with a return of her detached air.

No, no. Whatever you mean, it isn't true, dear. It was never a home. You've always preferred the Club or a barroom. And for me it's always been as lonely as a dirty room in a one-night stand hotel. In a real home one is never lonely. You forget I know from experience what a home is like. I gave up one to marry you—my father's home.

At once, through an association of ideas she turns to Edmund. Her manner becomes tenderly solicitous, but there is the strange quality of detachment in it.

I'm worried about you, Edmund. You hardly touched a thing at lunch. That's no way to take care of yourself. It's all right for me not to have an appetite. I've been growing too fat. But you must eat.

Coaxingly maternal.

Promise me you will, dear, for my sake.

EDMUND

Dully.

Yes, Mama.

MARY

Pats his cheek as he tries not to shrink away.

That's a good boy.

There is another pause of dead silence. Then the telephone in the front hall rings and all of them stiffen startledly.

TYRONE

Hastily.

I'll answer. McGuire[6] said he'd call me.

He goes out through the front parlor.

MARY

Indifferently.

McGuire. He must have another piece of property on his list that no one would think of buying except your father. It doesn't matter any more, but it's always seemed to me you father could afford to keep on buying property but never to give me a home.

She stops to listen as Tyrone's voice is heard from the hall.

TYRONE

Hello.

With forced heartiness.

Oh, how are you, Doctor?

Jamie turns from the window. Mary's fingers play more rapidly on the table top. Tyrone's voice, trying to conceal, reveals that he is hearing bad news.

I see—

Hurriedly.

Well, you'll explain all about it when you see him this afternoon. Yes, he'll be in without fail. Four o'clock. I'll drop in myself and have a talk with you before that. I have to go uptown on business, anyway. Goodbye, Doctor.

EDMUND

Dully.

That didn't sound like glad tiding.

Jamie gives him a pitying glance—then looks out the window again. Mary's face is terrified and her hands flutter distractedly. Tyrone comes in. The strain is obvious in his casualness as he addresses Edmund.

TYRONE

It was Doctor Hardy. He wants you to be sure and see him at four.

EDMUND

Dully.

What did he say? Not that I give a damn now.

MARY

Bursts out excitedly.

I wouldn't believe him if he swore on a stack of Bibles. You mustn't pay attention to a word he says, Edmund.

TYRONE

Sharply.

Mary!

MARY

More excitedly.

Oh, we all realize why you like him, James! Because he's cheap! But please don't try to tell me! I know all about Doctor Hardy. Heaven knows I ought to after all these years. He's an ignorant fool! There should be a law to keep men like him from practicing. He hasn't the slightest idea—When you're in agony and half insane, he sits and holds your hand and delivers sermons on will power!

Her face is drawn in an expression of intense suffering by the memory. For the moment, she loses all caution. With bitter hatred.

He deliberately humiliates you! He makes you beg and plead! He treats you like a criminal! He understands nothing! And yet it was exactly the same type of cheap quack who first gave you the medicine—and you never knew what it was until too late! [7]

Passionately.

I hate doctors! They'll do anything—anything to keep you coming to them. They'll sell their souls! What's worse, they'll sell yours, and you never know it till one day you find yourself in hell!

EDMUND

Mama! For God's sake, stop talking.

TYRONE

Shakenly.

Yes, Mary, it's no time—

MARY

Suddenly is overcome by guilty confusion—stammers.

I—Forgive me, dear. You're right. It's useless to be angry now.

There is again a pause of dead silence. When she speaks again, her face has cleared and is calm, and the quality of uncanny detachment is in her voice and manner.

I'm going upstairs for a moment, if you'll excuse me. I have to fix my hair.

She adds smilingly.

That is if I can find my glasses. I'll be right down.

TYRONE

As she starts through the doorway—pleading and rebuking.

Mary!

MARY

Turns to stare at him calmly.

Yes, dear? What is it?

TYRONE

Helplessly.

Nothing.

MARY

With a strange derisive smile.

You're welcome to come up and watch me if you're so suspicious.

TYRONE

As if that could do any good! You'd only postpone it. And I'm not your jailor. This isn't a prison.

MARY

No. I know you can't help thinking it's a home.

She adds quickly with a detached contrition.

I'm sorry, dear. I don't mean to be bitter. It's not your fault.

She turns and disappears through the back parlor. The three in the room remain silent. It is as if they were waiting until she got upstairs before speaking.

JAMIE

Cynically brutal.

Another shot in the arm!

EDMUND

Angrily.

Cut out that kind of talk!

TYRONE

Yes! Hold your foul tongue and your rotten Broadway loafer's lingo! Have you no pity or decency?

Losing his temper.

You ought to be kicked out in the gutter! But if I did it, you know damned well who'd weep and plead for you, and excuse you and complain till I let you come back.

JAMIE

A spasm of pain crosses his face.

Christ, don't I know that? No pity? I have all the pity in the world for her. I understand what a hard game to beat she's up against—which is more than you ever have! My lingo didn't mean I had no feeling. I was merely putting bluntly what we all know, and have to live with now, again.[8]

Bitterly.

The cures are no damned good except for a while. The truth is there is no cure and we've been saps to hope—

Cynically.

They[9] never come back!

EDMUND

Scornfully parodying his brother's cynicism.

They never come back! Everything is in the bag! It's all a frame-up! We're all fall guys and suckers and we can't beat the game!

Disdainfully.

Christ, if I felt the way you do—!

JAMIE

Stung for a moment—then shrugging his shoulders, dryly.

I thought you did. Your poetry isn't very cheery. Nor the stuff you read and claim you admire.

He indicates the small bookcase at rear.

Your pet with the unpronounceable name, for example.

EDMUND

Nietzsche.[10] You don't know what you're talking about. You haven't read him.

JAMIE

Enough to know it's a lot of bunk!

TYRONE

Shut up, both of you! There's little choice between the philosophy you learned from Broadway loafers, and the one Edmund got from his books. They're both rotten to the core. You've both flouted the faith you were born and brought up in—the one true faith of the Catholic Church—and your denial has brought nothing but self-destruction!

His two sons stare at him contemptuously. They forget their quarrel and are as one against him on this issue.

EDMUND

That's the bunk, Papa!

JAMIE

We don't pretend, at any rate.

Caustically.

I don't notice you've worn any holes in the knees of your pants going to Mass.

TYRONE

It's true I'm a bad Catholic in the observance, God forgive me. But I believe!

Angrily.

And you're a liar! I may not go to church but every night and morning of my life I get on my knees and pray!

EDMUND

Bitingly.

Did you pray for Mama?

TYRONE

I did. I've prayed to God these many years for her.

EDMUND

Then Nietzsche must be right.

He quotes from Thus Spake Zarathustra. [11]

"God is dead: of His pity for man hath God died."

TYRONE

Ignores this.

If your mother had prayed, too—She hasn't denied her faith, but she's forgotten it, until now there's no strength of the spirit left in her to fight against her curse.

Then dully resigned.

But what's the good of talk? We've lived with this before and now we must again. There's no help for it.

Bitterly.

Only I wish she hadn't led me to hope this time. By God, I never will again!

EDMUND

That's a rotten thing to say, Papa!

Defiantly.

Well, I'll hope! She's just started. It can't have got a hold on her yet. She can still stop. I'm going to talk to her.

JAMIE

Shrugs his shoulders.

You can't talk to her now. She'll listen but she won't listen. She'll be here but she won't be here. You know the way she gets.

TYRONE

Yes, that's the way the poison acts on her always. Every day from now on, there'll be the same drifting away from us until by the end of each night—

EDMUND

Miserably.

Cut it out, Papa!

He jumps up from his chair.

I'm going to get dressed.

Bitterly, as he goes.

I'll make so much noise she can't suspect I've come to spy on her.

He disappears through the front parlor and can be heard stamping noisily upstairs.

JAMIE

After a pause.

What did Doc Hardy say about the Kid?

TYRONE

Dully.

It's what you thought. He's got consumption.

JAMIE

God damn it!

TYRONE

There is no possible doubt, he said.

JAMIE

He'll have to go to a sanatorium.

TYRONE

Yes, and the sooner the better, Hardy said, for him and everyone around him. He claims that in six months to a year Edmund will be cured, if he obeys orders.

He sighs—gloomily and resentfully.

I never thought a child of mine—It doesn't come from my side of the family. There wasn't one of us that didn't have lungs as strong as an ox.

JAMIE

Who gives a damn about that part of it! Where does Hardy want to send him?

TYRONE

That's what I'm to see him about.

JAMIE

Well, for God's sake, pick out a good place and not some cheap dump!

TYRONE

Stung.

I'll send him wherever Hardy thinks best!

JAMIE

Well, don't give Hardy your old over-the-hills-to-the-poorhouse song about taxes and mortgages. [12]

TYRONE

I'm no millionaire who can throw money away! Why shouldn't I tell Hardy the truth?

JAMIE

Because he'll think you want him to pick a cheap dump, and because he'll know it isn't the truth—especially if he hears afterwards you've seen McGuire and let that flannel-mouth, gold-brick merchant sting you with another piece of bum property!

TYRONE

Furiously.

Keep your nose out of my business!

JAMIE

This is Edmund's business. What I'm afraid of is, with your Irish bogtrotter idea that consumption is fatal, you'll figure it would be a waste of money to spend any more than you can help.

TYRONE

You liar!

JAMIE

All right. Prove I'm a liar. That's what I want. That's why I brought it up.

TYRONE

His rage still smouldering.

I have every hope Edmund will be cured. And keep your dirty tongue off Ireland! You're a fine one to sneer, with the map of it on your face![13]

JAMIE

Not after I wash my face.

Then before his father can react to this insult to the Old Sod, he adds dryly, shrugging his shoulders.

Well, I've said all I have to say. It's up to you.

Abruptly.

What do you want me to do this afternoon, now you're going uptown? I've done all I can do on the hedge until you cut more of it. You don't want me to go ahead with your clipping, I know that.

TYRONE

No. You'd get it crooked, as you get everything else.

JAMIE

Then I'd better go uptown with Edmund. The bad news coming on top of what's happened to Mama may hit him hard.

TYRONE

Forgetting his quarrel.

Yes, go with him, Jamie. Keep up his spirits, if you can.

He adds caustically.

If you can without making it an excuse to get drunk!

JAMIE

What would I use for money? The last I heard they were still selling booze, not giving it away.

He starts for the front-parlor doorway.

I'll get dressed.

He stops in the doorway as he sees his mother approaching from the hall, and moves aside to let her come in. Her eyes look brighter, and her manner is more detached. This change becomes more marked as the scene goes on.

MARY

Vaguely.

You haven't seen my glasses anywhere, have you, Jamie?

She doesn't look at him. He glances away, ignoring her question but she doesn't seem to expect an answer. She comes forward, addressing her husband without looking at him.

You haven't seen them, have you, James?

Behind her Jamie disappears through the front parlor.

TYRONE

Turns to look out the screen door.

No, Mary.

MARY

What's the matter with Jamie? Have you been nagging at him again? You shouldn't treat him with such contempt all the time. He's not to blame. If he'd been brought up in a real home, I'm sure he would have been different.

She comes to the windows at right—lightly.

You're not much of a weather prophet,[14] dear. See how hazy it's getting. I can hardly see the other shore.

TYRONE

Trying to speak naturally.

Yes, I spoke too soon. We're in for another night of fog, I'm afraid.

MARY

Oh, well, I won't mind it tonight.

TYRONE

No, I don't imagine you will, Mary.

MARY

Flashes a glance at him—after a pause.

I don't see Jamie going down to the hedge. Where did he go?

TYRONE

He's going with Edmund to the Doctor's. He went up to change his clothes.

Then, glad of an excuse to leave her.

I'd better do the same or I'll be late for my appointment at the Club.

He makes a move toward the front parlor doorway, but with a swift impulsive movement she reaches out and clasps his arm.

MARY

A note of pleading in her voice.

Don't go yet, dear. I don't want to be alone.

Hastily.

I mean, you have plenty of time. You know you boast you can dress in one-tenth the time it takes the boys.

Vaguely.

There is something I wanted to say. What is it? I've forgotten. I'm glad Jamie is going uptown. You didn't give him any money, I hope.

TYRONE

I did not.

MARY

He'd only spend it on drink and you know what a vile, poisonous tongue he has when he's drunk. Not that I would mind anything he said tonight, but he always manages to drive you into a rage, especially if you're drunk, too, as you will be.

TYRONE

Resentfully.

I won't. I never get drunk.

MARY

Teasing indifferently.

Oh, I'm sure you'll hold it well. You always have. It's hard for a stranger to tell, but after thirty-five years of marriage—

TYRONE

I've never missed a performance in my life. That's the proof!

Then bitterly.

If I did get drunk it is not you who should blame me. No man has ever had a better reason.

MARY

Reason? What reason? You always drink too much when you go to the Club, don't you? Particularly when you meet McGuire. He sees to that. Don't think I'm finding fault, dear. You must do as you please. I won't mind.

TYRONE

I know you won't.

He turns toward the front parlor, anxious to escape.

I've got to get dressed.

MARY

Again she reaches out and grasps his arm—pleadingly.

No, please wait a little while, dear. At least, until one of the boys comes down. You will all be leaving me so soon.

TYRONE

With bitter sadness.

It's you who are leaving us, Mary.[15]

MARY

I? That's a silly thing to say, James. How could I leave? There is nowhere I could go. Who would I go to see? I have no friends.

TYRONE

It's your own fault—

He stops and sighs helplessly—persuasively.

There's surely one thing you can do this afternoon that will be good for you, Mary. Take a drive in the automobile. Get away from the house. Get a little sun and fresh air.

Injuredly.

I bought the automobile for you. You know I don't like the damned things. I'd rather walk any day, or take a trolley.

With growing resentment.

I had it here waiting for you when you came back from the sanatorium. I hoped it would give you pleasure and distract your mind. You used to ride in it every day, but you've hardly used it at all lately. I paid a lot of money I couldn't afford, and there's the chauffeur I have to board and lodge and pay high wages whether he drives you or not.

Bitterly.

Waste! The same old waste that will land me in the poorhouse in my old age! What good did it do you? I might as well have thrown the money out the window.

MARY

With detached calm.

Yes, it was a waste of money, James. You shouldn't have bought a secondhand automobile. You were swindled again as you always are, because you insist on secondhand bargains in everything.

TYRONE

It's one of the best makes! Everyone says it's better than any of the new ones!

MARY

Ignoring this.

It was another waste to hire Smythe, who was only a helper in a garage and had never been a chauffeur. Oh, I realize his wages are less than a real chauffeur's, but he more than makes up for that, I'm sure, by the graft he gets from the garage on repair bills. Something is always wrong. Smythe sees to that, I'm afraid.

TYRONE

I don't believe it! He may not be a fancy millionaire's flunky but he's honest! You're as bad as Jamie, suspecting everyone!

MARY

You mustn't be offended, dear. I wasn't offended when you gave me the automobile. I knew you didn't mean to humiliate me. I knew that was the way you had to do everything. I was grateful and touched. I knew buying the car was a hard thing for you to do, and it proved how much you loved me, in your way, especially when you couldn't really believe it would do me any good.

TYRONE

Mary!

He suddenly hugs her to him—brokenly.

Dear Mary! For the love of God, for my sake and the boys' sake and your own, won't you stop now?[16]

MARY

Stammers in guilty confusion for a second.

I—James! Please!

Her strange, stubborn defense comes back instantly.

Stop what? What are you talking about?

He lets his arm fall to his side brokenly. She impulsively puts her arm around him.

James! We've loved each other! We always will! Let's remember only that, and not try to understand what we cannot understand, or help things that cannot be helped—the things life has done to us we cannot excuse or explain.

TYRONE

As if he hadn't heard—bitterly.

You won't even try?

MARY

Her arms drop hopelessly and she turns away—with detachment.

Try to go for a drive this afternoon, you mean?[17] Why, yes, if you wish me to, although it makes me feel lonelier than if I stayed here. There is no one I can invite to drive with me, and I never know where to tell Smythe to go. If there was a friend's house where I could drop in and laugh and gossip awhile. But, of course, there isn't. There never has been.

Her manner becoming more and more remote.

At the Convent I had so many friends. Girls whose families lived in lovely homes. I used to visit them and they'd visit me in my father's home. But, naturally, after I married an actor—you know how actors were considered in those days—a lot of them gave me the cold shoulder. And then, right after we were married, there was the scandal of that woman who had been your mistress, suing you. From then on, all my old friends either pitied me or cut me dead. I hated the ones who cut me much less than the pitiers.

TYRONE

With guilty resentment.

For God's sake, don't dig up what's long forgotten. If you're that far gone in the past already, when it's only the beginning of the afternoon, what will you be tonight?

MARY

Stares at him defiantly now.

Come to think of it, I do have to drive uptown. There's something I must get at the drugstore.

TYRONE

Bitterly scornful.

Leave it to you to have some of the stuff hidden, and prescriptions for more! I hope you'll lay in a good stock ahead so we'll never have another night like the one when you screamed for it, and ran out of the house in your nightdress half crazy, to try and throw yourself off the dock!

MARY

Tries to ignore this.

I have to get tooth powder and toilet soap and cold cream—

She breaks down pitiably.

James! You mustn't remember! You mustn't humiliate me so!

TYRONE

Ashamed.

I'm sorry. Forgive me, Mary!

MARY

Defensively detached again.

It doesn't matter. Nothing like that ever happened. You must have dreamed it.

He stares at her hopelessly. Her voice seems to drift farther and farther away.

I was so healthy before Edmund was born. You remember, James. There was't a nerve in my body. Even traveling with you season after season, with week after week of one-night stands, in trains without Pullmans, in dirty rooms of filthy hotels, eating bad food, bearing children in hotel rooms, I still kept healthy. But bearing Edmund was the last straw. I was so sick afterwards, and that ignorant quack of a cheap hotel doctor—All he knew was I was in pain. It was easy for him to stop the pain.

TYRONE

Mary! For God's sake, forget the past!

MARY

With strange objective calm.

Why? How can I? The past is the present, isn't it? It's the future, too. We all try to lie out of that but life won't let us. [18]

Going on.

I blame only myself. I swore after Eugene died I would never have another baby. I was to blame for his death. If I hadn't left him with my mother to join you on the road, because you wrote telling me you missed me and were so lonely, Jamie would never have been allowed, when he still had measles, to go in the baby's room.

Her face hardening.

I've always believed Jamie did it on purpose. He was jealous of the baby. He hated him.

As Tyrone starts to protest.

Oh, I know jamie was only seven, but he was never stupid. He'd been warned it might kill the baby. He knew. I've never been able to forgive him for that.

TYRONE

With bitter sadness.

Are you back with Eugene now? Can't you let our dead baby rest in peace?

MARY

As if she hadn't heard him.

It was my fault. I should have insisted on staying with Eugene and not have let you persuade me to join you, just because I loved you. Above all, I shouldn't have let you insist I have another baby to take Eugene's place, because you thought that would make me forget his death. I knew from experience by then that children should have homes to be born in, if they are to be good children, and women need homes, if they are to be good mothers. I was afraid all the time I carried Edmund. I knew something terrible would happen. I knew I'd proved by the way I'd left Eugene that I wasn't worthy to have another baby, and that God would punish me if I did. I never should have borne Edmund.

TYRONE

With an uneasy glance through the front parlor.

Mary! Be careful with your talk. If he heard you he might think you never wanted him. He's feeling bad enough already without—

MARY

Violently.

It's a lie! I did want him! More than anything in the world! You don't understand! I meant, for his sake. He has never been happy. He never will be. Nor healthy. He was born nervous and too sensitive, and that's my fault. And now, ever since he's been so sick I've kept remembering Eugene and my father and I've been so frightened and guilty—[19]

Then, catching herself, with an instant change to stubborn denial.

Oh, I know it's foolish to imagine dreadful things when there's no reason for it. After all, everyone has colds and gets over them.[20]

Tyrone stares at her and sighs helplessly. He turns away toward the front parlor and sees Edmund coming down the stairs in the hall.

TYRONE

Sharply, in a low voice.

Here's Edmund. For God's sake try and be yourself—at least until he goes! You can do that much for him!

He waits, forcing his face into a pleasantly paternal expression. She waits frightenedly, seized again by a nervous panic, her hands fluttering over the bosom of her dress, up to her throat and hair, with a distracted aimlessness. Then, as Edmund approaches the doorway, she cannot face him. She goes swiftly away to the windows at left and stares out with her back to the front parlor. Edmund enters. He has changed to a ready-made bhue serge suit, high stiff collar and tie, black shoes.

With an actor's heartiness.

Well! You look spic and span. I'm on my way up to change, too.

He starts to pass him.

EDMUND

Dryly.

Wait a minute, Papa. I hate to bring up disagreeable topics, but there's the matter of carfare. I'm broke.

TYRONE

Starts automatically on a customary lecture.

You'll always be broke until you learn the value—

Checks himself guiltily, looking at his son's sick face with worried pity.

But you've been learning, lad. You worked hard before you took ill. You've done splendidly. I'm proud of you.

He pulls out a small roll of bills from his pants pocket and carefully selects one. Edmund takes it. He glances at it and his face expresses astonishment. His father again reacts customarily—sarcastically.

Thank you.

He quotes.

"How sharper than a serpent's tooth it is—" [21]

EDMUND

"To have a thankless child." I know. Give me a chance, Papa. I'm knocked speechless. This isn't a dollar. It's a ten spot. [22]

TYRONE

Embarrassed by his generosity.

Put it in your pocket. You'll probably meet some of your friends uptown and you can't hold your end up and be sociable with nothing in your jeans.

EDMUND

You meant it? Gosh, thank you, Papa.

He is genuinely pleased and grateful for a moment—then he stares at his father's face with uneasy suspicion.

But why all of a sudden—?

Cynically.

Did Doc Hardy tell you I was going to die?

Then he sees his father is bitterly hurt.

No! That's a rotten crack. I was only kidding, Papa.

He puts an arm around his father impulsively and gives him an affectionate hug.

I'm very grateful. Honest, Papa.

TYRONE

Touched, returns his hug.

You're welcome, lad.

MARY

Suddenly turns to them in a confused panic of frightened anger.

I won't have it!

She stamps her foot.

Do you hear, Edmund! Such morbid nonsense! Saying you're going to die! It's the books you read! [23] Nothing but sadness and death! Your father shouldn't allow you to have them. And some of the poems you've written yourself are even worse! You'd think you didn't want to live! A boy of your age with everything before him! It's just a pose you get out of books! You're not really sick at all!

TYRONE

Mary! Hold your tongue!

MARY

Instantly changing to a detached tone.

But, James, it's absurd of Edmund to be so gloomy and make such a great to-do about nothing.

Turning to Edmund but avoiding his eyes—teasingly affectionate.

Never mind, dear. I'm on to you.

She comes to him.

You want to be petted and spoiled and made a fuss over, isn't that it? You're still such a baby.

She puts her arm around him and hugs him. He remains rigid and unyielding. Her voice begins to tremble.

But please don't carry it too far, dear. Don't say horrible things. I know it's foolish to take them seriously but I can't help it. You've got me—so frightened.

She breaks and hides her face on his shoulder, sobbing. Edmund is moved in spite of himself. He pats her shoulder with an awkward tenderness.

EDMUND

Don't, mother.

His eyes meet his father's.

TYRONE

Huskily—clutching at hopeless hope.

Maybe if you asked your mother now what you said you were going to—[24]

He fumbles with his watch.

By God, look at the time! I'll have to shake a leg.

He hurries away through the front parlor. Mary lifts her head. Her manner is again one of detached motherly solicitude. She seems to have forgotten the tears which are still in her eyes.

MARY

How do you feel, dear?

She feels his forehead.

Your head is a little hot, but that's just from going out in the sun. You look ever so much better than you did this morning.

Taking his hand.

Come and sit down. You mustn't stand on your feet so much. You must learn to husband your strength.

She gets him to sit and she sits sideways on the arm of his chair, an arm around his shoulder, so he cannot meet her eyes.

EDMUND

Starts to blurt out the appeal he now feels is quite hopeless.

Listen, Mama—

MARY

Interrupting quickly.

Now, now! Don't talk. Lean back and rest.

Persuasively.

You know, I think it would be much better for you if you stayed home this afternoon and let me take care of you. It's such a tiring trip uptown in the dirty old trolley on a hot day like this. I'm sure you'd be much better off here with me.

EDMUND

Dully.

You forget I have an appointment with Hardy.

Trying again to get his appeal started.

Listen, Mama—

MARY

Quickly.

You can telephone and say you don't feel well enough.

Excitedly.

It's simply a waste of time and money seeing him. He'll only tell you some lie. He'll pretend he's found something serious the matter because that's his bread and butter.

She gives a hard sneering little laugh.

The old idiot! All he knows about medicine is to look solemn and preach will power!

EDMUND

Trying to catch her eyes.

Mama! Please listen! I want to ask you something! You—You're only just started. You can still stop. You've got the will power! We'll all help you. I'll do anything! Won't you, Mama?

MARY

Stammers pleadingly.

Please don't—talk about things you don't understand!

EDMUND

Dully.

All right, I give up. I knew it was no use.

MARY

In blank denial now.

Anyway, I don't know what you're referring to. But I do know you should be the last one—Right after I returned from the sanatorium, you began to be ill. The doctor there had warned me I must have peace at home with nothing to upset me, and all I've done is worry about you.

Then distractedly.

But that's no excuse! I'm only trying to explain. It's not an excuse!

She hugs him to her—pleadingly.

Promise me, dear, you won't believe I made you an excuse.

EDMUND

Bitterly.

What else can I believe?

MARY

Slowly takes her arm away—her manner remote and objective again.

Yes, I suppose you can't help suspecting that.

EDMUND

Ashamed but still bitter.

What do you expect?

MARY

Nothing, I don't blame you. How could you believe me—when I can't believe myself? I've become such a liar. I never lied about anything once upon a time. Now I have to lie, especially to myself. But how can you understand, when I don't myself. I've never understood anything about it, except that one day long ago I found I could no longer call my soul my own. [25]

She pauses—then lowering her voice to a strange tone of whispered confidence.

But some day, dear, I will find it again—some day when you're all well, and I see you healthy and happy and successful, and I don't have to feel gulity any more—some day when the Blessed Virgin Mary forgives me and gives me back the faith in Her love and pity I used to have in my convent days, and I can pray to Her again—when She sees no one in the world can believe in me even for a moment any more, then She will believe in me, and with Her help it will be so easy. I will hear myself scream with agony, and at the same time I will laugh because I will be so sure of myself.

Then as Edmund remains hopelessly silent, she adds sadly.

Of course, you can't believe that, either.

She rises from the arm of his chair and qoes to stare out the windows at right with her back to him—casually.

Now I think of it, you might as well go uptown. I forgot I'm taking a drive. I have to go to the drugstore. [26] You would hardly want to go there with me. You'd be so ashamed.

EDMUND

Brokenly.

Mama! Don't!

MARY

I suppose you'll divide that ten dollars your father gave you with Jamie. You always divide with each other, don't you? Like good sports. Well, I know what he'll do with his share. Get drunk someplace where he can be with the only kind of woman he understands or likes.

She turns to him, pleading frightenedly.

Edmund! Promise me you won't drink! It's so dangerous! You know Doctor Hardy told you—

EDMUND

Bitterly.

I thought he was an old idiot.

MARY

Pitifully.

Edmund!

Jamie's voice is heard from the front hall,

"Come on, Kid, let's beat it."

Mary's manner at once becomes detached again.

Go on, Edmund. Jamie's waiting.

She goes to the front-parlor doorway.

There comes your father downstairs, too.

Tyrone's voice calls,

"Come on, Edmund."

MARY

Kisses him with detached affection.

Goodbye, dear. If you're coming home for dinner, try not to be late. And tell your father. You know what Bridget is.

He turns and hurries away. Tyrone calls from the hall, "Goodbye, Mary," *and then Jamie,* "Goodbye, Mama." *She calls back.*

Goodbye.

The front screen door is heard closing after them. She comes and stands by the table, one hand drumming on it, the other fluttering up to pat her hair. She stares about the room with frightened, forsaken eyes and whispers to herself.

It's so lonely here.

Then her face hardens into bitter self-contempt.

You're lying to yourself again. You wanted to get rid of them. Their contempt and disgust aren't pleasant company. You're glad they're gone.

She gives a little despairing laugh.

Then Mother of God, why do I feel so lonely?

CURTAIN

〔注释〕

1. 指蒂龙家消夏别墅的起居室，约中午1时30分。本剧的地点是奥尼尔以其父亲在康涅狄格购置的别墅为蓝本的。奥尼尔的舞台指示是他剧作的重要组成部分，常意味深长。

2. 这时詹姆斯已发现玛丽又开始吸毒了。

3. 蒂龙家的厨师，同女仆 Cathleen 和司机 Smythe 一样，是蒂龙先生廉价雇来的。

4. 这是贯穿于本剧的线索之一：蒂龙夫人和孩子们需要一个真正的家。蒂龙在国内巡回演出，常住二流旅馆。

5. 蒂龙想说："在你开始吸毒前"。

6. McGuire：一个商人，常骗蒂龙买他的地产。

7. 指象哈代一样的庸医用吗啡为玛丽治病，使她染上吸毒的恶习。

8. 这一段表明了杰米对母亲的感情，尽管她出语刻薄。

9. They＝the better days.

10. Nietzsche：尼采（Friedrich Nietzsche，1844～1900），德国哲学家，学者。

11. *Thus Spake Zarathustra*：《查拉图什特拉如是说》(1884)，尼采著。

12. 詹姆斯童年饥寒交迫，很小便辍学做工。贫困的经历使他成为一个吝啬鬼。

13. with the map of it upon you：爱尔兰人面部特征明显。

14. 蒂龙在第1幕说过，"Take a look out of the window, Mary, There is no fog in the harbour. I'm sure the spell of it we've had is over now."而现在起雾了，玛丽故出此语。在本剧中，雾有很深的象征意义。在第1幕詹姆斯说上述话时，他的心里充满了对玛丽的希望。而现在雾霭蒙蒙，意味着忧虑、痛苦的开始。

15. 蒂龙指玛丽终将为毒品所控制，生活在自我隔绝的世界里而不能自拔。

16. 指停止吸毒。

17. 玛丽在故意岔开话题。

18. 这是本剧最重要的对白之一。

19. 玛丽的父亲死于肺结核。她对埃德蒙的担惊和内疚导致了她重新吸毒。

20. 玛丽努力使自己想埃德蒙患的是感冒。

21. 蒂龙是一位有名的演员，常情不自禁地背诵以前演过的戏的台词，以表达自己的感情。"How sharper than a serpent's tooth is/To have a thankless child"出自莎士比亚的《李尔王》第1幕第4场。

22. It's a ten spot：这是10元钱的钞票。

23. 埃德蒙深受叔本华（Schopenhauer）、尼采（Nietzsche）、波德莱尔（Charles Baudelaire）、史文朋（Swinburne）、王尔德（Oscar Wilde）等思想家和诗人的影响。本剧一开始，奥尼尔就曾把他和他父亲的藏书做过对比。

24. 指埃德蒙曾打算自己请求母亲停止吸毒。

25. 这是玛丽的自白。

26. 他要去买毒品。

T. S. ELIOT

〔作者介绍〕

T. S. 艾略特（T. S. Eliot，1888～1965），美国著名诗人、剧作家、评论家，出生在他祖父创立华盛顿大学的圣路易斯，自幼受到良好的古典文学教育，1906年入哈佛大学学习，在著名学者桑特亚那（George Santayana，1863～1952）、欧文·巴比特（Irving Babbitt，1865～1933）及巴雷特·温德尔（Barrett Wendell，1855～1921）等的指导下苦读，接受他们的启蒙影响，巴比特的“过去可被用来衡量、约束、丰富现在”的思想对他感染尤深。业余他首次阅读但丁之作，但丁后来成为他最推崇的诗人。他还研读了善以讽刺笔触描写现代城市风貌的法国诗人拉法格（Jules Laforgue），这位诗人赋予他一种在英诗中显得新颖而富独创性的风格。1911年他写成具有强烈现代色调的《J. 阿尔弗雷德·普鲁弗洛克的情歌》（“The Love Song of J. Alfred Prufrock”）一诗。艾略特获得文学学士、硕士学位，开始攻读博士学位，并在巴黎大学、牛津大学等处深造以后，于1915年在英国定居，以教书、做银行职员、为书局撰写书评为生，同时继续诗歌创作。英国现代派作家弗吉尼亚·沃尔夫（Virginia Woolf，1882～1941）等人曾努力募捐，以使诗人能全力以赴从事创作。这期间艾略特的诗歌在运用鲜明的感官意象、极其灵活的语调以及具有高度表达能力的节奏方面，都表现出独特的风格。1920年他发表《小老头》（“Gerontion”）一诗，1922年发表具有划时代意义的长诗《荒原》（*The Waste Land*），描绘了战后欧洲的精神危机，读来好象“迷惘的一代”的宣言书一般。《荒原》奠定了艾略特在美国诗坛首屈一指的地位。《空心人》（“The Hollow Men”）于1925年问世，其悲观情绪不亚于《荒原》。1917至1919年间担任《自我主义者》（*The Egoist*）编辑，1922年创立《标准》（*The Criterion*）杂志，并任编辑至1939年。《圣灰节》（*Ash-Wednesday*，1930）及《四个四重奏》（*Four Quartets*，1943）的发表标志着艾略特在思想上已转向保守。

艾略特还是一位剧作家。他对诗剧的兴趣可追溯到他在哈佛读书时期。他写诗剧惯用的形式是戏剧独白。20 年代艾略特又潜心研究了古罗马悲剧作家塞尼加（Seneca，？～65 A. D.）的剧作传统。他的剧作包括《力士斯威尼》（*Sweeney Agonistes*，1932）、《大教堂凶杀案》（*Murder in the Cathedral*，1935）、《鸡尾酒会》（*The Cocktail Party*，1950）及《机要秘书》（*The Confidential Clerk*，1954）等。艾略特写诗剧的目的之一在于扩大他的作品的读者面。

艾略特也是一位杰出的评论家。他善于以精辟和富有权威性的语言表达其他人经常想到和提到、然而不能准确讲出的论点。做为一个文学理论家，艾略特有时思想混乱、自相矛盾，不象约翰逊（Samuel Johnson，1709～1784）、柯勒律治（Samuel Taylor Coleridge，1772～1834）或阿诺德（Matthew Arnold，1822～1888）那样具有独特见解，那样别开生面；但是说他是美国文学评论史上最成功的"文学独裁者"，在相当一段时间内左右了文坛的动向，也绝不过分。在他的评论的影响下，弥尔顿和 19 世纪英国浪漫诗人被重新评价，堂恩（John Donne，1573～1631）及其"玄学诗派"、但丁和法国象征主义诗人的作品读者剧增，他还使人们认识到过去时代的文学的活力以及到英国文学以外的文学世界里汲取营养的必要性。艾略特的评论文集包括《神木》(*The Sacred Wood*)、《风格及秩序论文集》（*Essays on Style and Order*）、《伊丽莎白论文集》(*Elizabethan Essays*)、《古今文集》(*Essays Ancient and Modern*)、《诗歌的用途和评论的用途》（*The Use of Poetry and the Use of Criticism*）及《拜异教之神》(*After Strange Gods*) 等。

艾略特是本世纪 20 年代以后最有影响的美国诗人。在他的同时与以后，有相当一批作家出现，描绘西方现代"社会荒原"的面貌，这些作家被后世称为"荒原作家"。艾略特敏锐地感到现代生活经历的徒劳无益与零乱芜杂，真切地看到现代社会的可怕与可憎。现代诗人麦克利什（Archibald Macleish，1892～1982）说，艾略特的五、六十行诗比所有社会批评家对现代世界混乱状态的刻画都深刻得多。这样，艾略特便无形中成为一代"荒原作家"的领袖。1927 年，艾略特加入英国国籍。同年，他宣称自己是"文学上的古典主义者，宗教上的英国国教—天主教教徒，政治上忠于皇室"，公开转向保守，这伤害了他许多崇拜者的感情，招致了强烈的指责，犹如晚年的华兹华斯(William Wordsworth，1770～1850）被人斥骂为"垮掉的领袖"一样。诚然，艾略特做为一个伟大的诗人，最终还是超越了政治和宗教甚至文学理论的局限，他在诗歌创作方面独辟蹊径，他的文风对英美诗坛的影响直至 50 年代后期方见减弱，时至今日仍是一股不可抵估的传统力量。艾略特 1948 年获诺贝尔文学奖。

艾略特的诗一般较难懂，这一方面固然是诗中形象和意象系列的不连惯性所致，另一方面也是由于诗人喜欢旁征博引的缘故。因此，许多关于艾略特的评论集中在考证他的引语的来源上。理解艾略特的诗歌，首先应注意到，他的诗是一种持续的复杂的思想流动，一种过去和目前的记忆的混合。艾略特的基本思想特点在于，过去可以决定现在，而现在又可以决定未来，记忆可以"打捞"起很久以前的事件和感情，使之成为现实的一部分。艾略特说过，"在某些人的头脑中，某些从读书和生活中获得的记忆变得富有感情意义。所有这些都可以运用，虽有伤于明晰，但能达到强度。"艾略特将这一概念引伸为"客观相关物"，即如他所言，"成为表达一种特别感情的方式的一组物体、一连串事件"，客观物成为比喻或象征物；在艾略特诗中，比喻和象征一般代替直接的陈述。此外还应看到，艾略特虽在文学、政治和宗教方面倾向保守和传统，然而他的技巧革新、他在诗歌语言和形式方面的尝试却毫不保守和因袭旧规。如果他的思想似有一个保守的外框，框内的图画却有时近似毕加索（Pablo Picasso）或达利（Salvador Dali）在大约同一时期所进行的绘画革新式样。做为诗人，艾略特颇受法国象征主义、詹姆斯·乔伊斯（James Joyce）的名著《尤利西斯》（*Ulysses*）及美国诗人埃兹拉·庞德的影响。艾略特的代表作《荒原》——它标志着现代英美诗歌的一场革命——在表达意识方面，在表达意识把貌似互不衔接的见闻、物体、感觉、经历等相连成有机整体方面，明显地师法了乔伊斯的现代派革新；而这首诗是经过庞德的修改后才问世的。

艾略特堪称为一代诗圣。没有他的努力，英美诗坛便不会有今天的面貌。读他的作品是了解现代英美诗歌的钥匙。

The Love Song of J. Alfred Prufrock

〔作品介绍〕

《J. 阿尔弗雷德·普鲁弗洛克的情歌》（"The Love Song of J. Alfred Prufrock"）发表于 1917 年，现已成为美国文学经典作品之一。

它描写了一个悒郁不乐、无所作为、颇具悲剧性的 20 世纪西方知识分子的形象。普鲁弗洛克的悲剧性缺陷是他的胆怯，他致命的"天罚"是他的理想主义。他谙知一切，但却一事无成；被挟持在生与死两个世界之间，他的归宿却未定；他内心有炽热的爱，却又不敢向他的所爱启齿。普鲁弗洛克对生活已绝望，他洞悉生活的空虚，却未发现可以替代或填补之物。感情上的矛盾和失意贯穿于全诗的始终，使之包孕丰富，回味无穷。

本诗的结构同它所表达的感情与情绪密切相关。全诗可看做是一种内心独白。它描述许多貌似互不相关的场面、事件和形象，诗人似乎随意由一个场面移向另外一个，由一种想法飞跃至另外一种，过渡突兀，衔接纷乱，充满矛盾和奇怪的并列或穿插。然而仔细寻味便会发现《情歌》杂而不乱，错落有致。诗中各种内容的联系多非逻辑性的，而是以所要表达的感情或情绪为转移的联想为贯穿始末的线索；这一线索将貌似无关但却表现同一种感情的许多意象串接在一个有机体中。艾略特擅长通过比喻或象征来表达思想。《情歌》是记忆、观察、冥想和评论的混合体，这些因素多以某种象征或意象出现，而一种特殊的意象又成为一种特殊的感情的表达方式。甚至诗中的标点符号也独具匠心，尤其在诗的关键转折部份，用法既出人意料，作用也不同寻常。这种委婉的表达方式对揭示一个犹柔寡断、沉吟不决的人的内心状貌无疑是最合适不过了。

做为内心独白，《情歌》似受惠于英国诗人勃朗宁（Robert Browning，1812～1889）。它也把法国诗人拉法格（Jules Laforgue，1860～1887）的自嘲手法运用于严肃的目的上。这首诗又有浓郁的詹姆斯（Henry James，1843～1916）的风采，特别是在文字方面。詹姆斯的小说《戴黑纱的科妮莉亚》（"Crapy Cornelia，" 1909）或许为艾略特提供了这首诗的轮廓。詹姆斯的小说讲的是一位独身的中年人走访一位年轻女人，欲向她求婚，但考虑到他们之间的不同之处便中途改变初衷。这篇作品的开首几章可能为艾略特提供了一些点缀性细节，而它的结尾，中年人和他的寡妇朋友科妮莉亚所说的"我老了"，又极可能成为艾略特诗中第120行"我已老了"的底本。

The Love Song of J. Alfred Prufrock

S'io credesse che mia risposta fosse
A persona che mai tornasse al mondo,
Questa fiamma staria senza piu scosse.
Ma perciocche giammai di questo fondo
Non torno vivo alcun, s'i'odo il vero,
Senza tema d'infamia ti rispondo.

Let us go then, you and I,
When the evening is spread out against the
　　sky
Like a patient etherised upon a table;
Let us go, through certain half-deserted
　　streets,
The muttering retreats

Of restless nights in one-night cheap hotels
And sawdust restaurants with oyster-shells:
Streets that follow like a tedious argument
Of insidious intent
To lead you to an overwhelming ques-
tion…

Oh, do not ask, "What is it?"
Let us go and make our visit.

In the room the women come and go
Talking of Michelangelo.

The yellow fog that rubs its back upon the
window-panes,
The yellow smoke that rubs its muzzle on
the window-panes
Licked its tongue into the corners of the
evening,
Lingered upon the pools that stand in drains,
Let fall upon its back the soot that falls from
chimneys,
Slipped by the terrace, made a sudden
leap,
And seeing that it was a soft October night,
Curled once about the house, and fell asleep.

And indeed there will be time
For the yellow smoke that slides along the
street,
Rubbing its back upon the window-panes;
There will be time, there will be time
To prepare a face to meet the faces that
you meet;
There will be time to murder and create,
And time for all the works and days of
hands

That lift and drop a question on your
plate;
Time for you and time for me,
And time yet for a hundred indecisions,
And for a hundred visions and revisions,
Before the taking of a toast and tea.

In the room the women come and go
Talking of Michelangelo.

And indeed there will be time
To wonder, "Do I dare?" and, "Do I dare?"
Time to turn back and descend the stair,
With a bald spot in the middle of my
hair—
(They will say: "How his hair is growing
thin!")
My morning coat, my collar mounting
firmly to the chin,
My necktie rich and modest, but asserted by
a simple pin—
(They will say: "But how his arms and legs
are thin!")
Do I dare
Disturb the universe?
In a minute there is time
For decisions and revisions which a minute
will reverse.

For I have known them all already, known
them all:
Have known the evenings, mornings, after-
noons,
I have measured out my life with coffee
spoons;
I know the voices dying with a dying fall
Beneath the music from a farther room.

So how should I presume?

And I have known the eyes already, known them all—
The eyes that fix you in a formulated phrase,
And when I am formulated, sprawling on a pin,
When I am pinned and wriggling on the wall,
Then how should I begin
To spit out all the butt-ends of my days and ways?
And how should I presume?

And I have known the arms already, known them all—
Arms that are braceleted and white and bare
(But in the lamplight, downed with light brown hair!)
Is it perfume from a dress
That makes me so digress?
Arms that lie along a table, or wrap about a shawl.
And should I then presume?
And how should I begin?

• • • • •

Shall I say, I have gone at dusk through narrow streets
And watched the smoke that rises from the pipes
Of lonely men in shirt-sleeves, leaning out of windows?…

I should have been a pair of ragged claws
Scuttling across the floors of silent seas.

• • • • •

And the afternoon, the evening, sleeps so

peacefully!
Smoothed by long fingers,
Asleep…tired…or it malingers,
Stretched on the floor, here beside you and
me.
Should I, after tea and cakes and ices,
Have the strength to force the moment to
its crisis?
But though I have wept and fasted, wept
and prayed,
Though I have seen my head (grown
slightly bald) brought in upon a
platter,
I am no prophet—and here's no great mat-
ter;
I have seen the moment of my greatness
flicker,
And I have seen the eternal Footman hold
my coat, and snicker,
And in short, I was afraid.

And would it have been worth it, after all,
After the cups, the marmalade, the tea,
Among the porcelain, among some talk of
you and me,
Would it have been worth while,
To have bitten off the matter with a smile,
To have squeezed the universe into a ball
To roll it toward some overwhelming ques-
tion,
To say: "I am Lazarus, come from the dead,
Come back to tell you all, I shall tell you
all" —
If one, settling a pillow by her head,
Should say: "That is not what I meant
at all;
That is not it, at all."

And would it have been worth it, aftrer all,
Would it have been worth while,
After the sunsets and the dooryards and the
sprinkled streets,
After the novels, after the teacups, after the
skirts that trail along the floor—
And this, and so much more?—
It is impossible to say just what I mean!
But as if a magic lantern threw the nerves
in patterns on a screen:
Would it have been worth while
If one, settling a pillow or throwing off a
shawl,
And turning toward the window, should
say:
"That is not it at all,
That is not what I meant at all."

.....

No! I am not Prince Hamlet, nor was meant
to be;
Am an attendant lord, one that will do
To swell a progress, start a scene or two,
Advise the prince; no doubt, an easy tool,
Deferential, glad to be of use,
Politic, cautious, and meticulous;
Full of high sentence, but a bit obtuse;
At times, indeed, almost ridiculous—
Almost, at times, the Fool.

I grow old…I grow old…
I shall wear the bottoms of my trousers
rolled.

Shall I part my hair behind? Do I dare to
eat a peach?
I shall wear white flannel trousers, and walk

upon the beach.
I have heard the mermaids singing, each to each.

I do not think that they will sing to me.

I have seen them riding seaward on the waves
Combing the white hair of the waves blown back
When the wind blows the water white and black.

We have lingered in the chambers of the sea
By sea-girls wreathed with seaweed red and brown
Till human voices wake us, and we drown.

〔注释〕

题解：顾名思义，既为情歌，就应有情歌的韵味，但读了本诗，直到中间才发现作者提到爱情，而且也是轻描淡写，没有炽烈的感情，该诗的讽刺意味由此可见一斑。Prufrock 一名取自密苏里州圣路易市一位家具店主的名字；J. Alfred 听去颇风流，给人一种门阀高贵的感觉。

序诗解：意大利文，取自但丁《地狱篇》第28章（*Inferno*，XXVIII），英文译文如下：

If I thought that I were making
Answer to one that might return to view
The world, this flame should evermore cease shaking.
But since from this abyss, if I hear true,
None ever came alive, I have no fear
Of infamy, but give thee answer due.

这是《地狱篇》中吉多·蒙特费尔特罗（Guido da Montefeltro）同过访地狱的诗人但丁讲话。吉多因欺骗罪而在第8层地狱受熬煎，他全身被火焰包围，在但丁询问他的名字时，对诗人讲了上述一番话。艾略特诗的序诗是其诗作的有机组成部分。本诗的序诗可在3种意义上同诗本身相关联。其一，倘把全诗视为普鲁弗洛克的内心独白或冥想，那么他和吉多一样在欺骗人的理智；再者，倘把内心独白中的"you"视为普鲁弗洛克性格中被压抑的一面，那末普鲁弗洛克又和吉多一样自由地暴露自己的本来面目而又不必为隐私的公开而担心；第三，普鲁弗洛克也和吉多一样处在地狱般的景况中，受到疑惧和犹豫不定的情绪的折磨。

第1行：令人忆起英国诗人勃朗宁的诗作《我最后一位公爵夫人》（“My Last Duchess”）中的一句：“Nay，we'll go down together.”艾略特在运用“戏剧独白”技巧方面颇受勃朗宁的影响。“you”的所指众说纷纭：一说为一般的读者；艾略特称指“一位没有说出其名姓的男友”；更多的人认为“you”指普鲁弗洛克个性的另一面，他内心受压抑的情欲同标志他的表面性格与身分的“I”的对立的统一。“then”表示“you”不愿随“I”去走访。

第3～4行：走访的时间为傍晚。“etherised”指人受麻醉以后处于生死之间的状态，暗喻普鲁弗洛克的虽生犹死之状，显示他希冀以强力从痛苦里解脱的愿望。

第4～7行：走访的路线通过城市的贫区。凄凉污秽的街道、旅店和餐馆，反映出走访人的寂寞、孤苦、不安及抑郁的心境。“sawdust restaurants”：以锯末铺地的低级餐馆；“with oyster-shells”：地板上扔满牡蛎壳，宛如海底一般，暗喻普鲁弗洛克的感情受到淹没和压抑。

第8～10行：走向表面望去曲折而无条理的街道恰反映出走访者内心的矛盾和踌躇（a tedious argument），内心的这一斗争既毫无休止和乏味，又似居心不良，因为它企图把人引向一个极其棘手的问题。“insidious”和“overwhelming”二字逼真地描写出走访者的畏惧心理。这种“压倒一切的重大问题”到底是什么，诗人一直没有指明。第10行的省略号表明讲话人谈虎色变，一触到本质“问题”（question）感情上便出现阻滞，因而避而不谈。于是：

第11～12行：在“you”要求说明时，他反嗔它话多。走访在进行，但其真正目的却未讲清楚。

第13～14行：走访的地方。走访者在“问题”的搅扰中忆起他曾走访过的地方，忆起在那里百无聊赖的上流社会的女人们虽一无所知却大言不惭地谈论意大利艺术大师米开朗基罗（Michelangelo，1475～1564）。后者是一位具有非凡魄力和影响的雕塑大师，愚懦的普鲁弗洛克听到女人对他的赞美声便自惭形秽，觉得自己达不到女人的理想。故这两句诗也表现出讲话人的畏惧心情。可以想像，普鲁弗洛克迄今可能依然坐在他的屋内，向四方张望。

第15～22行：他的思绪又折回到眼前的场面中来。黄昏的雾宛如猫一般蜷伏在房子的四周，雾似猫的形象反映出讲话人的精神状态：猫象征性欲，也标志着怠惰，讲话人虽有情欲，但无勇气行动；于是像猫一样昏昏沉沉，无所作为。

第23～34行：雾气消散（第24～25行），讲话人又想到时间迫切，但他依然趔趄不前，在分秒的拖延中苟且偷安。他需要时间准备好会见女人时的面部表情（即脸谱），这表示出他的紧张和惧怕心情（第27行），脸谱变了又变（第28行），时间愈近，他心情愈紧张。“works and days”暗引公元前8世纪希腊诗人赫希俄德（Hesiod）的诗作《历书》(*Works and Days*)；《历书》教人以做工的必要性。既然普鲁弗洛克整日沉湎于幻梦而一事无成，在咖啡与茶点中打发日子，对“问题”迟疑不决（Lift and drop a question on your plate），这种人的一双手的作为和赫希俄德的《历书》的教诲大相径庭，将两者同日而语，讽刺意味极浓（第29～30行）。茶点时间濒临，做决定的时间即到，气氛愈益紧张（第31～34行）。

第35～36行：他所害怕会见的女人又浮现在他的脑海。这两句诗的再现具有迭句的艺术效果，足见普鲁弗洛克终日为其所累、无法解脱的痛苦状。

第38行：他对自己的勇气首次提出明确的怀疑，他的畏惧明朗化、具体化了，他又要打退堂鼓。

第39行：攀登楼梯的意象表明他害怕做出努力的心理。

第40～44行：这位上流绅士派头和打扮的中年人有点秃顶，头发已开始稀疏，细腿细胳膊的，女人对他的长相会有什么看法呢?不会对他嘲笑吗?想到这里，他有点自卑了。

第45～46行：向女人求爱的简单问题因他的高度紧张而显得如搅乱宇宙的秩序一样严重，仿佛它会破坏他的整个一生一样。“Disturb the universe”为夸张手法，清楚地显示出受到惊吓的自我意识的脆弱。

第47～48行：仍在痛苦中延宕。

第49～50行：普鲁弗洛克在想象中逐步接近女人的住宅。

第51行：他想到了在咖啡和闲谈中所打发的无聊的时光，表明他对自己所处的上流社会生活的漫无目的、毫无意义及其它愚昧和含光混世的不满。普鲁弗洛克的浪漫主义和理想主义由此可见一斑。

第52～53行：普鲁弗洛克在想象中又接近女人一步；他听到了声音。

第54行：So how should I presume?＝So how should I presume to propose or to raise this overwhelming question?

第55～58行：普鲁弗洛克害怕女人们用固定的眼光看待他；用预先想好的语言（formulated phrase）来和他周旋。在这种环境中，他想象自己已成为一只被钉在墙上做标本的昆虫，在痛苦中扑翅扭动挣扎（第57～58行）。

第59～60行：感情色彩强烈的比喻。在上流社会交际场合吐出烟蒂，显然有失体统，但也可表示厌烦一切的普鲁弗洛克的一种反抗；然而，怯弱的普鲁弗洛克似乎连这种勇气也没有，故有“Then how should I begin…?”的问题在他脑际辗转。days and ways：泛指他的日常生活和习惯；butt-ends，烟蒂，转喻臀部，暗指折磨他的女人；To spit out 有“甩掉”或“摆脱”之内含。普鲁弗洛克欲挣脱使他生活黯然失色的女人。他对眼前女人和厌恶是他的理想主义的一种表现。

第63～64行：手臂做为性爱的象征，表明普鲁弗洛克在冥想中对女人产生了片刻的然而却浓厚的兴趣，欲火仍在他胸中闪动。downed 指“覆盖着…细毛”，是情欲的客观化。

第65～66行：未能尽兴，他推托说是衣服上的香水打搅了他的情致，欲火冷却。暗喻性生活的失败，普鲁弗洛克性能不足。

第67～69行：依然柔情缠绵，但又举棋不定，欲言又止，在紧张气氛中诗意渐臻高潮。

第70～72行：高潮终于到来，他终于开口了，然而却未说完。在说过一句试探性的“shall I say”之后，他的心理阻滞再次出现，于是他又退避三舍，回到原处，本诗第1节的景象复又出现在读者面前。

第73～74行：螃蟹的形象表明，普鲁弗洛克已觉察到自己缺乏螃蟹那种无所顾忌的动物本能，那种没有思虑打搅的“胃口”。倘若他如螃蟹一样愚钝，或许他不会象现在这样痛苦地瞻前顾后地生活了。这一形象也可能表明，对生活已经失望的普鲁弗洛克在尴尬处境中自我安慰，以自己可在感情上自足、不必借助社交来为自己的性失意辩解。他也可以像螃蟹一样独立，摒弃一切忧虑过安静日子。

第75～78行：危机已过，心绪缓和下来，睡眠的形象表明气氛已明显地宽松下来。傍晚被描绘成如猫一样或酣睡或懒怠。“you and me”：可能指普鲁弗洛克的内心和外形这两个分裂的侧面。

第79～80行：他依然想做努力，但依然怀疑自己的能力。“To force the moment to its crisis”指向女人求爱。

第81～86行：“…my head…brought in upon a platter”以夸格的手法勾勒出普鲁弗洛克在茶会上极度的尴尬与不安。head upon a platter 暗喻施洗礼的约翰（John the Baptist)。据《圣经·马太福音》第14章记载，犹太国王希律(Herod）把先知施洗者约翰杀死在狱中，斩其首级置于盘上赠给继女莎乐美(Salome)，以取悦于其母——他的续弦夫人希罗底（Herodia)；这段故事后来成为英国作家王尔德（Oscar Wilde，1854～1900）的作品《莎乐美》的素材。施洗礼的约翰是一位精力旺盛、使命感极强的人，普鲁弗洛克一联想到他便立即声明，“我不是先知”(第83行)，这种联想仅起到披露和嘲笑他的弱点的作用，他如果曾有片刻的得意感，那也即刻消失了(第84行)，社会命运这位永恒的仆人帮他穿衣时也嘲笑他的低能和失败（第85行)。胆怯征服了他的情欲，他坦率承认他的怯弱（第86行)。

第87～98行：失败后他开始为自已做辩解。“To have bitten off the matter with a smile”(第91行)：拙劣的求婚方式；“the matter”，指求婚；“To squeeze the universe into a ball…”（第92～93行)：夸大的手法，意鼓足勇气求婚；这一意象似引自安德鲁·马维尔（Andrew Marvell，1621～1678）的诗作《致腼腆的情人》（“To His Coy Mistress”)：“Let us roll all our strength and all/Our sweetness up into one ball”，这里显然有情爱的意味。“I am Lazarus，come from the dead”(第94行)：拉撒路的典故取自《圣经》。据《约翰福音》第11章，拉

撒路死去被埋葬4天后，耶稣让他起死回生；暗喻普鲁弗洛克本性中情欲的一面虽受压抑（如拉撒路被埋葬），但是却不能象拉撒路一样得以复活。"to tell…all—"：另据《路加福音》第16章，耶稣在"财主和拉撒路"一寓言中讲，乞丐拉撒路死后躺在犹太始祖亚伯拉罕的怀抱中享福，财主死后却在阴间受苦，他苦求亚伯拉罕打发拉撒路回人间告诉他所有的家人改邪归正，以免死后受苦难，暗喻上流社会生活已失去意义，即便普鲁弗洛克象拉撒路从阴司回到人间一样告诉他们他的见闻，他们也不会理解，故第95行末的破折号表示他欲言又止的心理状态。第96～98行：普鲁弗洛克担心女人会委婉地拒绝他的要求。他害怕误解女人，害怕别人嘲笑，"怕"控制了他的举止言行。

第101～103：进一步描写普鲁弗洛克所属的上流社会的毫无意义的生活，理想主义者普鲁弗洛克认识到了它的无聊。

第104行：他无法讲清自己的意图。

第105行：他的畏惧，他的敏感及紧张，在一想到女人的拒绝时，便宛如幻灯把图案映射在银幕上一样清楚地表现出来。

第111～119行：在把自己比做先知施洗礼的约翰和圣经人物拉撒路后，普鲁弗洛克继续在类似的自嘲中苟且偷安，回避实质性问题。他意识到自己和莎士比亚悲剧《哈姆雷特》(*Hamlet*）中的丹麦王子略有相似之处，但他诚实地自我否定了这种比较，因为哈姆雷特王子最终还是做成了一件事情，而他却一事无成（第111行）。他最多是一场戏中开场或扫边的配角；象《哈姆雷特》剧中的 Polonius，Rosenkrantz 或 Osric 一样，或索性是伊丽莎白时代的悲剧中所必有的插科打诨的丑角。普鲁弗洛克承认自己无能、无力的状况。因此，

第120～125行：他发出失意和精神疲乏的长叹。他接受了社会命运的安排，承认他的失败，但他决心在衣着和打扮上随心所欲，不再考虑什么"压倒一切的重大问题"，不再考虑是否遮盖一下他的秃顶，或敢不敢吃禁果的问题了（peach 令人忆起《圣经·创世纪》中亚当和夏娃被禁止采吃的"知识树"果实），他将摆脱上流社会清规戒律，到海滨去散心，听美人鱼迷人的歌声，可惜这歌却不是为他而唱的。"The mermaids singing"可能暗指希腊神话中半人半鸟的海妖塞壬（the sirens），据说塞壬们常用美妙的歌声诱引过路的航海者而使航船触礁遇难，塞壬是爱和怕相结合的象征。

第126～131行：普鲁弗洛克又陷入美人鱼的诱惑中。他又开始幻想。海的形象展示出他对理想的美、爱情和生机的向往，他的这种痴梦使他无法有效地"参与"现实生活。流水的形象表示任其自然的松弛状态，在海底的美好时光标志着普鲁弗洛克的受压抑的一面在冥想中得到满足。然而好景不长，现实（human voices）把他从梦幻中唤醒，"我们"——即表示他分裂的本性中的两面"you"和"I"——又合而为一，复又淹没在无聊的现实中。普鲁弗洛克坐在原地，依然故我。

海底的美景也可有另外一种理解。海底的生活一般被认为与“死”同义。然而诗人似乎在说，死实际又是生，人们一般认为的生者可能却是死的。弦外之音在于说明普鲁弗洛克及其上流社会实际处于一种虽生犹死的状态。

The Waste Land

〔作品介绍〕

1921年秋，艾略特在庞德为他取得的一项基金（Bel Esprit Fund）的资助下，到瑞士西部的洛桑（Lausanne）休养，其间写成《荒原》（*The Waste Land*）初稿。回伦敦前，他在巴黎逗留期间拜访庞德，把诗稿留他审阅。庞德挥笔把篇幅削减近一半。艾略特深为叹服，故在发表之际将此诗敬献给他：“献给埃兹拉·庞德/最卓越的匠人”（For Ezra Pound il miglior fabbro）；“il miglior fabbro”引自但丁《炼狱章》（*Purgatorio*）第76节第117行。约在1922年底，艾略特将标示着他本人的修改及庞德的审校文字的原稿送其友约翰·奎因（John Quinn），奎因1924年7月逝世后，原稿便失踪近40年，1963年方重见天日，成为传世奇珍。《荒原》最初刊载在1922年10月的英国《标准》（*The Criterion*）及同年11月的美国《日轨》（*The Dial*）两杂志上。

《荒原》的内涵在其序诗内有所体现。最初，艾略特援引英国作家康拉德（Joseph Conrad，1857～1924）所著《黑暗的中心》（*The Heart of Darkness*，1902）里一个名为库尔茨的人物的临终叫喊声“可怕！可怕！”做其诗序，庞德不以为然，指出康拉德的地位尚不足以服众，艾略特于是转引古罗马讽刺家佩特罗尼斯（Petronius，公元1世纪）所著的《风流韵事记》（*Satyricon*，XIVIII）里的一段话：“因为我亲眼见到古米的西比尔吊在一只玻璃瓶里，当孩子们问她，‘西比尔，你想要什么？’她总是回答说，‘我想死。’”据希腊神话，古米的西比尔是女预言家，是她宣布神谕的圣洞的保护神，又是冥府的守卫。曾爱她的太阳神阿波罗施予她预言能力，但她忘记向太阳神要永恒的青春和健康。她被关在瓶中枯而不死的形象，是荒原人虽生犹死的最好写照。如果说艾略特的早期诗歌充满失望、无能为力、百无聊赖的情绪，那么，《荒原》所表达的则是绝望和死的愿望。在荒原上，生活业已失去意义，存在的痛苦需要死的麻醉，生的意志亦已枯竭。死的愿望固然表示自我毁灭和否定生活，然而逃脱荒原的欲望又体观出对生活的肯定态度。身处荒原的诗人，感官虽已因生活力的干枯而麻木，但依然能对肥沃的、美丽的、克服荒芜的事物做出反应。荒原固然满目荒凉，但人尚未冷漠和绝望到自我毁灭的地步。“古米的西比尔”又有痛苦挣扎以求解脱的一层蕴涵。

艾略特说，他在《荒原》一诗的题目、规划及其象征手法方面，曾受益于弗雷泽（James Frazer，1854～1941）的《金枝》（*The Golden Bough*）和魏士登女士（Jessie L. Weston，1850～1928）的《从仪式到传说》（*From Ritual to Romance*）。弗雷泽毕生从事祭仪、神话和宗教之间的关系的研究，他对祈丰仪式（vegetation ritual）及繁殖神（Fertility God）的见解尤令艾略特感兴趣。弗雷泽指出，古代民族把四季交替及年景丰歉同繁殖神的健康相连。繁殖神健壮，性能力强，便春光明媚、风调雨顺、大地丰茂；神如死亡或性能力减弱，便冬寒、干旱，万物凋谢。古人每年象征性地杀死和埋葬繁殖神，后再庆祝他的“复活”，以祈求五谷丰登，这便是祈丰仪式。魏士登女士主要考证圣杯（The Holy Grail）故事的原委，认为它是祈丰仪式的变种。圣杯的传说有多种，其大意是古代有渔王（Fisher King）冒犯天威，上帝动怒，伤其阴部以示惩罚。渔王阳萎，王国遂成荒芜不毛之地。为使国王康复、大地回春，骑士们出发寻找圣杯。据传圣杯是耶稣在最后的晚餐上用过的杯子，也是圣徒约瑟（Joseph of Arimathaea）用以接被钉在十字架上的耶稣之血的杯子。寻觅圣杯的人并非一定要拿到圣杯，但是他必须找对地点，提问有关圣杯的正确问题；正确的提问便能治愈受伤的国王，恢复大地的生机；否则一切皆为徒劳。魏士登女士指出，圣杯故事后来同亚瑟王传奇（the Arthurian Legends）联系在一起：渔王的国土荒芜达千年之久，直到亚瑟王时代方有诸如高文、帕西瓦尔、兰斯洛特、加兰等圆桌骑士外出寻觅圣杯。魏士登女士的著作直接影响了艾略特的创作构思过程。《荒原》显然得名于渔王阴部受伤、王国变做荒原的情节。全诗的潜在线索是骑士寻找圣杯；诗的突出特点之一是性爱的失意，这是寻杯努力已失败的标志，是荒原人精神贫乏的体现。在为《荒原》所做的注释中，艾略特建议读者阅读一下《金枝》及《从仪式到传说》两书，以加深对诗的理解。

《荒原》由一系列宛如诗画的幻景和短述组成，语言遒劲而优雅，感情充沛而强烈。季节的更替，过去的回忆，无能的女相士，地狱般的普鲁弗鲁克式（Prufrockian）的伦敦城，酒巴间的闲话，无精打彩的女打字员与“满脸疙瘩”的青年人的交媾等等画面，透过预言家铁瑞西斯（Tiresias）的意识，投射在读者的面前。泰晤士河水，载着它的污秽的漂浮物及其历史的记忆，在城内流过；伫立在岸边的诗人仿佛哈姆雷特（Hamlet）一样，在观察和沉思，迦太基在火中被夷为平地的历史又浮现在他的脑际，他用抒情的诗笔以水的乐声为被淹死的腓尼基水手弗莱巴斯作挽歌。之后传来雷的神秘声音，出现标示世界与灵魂荒原的枯朽和死亡的各种可怕形象，同时又闪现出祈求雨水和永恒安定的希望。

这些相互之间似不关联的内容，恰好反映出西方现代人的思维特点：他们缺乏信仰，对生活已失去整体感，世界呈现出一片混乱、脱节、支离破碎之状。上帝似乎已丢下他的创造物而离去，宇宙没有了中心，生活失掉了意义，人已失去安全感，绝望情绪便油然而生。《荒原》正是本世纪初西方这种精神状貌的逼真写照，是欧美有识之士运用艺术手段解救西方精神危机的努力的重要体现。

《荒原》难解，世人皆知。其原因之一是作者通篇用典，掌故之多，历史覆盖面之广，令人望而生畏。所用文字多达7种，某些文字包孕深邃，难以钩探。最费神的要推圣杯故事在诗内的体现。谁为渔王，谁为骑士，经常变幻，不易捉摸。诗的说话人“我”的身份迄今依然众说纷纭。费迪南王子和渔王本人都有似“我”之处，诗人的意识贯穿首尾，也有“我”的意味。艾略特指出，铁瑞西斯博古通今，洞彻事理，是诗的讲话人。铁瑞西斯是精神敏锐、感情——性能力——萎蔫的典范。这个神话人物具有重要的人类学意义。据奥维德《变形记》讲，主神朱庇特同妻子朱诺在关于男女交媾谁最快活的问题上争论不休，请曾变成过女人的铁瑞西斯做仲裁。铁瑞西斯赞同主神的观点，认为女人受益最多。朱诺怒不可遏，使他双目失明。主神出于怜悯，施予他以先知的能力。艾略特在一尾注中指出，铁瑞西斯虽身处旁观地位，并非诗内人物，但却是全诗最重要的成员。铁瑞西斯观察人世事态，一切人、事都通过他的脑海而交融在一起，全诗宛如他的“意识流”，穿流过他的意识的历史框架。“铁瑞西斯所见到的”把诗中各不相关的事物联结成为有机的统一整体。艾略特对铁瑞西斯的尾注也有欠妥之处。铁瑞西斯不仅是“旁观者”，而且是他这时忆起的行动的参与者。他参与了卜卦、女打字员、荒原跋涉等事件，在诗的开首、中间和结尾处，他担任了不可或缺的综述评论者的角色。在他的头脑中，一切都在交织混合。一切在这位古先知意识的迷宫中呈现出超越时间和地点的限囿的永恒状态。《荒原》一诗已成为传世佳作，时间的流逝也不能磨灭其永恒的光辉，原因之一便在于此。

全诗共5部分，下面选注的是第1部分。这一部分的题目“埋葬死者”是英国国教的《祈祷书》内悼念死者仪式的标题。在这一礼仪中，圣保罗宣布说，死者将复活，不会腐败，我们将会变化。因此，仪式的基调是再生。

The Waste Land

‘Nam Sibyllam quidem Cumis ego ipse oculis meis vidi in ampulla pendere, et cum illi pueri dicerent: Σιβυλλα Τί θέλεις; respondebat illa: ἀποθανεῖν θέλω.’

For Ezra Pound

il miglior fabbro.

I THE BURIAL OF THE DEAD

April is the cruellest month, breeding
Lilacs out of the dead land, mixing
Memory and desire, stirring
Dull roots with spring rain.
Winter kept us warm, covering
Earth in forgetful snow, feeding
A little life with dried tubers.
Summer surprised us, coming over the Starnbergersee
With a shower of rain; we stopped in the colonnade,
And went on in sunlight, into the Hofgarten,
And drank coffee, and talked for an hour.
Bin gar keine Russin, stamm' aus Litauen, echt deutsch.
And when we were children, staying at the archduke's,
My cousin's, he took me out on a sled,
And I was frightened. He said, Marie,
Marie, hold on tight. And down we went.
In the mountains, there you feel free.
I read, much of the night, and go south in the winter.

What are the roots that clutch, what branches grow
Out of this stony rubbish? Son of man,
You cannot say, or guess, for you know only
A heap of broken images, where the sun beats,
And the dead tree gives no shelter, the cricket no relief,
And the dry stone no sound of water. Only
There is shadow under this red rock,
(Come in under the shadow of this red rock),
And I will show you something different from either
Your shadow at morning striding behind you
Or your shadow at evening rising to meet you;
I will show you fear in a handful of dust.
Frisch weht der Wind
Der Heimat zu

Mein Irisch Kind,
Wo weilest du?
'You gave me hyacinths first a year ago;
'They called me the hyacinth girl.'
—Yet when we came back, late, from the hyacinth garden,
Your arms full, and your hair wet, I could not
Speak, and my eyes failed, I was neither
Living nor dead, and I knew nothing,
Looking into the heart of light, the silence.
Oed' und leer das Meer.

Madame Sosostris, famous clairvoyante,
Had a bad cold, nevertheless
Is known to be the wisest woman in Europe,
With a wicked pack of cards. Here, said she,
Is your card, the drowned Phoenician Sailor,
(Those are pearls that were his eyes. Look!)
Here is Belladonna, the Lady of the Rocks,
The lady of situations.
Here is the man with three staves, and here the Wheel,
And here is the one-eyed merchant, and this card,
Which is blank, is something he carries on his back,
Which I am forbidden to see. I do not find
The Hanged Man. Fear death by water.
I see crowds of people, walking round in a ring.
Thank you. If you see dear Mrs. Equitone,
Tell her I bring the horoscope myself:
One must be so careful these days.

Unreal City,
Under the brown fog of a winter dawn,
A crowd flowed over London Bridge, so many,
I had not thought death had undone so many.
Sighs, short and infrequent, were exhaled,
And each man fixed his eyes before his feet.
Flowed up the hill and down King William Street,
To where Saint Mary Woolnoth kept the hours

With a dead sound on the final stroke of nine.
There I saw one I knew, and stopped him, crying: 'Stetson!
'You who were with me in the ships at Mylae!
'That corpse you planted last year in your garden,
'Has it begun to sprout? Will it bloom this year?
'Or has the sudden frost disturbed its bed?
'O keep the Dog far hence, that's friend to men,
'Or with his nails he'll dig it up again!
'You! hypocrite lecteur!—mon semblable, —mon frère!'

〔注释〕

第1～4行：四月春光明媚，万物复苏，是最美好的季节。然而，荒原上的人并不为冬去春来，大地的复苏而高兴，因为这提醒他们死的“安稳”已消失，生的周期又开始了。他们喜欢毫无生机的冬季，“冬眠”和“春生”在其认识中恰巧倒置过来，故曰 the cruellest。这种倒置不仅赋予强调复活的“埋葬死者”仪式和《埋葬死者》章以讽刺的内涵，而且是理解《荒原》全诗的钥匙。breeding 具有“breeding evil”的奇特蕴含。the dead land：在铁瑞西斯看来，春天虽到，大地依然如在冬季时一般死气沉沉，dead 一字寒气逼人。mixing/Memory and desire：铁瑞西斯（或荒原人）有生的欲望，无生的行动，往昔业已逝去，欲望和回忆在这种境况里混合起来。dull：开始发芽的根并非新鲜有力，而是无精打采，给人一种精疲力竭、老朽衰颓的感觉。

第5～7行：冬寒不能使人暖和；铁瑞西斯在以怀念之情回顾荒凉和死亡统治的冬季(第5行)。他满足于让冬雪把他覆盖，因为冬雪掩埋了春天此时又使之复活的感情，使他在忘却中苟活。一度精力旺盛、现在感情萎蔫、精神沮丧的铁瑞西斯受着欲望和回忆的熬煎。feeding/A little life with dried tubers：借用19世纪英国诗人詹姆斯·汤姆森（James Thomson，1834～1882）所写的《致我们的死去的女人》（“To Our Ladies of Death”）一诗中的诗句改写而成；汤姆森的诗说：

Our Mother feedeth thus our little life,
That we in turn may feed her with our death.

用干枯的块茎喂养的生命貌似活着，实际已死。

第8～18行：记忆把铁瑞西斯由一般回忆带回到过去的一个春天，那时他尚年轻，复活的季节带来滋养生命的雨露和阳光，他立在慕尼黑附近的斯丹卜格西（Starbergersee）湖畔，一个名叫玛丽的立陶宛女郎的声音出现在他的记忆中，她是在复述幼时一次充满畏惧、兴奋和对自由的渴望的感情经历。玛丽对山的喜爱（欲望）同充满畏惧的记忆混合在一起，她的生活并非进取和满足，而是一种失意和隐遁。Hofgarten：慕尼黑的一个公园。Bin gar keine Russin，stamm' aus Litauen，echt deutsch：德文，“我不是俄国人。我出生在立陶宛，是纯粹德国血统”；最后一句表现出艾略特思想中存在的反犹太人的倾向。at the arch-duke's，/My cousin's：据说玛丽为伯爵夫人，奥地利女王伊丽莎白的侄女，曾写过回忆录《我的过去》，描绘第一次世界大战后奥国贵族因战败而破落的景况。艾略特曾和伯爵夫人谈话，本段诗便根据这一亲身经历写成。

第19～24行：在死比生更受人欣赏的世界里，“抓住不放的根”和“从这堆石垃圾中”长出的树枝都成为一种骇人的异常现象。这里有的只是“一堆被打碎的日象”和生活被摧毁后的混乱状态，太阳直射在大地上，在无水的情况下，它不仅不是生活的源泉，而且成为无情的摧毁者。这种一片荒凉的景象酷似《旧约全书》中《以西结书》、《以赛亚书》、《传道书》、《约伯记》以及《新约全书》里《路加福音》中某些章节所记述的某些情节。

第19～20行：这是铁瑞西斯在讲话，他把自己没有爱情、苍凉凄迷的内心现实和玛丽与他本人的快活回忆相映衬。the roots…branches…this stony rubbish：似取自《约伯记》第8章第11～17节：“蒲草没有泥、岂能发长。芦荻没有水，岂能生发。尚青的时候、还没有割下、比百样的草先枯槁。凡忘记上帝的人、景况也是这样。不虔诚人的指望要灭没……他在日光之下发青、蔓子爬满了园子。他的根盘绕石堆、扎入石地。”Son of man：意“人子”，据艾略特原注，此词取自于《以西结书》第2章和第37章；事实上，“人子”是《以西结书》48章内上帝对以西结的称呼。据《圣经》载，以西结是生活在公元前6世纪的以色列先知。其时以色列人处于亚述国和巴比伦国的奴役之下，开始偶像崇拜。上帝于是选中以西结为其先知，命他去规劝以色列人改邪归正。上帝对他说：“人子阿、你站起来我要和你说话”（《以西结书》第2章第1节）。耶稣基督也以“人子”自称。

第22行．A heap of broken images，亦援引自《以西结书》(6：4)，上帝命以西结对以色列人说：“你们的祭坛必然荒凉，你们的日像必被打碎……”后来上帝果然实行了他预言的警告。

第23行：the dead tree 引自《路加福音》(23：31）中走向十字架的耶稣对为他号啕痛哭的人所说的话：“那枯干的树、将来怎么样呢。”the cricket，艾略特原著说：“参阅《传道书》第12章第5节（“人怕高处、路上有惊慌、杏树开花、蚱蜢成为重担、人所愿的也都废掉……”）

第24行：参照第19～20行中“the roots…rubbish”注。

第25～26行：red rock 似取自《新约全书》，《马太福音》(27：59)、《马可福音》(15：46)、《路加福音》(23：53，24：1）及《约翰福音》(20：1)。这些章节都提到耶稣死后被亚马利太的约瑟 (Joseph of Arimathaea) 葬在石墓里，墓口顶上一块石头。亚马利太的约瑟是保存圣杯——耶稣在最后的晚餐上用过的杯——的人，于是引出圣杯和寻找圣杯的主题。“Rock”也可能有“圣彼得之石”的含义（《马太福音》16：16、16：18)。泛指基督教信仰。shadow

似引自《约伯记》："As a servant earnestly desireth the shadow…"（7：2），"For we are but of yesterday and know nothing，because our days upon earth are a shadow："（8：9）；亦可能指17世纪英国诗人堂恩（John Donne，1571或1572～1631）的"A Lecture upon the Shadow"。

第27～29行：似引自英国伊丽莎白时代剧作家博蒙特（Francis Beaumont，1584～1616）与弗莱彻（John Fletcher，1579～1625）合写的剧《菲拉斯特》（*Philaster*）。该剧第3幕第2场写菲拉斯特怀疑公主阿瑞修莎与人私通，盛怒之下向她发泄自己对女人的怨愤说：

…how that foolish man，
That reads the story of a woman's face
And dies believing it，is lost for ever；
How all the good you have is but a shadow，
I' the morning with you，and at night behind you
Past and forgotton.

"影子"这一象征在某种意义上可以说和性关系、女人相关。讲话人铁瑞西斯似在回忆往日他年轻力壮时做过的事，那时他不象渔王，而是和一名寻求圣杯的武士一样，同女人有过交往。"影子"所象征的似是性关系的失意。在《荒原》诗内，性生活的失败引起对死的畏惧心理。因此为下一行诗埋下伏笔。

第30行：畏惧的心情用"一把土"的形象表达出来。这一形象令人联想到《圣经》。在《创世纪》（3：19）中上帝对犯戒的亚当说："你本是尘土、仍要归于尘土。"在《传道书》（12：7-8）中传道者在形容"衰败的日子"、"毫无喜乐的那些年日"的可怕情景时说："尘土仍归于地、灵仍归于赐灵的上帝"，"虚空的虚空、凡事都是虚空。"

第31～42行：在荒原上，肉体爱的失意象征精神的空虚或死亡。这10余行诗描述了两次肉体爱的失败，同前面玛丽的经历相呼应。

第31～34行：德文，英译文为：

Fresh blows the wind
To the homeland
My Irish child
Where are you waiting?

引自德国作曲家华格纳（Richard Wagner，1813～1883）的歌剧《特利斯坦和伊索尔德》（*Tristan and Isolde*）的第1幕第5～8行。特利斯坦和伊索尔德的爱情悲剧是亚瑟王传奇故事的重要组成部份。特利斯坦是亚瑟王的一名圆桌骑士，康沃尔国王马克的侄子。马克王钟爱爱尔兰国王之女伊索尔德公主，便派他前去迎亲，归途中俩人误饮爱情酒，于是深深相爱起来。回到康沃尔后，国王与伊索尔德完婚，但她与特利斯坦柔情不断，终被国王发现，特利斯坦被遣回家乡布列坦尼。后负伤，临终前渴望公主前去一见，屡派仆人去海边观望，然而大海空旷，不见一帆。后待公主赶至，他已卒世，公主也自尽。华格纳歌剧的第1幕描写年轻情人离开爱尔兰乘船回康沃尔的情景。第31行～34行是航程中水手所唱的歌颂爱情和希望的情歌。后面第42行为德文，引自华格纳同一歌剧第3幕第24行，英译文为"vast and void is the sea"，为仆人自海边归来报告不见公主踪影的话，内含凄怆与死亡之意，开首时的希望和爱情已成泡影。

第35～42行：特利斯坦和伊索尔德的遭遇引出风信子姑娘在花园的场面，情歌第4句所提出的充满爱和希望的问题，"where are you waiting?"在这几行得到否定性的回答。风信子姑娘在花园的场面以对爱的期望开始，以失意和沉寂结束。在这里，读者听到铁瑞西斯对年轻时的一次经历的回忆。风信子是以古希腊繁殖神风信子（Hyacinthus）命名的花。据艾略特读过的詹姆斯·弗雷泽（James Frazer，1854～1941）所著的《金枝》（*The Golden Bough*）第5卷第2册第7章讲，风信子神是爱情的牺牲品。这里所说的风信子姑娘是曾接受铁瑞西斯所赠的风信子花的姑娘。风信子姑娘象征浪漫的爱情及肉体爱的快乐；然而她又具有圣洁的气质和风度，宛如亚瑟王传奇中手托圣杯的神女一样。如传奇中的渔王一样，铁瑞西斯同女郎在水清花茂的地方相遇，但是希望没有实现，爱情没有成功。倘若他照圣杯传说向姑娘提出恰当的问题，他便完成了骑士寻觅圣杯的重任，渔王便可康复，国土便可重新肥沃起来。但在风信子花园同姑娘相会时，他却呆若木人，虽生犹死，未能接受献给他的爱情。体现爱和美的风信子花是邀请荒原人铁瑞西斯共享爱情的象征，荒原人既无力接受女郎的"馈赠"，也无法面对圣爱之光，肉体爱和精神爱都已失败。第35～36行为风信子女郎对铁瑞西斯的讲话。第37～41行为铁瑞西斯的回忆。第39～40行：neither/Living nor dead 似引自但丁《地狱章》（*Inferno*，XXXIV，25）："Io non morii e non rimasi vivo"。第41行：the heart of light 似引自但丁《天堂章》（*Paradiso*，XII，28）："del cordell' una delle luci nuove"。

荒原女郎因此在瞬间颇似圣女（blessèd lady），令人忆起但丁的比阿特里斯（Beatrice），然而场面倏忽即逝，余下的只有空旷的大海，如歌剧《特利斯坦和伊索尔德》里仆人回报的状况一样（第42行）。"光的中心"（The heart of light）及"一片沉寂"的内涵尚待阐明，风信子花园场面在《荒原》诗第2章内仍将说到。荒原人面对春季到来、万象更新而表现出的灰暗精神状态，荒原上一片荒芜、毫无生机的状貌，可在风信子花园的经历中寻觅到其产生的原因：荒原人无力享受肉体爱和精神爱，而从宗教意义讲，爱情即信仰。荒原人的病根乃在于他们的信仰危机。这是《荒原》的基本主题。

第43行：Madame Sosostris，荒原上的女相士，Sosostris 为男子名，为古埃及第12王朝的国王；此名取自英国作家赫胥黎（Aldous Huxley，1894～1963）的小说《铅黄》（*Crome Yellow*）中一段风趣场面的描写。在《铅黄》中，凶狠的斯科根先生在银行假日的慈善集市上，把自己妆扮成吉卜赛女相士，自称为“埃克巴坦城（古大米狄亚国首都——笔者）的女巫索索斯特里斯”。索索斯特里斯夫人的存在表明，荒原上也有神谕传布者，但是他们的魔力和见地也因患重感冒（第44行）而削弱了许多。索索斯特里斯夫人是心理算命相士，她或许能诠释上面所说的“一片沉寂”（第41行）的蕴含。她也可能是风信子女郎的一种滑稽脸谱，一种不同一般的圣杯神女；当然，她是骗子，她的举动具有浓厚的颓废性。圣杯传说有多种，其一讲到，在武士未能提出正确的问题以后，年轻的圣杯神女便成为苍老的巫婆。

第45行：“the wisest woman in Europe”一词语是对现代欧洲宗教与精神生活面貌的尖刻讥讽。

第46行：a wicked pack of cards 即太洛牌（the Tarot pack of cards）。据魏士登女士讲，太洛牌共78张，分做4类，即杯（cup，chalice 或 goblet），相当于红桃；戟（lance，wand 或 sceptre），相当于方块；剑（sword），相当于黑桃；碟（dish），相当于梅花。魏士登女士似乎认为，太洛牌同古埃及寺庙所遗留的装饰或标示尼罗河水定期升降的古埃及皇历有密切关系；她还认为纸牌和中国古代传说尧舜时期洪水过后做为纪念的碑石的表面图案也有联系，这块石碑表面分成若干小面，其大小和数目与太洛纸牌相同。这些纸牌可能曾被用来预报河水的升涨或降落，标示繁殖季节的来去；在这一意义上，纸牌又和圣杯传说中的圣杯城的标志——戟与杯——相似，戟与杯是繁殖力的象征，戟代表雄，杯代表雌，两者的连结是生命力的体现。魏士登女士说，这种纸牌由神秘的吉卜赛人传入欧洲；这些吉卜赛人今日依然以此牌作占卜用。艾略特在诗内提及太洛纸牌目的有二：一为表达他的讽刺意味，“沉寂”或生活的意义只能由一位无能的女相士借助于同样无能的纸牌来加以诠解，现代西方的滑稽不言而喻。二是借机介绍一些诗中即将出现的人物。“Here, said she,”女相士对铁瑞西斯讲话。

第47行：your 指铁瑞西斯的。the drowned Phoenician Sailor：腓尼基水手，太洛牌里没有这样一张；它象征没有爱情的死，或走向再生的努力，这种努力由于女相士的“要怕水中之死”（第55行）的“劝告”而注定失败。据《圣经》，“水中之死”是标志复活的一种洗礼。

第48行：引自莎士比亚《暴风雨》（*The Tempest*）第1幕第2场第398行：“这些珍珠曾是他的眼睛。”情节是这样的：米兰王及其子腓迪南在船翻之后漂流到同一海岛的不同地点。腓迪南王子正急于打听父王的下落，忽然听到一个精灵的歌声。使他闻声寻父。本行诗便是歌声中的一句。米兰王虽海上遇难，但大难不死，经过大海的洗礼，痛改前非，又获新生。眼睛变做珍珠象征再生。本行为第55行“水中之死”埋下伏笔。

第49～50行：Belladonna，意大利文，意为“美丽的女人，”代表爱情的变态，精神的萎靡，是一种将男人诱向毁灭的“致命女人”。the Lady of the Rocks：岩石的夫人，由达·芬奇的《岩石的夫人》一画沿袭而来。Belladonna 又可能是

《荒原》第2章《弈棋》中的女王。

第51行：the man with three staves：手持3根杖的人，指太洛牌中的教皇（the Pope）。艾略特称，他武断地把他和渔王联结起来。“3根杖”又可能意味着《荒原》第5章内佛的3项训谕，因而体现出全诗所赖以存在的宗教和道德标准。the wheel 为太洛牌中的一张，在第56行中有“命运之轮”的含义。

第52行：the one-eyed merchant，独眼商人，太洛牌里的 Fool，随后他又出现在第3章内，为士麦那商人尤金尼地菲先生。

第52～55行：the card…to see 可能是“被绞死的人”（the Hanged Man），太洛牌里确有此张；他背上的东西可能是十字架。根据《圣经》受难的耶稣未被奔往埃摩司去的使徒辨认出来。艾略特称，他把“被绞死的人”同耶稣（即本诗第5章内“戴斗篷的人”）联系起来。换言之，“被绞死的人”就是耶稣，象征铁瑞西斯或渔王的最后康复或再生。索索斯特里斯夫人身人所体现的讽刺意义在于，荒原人不能理解高尚的事物，故“这张牌/是张白牌，他的背上背着一种/不准我看的东西。我找不到/‘被绞死的人’。”

第56行：女相士所见到的荒原人群正在“命运之轮”上旋转，精神空虚，毫无目的性。荒原人群很滑稽地酷似传说中显示咒符的圣杯队伍。

第57行：Mrs. Equitone 又可能是第2章里那位“神经质女人”；Equitone 一字意“单调”、“平淡”，表明荒原人生活的百无聊赖。

第59行：言外之意显而易见；这年头如不小心，太洛牌的智慧便会误入庸人之手；具有辛棘的讽刺意味的是，女相士本人也俗不可耐。

第60～68行：unreal city，虚渺的城；艾略特称，他指的是法国作家波德莱尔（Charles Baudelaire，1821～1867）《七个老人》（“Les Sept vieillard”）一诗中所描绘的城：“这拥挤的城，充满迷梦的城，/那里的鬼魂在白昼招呼行人。”当索索斯特里斯夫人望见的人群川流不息地“流过伦敦桥”（第62行），每个人的目光都盯着自己的足前（第65行），象波德莱尔诗里的老人那样，在冬日清晨棕色雾笼罩下的伦敦城（第61行），显然象征着幽暗和毁灭的地狱，是死灵魂之城，是但丁《地狱章》第3节、第4节所描绘的地狱边缘，是世俗的、精神愚昧的人的处所。这些人乃是道地的行尸走肉，故曰“我没想到死亡毁了这么多人”（第63行）；这句诗实际是对但丁《地狱章》第3节第55～57行的改写，但丁描写地狱边缘的灵魂说：“这样长的一行人，/我从未想到/死亡毁了这么多人。”伦敦人生活单调乏味，他们日复一日，按时沿着固定的路线越过小丘、经过威廉王大街（第66行），到达座落在这条街上的圣玛利鸟尔诺斯教堂（第67行），这教堂似有圣杯城的意味。钟打9点，这死的声音标志着一天的工作开始（第68行），人们又进入百无聊赖、毫无意义的一天；9点的钟声为“死的声音”还有一种内涵，据《圣经》讲，耶稣在十字架上是于9点咽气的（《路加福音》23：44）。难怪市民们走起路来无精打采，长吁短叹，宛如亡魂，原来他们真是在人间地狱行进。

第69行：Stetson，斯特逊，泛指荒原人。在荒原上，千人一面，诗中的“我”既是旁观者，又是人群中的一员。“我”认出的名叫斯特逊的人可以是任何一位荒原居民，甚至也可以是“我”。

第70行：Mylae，迈里，公元前260年在布尼战争中（The Punic Wars）罗马人战胜迦太基人的一次海战地点，位于西西里岛东北部。讲话人在说到“迈里的船”时，恰切地把自己同腓尼基水手联系起来。

第71行：that corpse，指被杀死的繁殖神；据弗雷泽说，古时人们相信象征性地杀死并埋葬此神，再庆祝他的复活，可确保五谷丰登、人畜繁盛。这儿可能指古埃及繁殖神奥里西斯（Orisis），该神的3个男生殖器同“手持3根杖的人”又似一脉相承。your garden，同前面风信子花园相呼应，令人忆起那里发生的肉体和精神的失意及不快。

第72行：sprout 及 bloom 象征“复活”，那将是精神上的“再生”。

第73行：the sudden frost，指说话人或荒原居民的精神麻木，拒绝新生的任何标示。

第74～75行：对约翰·韦卜斯特（John Webster，1580～1625）所著的《白魔》中的挽歌的改写，韦氏的原文是：“But keep the wolf far thence，that's foe to man，/For with his nails he'll dig them up again”（第5幕第4场第97～98行）。the Dog，指天狼星（Sirius），是涨潮的标志，因此有益于生长，“它是人的朋友”。艾略特在另一首诗《在夜莺群中的斯威尼》（“Sweeney Among the Nightingales”）亦提及此星。竭力不让天狼星去掘出神从而加速复活的进程，是荒原人惧怕再生的又一例证。至此，本章内容首尾呼应，周而复始，荒原人精神之麻木状，可见其端倪。

第76行：引自波德莱尔《恶之花》（“Les Fleurs du mal”）的序诗《致读者》最后一行，英译文为：“you！hypocrite reader！—my likeness，—my brother！”《致读者》把无聊写成人之极恶，读者也知道这一点，他们却还帮闲凑趣，故曰“虚伪”。

e • e • cummings

〔作者介绍〕

卡明斯（e • e • cummings，1894～1962），美国诗人，出生于马萨诸塞州，其父曾在哈佛大学任教，卡明斯自幼深爱传统文化的熏陶。在哈佛学习期间，他对英国文学极感兴趣，涉猎颇深。诸如玄学派诗人，济慈（John Keats，1795～1821）、丁尼生（Alfred Tennyson，1809～1892）、前拉菲尔派，史文朋以及19世纪90年代的唯美派诗人等，都对他产生过影响。他对自由体诗的喜爱使他在诗风上向现代诗歌的革新靠近。卡明斯又是一位现代画家，对后印象派及立体派的绘画，对塞尚（Cezanne，1839～1906）毕加索（Picasso，1881～1973）及其它现代派绘画大师崇尚不已。当时弥漫在文学艺术界的时代叛逆精神激励了卡明斯在诗歌创作上大胆尝试，向传统挑战，打破传统形式的束缚，充分表现自已的独特风格。

卡明斯对美国作家多斯·帕索斯所说的“机器”非常反感，憎恶现代社会对人性的扭曲。他家里没有收音机和电视机等现代设施；他一生只有一次被正式雇用，为时也只有3个月。生命对他太宝贵了，不能将其耗费在名利上面。他一生献身艺术，热爱和维护人的尊严，对尘世的得失颇为恬淡。

卡明斯在哈佛学习期间所写的诗，格律皆属传统形式。1916年离开哈佛以后，他的诗作在内容和形式上都显示出一种悖逆传统的创造性飞跃。他几乎完全打破了诗歌在句法、拼写、标点、行距、用字等方面的规范和要求。他开始创作结构奇异、表现“诗意浅薄”的题材，如随便的交谈，乏味的议论，城镇印象等，诗的格调也变幻无常。第一次世界大战以后，卡明斯自欧洲返美，写出了许多优秀作品，其中一些是关于性爱的，韵味极浓；另外一些是出色的立体派（cubism）诗歌。1918至1920年间，他创作了许多爱情诗和写景篇什，并对宗教布道进行了尖锐的讽刺。

在20年代，卡明斯以立体派和达达派（Dadaism）的风格指导创作，运用异乎寻常的词语和结构，挖掘视觉在诗歌创作和欣赏中的潜力，独特的卡明斯风格脱颖而出。在他一生的最后30余年中，他的“文字游戏”越来越成熟，越来越抑扬有致。卡明斯珍视活力，歌咏个性，反对“集体”，反对盲目因袭传统。他描写爱情和性欲；他的自然诗表明他对世界、特别是对童稚天真世界的热爱；这个世界的朴实、纯真和快乐在他的诗作中表现得淋漓尽致。他的某些诗看在宛如朦胧的画面，把某种意境和现象成功地通过视觉传达给读者：他在诗歌领域内所进行的革命之激进程度，在美国诗歌史上堪称前所未有，但有时也难免失之偏颇。

卡明斯的诗集有《郁金香和烟囱》(*Tulips and Chimneys*, 1923)，《诗四十一首》(*XLI Poems*, 1925)、《是5》(*is* 5, 1926)、《不谢》(*No thanks*, 1935)以及《全集：1913～1962》(*Complete Poems*: 1913～1926)。卡明斯还写了一些剧本，如《他》(*him*, 1927) 及《圣诞老人》(*Santa Claus*, 1946)。他的散文著作《巨大的房间》(*The Enormous Room*, 1922) 叙述的是他在第一次世界大战期间曾被蒙冤监禁4个多月的经历。《艾米》(*Eimi*, 1933) 记述的是他在俄国的经历。1952至1953年间他还在哈佛大学做过讲演，讲演辞后来被收在《六个非讲座》(*six nonlectures*) 一书中。

本书选注的是他的两首名诗。

in Just

〔**作品介绍**〕

这首诗是《郁金香一烟囱》诗集中《天真之歌》里的一首。它所表现的是春天到来之际大地复苏的欢快景象。一群孩子正在快活地玩耍，看到前面来了一位跛足的卖汽球者，更使他们感到无比欢欣。大自然的春色和人类的欢娱交相映衬，诗的形式也极好地表达了这种意境：男女儿童的名字挤在一起，让人感到他们欢呼雀跃的情景，大量运用跨行的手法暗示出自然界的勃勃生机与运动，逐渐消隐下去的结尾又给人以回味不尽、余音袅袅之感。

in Just-

in Just-
spring   when the world is mud-
luscious[1] the little

lame balloonman

whistles   far   and wee

and eddieandbill[2] come
running from marbles and
piracies[3] and it's
spring

when the world is puddle-wonderful

the queer
old balloonman whistles
far   and   wee
and bettyandisbel[4] come dancing

from hop-scotch and jump-rope[5] and

it's
spring
and
    the

        goat-footed

ballonMan   whistles

                far
                and
                wee

〔注释〕

1. when the world is mud-luscious：到处都散溢着湿润泥土的浓郁气息的时候。

2. eddieandbill：Eddie and Bill：两个男孩的名字。

3. marbles and piracies：孩子们弹石子和扮强盗的游戏。

4. bettyandishel：Betty and Isabel：两个女孩子的名字。

5. hop-scotch and jump-rope：跳房子和跳绳等游戏。

O sweet spontaneous

〔作品介绍〕

这首诗歌颂大地的永生力量，挞伐人类对它的摧残。诗中列举了昏聩的哲学、愚亡的科学与伪善而又贫瘠的宗教；然而，大地总是以生机盎然的春天回敬这些。

O sweet spontaneous

O sweet spontaneous
earth how often have
the
doting

          fingers of
prurient philosophers pinched
and
poked

thee
，has the naughty thumb
of science prodded
thy

     beauty   . how
often have religions taken
thee upon their scraggy knees
squeezing and

buffeting thee that thou mightest conceive [1]
gods

(but
true

to the incomparable
couch of death thy
rhythmic
lover[2]

thou answerest
them only with

spring)

〔注释〕

1. conceive：信仰之意。

2. …the incomparable/couch of death thy/rhythmic lover：意周而复始的冬季，大地万物的凋零。

LANGSTON HUGHES

〔作者介绍〕

兰斯顿·休斯（Langston Hughes，1902～1967）是美国现代优秀黑人诗人、小说家和剧作家，"哈莱姆文艺复兴"（Harlem Renaissance）的杰出代表。

休斯出生在美国密苏里州的乔普林，自幼聪颖好学，广读博览。早在克利弗兰上中学时就开始写诗，显示出文学创作的才能。1921年，入纽约哥伦比亚大学，一年后辍学，开始独立谋生。先后在货轮上当过水手，在巴黎夜总会做过厨师，在华盛顿一家旅馆做过勤杂工。在华盛顿，他遇到诗人维切尔·林赛（Vachel Lindsay，1879～1931），林赛很赏识他的诗才，鼓励他"多思考，多研究，多写作"，立志献身文学事业。1926年在小说家卡尔·万·维奇顿（Carl Van Vechten，1880～1966）的帮助下出版第一部诗集《委靡的布鲁斯》（*The Weary Blues*）。1927年第二部诗集《献给犹太人的好衣裳》（*Fine Clothes to the Jew*）出版，同年兰斯顿入宾州林肯大学就读，1929年毕业，开始职业作家的生活。

休斯是一个多才多艺的作家，他一生创作大量各种体裁的文学作品，包括十几部诗集，长篇小说《不是没有笑声》（*Not Without Laughter*，1930），短篇小说集《白人的行经》（*The Ways of White Folks*，1934），讽刺小品集三部曲《辛普尔倾吐衷情》（*Simple Speaks of His Mind*，1950），《辛普尔的高明》（*The Best of Simple*，1961），《辛普尔的山姆叔叔》（*Simple's Uncle Tom*，1965）。辛普尔三部曲塑造出美国文学中一个令人难忘的可爱的人物形象。他还写了自传《大海》（*The Big Sea*，1940），《我徘徊，我彷徨》（*I Wonder as I Wander*，1956），以及一些剧本和儿童文学作品。晚年他编辑了大量黑人作家的作品。

"哈莱姆文艺复兴"是本世纪20年代出现在美国文坛上的一个具有重要意义的运动。一批有才智的黑人作家第一次在文学界露面，讴歌黑人的觉醒及充满活力的美国黑人文化。休斯是这一"文艺复兴"的中坚人物。他以极大的同情描写美国黑人的苦难生活和悲惨命运，抨击白人统治者的种族岐视政策，启发黑人群众的觉悟和自豪感。他的诗发出了黑人要求自由，平等和民主的呼声，在启蒙黑人觉悟方面发挥了重要作用。体斯反对种族岐视的坚定立场以及他在文学创作上的卓越成就使他早在20年代就荣获“哈莱姆桂冠诗人”的称号。

在美国黑人斗争史上，休斯的影响是很大的。在某种意义上，五、六十年代在美国蓬勃兴起的“民权运动”是以休斯、杜波依斯等作家为中坚的“哈莱姆文艺复兴”运动的继续和发展。

休斯作品的主题远远超出种族问题的界线。他向往十月革命后的苏联，颂扬新的苏维埃政权；他同情中国革命，写过战斗号角般的诗篇，号召被压迫的中国人民起来争取自由；他到过内战时期的西班牙，用大量事实揭露弗朗哥反动政权勾结法西斯势力，对西班牙人民所犯下的罪行。

休斯的诗歌朴实清新，体现了惠特曼、桑德堡和黑人诗人登巴（Paul Laurence Dunbar，1872～1906）的自由体诗歌的特色。他继承了黑人民歌和爵士乐的优良传统，作品节奏明快，很多诗被谱上乐曲，广为传唱。

休斯的文学创作为美国黑人现实主义文学的发展开避了道路。

The Negro Speaks of Rivers

〔**作品介绍**〕

《黑人谈河》（“The Negro Speaks of Rivers”）是兰斯顿·休斯学生时代写的作品。

休斯17岁时中学毕业，为了生计，母亲希望他做工帮助维持家庭生活，而离婚后远居墨西哥的父亲希望他上大学，并来信要他亲赴墨西哥讨论升学问题。兰斯顿本来就想摆脱这个家庭，最好的办法就是去上学，于是他决定去墨西哥会见父亲。母亲没有为他送行，他怀着沉重的心情登上了火车。当火车缓缓地通过密西西比河的一座大桥时，他从车窗望着湍急的河水，思索着密西西比河对于黑人意味着什么。早年非洲的黑人被奴隶贩子运往美国南方的新奥尔良一带，再沿密西西比河北上被卖到沿岸各地。他又记起林肯曾乘坐木筏沿河南下到新奥尔良，沿途目睹奴隶们生活的惨状，决心从美国的生活中铲除奴隶制。休斯同时还想到哺育人类文明和黑人文化的别的河流——刚果河，尼日尔河，尼罗河等。想着想着，一个诗句便油然而生，“我了解河流”。他顺手从衣袋里掏出一个信封，只用了10分钟便写出这首有名的

《黑人谈河》。

The Negro Speaks of Rivers

I've known rivers：
I've known rivers ancient as the world and older than the flow of
human blood in human veins.

My soul has grown deep like the rivers.

I bathed in the Euphrates when dawns were young.
I built my hut near the Congo and it lulled me to sleep.
I looked upon the Nile and raised the pyramids above it.
I heard the singing of Mississippi when Abe Lincoln went down
to New Orleans, and I've seen its muddy bosom turn all
golden in the sunset.
I've known rivers：
Ancient, dusky rivers.

My soul has grown deep like the rivers.

As I Grew Older

〔作品介绍〕

《我长大的时候》（"As I Grew Older"）是兰斯顿·休斯早期用自由体写的一首短诗，收在1926年出版的第1本诗集《萎靡的布鲁斯》里。诗人站在被压迫黑人的立场，运用比喻、象征和浪漫主义的手法抒发对种族歧视和种族隔离的愤懑心情，号召黑人依靠自己的力量起来斗争，冲破黑暗去迎接光明和自由。这首诗充分表达了诗人对未来的憧憬。

As I Grew Older

It was a long time ago.
I have almost forgotten my dream.[1]
But it was there then,
In front of me,
Bright as a sun—
My dream.

And then the wall rose,
Rose slowly,
Slowly,
Between me and my dream.
Rose slowly, slowly,
Dimming,
Hiding,
The light of my dream.
Rose until it touched the sky—
The wall.[2]

Shadow.
I am black.

I lie down in the shadow.
No longer the light of my dream before me,
Above me.
Only the thick wall.
Only the shadow.

My hands!
My dark hands!
Break through the wall!
Find my dream!
Help me to shatter this darkness,
To smash this night,

To break this shadow
Into a thousand lights of sun,
Into a thousand whirling dreams
of sun!

〔注释〕

1. My dream："我的梦"在这首短诗里多次出现。在休斯的诗里，"我的梦"是一个重复出现的主题。在另一首短诗《梦的变幻》（"Dream Variations"）里，他这样写到：

张开我的双臂，
在充满阳光的地方，
翩翩起舞，旋转如风，
直到白昼消失。
然后，当温柔的夜——
象我一样黑的夜——降临时，
在凉爽的夜晚，
坐在一棵大树下休息，
这就是我的梦。

诗人对光明、自由与欢乐的憧憬直接影响了五、六十年代美国黑人民权运动。1963年8月28日，当黑人民权运动领袖马丁·路德·金率领25万人的游行队伍向首都华盛顿挺进，发表著名的演讲时说："我有一个梦，我梦想终有一天偏见与隔离的罪恶会被消灭。"他的梦和休斯的梦一脉相承。

2. the wall：象征种族隔离。

Ballad of the Landlord

〔作品介绍〕

《房东小调》（"Ballad of the Landlord"）是一首政治讽刺诗。60年代，在美国波士顿一所黑人学校里，一个教师因为在课堂上讲授这首诗而被教育当局解雇。

Ballad of the Landlord

Landlord, landlord,
My roof has sprung a leak.
Don't you'member I told you about it
Way last week?

Landlord, landlord,
These steps is broken down.
When you come up yourself
It's a wonder you don't fall down.

Ten Bucks you say I owe you?
Ten Bucks you say is due?
Well, that's Ten Bucks more'n I'll pay you
Till you fix this house up new.

What? You gonna get eviction orders?
You gonna cut off my hcat?
You gonna take my furniture and
Throw it in the street?

Um-huh! You talking high and mighty.
Talk on—till you get through.
You ain't gonna be able to say a word
If I land my fist on you.

Police! Police!
Come and get this man!
He's trying to ruin the government
And overturn the land!

Copper's whistle!
Patrol bell!
Arrest.

Precinct Station.
Iron cell.
Headlines in press:

MAN THREATENS LANDLORD

• •
•

TENANT HELD NO BAIL

• •
•

JUDGE GIVES NEGRO 90 DAYS IN COUNTY JAIL

F. Scott Fitzgerald

〔作者介绍〕

弗·司各特·菲茨杰拉德（F. Scott Fitzgerald，1896～1940），美国著名小说家。他生于明尼苏达州的首府圣保罗。父亲属于上流阶层，母亲是爱尔兰移民的后裔。父母虽不富裕，但仍送他入私立学校学习。他17岁进普林斯顿大学，对写作和体育极感兴趣。在普林斯顿，他结识了埃德蒙·威尔逊（Edmund Wilson），威尔逊后来成为有影响的文学评论家和作家。这时，菲茨杰拉德开始向文学杂志投稿。1917年他离校入伍，被派驻亚拉巴马州首府蒙哥马利任陆军中尉，但未出国参战。在营地他利用业余时间写了小说《浪漫的利已主义者》（*The Romantic Egoist*）的初稿。在这期间，他爱上了一位法官的年轻貌美的女儿泽尔达·赛尔（Zelda Sayre）。她答应他只要有足够的钱让她过舒适日子，便愿意嫁给他。于是他们订婚了。1919年他退伍后去纽约，想赚大钱以博得泽尔达的欢心，但失望了。他立即回到圣保罗致力于创作。他大力修改了在大学期间创作的《浪漫的利已主义者》书稿。这本小说于1920年以《人间天堂》（*This Side of Paradise*）为名出版，轰动一时，他也一下子成为蜚声文坛的作家，就在这一年他和泽尔达结婚。他们在20年代初来到纽约，出入上层社会，过着豪华奢侈的生活。他们成为美国人所向往的年轻、富有、美貌和幸福的象征。1924年他们到了法国，一时又成为巴黎文艺界的重要人物。至此，菲茨杰拉德如愿以偿了。

这位年轻小说家在得意之余妙笔生花，接连发表了《轻佻女郎与哲学家》（*Flappers and Philosophers*，1921），《爵士乐时代的故事》（*Tales of the Jazz Age*，1922），以及《漂亮冤家》（*The Beautiful and Damned*，1922）。这一对年轻夫妇出入美国和欧洲的高级旅馆，经常大摆筵席，俾昼作夜，挥霍无度。由于入不敷出，菲茨杰拉德也曾为了迎合读者写些畅销的故事以获取高额稿酬来支撑局面。他的一篇名为《大如里兹饭店的钻石》（“The Diamond as Big as the Ritz”）的短篇小说，把对金钱的迫切需要描述得淋漓尽致。在巴黎，作为

"迷惘的一代"的发言人，菲茨杰拉德完成了他的代表作《大人物盖茨比》(*The Great Gatsby*，1925)，次年《一代悲哀的年轻人》(*All the Sad Young Men*，1926)短篇小说集发表了。《大人物盖茨比》虽然获得了T. S. 艾略特和埃德蒙·威尔逊的称赞，但是公众反应一般。菲茨杰拉德后来返美，曾想创作一部好莱坞喜剧但事不如意，又终于在1928年去欧洲。他感到灵感在枯竭，才华在流逝，将会变得默默无闻的预感的威胁开始袭击他的沉重的心。与此同时，他家庭生活的不幸开始了。他们夫妇间的争吵愈益激烈，后来泽尔达终于住进了精神病院，对此菲茨杰拉德感到内疚。他的《夜色温柔》(*Tender Is the Night*)一书在他长期无声无息之后于1934年问世，戏剧性地再现了他同妻子间的一些痛苦经历。

菲茨杰拉德一生的最后几年靠为好莱坞撰写剧本维持生计。为让妻子住进最好的医院，供女儿读最好的学校，他不辞劳累地工作着。他孤独寂寞，常以酒浇愁。

菲茨杰拉德代表着美国文化史上一个关键时期，他以熟练的笔描述了这个被称为"爵士乐"和"金元"的时代。他的天才和伟大正在于：他本能地把自身的经历同美国的经历等同起来，于无意中反映出时代的脉搏和面貌。他生活在战后美国的经济繁荣时期，既体验到"喧嚣的20年代"——"爵士乐时代"的表面繁荣，又预感到它的好景不长。这种认识贯穿在他的作品中，使他成为"爵士乐时代"的代言人。细读他的故事便会发现一种基本格式：开首总有梦想，随之便是奋斗，到头来却是失意和绝望——这恰是"现代美国神话"的格调。到本世纪初，敏感的人们已意识到，"美国梦"业已破灭。菲茨杰拉德的处女作《人间天堂》以他本人在普林斯顿大学期间的经历为素材，描绘他的功败垂成之感，同时也揭示出"爵士乐时代"的年轻一代成人以后发现"神仙都已死去，战争都已打完，对人的一切信心都已受到震撼"的失望与灰暗心理。《轻佻女郎与哲学家》写的是以菲茨杰拉德夫妇的形象为代表的战后美国青年的"摩登"生活，而《漂亮冤家》则透露出这种生活颓朽的一面。如果说《大人物盖茨比》的实质是关于美国经历的神话，那么，《夜色温柔》则是一部带有自传性的小说。它探索了一种酷似作者所经历的感情与精神的崩溃过程。《最后的一个巨头》(*The Last Tycoon*，1941)是揭露好莱坞电影业腐败现象的一部作品，虽然是片断（约6万字），但也足以显出是作者创作顶峰时期之作，表明作者在悲惨的遭遇之后对人生的了解更加深刻，从而达到了平心静气的境界。这本小说表达了作者对西方已腐朽和堕落的敏锐感觉。菲茨杰拉德在给女儿的一封信中说，"美国是一轮从未升起来的月亮"，这一隐喻概括总结了作家全部作品的主题。

菲茨杰拉德首先是属于20年代的。20年代的结束在一定程度上也意味着他的创作生涯的终结。他曾是这个"爵士乐时代"的命名者和象征。其后他所写的作品大部都可以说是他给自己写的"讣告"。诚然，随着时间的推移，人们也愈益清楚地认识到菲茨杰拉德的佳作又具有一种伟大的永恒的性质。这是近半个世纪以来他在美国文学史上的地位逐步升高的重要原因。回顾他的创作生涯后期及他去世以后10余年间，他曾长期湮没无闻，无人问津。到40年代末和50年代初，菲茨杰拉德才开始“复活”。诸如爱德蒙·威尔逊、马尔科姆·考利（Malcolm Cowley，1898～）和亚瑟·米兹纳（Arthur Mizener，1907～）著名作家和评论家在“发掘”这位被埋没的作家方面做出了贡献。菲茨杰拉德的声望愈来愈高，今天已成为和海明威与福克纳（William Faulkner，1897～1962）比肩齐名的小说家。

即使是在日趋“崩溃”的年月里，菲茨杰拉德也一直是一位严肃的、一丝不苟的艺术家。读他的作品会情不自禁地感到作者既是他所描述的生活现实的参加者，又是清醒地认识那种现实弊病的冷眼旁观者。这种“双重观点”及两者间所存在的张力常常产生一种强烈的讽刺意味。马尔科姆·考利评论时说，“他的所有小说仿佛在描写一场大型舞会。他带着……最漂亮的女郎前去参加……而在同时他又似站在舞厅外面，一个中西部的少年，鼻子贴在玻璃上面，捉摸着门票有多贵，是谁雇的乐队。”这种亲历与旁观的结合是菲茨杰拉德的作品蕴含遥深的基本原因。菲茨杰拉德的文字流畅，语感敏锐。他的优秀作品遣词用字总能恰到好处，细节的描写总能适可而止，情绪、思想和语调总能惬当相宜。他的笔触时而简括，时而细腻，用以确切地描述行动，塑造性格，渲染气氛。一般说来，他笔意轻捷而饶变化，语似浅而味浓，于平淡中见奇崛，点染景色而意在传情，说明作家的想像和富有诗意的艺术感都已臻精深圆熟的境界，让人读来确有一种字正腔圆、余音绕梁的美感。

The Great Gatsby

〔作品介绍〕

《大人物盖茨比》（*The Great Gatsby*）和马克·吐温的《哈克·费恩历险记》一样，是关于美国国情的一种寓言，它又和海明威的《太阳照样升起》（*The Sun Also Rises*）一样，以无出其右的艺术形式确切地再现了时代的风貌。盖茨比的故事包含着至本世纪初的全部美国经历。杰伊·盖茨比是有理想的年轻人，他心中的情人黛西代表着他对生活的憧憬。为博取这位富家漂亮小姐的爱情，他不惜用5年时间积财致富，耗费巨资买下一幢豪华别墅。他挥金如土，经常举行丰盛的酒宴，热切期待着业已嫁给富家纨绔子弟汤姆的黛西前来相会，希望复活他们之间已失去的旧情。黛西最后果然露面，但她俗不可耐的举止言谈使盖茨比颇感失望。盖茨比的期望落空了。梦想破灭，百无聊赖的盖茨比最后成为自私的黛西的牺牲品。美国曾幻想在新世界重建伊甸园，创造新的黄金时代，本世纪初资本主义机械文明的高度发展，使这种梦想成为泡影。在这个意义上讲，《大人物盖茨比》乃是关于美国的一种文化—历史性的寓言故事。

小说又简明地反映出20年代美国的精神面貌。它是“爵士乐时代”的总结。T. S. 艾略特称之为“荒原”的现代欧美精神世界，在《大人物盖茨比》中也得到形象的体现。纽约及其所代表的美国东部是这片荒原的贴切的象征。小说的关键情节发生在一片荒凉的灰尘之谷，这儿到处是一片昏暗，人宛如在地狱中一般被“尘烟完全罩住和吞噬了”（中译文引自范岳译《大人物盖茨比》，辽宁人民出版社，1983）。广告招牌上画的T. J. 埃克尔伯格医生的蓝色眼睛，瞳仁足有一码高，象上帝一样窥视着死气沉沉的人间。那副釉彩业已褪落的无精打采的眼睛又让人感到上帝已抛下他的造物离去。小说指出，东部恰似西班牙古代画家格雷科所描绘的一幅夜景：阴霾的苍穹笼罩着大地，天边的月亮暗淡无光，令人感到恐怖和不安。小说哀叹社会变态已经超出人们所能矫正的程度。

小说主人公盖茨比的形象具有妙不可言的艺术效果。一方面，盖茨比的性格带有浓厚的浪漫色彩。他相信人可以恢复过去的美好岁月，重享青春和爱情的幸福时刻，对未来充满希望。他生活目标专一，对理想忠贞不贰，具有浑浑噩噩的现代人中不可多得的高贵和天真。年轻时他严于律己，自强不息，遵循着酷似本杰明·富兰克林和亚伯拉罕·林肯的修身规范。他的成功的事实足以表明，倘若他生在18世纪，他会成为富兰克林第二，可惜他生不逢辰，事与愿违。但在另一方面，盖茨比为实现理想而采取的手段却丝毫没有高贵和天真之处。他靠非法走私而攫取巨额财产，这就不仅使他本身堕落，也直接或间接地导致他人的堕落，就这一点说，似又不值得小说用那样浓重的笔墨来加以赞扬。相信金钱可以实现理想——这是美国这个国家的矛盾形象的突出特征：盖茨比在美国历史的一个阶段成了它的杰出象征。

故事叙述者卡拉韦形象的塑造也独具匠心。卡拉韦似乎体现着他的种族的道德和良心，他诙谐地称自己的“向导、引路人、拓荒者”，希望世界穿上军装永远处于“精神立正”的严肃姿态，同时又念念不忘人“天生就有区别”的基本认识。他冷眼旁观，独清独醒，对所见所闻持不即不离的态度。这就是故事的思想与结构的中心所在。卡拉韦的神态和感情的高度坚持不懈的集中使情节的发展得到严谨的控制和加强，使小说取得一种神妙的戏剧性效果。第一人称的叙事角度使故事能有条不紊地深入展开，读者常有先是累石蓄势、悬疑不决，突然又感到“踏破铁鞋无觅处，得来全不费工夫”之感。

《大人物盖茨比》的内涵之所以如此耐人寻味，重要原因之一是它运用《圣经》的某些故事做铺垫。盖茨比在许多方面和耶稣相似。纵观盖茨比的生活，可辨认出3个明显的阶段——立志、死难、复活，这在轮廓或性质上都似耶稣的生活经历。例如，盖茨比的更改姓名（实际上是否认自己的贫贱的父母），他被称为“上帝的儿子”，“应当以他父亲的事为念”，这同《新约全书·路加福音》所记12岁的耶稣私自离家去耶路撒冷神殿的举止言行极其相似。又如盖茨比去世前的痛苦经历、去世后众叛亲离、然后又在其挚友的回忆中“复活”，细味起来，这和《圣经》福音书中所记载的耶稣殉难前最后一周的情况——犹大的背叛、耶稣的遭受诬告和审讯、门徒的惶恐和逃匿、群众对他的亵渎和判处以及死后的复活等等，都相切近。当然，如前所说，盖茨比的生活又具有双重性，这同耶稣的单纯的高贵和理想主义又互相映衬，在客观上便产生出一种出人意表的讽刺意味：以盖茨比为代表的美国人不顾现实的局限，一味追求虚渺的但令人神往的幻想，但又相信物质主义，到头来得到的不是崇高的理想，而却是“一种庞大的、低级的、俗不可耐的美”。这样，作者通过《圣经》的典故，不仅加强了人物性格的刻划和故事情节的叙述，而且加深了作品的社会意义，诱使读者去反复琢磨和想象，从而收到弦外之音的艺术效果。

下面选注的是本书最后一章——第9章。

The Great Gatsby

CHAPTER Ⅸ

After two years I[1] remember the rest of that day, and that night and the next day, only as an endless drill of police and photograhers and newspapermen in and out of Gatsby's front door. A rope stretched across the main gate and a policeman by it kept out the curious, but little boys soon discovered that they could enter through my yard, and there were always a few of them clustered open-mouthed about the pool. Someone with a positive manner, perhaps a detective, used the expression "madman" as he bent over Wilson's body[2] that afternoon, and the adventitious authority of his voice set the key for the newspaper reports next morning.

Most of those reports were a nightmare—grotesque, circumstantial, eager, and untrue. When Michaelis'[3] testimony at the inquest brought to light Wilson's suspicions of his wife I thought the whole tale would shortly be served up in racy pasquinade—but Catherine,[4] who might have said anything, didn't say a word. She showed a surprising amount of character about it too—looked at the coroner with determined eyes under that corrected brow of hers, and swore that her sister had never seen Gatsby, that her sister was completely happy with her husband, that her sister had been into no mischief whatever. She convinced herself of it, and cried into her handkerchief, as if the very suggestion was more than she could endure. So Wilson was reduced to a man "deranged by grief" in order that the case might remain in its simplest form. And it rested there.

But all this part of it seemed remote and unessential. I found myself on Gatsby's side, and alone. From the moment I telephoned news of the catastrophe to West Egg Village,[5] every surmise about him, and every practical question, was referred to me. At first I was surprised and confused; then, as he lay in his house and didn't move or breathe or speak, hour upon hour, it grew upon me that I was responsible, because no one else was interested—interested, I mean, with that intense personal interest to which everyone has some vague right at the end.

I called up Daisy[6] half an hour after we found him, called her instinctively and without hesitation. But she and Tom[7] had gone away early that afternoon, and taken baggage with them.

"Left no address?"

"No."

"Say when they'd be back?"

"No."

"Any idea where they are? How I could reach them?"

"I don't know. Can't say."

I wanted to get somebody for him. I wanted to go into the room where he lay and reassure him: "I'll get somebody for you, Gatsby. Don't worry. Just trust me and I'll get somebody for you——"

Meyer Wolfsheim's[8] name wasn't in the phone book. The butler gave me his offce address on Broadway, and I called Information, but by the time I had the number it was long after five, and no one answered the phone.

"Will you ring again?"

"I've rung them three times."

"It's very important."

"Sorry. I'm afraid no one's there."

I went back to the drawing room and thought for an instant that they were chance visitors, all these official people who suddenly filled it. But, as they drew back the sheet and looked at Gatsby with unmoved eyes, his protest continued in my brain:

"Look here, old sport, you've got to get somebody for me. You've got to try hard. I can't go through this alone."

Someone started to ask me questions, but I broke away and going upstairs looked hastily through the unlocked parts of his desk—he'd never told me definitely that his parents were dead. But there was nothing—only the picture of Dan Cody,[9] a token of forgotten violence, staring down from the wall.

Next morning I sent the butler to New York with a letter to Wolfsheim, which asked for information and urged him to come out on the next train. That request seemed superfluous when I wrote it. I was sure he'd start when he saw the newspapers, just as I was sure there'd be a wire from Daisy before noon—but neither a wire nor Mr. Wolfsheim arrived; no one arrived except more police and photographers and newspapermen. When the butler brought back Wolfsheim's answer I began to have a feeling of defiance, of scornful solidarity between Gatsby and me against them all.

> Dear Mr. Carraway. This has been one of the most terrible shocks of my life to me I hardly can believe it that it is true at all. Such a mad act as that man did should make us all think. I cannot come down now as I am tied up in some very important business and cannot get mixed up in this thing now. If there is anything I can do a little later let me know in a letter by Edgar. I hardly know where I am when I hear about a thing like this and am completely knocked down and out.
>
> Yours truly
>
> MEYER WOLFSHEIM

and then hasty addenda beneath:

> Let me know about the funeral etc do not know his family at all.

When the phone rang that afternoon and longdistance said Chicago was calling I thought this would be Daisy at last. But the connection came through as a man's voice, very thin and far away.

"This is Slagle[10] speaking..."

"Yes?" The name was unfamiliar.

"Hell of a note, isn't it? Get my wire?"

"There haven't been any wires."

"Young Parke's[11] in trouble," he said rapidly. "They[12] picked him up when he handed the bonds over the counter. They got a circular from New York giving'em the numbers just five minutes before. What d'you know about that, hey? You never can tell in these hick towns——"

"Hello!" I interrupted breathlessly. "Look here—this isn't Mr. Gatsby. Mr. Gatsby's dead."

There was a long silence on the other end of the wire, followed by an exclamation...then a quick squawk as the connection was broken.

I think it was on the third day that a telegram signed Henry C. Gatz arrived from a town in Minnesota. It said only that the sender was leaving immediately and to postpone the funeral until he came.

It was Gatsby's father, a solemn old man, very helpless and dismayed, bundled up in a long cheap ulster against the warm September day. His eyes leaked continuously with excitement, and when I took the bag and umbrella from his hands he began to pull so incessantly at his sparse gray beard that I had difficulty in getting off his coat. He was on the point of collapse, so I took him into the music room and made him sit down while I sent for something to eat. But he wouldn't eat, and the glass of milk spilled from his trembling hand.

"I saw it in the Chicago newspaper," he said. "It was all in the Chicago newspaper. I started right away."

"I didn't know how to reach you."

His eyes, seeing nothing, moved ceaselessly about the room.

"It was a madman," he said. "He must have been mad."

"Wouldn't you like some coffee?" I urged him.

"I don't want anything. I'm all right now, Mr. ——"

"Carraway."

"Well, I'all right now. Where have they got Jimmy?"

I took him into the drawing room, where his son lay, and left him there. Some little boys had come up on the steps and were looking into the hall; when I told them who had arrived, they went reluctantly away.

After a little while Mr. Gatz opened the door and came out, his mouth ajar, his face flushed slightly, his eyes leaking isolated and unpunctual tears. He had reached an age where death no longer has the quality of ghastly surprise, and when he looked around him now for the first time and saw the height and splendor of the hall and the great rooms opening out from it into other rooms, his grief began to be mixed with an awed pride. I helped him to a bedroom upstairs; while he took off his coat and vest I told him that all arrangements had been deferred until he came.

"I didn't know what you'd want, Mr. Gatsby——"

"Gatz is my name"

"—Mr. Gatz. I thought you might want to take the body West."

He shook his head.

"Jimmy always liked it better down East. He rose up to his position in the East. Were you a friend of my boy's, Mr. ——?"

"We were close friends."

"He had a big future before him, you know. He was only a young man, but he had a lot of brain power here."

He touched his head impressively, and I nodded.

"If he'd of lived,[13] he'd of been a great man. A man like James J. Hill.[14] He'd of helped build up the country."

"That's true," I said, uncomfortably.

He fumbled at the embroidered coverlet, trying to take it from the bed, and lay down stiffly—was instantly asleep.

That night an obviously frightened person called up, and demanded to know who I was before he would give his name.

"This is Mr. Carraway," I said.

"Oh!" He sounded relieved. "This is Klipspringer."[15]

I was relieved too, for that seemed to promise another friend at Gatsby's grave. I didn't want it to be in the papers and draw a sightseeing crowd, so I'd been calling up a few people myself. They were hard to find.

"The funeral's tomorrow," I said. "Three o'clock, here at the house. I wish you'd tell anybody who'd be interested."

"Oh, I will," he broke out hastily. "Of course I'm not likely to see anybody, but if I do."

His tone made me suspicious.

"Of course you'll be there yourself."

"Well, I'll certainly try. What I called up about is——"

"Wait a minute," I interrupted. "How about saying you'll come?"

"Well, the fact is—the truth of the matter is that I'm staying with some people up here in Greenwich,[16] and they rather expect me to be with them tomorrow. In fact, there's a sort of picnic or something. Of course I'll do my very best to get away."

I ejaculated an unrestrained "Huh!" and he must have heard me, for he went on nervously:

"What I called up about was a pair of shoes I left there. I wonder if it'd be too much trouble to have the butler send them on. You see, they're tennis shoes, and I'm sort of helpless without them. My address is care of B. F. ——"

I didn't hear the rest of the name, because I hung up the receiver.

After that I felt a certain shame for Gatsby—one gentleman to whom I telephoned implied that he had got what he deserved. However, that was my fault, for he was one of those who used to sneer most bitterly at Gatsby on the courage of Gatsby's liquor, and I should have known better than to call him.

The morning of the funeral I went up to New York to see Meyer Wolfsheim; I couldn't seem to reach him any other way. The door that I pushed open, on the advice of an elevator boy, was marked "The Swastika Holding Company," and at first there didn't seem to be anyone inside. But when I'd shouted "hello" several times in vain, an argument broke out behind a partition, and presently a lovely Jewess appeared at an interior door and scrutinized me with black hostile eyes.

"Nobody's in," she said. "Mr. Wolfsheim's gone to Chicago."

The first part of this was obviously untrue, for someone had begun to whistle "The Rosary," tunelessly, inside.

"Please say that Mr. Carraway wants to see him."

"I can't get him back from Chicago, can I?"

At this moment a voice, unmistakably Wolfsheim's, called "Stella!" from the other side of the door.

"Leave your name on the desk," she said quickly. "I'll give it to him when he gets back."

"But I know he's there."

She took a step toward me and began to slide her hands indignantly up and down her hips.

"You young men think you can force your way in here any time," she scolded. "We're getting sickantired[17] of it. When I say he's in Chicago, he's in Chic*ago*."

I mentioned Gatsby.

"Oh-h!" She looked at me over again. "Will you just—what was your name?"

She vanished. In a moment Meyer Wolfsheim stood solemnly in the doorway, holding out both hands. He drew me into his office, remarking in a reverent voice that it was a sad time for all of us, and offered me a cigar.

"My memory goes back to when first I met him," he said. "A young major just out of the army and covered over with medals he got in the war. He was so hard up he had to keep on wearing his uniform because he couldn't buy some regular clothes. First time I saw him was when he come[18] into Winebrenner's poolroom at Forty-third Street and asked for a job. He hadn't eat[19] anything for a couple of days. 'Come on have some lunch with me,' I said. He ate more than four dollars' worth of food in half an hour."

"Did you start him in business?" I inquired.

"Start him! I made him."

"Oh."

"I raised him up out of nothing, right out of the gutter. I saw right away he was a fine-appearing, gentlemanly young man, and when he told me he was an Oggsford[20] I knew I could use him good. I got him to join up in the American Legion[21] and he used to stand high there. Right off he did some work for a client of mine up to Albany.[22] We were so thick like that in everything"—he held up two bulbous fingers—"always together."

I wondered if this partnership had included the world's series transaction in 1919.[23]

"Now he's dead," I said after a moment. "You were his closest friend, so I know you'll want to come to his funeral this afternoon."

"I'd like to come."

"Well, come then."

The hair in his nostrils quivered slightly, and as he shook his head his eyes filled with tears.

"I can't do it—I can't get mixed up in it," he said.

"There's nothing to get mixed up in. It's all over now."

"When a man gets killed I never like to get mixed up in it in any way. I keep out. When I was a young man it was different—if a friend of mine died, no matter how, I stuck with them to the end. You may think that's sentimental, but I mean it—to the bitter end."

I saw that for some reason of his own he was determined not to come, so I stood up.

"Are you a college man?" he inquired suddenly.

For a moment I thought he was going to suggest a "gonnegtion,"[24] but he only nodded and shook my hand.

"Let us learn to show our friendship for a man when he is alive and not after he is dead," he suggested. "After that, my own rule is to let everything alone."

When I left his office the sky had turned dark and I got back to West Egg in a drizzle. After changing my clothes I went next door and found Mr. Gatz walking up and down excitedly in the hall. His pride in his son and in his son's possessions was continually increasing and now he had something to show me.

"Jimmy sent me this picture." He took out his wallet with trembling fingers. "Look there."

It was a photograph of the house, cracked in the corners and dirty with many hands. He pointed out every detail to me eagerly. "Look there!" and then sought admiration from my eyes. He had shown it so often that I think it was more real to him now than the house itself.

"Jimmy sent it to me. I think it's a very pretty picture. It shows up well."

"Very well. Had you seen him lately?"

"He come out[25] to see me two years ago and bought me the house I live in now. Of course we was broke up when he run off from home,[26] but I see now there was a reason for it. He knew he had a big future in front of him. And ever since he made a success he was very generous with me."

He seemed reluctant to put away the picture, held it for another minute, lingeringly, before my eyes. Then he returned the wallet and pulled from his pocket a ragged old copy of a book called *Hopalong Cassidy.*[27]

"Look here, this is a book he had when he was a boy. It just shows you."

He opened it at the back cover and turned it around for me to see. On the last flyleaf was printed the word SCHEDULE,[28] and the date September 12, 1906. And underneath:

Rise from bed	6.00	A.M.
Dumbbell exercise and wall-scaling	6.15—6.30	"
Study electricity, etc.	7.15—8.15	"
Work	8.30—4.30	P.M.
Baseball and sports	4.30—5.00	"
Practice elocution, poise and how to attain it	5.00—6.00	"
Study needed inventions	7.00—9.00	"

GENERAL RESOLVES

No wasting time at Shafters or [a name, indecipherable]
No more smokeing or chewing.
Bath every other day
Read one improving book or magazine per week
Save $5.00 [crossed out] $3.00 per week
Be better to parents

"I come across[29] this book by accident," said the old man. "It just shows you, don't it?

"Jimmy was bound to get ahead. He always had some resolves like this or something. Do you notice what he's got about improving his mind? He was always great for that. He told me I et[30] like a hog once, and I beat him for it."

He was reluctant to close the book, reading each item aloud and then looking eagerly at me. I think he rather expected me to copy down the list for my own use.

A little before three the Lutheran[31] minister arrived from Flushing, and I began to look involuntarily out the windows for other cars. So did Gatsby's father. And as the time passed and the servants came in and stood waiting in the hall, his eyes began to blink anxiously, and he spoke of the rain in a worried, uncertain way. The minister glanced several times at his watch, so I took him aside and asked him to wait for half an hour. But it wasn't any use. Nobody came.

About five o'clock our procession of three cars reached the cemetery and stopped in a thick drizzle beside the gate—first a motor hearse, horribly black and wet, then Mr. Gatz and the minister and I in the limousine, and a little later four or five servants and the postman from West Egg, in Gatsby's station wagon, all wet to the skin. As we started through the gate into the cemetery I heard a car stop and then the sound of someone splashing after us over the soggy ground. I looked around. It was the man with owl-eyed glasses[32] whom I had found marveling over Gatsby's books in the library one night three months before.

I'd never seen him since then. I don't know how he knew about the funeral, or even his name. The rain poured down his thick glasses, and he took them off and wiped them to see the protecting canvas unrolled from Gatsby's grave.

I tried to think about Gatsby then for a moment, but he was already too far away, and I could only remember, without resentment, that Daisy hadn't sent a message or a flower. Dimly I heard someone murmur "Blessed are the dead that the rain falls on," and then the owl-eyed man said "Amen to that," in a brave voice.

We straggled down quickly through the rain to the cars. Owl Eyes spoke to me by the gate.

"I couldn't get to the house," he remarked.

"Neither could anybody else."

"Go on!" He started. "Why, my God! they used to go there by the hundreds."

He took off his glasses and wiped them again, outside and in.

"The poor son-of-a-bitch," he said.

One of my most vivid memories is of coming back West from prep school and later from college at Christmas time. Those who went farther than Chicago would gather in the old dim Union Station at six o'clock of a December evening, with a few Chicago friends, already caught up into their own holiday gaieties, to bid them a hasty good-by. I remember the fur coats of the girls returning from Miss This-or-That's[33] and the chatter of frozen breath and the hands waving overhead as we caught sight of old acquaintances, and the matchings of invitations: "Are you going to the Ordways'? the Herseys'? the Schultzes'?" and the long green tickets clasped tight in our gloved hands. And last the murky yellow cars of the Chicago, Milwaukee[34] & St. Paul[35] Railroad looking cheerful as Christmas itself on the tracks beside the gate.

When we pulled out into the winter night and the real snow, our snow, began to stretch out beside us and twinkle against the windows, and the dim lights of small Wisconsin[36] stations moved by, a sharp wild brace came suddenly into the air. We drew in deep breaths of it as we walked back from dinner through the cold vestibules, unutterably aware of our identity with this country for one strange hour, before we melted indistinguishably into it again.

That's my Middle West[37]—not the wheat or the prairies or the lost Swede towns, but the thrilling returning trains of my youth, and the street lamps and sleigh bells in the frosty dark and the shadows of holly wreaths thrown by lighted windows on the snow. I am part of that, a little solemn with the feel of those long winters, a little complacent from growing up in the Carraway house in a city where dwellings are still called through decades by a family's name. I see now that this has been a story of the West, after all—Tom and Gatsby, Daisy and Jordan and I, were all Westerners, and perhaps we possessed some deficiency in common which made us subtly unadaptable to Eastern life.

Even when the East excited me most, even when I was most keenly aware of its superiority to the bored, sprawling, swollen towns beyond the Ohio.[38] with their interminable inquisitions which spared only the children and the very old—even then it had always for me a quality of distortion. West Egg, especially, still figures in my more fantastic dreams. I see it as a night scene by El Greco:[39] a hundred houses, at once conventional and grotesque, crouching under a sullen, overhanging sky and a lusterless moon. In the foreground four solemn men in dress suits are walking along the sidewalk with a stretcher on which lies a drunken woman in a white evening dress. Her hand, which dangles over the side, sparkles cold with jewels. Gravely the men turn in at a house—the wrong house. But no one knows the woman's name, and no one cares.

After Gatsby's death the East was haunted for me like that, distorted beyond my eyes' power of correction. So when the blue smoke of brittle leaves was in the air and the wind blew the wet laundry stiff on the line I decided to come back home.[40]

There was one thing to be done before I left, an awkward, unpleasant thing that perhaps had better have been let alone. But I wanted to leave things in order and not just trust that obliging and indifferent sea to sweep my refuse away. I saw Jordan Baker[41] and talked over and around what had happened to us together and what had happened afterward to me, and she lay perfectly still, listening, in a big chair.

She was dressed to play golf, and I remember thinking she looked like a good illustration, her chin raised a little jauntily, her hair the color of an autumn leaf, her face the same brown tint as the fingerless glove on her knee. When I had finished she told me without comment that she was engaged to another man. I doubted that, though there were several she could have married at a nod of her head, but I pretended to be surprised. For just a minute I wondered if I wasn't making a mistake, then I thought it all over again quickly and got up to say good-by.

"Nevertheless you did throw me over," said Jordan suddenly. "You threw me over on the telephone. I don't give a damn about you now, but it was a new experience for me, and I felt a little dizzy for a while."

We shook hands.

"Oh, and do you remember"—she added—"a conversation we had once about driving a car?"

"Why—not exactly."

"You said a bad driver was only safe until she met another bad driver? Well, I met another bad driver, didn't I? I mean it was careless of me to make such a wrong guess. I thought you were rather an honest, straightforward person. I thought it was your secret pride."

"I'm thirty," I said. "I'm five years too old to lie to myself and call it honor."

She didn't answer. Angry, and half in love with her, and tremendously sorry, I turned away.

One afternoon late in October I saw Tom Buchanan. He was walking ahead of me along Fifth Avenue in his alert, aggressive way, his hands out a little from his body as if to fight off interference, his head moving sharply here and there, adapting itself to his restless eyes. Just as I slowed up to avoid overtaking him he stopped and began frowning into the windows of a jewelry store. Suddenly he saw me and walked back, holding out his hand.

"What's the matter, Nick? Do you object to shaking hands with me?"

"Yes. You know what I think of you."

"You're crazy, Nick," he said quickly. "Crazy as hell. I don't know what's the matter with you."

"Tom," I inquired, "what did you say to Wilson that afternoon?"

He stared at me without a word, and I knew I had guessed right about those missing hours. I started to turn away, but he took a step after me and grabbed my arm.

"I told him the truth," he said. "He came to the door while we were getting ready to leave, and when I sent down word that we weren't in he tried to force his way upstairs. He was crazy enough to kill me if I hadn't told him who owned the car. His hand was on a revolver in his pocket every minute he was in the house—" He broke off defiantly. "What if I did tell him? That fellow had it coming to him. [42] He threw dust into your eyes just like he did in Daisy's, but he was a tough one. He ran over Myrtle like you'd run over a dog and never even stopped his car."

There was nothing I could say, except the one unutterable fact that it wasn't true.

"And if you think I didn't have my share of suffering—look here, when I went to give up that flat and saw that damn box of dog biscuits sitting there on the sideboard, I sat down and cried like a baby. By God it was awful——"

I couldn't forgive him or like him, but I saw that what he had done was, to him, entirely justified. It was all very careless and confused. They were careless people, Tom and Daisy—they smashed up things and creatures and then retreated back into their money or their vast carelessness, or whatever it was that kept them together, and let other people clean up the mess they had made.... [43]

I shook hands with him; it seemed silly not to, for I felt suddenly as though I were talking to a child. Then he went into the jewelry store to buy a pearl necklace—or perhaps only a pair of cuff buttons—rid of my provincial squeamishness forever.[44]

Gatsby's house was still empty when I left—the grass on his lawn had grown as long as mine. One of the taxi drivers in the village never took a fare past the entrance gate without stopping for a minute and pointing inside; perhaps it was he who drove Daisy and Gatsby over to East Egg[45] the night of the accident, and perhaps he had made a story about it all his own. I didn't want to hear it and I avoided him when I got off the train.

I spent my Saturday nights in New York, because those gleaming, dazzling parties of his were with me so vividly that I could still hear the music and the laughter, faint and incessant, from his garden, and the cars going up and down his drive. One night I did hear a material[46] car there, and saw its lights stop at his front steps. But I didn't investigate. Probably it was some final guest who had been away at the ends of the earth and didn't know that the party was over.[47]

On the last night, with my trunk packed and my car sold to the grocer, I went over and looked at that huge incoherent failure of a house[48] once more. On the white steps an obscene word, scrawled by some boy with a piece of brick, stood out clearly in the moonlight, and I erased it, drawing my shoe raspingly along the stone.[49] Then I wandered down to the beach and sprawled out on the sand.

Most of the big shore places were closed now and there were hardly any lights except the shadowy, moving glow of a ferryboat across the Sound.[50] And as the moon rose higher the inessential houses began to melt away until gradually I became aware of the old island here that flowered once for Dutch sailors' eyes—a fresh, green breast of the new world. Its vanished trees, the trees that had made way for Gatsby's house, had once pandered in whispers to the last and greatest of all human dreams; for a transitory enchanted moment man must have held his breath in the presence of this continent, compelled into an aesthetic contemplation he neither understood nor deired, face to face for the last time in history with something commensurate to his capacity for wonder.

And as I sat there brooding on the old, unknown world, I thought of Gatsby's wonder[51] when he first picked out the green light at the end of Daisy's dock.[52] He had come a long way to this blue lawn, and his dream must have seemed so close that he could hardly fail to grasp it. He did not know that it was already behind him, somewhere back in that vast obscurity beyond the city, where the dark fields of the republic rolled on under the night.

Gatsby believed in the green light, the orgiastic future that year by year recedes before us. It eluded us then, but that's no matter—tomorrow we will run faster, stretch out our arms farther . . . . And one fine morning——

So we beat on, boats against the current, borne back ceaselessly into the past.

〔注释〕

1. I：即尼克·卡拉韦（Nick Carraway），故事的叙述人。

2. Wilson's body：威尔逊的尸体。Wilson 即乔治·威尔逊。他经营一个汽车买卖和修理业务的汽车修理行（见第2章），其妻因车祸丧生。他听信妻子的情夫汤姆的谎言，误认为盖茨比为肇祸者，因此将他杀死，后自尽。

3. Michaelis：一个开咖啡馆的年轻的希腊人，乔治·威尔逊的邻居，曾目睹汽车辗死乔治的妻子默特尔（见第2章）。

4. Catherine：Myrtle 的妹妹（见第2章）。

5. West Egg Village：西卵镇，是书中主人公盖茨比（Gatsby）和故事叙述者尼克·卡拉韦住的地方。

6. Daisy：黛西，出身富家的漂亮小姐，原为盖茨比的情人，后嫁给花花公子汤姆。

7. Tom：即汤姆·布坎南（Tom Buchanan），黛西的丈夫（参看注释2）。

8. Meyer Wolfsheim：一个与盖茨比合伙做非法生意的人（见第4章）。

9. Dan Cody：小说中一个数次被提到但从未露面的人物。他靠开发金银矿发迹。盖茨比年轻时曾在他手下工作过。Dan Cody 这一名字使人想起西部的著名人物 Daniel Boone 和 Buffalo Bill Cody 及他们所代表的开拓精神。

10. Slagle：盖茨比做非法生意的伙伴。

11. Parke：盖茨比做非法生意的伙伴。

12. They：指警察局。

13. If he'd of lived, …a great man：应为 If he'd lived, he'd have been a great man。口语中或未受过教育者的话中常有不合语法的语句。

14. James J. Hill：詹姆斯·J·希尔（1838～1916），美国的铁路大王。

15. Klipspringer：一个常到盖茨比家长住的人，有盖茨比家的"寄宿者"之称。

16. Greenwich：格林尼治，美国康涅狄格州西南部一城市，濒临长岛海峡。

17. sickantired＝sick and tired.

18. when he come：应为 when he came。

19. He hadn't eat：应为 He hadn't eaten。

20. an Oggsford：应为 an Oxford，牛津大学毕业生。

21. The American Legion：美国退伍军人协会。

22. Albany：奥本尼，美国纽约州的首府。

23. the world's series transaction in 1919：1919 年世界棒球赛的那项交易，小说的第 4 章曾提到此事。盖茨比曾对尼克说，"He's the man who fixed the world's series back in 1919."（"他是远在 1919 年操纵过世界棒球比赛的人。"）

24. gonnegtion：应为 connection。

25. He come out：应为 He came out。

26. of course we was broke up when he run off from home：应为 Of course we were broken up when he ran off from home。

27. *Hopalong Cassidy*：书名，《牛仔卡西迪》。Hopalong 意为"跛子"；Cassidy 为人名。

28. SCHEDULE：作息时间表。这个作息时间表及后面的个人总守则与本杰明·富兰克林《自传》中所谈的修身要求极相似。富兰克林认为通过艰苦劳动、节约和诚实，穷人可以从贫困的桎梏下解放自己。盖茨比的故事很有美国成功故事的意味。然而时过境迁，富兰克林一生所体现的"美国梦"到盖茨比时代业已破灭。

29. come across：应为 came across。

30. I et：应为 I ate。

31. Lutheran：路德教派的。马丁·路德（Martin Luther）为 16 世纪德国宗教改革运动的倡导者、基督教新教路德教派的创始人。

32. the man with owl-eyed glasses：这是一个肥胖的中年人，盖茨比生前宴会上不邀自来的"客人"之一（见本书第 3 章）。他的古怪的眼镜令人想起竖立在灰尘之谷旁眼镜广告牌上那一双俯瞰下面灰堆般的昏暗世界的眼睛——T. J. 埃克尔伯格医生的眼睛。在汽车修理店的威尔逊看来，这是"上帝"的眼睛。因此，这位中年人参加葬礼，便具有盖茨比的"精神之父"出席的意味。这和耶稣的死难情景相近。

33. Miss This-or-That's：指当时以某某小姐为名字的女子学校。

34. Milwaukee：密尔沃基，美国威斯康星州一城市。

35. St Paul：圣保罗，美国明尼苏达州之首府。

36. Wisconsin：美国威斯康星州。

37. Middle West：美国的中西部，亦做 Midwest。

38. the Ohio：美国东部一河流，注入密西西比河。

39. El Greco：艾尔格雷考（1541～1614），西班牙画家。

40. 本段及上一段的描绘和第2章对灰尘之谷的描写相呼应。在菲茨杰拉德笔下，美国东部宛如地狱一般。

41. Jordan Baker：乔丹・贝克，黛西・布坎南的女友，与故事的叙述者卡拉韦有一段若即若离的爱情关系。

42. That fellow had it coming to him：那家伙是咎由自取。That fellow 指盖茨比。

43. 此段表明菲茨杰拉德对华贵之家的态度是既羡慕又鄙夷，鄙夷多于羡慕。在他笔下，豪富本身意味着堕落，也诱致他人堕落。他的短篇小说《有钱人家的孩子》（"The Rich Boy"）是对这段话的脚注。

44. rid of my …for ever：在这里，作者的自贬中孕含着对虚伪、自私、金钱凌驾一切的现代文明的尖刻讽刺。

45. East Egg：东卵镇，小说中汤姆和黛西居住过的地方。

46. material：意"真的"。

47. the party was over：筵席已散。卡拉韦回首往事，百感交集，凄楚之情跃于纸上。同第3章"宴会已开始"遥相呼应，哀叹人生的荣枯浮沉。

48. that huge incoherent failure of a house：被遗弃的房子成为盖茨比生涯的象征：那是离奇、矛盾、失败的一生。

49. 和对汤姆夫妇的态度相反，卡拉韦始终设法维护盖茨比的声誉。卡拉韦虽然说他"鄙夷"盖茨比所代表的一切，但他毕竟更推崇他对人生前景的高度敏感，和对未来充满希望的天赋。卡拉韦认为他"从没见过别人身上具备这种特点，恐怕将来也是难以看到的"（见第1章）。

50. the Sound：指长岛海峡（Long Island Sound），位于美国康涅狄格州与长岛之间。

51. I thought of Gatsby's wonder…：这里卡拉韦回忆起过去。盖茨比的海滨住宅昔日人声鼎沸，今日落寞、凄清，人亡物在，使卡拉韦感伤不已。在他对老友的怀念中几乎下意识地把盖茨比同几百年前来长岛定居的荷兰移民及美国的过去联结并等同起来。这种联结和等同可以看做是盖茨比的一种"复活"。盖茨比曾相信往昔可以失而复得，曾竭力恢复业已逝去的美好的过去，卡拉韦认为他所体现的美国梦并未幻灭，他的富于理想色彩的浪漫精神应该永存。这种"复活"又令人忆起耶稣遇难3日后以在人间显身的《圣经》故事。

52. the green light at the end of Daisy's dock：Daisy's dock 暗喻，盖茨比的梦想；green light 形容他对理想可以实现的信念。

WILLIAM FAULKNER

〔作者介绍〕

福克纳（William Faulkner，1897～1962）是美国现代著名小说家。他出生在南方新奥本尼市一个历史悠久的家庭。南方的兴衰荣枯成为他作品的主题；他的家庭成员，包括他的曾祖、祖父、父亲及兄弟，都成为他小说人物的原型。

第一次世界大战早期，福克纳曾到加拿大参加英国空军。回国后在密西西比大学就读1年，做过银行职员及多种杂工。这期间他结识了饱读古典及现代文学名著的菲尔·斯通（Phil Stone），在斯通的启迪和帮助下，他了解到美国文坛新星庞德及弗罗斯特等人的创作情况，并于1924年出版了诗集《玉石收神》（*The Marble Faun*）。又经斯通的引荐，他在新奥尔良谒见舍伍德·安德森，在后者的指点下，创作和出版了第一部小说《士兵的报酬》（*Soldier's Pay*，1926）。在新奥尔良，他还听到乔伊斯（James Joyce，1882～1941）、康拉德（Joseph Conrad，1857～1824）及弗洛伊德（Sigmund Freud，1856～1939）等人的大名。1925年他赴欧洲旅行，见到他崇拜的乔伊斯，并对现代派绘画产生了兴趣。

福克纳的第2部小说《蚊群》（*Mosquitoes*，1927）并未引起注意；1929年出版的《沙特里斯》（*Sartoris*）却表现出作家的创作已渐臻成熟。在这部小说里，他第一次描绘他日后一直努力表现的虚构的"约克那帕特法县"，开始展露他的独特宇宙的状貌。他的《喧哗与骚动》（*The Sound and the Fury*，1929）标志着他已成为美国现代主要作家。1930年，《我弥留之际》（*As I Lay Dying*）问世，福克纳开始为自己的声名不振担心。次年他出版了旨在刺激读者而引人注目的《圣殿》（*Sanctuary*），由于该书情节引人入胜，描写细腻，在一定程度上扩大了他的影响。其后10余年中，他致力于在作品中描状"约克那帕特法县"，《八月之光》（*Light in August*，1932）、《押沙龙，押沙龙！》（*Absalom，Absalom!*，1936）及《去吧，摩西》（*Go Down，Moses*，1942）等相继问世，都堪称美国文学的上乘之作。评论界开始承认他在文坛的地位，但在整个40年代，没有出现关于他的作品的严肃评论文章，某些作品业已绝版。1946年是福克纳文学生涯的转折点。著名文学批评家马尔科姆·考利编辑了他的作品选集，并撰文详细介绍他的著作。这使世人得以赏识他那独特精湛的艺术。一个文学巨匠几十年的苦心终于得到世界的理解。他获得了1949年诺贝尔文学奖。

福克纳共创作了18部小说和3部短篇小说集。他的作品多以美国南方的历史为题材。他探讨过去的兴趣时常达到入魔的程度。印第安人的时代、白人的出现、资本主义制度和奴隶制的建立、以剥夺红色人种和压榨黑人为基础的南方特殊文化的形成、白人梦幻的破灭等等，都在福克纳的作品中有所反映。他以浓重的笔墨描写“约克那帕特法县”的演进，再现出南方的兴衰史。平凡的史料在福克纳的笔下突然具备了一种神话性质，令人感到故事业已超出美国南方的范畴。他讲述的是人的梦想、勇气、成功与最后失败的故事，表现的是人生内在的格局或模式。其目的似乎在于利用南方历史谈论过去和今天人与生活的关系等重大问题。因此，读者有时会不由自主地意识到，他笔下的美国南方历史是人类经历的一个缩影。这是福克纳的作品耐人寻味的根本所在。

福克纳的作品所描述的多是发生在南方的悲剧故事。如沙特里斯家族、康普生家族、塞特潘家族及麦卡斯林家族的白人移民，在暴力、流血、压迫、乱伦、不义的基础上建立起一个没有人性的社会，并竭力维护它，妄图使之永世长存。这个社会的罪恶根基受到美国内战的震撼，战后，一切复辟的努力都以惨败告终。“现代工业文明”长驱直入，南方于是衰颓下去。这是福克纳全部作品的故事轮廓。福克纳认为，现代人已失去爱和感情，失去人的同情心，生活因而失去意义，世界已成为精神贫乏的虚无之地。恰如《喧哗与骚动》一书中康普生先生所说，给生活强涂上一层道德与信仰的色彩是无助于事的，这不仅因为现实生活无法达到这些标准，而且这种标准本身就没有意义。童贞没有意义。人的一切价值标准也毫无意义。生活中的一切，包括人、人的梦想，都不稳定，都会在钟表的小齿轮的咔嗒声中消逝。抗拒时间的威力是徒劳无益的。时间将吞噬一切，人的痛苦也不例外。康普生于是以酒浇愁，而他的理想主义者的儿子昆廷则企图以自尽来阻止时间的前进，以期保持他年轻的理想世界原封不动。虚无主义和绝望情绪弥漫着“喧哗与骚动”的整个世界。

《押沙龙，押沙龙!》和《去吧，摩西》讲述的是两个典型的南方悲剧故事。前者描述一个雄心勃勃要发家立业、一生惨淡经营却只落得失意潦倒下场的人的故事。托马斯·塞德潘胸怀宏图，立志要摆脱贫贱的社会地位，登上社会的顶端，并决心建造一座豪华的宅第做为他发迹的象征。他单身出走西印度群岛，同一有黑人血统的女人结婚，生一子名查尔斯·邦；后来他抛弃了妻和子，回到美国，以剥削黑人的血汗所得建造了房子，后又结婚，生一子名亨利，一女名裘迪丝。光阴荏苒，查尔斯来到美国，同裘迪丝相爱，亨利气急败坏，杀查尔斯而酿成兄弟自相残杀的悲剧。塞德潘拒不承认查尔斯为骨肉，是父子为敌的典型。兄弟阋墙、父子反目、兄妹乱伦，这些在作者看来无疑导致了塞德潘的家族和个人悲剧。福克纳旨在表明，人的堕落、人心目中的恨压倒爱，是使现代文明解体的根本原因。

《去吧，摩西》一书由7个相互连接的故事构成。作者对白人和黑人两个种族之间充满痛苦和耻辱的关系进行了严肃的探讨。白人庄园主卡洛沙斯·麦卡斯林同女黑奴尤妮斯私通，生一女名托密，20年后托密长大成人，老麦卡斯林大发兽性，把她奸污，生一子名叫“托密的托尔”。尤妮斯闻知后自尽。麦卡斯林的孪生子承继了建立在剥削黑人和印第安人的不义基础上的家产以后，曾天良萌发而销毁某些黑人的卖身契，使他们获得人身自由。但麦卡斯林家族的罪恶仍同这个家族并存着。后来传到第3代艾克·麦卡斯林，终于无法维持下去。艾克逐渐了解到自己丑恶的家史，了解到生活在这个家族里的黑人及一些白人世世代代所遭受的苦难，决定摈弃家产，离群索居，悉心忏悔以求获得新生。

福克纳认为，现代人的通病在于理性有余而感情不足，因而生活呈现出虚无的荒诞状态，医治的良药在于恢复人的自然状态。在他所描绘的现代人的精神荒原里，又常有“自然人”和他们的“净土”出现，他们代表着一种新的、不同以往的价值观和生活态度。例如在已失去生活气息的康普生一家里，黑人女管家迪尔西则心地善良，充满了爱与同情。她虽然只是一个女仆，但她是这个摇摇欲坠的家族的精神支柱。她取代了康普生夫人的地位，照料她的全家及子女，只有她把白痴本吉当做有血肉的人加以照顾。倘若没有她的努力，康氏家族早已不复存在。迪尔西的力量源于她的纯朴自然的感情，源于她对生活和他人“自然的反应。所以她最了解康家的困境，最清楚这个家族必然没落的原因：“我已看到开始和结尾……我看过它的开始，现在又看到结尾。”作者通过这一艺术形象似在表明，人要获得新生，就必须恢复业已失去的爱和同情。

在《八月之光》这部小说中，莉娜的故事所阐明的价值观和人生观，与小说的主要人物的生活态度迥然不同。莉娜是一个信仰虔诚、心地纯朴的村女。她拖着怀孕的身子，从亚拉巴马搭车到杰佛逊去，坚信上帝会照料她，把她指引到腹中孩子的父亲那里去。一路上人人都向她伸出热情援助之手。她宛如圣徒一样天真、纯朴、执著。她的生活和乔安娜·伯登等人毫无意义的生活形成鲜明对比。

福克纳笔下另外一个感人的“自然人”形象是《去吧，摩西》一书中的萨姆。这个人生活在天然森林中，保持着现代人心灵中已渐消逝的自然感情。他在深林中不仅洁身自好，而且培育象艾克·麦卡斯林这样的现代人同自然融为一体，使之具备正义、怜悯、勇敢、荣誉感等已从康普生及塞德潘家族生活中消失的基本品德，把他从现代文明深渊的边缘拯救回来。

福克纳写作的目的在于促使人们对生活采取肯定态度，这一点在他的诺贝尔文学奖获奖演说中谈得很清楚。他认为，好的文学作品应当描写人的精神问题，描写老的、感情的真理，普遍的真理，否则任何故事都是倏忽即逝、厄运难逃的。他所讲的真理包括爱、荣誉感、自豪感、同情心和牺牲精神。福克纳拒不接受关于人的命运的悲观论点。他认为人不仅能持久，而且必定成为胜利者。人有灵魂，有同情心、牺牲精神及美好的心灵，因而是不朽的。诗人的责任，作家的责任，在于描写这些东西，以便振作人们的精神，提醒人们铭记曾经造就了他们光荣历史的那些品质——勇敢、荣誉感、希望、自豪感、怜悯、同情及牺牲精神，以帮助人们永恒长存。福克纳的这番讲话发表之后，他的读者曾为之一惊。讲话从内容到语调都比他的带有浓郁自然主义色调和虚无主义特征的悲观小说显得更肯定、更乐观，使他在读者的心目中突然变成一位"道德英雄"。这篇讲话对福克纳后来的作品影响更大，这可以从他的《寓言》(*A Fable*，1954) 这部象征性很强的作品中清楚地看出来。

福克纳在技巧方面是一位大胆的尝试者。为更好地表达自己的思想，他悉心努力，逐步形成了自己独特的创作风格。福克纳不仅潜心观察和研究人以及人的生活，而且也是一位象亨利·詹姆斯那样的自觉的艺术家。阅读他的小说，读者会感到，作者在动笔之前，便已把全部内容的腹稿打好，已经预见到故事的发展过程及结局，因而能够熟练地安排情节的先后顺序而不致混乱，能够象胸有成竹的常胜将军那样指挥自如地支配素材。福克纳的作品不容易读，其原因之一便在于他不平铺直叙地讲故事，"倒插笔"屡屡出现，而"真相"又迟迟不见。他的书往往要读两遍以上方可品尝出其真实的味道。这是福克纳的精湛创作方法的突出标志之一。

福克纳认为，作家的艺术领域囊括人的一切言行、希望和真理，作家的首要责任在于探索及表现人生内在的无限的发展可能性。欲达此目的，作家应赋予其所刻划的人物以最大限度的独立性；换言之，作家在叙事中的干预愈少愈好。福克纳极重视人物性格的塑造，这是他表现人的多侧面性的关键所在。他似乎具备一种惊人的天赋，能把人物刻画得有血有肉，栩栩如生。对他来说，他的小说人物是真实而常在的，他的头脑中挤满了这些呼之欲出的人。他赋予他们以最大限度的独立性，而自己则满足于扮演一个旁观兼记录者的角色，时刻准备着仔细观察，再现他们的复杂生活及性格。这些人物可能具有其独特之处，甚至自相矛盾，可是这在作者看来是自然的，因为生活本身并不总是合乎逻辑的。福克纳以能创作出逼真的虚构世界而洋洋自得。他说："对我来说，他们（指小说中的人物——笔者）是人，他们象我一样老起来……我现在对人的了解比我起初所想的要多，他们已做为人清楚地立在我面前。"

福克纳运用了一些手法以保证人物的独立性。其中最重要的一种首推

“作家的超脱”。这是文学艺术家所做的一种明显的努力，坚决克制自己不插足于人物和读者之间去充当解说者的角色。作者让人物用自己的言行表明自己的特点，让读者发挥自己的智力和美学鉴赏能力，直接体会艺术品的价值。诚然，读者有时确实能听一个无名氏的声音，但那是作者自己和故事间保持某种距离而提出的一处合情合理但并非结论性的观点。此外，福克纳还善于通过一个不可靠的叙事者去讲述故事，这位叙事者时刻准备纠正自己观察上的错误或缺陷；他还善于通过多位叙事者讲述故事，这些叙事者相互矛盾、纠正或补充。这种多角度的叙述方法（multiple points of view）是传统小说中少见的。另外，他还打破了传统的时空观念，所以在他的小说中常有时间和地点都相异的场面并列出现，使读者认识到故事的同步和发展这两个特点。这些以及其他一些不能在此一一列举的技巧都有益于造就“作者超脱”的效果，保证最大限度地展示人物性格发展的特征。

福克纳一生孜孜不倦地进行技巧革新的尝试。他的小说可以分成几个不同的类型。一种是故事类，如《不可征服的》（*The Unvanquished*，1938）、《去吧，摩西》及《骑士的一着》（*Knight's Gambit*，1949）等，重点放在一件事或一个人某一最富启示性的时刻，故事常沿某种框架（如爱情、金钱、死亡等）而发展，虽然这种框架同人心的愿望或矛盾可能关系不大；另一种是平列类，如《喧哗和骚动》及《我弥留之际》等，通过人物内心独白（意识流手法）来表现一种思想状态或情绪；另外还有相对类，如《野棕榈》（*The Wild Palms*，1939）及《八月之光》等，常有两条故事线索表现不同的内涵，从对照中突出某种主题思想；以及诸如《押沙龙，押沙龙！》等把短篇小说的优点同长篇小说所表现的生活深度及复杂程度相结合的综合类，等等。这些都表明作为艺术家的福克纳对艺术的执着及刻意追求。

福克纳的语言很耐人琢磨。他的句子有时没有大写，没有标点符号，特别是较长的句子，让人感到是一种文字的奇特堆积，一部分同另一部分中间没有必要的联系。这是造成阅读困难的原因。此外还要说到福克纳的代词的用法。在不少情况下，这些词的所指不清楚，因而导致人物或情节方面的模糊甚至混淆。另一方面，福克纳不愧为一位文字大师。他的作品里既包含有日常口语、地区方言，又有规范的文学语言等多种级别的文字。他的一些段落读来朗朗上口，富有诗的格调。

福克纳的想象力异常丰富。如前所说，他把自己的作品根植于美国南部历史的土壤之中，创造出一种独特的文学氛围，最终则超越具体的人或事的局限而触及具有普遍性的问题。他的小说逐步向神话的境界移动，后来竟把人生的一个真实而简单的故事提高和渲染到一种神话系统的高度。他所关心的向来是做为整体的人的状况和处境；因而仅仅把他看作是南方小说家是不足的。

Light in August

〔作品介绍〕

《八月之光》(*Light in August*, 1932)是代表福克纳小说创作最高成就的作品之一。它通过描述和分析南方现代生活的状况，揭示出现代人对生活缺乏肯定态度的窘境。

小说的主人公乔·克里斯马斯是对生活采取否定态度的典型代表。他一生最大的苦恼是不知自己的身份，不能确定自己的归属。他的生母未婚便怀了他，他的父亲从未露过面，但有可能有黑人血统。外祖父种族偏见严重，在母亲生他时拒不请医生前来助产，致使母亲死于分娩。外祖父随后便把他遗弃在一家冷漠的孤儿院里。后来麦吉辰一家收养了他，但养父过于严苛，养母的同情和爱也不能温暖他的冰冷的心。乔于是杀了养父外逃。此后他一身孤寂，举目无亲，拒不爱他人，也不接受他人之爱。除在他一生最后几天内曾朦胧产生同世人应达成谅解的愿望以外，他在世上全然以一副局外人的面貌出现。他的世界一片空虚。他曾和乔安娜·伯登有过儿女之情，但他的血统使他无法正常地去生活、去爱。他虽然看去和白人一样，但他宁愿把自己说成是黑人：他的心态已发生变异，他期望受到歧视和拒绝。后来他杀了乔安娜，烧了她的房子，自己遭到追捕，最后被村人杀死。他的生活充溢着冷漠、敌意、报复等否定性的感情和心理。

小说还展现了一幅栩栩如生的人物画卷。其中有精神贫乏的乔安娜，有与世隔绝的盖尔·海托华，有宗教、种族偏执狂的海因斯（主人公的外祖父），有嗜血的珀西·格里姆，有对生活充满希望的莉娜和拜伦等，不一而足。尤其值得称道的是小说的结构。《八月之光》有两条故事线索贯穿其中，一条是主线，沿着乔·克里斯马斯的故事延伸；一条是陪衬，表现的对象是莉达和拜伦。乔是否定生活的代表，莉达则是对生活持肯定态度的典型。小说以莉达搭车离家寻“夫”开始，又以她和拜伦的喜剧终结，两条线索仅通过拜伦这一人物取得一种不即不离的联系，既收到良好的对比和衬托效果，联结的处理手法又极巧妙。

小说共21章，叙述的主要特点是倒叙、追述和转述。例如主人公克里斯马斯的故事就明显体现出这一特征。第1章末尾“There's a house burning”一句，把主人公杀人烧屋的事引出，第2章、第4章通过别人转述他初到镇上的情景，第5章追述他和乔安娜同居的状况，第6章追述他的孤儿院生活，第

7、8、9章追述他的青少年生活，第10、11、12、13章讲他杀养父后流浪15年，后到镇上和乔安娜同居的事情。至此，小说方回到第1、2两章所开始的起点上，倒叙和追述方告结束。第14章以后说他被捕、逃走、以及被追杀的情节，作者多采用插述或转述的手法，很少有直接的勾勒。另外，关于牧师海托华和主人公的外祖父母的故事，也多采用同样的写作方法：海托华的现状在第3章表现出后，直到第20章才全盘托出；主人公的外祖父母首次在第6章简述后，直到第17、18章才讲述始末。这部小说的创作技巧是作者丰富想象力的卓越体现。

这里选注的是小说第12章。

Light in August

CHAPTER XII

In this way the second phase[1] began. It was as though he had fallen into a sewer. As upon another life he looked back upon that first hard and manlike surrender,[2] that surrender terrific and hard, like the breaking down of a spiritual skeleton the very sound of whose snapping fibers could be heard almost by the physical ear, so that the act of capitulation was anticlimax, as when a defeated general on the day after the last battle, shaved overnight and with his boots cleaned of the mud of combat, surrenders his sword to a committee.

The sewer ran only by night. The days were the same as they had ever been. He went to work at half past six in the morning. He would leave the cabin without looking toward the house at all. At six in the evening he returned, again without even looking toward the house. He washed and changed to the white shirt and the dark creased trousers and went to the kitchen and found his supper waiting on the table and he sat and ate it, still without having seen her at all. But he knew that she was in the house and that the coming of dark within the old walls was breaking down something and leaving it corrupt with waiting. He knew how she had spent the day; that her days also were no different from what they had always been, as if in her case too another person had lived them. All day long he would imagine her, going about her housework, sitting for that unvarying period at the scarred desk, or talking, listening, to the negro women who came to the house from both directions up and down the road, following paths which had been years in the wearing and which radiated from the house like wheelspokes. What they talked about to her he did not know, though he had watched them approaching the house in a manner not exactly secret, yet purposeful, entering usually singly though sometimes in twos and threes, in their aprons and headrags and now and then with a man's coat thrown about their shoulders, emerging again and returning down the radiating paths not fast and yet not loitering. They would be brief in his mind, thinking *Now she is doing this. Now she is doing that* not thinking much about her. He believed that during the day she thought no more about him than he did about her, too. Even when at night, in her dark bedroom, she insisted on telling him in tedious detail the trivial matters of her day and insisted on his telling her of his day in turn, it was in the fashion of lovers: that imperious and insatiable demand that the trivial details of both days be put into words, without any need to listen to the telling. Then he would finish his supper and go to her where she waited. Often he would not hurry. As time went on and the novelty of the second phase began to wear off and become habit, he would stand in the kitchen door and look out across the dusk and see, perhaps with foreboding and premonition, the savage and lonely street which he had chosen of his own will, waiting for him, thinking *This is not my life. I dont belong here.*

At first it shocked him: the abject fury of the New England glacier exposed suddenly to the fire of the New England biblical hell.[3] Perhaps he was aware of the abnegation in it: the imperious and fierce urgency that concealed an actual despair at frustrate and irrevocable years, which she appeared to attempt to compensate each night as if she believed that it would be the last night on earth by damning herself forever to the hell of her forefathers, by living not alone in sin but in filth. She had an avidity for the forbidden wordsymbols; an insatiable appetite for the sound of them on his tongue and on her own. She revealed the terrible and impersonal curiosity of a child about forbidden subjects and objects; that rapt and tireless and detached interest of a surgeon in the physical body and its possibilities. And by day he would see the calm, coldfaced, almost manlike, almost middleaged woman who had lived for twenty years alone, without any feminine fears at all, in a lonely house in a neighborhood populated, when at all, by negroes, who spent a certain portion of each day sitting tranquilly at a desk and writing tranquilly for the eyes of both youth and age the practical advice of a combined priest and banker and trained nurse.

During that period (it could not be called a honeymoon) Christmas watched her pass through every avatar of a woman in love. Soon she more than shocked him: she astonished and bewildered him. She surprised and took him unawares with fits of jealous rage. She could have had no such experience at all, and there was neither reason for the scene nor any possible protagonist: he knew that she knew that. It was as if she had invented the whole thing deliberately, for the purpose of playing it out like a play. Yet she did it with such fury, with such convincingness and such conviction, that on the first occasion he thought that she was under a delusion and the third time he thought that she was mad. She revealed an unexpected and infallible instinct for intrigue. She insisted on a place for concealing notes, letters. It was in a hollow fence post below the rotting stable. He never saw her put a note there, yet she insisted on his visiting it daily; when he did so, the letter would be there. When he did not and lied to her, he would find that she had already set traps to catch him in the lie; she cried, wept.

Sometimes the notes would tell him not to come until a certain hour, to that house which no white person save himself had entered in years and in which for twenty years now she had been all night alone; for a whole week she forced him to climb into a window to come to her. He would do so and sometimes he would have to seek her about the dark house until he found her, hidden, in closets, in empty rooms, waiting, panting, her eyes in the dark glowing like the eyes of cats. Now and then she appointed trysts beneath certain shrubs about the grounds, where he would find her naked, or with her clothing half torn to ribbons upon her, in the wild throes of nymphomania, her body gleaming in the slow shifting from one to another of such formally erotic attitudes and gestures as a Beardsley of the time of Petronius[4] might have drawn. She would be wild then, in the close, breathing halfdark without walls, with her wild hair, each strand of which would seem to come alive like octopus tentacles, and her wild hands and her breathing: "Negro! Negro! Negro!"

Within six months she was completely corrupted. It could not be said that he corrupted her. His own life, for all its anonymous promiscuity, had been conventional enough, as a life of healthy and normal sin usually is. The corruption came from a source even more inexplicable to him than to her. In fact, it was as though with the corruption which she seemed to gather from the air itself, she began to corrupt him. He began to be afraid. He could not have said of what. But he began to see himself as from a distance, like a man being sucked down into a bottomless morass. He had not exactly thought that yet. What he was now seeing was the street lonely, savage, and cool. That was it: cool; he was thinking, saying aloud to himself sometimes, "I better move. I better get away from here."

But something held him, as the fatalist can always be held: by curiosity, pessimism, by sheer inertia. Meanwhile the affair went on, submerging him more and more by the imperious and overriding fury of those nights. Perhaps he realised that he could not escape. Anyway, he stayed, watching the two creatures that struggled in the one body like two moongleamed shapes struggling drowning in alternate throes upon the surface of a black thiek pool beneath the last moon. Now it would be that still, cold, contained figure of the first phase who, even though lost and damned, remained somehow impervious and impregnable; then it would be the other, the second one, who in furious denial of that impregnability strove to drown in the black abyss of its own creating that physical purity which had been preserved too long now even to be lost. Now and then they would come to the black surface, locked like sisters; the black waters would drain away. Then the world would rush back: the room, the walls, the peaceful myriad sound of insects from beyond the summer windows where insects had whirred for forty years. She would stare at him then with the wild, despairing face of a stranger; looking at her then he paraphrased himself: "She wants to pray, but she dont know how to do that either."

She had begun to get fat.

The end of this phase was not sharp, not a climax, like the first. It merged into the third phase so gradually that he could not have said where one stopped and the other began. It was summer becoming fall, with already, like shadows before a westering sun, the chill and implacable import of autumn cast ahead upon summer; something of dying summer spurting again like a dying coal, in the fall. This was over a period of two years. He still worked at the planing mill, and in the meantime he had begun to sell a little whiskey, very judiciously, restricting himself to a few discreet customers none of whom knew the others. She did not know this, although he kept his stock hidden on the place and met his clients in the woods beyond the pasture. Very likely she would not have objected. But neither would Mrs McEachern have objected to the hidden rope;[5] perhaps he did not tell her for the same reason that he did not tell Mrs McEachern. Thinking of Mrs McEachern and the rope, and of the waitress whom he had never told where the money came from which he gave to her, and now of his present mistress and the whiskey, he could almost believe that it was not to make money that he sold the whiskey but because he was doomed to conceal always something from the women who surrounded him. Meanwhile he would see her from a distance now and then in the daytime, about the rear premises, where moved articulate beneath the clean, austere garments which she wore that rotten richness ready to flow into putrefaction at a touch, like something growing in a swamp, not once looking toward the cabin or toward him. And when he thought of that other personality that seemed to exist somewhere in physical darkness itself, it seemed to him that what he now saw by daylight was a phantom of someone whom the night sister had murdered and which now moved purposeless about the scenes of old peace, robbed even of the power of lamenting.

Of course the first fury of the second phase could not last. At first it had been a torrent; now it was a tide, with a flow and ebb. During its flood she could almost fool them both. It was as if out of her knowledge that it was just a flow that must presently react was born a wilder fury, a fierce denial that could flag itself and him into physical experimentation that transcended imagining, carried them as though by momentum alone, bearing them without volition or plan. It was as if she knew somehow that time was short, that autumn was almost upon her, without knowing yet the exact significance of autumn. It seemed to be instinct alone: instinct physical and instinctive denial of the wasted years. Then the tide would ebb. Then they would be stranded as behind a dying mistral, upon a spent and satiate beach, looking at one another like strangers, with hopeless and reproachful (on his part with weary: on hers with despairing) eyes.

But the shadow of autumn was upon her. She began to talk about a child, as though instinct had warned her that now was the time when she must either justify or expiate. She talked about it in the ebb periods. At first the beginning of the night was always a flood, as if the hours of light and of separation had damned up enough of the wasting stream to simulate torrent for a moment at least. But after a while the stream became too thin for that: he would go to her now with reluctance, a stranger, already backlooking; a stranger he would leave her after having sat with her in the dark bedroom, talking of still a third stranger. He noticed now how, as though by premeditation, they met always in the bedroom, as though they were married. No more did he have to seek her through the house; the nights when he must seek her, hidden and panting and naked, about the dark house or among the shrubbery of the ruined park were as dead now as the hollow fencepost below the barn.

That was all dead: the scenes, the faultlessly played scenes of secret and monstrous delight and of jealousy. Though if she had but known it now, she had reason for jealousy. He made trips every week or so, on business, he told her. She did not know that the business took him to Memphis, where he betrayed her with other women, women bought for a price. She did not know it. Perhaps in the phase in which she now was she could not have been convinced, would not have listened to proof, would not have cared. Because she had taken to lying sleepless most of the night, making up the sleep in the afternoons. She was not sick; it was not her body. She had never been better; her appetite was enormous and she weighed thirty pounds more than she had ever weighed in her life. It was not that that kept her awake. It was something out of the darkness, the earth, the dying summer itself: something threatful and terrible to her because instinct assured her that it would not harm her; that it would overtake and betray her completely, but she would not be harmed: that on the contrary, she would be saved, that life would go on the same and even better, even less terrible. What was terrible was that she did not want to be saved. "I'm not ready to pray yet," she said aloud, quietly, rigid, soundless, her eyes wide open, while the moon poured and poured into the window, filling the room with something cold and irrevocable and wild with regret. "Dont make me have to pray yet. Dear God, let me be damned a little longer, a little while." She seemed to see her whole past life, the starved years, like a gray tunnel, at the far and irrevocable end of which, as unfading as a reproach, her naked breast of three short years ago ached as though in agony, virgin and crucified; "Not yet, dear God. Not yet, dear God."

So when he now came to her, after the passive and cold and seemly transports of sheer habit she began to speak of a child. She talked about it impersonally at first, discussing children. Perhaps it was sheer and instinctive feminine cunning and indirection, perhaps not. Anyway, it was some time before he discovered with a kind of shock that she was discussing it as a possibility, a practical thought. He said No at once.

"Why not?" she said. She looked at him, speculative. He was thinking fast, thinking *She wants to be married. That's it. She wants a child no more than I do* 'It's just a trick,' he thought. 'I should have known it, expected it. I should have cleared out of here a year ago.' But he was afraid to tell her this, to let the word marriage come between them, come aloud, thinking, 'She may not have thought of it, and I will just put the notion in her head.' She was watching him. "Why not?" she said. And then something in him flashed *Why not? It would mean ease, security, for the rest of your life. You would never have to move again. And you might as well be married to her as this* thinking, 'No. If I give in now, I will deny all the thirty years that I have lived to make me what I chose to be.' He said:

"If we were going to have one, I guess we would have had one two years ago."

"We didn't want one then."

"We dont want one now, either," he said.

That was in September. Just after Christmas she told him that she was pregnant. Almost before she ceased to speak, he believed that she was lying. He discovered now that he had been expecting her to tell him that for three months. But when he looked at her face, he knew that she was not. He believed that she also knew that she was not. He thought, 'Here it comes. She will say it now: marry. But I can at least get out of the house first.'

But she did not. She was sitting quite still on the bed, her hands on her lap, her still New England face (it was still the face of a spinster: prominently boned, long, a little thin, almost manlike: in contrast to it her plump body was more richly and softly animal than ever) lowered. She said, in a tone musing, detached, impersonal: "A full measure. Even to a bastard negro child. I would like to see father's and Calvin's[6] faces. This will be a good time for you to run, if that's what you want to do. "But it was as though she were not listening to her own voice, did not intend for the words to have any actual meaning: that final upflare of stubborn and dying summer upon which autumn, the dawning of halfdeath, had come unawares. 'It's over now,' she thought quietly; 'finished.' Except the waiting, for one month more to pass, to be sure; she had learned that from the negro women, that you could not always tell until after two months. She would have to wait another month, watching the calendar. She made a mark on the calendar to be sure, so there would be no mistake; through the bedroom window she watched that month accomplish. A frost had come, and some of the leaves were beginning to turn. The marked day on the calendar came and passed; she gave herself another week, to be doubly sure. She was not elated, since she was not surprised. "I am with child," she said, quietly, aloud.

'I'll go tomorrow,' he told himself, that same day. 'I'll go Sunday,' he thought. 'I'll wait and get this week's pay, and then I am gone.' He began to look forward to Saturday, planning where he would go. He did not see her all that week. He expected her to send for him. When he entered or left the cabin he would find himself avoiding looking toward the house, as he had during the first week he was there. He did not see her at all. Now and then he would see the negro women, in nondescript garments against the autumn chill, coming or going along the worn paths, entering or leaving the house. But that was all. When Saturday came, he did not go. 'Might as well have all the jack I can get,' he thought. 'If she aint anxious for me to clear out, no reason why I should be. I'll go next Saturday.'

He stayed on. The weather remained cold, bright and cold. When he went to bed now in his cotton blanket, in the draughty cabin, he would think of the bedroom in the house, with its fire, its ample, quilted, lintpadded covers. He was nearer to selfpity than he had ever been. 'She might at least send me another blanket,' he thought. So might he have bought one. But he did not. Neither did she. He waited. He waited what he thought was a long time. Then one evening in February he returned home and found a note from her on his cot. It was brief; it was an order almost, directing him to come to the house that night. He was not surprised. He had never yet known a woman who, without another man available, would not come around in time. And he knew now that tomorrow he would go. 'This must be what I have been waiting for,' he thought; 'I have just been waiting to be vindicated.' When he changed his clothes, he shaved also. He prepared himself like a bridegroom, unaware of it. He found the table set for him in the kitchen, as usual; during all the time that he had not seen her, that had never failed. He ate and went upstairs. He did not hurry. 'We got all night,' he thought. 'It'll be something for her to think about tomorrow night and the next one, when she finds that cabin empty.' She was sitting before the fire. She did not even turn her head when he entered. "Bring that chair up with you," she said.

This was how the third phase began. It puzzled him for a while, even more than the other two. He had expected eagerness, a kind of tacit apology; or lacking that, an acquiescence that wanted only to be wooed. He was prepared to go that length, even. What he found was a stranger who put aside with the calm firmness of a man his hand when at last and in a kind of baffled desperation he went and touched her. "Come on," he said, "if you have something to tell me. We always talk better afterward. It wont hurt the kid, if that's what you have been afraid of."

She stayed him with a single word; for the first time he looked at her face: he looked upon a face cold, remote, and fanatic. "Do you realise," she said, "that you are wasting your life?" And he sat looking at her like a stone, as if he could not believe his own ears.

It took him some time to comprehend what she meant. She did not look at him at all. She sat looking into the fire, her face cold, still, brooding, talking to him as if he were a stranger, while he listened in outraged amazement. She wanted him to take over all her business affairs—the correspondence and the periodical visits—with the negro schools. She had the plan all elaborated. She recited it to him in detail while he listened in mounting rage and amazement. He was to have complete charge, and she would be his secretary, assistant: they would travel to the schools together, visit in the negro homes together; listening, even with his anger, he knew that the plan was mad. And all the while her calm profile in the peaceful firelight was as grave and tranquil as a portrait in a frame. When he left, he remembered that she had not once mentioned the expected child.

He did not yet believe that she was mad. He thought that it was because she was pregnant, as he believed that was why she would not let him touch her. He tried to argue with her. But it was like trying to argue with a tree: she did not even rouse herself to deny, she just listened quietly and then talked again in that level, cold tone as if he had never spoken. When he rose at last and went out he did not even know if she was aware that he had gone.

He saw her but once more within the next two months. He followed his daily routine, save that he did not approach the house at all now, taking his meals downtown again, as when he had first gone to work at the mill. But then, when he first went to work, he would not need to think of her during the day; he hardly ever thought about her. Now he could not help himself. She was in his mind so constantly that it was almost as if he were looking at her, there in the house, patient, waiting, inescapable, crazy. During the first phase it had been as though he were outside a house where snow was on the ground, trying to get into the house; during the second phase he was at the bottom of a pit in the hot wild darkness; now he was in the middle of a plain where there was no house, not even snow, not even wind.

He began now to be afraid, whose feeling up to now had been bewilderment and perhaps foreboding and fatality. He now had a partner in his whiskey business: a stranger named Brown[7] who had appeared at the mill one day early in the spring, seeking work. He knew that the man was a fool, but at first he thought, 'At least he will have sense enough to do what I tell him to do. He wont have to think himself at all'; it was not until later that he said to himself: 'I know now that what makes a fool is an inability to take even his own good advice.' He took Brown because Brown was a stranger and had a certain cheerful and unscrupulous readiness about him, and not overmuch personal courage, knowing that in the hands of a judicious man, a coward within his own limitations can be made fairly useful to anyone except himself.

His fear was that Brown might learn about the woman in the house and do something irrevocable out of his own unpredictable folly. He was afraid that the woman, since he had avoided her, might take it into her head to come to the cabin some night. He had not seen her but once since February. That was when he sought her to tell her that Brown was coming to live with him in the cabin. It was on Sunday. He called her, and she came out to where he stood on the back porch and listened quietly. "You didn't have to do that," she said. He didn't understand then what she meant. It was not until later that thinking again flashed, complete, like a printed sentence: *She thinks that I brought him out here to keep her off. She believes that I think that with him there, she wont dare come down to the cabin; that she will have to let me alone*

Thus he put his belief, his fear of what she might do, into his own mind by believing that he had put it into hers. He believed that, since she had thought that, that Brown's presence would not only not deter her: it would be an incentive for her to come to the cabin. Bacause of the fact that for over a month now she had done nothing at all, made no move at all, he believed that she might do anything. Now he too lay awake at night. But he was thinking, 'I have got to do something. There is something that I am going to do.'

So he would trick and avoid Brown in order to reach the cabin first. He expected each time to find her waiting. When he would reach the cabin and find it empty, he would think in a kind of impotent rage of the urgency, the lying and the haste, and of her alone and idle in the house all day, with nothing to do save to decide whether to betray him at once or torture him a little longer. By ordinary he would not have minded whether Brown knew about their relations or not. He had nothing in his nature of reticence or of chivalry toward women. It was practical, material. He would have been indifferent if all Jefferson knew he was her lover: it was that he wanted no one to begin to speculate on what his private life out there was because of the hidden whiskey which was netting him thirty or forty dollars a week. That was one reason. Another reason was vanity. He would have died or murdered rather than have anyone, another man, learn what their relations had now become. That not only had she changed her life completely, but that she was trying to change his too and make of him something between a hermit and a missionary to negroes. He believed that if Brown learned the one, he must inevitably learn the other. So he would reach the cabin at last, after the lying and the hurry, and as he put his hand on the door, remembering the haste and thinking that in a moment he would find that it had not been necessary at all and yet to neglect which precaution he dared not, he would hate her with a fierce revulsion of dread and impotent rage. Then one evening he opened the door and found the note on the cot.

He saw it as soon as he entered, lying square and white and profoundly inscrutable against the dark blanket. He did even stop to think that he believed he knew what the message would be, would promise. He felt no eagerness; he felt relief. 'It's over now,' he thought, not yet taking up the folded paper. 'It will be like it was before now. No more talking about niggers and babies. She has come around. She has worn the other out, seen that she was getting nowhere. She sees now that what she wants, needs, is a man. She wants a man by night; what he does by daylight does not matter.' He should have realised then the reason why he had not gone away. He should have seen that he was bound just as tightly by that small square of still undivulging paper as though it were a lock and chain. He did not think of that. He saw only himself once again on the verge of promise and delight. It would be quieter though, now. They would both want it so; besides the whiphand which he would now have. 'All that foolishness,' he thought, holding the yet unopened paper in his hands; 'all that damn foolishness. She is still she and I am still I. And now, after all this damn foolishness'; thinking how they would both laugh over it tonight, later, afterward, when the time for quiet talking and quiet laughing came: at the whole thing, at one another, at themselves.

He did not open the note at all. He put it away and washed and shaved and changed his clothes, whistling while he did so. He had not finished when Brown came in. "Well, well, well," Brown said. Christmas said nothing. He was facing the shard of mirror nailed to the wall, knotting his tie. Brown had stopped in the center of the floor: a tall, lean, young man in dirty overalls, with a dark, weakly handsome face and curious eyes. Beside his mouth there was a narrow scar as white as a thread of spittle. After a while Beown said: "Looks like you are going somewhere."

"Does it?" Christmas said. He did not look around. He whistled monotonously but truely: something in minor, plaintive and negroid.

"I reckon I wont bother to clean up none," Brown said, "seeing as you are almost ready."

Christmas looked back at him. "Ready for what?"

"Aint you going to town?"

"Did I ever say I was?" Christmas said. He turned back to the glass.

"Oh," Brown said. He watched the back of Christmas's head. "Well, I reckon from that that you're going on private business." He watched Christmas. "This here's a cold night to be laying around on the wet ground without nothing under you but a thin gal."

"Aint it, though?" Christmas said, whistling, preoccupied and unhurried. He turned and picked up his coat and put it on, Brown still watching him. He went to the door. "See you in the morning," he said. The door did not close behind him. He knew that Brown was standing in it, looking after him. But he did not attempt to conceal his purpose. He went on toward the house. 'Let him watch,' he thought. 'Let him follow me if he wants to.'

The table was set for him in the kitchen. Before sitting down he took the unopened note from his pocket and laid it beside his plate. It was not enclosed, not sealed; it sprang open of its own accord, as though inviting him, insisting. But he did not look at it. He began to eat. He ate without haste. He had almost finished when he raised his head suddenly, listening. Then he rose and went to the door through which he had entered, with the noiselessness of a cat, and jerked the door open suddenly. Brown stood just outside, his face leaned to the door, or where the door had been. The light fell upon his face and upon it was an expression of intent and infantile interest which became surprise while Christmas looked at it, then it recovered, falling back a little. Brown's voice was gleeful though quiet, cautious, conspiratorial, as if he had already established his alliance and sympathy with Christmas, unasked, and without waiting to know what was going on, out of loyalty to his partner or perhaps to abstract man as opposed to all woman. "Well, well, well," he said. "So this is where you tomcat to every night. Right at our front door, you might say—"

Without saying a word Christmas struck him. The blow did not fall hard, because Brown was already in innocent and gleeful backmotion, in midsnicker as it were. The blow cut his voice short off; moving, springing backward, he vanished from the fall of light, into the darkness, from which his voice came, still not loud, as if even now he would not jeopardise his partner's business, but tense now with alarm, astonishment: "Dont you hit me!" He was the taller of the two: a gangling shape already in a ludicrous diffusion of escape as if he were on the point of clattering to earth in complete disintegration as he stumbled backward before the steady and still silent advance of the other. Again Brown's voice came, high, full of alarm and spurious threat: "Dont you hit me!" This time the blow struck his shoulder as he turned. He was running now. He ran for a hundred yards before he slowed, looking back. Then he stopped and turned. "You durn yellowbellied wop," he said, in a tentative tone, jerking his head immediately, as if his voice had made more noise, sounded louder, than he had intended. There was no sound from the house; the kitchen door was dark again, closed again. He raised his voice a little: "You durn yellowbellied wop! I'll learn you who you are monkeying with." There came no sound anywhere. It was chilly. He turned and went back to the cabin, mumbling to himself.

When Christmas reentered the kitchen he did not even look back at the table on which lay the note which he had not yet read. He went on through the door which led into the house and on to the stairs. He began to mount, not fast. He mounted steadily; he could now see the bedroom door, a crack of light, firelight, beneath it. He went steadily on and put his hand upon the door. Then he opened it and he stopped dead still. She was sitting at a table, beneath the lamp. He saw a figure that he knew, in a severe garment that he knew—a garment that looked as if it had been made for and worn by a careless man. Above it he saw a head with hair just beginning to gray drawn gauntly back to a knot as savage and ugly as a wart on a diseased bough. Then she looked up at him and he saw that she wore steelrimmed spectacles which he had never seen before. He stood in the door, his hand still on the knob, quite motionless. It seemed to him that he could actually hear the words inside him: *You should have read that note. You should have read that note* thinking, 'I am going to do something. Going to do something.'

He was still hearing that while he stood beside the table on which papers were scattered and from which she had not risen, and listened to the calm enormity which her cold, still voice unfolded, his mouth repeating the words after her while he looked down at the scattered and enigmatic papers and documents and thinking fled smooth and idle, wondering what this paper meant and what that paper meant. "To school," his mouth said.

"Yes," she said. "They will take you. Any of them will. On my account. You can choose any one you want among them. We wont even have to pay."

"To school," his mouth said. "A nigger school. Me."

"Yes. Then you can go to Memphis. You can read law in Peebles's office. He will teach you law. Then you can take charge of all the legal business. All this, all that he does, Peebles does."

"And then learn law in the office of a nigger lawyer," his mouth said.

"Yes. Then I will turn over all the business to you, all the money. All of it. So that when you need money for yourself you could…you would know how; lawyers know how to do it so that it…You would be helping them up out of darkness and none could accuse or blame you even if they found out…even if you did not replace…but you could replace the money and none would ever know . . . ."

"But a nigger college, a nigger lawyer," his voice said, quiet, not even argumentative; just promptive. They were not looking at one another; she had not looked up since he entered.

"Tell them," she said.

"Tell niggers that I am a nigger too?" She now looked at him. Her face was quite calm. It was the face of an old woman now.

"Yes. You'll have to do that. So they wont charge you anything. On my account."

Then it was as if he said suddenly to his mouth: 'Shut up. Shut up that drivel. Let me talk.' He leaned down. She did not move. Their faces were not a foot apart: the one cold, dead white, fanatical, mad; the other parchment-colored, the lip lifted into the shape of a soundless and rigid snarl. He said quietly: "You're old. I never noticed that before. An old woman. You've got gray in your hair." She struck him, at once, with her flat hand, the rest of her body not moving at all. Her blow made a flat sound; his blow as close upon it as echo. He struck with his fist, then in that long blowing wind he jerked her up from the chair and held her, facing him, motionless, not a flicker upon her still face, while the long wind of knowing rushed down upon him. "You haven't got any baby," he said. "You never had one. There is not anything the matter with you except being old. You just got old and it happened to you and now you are not any good anymore. That's all that's wrong with you." He released her and struck her again. She fell huddled onto the bed, looking up at him, and he struck her in the face again and standing over her he spoke to her the words which she had once loved to hear on his tongue, which she used to say that she could taste there, murmurous, obscene, caressing. "That's all. You're just worn out. You're not any good anymore. That's all."

She lay on the bed, on her side, her head turned and looking up at him across her bleeding mouth. "Maybe it would be better if we both were dead," she said.

He could see the note lying on the blanket as soon as he opened the door. Then he would go and take it up and open it. He would now remember the hollow fencepost as something of which he had heard told, as having taken place in another life from any that he had ever lived. Because the paper, the ink, the form and shape, were the same. They had never been long; they were not long now. But now there was nothing evocative of unspoken promise, of rich and unmentionable delights, in them. They were now briefer than epitaphs and more terse than commands.

His first impulse would be to not go. He believed that he dared not go. Then he knew that he dared not fail to go. He would not change his clothes now. In his sweatstained overalls he would traverse the late twilight of May and enter the kitchen. The table was never set with food for him now. Sometimes he would look at it as he passed and he would think, 'My God. When have I sat down in peace to eat.' And he could not remember.

He would go on into the house and mount the stairs. Already he would be hearing her voice. It would increase as he mounted and until he reached the door to the bedroom. The door would be shut, locked; from beyond it the monotonous steady voice came. He could not distinguish the words; only the ceaseless monotone. He could not distinguish the words; only the ceaseless monotone. He dared not try to distinguish the words. He did not dare let himself know what she was at. So he would stand there and wait, and after a while the voice would cease and she would open the door and he would enter. As he passed the bed he would look down at the floor beside it and it would seem to him that he could distinguish the prints of knees and he would jerk his eyes away as if it were death that they had looked at.

Likely the lamp would not yet be lighted. They did not sit down.

Again they stood to talk, as they used to do two years ago; standing in the dusk while her voice repeated its tale: "…not to school, then, if you dont want to go…Do without that…Your soul. Expiation of…" And he waiting, cold, still, until she had finished: "…hell…forever and ever and ever…"

"No," he said. And she would listen as quietly, and he knew that she was not convinced and she knew that he was not. Yet neither surrendered; worse: they would not let one another alone; he would not even go away. And they would stand for a while longer in the quiet dusk peopled, as though from their loins, by a myriad ghosts of dead sins and delights, looking at one another's still and fading face, weary, spent, and indomitable.

Then he would leave. And before the door had shut and the bolt had shot to behind him, he would hear the voice again, monotonous, calm, and despairing, saying what and to what or whom he dared not learn nor suspect. And as he sat in the shadows of the ruined garden on that August night three months later and heard the clock in the courthouse two miles away strike ten and then eleven, he believed with calm paradox that he was the volitionless servant of the fatality in which he believed that he did not believe. He was saying to himself I had to do it already in the past tense; *I had to do it. She said so herself*

She had said it two nights ago. He found the note and went to her. As he mounted the stairs the monotonous voice grew louder, sounded louder and clearer than usual. When he reached the top of the stairs he saw why. The door was open this time, and she did not rise from where she knelt beside the bed when he entered. She did not stir; her voice did not cease. Her head was not bowed. Her face was lifted, almost with pride, her attitude of formal abjectness a part of the pride, her voice calm and tranquil and abnegant in the twilight. She did not seem to be aware that he had entered until she finished a period. Then she turned her head. "Kneel with me," she said.

"No," he said.

"Kneel," she said. "You wont even need to speak to Him yourself. Just kneel. Just make the first move."

"No," he said. "I'm going."

She didn't move, looking back and up at him. "Joe," she said, "will you stay? Will you do that much?"

"Yes," he said. "I'll stay. But make it fast."

She prayed again. She spoke quietly, with that abjectness of pride. When it was necessary to use the symbolwords which he had taught her, she used them, spoke them forthright and without hesitation, talking to God as if He were a man in the room with two other men. She spoke of herself and of him as of two other people, her voice still, monotonous, sexless. Then she ceased. She rose quietly. They stood in the twilight, facing one another. This time she did not even ask the question; he did not even need to reply. After a time she said quietly:

"Then there's just one other thing to do."

"There's just one other thing to do," he said.

'So now it's all done, all finished,' he thought quietly, sitting in the dense shadow of the shrubbery, hearing the last stroke of the far clock cease and die away. It was a spot where he had overtaken her, found her on one of the wild nights two years ago. But that was in another time, another life. Now it was still, quiet, the fecund earth now coolly suspirant. The dark was filled with the voices, myriad, out of all time that he had known, as though all the past was a flat pattern. And going on: tomorrow night, all the tomorrows, to be a part of the flat patten, going on. He thought of that with quiet astonishment: going on, myriad, familiar, since all that had ever been was the same as all that was to be, since tomorrow to-be and had-been would be the same.[8] Then it was time.

He rose. He moved from the shadow and went around the house and entered the kitchen. The house was dark. He had not been to the cabin since early morning and he did not know if she had left a note for him or not, expected him or not. Yet he did not try for silence. It was as if he were not thinking of sleep, of whether she would be asleep or not. He mounted the stairs steadily and entered the bedroom. Almost at once she spoke from the bed. "light the lamp," she said.

"It wont need any light," he said.

"Light the lamp."

"No," he said. He stood over the bed. He held the razor in his hand. But it was not open yet. But she did not speak again and then his body seemed to walk away from him. It went to the table and his hands laid the razor on the table and found the lamp and struck the match. She was sitting up in the bed, her back against the headboard. Over her nightdress she wore a shawl drawn down across her breast. Her arms were folded upon the shawl, her hands hidden from sight. He stood at the table. They looked at one another.

"Will you kneel with me?" she said. "I dont ask it."

"No," he said.

"I dont ask it. It's not I who ask it. Kneel with me."

"No."

They looked at one another. "Joe," she said, "for the last time. I dont ask it. Remember that. Kneel with me."

"No," he said. Then he saw her arms unfold and her right hand come forth from beneath the shawl. It held an old style, single action, cap-and-ball revolver almost as long and heavier than a small rifle. But the shadow of it and of her arm and hand on the wall did not waver at all, the shadow of both monstrous, the cocked hammer monstrous, back-hooked and viciously poised like the arched head of a snake; it did not waver at all. And her eyes did not waver at all. They were as still as the round black ring of the pistol muzzle. But there was no heat in them, no fury. They were calm and still as all pity and all despair and all conviction. But he was not watching them. He was watching the shadowed pistol on the wall; he was watching when the cocked shadow of the hammer flicked away.

Standing in the middle of the road, with his right hand lifted full in the glare of the approaching car, he had not actually expected it to stop. Yet it did, with a squealing and sprawling suddenness that was almost ludicrous. It was a small car, battered and old. When he approached it, in the reflected glare of the headlights two young faces seemed to float like two softcolored and aghast balloons, the nearer one, the girl's, back-shrunk in a soft, wide horror. But Christmas did not notice this at the time. "How about riding with you, as far as you go?" he said. They said nothing at all, looking at him with that still and curious horror which he did not notice So he opened the door to enter the rear seat.

When he did so, the girl began to make a choked wailing sound which would be much louder in a moment, as fear gained courage as it were. Already the car was in motion; it seemed to leap forward, and the boy, without moving his hands from the wheel or turning his head toward the girl hissed: "Shut up! Hush! It's our only chance! Will you hush now?"Christmas did not hear this either. He was sitting back now, completely unaware that he was riding directly behind desperate terror. He only thought with momentary interest that the small car was travelling at a pretty reckless speed for a narrow country road.

"How far does this road go?" he said.

The boy told him, naming the same town which the negro boy had named to him on that afternoon three years ago,[9] when he had first seen Jefferson. The boy's voice had a dry, light quality. "Do you want to go there, cap'm?"

"All right," Christmas said. "Yes. Yes. That will do. That will suit me. Are you going there?"

"Sure," the boy said, in that light, flat tone. "Wherever you say." Again the girl beside him began that choked, murmurous, small-animallike moaning; again the boy hissed at her, his face still rigidly front, the little car rushing and bouncing onward: "Hush! Shhhhhhhhhh. Hush! Hush!" But again Christmas did not notice. He saw only the two young, rigidly forwardlooking heads against the light glare, into which the ribbon of the road rushed swaying and fleeing. But he remarked both them and the fleeing road without curiosity; he was not even paying attention when he found that the boy had apparently been speaking to him for some time; how far they had come or where they were he did not know. The boy's diction was slow now, recapitulant, each word as though chosen simply and carefully and spoken slowly and clearly for the ear of a foreigner: "Listen, cap'm. When I turn off up here. It's just a short cut. A short cutoff to a better road. I am going to take the cutoff. When I come to the short cut. To the better road. So we can get there quicker. See?"

"All right," Christmas said. The car bounced and rushed on, swaying on the curves and up the hills and fleeing down again as if the earth had dropped from under them. Mail boxes on posts beside the road rushed into the lights and flicked past. Now and then they passed a dark house. Again the boy was speaking:

"Now, this here cutoff I was telling you about. It's right down here. I'm going to turn into it. But it dont mean I am leaving the road. I am just going a little way across to a better road. See?

"All right," Christmas said. Then for no reason he said: "You must live around here somewhere."

Now it was the girl who spoke. She turned in the seat, whirling, her small face wan with suspense and terror and blind and ratlike desperation: “We do!” she cried. “We both do! Right up yonder! And when my pappy and brothers—” Her voice ceased, cut short off; Christmas saw the boy's hand clapped upon her lower face and her hands tugging at the wrist while beneath the hand itself her smothered voice choked and bubbled. Christmas sat forward.

“Here,” he said. “I'll get out here. You can let me out here.”

“Now you've done it!” the boy cried, too, thinly, with desperate rage too. “If you'd just kept quiet—”

“Stop the car,” Christmas said. “I aint going to hurt either of you. I just want to get out.” Again the car stopped with sprawling suddenness. But the engine still raced, and the car leaped forward again before he was clear of the step; he had to leap forward running for a few steps to recover his balance. As he did so, something heavy and hard struck him on the flank. The car rushed on, fading at top steed. From it floated back the girl's shrill wailing. Then it was gone; the darkness, the now impalpable dust, came down again, and the silence beneath the summer stars. The object which had struck him had delivered an appreciable blow; then he discovered that the object was attached to his right hand. Raising the hand, he found that it held the ancient heavy pistol. He did not know that he had it; he did not remember having picked it up at all, nor why. But there it was. ‘And I flagged that car with my right hand,’ he thought. ‘No wonder she…they…’ He drew his right hand back to throw, the pistol balanced upon it. Then he paused, and he struck a match and examined the pistol in the puny dying glare. The match burned down and went out, yet he still seemed to see the ancient thing[10] with its two loaded chambers: the one upon which the hammer had already fallen and which had not exploded, and the other upon which no hammer had yet fallen but upon which a hammer had been planned to fall. ‘For her and for me,’ he said. His arm came back, and threw. He heard the pistol crash once through undergrowth. Then there was no sound again. ‘For her and for me.’

〔注释〕

1. the second phase：指 Christmas 和 Joanna 之间同居关系发展的第 2 阶段。关于两者之间关系发生及发展过程的第 1 阶段的情况，参阅小说第 10 章后半部分及第 11 章。

2. that first hard and manlike surrender：指 Christmas 经过激烈的思想斗争后和 Joanna 终于暗中同居：这是他生活中第一次和一个女人如此亲近。

3. the abject fury of the New England glacier exposed suddenly to the fire of the New England biblical hell：据小说第 11 章内 Joanna 的自述，她祖上为新英格兰籍，笃信新教美以美派（Methodism）所说的“地狱之火”（hellfire），故曰“the fire of…hell”；此处亦有尖刻的讽刺性引伸，转喻内涵丰富，一言 Joanna 做爱的狂热状，一言她的自取毁灭。the New England glacier：指压抑感情而独居达 20 余年的 Joanna 的冷漠貌。

4. a Beardsley of the time of petronius：Beardsley 指 19 世纪英国插图画家奥博利·比尔兹利（Aubrey Beardsley，1872～1898），其画中有令人瞠目的女性肉感。Petronius 指古罗马作家佩特罗尼乌斯（petronius Arbiter，?～66），他生活在荒淫的罗马皇帝尼禄在位的年代，当时社会上享乐成风，他本人是十足的浪荡公子，著有《萨蒂利孔》一书，记录当时的淫秽之风。

5. the hidden rope：乔 17 岁时夜里和一个妓女——一小店女招待幽会，因恐养父母（the McEacherns）发现，故私藏一绳，深夜启窗缘绳而下。详见小说第 8 章。

6. Calvin：指 Calvin Burden，乔安娜的同父异母哥哥，在一次关于种族的争论中被南方白人杀死。详见小说第 11 章。

7. He now had a partner…a stranger named Brown…关于 Christmas 贩卖威士忌的活动，以及布朗入伙的情形，详见小说第 5 章；布朗曾是莉娜的情人，关于这一点，详见小说的第 2、3、4 章。

8. since all that had ever been…would be the same：作者化用了《圣经·传道书》第 1 章第 9、10 两节的主旨，以表达小说主人公所体现的虚无主义思想。《传道书》第 9、10 两节的原义是："The thing that hath been, it *is that* which shall be; and that which is done *is* that which shall be done: and *there is* no new *thing* under the sun. Is there *any* thing whereof it may be said, See, this *is* new? it hath been already of old time, which was before us."

9. the negro boy…three years ago：指 Christmas 打死养父之后到处流浪，长达 15 年，后来到达杰佛逊（Jefferson）镇，在路边向一黑人男孩打听情况。详见小说第 10 章。

10. the ancient thing：乔安娜的枪已太旧，她未能杀死 Christmas，反被他所杀。Christmas 然后放火烧屋，落荒而逃，后被追捕者杀死。详见小说第 14、19 两章。

ERNEST HEMINGWAY

〔作者介绍〕

海明威（Ernest Hemingway，1899～1961）是美国现代著名小说家，本世纪世界公认的优秀作家之一。他出生在美国伊利诺州的奥克帕克。母亲是音乐教师，父亲是内科医生。在父亲的影响下，海明威自幼喜爱打猎、钓鱼，性格勇敢，好冒险。后来渔猎成为他文学创作的重要题材。

中学毕业后，他当了6个月的《堪萨斯城星报》见习记者。报社编辑部指示记者"尽量不用形容词"，写"短句"和"短小的开头段落"，使用"生动有力的文字"。他在新闻写作方面得到的锻炼为他后来逐渐形成的独特文风打下了基础。海明威后来回忆说："这些是学到的关于写作的最好准则"。

第一次世界大战爆发以后，海明威志愿参加美国红十字会组织的战地救护队，在意大利前线当救护车司机。他表现英勇，在战斗中受伤，是第一个在意大利受伤的美国人，曾受到意大利政府的嘉奖。他的这段经历为他后来创作《太阳照样升起》(*The Sun Also Rises*，1926)，《永别了，武器》(*A Farewell to Arms*，1929）以及很多短篇小说提供了丰富的素材。

1921年，海明威作为加拿大《多伦多星报》记者前往巴黎，结识了格特鲁德·斯泰因、艾兹拉·庞德和司格特·菲茨杰拉德等美国文坛名家，在写作上得到他们的鼓励和指导。侨居巴黎的几年是海明威文学生涯的启蒙时期，后来，他放弃记者的采访工作，专心从事写作。

1923年，他发表《三篇短篇小说和十首诗》(*Three Stories and Ten Poems*)，没有引起批评界的注意。1925年，他发表了短篇小说集《在我们的时代里》(*In Our Time*)，其中共收集16个短篇小说，每篇附一个小品。书中很多篇章是描写一个名叫尼克·亚当斯的少年，他的童年和海明威的童年相类似；他目睹过暴力和死亡（如《印第安营寨》)；在战争中负伤；复员后发现自己的思想与现实生活格格不入，于是以终日垂钓消磨时光。他怀着对社会的疑虑和恐怖从少年步入青年。天真已不复存在，生活中充满了冷漠与无情。海明威在这本集子里创造了一种崭新的文体，他以冷峻、客观和不动声色的叙述，描绘一幅幅真实的生活画面。英国著名小说家D. H. 劳伦斯（David Herbert Lawrence）说："这些素描似的作品简短、尖锐而生动，多数都很精彩。"这部作品的出版标志着具有独特写作风格的海明威已经登上美国文坛。

1926年，海明威的第1部长篇小说《太阳照样升起》问世。这是一部成名作，确立了海明威在美国文坛上小说家的地位。美国著名文学批评家艾德蒙·威尔逊（Edmund Wilson）说："在海明威一代人的作品中，《太阳照样升起》是最好的一部小说。"它描写第一次世界大战以后，一群英美青年流落巴黎时的生活情形。他们之中有的人曾相信，第一次世界大战将是"结束战争"的战争，"拯救世界民主"的战争，他们怀着"崇高"的理想和青年人的热情上了前线。但战争的残酷现实使他们的理想化为泡影，对传统的道德标准和价值观念产生怀疑。他们迷惘、惆怅，逃避现实，沉湎于饮酒、谈情、垂钓和观看拳击、斗牛之中，以此掩盖内心的苦闷和空虚，但终究不能医治战争给他们造成的心理创伤。

主人公杰克·巴恩斯在战争中负伤，失去性爱能力。他孑然一身，侨居他乡，内心痛苦，常常夜不成眠。他默默地忍受着这一切，以一种"绝望中的勇气"，尽量象正常人一样生活，并努力想在他的朋友之中建立起正常的生活秩序。最后，在西班牙斗牛场上找到了他所崇拜的英雄，在年轻的斗牛士身上发现了人的尊严和勇敢精神。

女主人公勃莱特·艾施莉是战后出现在美国生活中的"新女性"的典型。她虽然吸烟、喝酒、跳舞、赴会，生活放荡不羁，实际上她也是一次大战的牺牲品。但同时她也是一个心地善良、乐于助人、从无害人之心的女人。在小说结尾处，当斗牛士罗梅罗向她求婚时，她拒绝了。她对杰克说："我不作专门坑害年轻人的淫妇。"

海明威自己很喜欢这部小说，称它是一部"最富教育意义的书"。有一次，一个教师告诉他，他的学生们正在读《永别了，武器》，海明威说："让他们读《太阳照样升起》，那是一本好书。"

3年以后，他完成另一部以第一次世界大战为背景的反战小说《永别了，武器》。

30年代经济萧条时期，他离开美国到各地做冒险旅行。这期间他先后写了以斗牛和打猎为主题的"非虚构"作品《午后之死》（*Death in the Afternoon*, 1932），《非洲的青山》（*Green Hills of Africa*, 1935）。此外还有《胜者无所得》（*Winner Take Nothing*, 1933）和描写弗罗里达水上走私者生活的《富有与贫穷》（*To Have and Have Not*, 1937）。

如果说30年代初海明威的左派朋友批评他在作品里回避写政治主题，那么从1937年写的《富有与贫穷》开始直到1940年完成的《丧钟为谁而鸣》（*For Whom the Bell Tolls*），他已经从关心个人命运转到关心社会前途。在前一本书里，作者通过一个生命垂危的人物的口述，说明一个人单枪匹马、赤手空拳是不会有任何作为的。这标志海明威悲剧观的转变。在这以前，海明威企图通过自己的作品说明，在当今世界里，人除照料自己免遭厄运之外别无他为。在他的笔下，从尼克·亚当斯到亨利上尉都是具有同运命抗衡的坚强意志和傲岸性格的人。他们相信，生存的力量和勇气来自自身，因而既不乞求于上帝，也不依靠集体的力量。第一次世界大战以后，作为“迷惘的一代”的代表人物，海明威的思想经历了一个消极、迷惘的危机。这个时期他的作品充满了玩世不恭和悲观失望的情绪。《太阳照样升起》和《永别了，武器》就存在严重的虚无主义和和平主义的反战倾向，主人公也多是消极的，他们在逆境与苦闷中努力寻求个人的出路，而最终仍满怀苦恼与不幸。《富有与贫穷》，特别是《丧钟为谁而鸣》的问世反映了海明威世界观的微妙变化。

1936 年西班牙内战爆发，海明威以记者身分赴西班牙前线。他支持当时的共和政府，反对以弗朗哥为首的法西斯叛乱分子。这时的海明威在强烈的社会责任感的感召下，将自己作家 的才华和反法西斯的正义事业溶合在一起。《丧钟为谁而鸣》是以西班牙内战为背景正面描写战争的一部重要长篇小说。主人公罗伯特·乔丹是美国人，为帮助西班牙共和政府作战，被派往弗朗哥反动势力和法西斯分子占领的后方，在当地游击队的配合下执行炸桥任务。负伤后，在生命垂危之际仍然想着再多消灭一个敌人。最后，为西班牙人民自由与民主的正义事业献出年轻的生命。《丧钟为谁而鸣》塑造了一个崭新的艺术形象，就其思想意义讲，和海明威的早期作品比较，它代表着一个质的变化。这部小说主题的飞跃与海明威热爱西班牙人民、反对法西斯的立场有直接关系。

此后 10 年内海明威几乎没有写书，直到 50 年代初他才又出版了几本小说，其中以《老人与海》(*The Old Man and the Sea*，1952) 最为成功。

这是关于一个古巴老人的故事。老渔民桑提亚哥出海打鱼，一连 84 天一无所获，但在第 85 天上他捉到一条比船身还长的马林鱼，经过三天两夜的搏斗终于制服了它。在返航途中，一群鲨鱼尾随而来，将鱼肉吃光。当老人把鱼拖到岸边时，马林鱼只剩下一个骨架，完全失去了它的雄姿与风采。疲惫不堪的桑提亚哥在梦中仍不忘雄狮。

小说通过对桑提亚哥在海上经历的描写塑造了一个饱经风浪、意志如钢的老渔民的形象。他一生与大海搏斗，非但没有被它吞噬，反而能象与之溶为一体那样驾驭它，小说用了很多笔墨描写老人与马林鱼周旋的场面，成功的塑造了老人坚韧不拔、临危不惧的性格。他没有因为 84 天没交好运而抱怨，也没有因为与马林鱼拼搏三天两夜所经受的折磨而悔恨。“但人不是为被打败而生。人可以被毁灭，可不能被打败”。小说还通过描述老人对马林鱼的赞赏揭示了他性格方面更深的美学内涵。当他看到马林鱼的身躯如此之大，身姿如此壮观时，他兴奋不已。他敬重它，认为它是一个值得与之交战的对手。他对马林鱼说："你会把我干掉的，鱼儿…但是你有这个权利。我从未见过比你更雄伟，更漂亮，更沉着或更高尚的鱼。兄弟，来来来，把我干掉吧！咱们两个不论谁干掉谁我都不在乎。"这哪里是一个以打鱼为生的渔民的心理，这里所描写的简直是一个大自然的美充满深情而又怀有极高鉴赏能力的美学家的思想境界。最后，当他拖着疲惫的身躯进入梦乡时，他的脑海里仍然充满了雄风、力量和威严，准备与世界上的任何强者对峙。在某种意义上讲，《老人与海》概括地总结了海明威的思想发展过程。小说开首的桑提亚哥是典型的早期海明威小说主人公的形象；但是后来他逐渐体会到人际间的友爱、人与大自然间的和谐，因而对周围的人和物、甚至对他的敌手马林鱼也产生了感情。在他的坚强中增加了湿润的色调。

在海明威死后出版的《流动的节》(*Movable Feast*, 1964）是他20年代在巴黎生活的回忆录，是一部优秀的散文作品。此外还有《海流中的岛屿》(*Islands in the Stream*, 1970）和《伊甸园》(*Garden of Eden*, 1986)。第一次世界大战以后，美国文学界涌现出一批年轻作家，他们多数遭受战争的劫难，心灵受过不同程度的创伤。战争割断了他们同旧的价值观念的联系，而时间又未能赋予他们新的思想以适应战后残酷的现实，他们感到"迷惘"。因此，美国作家格特鲁德·斯泰因说他们是"迷惘的一代"，而海明威则是这一代人的代表作家。

海明威的文学生涯是和战争紧密联系在一起的，因此，他也是本世纪描写战争的最出色的作家。早期的海明威有严重的虚无主义情绪和悲观主义倾向。在他看来，以流血、残酷和背信弃义为特点的现代战争，是现代生活空虚状态的最高体现。他的几部主要作品都是以战争为背景，描写战争给人们造成的精神创伤的。20年代完成的《太阳照样升起》、《永别了，武器》以及一些短篇小说就属于这一类。他在这些作品中所塑造的人物多是在生活中失去理想、精神苦闷、悲观失望的小资产阶级知识分子。战争破坏了传统的信念和伦理，也毁坏了他们的个人幸福。在一个荒诞无稽的世界里生活，人需要勇气、尊严和风度。因此，海明威式的主人公都表现出性格坚强的一面。尽管他们的生活被爱情的悲剧和死亡的阴影所笼罩，但他们具有一种本世纪初英国哲学家贝特兰·罗素（Bertrand Russell, 1872～1970）所说的"绝望中的勇气"，能在失败中保持尊严，在压力下不失风度。这种"压力下的风度"几乎在他所有的作品中都有反映。

罗伯特·乔丹、桑提亚哥、杰克·巴思斯、弗瑞德里克·亨利以及短篇小说《不败者》("The Undefeated"）的主人公，都在重压之下表现出非凡的勇气和优雅的风度。他们单枪匹马与自己不理解的力量对抗，注定以失败告终；但他们遵照"荣誉的准则"，依靠自己生存，表现出"大丈夫气概"。胜负并不重要，斗争就是一切，在斗争中人才能表现出自己的"人格"。海明威的典型人物多是百折不挠的血性汉子，他们不动声色，但临危不惧，随遇而安。他们渴望得到现代生活无法提供的秩序和安全感，因为他们心头充满了绝望情绪。但是他们又多在富于刺激性的生活中吸取补偿空虚的滋养。于是典型的“海明威场面”不是暴力、犯罪、混乱与残酷，就是狂歌豪饮或偷情做爱，尽情寻欢作乐。典型的海明威式主人公都具有一种浓重的存在主义色调。

在美国文学史上，海明威是一位具有独特风格的作家。他先后受教于舍伍德·安德森和斯泰因，认真研读了马克·吐温的《哈克贝利·芬历险记》等著作，经过自己多年的不断探索和创作实践，一改过去那种冗陈繁赘的旧文风，发展了美国文学口语化的新文风，给20世纪美国文学带来了生气。有人说海明威在巴黎期间和斯泰因、庞德、乔伊斯共同发起了文风和文学语言的一次革命，这话是有道理的。

海明威写作力求真实，主张用简明生动的语言具体描述真实的生活画面，创造一种意境，让读者自己去体会，从而使作品产生很强的艺术感染力。他主张“写你知道的一句最真实的话……我宁肯把那些花里胡哨的装饰品通通砍掉，就用我写的第一个真实、朴素的陈述句作为开头”。

他还主张省略，他说，“如果一个散文作家对于他想写的东西心中有数，那么他可以省略他知道的东西，读者呢，只要他写的真实，会强烈地感受到他所省略的地方，好象作者已经写出来似的”。他在谈及《老人与海》的创作时说，他本来可以把它写成一本上千页的大书，而在他省去了与主题无关的情节和内容以后，剩下的只是一本用洗炼的语言浓缩成的信息含量宏丰的小书，读起来犹如冰山似的深沉稳重。因此，海明威的文章以简朴、凝炼，表达准确、直接了当，貌似单纯、实则包孕丰富的特点而著称。

然而，海明威的文风又不单是写作技巧问题；他的文风服从作品主题和塑造人物性格的需要。在海明威的作品里，文风和主题往往是不可分的统一体。

由于他在文学创作上所取得的巨大成就以及他的作品所产生的世界性的影响，1954年，海明威获得诺贝尔文学奖。

晚年海明威曾宣称另一部数十万言的文学巨著即将问世。事实上这只是他个人的愿望，因为他的创作源泉已经枯竭。这件事深深挫伤了他的自尊心，兼之他又疾病缠身，便于1961年7月以猎枪自杀，结束了他的一生。海明威的死标志着美国文学史上一个时代的终结。

A Farewell to Arms

〔作品介绍〕

《永别了，武器》(*A Farewell to Arms*) 发表于 1929 年。

第一次世界大战期间在意大利服役的美国上尉弗德里克·亨利在执行任务中负伤，被送往米兰一家医院治疗，和英国女护士凯瑟琳·伯克利产生爱情。后亨利重返前线，适逢奥军发起进攻。在随意军撤退途中，亨利被诬为敌方间谍而被捕。在被处决之前，他伺机逃跑成功。到米兰后，凯瑟琳已离开米兰去斯特利萨。亨利赶到那里同她相聚，两人感慨万端。他们同住在一家旅馆里，度过一段缠绵的美好时光。一天夜里，旅馆服务员突然跑来告诉他，因亨利逃跑，意军宪兵队正在追捕他。于是他们连夜划船逃到瑞士。在那里，他们等待着孩子出生，向往着幸福的生活。但出人意料，凯瑟琳在难产中死去，孩子在母体中便已断气。亨利告别了凯瑟琳遗体，独自一人在雨中走回旅馆。

《永别了，武器》突出描写战争中的爱情悲剧。全书充满了反战情绪。在亨利所在的救护队里，从军官到士兵无不诅咒这场“肮脏”的战争，盼望它尽早结束。亨利更是如此，他在战场上的亲身经历使他认识到美国统治者所宣扬的“拯救世界民主”是一句骗人的口号。实际上，战争就象屠宰场一样，人们相互残杀，到处是流血和死亡。正象他自己说的：“神圣，光荣和牺牲等空洞的字眼使我感到难为情”。“这场战争和我没有一点关系……我祈祷上帝让它结束”。

他憎恨战争，希望在爱情中找到和平和幸福，从孤独和恐怖中摆脱出来。战争不堪忍受，已经得到的爱情和幸福也瞬息即逝，等待他的只有两种命运：一是走投无路，一是唤起人的尊严和勇气，正视悲剧，默默地忍受痛苦。作为典型的海明威式主人公的亨利选择了后者。亨利的悲剧既是个人的，也是社会性的。

小说《永别了，武器》反映了战后普遍存在于西方资本主义世界的失望情绪；到了 30 年代经济萧条时期，这种情绪更是有增无减，从而加剧了资本主义世界的思想危机。

这里选注的是本书第 1 章的前 6 节。

A Farewell to Arms

BOOK I

1

In the late summer of that year we lived in a house in a village that looked across the river and the plain to the mountains. In the bed of the river there were pebbles and boulders, dry and white in the sun, and the water was clear and swiftly moving and blue in the channels. Troops went by the house and down the road and the dust they raised powdered the leaves of the trees. The trunks of the trees too were dusty and the leaves fell early that year and we saw the troops marching along the road and the dust rising and leaves, stirred by the breeze, falling and the soldiers marching and afterward the road bare and white except for the leaves.

The plain was rich with crops; there were many orchards of fruit trees and beyond the plain the mountains were brown and bare. There was fighting in the mountains and at night we could see the flashes from the artillery. In the dark it was like summer lightning, but the nights were cool and there was not the feeling of a storm coming.

Sometimes in the dark we heard the troops marching under the window and guns going past pulled by motor-tractors. There was much traffic at night and many mules on the roads with boxes of ammunition on each side of their pack-saddles and gray motor trucks that carricd men, and other trucks with loads covered with canvas that moved slower in the traffic. There were big guns too that passed in the day drawn by tractors, the long barrels of the guns covered with green branches and green leafy branches and vines laid over the tractors. To the north we could look across a valley and see a forest of chestnut trees and behind it another mountain on this side of the river. There was fighting for that mountain too, but it was not successful, and in the fall when the rains came the leaves all fell from the chestnut trees and the branches were bare and the trunks black with rain. The vineyards were thin and bare-branched too and all the country wet and brown and dead with the autumn. There were mists over the river and clouds on the mountain and the trucks splashed mud on the road and the troops were muddy and wet in their capes; their rifles were wet and under their capes the two leather cartridge-boxes on the front of the belts, gray leather boxes heavy with the packs of clips of thin, long 6. 5mm. cartridges, bulged forward under the capes so that the men, passing on the road, marched as though they were six months gone with child.

There were small gray motor cars that passed going very fast; usually there was an officer on the seat with the driver and more officers in the back seat. They splashed more mud than the camions even and if one of the officers in the back was very small and sitting between two generals, he himself so small that you could not see his face but only the top of his cap and his narrow back, and if the car went especially fast it was probably the King[1]. He lived in Udine and came out in this way nearly every day to see how things were going, and things went very badly.

At the start of the winter came the permanent rain and with the rain came the cholera. But it was checked and in the end only seven thousand died of it in the army.[2]

2

THE next year there were many victories. The mountain that was beyond the valley and the hillside where the chestnut forest grew was captured and there were victories beyond the plain on the plateau to the south and we crossed the river in August and lived in a house in Gorizia that had a fountain and many thick shady trees in a walled garden and a wistaria vine purple on the side of the house. Now the fighting was in the next mountains beyond and was not a mile away. The town was very nice adn our house was very fine. The river ran behind us and the town had been captured very handsomely but the mountains beyond it could not be taken and I was very glad the Austrians[3] seemed to want to come back to the town some time, if the war should end, because they did not bombard it to destroy it but only a little in a military way. People lived on in it and there were hospitals and cafés and artillery up side streets and two bawdy houses, one for troops and one for officers, and with the end of the summer, the cool nights, the fighting in the mountains beyond the town, the shell-marked iron of the railway bridge, the smashed tunnel by the river where the fighting had been, the trees around the square and the long avenue of trees that led to the square; these with there being girls in the town, the King passing in his motor car, sometimes now seeing his face and little long necked body and gray beard like a goat's chin tuft; all these with the sudden interiors of houses that had lost a wall through shelling, with plaster and rubble in their gardens and sometimes in the street, and the whole thing going well on the Carso[4] made the fall very different from the last fall when we had been in the country. The war was changed too.

The forest of oak trees on the mountain beyond the town was gone. The forest had been green in the summer when we had come into the town but now there were the stumps and the broken trunks and the ground torn up, and one day at the end of the fall when I was out where the oak forest had been I saw a cloud coming over the mountain. It came very fast and the sun went a dull yellow and then everything was gray and the sky was covered and the cloud came on down the mountain and suddenly we were in it and it was snow. The snow slanted across the wind, the bare ground was covered, the stumps of trees projected, there was snow on the guns and there were paths in the snow going back to the latrines behind trenches.

Later, below in the town, I watched the snow falling, looking out of the window of the bawdy house, the house for officers, where I sat with a friend and two glasses drinking a bottle of Asti,[5] and, looking out at the snow falling slowly and heavily, we knew it was all over for that year. Up the river the mountains had not been taken; none of the mountains beyond the river had been taken. That was all left for next year. My friend saw the priest from our mess going by in the street, walking carefully in the slush, and pounded on the window to attract his attention. The priest looked up. He saw us and smiled. My friend motioned for him to come in. The priest shook his head and went on. That night in the mess after the spaghetti course, which every one ate very quickly and seriously, lifting the spaghetti on the fork until the loose strands hung clear then lowering it into the mouth, or else using a continuous lift and sucking into the mouth, helping ourselves to wine from the grass-covered gallon flask; it swung in a metal cradle and you pulled the neck of the flask down with the forefinger and the wine, clear red, tannic and lovely, poured out into the glass held with the same hand; after this course, the captain commenced picking on the priest.

The priest was young and blushed easily and wore a uniform like the rest of us but with a cross in dark red velvet above the left breast pocket of his gray tunic. The captain spoke pidgin Italian for my doubtful benefit, in order that I might understand perfectly, that nothing should be lost.

"Priest to-day with girls," the captain said looking at the priest and at me. The priest smiled and blushed and shook his head. This captain baited him often.

"Not true?" asked the captain. "To-day I see priest with girls."

"No," said the priest. The other officers were amused at the baiting.

"Priest not with girls," went on the captain. "Priest never with girls," he explained to me. He took my glass and filled it, looking at my eyes all the time, but not losing sight of the priest.

"Priest every night five against one." Every one at the table laughed. "You understand? Priest every night five against one." He made a gesture and laughed loudly. The priest accepted it as a joke.

"The Pope wants the Austrians to win the war," the major said. "He loves Franz Joseph.[6] That's where the money comes from. I am an atheist."

"Did you ever read the 'Black Pig'?" asked the lieutenant. "I will get you a copy. It was that which shook my faith."

"It is a filthy and vile book," said the priest. "You do not really like it."

"It is very valuable," said the lieutenant. "It tells you about those priests. You will like it," he said to me. I smiled at the priest and he smiled back across the candle-light. "Don't you read it," he said.

"I will get it for you," said the lieutenant.

"All thinking men are atheists," the major said. "I do not believe in the Free Masons[7] however."

"I believe in the Free Masons," the lieutenant said. "It is a noble organization." Some one came in and as the door opened I could see the snow falling.

"There will be no more offensive now that the snow has come," I said.

"Certainly not," said the major. "You should go on leave. You should go to Rome, Naples, Sicily——"

"He should visit Amalfi," said the lieutenant. "I will write you cards to my family in Amalfi. They will love you like a son."

"He should go to Palermo."

"He ought to go to Capri."

"I would like you to see Abruzzi and visit my family at Capracotta," said the priest.

"Listen to him talk about the Abruzzi. There's more snow there than here. He doesn't want to see peasants. Let him go to centres of culture and civilization."

"He should have fine girls. I will give you the addresses of places in Naples. Beautiful young girls—accompanied by their mothers. Ha! Ha! Ha!" The captain spread his hand open, the thumb up and fingers outspread as when you make shadow pictures. There was a shadow from his hand on the wall. He spoke again in pidgin Italian. "You go away like this," he pointed to the thumb, "and come back like this," he touched the little finger. Every one laughed.

"Look," said the captain. He spread the hand again. Again the candle-light made its shadows on the wall. He started with the upright thumb and named in their order the thumb and four fingers, "soto-tenente (the thumb), tenente (first finger), capitano (next finger), maggiore (next to the little finger), and tenente-colonello (the little finger). You go away soto-tenente! You come back soto-colonello!" They all laughed. The captain was having a great success with finger games. He looked at the priest and shouted, "Every night priest five against one!" They all laughed again.

"You must go on leave at once," the major said.

"I would like to go with you and show you things," the lieutenant said.

"When you come back bring a phonograph."

"Bring good opera disks."

"Bring Caruso."

"Don't bring Caruso. He bellows."

"Don't you wish you could bellow like him?"

"He bellows. I say he bellows!"

"I would like you to go to Abruzzi," the priest said. The others were shouting. "There is good hunting. You would like the people and though it is cold it is clear and dry. You could say with my family. My father is a famous hunter."

"Come on," said the captain. "We go whorehouse before it shuts."

"Good-night," I said to the priest.

"Good-night," he said.

3

WHEN I came back to the front we still lived in that town. There were many more guns in the country around and the spring had come. The fields were green and there were small green shoots on the vines, the trees along the road had small leaves and a breeze came from the sea. I saw the town with the hill and the old castle above it in a cup in the hills with the mountains beyond, brown mountains with a little green on their slopes. In the town there were more guns, there were some new hospitals, you met British men and sometimes women, on the street, and a few more houses had been hit by shell fire. It was warm and like the spring and I walked down the alleyway of trees, warmed from the sun on the wall, and found we still lived in the same house and that it all looked the same as when I had left it. The door was open, there was a soldier sitting on a bench outside in the sun, and ambulance was waiting by the side door and inside the door, as I went in, there was the smell of marble floors and hospital. It was all as I had left it except that now it was spring. I looked in the door of the big room and saw the major sitting at his desk, the window open and the sunlight coming into the room. He did not see me and I did not know whether to go in and report or go upstairs first and clean up. I decided to go on upstairs.

The room I shared with the lieutenant Rinaldi looked out on the courtyard. The window was open, my bed was made up with blankets and my things hung on the wall, the gas mask in an oblong tin can, the steel helmet on the same peg. At the foot of the bed was my flat trunk, and my winter boots, the leather shiny with oil, were on the trunk. My Austrian sniper's rifle with its blued octagon barrel and the lovely dark walnut, cheek-fitted, *schutzen* stock, hung over the two beds. The telescope that fitted it was, I remembered, locked in the trunk. The lieutenant, Rinaldi, lay asleep on the other bed. He woke when he heard me in the room and sat up.

"Ciaou!" he said. "What kind of time did you have?"

"Magnificent."

We shook hands and he put his arm around my neck and kissed me.

"Oughf," I said.

"You're dirty," he said. "You ought to wash. Where did you go and what did you do? Tell me everything at once."

"I went everywhere. Milan, Florence, Rome, Naples, Villa San Giovanni, Messina, Taormina——"

"You talk like a time-table. Did you have any beautiful adventures?"

"Yes."

"Where?"

"Milano, Firenze, Roma, Napoli——"

"That's enough. Tell me really what was the best."

"In Milano."

"That was because it was first. Where did you meet her? In the Cova? Where did you go? How did you feel? Tell me everything at once. Did you stay all night?"

"Yes."

"That's nothing. Here now we have beautiful girls. New girls never been to the front before."

"Wonderful."

"You don't believe me? We will go now this afternoon and see. And in the town we have beautiful English girls. I am now in love with Miss Barkley. I will take you to call. I will probably marry Miss Barkley."

"I have to get washed and report. Doesn't anybody work now?"

"Since you are gone we have nothing but frostbites, chilblains, jaundice, gonorrhea, self-inflicted wounds, pneumonia and hard and soft chancres. Every week some one gets wounded by rock fragments. There are a few real wounded. Next week the war starts again. Perhaps it start again. They say so. Do you think I would do right to marry Miss Barkley—after the war of course?"

"Absolutely," I said and poured the basin full of water.

"To-night you will tell me everything," said Rinaldi. "Now I must go back to sleep to be fresh and beautiful for Miss Barkley."

I took off my tunic and shirt and washed in the cold water in the basin. While I rubbed myself with a towel I looked around the room and out the window and at Rinaldi lying with his eyes closed on the bed. He was good-looking, was my age, and he came from Amalfi. He loved being a surgeon and we were great friends. While I was looking at him he opened his eyes.

"Have you any money?"

"Yes."

"Loan me fifty lire."

I dried my hands and took out my pocket-book from the inside of my tunic hanging on the wall. Rinaldi took the note, folded it without rising from the bed and slid it in his breeches pocket. He smiled, "I must make on Miss Barkley the impression of a man of sufficient wealth. You are my great and good friend and financial protector."

"Go to hell," I said.

That night at the mess I sat next to the priest and he was disappointed and suddenly hurt that I had not gone to the Abruzzi. He had written to his father that I was coming and they had made preparations. I myself felt as badly as he did and could not understand why I had not gone. It was what I had wanted to do and I tried to explain how one thing had led to another and finally he saw it and understood that I had really wanted to go and it was almost all right. I had drunk much wine and afterward coffee and Strega and I explained, winefully, how we did not do the things we wanted to do; we never did such things.

We two were talking while the others argued. I had wanted to go to Abruzzi. I had gone to no place where the roads were frozen and hard as iron, where it was clear cold and dry and the snow was dry and powdery and hare-tracks in the snow and the peasants took off their hats and called you Lord and there was good hunting. I had gone to no such place but to the smoke of cafés and nights when the room whirled and you needed to look at the wall to make it stop, nights in bed, drunk, when you knew that that was all there was, and the strange excitement of waking and not knowing who it was with you, and the world all unreal in the dark and so exciting that you must resume again unknowing and not caring in the night, sure that this was all and all and all and not caring. Suddenly to care very much and to sleep to wake with it sometimes morning and all that had been there gone and everything sharp and hard and clear and sometimes a dispute about the cost. Sometimes still pleasant and fond and warm and breakfast and lunch. Sometimes all niceness gone and glad to get out on the street but always another day starting and then another night. I tried to tell about the night and the difference between the night and the day and how the night was better unless the day was very clean and cold and I could not tell it; as I cannot tell it now. But if you have had it you know. He had not had it but he understood that I had really wanted to go to the Abruzzi but had not gone and we were still friends, with many tastes alike, but with the difference between us. He had always known what I did not know and what, when I learned it, I was always able to forget. But I did not know that then, although I learned it later. In the meantime we were all at the mess, the meal was finished, and the argument went on. We two stopped talking and the captain shouted, "Priest not happy. Priest not happy without girls."

"I am happy," said the priest.

"Priest not happy. Priest wants Austrians to win the war," the captain said. The others listened. The priest shook his head.

"No," he said.

"Priest wants us never to attack. Don't you want us never to attack?"

"No. If there is a war I suppose we must attack."

"Must attack. Shall attack!"

The priest nodded.

"Leave him alone," the major said. "He's all right."

"He can't do anything about it anyway," the captain said. We all got up and left the table.

4

THE battery in the next garden woke me in the morning and I saw the sun coming through the window and got out of the bed. I went to the window and looked out. The gravel paths were moist and the grass was wet with dew. The battery fired twice and the air came each time like a blow and shook the window and made the front of my pajamas flap. I could not see the guns but they were evidently firing directly over us. It was a nuisance to have them there but it was a comfort that they were no bigger. As I looked out at the garden I heard a motor truck starting on the road. I dressed, went downstairs, had some coffee in the kitchen and went out to the garage.

Ten cars were lined up side by side under the long shed. They were top-heavy, blunt-nosed ambulances, painted gray and built like moving-vans. The mechanics were working on one out in the yard. Three others were up in the mountains at dressing stations.

"Do they ever shell that battery?" I asked one of the mechanics.

"No, Signor Tenente. It is protected by the little hill."

"How's everything?"

"Not so bad. This machine is no good but the others march." He stopped working and smiled. "Were you on permission?"

"Yes."

He wiped his hands on his jumper and grinned. "You have a good time?" The others all grinned too.

"Fine," I said. "What's the matter with his machine?"

"It's no good. One thing after another."

"What's the matter now?"

"New rings."

I left them working, the car looking disgraced and empty with the engine open and parts spread on the work bench, and went in under the shed and looked at each of the cars. They were moderately clean, a few freshly washed, the others dusty. I looked at the tires carefully, looking for cuts or stone bruises. Everything seemed in good condition. It evidently made no difference whether I was there to look after things or not. I had imagined that the condition of the cars, whether or not things were obtainable, the smooth functioning of the business of removing wounded and sick from the dressing stations, hauling them back from the mountains to the clearing station and then distributing them to the hospitals named on their papers, depended to a considerable extent on myself. Evidently it did not matter whether I was there or not.

"Has there been any trouble getting parts?" I asked the sergeant mechanic.

"No, Signor Tenente."

"Where is the gasoline park now?"

"At the same place."

"Good," I said and went back to the house and drank another bowl of coffee at the mess table. The coffee was a pale gray and sweet with condensed milk. Outside the window it was a lovely spring morning.

There was that beginning of a feeling of dryness in the nose that meant the day would be hot later on. That day I visited the posts in the mountains and was back in town late in the afternoon.

The whole thing seemed to run better while I was away. The offensive was going to start again I heard. The division for which we worked were to attack at a place up the river and the major told me that I would see about the posts for during the attack. The attack would cross the river up above the narrow gorge and spread up the hillside. The posts for the cars would have to be as near the river as they could get and keep covered. They would, of course, be selected by the infantry but we were supposed to work it out. It was one of those things that gave you a false feeling of soldiering.

I was very dusty and dirty and went up to my room to wash. Rinaldi was sitting on the bed with a copy of Hugo's English grammar. He was dressed, wore his black boots, and his hair shone.

"Splendid," he said when he saw me. "You will come with me to see Miss Barkley."

"No."

"Yes. You will please come and make me a good impression on her."

"All right. Wait till I get cleaned up."

"Wash up and come as you are."

I washed, brushed my hair and we started.

"Wait a minute," Rinaldi said. "Perhaps we should have a drink." He opened his trunk and took out a bottle.

"Not Strega," I said.

"No. Grappa."

"All right."

He poured two glassed and we touched them, first fingers extended. The grappa was very strong.

"Another?"

"All right," I said. We drank the second grappa, Rinaldi put away the bottle and we went down the stairs. It was hot walking through the town but the sun was starting to go down and it was very pleasant. The British hospital was a big villa built by Germans before the war. Miss Barkley was in the garden. Another nurse was with her. We saw their white uniforms through the trees and walked toward them. Rinaldi saluted. I saluted too but more moderately.

"How do you do?" Miss Barkley said. "You're not an Italian, are you?"

"Oh, no."

Rinaldi was talking with the other nurse. They were laughing.

"What an odd thing—to be in the Italian army."

"It's not really the army. It's only the ambulance."

"It's very odd though. Why did you do it?"

"I don't know," I said. "There isn't always an explanation for everything."

"Oh, isn't there? I was brought up to think there was."

"That's awfully nice."

"*Do* we have to go on and talk this way?"

"No," I said.

"That's a relief. Isn't it?"

"What is the stick?" I asked. Miss Barkley was quite tall. She wore what seemed to me to be a nurse's uniform, was blonde and had a tawny skin and gray eyes. I thought she was very beautiful. She was carrying a thin rattan stick like a toy riding-crop, bound in leather.

"It belonged to a boy who was killed last year."

"I'm awfully sorry."

"He was a very nice boy. He was going to marry me and he was killed in the Somme."

"It was a ghastly show."

"Were you there?"

"No."

"I've heard about it," she said. "There's not really any war of that sort down here. They sent me the little stick. His mother sent it to me. They returned it with his things."

"Had you been engaged long?"

"Eight years. We grew up together."

"And why didn't you marry?"

"I don't know," she said. "I was a fool not to. I could have given him that anyway. But I thought it would be bad for him."

"I see."

"Have you ever loved any one?"

"No," I said.

We sat down on a bench and I looked at her.

"You have beautiful hair," I said.

"Do you like it?"

"Very much."

"I was going to cut it all off when he died."

"No."

"I wanted to do something for him. You see I didn't care about the other thing and he could have had it all. He could have had anything he wanted if I would have known. I would have married him or anything. I know all about it now. But then he wanted to go to war and I didn't know."

I did not say anything.

"I didn't know about anything then. I thought it would be worse for him. I thought perhaps he couldn't stand it and then of course he was killed and that was the end of it."

"I don't know."

"Oh, yes," she said. "That's the end of it."

We looked at Rinaldi talking with the other nurse.

"What is her name?"

"Ferguson. Helen Ferguson. Your friend is a doctor, isn't he?"

"Yes. He's very good."

"That's splendid. You rarely find any one any good this close to the front. This is close to the front, isn't it?"

"Quite."

"It's a silly front," she said. "But it's very beautiful. Are they going to have an offensive?"

"Yes."

"Then we'll have to work. There's no work now."

"Have you done nursing long?"

"Since the end of 'fifteen. I started when he did. I remember having a silly idea he might come to the hospital where I was. With a sabre cut, I suppose, and a bandage around his head. Or shot through the shoulder. Something picturesque."

"This is the picturesque front," I said.

"Yes," she said. "People can't realize what France is like. If they did, it couldn't all go on. He didn't have a sabre cut. They blew him all to bits."

I didn't say anything.

"Do you suppose it will always go on?"

"No."

"What's to stop it?"

"It will crack somewhere."

"We'll crack. We'll crack in France. They can't go on doing things like the Somme and not crack."

"They won't crack here," I said.

"You think not?"

"No. They did very well last summer."

"They may crack," she said. "Anybody may crack."

"The Germans too."

"No," she said. "I think not."

We went over toward Rinaldi and Miss Ferguson.

"You love Italy?" Rinaldi asked Miss Ferguson in English.

"Quite well."

"No understand," Rinaldi shook his head.

"Abbastanza bene," I translated. He shook his head.

"That is not good. You love England?"

"Not too well. I'm Scotch, you see."

Rinaldi looked at me blankly.

"She's Scotch, so she loves Scotland better than England," I said in Italian.

"But Scotland is England."

I translated this for Miss Ferguson.

"Pas encore," said Miss Ferguson.

"Not really?"

"Never. We do not like the Engligh."

"Not like the English? Not like Miss Barkley?"

"Oh, that's different. You mustn't take everything so literally."

After a while we said good-night and left. Walking home Rinaldi said, "Miss Barkley prefers you to me. That is very clear. But the little Scotch one is very nice."

"Very," I said. I had not noticed her. "You like her?"

"No," said Rinaldi.

5

THE next afternoon I went to call on Miss Barkley again. She was not in the garden and I went to the side door of the villa where the ambulances drove up. Inside I saw the head nurse, who said Miss Barkley was on duty— "there's a war on, you know."

I said I knew.

"You're the American in the Italian army?" she asked.

"Yes, ma'am."

"How did you happen to do that? Why didn't you join up with us?"

"I don't know," I said. "Could I join now?"

"I'm afraid not now. Tell me. Why did you join up with the Italians?"

"I was in Italy," I said, "and I spoke Italian."

"Oh," she said. "I'm learning it. It's beautiful language."

"Somebody said you should be able to learn it in two weeks."

"Oh, I'll not learn it in two weeks. I've studied it for months now. You may come and see her after seven o'clock if you wish. She'll be off then. But don't bring a lot of Italians."

"Not even for the beautiful language?"

"No. Nor for the beautiful uniforms."

"Good evening," I said.

"A rivederci, Tenente."

"A rivederla." I saluted and went out. It was impossible to salute foreigners as an Italian, without embarrassment. The Italian salute never seemed made for export.

The day had been hot. I had been up the river to the bridgehead at Plava. It was there that the offensive was to begin. It had been impossible to advance on the far side the year before because there was only one road leading down from the pass to the pontoon bridge and it was under machine-gun and shell fire for nearly a mile. It was not wide enough either to carry all the transport for an offensive and the Austrians could make a shambles out of it. But the Italians had crossed and spread out a little way on the far side to hold about a mile and a half on the Austrian side of the river. It was a nasty place and the Austrians should not have let them hold it. I suppose it was mutual tolerance because the Austrians still kept a bridgehead further down the river. The Austrian trenches were above on the hillside only a few yards from the Italian lines. There had been a little town but it was all rubble. There was what was left of a railway station and a smashed permanent bridge that could not be repaired and used because it was in plain sight.

I went along the narrow road down toward the river, left the car at the dressing station under the hill, crossed the pontoon bridge, which was protected by a shoulder of the mountain, and went through the trenches in the smashed-down town and along the edge of the slope. Everybody was in the dugouts. There were racks of rockets standing to be touched off to call for help from the artillery or to signal with if the telephone wires were cut. It was quiet, hot and dirty. I looked across the wire at the Austrian lines. Nobody was in sight. I had a drink with a captain that I knew in one of the dugouts and went back across the bridge.

A new wide road was being finished that would go over the mountain and zig-zag down to the bridge. When this road was finished the offensive would start. It came down through the forest in sharp turns. The system was to bring everything down the new road and take the empty trucks, carts and loaded ambulances and all returning traffic up the old narrow road. The dressing station was on the Austrian side of the river under the edge of the hill and stretcher-bearers would bring the wounded back across the pontoon bridge. It would be the same when the offensive started. As far as I could make out the last mile or so of the new road where it started to level out would be able to be shelled steadily by the Austrians. It looked as though it might be a mess. But I found a place where the cars would be sheltered after they passed that last bad-looking bit and could wait for the wounded to be brought across the pontoon bridge. I would have liked to drive over the new road but it was not yet finished. It looked wide and well made with a good grade and the turns looked very impressive where you could see them through openings in the forest on the mountain side. The cars would be all right with their good metal-to-metal brakes and anyway, coming down, they would not be loaded. I drove back up the narrow road.

Two carabinieri held the car up. A shell had fallen and while we waited three others fell up the road. They were seventy-sevens and came with a whishing rush of air, a hard bright burst and flash and then gray smoke that blew across the road. The carabinieri waved us to go on. Passing where the shells had landed I avoided the small broken places and smelled the high explosive and the smell of blasted clay and stone and freshly shattered flint. I drove back to Gorizia and our villa and, as I said, went to call on Miss Barkley, who was on duty.

At dinner I ate very quickly and left for the villa where the British had their hospital. It was really very large and beautiful and there were fine trees in the grounds. Miss Barkley was sitting on a bench in the garden. Miss Ferguson was with her. They seemed glad to see me and in a little while Miss Ferguson excused herself and went away.

"I'll leave you two," she said. "You get along very well without me."

"Don't go, Helen," Miss Barkley said.

"I'd really rather. I must write some letters."

"Good-night," I said.

"Good-night, Mr. Henry."

"Don't write anything that will bother the censor."

"Don't worry. I only write about what a beautiful place we live in and how brave the Italians are."

"That way you'll be decorated."

"That will be nice. Good-night, Catherine."

"I'll see you in a little while," Miss Barkley said. Miss Ferguson walked away in the dark.

"She's nice," I said.

"Oh, yes, she's very nice. She's a nurse."

"Aren't you a nurse?"

"Oh, no. I'm something called a V. A. D. [8] We work very hard but no one trusts us."

"Why not?"

"They don't trust us when there's nothing going on. When there is really work they trust us."

"What is the difference?"

"A nurse is like a doctor. It takes a long time to be. A V. A. D. is a short cut."

"I see."

"The Italians didn't want women so near the front. So we're all on very special behavior. We don't go out."

"I can come here though."

"Oh, yes. We're not cloistered."

"Let's drop the war."

"It's very hard. There's no place to drop it."

"Let's drop it anyway."

"All right."

We looked at each other in the dark. I thought she was very beautiful and I took her hand. She let me take it and I held it and put my arm around under her arm.

"No," she said. I kept my arm where it was.

"Why not?"

"No."

"Yes," I said. "Please." I leaned forward in the dark to kiss her and there was a sharp stinging flash. She had slapped my face hard. Her hand had hit my nose and eyes, and tears came in my eyes from the reflex.

"I'm so sorry," she said. I felt I had a certain advantage.

"You were quite right."

"I'm dreadfully sorry," she said. "I just couldn't stand the nurse's-evening-off[9] aspect of it. I didn't mean to hurt you. I did hurt you, didn't I?"

She was looking at me in the dark. I was angry and yet certain, seeing it all ahead like the moves in a chess game.

"You did exactly right," I said. "I don't mind at all."

"Poor man."

"You see I've been leading a sort of a funny life. And I never even talk English. And then you are so very beautiful." I looked at her.

"You don't need to say a lot of nonsense. I said I was sorry. We do get along."

"Yes," I said. "And we have gotten away from the war."

She laughed. It was the first time I had ever heard her laugh. I watched her face.

"You are sweet," she said.

"No, I'm not."

"Yes. You are a dear. I'd be glad to kiss you if you don't mind."

I looked in her eyes and put my arm around her as I had before and kissed her. I kissed her hand and held her tight and tried to open her lips; they were closed tight. I was still angry and as I held her suddenly she shivered. I held her close against me and could feel her heart beating and her lips opened and her head went back against my hand and then she was crying on my shoulder.

"Oh, darling," she said. "You will be good to me, won't you?"

What the hell, I thought. I stroked her hair and patted her shoulder. She was crying.

"You will, won't you?" She looked up at me. "Because we're going to have a strange life."

After a while I walked with her to the door of the villa and she went in and I walked home. Back at the villa I went upstairs to the room. Rinaldi was lying on his bed. He looked at me.

"So you make progress with Miss Barkley?"

"We are friends."

"You have that pleasant air of a dog in heat."

I did not understand the word.

"Of a what?"

He explained.

"You," I said, "have that pleasant air of a dog who—"

"Stop it," he said. "In a little while we would say insulting things." He laughed.

"Good-night," I said.

"Good-night, little puppy."

I knocked over his candle with the pillow and got into bed in the dark.

Rinaldi picked up the candle, lit it and went on reading.

6

I WAS away for two days at the posts. When I got home it was too late and I did not see Miss Barkley until the next evening. She was not in the garden and I had to wait in the office of the hospital until she came down. There were many marble busts on painted wooden pillars along the walls of the room they used for an office. The hall too, that the office opened on, was lined with them. They had the complete marble quality of all looking alike. Sculpture had always seemed a dull business—still, bronzes looked like something. But marble busts all looked like a cemetery. There was one fine cemetery though—the one at Pisa.

Genoa was the place to see the bad marbles. This had been the villa of a very wealthy German and the busts must have cost him plenty. I wondered who had done them and how much he got. I tried to make out whether they were members of the family or what; but they were all uniformly classical. you could not tell anything about them.

I sat on a chair and held my cap. We were supposed to wear steel helmets even in Gorizia but they were uncomfortable and too bloody theatrical in a town where the civilian inhabitants had not been evacuated. I wore one when we went up to the posts and carried an English gas mask. We were just beginning to get some of them. They were a real mask. Also we were required to wear an automatic pistol; even doctors and sanitary officers. I felt it against the back of the chair. You were liable to arrest if you did not have one worn in plain sight. Rinaldi carried a holster stuffed with toilet paper. I wore a real one and felt like a gunman until I practised firing it. It was an Astra 7.65 caliber with a short barrel and it jumped so sharply when you let it off that there was no question of hitting anything. I practised with it, holding below the target and trying to master the jerk of the ridiculous short barrel until I could hit within a yard of where I aimed at twenty paces and then the ridiculousness of carrying a pistol at all came over me and I soon forgot it and carried it flopping against the small of my back with no feeling at all except a vague sort of shame when I met English-speaking people. I sat now in the chair and an orderly of some sort looked at me disapprovingly from behind a desk while I looked at the marble floor, the pillars with the marble busts, and the frescoes on the wall and waited for Miss Barkley. The frescoes were not bad. Any frescoes were good when they started to peel and flake off.

I saw Catherine Barkley coming down the hall, and stood up. She did not seem tall walking toward me but she looked very lovely.

"Good-evening, Mr. Henry," she said.

"How do you do?" I said. The orderly was listening behind the desk.

"Shall we sit here or go out in the garden?"

"Let's go out. It's much cooler."

I walked behind her out into the garden, the orderly looking after us. When we were out on the gravel drive she said, "Where have you been?"

"I've been out on post."

"You couldn't have sent me a note?"

"No," I said. "Not very well. I thought I was coming back."

"You ought to have let me know, darling."

We were off the driveway, walking under the trees. I took her hands, then stopped and kissed her.

"Isn't there anywhere we can go?"

"No," she said. "We have to just walk here. You've been away a long time."

"This is the third day. But I'm back now."

She looked at me, "And you do love me?"

"Yes."

"You did say you loved me, didn't you?"

"Yes," I lied. "I love you." I had not said it before.

"And you call me Catherine?"

"Catherine." We walked on a way and were stopped under a tree.

"Say, 'I've come back to Catherine in the night.'"

"I've come back to Catherine in the night."

"Oh, darling, you have come back, haven't you?"

"Yes."

"I love you so and it's been awful. You won't go away?"

"No. I'll always come back."

"Oh, I love you so. Please put your hand there again."

"It's not been away." I turned her so I could see her face when I kissed her and I saw that her eyes were shut. I kissed both her shut eyes. I thought she was probably a little crazy. It was all right if she was. I did not care what I was getting into. This was better than going every evening to the house for officers where the girls climbed all over you and put you cap on backward as a sign of affection between their trips upstairs with brother officers. I knew I did not love Catherine Barkley nor had any idea of loving her. This was a game, like bridge, in which you said things instead of playing cards. Like bridge you had to pretend you were playing for money or playing for some stakes. Nobody had mentioned what the stakes were. It was all right with me.

"I wish there was some place we could go," I said. I was experiencing the masculine difficulty of making love very long standing up.

"There isn't any place," she said. She came back from wherever she had been.

"We might sit there just for a little while."

We sat on the flat stone bench and I held Catherine Barkley's hand. She would not let me put my arm around her.

"Are you very tired?" she asked.

"No."

She looked down at the grass.

"This is a rotten game we play, isn't it?"

"What game?"

"Don't be dull."

"I'm not, on purpose."

"You're a nice boy," she said. "And you play it as well as you know how. But it's a rotten game."

"Do you always know what people think?"

"Not always. But I do with you. You don't have to pretend you love me. That's over for the evening. Is there anything you'd like to talk about?"

"But I do love you."

"Please let's not lie when we don't have to. I had a very fine little show and I'm all right now. You see I'm not mad and I'm not gone off. It's only a little sometimes."

I pressed her hand, "Dear Catherine."

"It sounds very funny now- Catherine. You don't pronounce it very much alike. But you're very nice. You're a very good boy."

"That's what the priest said."

"Yes, you're very good. And you will come and see me?"

"Of course."

"And you don't have to say you love me. That's all over for a while." She stood up and put out her hand. "Good-night."

I wanted to kiss her.

"No," she said. "I'm awfully tired."

"Kiss me, though," I said.

"I'm awfully tired, darling."

"Kiss me."

"Do you want to very much?"

"Yes."

We kissed and she broke away suddenly. "No. Good-night, please, darling." We walked to the door and I saw her go in and down the hall. I liked to watch her move. She went on down the hall. I went on home. It was a hot night and there was a good deal going on up in the mountains. I watched the flashes on San Gabriele.

I stopped in front of the Villa Rossa. The shutters were up but it was still going on inside. Somebody was singing. I went on home. Rinaldi came in while I was undressing.

"Ah, ha!" he said. "It does not go so well. Baby is puzzled."

"Where have you been?"

"At the Villa Rossa. It was very edifying, baby. We all sang. Where have you been?"

"Calling on the British."

"Thank God I did not become involved with the British."

〔注释〕

1. the King：指意大利国王。

2. …only seven thousand died of it in the army：海明威的含蓄笔法（understatement）。这是对战争的无情抨击，在平淡无奇的文字下面饱含激愤的情绪。

3. the Austrians：第一次世界大战主要是以英、法、俄为首的协约国和以德、奥为首的同盟国双方交战。战争初期意大利保持中立，后来协约国利用意大利和奥匈国在巴尔干领土问题上的矛盾，将意大利争取到协约国一方（1915）。小说开头描写的是意大利军队抵抗奥军入侵的情形。

4. the Carso：位于南斯拉夫西南部，亚得里亚海东北方的一个高原地。

5. Asti：意大利西南部一村镇，此处指该地产的酒。

6. Franz Joseph：奥地利皇帝，匈牙利国王，其名字也拼作 Francis Joseph.

7. Free Masons：共济会，国际性秘密组织，目前世界各国约有 600 万会员。其宗旨是从事友爱、互助和慈善事业等活动。

8. V. A. D.：Volunteer Aid Detachment，志愿辅助服务队。

9. the nurse's-evening-off：闲暇时的女护士往往被看作是男性猎取的对象。

John Dos Passos

〔作者介绍〕

约翰·多斯·帕索斯（John Dos Passos，1896～1970），美国小说家，社会历史学家。他生于芝加哥一个葡萄牙移民家庭，1916年毕业于哈佛大学，赴西班牙学建筑，但随后就赴法参加第一次世界大战，在法国救护车队做司机。大战结束之后，他成为新闻工作者，积极参与当时重要的社会政治活动，报导过震惊世界的萨科—范泽蒂案件以及30年代经济危机的状况，写了关于墨西哥农民惨遭剥削及肯塔基洲大企业里劳资间尖锐纠纷的文章。多斯·帕索斯是本世纪美国文学史上的一位奇特人物：在所有与动荡的现代美国生活联系紧密的主要作家中，他在思想上经历了自左向右的最突出的激烈转变。他是从描绘下层人的境遇开始他的写作生涯的，1917年，他曾自称是"红色的激进的革命者"。他的作品在很长的时期内（可以说自开始到30年代中期）具有明显的、甚至共产主义的倾向，美国共产党曾一度视他为同路人。1936年他因对共产主义失望而开始右倾，成为"新经济政策"的支持者，认为共产党是反对美国民主的力量。与此同时，他对资本主义的抨击仍然非常强烈，直到50年代，他向保守思想的转变才最后完成。多斯·帕索斯后期竟对大企业表现出赞许态度，支持美国对越南的侵略战争。

多斯·帕索斯是一位多产作家。在20年代至70年代的半个世纪里，他坚持以文学形式反映那些对现代美国产生了深远影响的社会和政治事件，写出了小说、剧本、报告文学、游记及散文等。他的著名作品有：《三个士兵》（*Three Soldiers*，1921），《曼哈顿中转站》（*Manhattan Transfer*，1925），《美国》（*U. S. A.*）三部曲——《北纬四十二度》（*The Forty-Second Parallel*，1930）、《一九一九》（*1919*，1932）、《赚大钱》（*The Big Money*，1936）、《哥伦比亚特区》（*District of Columbia*）三部曲——《一个年轻人的冒险》（*The Adventures of a Young Man*，1939）、《第一号》（*Number One*，1943）、《伟大的计划》（*The Grand Design*，1949），《托马斯·杰佛逊的思想和感情》（*The Head and Heart of Thomas*

Jefferson，1954)，《最美好的年代》(*The Best Times*，1967) 等。

贯穿于多斯·帕索斯作品的中心思想是庞大无情的社会对个人的摧残，中心意象是侏儒般的个人和巨兽般的“国家”相互抗衡。他把自己装扮成一位旁观者，力求准确地报导他的所见所闻。他对生活的看法远非乐观，评论家称他的作品是“绝望的小说”。他认为，在美国这样的国家里，人们必须坚持不懈的抵制一切主张以自由为代价换取进步的思想的力量，以保证个人的有限度的发展，保持人的有限度的尊严，在个人和社会机器之间达到某种有限的平衡。

多斯·帕索斯在写作技巧方面是一位大胆的革新者、尝试者。他汲取了印象派绘画、试验性电影以及“意识流”小说等的艺术特长，创造出自己独特的叙事方法。这一点在他的代表作《美国》三部曲中表现尤为突出。他在创作方法上的成就为他在美国文学史上赢得了一席重要之地。

U. S. A.

〔**作品介绍**〕

《美国》(*U. S. A.*) 三部曲可以说是美国30年代最引人注目的文学作品。它以自己独特的风格勾画出一幅美国本世纪初30年间里政治、经济、文化等各个侧面的社会风物图。它的第1部叫《北纬四十二度》，(*The 42nd Parallel*) 描述了美国资本主义“机器”的形成过程以及它对个人的专制和摧残；《一九一九年》(*1919*) 是第一次世界大战中美国社会生活的记录，继续描写第1部小说中提到的“非人格化”过程，为下一部小说《赚大钱》(*The Big Money*) 记述“繁荣”的20年代奠定基础。三部曲从本世纪开始说起，1927年以萨科—范泽蒂事件结尾，用比较精确的文笔，再现出美国自“镀金时代”便开始的演进过程。这几十年是社会主义运动遭受挫折、大资本企业获得胜利的年代。各个阶层的人都受到“机器”的控制，人的发展受到严重阻碍。社会生活中弥漫着一股强烈的绝望情绪：在三部曲所描绘的世界里，“鸟不歌唱，花不开放，空气几乎不能呼吸”。

在《美国》三部曲里，思想居主宰地位。作者用人物体现思想，人物有时近公式化。这是描述了11位主要人物及30余位次要人物的生活的“群体小说”，其中心意图在于揭露资本主义“机器”如何左右个人身心发展的社会现实。书中的人物，不管他们属于哪个阶层，都无一例外地承受着“机器”的压力，他们的胜败得失都以他们对“机器”的态度为转移。例如代表大企业的J·沃德·穆尔豪斯意识到“机器”的活动规律，按照它的要求行动，自觉地顺从它的意志，因而成为它的代言人。穆尔豪斯在物质上成功，而在精神上则彻底堕落。理查德·埃尔斯沃思·萨维奇也属于这个阶层。他开始是一个理想主义者，逐步了解到他所处的社会制度的性质，学习到如何遵从它并利用它。埃利诺·斯托达德的情况则很不同。她本能地追求寄生性的“幸福”，不意间接受了“机器”的专制，并尽力利用它达到自己的目的。她经过了女人堕落的各个阶段；虽然在物质上她得到了某种满足，但所付出的人格代价是沉重的。

《美国》三部曲对下层人民的刻划具有一种动人的伤感色调。珍妮·威廉斯、迈克·麦克里里及查理·安德逊3人的生活体现出工人阶级的不同经历。珍妮来自工人阶级，但却想方设法摆脱这个阶级。她认为她所处的世界是最好的，一心想利用一切她能利用的机会。她热衷于等级的划分，后来竟和包括她的弟弟在内的阶级兄弟断绝往来。迈克·麦克里里可以说是工人阶级的先进代表，起初颇有一股改善自己阶级地位和命运的强烈使命感。后来他到墨西哥参加革命，和一个女人相遇，境遇愈来愈好，便和革命运动失去关系。他的经历似乎说明，人一旦富有起来，思想便动摇，革命就结束了。查理·安德逊由于不能承受“机器”的压力，虽然接受了它的专制地位，也避免不了成为其受害者的命运。小说中还提到玛丽·弗伦奇，她和共产党人联系紧密，坚决反对“机器”；作者似又同时暗示，她并未意识到共产主义有可能是危及个人自由的另外一种“机器”（这种思想作者后来在其《一个年轻人的冒险》一书中进一步作了发挥）。此外还有决心要“机器”摧毁自己的本·康普顿，他是一名社会主义鼓动家。

《美国》三部曲表现出多斯·帕索斯的创新精神。他在写作中运用了前所未有的手法和技巧。在对不同人物生活经历的叙述中间，他巧妙地引进了“新闻片”、“人物肖像”及“摄影机眼”等手法。“新闻片”包含有报纸标题、新闻报导节录、流行歌曲片段等。这些反映出社会的动荡情况，以及人物所处时代的精神状貌，也给读者一种时间概念。“人物肖像”写的是曾为人类做出贡献的著名美国人的生平小传，这些人包括工人领袖、科学家、政客、工业和金融巨头等，如尤金·戴博斯、路德·伯班克、卡内基、爱迪生、约翰·理德、西奥多·罗斯福、摩根、福特等。这些人的生活和普通人形成对比，帮助读者加深对后者的经历的理解。“摄影机眼”记录的是一个四面移动的人的头脑在观望大千世界生活状况之后的反应和思考及其思想成熟的情况。在这里读者接触到的是思想和见解，有时是零散的，作者用印象派或意识流手法写出，某些主题或思想一再重复出现，旨在加深读者的思想认识。此外，多斯·帕索斯的语言简练，意象感人，富有节奏感，结构多排比句，具有典型的口语风格。他是独具特点的文体家。

《美国》三部曲给人一种零乱庞杂之感。文件、事件、现代生活杂乱无章，容易令人只见混乱，不见秩序；只见脱节，不见联系；只见不同和差别，不见一致和统一。然而，读者阅后却能得到一个完整的印象，即资本主义“机器”在进行着无情的控制：这是三部曲和艾略特的《荒原》、庞德的《诗章》在结构上极相似之处。

《美国》三部曲奠定了多斯·帕索斯在美国文学史上的地位。

U. S. A.

PREFACE[1]

The young man walks fast by himself through the crowd that thins into the night streets; feet are tired from hours of walking; eyes greedy for warm curve of faces, answering flicker of eyes, the set of a head, the lift of a shoulder, the way hands spread and clench; blood tingles with wants; mind is a beehive of hopes buzzing and stinging; muscles ache for the knowledge of jobs, for the roadmender's pick and shovel work, the fisherman's knack with a hook when he hauls on the slithery net from the rail of the lurching trawler, the swing of the bridgeman's arm as he slings down the whitehot rivet, the engineer's slow grip wise on the throttle, the dirtfarmer's use of his whole body when, whoaing the mules, he yanks the plow from the furrow. The young man walks by himself searching through the crowd with greedy eyes, greedy ears taut to hear, by himself, alone.

The streets are empty. People have packed into subways, climbed into streetcars and buses; in the stations they've scampered for suburban trains; they've filtered into lodgings and tenements, gone up in elevators into apartmenthouses. In a showwindow two sallow windowdressers in their shirtsleeves are bringing out a dummy girl in a red evening dress, at a corner welders in masks lean into sheets of blue flame repairing a cartrack, a few drunk bums shamble along, a sad streetwalker fidgets under an arclight. From the river comes the deep rumbling whistle of a steamboat leaving dock. A tug hoots far away.

The young man walks by himself, fast but not fast enough, far but not far enough (faces slide out of sight, talk trails into tattered scraps, footsteps tapfainter in alleys); he must catch the last subway, the streetcar, the bus, run up the gangplanks of all the steamboats, register at all the hotels, work in the cities, answer the wantads, learn the trades, take up the jobs, live in all the boardinghouses, sleep in all the beds. One bed is not enough, one job is not enough, one life is not enough. At night, head swimming with wants, he walks by himself alone.

No job, no woman, no house, no city.

Only the ears busy to catch the speech are not alone; the ears are caught tight, linked tight by the tendrils of phrased words, the turn of a joke, the singsong fade of a story, the gruff fall of a sentence; linking tendrils of speech twine through the city blocks, spread over pavements, grow out along broad parked avenues, speed with the trucks leaving on their long night runs over roaring highways, whisper down sandy byroads past wornout farms, joining up cities and fillingstations, roundhouses, steamboats, planes groping along airways; words call out on mountain pastures, drift slow down rivers widening to the sea and the hushed beaches.

It was not in the long walks through jostling crowds at night that he was less alone, or in the training camp at Allentown, or in the day on the docks at Seattle, or in the empty reek of Washington City hot boyhood summer nights, or in the meal on Market Street,[2] or in the swim off the red rocks at San Diego, or in the bed full of fleas in New Orleans, or in the cold razorwind off the lake, or in the gray faces trembling in the grind of gears in the street under Michigan Avenue,[3] or in the smokers of limited expresstrains, or walking across country, or riding up the dry mountain canyons, or the night without a sleepingbag among frozen beartracks in the Yellowstone, or canoeing Sundays on the Quinnipiac;[4]

but in his mother's words telling about longago, in his father's telling about when I was a boy, in the kidding stories of uncles, in the lies the kids told at school, the hired man's yarns, the tall tales the doughboys told after taps;

it was the speech that clung to the ears, the link that tingled in the blood; U. S. A.

U. S. A. is the slice of a continent. U. S. A. is a group of holding companies, some aggregations of trade unions, a set of laws bound in calf, a radio network, a chain of moving picture theatres, a column of stock—quotations rubbed out and written in by a Western Union boy on a blackboard, a publiclibrary full of old newspapers and dogeared historybooks with protests scrawled on the margins in pencil U. S. A. is the world's greatest rivervalley fringed with mountains and hills, U. S. A. is a set of bigmouthed officials with too many bankaccounts. U. S. A. is a lot of men buried in their uniforms in Arlington Cemetery. [5] U. S. A. is the letters at the end of an address when you are away from home. But mostly U. S. A. is the speech of the people.

The 42nd Parallel

PROTEUS [6]

Steinmetz was a hunchback,
son of a hunchback lithographer.

He was born in Breslau in eighteen sixtyfive, graduated with highest honors at seventeen from the Breslau Gymnasium, [7] went to the University of Breslau to study mathematics;

mathematics to Steinmetz was muscular strength and long walks over the hills and the kiss of a girl in love and big evenings spent swilling beer with your friends;

on his broken back he felt the topheavy weight of society the way workingmen felt it on their straight backs, the way poor students felt it, was a member of a socialist club, editor of a paper called *The People's Voice*.

Bismarck[8] was sitting in Beriln like a big paper-weight to keep the new Germany feudal, to hold down the empire for his bosses the Hohenzollerns[9].

Steinmetz had to run off to Zurich for fear of going to jail; at Zurich his mathematics woke up all the professors at the Polytechnic;

but Europe in the eighties was no place for a penniless German student with a broken back and a big head filled with symbolic calculus and wonder about electricity that is mathematics made power and a socialist at that.

With a Danish friend he sailed for America steerage on an old French line boat *La Champagne*,

lived in Brooklyn at first and commuted to Yonkers[10] where he had a twelvedollar a week job with Rudolph Eichemeyer[11] who was a German exile from fortyeight an inventor and electrician and owner of a factory where he made hatmaking machinery and electrical generators.

In Yonkers he [Steinmetz] worked out the theory of the Third Harmonics [12]

and the law of hysteresis which states in a formula the hundredfold relations between the metallic heat, density, frequency when the poles change places in the core of a magnet under an alternating current.

It is Steinmetz's law of hysteresis that makes possible all the transformers that crouch in little boxes and gableroofed houses in all the hightension lines all over everywhere. The mathematical symbols of Steinmetz's law are the patterns of all transformers everywhere.

In eighteen ninetytwo when Eichemeyer sold out to the corporation that was to form General Electric,[13] Steinmetz was entered in the contract along with other valuable apparatus. All his life Steinmetz was a piece of apparatus belonging to General Electric.

First his laboratory was at Lynn, then it was moved and the little hunchback with it to Schenectady, the electric city.

General Electric humored him, let him be a socialist, let him keep a greenhouseful of cactuses lit up by mercury lights, let him have alligators, talking crows and a gila monster for pets and the publicity department talked up the medicine man[14] who knew the symbols that opened up the doors of Ali Baba's cave.[15]

Steinmetz jotted a formula on his cuff and next morning a thousand new powerplants had sprung up and the dynamos sang dollars and the silence of the transformers was all dollars,

and the publicity department poured oily stories into the ears of the American public every Sunday and Steinmetz became the little parlor magician,

who made a toy thunderstorm in his laboratory and made all the toy trains run on time and the meat stay cold in the icebox and the lamp in the parlor and the great lighthouses and the searchlights and the revolving beams of light that guide airplanes at night towards Chicago, New York, St. Louis, Los Angeles,[16]

and they let him be a socialist and believe that human Society could be improved the way you can improve a dynamo and they let him be pro-German and write a letter offering his services to Lenin because mathematicians are so impractical who make up formulas by which you can build powerplants, factories, subway systems, light, heat, air, sunshine but not human relations that affect the stockholders' money and the directors' salaries.

Steinmetz was a famous magician and he talked to Edison[17] tapping with the Morse code on Edison's knee

because Edison was so very deaf

and he went out West

to make speeches that nobody understood

and he talked to Bryan[18] about God on a railroad train

and all the reporters stood round while he and Einstein[19]

met face to face,

but they couldn't catch what they said

and Steinmetz was the most valuable piece of apparatus General Electric had

until he wore out and died.

1919

NEWSREEL XLIII[20]

the placards borne by the radicals were taken away from them, their clothing torn and eyes blackened before the service and ex-service men had finished with them

34 Die After Drinking Wood Alcohol Trains in France May Soon Stop Gerard Throws His Hat into the Ring[21]

SUPREME COURT DASHES LAST HOPE OF MOIST MOUTH[22]

LIFE BOAT CALLED BY ROCKET SIGNALS SEARCHES IN VAIN FOR SIXTEEN HOURS

America I love you
You're like a sweetheart of mine

LES GENS SAGES FUIENT LES REUNIONS POLITIQUES[23]

WALLSTREET CLOSES WEAK: FEARS TIGHT MONEY

From ocean to ocean
For you my devotion
Is touching each boundary line

LITTLE CARUSO[24] EXPECTED

his mother, Mrs. W. D. McGillicudy said: "My first husband was killed while crossing tracks in front of a train, my second husband was killed in the same way and now it is my son

Just like a little baby
Climbing its mother's knee

MACHINEGUNS MOW DOWN MOBS IN KNOXVILLE[25]

America I love you

Aviators Lived for Six Days on Shellfish

the police compelled the demonstrators to lower these flags and ordered the convention not to exhibit any red emblems save the red in the starry banner of the United States; it may not be indiscreet to state, however, in any case it cannot dim his glory, that General Pershing[26] was confined to his stateroom through seasickness when the message arrived. Old Fellow of 89 Treasures Chewinggum as Precious Souvenir Couldn't Maintain His Serenity In Closing League Debates

And there's a hundred million others like me

THE CAMERA EYE (50)[27]

they have clubbed us off the streets they are stronger they are rich they hire and fire the politicians the newspapereditors the old judges the small men with reputations the collegepresidents the ward-heelers (listen businessmen collegepresidents judges America will not forget her betrayers) they hire the men with guns the uniforms the policecars the patrolwagons

all right you have won you will kill the brave men our friends tonight

there is nothing left to do we are beaten we the beaten crowd together in these old dingy schoolrooms on Salem Street shuffle up and down the gritty creaking stairs sit hunched with bowed heads on benches and hear the old words of the haters of oppression made new in sweat and agony tonight

our work is over the scribbled phrases the nights typing releases the smell of the printshop the sharp reek of newprinted leaflets the rush for Western Union stringing words into wires the search for stinging words to make you feel who are your oppressors America

America our nation has been beaten by strangers who have turned our language inside out who have taken the clean words our fathers spoke and made them slimy and foul

their hired men sit on the judge's bench they sit back with their feet on the tables under the dome of the State House they are ignorant of our beliefs they have the dollars the guns the armed forces the power-plants

they have built the electricchair and hired the executioner to throw the switch

all right we are two nations

America our nation has been beaten by strangers who have bought the laws and fenced off the meadows and cut down the woods for pulp and turned our pleasant cities into slums and sweated the wealth out of our people and when they want to they hire the executioner to throw the switch

but do they know that the old words of the immigrants are being renewed in blood and agony tonight do they know that the old American speech of the haters of oppression is new tonight in the mouth of an old woman from Pittsburgh of a husky boilermaker from Frisco who hopped freights clear from the Coast to come here in the mouth of a Back Bay socialworker in the mouth of an Italian printer of a hobo from Arkansas the language of the beaten nation is not forgotten in our ears tonight

the men in the deathhouse made the old words new before they died

If it had not been for these things, I might have lived out my life talking at streetcorners to scorning men. I might have died unknown, unmarked, a failure. This is our career and our triumph. Never in our full life can we hope to do such work for tolerance, for justice, for man's understanding of man as now we do by an accident. [28]

now their work is over the immigrants haters of oppression lie quiet in black suits in the little undertaking parlor in the North End the city is quiet the men of the conquering nation are not to be seen on the streets

they have won why are they scared to be seen on the streets? on the streets you see only the downcast faces of the beaten the streets belong to the beaten nation all the way to the cemetery where the bodies of the immigrants are to be burned we line the curbs in the drizzling rain we crowd the wet sidewalks elbow to elbow silent pale looking with scared eyes at the coffins

we stand defeated America

VAG[29]

The young man waits at the edge of the concrete, with one hand he grips a rubbed suitcase of phony leather, the other hand almost making a fist, thumb up

that moves in ever so slight an arc when a cars slithers past, a truck roars, clatters; the wind of cars passing ruffles his hair, slaps grit in his face.

Head swims, hunger has twisted the belly tight,

he has skinned a heel through the torn sock, feet ache in the broken shoes, under the threadbare suit carefully brushed off with the hand, the torn drawers have a crummy feel, the feel of having slept in your clothes; in the nostrils lingers the staleness of discouraged carcasses crowded into a transient camp, the carbolic stench of the jail, on the taut cheeks the shamed flush from the boring eyes of cops and deputies, railroadbulls (they eat three squares a day, they are buttoned into wellmade clothes, they have wives to sleep with, kids to play with after supper, they work for the big men who buy their way, they stick their chests out with the sureness of power behind their backs). Git the hell out, scram! Know what's good for you, you'll make yourself scarce. Gittin' tough, eh? Think you kin take it, eh?

The punch in the jaw, the slam on the head with the nightstick, the wrist grabbed and twisted behind the back, the big knee brought up sharp into the crotch,

the walk out of town with sore feet to stand and wait at the edge of the hissing speeding string of cars where the reek of ether and lead and gas melts into the silent grassy smell of the earth.

Eyes black with want seek out the eyes of the drivers, a hitch, a hundred miles down the road.

Overhead in the blue a plane drones. Eyes follow the silver Douglas[30] that flashes once in the sun and bores its smooth way out of sight into the blue.

(The transcontinental passengers sit pretty, big men with bankaccounts, highly paid jobs, who are saluted by doormen; telephonegirls say goodmorning to them. Last night after a fine dinner, drinks with friends, they left Newark. Roar of climbing motors slanting up into the inky haze. Lights drop away. An hour staring along a silvery wing at a big lonesome moon hurrying west through curdling scum. Beacons flash in a line across Ohio.

At Cleveland the plane drops banking in a smooth spiral, the string of lights along the lake swings in a circle. Climbing roar of the motors again; slumped in the soft seat drowsing through the flat moonlight night.

Chi. A glimpse of the dipper. Another spiral swoop from cool into hot air thick with dust and the reek of burnt prairies.

Beyond the Mississippi dawn creeps up behind through the murk over the great plains. Puddles of mist go white in the Iowa hills, farms, fences, silos, steel glint from a river. The blinking eyes of the beacons reddening into day. Watercourses vein the eroded hills.

Omaha. Great cumulus clouds, from coppery churning to creamy to silvery white, trail brown skirts of rain over the hot plains. Red and yellow badlands, tiny horned shapes of cattle.

Cheyenne. The cool high air smells of sweetgrass.

The tightbaled clouds to westward burst and scatter in tatters over the strawcolored hills. Indigo mountains jut rimrock. The plane breasts a huge crumbling cloudbank and toboggans over bumpy air across green and crimson slopes into the sunny dazzle of Salt Lake.

The transcontinental passenger thinks contracts, profits, vacation-trips, mighty continent between Atlantic and Pacific, power, wires humming dollars, cities jammed, hills empty, the indiantrail leading into the wagonroad, the macadamed pike, the concrete skyway; trains, planes: history the billiondollar speedup,

and in the bumpy air over the desert ranges towards Las Vegas

sickens and vomits into the carton container the steak and mushrooms he ate in New York. No matter, silver in the pocket, greenbacks in the wallet, drafts, certified checks, plenty restaurants in L. A.)[31]

The young man waits on the side of the road; the plane has gone; thumb moves in a small arc when a car tears hissing past. Eyes seek the driver's eyes. A hundred miles down the road. Head swims, belly tightens, wants crawl over his skin like ants:

went to school, books said opportunity, ads promised speed, own your home, shine bigger than your neighbor, the radiocrooner whispered girls, ghosts of platinum girls coaxed from the screen, millions in winnings were chalked up on the boards in the offices, paychecks were for hands willing to work, the cleared desk of an executive with three telephones on it;

waits with swimming head, needs knot the belly, idle hands numb, beside the speeding traffic.

A hundred miles down the road.

〔注释〕

1. 这是1938年发表的《美国》三部曲的前言。
2. Market Street：市场街，位于旧金山。
3. Michigan Avenue：密执安道，位于芝加哥市。
4. Quinnipiac：奎尼匹亚克河，位于康涅狄格州。
5. Arlington Cemetery：弗吉尼亚州阿灵顿国家公墓。
6. Proteus：摘自《北纬四十二度》一书，为施泰因梅茨（Charles Proteus

Steinmetz，1865～1923）的小传。施泰因梅茨是世界一流发明家，生于德国，原名为 Karl August Steinmetz，1889 年因持不同政见被迫移居美国，易名为 Charles Proteus Steinmetz。他在电气理论方面成就卓著，有三大贡献：(1) 提出了磁带损失的新定律；(2) 创立了计算交流电路的实用方法；(3) 研究了电的瞬变现象理论。施泰因梅茨在学生时代便参加社会主义运动，在政治上致力于教育改革，是一位有社会觉悟的科学家。

7. the Breslau Gymnasium：布雷斯劳大学预科学校。

8. Bismarck：俾斯麦（Otto von Bismarck，1815～1898），统一后德国第一任首相（1871～1890），以高压政策著称。

9. the Hohenzollerns：自 1871 年至 1918 年统治德国的霍亨索伦王朝。

10. Yonkers：扬克斯城，位于纽约市附近。

11. Rudolph Eidnemeyer：（1831～1895），德国发明家。德国 1848 年革命失败后，于 1850 年移居美国。

12. the Third Harmonics：第三谐波。

13. General Electric：通用电气公司。

14. the wizard，the medicine man：指施泰因梅茨，意为他所巫师一样奇迹般地进行发明创造。

15. Ali Baba's cave：阿里·巴巴，《天方夜谭》(*Arabian Nights*) 中的一个人物，他用“芝麻开门”的咒语打开了四十大盗宝洞的门。

16. who made... Los Angeles：意指施泰因梅茨的实验结果立即在电力工业上产生了巨大影响。

17. Edison：爱迪生（Thomas Alva Edison，1847～1931），美国发明家。

18. Bryan：布赖恩（William Jennings Bryan，1860～1925），美国政治家、基督教原教旨主义捍卫者。

19. Einstein：爱因斯坦（Albert Einstein，1879～1955），相对论发明者。

20. Newsreel XLIII：“新闻片 43”，摘自《一九一九》一书。

21. Gerard Throws His Hat into the Ring：Gerard 指詹姆士·沃森·杰拉德（James Watson Garard，1867～1951），美国律师、驻德国大使（1913～1917）。1919 年他宣布要争取被提名为民主党总统后选人，以参加 1920 年总统选举，后被詹姆斯·M·考克斯（James M. Cox）击败，考克斯也未当选，败于共和党候选人沃伦·G·哈丁（Warren G. Harding）之手。此句指杰拉德宣布参加提名竞争一事。

22. Supreme…Mouth：指美国最高法院承认禁酒法案合法性的决定。1918 年 10 月美国国会通过禁酒法，1919 年 1 月批准生效。moistmouth：饮酒者。

23. Les…Politiques：法文，意为“聪明的人不参加政治集会”。

24. Little Caruso：意大利男高音歌唱家思里科·卡鲁索（1873～1921）的女儿格罗里亚·卡鲁索（Gloria Caruso），她生于 1919 年 12 月。

25. Machineguns…Knoxville：指镇压 1919 年 8 月 31 日至 9 月 1 日发生在田纳西州诺克斯雅尔市的种族骚乱事件。

26. General Pershing：美国陆军元帅潘兴（John Joseph Pershing，1860～1948）。

27. The Camera Eye（50）：摘自《赚大钱》一书；这一段谈的是作家本人本世纪 20 年代在波士顿的工作经历，当时他在萨科—茨泽蒂辩护委员会工作。

28. If... accident：1927 年 4 月 9 日茨泽蒂被判死刑后所发表的声明中的一段。

29. 此段选自《美国》三部曲第 3 部《赚大钱》（*The Big Money*）的结尾。Vag，美俚，意“vagrant”、“vagabond”。

30. Douglas：“道格拉斯号”飞机。

31. L. A.：Los Angels.

HART CRANE

〔作者介绍〕

哈特·克兰（Hart Crane，1899～1932），美国诗人。出生在俄亥俄州一个糖果制造商家庭，幼时因父母分居，随外祖父居住在古巴以南的派因斯岛上。诗人幼年和青少年时期的这种经历对其成长和创作都极为重要：他的诗中有童年的痛苦，也有对异国自然风光的缅怀。他父母的最后离婚加剧了他的心态的变异。后来他曾在父亲的公司里短期任职。

克兰 13 岁开始诗歌创作，17 岁发表第一首诗。他发表在《小杂志》（*Little Review*）上的早期诗歌，表现出伊丽莎白文学和法国象征主义的特点，记录了他的紧张的精神状态和同性恋倾向。由于在贫穷和疲顿的条件下竭力继续和完善自己的诗歌创作，克兰愈来愈多地饮酒。后来他终于和家庭破裂，到纽约谋生，在那里，他结识了瓦尔多·弗兰克（Waldo Frank）、马尔科姆·考利（Malcolm Cowley）、艾伦·塔特（Allen Tate）等文学界人物。银行家奥托·卡恩（Otto Kahn）给他提供资助，以使他能专心致志地从事创作。他的第一部诗集《白色的房屋》（*White Buildings*）于 1926 年问世，评论界褒贬不一。他的主要作品《桥》（*The Bridge*）自构思（1924 年）到出版（1930 年），历时 7 年之久，同样未能获得评论界的一致赞许。这使他情绪沮丧。克兰长期以来精神不振。不安定的生活，父亲的死亡，他与母亲及后来与许多朋友的疏远，使人对未来失去信心的 30 年代大萧条等等，都给他渐趋脆弱的神经带来压力。1930 年克兰赴墨西哥旅行，计划在那里写一首有关墨西哥历史的长诗，同时使自己的精神得以松驰和镇定。不料，1932 年 4 月他在乘船自墨西哥回纽约的途中竟投海自尽，时年 32 岁。

克兰酷爱读书，对于诗人和诗歌很有独立见解。他曾在信中说过："我不太喜欢勃朗宁夫人。除我对这位女士的不喜欢外，我还不喜欢丁尼生、汤普逊、杰脱顿（Thomas Chatterson，1752～1770）、拜伦、穆尔、弥尔顿、以及其他几位……可是你大概已注意到，我的确是高兴地向往坡、惠特曼、莎士比亚、济慈、雪莱、柯勒律治、约翰·堂恩、约翰·韦伯斯特、马洛、波多莱尔、拉法格、但丁……”此外，现代诗坛巨匠T. S. 艾略特和埃兹拉·庞德对克兰的诗歌创作也产生过很大的影响。

《白色的楼房》诗集收入克兰早期诗作23首。其中主要的长诗《为浮士德和海伦的婚姻而作》(“For the Marriage of Faustus and Helen”)，对美、爱情和再生发表了见解，是对T. S. 艾略特的“文化悲观主义”的一种回答。歌德（Goethe，1749～1832）在他的诗剧《浮士德》(*Faust*) 中所提到的浮士德和海伦的结合，在诗人的意境中成为现代生活的象征，在诗人的作品中总是做为一种结构维系手段出现。其他的诗如《旅行》(“Voyages”)、《凭吊麦尔维尔墓》(“At Melville's Tomb”) 等，表现出诗人坚持运用大海做为一个复杂的意象的特点。《桥》是诗人对T. S. 艾略特《荒原》(*The Waste Land*) 的又一次回击。在这首诗中，克兰把桥视为生的象征，美国的理想的未来的象征。1933年，克兰的《诗集》(*Collected Poems*) 出版，1958年此书再版，1966年《哈特·克兰诗作全集及书信与散文选》(*The Complete Poems and Selected Letters and Prose*) 出版，收入了克兰早期及晚期未曾收入或散见在杂志里的诗作。

克兰的诗歌曾在评论界引起争论。30年代初期，一些主要评论家似乎认为他虽有天才，但运用不当，《桥》基本上是败笔。但自1937年起，不少评论家开始以新的眼光看待他的作品。这一年他的传记问世，1948年又有评传出版，1951年第一篇重新肯定《桥》的文章出现，1952年克兰书信结集出版。自那以后，包括著名评论家在内新写的专著和专论肯定了克兰在美国文学上的地位，他的声望逐渐提高。其诗作的精神与语言对他的同代人如霍勒斯·格雷戈里 (Horace Gregory) 及年轻一代如罗伯特·洛厄尔 (Robert Lowell)、迪伦·托马斯 (Dylan Thomas)、卡尔·夏皮诺 (Karl Shapiro) 及约翰·贝里曼 (John Berryman) 等都产生了一定的影响。今天，克兰已被视为本世纪美国最出色的诗人之一。

The Bridge

〔作品介绍〕

《桥》(*The Bridge*) 是克兰的代表作，是本世纪美国诗坛出现的著名长诗之一。1924年，克兰移居纽约，恰巧住在设计布鲁克林桥 (the Brooklyn Bridge) 的建筑师华盛顿·罗布林 (Washington Roebling) 曾居住过的房子里。他凭窗望桥，心有所动，遂萌创作讴歌大桥的长诗之意。此后经7年悉心写作，史诗般的《桥》终于在1930年问世。这首长诗可以说是自《荒原》问世以来用意最雄伟的诗作。克兰希望通过此诗对美国经历进行一种现代性、神话性综合，以期彻底了解这种经历，指出现在与过去的紧密关系以及未来的希望。他把布鲁克林桥视为“我们的肯定的未来、我们的独特的身分”的象征，从他同代作家所抨击的机械文明中看到未来。他在一封信中说：“我真正在搞的……是美国神话……我真正在写的是一首关于现代意识的史诗。”

这首长诗由一首序诗和8部分（共15首诗）组成。序诗《献给布鲁克林桥》（“To Brooklyn Bridge”）提出长诗的主题，令读者看到希望，又认识到存在的问题。《万福玛利亚》（“Ave Maria”）为第1部分，写的是哥伦布发现新大陆后回西班牙途中的思想活动；哥伦布显然是诗人自己的面具，把欧洲的过去与美国的现在两种敏感度结合在一起。第2部分是《坡哈坦的女儿》（*Powhatan's Daughter*），共包括5首诗：《海港的黎明》（“The Harbor Dawn”）、《凡·温克尔》（“Van Winkle”）、《河》（“The River”）《舞蹈》（“The Dance”）及《印第安纳》（“Indiana”）。坡哈坦的女儿——坡科杭塔丝（Pocohontas）是代表美洲大地的女神，她激励着美国人一代一代地前进。《海港的黎明》把女神介绍给读者；这一部分中其他几首诗进一步在不同层次上对女神的象征意义进行探讨，其间把许多个人的或民族的或神话性的记忆巧妙地联结在一起，如《凡·温克尔》谈到美国的一个传说，《河》谈到密西西比河同印第安人文化和白人文化的关系，《舞蹈》完全移向印第安主题，《印第安纳》则谈及印第安文化向白人文化的转移。

第3部分《卡蒂·沙克》（“Cutty Sark”）中心是诗人和一位老水手的谈话，末尾说到船的沉没和迷失。在第4部分《哈特拉斯角》（“Cape Hatteras”）中，诗人反对悲观思想，使自己成为新世界的代言人。第五部分《三支歌》（*Three Songs*）——《南方的混血女人》（“Southern Cross”）、《国家冬季花园》——（“National Winter Garden”）及《弗吉尼亚》（“Virginia”），组成一支关于女人的插曲，实际上是坡科杭塔丝主题不同形式的表现。第六部分《贵格山》（“Quaker Hill”），谈及美国生活的庸俗化，诗的情绪突然低沉下来。第七部分《隧道》（“The Tunnel”），在长诗中地位极其关键，写的是地铁中单调的动作，从听到的谈话片断，到地铁环境中普遍的肮脏状况，全诗的情绪达到最低点，读者宛如置身于地狱之中。长诗以《亚特兰提斯》（“Atlantis”）为结尾，充满赞美的激情，把亚特兰提斯视为神话时代的城市或未来的希望，其高调和《隧道》成鲜明对比，两者一起保证了《序诗》中的双重基调。纵观全诗，双重的基调是极其必要的。《万福玛利亚》中颇具威胁性的“海”的意象体现出宇宙的恐怖；还有《河》结尾部分的非人的历史演进，《隧道》所表现的野蛮，以及其他部分所提到的诗人自己青少年时期的不愉快经历等，都是追求肯定态度者应当充分加以考虑的必要因素。

《桥》是克兰努力写作的一首民族史诗，是诗人对《荒原》的一种回击，诗人认为《荒原》过于悲观，忽略了“精神方面的事件及可能性”。《桥》反映了诗人在不协调、无信仰的时代里寻找协调的愿望，反映了诗人竭力联结新与旧、东方与西方、人与上帝的愿望。长诗宛如一组阐述美国主要神话——坡科杭塔丝、里普·凡·温克尔、麦尔维尔、坡、惠特曼、哥伦布、地铁、亚特兰提斯——的巨幅交响乐章，充分表现出诗人的想象力，表现出诗人描绘人类追求协调、爱情及美的非凡能力。这首诗有的地方艰涩难懂，意象和象征满篇皆是，令人望而生畏，如不加详细的注释，读者会感到步履维艰。这应该说是它的缺点。

这里选注的是该诗第7部分《隧道》。

The Tunnel[1]

To Find the Western path
Right thro' the Gates of Wrath. [2]

BLAKE

Performances, assortments, résumés—
Up Times Square to Columbus Circle lights
Channel the congresses, nightly sessions,
Refractions of the thousand theatres, faces—
Mysterious kitchens. . . . You shall search them all.
Someday by heart you'll learn each famous sight
And watch the curtain lift in hell's despite;
You'll find the garden in the third act dead,
Finger your knees—and wish yourself in bed
With tabloid crime-sheets perched in easy sight.

Then let you reach your hat
and go.
As usual, let you—also
walking down—exclaim
to twelve upward leaving
a subscription praise
for what time slays.

Or can't you quite make up your mind to ride;
A walk is better underneath the L a brisk
Ten blocks or so before? But you find yourself
Preparing penguin flexions of the arms, —
As usual you will meet the scuttle yawn:
The subway yawns the quickest promise home.

Be minimum, then, to swim the hiving swarms
Out of the Square, the Circle burning bright—
Avoid the glass doors gyring at your right,
Where boxed alone a second, eyes take fright
—Quite unprepared rush naked back to light:
And down beside the turnstile press the coin
Into the slot. The gongs already rattle. [3]

And so
of cities you bespeak
subways, rivered under streets
and rivers. . . . In the car
the overtone of motion
underground, the monotone
of motion is the sound
of other faces, also underground—

"Let's have a pencil Jimmy—living now
at Floral Park
Flatbush—on the fourth of July—
like a pigeon's muddy dream—potatoes
to dig in the field—travlin the town—too—
night after night—the Culver line—the
girls all shaping up—it used to be—" [4]

Our tongues recant like beaten weather vanes.
This answer lives like verdigris, like hair
Beyond extinction, surcease of the bone;
And repetition freezes— "What[5]

"what do you want? getting weak on the links?
fandaddle daddy don't ask for change—IS THIS
FOURTEENTH? it's half past six she said—if
you don't like my gate why did you
swing on it, why *didja*
swing on it
anyhow—" [6]

And somehow anyhow swing—

The phonographs of hades in the brain
Are tunnels that re-wind themselves, and love
A burnt match skating in a urinal—[7]
Somewhere above Fourteenth TAKE THE EXPRESS
To brush some new presentiment of pain—

"But I want service in this office SERVICE
I said—after
the show she cried a little afterwards but—"

Whose head is swinging from the swollen strap?
Whose body smokes along the bitten rails,
Bursts from a smoldering bundle far behind
In back forks of the chasms of the brain,—
Puffs from a riven stump far out behind
In interborough fissures of the mind…? [8]

And why do I often meet your visage[9] here,
Your eyes like agate lanterns—on and on
Below the toothpaste and the dandruff ads?
—And did their riding eyes[10] right through your side,
And did their eyes like unwashed platters ride?
And Death, aloft, —gigantically down[11]
Probing through you—toward me, O evermore!
And when they dragged your retching flesh,
Your trembling hands that night through Baltimore—
That last night on the ballot rounds, did you

Shaking, did you deny the ticket, Poe? [12]

For Gravesend Manor[13] change at Chambers Street.
The platform hurries along to a dead stop.

The intent escalator lifts a serenade
Stilly
Of shoes, umbrellas, each eye attending its shoe, then
Bolting outright somewhere above where streets
Burst suddenly in rain.... The gongs recur: [14]
Elbows and levers, guard and hissing door.
Thunder is galvothermic here below.... The car
Wheels off. The train rounds, bending to a scream,
Taking the final level for the dive
Under the river—
And somewhat emptier than before,
Demented, for a hitching second, humps; then
Lets go.... Toward corners of the floor
Newspapers wing, revolve and wing.
Blank windows gargle signals through the roar. [15]

And does the Daemon take you home, also,
Wop washerwoman, with the bandaged hair?
After the corridors are swept, the cuspidors—
The gaunt sky-barracks cleanly now, and bare,
O Genoese, do you bring mother eyes and hands
Back home to children and to golden hair? [16]

Dæmon, demurring and eventful yawn!
Whose hideous laughter is a bellows mirth
—Or the muffled slaughter of a day in birth—
O cruelly to inoculate the brinking dawn
With antennae toward worlds that glow and sink; —
To spoon us out more liquid than the dim
Locution of the eldest star, and pack
The conscience navelled in the plunging wind,
Umbilical to call—and straightway die!

O caught like pennies beneath soot and steam,
Kiss of our agony thou gatherest;
Condensed, thou takest all—shrill ganglia
Impassioned with some song we fail to keep.[17]
And yet, like Lazarus, to feel the slope,
The sod and billow breaking, —lifting ground,
—A sound of waters bending astride the sky
Unceasing with some Word that will not die...![18]

* * *

A tugboat, wheezing wreaths of steam,
Lunged past, with one galvanic blare stove up the
River.
I counted the echoes assembling, one after one.
Searching, thumbing and midnight on the piers.
Lights, coasting, left the oily tympanum of waters;
The blackness somewhere gouged glass on a sky.[19]
And this thy harbor, O my City, I have driven under,[20]
Tossed from the coil of ticking towers[21].... Tomorrow,
And to be.... Here by the River that is East[22]—
Here at the waters' edge the hands[23] drop memory;
Shadowless in that abyss they unaccounting lie.
How far away the star has pooled the sea—
Or shall the hands be drawn away, to die?

Kiss of our agony Thou gatherest,
O Hand of Fire
gatherest—

〔注释〕

1. The Tunnel:《隧道》,指地铁。这首诗是《桥》诗中最成功的诗作之一,主要以描绘城市里的一种经历——乘坐地铁的经历而著称。地铁里的嘈杂声、断断续续的谈话声、盯人的目光、昏黄的灯光、每站必有的突然停车和起动、火车转弯等等令人可畏又可憎的景象,都被淋淳尽致地描绘出来。诗人自己称这首诗所表现的乃是一种"炼狱",其主题是"机械对人类的侵犯"。本诗所勾勒的地铁画面虽然令人感到沮丧,但在末尾部分,诗人提到了死而复生的圣经人物拉撒路，提到了永恒的神明以及使人纯洁的神圣的“火的手”，从而给予人们一种希望的曙光。

2. To Find…Wrath：引自英国诗人布莱克（William Blake，1757～1827）的《早晨》（“Morning”）一诗，这是开首两行。

3. 第1～30行：描写人们在散场后从百老汇剧场出来，走向地铁车站乘车回家的景状。assortments：五花八门的节目；resumé：短歌剧（一说做评论）；Up Times square to Columbus Circle：在纽约市内沿百老汇行进；congresses：人群；kitchens：指娱乐场地；tabloid crime-sheets perched in easy sight：放置在读者容易见到的地方的侦探插图读物；twelve upward：已过12点（午夜）；a subscription praise：预先已准备好的赞许，或习惯性的赞许，两字都有讽刺意味；the L＝the elevated train；penguin flexions of arms：手臂的笨拙、机械的弯曲（意准备取钱买票的动作）；scuttle：指地铁入口；Be minimum：尽量缩小体积；boxed：指在十字门内。

4. 第41～45行：在地铁里的乘客乱哄哄的谈话。Floral Park Flatbush：纽约市布鲁克林区一地名；Culver line：一交通线。

5. 第46～49行：诗人听后的反应。Our tongues…vanes：指乘客的你言我语，七零八乱，互不衔接，听后很有一种人们总在改口的感觉；This answer：指第49行的“what“，意思是由于人声嘈杂，不易听清他人讲话，听后只能以问一句“什么”做为回答；repetition freezes：一再重复地说“什么”，令人听了感到沮丧。

6. 第50～56行：乘客的零乱谈话。fandaddle daddy：糊涂的大爷；Fourteenth：第14街；didja＝did you.

7.、The phonographs…urinal：把地铁里的声音比做地狱之声，经常在头脑中回荡，令人非常厌恶；a burnt match skating in a urinal：一种引人厌恶的意象。

8. 第66～71行：写乘车时的状貌，巧妙地把景和情融为一体；the swollen strap：地铁中的皮带拉手，一只皮带上由于有多只手牵拉，故弯成满圆形(swollen)；a smoldering bundle：指地铁隧道，下文中“a riven stump”亦指隧道；back forks of the chasms of the brain：把地铁的状貌同人的头脑、精神巧妙相连，下文中“interborough fissures of the mind”意亦同此。

9. your visage：诗人在和埃德加·艾伦·坡（Edgar Allan Poe）讲话，坡的诗如《海底之城》（“The City in the Sea”）及《梦境》（“Dream-Land”）等描写死的国度，其阴沉的气氛和可怕的意象对克兰都有影响。本诗——《隧道》——便是适例。

10. their riding eyes：指乘客盯人的目光。

11. And Death，aloft，—gigantically down：化用坡的《海底之城》第28～29两行：“While from a proud tower in the town/Death looks gigantically

down.”

12. 第79～82行：坡在1849年10月7日选举日去世，故有人提出他的死和选举有关；the ticket：选票。

13. Gravesend manor：地铁站名；Chambers Street：地铁站名。

14. 第85～89行：换车的情景，自地下沿自动电梯上升到可以望到街面的部位，然后再下去。each eye…/Bolting outright somewhere above where streets/Burst suddenly in rain…：在再次下去乘车前，目光突然见到上面的街道，外面正下雨。

15. 第97～99行：车厢里的肮脏等令人厌恶的情况。Blank windows gargle signals through the roar：指车在隧道的轰鸣里行进，外面的信号不时从车窗里闪进来，好像车窗吐出的一样。

16. 第100～105行：通过女佣人的形象描绘乘车人回家时的心情。the Daemon：指地铁；the bandaged hair：系绷带的头，指洗衣妇人的头，泛指乘客的受刺激的头；Genoese：指洗衣妇，一说指由洗衣妇（南欧人）联想到的哥伦布（Christopher Columbus）。

17. 第106～118行：以地铁为象征，描绘机械文明对人的侵犯。To spoon…out…liquid：盛出液体物；liquid：引伸意为“没有希望”。the dim/Locution of the eldest star：晨星的听不清的话。like pennies：指乘客在车厢里拥挤的情况。thou：指地铁。

18. 第119～122行：诗人笔锋一转，把地铁向地面移动与再生、神明巧妙结合，令人见到希望。Lazarus：拉撒路，见《圣经·约翰福音》(11章43节～44节)：耶稣使拉撒路起死回生。to feel the slope：地铁在向地面徐徐上移。A sound of waters…sky：在地铁出口人们见到水天相连的景象。Word：神明。

19. The blackness…sky：在灰暗中，灯光照亮倒映在河里的天空，望去仿佛是一块一块的玻璃。

20. I have driven under：我曾在下面乘车。

21. the coil of ticking towers：钟楼的缠绕。

22. the River that is East：纽约的东河（the East River）。

23. the hands：钟楼的表针。

ALLEN TATE

〔作者介绍〕

1930 年，几位被称为“逃亡者”（ the Fugitives）派的南方作家合作出版了一本题为《我要坚持我的立场》(*I'll Take My Stand*）的书，欲以南方的农业经济和文化传统与飞速工业化及商业化的北方相抗衡。诗人和批评家艾伦·塔特（Allen Tate，1899～1979）便是此书的主要撰稿人之一。

塔特就读于田纳西州的万德比尔特（Vanderbilt）大学（1919～1922）。在学期间，他曾多次聆听新批评（New Criticism）主帅兰生（John Crowe Ransom）的教诲。塔特是有影响的《逃亡者》(*The Fugitives*) 杂志的编辑之一。大学毕业后，他边教学边创作和研究，过着“学者诗人”（scholar-poet）的生活。他曾在美国国内及欧洲的多所大学任教，对新批评的发展及其在诗歌教育中支配地位的确立和巩固发挥了重要作用。

作为新批评的主要倡导人之一，塔特反对传统文学批评中那种过于重视作者生平及历史背景、忽视作品本身价值、将其视为某种思想观念的传播工具的作法。他主张文学研究应深入探讨作品的遣词造句、结构、意象，通过周密的本文分析而挖掘出它的丰富内含。在诗歌创作中，他所表现的多是对稳定与和谐的社会生活秩序的憧憬以及由于现代信仰危机而引起的骚乱与恐慌。他在接受一位记者采访时曾说过，他的所有诗作都是关于“失去信仰的痛苦”。他认为文学批评家应具有“宗教的想象力”（religious imagination）。为了追寻这种在现实生活中无法找到的和谐与信念，1950 年他皈依了罗马天主教。

三、四十年代塔特曾做过几家杂志的编辑。他的作品主要包括：诗集《蒲柏先生及其他诗篇》(*Mr Pope and Other Poems*, 1928)，《诗集》(*Poems*, *1928～1931*, *1932*）《地中海及其他诗篇》（*The Mediterranean and Other Poems*, *1928*)《冬海》(*Winter Sea*, *1944*) 等，批评著作《关于诗及其思想的反动文章》(*Reactionary Essays on Poetry and Ideas*, *1936*)，《疯狂中的理性》(*Reason in Mad-*

ness, *1941*）以及小说《先辈》（*The Fathers*）。

塔特的诗形式严谨，内容深刻。他怀念欧洲文化，歌咏南方传统。他善于用典，诗笔迂回婉约，读来并非容易。

Ode to the Confederate Deed

〔作品介绍〕

《南方同盟烈士颂》是一首艰深晦涩的诗，是诗人的代表作。据作者本人说，它所表现的是充斥于现代社会中的自我中心论给人带来的悲剧性结局。自我中心论认为，人所生活和体验的一切，都是由我们本人创造出来的。塔特认为，自我中心论是西方社会走向衰落的症结所在。人与人以及人与传统之间的交流消失了，每个人都如诗中的螃蟹一样，漫无目标地生活在一个阴森、冷漠的、坟墓般的世界中，最后只能象本诗结尾的美洲虎那样，成为唯我独尊的牺牲品。

本诗所描写的是一个人凭吊一处南方将士墓地的情景。他望着面前紧闭的门，残破的墙，丛生的野草，想象着草下的白骨与甲胄，企图在脑际再现过去的伟大，然而终究未能做到。现代之风如此之强，保持传统和信仰已不可能。本诗并非写理想的过去，而着重写现代人已不能再体验过去传统的美好。塔特认为，自我崇拜乃是本世纪 20 年代人们的致命伤。

Ode to the Confederate Dead[1]

Row after row with strict impunity
The headstones yield their names to the element,[2]
The wind whirrs without recollection;[3]
In the riven troughs the splayed leaves[4]
Pile up, of nature the casual sacrament
To the seasonal eternity of death;
Then driven by the fierce scrutiny
Of heaven to their election in the vast breath,[5]
They sough the rumor of mortality.

Autumn is desolation in the plot
Of a thousand acres where these memories grow
From the inexhaustible bodies that are not
Dead, but feed the grass row after rich row. [6]
Think of the autumns that have come and gone! —
Ambitious November with the humors of the year, [7]
With a particular zeal for every slab, [8]
Staining the uncomfortable angels[9] that rot
On the slabs, a wing chipped here, an arm there:
The brute curiosity of an angel's stare[10]
Turns you, like them, to stone,
Transforms the heaving air
Till plunged to a heavier world below
You shift your sea-space blindly
Heaving, turnign like the blind crab. [11]

Dazed by the wind, only the wind
The leaves flying, plunge[12]

You know who have waited by the wall
The twilight certainty of an animal,
Those midnight restitutions of the blood
You know—the immitigable pines, the smoky frieze
Of the sky, the sudden call: you know the rage,
The cold pool left by the mounting flood,
Of muted Zeno and Parmenides. [13]
You who have waited for the angry resolution
Of those desires that should be yours tomorrow,
You know the unimportant shrift of death
And praise the vision[14]
And praise the arrogant circumstance
Of those who fall
Rank upon rank, hurrieS beyond decision—
Here by the sagging gate, stopped by the wall. [15]

Seeing, seeing only the leaves
Flying, plunge and expire

Turn your eyes to the immoderate past,[16]
Turn to the inscrutable infantry rising
Demons out of the earth—they will not last.
Stonewall, Stonewall, and the sunken fields of hemp,[17]
Shiloh, Antietam, Malvern Hill, Bull Run.[18]
Lost in that orient of the thick-and-fast
You will curse the setting sun.

  Cursing only the leaves crying
  Like an old man in a storm

You hear the shout, the crazy hemlocks point
With troubled fingers to the silence which
Smothers you, a mummy, in time.

          The hound bitch
Toothless and dying, in a musty cellar
Hears the wind only.

          Now that the salt of their blood[19]
Stiffens the saltier oblivion of the sea,
Seals the malignant purity of the flood,
What shall we who count our days and bow
Our heads with a commemorial woe
In the ribboned coats of grim felicity,
What shall we say of the bones, unclean,
Whose verdurous anonymity will grow?[20]
The ragged arms, the ragged heads and eyes
Lost in these acres of the insane green?[21]
The gray lean spiders come, they come and go;
In a tangle of willows without light
The singular screech-owl's tight
Invisible lyric seeds the mind
With the furious murmur of their chivalry.

  We shall say only the leaves
  Flying, plunge and expire

We shall say only the leaves whispering[22]
In the improbable mist of nightfall
That flies on multiple wing:
Night is the beginning and the end
And in between the ends of distraction
Waits mute speculation, the patient curse
That stones the eyes, or like the jaguar leaps[23]
For his own image in a jungle pool, his victim.
What shall we say who have knowledge
Carried to the heart? Shall we take the act
To the grave? Shall we, more hopeful, set up the grave
In the house? The ravenous grave?

Leave now
The shut gate and the decomposing wall:
The gentle serpent, green in the mulberry bush,
Riots with his tongue through the hush—
Sentinel of the grave who counts us all![24]

〔注释〕

1. Confederate Dead：指在美国南北战争中为南方同盟战死的将士。

2. headstones：墓碑。这两行意指排排墓碑上刻着死亡将士的名字，他们遭受了风吹雨打。

3. 风呼啸着，但却没有引起对往事的追忆。

4. riven troughs：指沟壑。此行连同下两行正常语序是：In the riven troughs the splayed leaves of nature, the casual sacrament, pile up to the seasonable eternity of death。seasonal eternity of death：树叶每年都要脱落、死亡，是季节性(seasonal)的，周而复始的永恒(eternity)。

5. the fierce scrutiny/of heaven（承上行）：大自然的可怕审视。their election：有些树叶被风吹起，似乎是经大自然严格审查后而被挑选出来的。vast breath：指秋风。此句连同下句意为树叶被秋风吹起，在空中呜咽。

6. the inexhaustible bodies that are not/Dead, but feed the grass row after rich row：可以理解为死去的将士并没有死亡，因为他们的尸体给草叶以营养，使之长得繁茂。

7. the humors of the year：指天气不佳。

8. 指秋风强劲，吹打墓碑。

9. the uncomfortable angels：墓碑上的天使图案。

10. the brute curiosity of an angel's stare：指天使怒视，不解其意。

11. 对以上这两节，塔特曾解释道："我们可以想象一个人于深秋时节站在联盟将士墓地的门前；树叶在飘落，他的第一个印象便是'有关死亡的信息'。在诗的第2节的开首，萧瑟的景象使他无法想象死亡会给大地带来新生这一传统的英雄主义的猜想。从这里到本节结尾，他深思着时间对万物的摧残，并以'盲目的螃蟹'结尾。螃蟹这一形象有运动，但无方向和力量，而且从人类的角度来看，无法将它用于任何有目的性的世界；在整篇诗中有两个被禁锢的自我的象征，螃蟹是比较晦涩的一个，……它为另一个更明确的象征——美洲虎打下了伏笔。螃蟹是对全诗中道德冲突的第一个揭示，这种冲突便是'现代知识分子'与世界的隔绝。"（见塔特《四十年论文集》第595～596页）

12. 塔特对这个重叠句做说明时说："风——叶句是在1930年，即诗的第一稿写成近5年以后才加入的……它使诗更有'节奏'，使读者在诗的主题的展开过程中有经常的停顿时间，使他有机会消化……"（见《疯狂中的理性》）。

13. Zeno：芝诺，Parmenides：巴门尼德斯，均为公元前6世纪古希腊哲学家。他们认为真实的宇宙是统一不变的整体，认为现实即存在，否认变化和运动。

14. the vision：即英雄主义的理想。

15. 塔特说这一节"写的是另外一种冲突。这是一种英雄主义的主题，而且不仅仅是道德上的英雄主义；它是一种辉煌的英雄主义，甚至将死从肉体上的腐烂升华为一种形式上的仪式：这种英雄主义是人类精神在整个社会中的形式冲溢……因此这一节的结构是如下两个主题冲突的客观组合，即已经衰颓的'积极信仰'和围绕我们的'破碎混乱'。……在沉思这一英雄主义的主题时，站在墓地门前的人从未抱有过他本人可达到这一英雄主义的幻想。（见《四十年论文集》第599页）。"此节是凭吊者企图再忆往事，几乎又能重温昔日的理想，然而终于未能如愿。诗中的"知道"（know）一字表达出这样的意思，"知道"之后便不能再通过遐思而"体验"；所以，凭吊者尽管努力想象将士不畏生死进攻时松柏、天空、树叶等的状貌，但是思路最终被随风飘逝的黄叶打断。

16. 之后，凭吊者再次追抚昔日的英雄人物与业绩，诸次战役的景状及一位南方将领的名字等又回荡在他的脑际。诗的重叠句表明，他还是不能追忆过去的理想，因为在传统业已不复存在的今天，过去已经一去不复返了。"the bound bitch"的形象是这种状况的逼真写照。

17. Stonewall：双关语，一指墓地的围墙，一指南方名将Stonewall Jackson（塔特1928年写过他的传记）。意指颓残的石墙把凭吊者和象征英雄主义的过去的将士无情地分隔开来。

18. 皆为美国内战期间发生过激烈战斗的地方。

19. 诗人的笔锋一转，开始描状吊唁死者的人群，面对草下白骨，他们对死又有什么可说呢？他们只能说，人人都会一死，肉体会分解，消逝在荒草中，猫头鹰叫声偶尔令人忆起往昔的英雄主义，然而落叶在随风飘逝，令人遐思。

20. verdurous anonymity：死者已全部化为绿色草地的一部分，失去了个人身份。

21. insane green：意指大地也似乎带有疯狂的特征。

22. 现代混乱的根源——自我崇拜，阻止人们同传统交融。恰似美洲虎冲向林中池塘捕食自己的倒影一样，现代人自我吞噬，自我毁灭。于是诗人请凭吊者还是远离墓地那紧闭的门和颓残的围墙。

23. jaguar：美洲虎。有关这一意象及其下一行的含义，塔特有如下评论："美洲虎的形象是本诗中纳西索斯主题的唯一直接表现，但不同的是，这里不是一位青年凝视着池水，而是一只猛兽注视着森林中的流水，然后跃入其中，自取灭亡。"（见《四十年论文选》，第 609 页）

24. "结尾中蛇的意象是一个古老的时间象征，我试图把它安置在桑树下使其显得平常可信，这是因为我希望蚕也或多或少地隐含于这种形象之中。但时间也是死亡。"（诗人原注，见《四十年论文选》第 600～601 页）。诗人想用蚕这一生命的象征来冲淡结尾那浓重的悲观情调，但这一企图虽然并不成功，因为读者所获得的最突出印象，便是时间将吞噬一切。塔特似乎也意识到了这一点，故说"时间也是死亡。"

John Steinbeck

〔作者介绍〕

约翰·斯坦贝克（John Steinbeck，1902～1968），美国小说家，生于加利福尼亚州的萨利纳斯。从小受父母的影响，喜读文学作品。1919至1925年间，入斯坦福大学，读英语专业。其间曾几次辍学，以做工所得，继续大学的课程学习。斯坦贝克经历丰富，曾从事筑路、采摘水果、捕鱼等体力劳动，以及丈量土地，新闻报导等工作。他十分熟悉加利福尼亚州农民和农业工人的生活，他在青、少年时期的经历和30年代经济危机时期的见闻，是他的优秀作品的基本素材。

斯坦贝克的第一本小说发表于1929年，题为《金杯》（*Cup of Gold*），此后20年期间是他文学创作的盛期。他在1961年出版的《我们的不满的冬天》（*The Winter of Our Discontent*）是他最后一部长篇小说。除长篇小说以外，他还从事剧本、短篇小说、游记、新闻等文章的写作。

他在30年代创作的作品，反映了当时处于经济危机困境中的农业工人的生活与斗争，十分出色。他在1936年发表的《胜负未决的战斗》（*In Dubious Battle*）便是一例，这是一本描写采摘水果的农业工人进行罢工斗争的小说，这场罢工斗争在农场主的破坏下以失败告终，小说反映了作者对农业工人处境的深刻同情。1937年出版的《鼠与人》（*Of Mice and Men*），以及同名剧本（在纽约上演）获得极大成功，确立了斯坦贝克在美国文坛上的地位，使他成为公认的作家。《鼠与人》描述了两个农业工人的生活遭遇：乔治和列尼是两个流动的季节工人，他们从一个农场到另一个农场劳动；从一种工作干到另外一种工作，梦寐以求的就是拥有一间小小的房子，一块土地，摆脱颠沛流离的艰苦，过自立、安定的生活。可是在他们的理想有可能实现的时候，列尼却成了飞来横祸的牺牲品。农场主的儿子是一个仗势欺人的公子，儿媳妇是一个水性杨花的女人，她有意勾引列尼，无意中列尼伤害了她的性命。家场主的儿子带领一批愤怒、盲从的人群追捕列尼，乔治不得不枪杀了处于绝境中的列尼。在现代社会中，乔治与列尼所追求的和平、宁静、自立、自足的美丽的理想，只不过是一种梦想而已。斯坦贝克在这部作品中所取得的艺术成就表现在他同小说中的人物保持了一定的距离，既不太远又不太近，使读者十分清楚地看到人物的活动，明确地理解作者的同情心所寄托的对象。

《愤怒的葡萄》(*The Grapes of Wrath*, 1938) 是斯坦贝克对美国文学的重大贡献，被誉为美国文化中的一个里程碑。

他在 1937 年发表的《红马驹》(*The Red Pony*, 1937) 是由 4 个故事组成的作品，描写一个天真烂漫的少年的成长。通过在自己父亲的农场中的亲身经历，他懂得了人生中错误和挫折的不可避免以及自然界的变幻无常。在《人民的领袖》(“The Leader of the People”) 这篇故事中，斯坦贝克颂扬了早年向西挺进的开拓者在创造美国历史中的功绩，强调人们团结合作的精神，也反映了早年移民同当地印第安人的冲突与残杀。故事还反映了老年人的怀旧情绪以及老一代人与新一代人之间缺乏相互理解的“代沟”问题。

他在 1942 年发表的《月落》(*The Moon Is Down*)，描写挪威人民反对纳粹占领的斗争，受到挪威人民的赞赏。后来，他获得了挪威的自由十字勋章。50 年代以后，斯坦贝克在文学创作方面的成就远不如前期巨大。《我们的不满的冬天》反映了现代社会中道德真空的现实。人们为了追求无所不能的、神圣的美元，而置道德原则于不顾。小说以长岛的一个地方为背景，在那里，贝克先生开办了一家银行。作者写道：“每天早上，人们象参加弥撒一样站在保险库前面，当时钟的指针转到 9 点钟的时候，保险柜发出一个清澈的声音，接着便是一阵吱……吱……吱的声响，他神秘地拨动数字号码，轻轻地转动保险柜的把手，圣殿般神圣的保险柜便开启了，贝克先生恭恭敬敬接受堆集在一起的钞票的敬礼”。

美国在 30 年代前期经历了严重的经济危机的打击，斯坦贝克是这个时期一位杰出的文学家。他本人是这一时期的时势所造成的作家，他的优秀作品是这一历史年代中社会变动的产物，具有强烈的时代气息，读起来使人感到跳动着的社会脉搏。斯坦贝克细心观察社会变动，同情在苦难中挣扎着的人们，表达他们的呼声，关心他们的反抗斗争。他一方面以尖刻的笔触针砭社会的弊端，一方面则强烈地表示对人生，人与人之间的友爱与勇气的信心。面对社会中残酷的非人化现实，他坚持寻求生活的意义和价值观。他歌颂生活，勇敢地展望生活前景；他认为尽管人在无情的世界面前显得渺小，尽管生活中充满了灾难和死亡，但是人们的生活欲望和勇气是不可战胜的，他们能够经受苦难而生存下去。

斯坦贝克的作品表明，他的思想体现着美国文化的几个鲜明的特征：爱默生的人性本善的观点；惠特曼的社会民主及实用主义哲学的核心——有效行动的思想。他对于城乡、今昔、劳资以及个人与集体的关系十分注意。他的几部优秀作品情节逼真，感情真挚、深厚，是美国的社会问题小说的重要组成部分。

他的不少作品的故事往往发生在加利福尼亚的乡村地区，具有浓郁的地方色彩和强烈的乡土气息；他熟悉和善于应用民间语言，纯朴而自然，富有诗意。然而，他所塑造的人物略显平板，他的后期作品，结构略显松散，缺乏创新精神。斯坦贝克于1962年获诺贝尔文学奖。

斯坦贝克的其他作品还有《天堂的牧场》(*The Pastures of Heaven*, 1932)、《托蒂亚平地》(*Tortilla Flat*, 1935)《长谷地》(*The Long Valley*, 1938)、《罐头厂街》(*Cannery Row*, 1945)、《珍珠》(*The Pearl*, 1947)、《任性的公共汽车》(*The Wayward Bus*, 1947) 以及《伊甸园以东》(*East of Eden*, 1952) 等。

The Grapes of Wrath

〔作品介绍〕

《愤怒的葡萄》(*The Grapes of Wrath*)是斯坦贝克的代表作品，出版于1938年。小说以30年代美国流动农业工人的生活遭遇以及他们为生存而进行的顽强斗争为题材，反映遭受严重经济危机打击的美国社会中大银行土地占有者与被剥夺了小块土地、从而沦为季节农工的农民之间的矛盾和斗争。人们称之为30年代的《汤姆叔叔的小屋》。它曾被斥为宣扬共产主义的政治小说，在俄克拉何马州等地方被列为禁书多年。但是时间和生活经验证明它是一本文学杰作，世界名著。它被翻译成多种文字出版，深受各国读者的欢迎。

小说以深切的同情，描绘了中西部的破产农民利用一辆破旧的卡车，离乡背井，餐风宿露，向西迁移，以加利福尼亚为目的地寻求生路的凄惨景象。长期居住在俄克拉何马州的汤姆·乔德一家与当地的一位牧师，面对着天灾人祸的威胁，在疾病与死亡的魔爪之下，扶老携幼，到被称为“天堂”、“乐土”的加利福尼亚州逃荒，最后却遭到当地农场主的歧视、虐待和无情的剥削。小说从头到尾，字字句句饱含着辛酸，渗透着血泪。作者义愤填膺地警告说：“当大多数的人处于冻馁之中的时候，他们就会强力夺取他们需要的一切。”作者对不公正的社会制度强加在人民头上的苦难进行了淋漓尽致的叙述以后说道：生活中存在着无法铲除的罪恶，控诉与谴责都无济于事。但是《愤怒的葡萄》坚信友爱与同情是新生活的起点。它是30年代中既把经济危机的苦难揭露无遗，又不渲染暴力仇恨的唯一的一部美国小说。

《愤怒的葡萄》的结构特色之一，是把叙述情节和论述观点两方面巧妙地结合为一体。全书共30章，其中16章为“插入章节”，约占小说总的篇幅的六分之一，穿插在乔德、威尔逊、温赖特等农家故事的叙述中间，说明乔德一家向西迁移的社会背景，(干旱、饥馑、生产废荒、加利福尼亚州的土地所有制，流动工人的境遇等)，同时阐述他们对于生活和社会的主张。这两个方面相辅相成，一张一弛；一唱一和，烘托渲染，推动故事向纵深发展。

小说结构的另外一个特点是，借鉴了《圣经·出埃及记》(“Exodus”)故事的构思轮廓。全书分成三大部分：前12章描述旱灾、农田荒芜、生活苦难；第13章至18章描绘三五成群的贫民结队西行的凄惨景象；最后12章叙述移民们到达加利福尼亚以后的遭遇与争取生存的斗争。假如我们把它同《出埃及记》的布局相比较，就发现十分相似：以色列人在埃及遭受奴役，于是在摩西带领之下脱离苦海，奔向“乐土”迦南；到了福地以后却又遇到当地人的抵制。此外小说中许多细节的描写，使它和《圣经》的相似之处更加突出。例如：书名《愤怒的葡萄》一词在《圣经》的《申命记》(“Deuteronomy”)、《耶利米书》(“Jeremiad”)、《启示录》(“Revelation”)等部分中都被多次提到。第17章很有《申命记》的味道。小说结尾部分的情节发人深省：罗丝用自己的奶水抢救一个生命垂危的老人，它和耶稣在最后的晚餐上所说的话相似。(耶稣说：“拿去吃吧，这是我的肉体。”)此外，牧师詹姆斯·凯丽的言论与行动和耶稣的言行相仿。此外小说的语言、文章笔法引人注目。用字简洁、句型工整、细节翔实，总结概括，交待明确。

不过，小说有时失于感情外露，某些人物性格比较呆滞，心理活动的刻划亦着墨不足。

这里选注的是小说的第1章和第4章。

The Grapes of Wrath

CHAPTER I

TO THE red country and part of the gray country of Oklahoma,[1] the last rains came gently, and they did not cut the scarred earth. The plows crossed and recrossed the rivulet marks. The last rains lifted the corn quickly and scattered weed colonies and grass along the sides of the roads so that the gray country and the dark red country began to disappear under a green cover. In the last part of May the sky grew pale and the clouds that had hung in high puffs for so long in the spring were dissipated. The sun flared down on the growing corn day after day until a line of brown spread along the edge of each green bayonet. The clouds appeared, and went away, and in a while they did not try any more.

The weeds grew darker green to protect themselves, and they did not spread any more. The surface of the earth crusted, a thin hard crust, and as the sky became pale, so the earth became pale, pink in the red country and white in the gray country.

In the water-cut gullies the earth dusted down in dry little streams. Gophers and ant lions started small avalanches. And as the sharp sun struck day after day, the leaves of the young corn became less stiff and erect; they bent in a curve at first, and then, as the central ribs of strength grew weak, each leaf tilted downward. Then it was June, and the sun shone more fiercely. The brown lines on the corn leaves widened and moved in on the central ribs. The weeds frayed and edged back toward their roots. The air was thin and the sky more pale; and every day the earth paled.

In the roads where the teams moved, where the wheels milled the ground and the hooves of the horses beat the ground, the dirt crust broke and the dust formed. Every moving thing lifted the dust into the air: a walking man lifted a thin layer as high as his waist, and a wagon lifted the dust as high as the fence tops, and an automobile boiled a cloud behind it. The dust was long in settling back again.

When June was half gone, the big clouds moved up out of Texas and the Gulf,[2] high heavy clouds, rain-heads. The men in the fields looked up at the clouds and sniffed at them and held wet fingers up to sense the wind. And the horses were nervous while the clouds were up. The rain-heads dropped a little spattering and hurried on to some other country. Behind them the sky was pale again and the sun flared. In the dust there were drop craters where the rain had fallen, and there were clean splashes on the corn, and that was all.

A gentle wind followed the rain clouds, driving them on northward, a wind that softly clashed the drying corn. A day went by and the wind increased, steady, unbroken by gusts. The dust from the roads fluffed up and spread out and fell on the weeds beside the fields, and fell into the fields a little way. Now the wind grew strong and hard and it worked at the rain crust[3] in the corn fields. Little by little the sky was darkened by the mixing dust, and the wind felt over the earth, loosened the dust, and carried it away. The wind grew stronger. The rain crust broke and the dust lifted up out of the fields and drove gray plumes into the air like sluggish smoke. The corn threshed the wind and made a dry, rushing sound. The finest dust did not settle back to earth now, but disappeared into the darkening sky.

The wind grew stronger, whisked under stones, carried up straws and old leaves, and even little clods, marking its course as it sailed across the fields. The air and the sky darkened and through them the sun shone redly, and there was a raw sting in the air. During a night the wind raced faster over the land, dug cunningly among the rootlets of the corn, and the corn fought the wind with its weakened leaves until the roots were freed by the prying wind and when each stalk settled wearily sideways toward the earth and pointed the direction of the wind.

The dawn came, but no day. In the gray sky a red sun appeared, a dim red circle that gave a little light, like dusk; and as that day advanced, the dusk slipped back toward darkness, and the wind cried and whimpered over the fallen corn.

Men and women huddled in their houses, and they tied handkerchiefs over their noses when they went out, and wore goggles to protect their eyes.

When the night came again it was black night, for the stars could not pierce the dust to get down, and the window lights could not even spread beyond their own yards. Now the dust was evenly mixed with the air, an emulsion of dust and air. Houses were shut tight, and cloth wedged around doors and windows, but the dust came in so thinly that it could not be seen in the air, and it settled like pollen on the chairs and tables, on the dishes. The people brushed it from their shoulders. Little lines of dust lay at the door sills.

In the middle of that night the wind passed on and left the land quiet. The dust-filled air muffled sound more completely than fog does. The people, lying in their beds, heard the wind stop. They awakened when the rushing wind was gone. They lay quietly and listened deep into the stillness. Then the roosters crowed, and their voices were muffled, and the people stirred restlessly in their beds and wanted the morning. They knew it would take a long time foor the dust to settle out of the air. In the morning the dust hung like fog, and the sun was as red as ripe new blood. All day the dust sifted down from the sky, and the next day it sifted down. An even blanket covered the earth. It settled on the corn, piled up on the tops of the fence posts, piled up on the wires; it settled on roofs, blanketed the weeds and trees.

The people came out of their houses and smelled the hot stinging air and covered their noses from it. And the children came out of the houses, but they did not run or shout as they would have done after a rain. Men stood by their fences and looked at the ruined corn, drying fast now, only a little green showing through the film of dust. The men were silent and they did ont move often. And the women came out of the houses to stand beside their men—to feel whether this time the men would break. The women studied the men's faces secretly, for the corn could go, as long as something else remained. The children stood near by, drawing figures in the dust with bare toes, and the children sent exploring senses out to see whether men and women would break. The children peeked at the faces of the men and women, and then drew careful lines in the dust with their toes. Horses came to the watering troughs and nuzzled the water to clear the surface dust. After a while the faces of the watching men lost their bemused perplexity and became hard and angry and resistant. Then the women knew that they were safe and that there was no break. Then they asked, What'll we do? And the men replied, I don't know. But it was all right. The women knew it was all right, and the watching children knew it was all right. Women and children knew deep in themselves that no misfortune was too great to bear if their men were whole. The women went into the houses to their work, and the children began to play, but cautiously at first. As the day went forward the sun became less red. It flared down on the dust-blanketed land. The men sat in the doorways of their houses; their hands were busy with sticks and little rocks. The men sat still—thinking—figuring.

CHAPTER Ⅳ

WHEN Joad heard the truck get under way, gear climbing up to gear and the ground throbbing under the rubber beating of the tires, he stopped and tured about and watched it until it disappeared. When it was out of sight he still watched the distance and the blue air-shimmer. Thoughtfully he took the pint from his pocket, unscrewed the metal cap, and sipped the whisky delicately, running his tongue inside the bottle neck, and then around his lips, to gather in any flavor that might have escaped him. He said experimentally, "There we spied a nigger—" and that was all he could remember. At last he turned about and faced the dusty side road that cut off at right angles through the fields. The sun was hot, and no wind stirred the sifted dust. The road was cut with furrows where dust had slid and settled back into the wheel tracks. Joad took a few steps, and the flourlike dust spurted up in front of his new yellow shoes, and the yellowness was disappearing under gray dust.

He leaned down and untied the laces, slipped off first one shoe and then the other. And he worked his damp feet comfortably in the hot dry dust until little spurts of it came up between his toes, and until the skin on his feet tightened with dryness. He took off his coat and wrapped his shoes in it and slipped the bundle under his arm. And at last he moved up the road, shooting the dust ahead of him, making a cloud that hung low to the ground behind him.

The right of way[1] was fenced, two strands of barbed wire on willow poles. The poles were crooked and badly trimmed. Whenever a crotch came to the proper height the wire lay in it, and where there was no crotch the barbed wire was lashed to the post with rusty baling wire. Beyond the fence, the corn lay beaten down by wind and heat and drought, and the cups where leaf joined stalk were filled with dust.

Joad plodded along, dragging his cloud of dust behind him. A little bit ahead he saw the high-domed shell of a land turtle, crawling slowly along through the dust, its legs working stiffly and jerkily. Joad stopped to watch it, and his shadow fell on the turtle. Instantly head and legs were withdrawn and the short thick tail clamped sideways into the shell. Joad picked it up and turned it over. The back was browngray, like the dust, but the underside of the shell was creamy yellow, clean and smooth. Joad shifted his bundle high under his arm and stroked the smooth undershell with his finger, and he pressed it. It was softer than the back. The hard old head came out and tried to look at the pressing finger, and the legs waved wildly. The turtle wetted on Joad's hand and struggled uselessly in the air. Joad turned it back upright and rolled it up in his coat with his shoes. He could feel it pressing and struggling and fussing under his arm. He moved ahead more quickly now, dragging his heels a little in the fine dust.

Ahead of him, beside the road, a scrawny, dusty willow tree cast a speckled shade. Joad could see it ahead of him, its poor branches curving over the way, its load of leaves tattered and scraggly as a molting chicken[2]. Joad was sweating now. His blue shirt darkened down his back and under his arms. He pulled at the visor of his cap and creased it in the middle, breaking its cardboard lining so completely that it could never look new again. And his steps took on new speed and intent toward the shade of the distant willow tree. At the willow he knew there would be shade, at least one hard bar of absolute shade thrown by the trunk, since the sun had passed its zenith. The sun whipped the back of his neck now and made a little humming in his head. He could not see the base of the tree, for it grew out of a little swale that held water longer than the level places. Joad speeded his pace against the sun, and he started down the declivity. He slowed cautiously, for the bar of absolute shade was taken. A man sat on the ground, leaning against the trunk of the tree. His legs were crossed and one bare foot extended nearly as high as his head. He did not hear Joad approaching, for he was whistling solemnly the tune of "Yes, Sir, That's My Baby."[3] His extended foot swung slowly up and down in the tempo. It was not dance tempo. He stopped whistling and sang in an easy thin tenor:

> "Yes, sir, that's my Saviour,
> Je—sus is my Saviour,
> Je—sus is my Saviour now.
> On the level[4]
> 'S not the devil,
> Jesus is my Saviour now."

Joad had moved into the imperfect shade of the molting leaves before the man heard him coming, stopped his song, and turned his head. It was a long head, bony, tight of skin, and set on a neck as stringy and muscular as a celery stalk. His eyeballs were heavy and protruding; the lids stretched to cover them, and the lids were raw and red. His cheeks were brown and shiny and hairless and his mouth full-humorous or sensual. The nose, beaked and hard, stretched the skin so tightly that the bridge showed white. There was no perspiration on the face, not even on the tall pale forehead. It was an abnormally high forehead, lined with delicate blue veins at the temples. Fully half of the face was above the eyes. His stiff gray hair was mussed back from his brow as though he had combed it back with his fingers. For clothes he wore overalls and a blue shirt. A denim coat with brass buttons and a spotted brown hat creased like a pork pie lay on the ground beside him. Canvas sneakers, gray with dust, lay near by where they had fallen when they were kicked off.

The man looked long at Joad. The light seemed to go far into his brown eyes, and it picked out little golden specks deep in the irises. The strained bundle of neck muscles stood out.

Joad stood still in the speckled shade. He took off his cap and mopped his wet face with it and dropped it and his rolled coat on the ground.

The man in the absolute shade uncrossed his legs and dug with his toes at the earth.

Joad said, "Hi. It's hotter'n hell on the road."

The seated man stared questioningly at him. "Now ain't you young Tom Joad-ol'Tom's boy?"

"Yeah," said Joad. "All the way. Goin' home now."

"You wouldn' remember me. I guess," the man said. He smiled and his full lips revealed great horse teeth. "Oh, no, you wouldn't remember. You was always too busy pullin' little girls' pigtails when I give you the Holy Sperit. You was all wropped up in yankin' that pigtail[5] out by the roots. You maybe don't recollect, but I do. The two of you come to Jesus at once' cause of that pigtail yankin'. Baptized both of you in the irrigation ditch at once. Fightin' an' yellin' like a couple a cats."

Joad looked at him with drooped eyes, and then he laughed. "Why, you're the preacher. You're the preacher. I jus' passed a recollection about you to a guy not an hour ago."

"I was a preacher," said the man seriously. "Reverend Jim Casy—was a Burning Busher.[6] Used to howl out the name of Jesus to glory. And used to get an irrigation ditch so squirmin' full of repented sinners half of 'em like to drownded. But not no more," he sighed. "Just Jim Casy now. Ain't got the call no more.[7] Got a lot of sinful idears—but they seem kinda sensible."

Joad said, "You're bound to get idears if you go thinkin' about stuff. Sure I remember you. You use ta give a good meetin'. I recollect one time you give a whole sermon walkin' around on your hands, yellin' your head off. Ma favored you more than anybody. An' Granma says you was just lousy with the spirit." Joad dug at his rolled coat and found the pocket and brought out his pint. The turtle moved a leg but he wrapped it up tightly. He unscrewed the cap and held out the bottle. "Have a little snort?"

Casy took the bottle and regarded it broodingly. "I ain't preachin' no more much. The sperit ain't in the people much no more; and worse'n that, the sperit ain't in me no more. 'Course now an' again the sperit gets movin' an' I rip out a meetin', or when folks sets out food I give 'em a grace,[8] but my heart ain't in it. I on'y do it' cause they expect it."

Joad mopped his face with his cap again. "You ain't too damn holy to take a drink, are you?" he asked.

Casy seemed to see the bottle for the first time. He tilted it and took three big swallows. "Nice drinkin' liquor," he said.

"Ought to be," said Joad. "That's fact'ry liquor. Cost a buck."

Casy took another swallow before he passed the bottle back. "Yes, sir!" hesaid. "Yes, sir!"

Joad tood the bottle from him, and in politeness did not wipe the neck with his sleeve before he drank. He squatted on his hams and set the bottle upright against his coat roll. His fingers found a twig with which to draw his thoughts on the ground. He swept the leaves from a square and smoothed the dust. And he drew angles and make little circles. "I ain't seen you in a long time," he said.

"Nobody seen me," said the preacher. "I went off alone, an' I sat and figured. The sperit's strong in me, on'y it ain't the same. I ain't so sure of a lot of things. "He sat up straighter against the tree. His bony hand dug its way like a squirrel into his overall pocket, brought out a black, bitten plug of tobacco. Carefully he brushed off bits of straw and gray pocket fuzz before he bit off a corner and settled the quid into his cheek. Joad waved his stick in negation when the plug was held out to him. The turtle dug at the rolled coat. Casy looked over at the stirring garment. "What you got there—a chicken? Yor'll smother it."

Joad rolled the coat up more tightly. "An old turtle," he said. "Picked him up on the road. An old bulldozer. Thought I'd take 'im to my little brother. Kids like turtles."

The preacher nodded his head slowly. "Every kid got a turtle some time or other. Nobody can't keep a turtle though. They work at it and work at it, and at last one day they get out and away they go—off somewheres. It's like me. I wouldn' take the good ol' gospel that was just layin' there to my hand. I got to be pickin' at it an' workin' at it until I got it all tore down. Here I got the sperit sometimes an' nothin' to preach about. I got the call to lead the people, an' no place to lead 'em."

"Lead 'em around and around," said Joad. "Sling' em in the irrigation ditch.[9] Tell 'em they'll burn in hell[10] if they don't think like you. What the hell you want to lead'em someplace for? Jus' lead' em." The straight trunk shade had stretched out along the ground. Joad moved gratefully into it and squatted on his hams and made a new smooth place on which to draw his thoughts with a stick. A thick-furred yellow shepherd dog came trotting down the road, head low, tongue lolling and dripping. Its tail hung limply curled, and it panted loudly. Joad whistled at it, but it only dropped its head an inch and trotted fast toward some definite destination. "Goin' someplace," Joad explained, a little piqued. "Goin' for home maybe."

The preacher could not be thrown from his subject. "Goin' someplace," he repeated. "That's right, he's goin' someplace. Me—I don't know where I'm goin'. Tell you what—I use ta get the people jumpin' an' talkin' in tongues, an' glory-shoutin' till they just fell down an' passed out. An'[11] some I'd baptize to bring 'em to.[12] An' then—you know what I'd do? I'd take one of them girls out in the grass, an' I'd lay with her. Done it ever' time. Then I'd feel bad, an' I'd pray an' pray, but it didn't do no good. Come the nex' time, them an' me was full of the sperit, I'd do it again. I figgered there just wasn't no hope for me, an' I was a damned ol' hypocrite. But I didn't mean to be."

Joad smiled and his long teeth parted and he licked his lips. "There ain't nothing like a good hot meetin' for pushin' 'em over," he asid. "I done that myself."

Casy leaned forward excitedly. "You see," he cried, "I seen it was that way, an' I started thinkin'." He waved his bony big-knuckled hand up and down in a patting gesture. "I got to thinkin' like this— 'Here's me preachin' grace. An' here's them people gettin' grace so hard they're jumpin' an' shoutin'. Now they say layin' up with a girl comes from the devil. But the more grace a girl got in her, the quicker she wants to go out in the grass.' An' I got to thinkin' how in hell, s'cuse me,[13] how can the devil get in when a girl is so full of the Holy Sperit that it's spoutin' out of her nose an' ears. You'd think that'd be one time when the devil didn't stand a snowball's chance[14] in hell. But there it was." His eyes were shining with excitement. He worked his cheeks for a moment and then spat into the dust, and the gob of spit rolled over and over, picking up dust until it looked like a round dry little pellet. The preacher spread out his hand and looked at his palm as though he were reading a book. "An' there's me," he went on softly. "There's me with all them people's souls in my han'—responsible an' feelin' my responsibility—an' ever' time, I lay with one of them girls." He looked over at Joad and his face looked helpless. His expression asked for help.

Joad carefully drew the torso of a woman in the dirt, breasts, hips, pelvis. "I wasn't never a preacher," he said. "I never let nothin' get by when I could catch it. An' I never had no idears about it except I was goddamn glad when I got one."

"But you wasn't a preacher," Casy insisted. "A girl was just a girl to you. They wasn't nothin' to you. But to me they was holy vessels. I was savin' their souls. An' here with all that responsibility on me I'd just get'em frothin' with the Holy Sperit, an' then I'd take'em out in the grass."

"Maybe I should of been a preacher,"[15] said Joad. He brought out his tobacco and papers and rolled a cigarette. He lighted it and squinted through the smoke at the preacher. "I been a long time without a girl," he said. "It's gonna take some catchin' up."

Casy continued, "It worried me till I couldn't get no sleep. Here I'd go to preachin' and I'd say, 'By God, this time I ain't gonna do it.' And right while I said it, I knowed I was."

"You should a got a wife," said Joad. "Preacher an' his wife stayed at our place one time. Jehovites[16] they was. Slep' upstairs. Held meetin's in our barnyard. Us kids would listen. That preacher's missus took a godawful poundin' after ever' night meetin'."

"I'm glad you tol' me," said Casy. "I use to think it was jus' me. Finally it give me such pain I quit an' went off by myself an' give her a damn good thinkin' about." He doubled up his legs and scratched between his dry dusty toes. "I says to myself, 'What's gnawin' you? Is it the screwin'?' An' I says, 'No, it's the sin.' An' I says, 'Why is it that when a fella ought to be just about mule-ass[17] proof against sin, an' all full up of Jesus,[18] why is it that's the time a fella gets fingerin' his pants buttons?'" He laid two fingers down in his palm in rhythm, as though he gently placed each word there side by side. "I says, 'Maybe it ain't a sin. Maybe it's just the way folks is. Maybe we been whippin' the hell out of ourselves for nothin'.' An' I thought how some sisters[19] took to beatin' theirselves with a three-foot shag of bobwire. An' I thought how maybe they liked to hurt themselves, an' maybe I liked to hurt myself. Well, I was layin' under a tree when I figured that out, and I went to sleep. And it come night, an' it was dark when I come to. They was a coyote squawkin' near by. Before I knowed it, I was sayin' out loud, 'The hell with it! There ain't no sin and there ain't no virtue. There's just stuff people do. It's all part of the same thing. And some of the things folks do is nice, and some ain't nice, but that's as far as any man got a right to say.'" He paused and looked up from the palm of his hand, where he had laid down the words.

Joad was grinning at him, but Joad's eyes were sharp and interested, too. "You give her a goin'-over," he said "You figured her out."

Casy spoke again, and his voice rang with pain and confusion. "I says, 'What's this call, this sperit?' An' I says,' It's love. I love people so much I'm fit to bust, sometimes.' An' I says, 'Don't you love Jesus?' Well, I thought an'thought, an' finally I says, 'No, I don't know nobody name' Jesus. I know a bunch of stories, but I only love people. An'sometimes I love 'em fit to bust, an' I want to make 'em happy, so I been preachin' somepin I thought would make 'em happy.' An' then—I been talkin' a hell of a lot. Maybe you wonder about me using bad words. Well, they ain't bad to me no more. They're jus' words folks use, an' they don't mean nothing bad with' em. Anyways, I'll tell you one more thing I thought out; an' from a preacher it's the most unreligious thing, and I can't be a preacher no more because I thought it an' I believe it."

"What's that?" Joad asked.

Casy looked shyly at him. "If it hits you wrong, don't take no offense at it, will you?"

"I don't take no offense 'cept a bust in the nose," said Joad. "What did you figger?"

"I figgered about the Holy Sperit and the Jesus road. I figgered, 'Why do we got to hang it on God or Jesus? Maybe,' I figgered, 'maybe it's all men an' all women we love; maybe that's the Holy Sperit—the human sperit—the whole shebang. Maybe all men got one big soul ever'body's a part of.' Now I sat there thinkin' it, an' all of a suddent—I knew it. I knew it so deep down that it was true, and I still know it."

Joad's eyes dropped to the ground, as though he could not meet the naked honesty in the preacher's eyes. "You can't hold no church[20] with idears like that," he said. "People would drive you out of the country with idears like that. Jumpin' an' yellin'. That's what folks like. Makes 'em feel swell. When Granma got to talkin' in tongues, you couldn't tie her down. She could knock over a full-growed deacon with her fist."

Casy regarded him broodingly. "Somepin I like to ast you," he said. "Somepin that been eatin' on me."

"Go ahead. I'll talk, sometimes."

"Well"—the preacher said slowly—"here's you that I baptized right when I was in the glory roof-tree. Got little hunks of Jesus jumpin' outa my mouth[21] that day. You won't remember 'cause[22] you was busy pullin' that pigtail."

"I remember," said Joad. "That was Susy Little. She bust my finger a year later."

"Well—did you take any good outa that baptizin'? Was your ways better?"

Joad thought about it. "No-o-o, can't say as I felt anything."

"Well—did you take any bad from it? Think hard."

Joad picked up the bottle and took a swig. "They wasn't nothing in it, good or bad. I just had fun." He handed the flask to the preacher.

He sighed and drank and looked at the low level of the whisky and took another tiny drink. "That's good," he said. "I got to worryin' about whether in messin' around maybe I done somebody a hurt."

Joad looked over toward his coat and saw the turtle, free of the cloth and hurrying away in the direction he had been following when Joad found him. Joad watched him for a moment and then got slowly to his feet and retrieved him and wrapped him in the coat again. "I ain't got no present for the kids," he said. "Nothin' but this ol' turtle."

"It's a funny thing," the preacher said. "I was thinkin' about ol' Tom Joad when you come along. Thinkin' I'd call in on him. I used to think he was a godless man. How is Tom?"

"I don' know how he is. I ain't been home in four years."

"Didn't he write to you?"

Joad was embarrassed. "Well, Pa wasn't no hand to write for pretty, or to write for writin'. He'd sign up him name as nice as anybody, an' lick his pencil. But Pa never did write no letters. He always says what he couldn' tell a fella with his mouth wasn't worth leanin' on no pencil about."

"Been out travelin' around?" Casy asked.

Joad regarded him suspiciously. "Didn' you hear about me? I was in all the papers."

"No—I never. What?" He jerked one leg over the other and settled lower against the tree. The afternoon was advancing rapidly, and a richer tone was growing on the sun.

Joad said pleasantly, "Might's well tell you now an' get it over with. But if you was still preachin' I wouldn't tell, fear you get prayin' over me." He drained the last of the pint and flung it from him, and the flat brown bottle skidded lightly over the dust. "I been in McAlester them four years."

Casy swung around to him, and his brows lowered so that his tall forehead seemed even taller. "Ain't wantin' to talk about it, huh? I won' ask you no questions, if you done something bad——"

"I'd do what I done—again," said Joad. "I killed a guy in a fight. We was drunk at a dance. He got a knife in me, an' I killed him with a shovel that was layin' there. Knocked his head plumb to squash."[23]

Casy's eyebrows resumed their normal level. "You ain't ashamed of nothin' then?"

"No," said Joad, "I ain't. I got seven years, account of he had a knife in me. Got out in four—parole."

"Then you ain't heard nothin' about your folks for four years?"

"Oh, I heard. Ma sent me a card two years ago, an' las' Christmus Granma sent a card. Jesus, the guys in the cell block laughed! Had a tree an' shiny stuff looks like snow. It says in po'try:[24]

> " 'Merry Christmus, purty child,[25]
> Jesus meek an' Jesus mild,
> Underneath the Christmus tree
> There's a gif' for you from me'.

I guess Granma never read it. Prob'ly got it from a drummer[26] an' picked out the one with the mos' shiny stuff on it. The guys in my cell block goddamn near died laughin'. Jesus Meek they called me after that. Granma never meant it funny; she jus' figgered it was so purty she wouldn' bother to read it. She lost her glasses the year I went up. Maybe she never did find 'em."

"How they treat you in McAlester?" Casy asked.

"Oh, awright. You eat regular, an' get clean clothes, and there's places to take a bath. It's pretty nice some ways. Makes it hard not havin' no women." Suddenly he laughed. "They was a guy paroled," he said. "'Bout a month he's back for breakin' parole. A guy ast him why he bust his parole. 'Well, hell,' he says. 'They got no conveniences at my old man's place. Got no 'lectric lights, got no shower baths. There ain't no books, an' the food's lousy.' Says he come back where they got a few conveniences an' he eats regular. He says it makes him feel lonesome out there in the open havin' to think what to do next. So he stole a car an' come back." Joad got out his tobacco and blew a brown paper free of the pack and rolled a cigarette. "The guy's right, too," he said. "Las' night, thinkin' where I'm gonna sleep, I got scared. An' I got thinkin' about my bunk, an' I wonder what the stir-bug[27] I got for a cell mate is doin'. Me an' some guys had a strang band goin'. Good one. Guy said we ought to go on the radio. An' this mornin' I didn' know what time to get up. Jus' laid there waitin' for the bell to go off."

Casy chuckled. "Fella can get so he misses the noise of a saw mill."

The yellowing, dusty, afternoon light put a golden color on the land. The cornstalks looked golden. A flight of swallows swooped overhead toward some waterhole. The turtle in Joad's coat began a new campaign of escape. Joad creased the visor of his cap. It was getting the long protruding curve of a crow's beak now. "Guess I'll mosey along,"[28] he said. "I hate to hit the sun, but it ain't so bad now."

Casy pulled himself together. "I ain't seen ol' Tom in a bug's age,"[29] he said. "I was gonna look in on him anyways. I brang Jesus to your folks for a long time, an' I never took up a collection[30] nor nothin' but a bite to eat."

"Come along," said Joad. "Pa'll be glad to see you. He always said you got too long a pecker for a preacher."[31] He picked up his coat roll and tightened it snugly about his shoes and turtle.

Casy gathered in his canvas sneakers and shoved his bare feet into them. "I ain't got your confidence," he said. "I'm always scared there's wire or glass under the dust. I don't know nothin' I hate so much as a cut toe."

They hesitated on the edge of the shade and then they plunged into the yellow sunlight like two swimmers hastening to get to shore. After a few fast steps they slowed to a gentle, thoughtful pace. The cornstalks threw gray shadows sideways now, and the raw smell of hot dust was in the air. The corn field ended and dark green cotton took its place, dark green leaves through a film of dust, and the bolls forming. It was spotty cotton, thick in the low places where water had stood, and bare on the high places. The plants strove against the sun. And distance, toward the horizon, was tan to invisibility. The dust road stretched out ahead of them, waving up and down. The willows of a stream lined across the west, and to the northwest a fallow section was going back to sparse brush. But the smell of burned dust was in the air, and the air was dry, so that mucus in the nose dried to a crust, and the eyes watered to keep the eyeballs from drying out.

Casy said, "See how good the corn come along until the dust got up. Been a dinger of a crop."[32]

"Ever' year," said Joad. "Ever' year I can remember, we had a good crop comin', an' it never come. Grampa says she was good the first five plowin's,[33] while the wild grass was still in her." The road dropped down a little hill and climbed up another rolling hill.

Casy said, "Ol' Tom's house can't be more'n a mile from here. Ain't she over that third rise?"[34]

"Sure," said Joad. "'Less somebody stole it, like Pa stole it."

"Your pa stole it?"

"Sure, got it a mile an' a half east of here an' drug it.[35] Was a family livin' there, an' they moved away. Grampa an' Pa an' my brother Noah like to took the whole house, but she wouldn' come. They only got part of her. That's why she looks so funny on one end. They cut her in two an' drug her over with twelve head of horses and two mules. They was goin' back for the other half an' stick her together a-gain, but before they got there Wink Manley come with his boys and stole the other half. Pa an' Gramp was pretty sore, but a little later them an' Wink got drunk together an' laughed their heads off about it. Wink, he says his house is at stud,[36] an' if we'll bring our'n over an' breed 'em we'll maybe get a litter of crap houses. Wink was a great ol' fella when he was drunk. After that him an' Pa an' Grampa was friends. Got drunk together ever' chance they got."

"Tom's a great one," Casy agreed. They plodded dustily on down to the bottom of the draw, and then slowed their steps for the rise. Casy wiped his forehead with his sleeve and put on his flat-topped hat again. "Yes," he repeated, "Tom was a great one. For a godless man he was a great one. I seen him in meetin' sometimes when the sperit got into him just a little, an' I seen him take ten-twelve foot jumps.[37] I tell you when ol' Tom got a dose of the Holy Sperit you got to move fast to keep from gettin' run down an' tromped. Jumpy as a stud horse in a box stall."[38]

They topped the next rise and the road dropped into an old water-cut, ugly and raw, a ragged course, and freshet scars cutting into it from both sides. A few stones were in the crossing. Joad minced across in his bare feet. "You talk about Pa," he said. "Maybe you never seen Uncle John the time they baptized him over to Polk's place.[39] Why, he got to plungin' an' jumpin'. Jumped over a feeny bush as big as a piana. Over he'd jump, an' back he'd jump, howlin' like a dog-wolf in moon time. Well, Pa seen him, an' Pa, he figgers he's the bes' Jesus-jumper in these parts. So Pa picks out a feeny bush 'bout twicet as big as Uncle John's feeny bush, and Pa lets out a squawk like a sow litterin' broken bottles, an' he takes a run at that feeny bush an' clears her an' bust his right leg. That took the sperit out of Pa. Preacher wants to pray it set, but Pa says, no, by God, he'd got his heart full of havin' a doctor.[40] Well, they wasn't a doctor, but they was a travelin' dentist, an' he set her. Preacher give her a prayin' over anyways."

They plodded up the little rise on the other side of the water-cut. Now that the sun was on the wane some of its impact was gone, and while the air was hot, the hammering rays were weaker. The strung wire on crooked poles still edged the road. On the right-hand side a line of wire fence strung out across the cotton field, and the dusty green cotton was the same on both sides, dusty and dry and dark green.

Joad pointed to the boundary fence. "That there's our line. We didn't really need no fence there, but we had the wire, an' Pa kinda liked her there. Said it give him a feelin' that forty was forty.[41] Wouldn't of had the fence if Uncle John didn' come drivin' in one night with six spools of wire in his wagon. He give 'em to Pa for a shoat. We never did know where he got that wire." They slowed for the rise, moving their feet in the deep soft dust, feeling the earth with their feet. Joad's eyes were inward on his memory. He seemed to be laughing inside himself. "Uncle John was a crazy bastard," he said. "Like what he done with that shoat." He chuckled and walked on.

Jim Casy waited impatiently. The story did not continue. Casy gave it a good long time to come out. "Well, what'd he do with that shoat?" he demanded at last, with some irritation.

"Huh? Oh!" Well, he killed that shoat right there, an' he got Ma to light up the stove. He cut out pork chops an' put 'em in the pan, an' he put ribs an' a leg in the oven. He et chops till the ribs was done, an' he et ribs till the leg was done. An' then he tore into that leg. Cut off big hunks of her an' shoved 'em in his mouth. Us kids hung around slaverin', an' he give us some, but he wouldn' give Pa none. By an' by he et so much he throwed up an' went to sleep. While he's asleep us kids an' Pa finished off the leg. Well, when Uncle John woke up in the mornin' he slaps another leg in the oven. Pa says, 'John, you gonna eat that whole damn pig?' An' he says, 'I aim to, Tom, but I'm scairt some of her'll spoil 'fore I get her et, hungry as I am for pork. Maybe you better get a plate an' gimme back a couple rolls of wire.' Well, sir, Pa wasn't no fool. He jus' let Uncle John go on an' eat himself sick of pig, an' when he drove off he hadn't et much more'n half. Pa says, 'Whyn't you salt her down?' But not Uncle John; when he wants pig he wants a whole pig, an' when he's through, he don't want no pig hangin' around. So off he goes, and Pa salts down what's left."

Casy said, "While I was still in the preachin' sperit I'd a made a lesson of that an' spoke it to you, but I don't do that no more. What you s'pose he done a thing like that for?"

"I dunno," said Joad. "He jus' got hungry for pork. Makes me hungry jus' to think of it. I had jus' four slices of roastin' pork in four years—one slice ever' Christmas."

Casy suggested elaborately, "Maybe Tom'll kill the fatted calf like for the prodigal in Scripture."[42]

Joad laughed scornfully. "You don't know Pa. If he kills a chicken most of the squawkin' will come from Pa, not the chicken. He don't never learn. He's always savin' a pig for Christmus and then it dies in September of bloat or somepin so you can't eat it. When Uncle John wanted pork he et pork. He had her."

They moved over the curving top of the hill and saw the Joad place below them. And Joad stopped. "It ain't the same," he said. "Looka that house. Somepin's happened. They ain't nobody there." The two stood and stared at the little cluster of buildings.

〔注释〕

Chapter Ⅰ

1. the red country and part of the grey country of Oklahoma：俄克拉何马州位于美国中南部，土壤呈红色，狂风起时，满天风沙，一片灰白色。

2. Texas and Gulf：得克萨斯州与墨西哥湾。

3. rain crust：因雨水而凝结成的坚硬泥块。

Chapter Ⅳ

1. the right of way：通过私人土地的公共通道。

2. a molting chicken，一只脱毛小鸡。

3. Yes, Sir, That's my baby：一首流行歌曲。凯西借用它的曲调，改换歌词，把"这是我的宝贝"改成"这是我的救世主"等。

4. On the level：诚实、可靠。

5. You was all wropped up in Yankin' that pigtail out by the roots：当时，你一个劲地揪着那条辫子，想把它连根揪掉。

6. a Burning Busher：一簇熊熊燃烧的灌木丛。语出《圣经·出埃及记》第3章。

7. Ain't got the call no more：不再担任牧师的职务了。

8. I give 'em a grace：我给他们做了一次感恩祷告。

9. Sling 'em in the irrigation ditch：在灌溉水渠里涤洗他们，指施行洗礼。

10. they'll burn in hell：基督教认为，一个人在世时作了孽，死后就要下地狱受硫磺烈火的煎熬。

11. talkin' in tongues：嘈杂地说话。

12. An' some I'd baptize to bring 'em to：有一些人我给他们受洗礼，使他们甦醒过来。

13. S'cuse me：即 excuse me。

14. the devil did'nt stand a snowball's chance：魔鬼碰不到一点机会。

15. I should of been a preacher：即 I should have been a preacher。

16. Jehovites：基督教的一个派别，相当于 Jehovits，是 Jehovah 的派生词。

17. mule-ass proof against sin：mule-ass 用来加强语气，污秽语。

18. ful up of Jesus：满脑子是耶稣基督的信条。

19. some sisters：某些修女。

20. you can't hold no church：你不能在教堂中任职。

21. Got little hunks of Jesus jumpin' outa my mouth：耶稣基督的片言只语，脱口而出。

22. 'cause：即 because。

23. knock his head plumb to squash：一下子就把他的脑袋砸烂。

24. in po'try：即 in poetry。

25. purty child：即 pretty child。

26. from a drummer：从一个流动小贩那里买来的。

27. the stir-bug：长期坐牢而神经不正常的人。

28. I'll mosey along：我该动身走了。

29. in a bug's age：很长时间。

30. I never took up a collection：我从来没有收过钱。

31. you got too long a pecker for a preacher：你说话太尖锐，当牧师不适合。

32. Being a dinger of a crop：庄稼曾经长得顶呱呱。

33. Grampa says she was good the first five plowin's. 即 Grampa says the land was good the five plowings.

34. Ain't she over that third rise? 翻过第 3 个斜坡不就是那座房子了吗？

35. An' drug it：即 and dragged it。

36. his house is at stud：他的房子象一匹种马，可以用来配种，意思是越来越大。

37. take ten-twelve foot jumps：他蹦得八丈高。

38. in a box stall：单独的马厩。

39. They baptized him over to Polk's place.：即 They baptized him at Polk's place。

40. he'd got his heart full of having a doctor：他执意要请一位医生治疗。

41. Pa kinda liked her there. Said it give him a feelin' that forty was forty：爸爸喜欢在那里没置围栏，这使他感到占有 40 英亩就是 40 英亩，一点也不少。

42. for the prodigal in Scripture：指浪子回头，受到他父亲热烈欢迎的故事。《圣经·路加福音》第 15 章。

THOMAS WOLFE

〔作者介绍〕

托马斯·沃尔夫（Thomas wolfe，1900～1938），美国小说家，生于北卡罗来纳州阿什维尔市。他自幼聪明过人，在中学时代就开始对写作感兴趣。15岁时，沃尔夫入北卡罗来纳大学读书，1920年毕业后赴哈佛大学，在乔治·皮尔斯·贝克尔（George Pierce Baker，1866～1935）的指导下学习戏剧写作，为时3年，获硕士学位。但是由于后来戏剧创作并不成功，他改写小说。1924至1930年间，他在纽约大学教英语，曾赴欧洲旅行，发表了第1部长篇小说《天使望故乡》（*Look Homeward*，*Angel*，1929），这部小说显示他深受德莱塞和乔伊斯的影响。他的第2部小说《时间与河流》（*Of Time and the River*），在某种意义上可以说是前书的续集。此书1935年出版后作者便在纽约定居。1935年至1936年间，他走访美国西海岸和南部以及德国，1937年回家乡阿什维尔。1938年因患脑结核去世。他的其他两部长篇小说《网与石》（*The Web and the Rock*）和《你再也不能回家》（*You Can't Go Home Again*），是从他的遗稿中选编而成的，分别于1939年和1940年出版。沃尔夫的其他著作有《远山》（*The Hills Beyond*，1941），一部短篇小说集及书信集等。

沃尔夫思想丰富，表达流畅，他相信语言的力量，相信艺术的"包容力"。传说他在纽约的住所内不停地写，用卡车把文稿运往编辑那里，编辑于是动手剪贴修整，用出租车送回。这说明沃尔夫的充沛的创造力。他的作品有一种天真发溢的韵味，一种浪漫主义的洒脱情调。沃尔夫的作品多是自传性质；他通过描述和剖析自己的生活经历而窥探他的时代和国家的本质。他在《一部小说的故事》（*The Story of a Novel*，1936）中说，"一切严肃的作品归根结底都应当是自传性的，一个人如想创作出有实在价值的东西，就必须从他自己的生活经历中撷取素材。"他的第一部小说实际上写的是他少年时代同父母兄弟一起生活、最后离家的经历。第2部小说继续第一部的线索，叙述他在哈佛大学读书，在纽约大学任教，赴欧旅行及返回故国的情况。《网与石》和《你再也不能回家》叙述了他的后半生及最后几年的生活。4部书的主人公虽然都已经过作者的艺术加工，但都可以说是他自己的艺术化身。沃尔夫后期注意了素材的取舍和表达的凝练，认识到“艺术品中的一切都经过艺术家的人格力量而变化和改观”，在艺术上达到一个新的高度。

沃尔夫是一个极有抱负的小说家，他要表现的是整个的美国生活。他有些象惠特曼，对美国梦曾满怀信心。在谈论自己的过程中，他发现了美国生活的节奏。随着30年代的经济萧条愈来愈严重，沃尔夫痛苦地认识到，美国也并非他所想象的那样伟大。沃尔夫的作品虽然有时给人一种冗长臃肿的感觉，但有浓郁的抒情意味，他那生动而具体的文字具有一种让读者通过各种感官欣赏事物的色、味、声、状的魅力。在他作品中洋溢着一种内在的活力，这是他能跻身于本世纪主要美国作家行列的重要原因。

The Lost Boy

〔作品介绍〕

《迷惑的孩子》(“The Lost Boy”)写成于30年代中期，首次发表在1937年11月的《红书》(*Red Book*)杂志上，后收入《远山》(*The Hills Beyond*)一书里。故事虽然仍带有自传性质，但反映出作者日渐关心作品的客观性：作者运用了4种富有戏剧性对比性质的叙事角度；过去、现在和永恒相互交织，表明作者对形式愈来愈感兴趣，对对立物的统一的认识也日益深刻。《迷惑的孩子》堪称沃尔夫的代表作。

这里选注的是故事的第1、2两节。

The Lost Boy

I

Light came and went and came again, the booming strokes of three o'clock beat out across the town in thronging bronze from the courthouse bell, light winds of April blew the fountain out in rainbow sheets, until the plume returned and pulsed, as Grover turned into the Square. He was a child, dark-eyed and grave, birthmarked upon his neck—a berry of warm brown—and with a gentle face, too quiet and too listening for his years. The scuffed boy's shoes, the thick-ribbed stockings gartered at the knees, the short knee pants cut straight with three small useless buttons at the side, the sailor blouse, the old cap battered out of shape, perched sideways up on top of the raven head, the old soiled canvas bag slung from the shoulder, empty now, but waiting for the crisp sheets of the afternoon—these friendly, shabby garments, shaped by Grover, uttered him. He turned and passed along the north side of the Square and in that moment saw the union of Forever and of Now.

Light came and went and came again, the great plume of the fountain pulsed and winds of April sheeted it across the Square in a rainbow gossamer of spray. The fire department horses drummed on the floors with wooden stomp, most casually, and with dry whiskings of their clean, coarse tails. The street cars ground into the Square from every portion of the compass and halted briefly like wound toys in their familiar quarter-hourly formula. A dray, hauled by a boneyard nag, rattled across the cobbles on the other side before his father's shop. The courthouse bell boomed out its solemn warning of immediate three, and everything was just the same as it had always been.

He saw that haggis of vexed shapes with quiet eyes—that hodgepodge of ill-sorted architectures that made up the Square, and he did not feel lost. For "Here," thought Grover, "here is the Square as it has always been—and papa's shop, the fire department and the City Hall, the fountain pulsing with its plume, the street cars coming in and halting at the quarter hour, the hardware store on the corner there, the row of old brick buildings on this side of the street, the people passing and the light that comes and changes and that always will come back again, and everything that comes and goes and changes in the Square, and yet will be the same again. And here," the boy thought, "is Grover with his paper bag. Here is old Grover, almost twelve years old. Here is the month of April, 1904. Here is the courthouse bell and three o'clock. Here is Grover on the Square that never changes. Here is Grover, caught upon this point of time."

It seemed to him that the Square, itself the accidental masonry of many years, the chance agglomeration of time and of disrupted strivings, was the center of the universe. It was for him, in his soul's picture, the earth's pivot, the granite core of changelessness, the eternal place where all things came and passed, and yet abode forever and would never change.

He passed the old shack on the corner—the wooden fire-trap where S. Goldberg ran his wiener stand. Then he passed the Singer place[1] next door, with its gleaming display of new machines. He saw them and admired them, but he felt no joy. They brought back to him the busy hum of housework and of women sewing, the intricacy of stitch and weave, the mystery of style and pattern, the memory of women bending over flashing needles, the pedaled tread, the busy whir. It was women's work; it filled him with unknown associations of dullness and of vague depression. And always, also, with a moment's twinge of horror, for his dark eye would always travel toward that needle stitching up and down so fast the eye could never follow it. And then he would remember how his mother once had told him she had driven the needle through her finger, and always, when he passed this place, he would remember it and for a moment crane his neck and turn his head away.

He passed on then, but had to stop again next door before the music store. He always had to stop by places that had shining perfect things in them. He loved hardware stores and windows full of accurate geometric tools. He loved windows full of hammers, saws, and planing boards. He liked windows full of strong new rakes and hoes, with unworn handles, of white perfect wood, stamped hard and vivid with the maker's seal. He loved to see such things as these in the windows of hardware stores. And he would fairly gloat upon them and think that some day he would own a set himself.

Also, he always stopped before the music and piano store. It was a splendid store. And in the window was a small white dog upon his haunches, with head cocked gravely to one side, a small white dog that never moved, that never barked, that listened attentively at the flaring funnel of a horn to hear "His Master's Voice" —a horn forever silent, and a voice that never spoke. And within were many rich and shining shapes of great pianos, an air of splendor and of wealth.

And now, indeed, he *was* caught, held suspended. A waft of air, warm, chocolate-laden, filled his nostrils. He tried to pass the white front of the little eight-foot shop; he paused, struggling with conscience; he could not go on. It was the little candy shop run by old Crocker and his wife. And Grover could not pass.

"Old stingy Crockers!" he thought scornfully. "I'll not go there any more. But—" as the maddening fragrance of rich cooking chocolate touched him once again— "I'll just look in the window and see what they've got." He paused a moment, looking with his dark and quiet eyes into the window of the little candy shop. The window, spotlessly clean, was filled with trays of fresh-made candy. His eyes rested on a tray of chocolate drops. Unconsciously he licked his lips. Put one of them upon your tongue and it just melted there, like honeydew. And then the trays full of rich home-made fudge. He gazed longingly at the deep body of the chocolate fudge, reflectively at maple walnut, more critically, yet with longing, at the mints, the nougatines, and all the other dainties.

"Old stingy Crockers!" Grover muttered once again, and turned to go. "I wouldn't go in *there* again."

And yet he did not go away. "Old stingy Crockers" they might be; still, they did make the best candy in town, the best, in fact, that he had ever tasted.

He looked through the window back into the little shop and saw Mrs. Crocker there. A customer had gone in and had made a purchase, and as Grover looked he saw Mrs. Crocker, with her little wrenny face, her pinched features, lean over and peer primly at the scales. She had a piece of fudge in her clean, bony, little fingers, and as Grover looked, she broke it, primly, in her little bony hands. She dropped a morsel down into the scales. They weighted down alarmingly, and her thin lips tightened. She snatched the piece of fudge out of the scales and broke it carefully once again. This time the scales wavered, went down very slowly, and came back again. Mrs. Crocker carefully put the reclaimed piece of fudge back in the tray, dumped the remainder in a paper bag, folded it and gave it to the customer, counted the money carefully and doled it out into the till, the pennies in one place, the nickels in another.

Grover stood there, looking scornfully. "Old stingy Crocker—afraid that she might give a crumb away!"

He grunted scornfully and again he turned to go. But now Mr. Crocker came out from the little partitioned place where they made all their candy, bearing a tray of fresh-made fudge in his skinny hands. Old Man Crocker rocked along the counter to the front and put it down. He really rocked along. He was a cripple. And like his wife, he was a wrenny, wizened little creature, with bony hands, thin lips, a pinched and meager face. One leg was inches shorter than the other, and on this leg there was an enormous thick-soled boot, with a kind of wooden, rocker-like arrangement, six inches high at least, to make up for the deficiency. On this wooden cradle Mr. Crocker rocked along, with a prim and apprehensive little smile, as if he were afraid he was going to lose something.

"Old stingy Crocker!" muttered Grover. "Humph! He wouldn't give you anything!"

And yet—he did not go away. He hung there curiously, peering through the window, with his dark and gentle face now focused and intent, alert and curious, flattening his nose against the glass. Unconsciously he scratched the thick-ribbed fabric of one stockinged leg with the scuffed and worn toe of his old shoe. The fresh, warm odor of the new-made fudge was delicious. It was a little maddening. Half consciously he began to fumble in one trouser pocket, and pulled out his purse, a shabby worn old black one with a twisted clasp. He opened it and prowled about inside.

What he found was not inspiring—a nickel and two pennies and—he had forgotten them—the stamps. He took the stamps out and unfolded them. There were five twos, eight ones, all that remained of the dollar-sixty-cents' worth which Reed, the pharmacist, had given him for running errands a week or two before.

"Old Crocker," Grover thought, and looked somberly at the grotesque little form as it rocked back into the shop again, around the counter, and up the other side. "Well—" again he looked indefinitely at the stamps in his hand— "he's had all the rest of them. He might as well take these."

So, soothing conscience with this sop of scorn, he went into the shop and stood looking at the trays in the glass case and finally decided. Pointing with a slightly grimy finger at the fresh-made tray of chocolate fudge, he said, "I'll take fifteen cents' worth of this, Mr. Crocker." He paused a moment, fighting with embarrassment, then he lifted his dark face and said quietly, "And please, I'll have to give you stamps again."

Mr. Crocker made no answer. He did not look at Grover. He pressed his lips together primly. He went rocking away and got the candy scoop, came back, slid open the door of the glass case, put fudge into the scoop, and, rocking to the scales, began to weigh the candy out. Grover watched him as he peered and squinted, he watched him purse and press his lips together, he saw him take a piece of fudge and break it in two parts. And then old Crocker broke two parts in two again. He weighed, he squinted, and he hovered, until it seemed to Grover that by calling *Mrs.* Crocker stingy he had been guilty of a rank injustice. But finally, to his vast relief, the job was over, the scales hung there, quivering apprehensively, upon the very hair-line of nervous balance, as if even the scales were afraid that one more move from Old Man Crocker and they would be undone.

Mr. Crocker took the candy then and dumped it in a paper bag and, rocking back along the counter toward the boy, he dryly said: "Where are the stamps?" Grover gave them to him. Mr. Crocker relinquished his claw-like hold upon the bag and set it down upon the counter. Grover took the bag and dropped it in his canvas sack, and then remembered. "Mr. Crocker—" again he felt the old embarrassment that was almost like strong pain— "I gave you too much," Grover said. "There were eighteen cents in stamps. You—you can just give me three ones back."

Mr. Crocker did not answer. He was busy with his bony little hands, unfolding the stamps and flattening them out on top of the glass counter. When he had done so, he peered at them sharply for a moment, thrusting his scrawny neck forward and running his eye up and down, like a bookkeeper who totes up rows of figures.

When he had finished, he said tartly: "I don't like this kind of business. If you want candy, you should have the money for it. I'm not a post office. The next time you come in here and want anything, you'll have to pay me money for it."

Hot anger rose in Grover's throat. His olive face suffused with angry color. His tarry eyes got black and bright. He was on the verge of saying: "Then why did you take my other stamps? Why do you tell me now, when you have taken all the stamps I had, that you don't want them?"

But he was a boy, a boy of eleven years, a quiet, gentle, gravely thoughtful boy, and he had been taught how to respect his elders. So he just stood there looking with his tar-black eyes. Old Man Crocker, pursing at the mouth a little, without meeting Grover's gaze, took the stamps up in his thin, parched fingers and, turning, rocked away with them down to the till.

He took the twos and folded them and laid them in one rounded scallop, then took the ones and folded them and put them in the one next to it. Then he closed the till and started to rock off, down toward the other end. Grover, his face now quiet and grave, kept looking at him, but Mr. Crocker did not look at Grover. Instead he began to take some stamped cardboard shapes and fold them into boxes.

In a moment Grover said, "Mr. Crocker, will you give me the three ones, please?"

Mr. Crocker did not answer. He kept folding boxes, and he compressed his thin lips quickly as he did so. But Mrs. Crocker, back turned to her spouse, also folding boxes with her birdlike hands, muttered: "Hm! *I'd* give him nothing!"

Mr. Crocker looked up, looked at Grover, said, "What are you waiting for?"

"Will you give me the three ones, please?" Grover said.

"I'll give you nothing," Mr. Crocker said.

He left his work and came rocking forward along the counter. "Now you get out of here! Don't you come in here with any more of those stamps," said Mr. Crocker.

"I should like to know where he gets them—that's what I should like to know," said Mrs. Crocker.

She did not look up as she said these words. She inclined her head a little to the side, in Mr. Crocker's direction, and continued to fold the boxes with her bony fingers.

"You get out of here!" said Mr. Crocker. "And don't you come back here with any stamps.... Where did you get those stamps?" he said.

"That's just what *I've* been thinking," Mrs. Crocker said. "*I've* been thinking all along."

"You've been coming in here for the last two weeks with those stamps," said Mr. Crocker. "I don't like the look of it. Where did you get those stamps?" he said.

"That's what *I've* been thinking," said Mrs. Crocker, for a second time.

Grover had got white underneath his olive skin. His eyes had lost their luster. They looked like dull, stunned balls of tar. "From Mr. Reed," he said. "I got the stamps from Mr. Reed." Then he burst out desperately. "Mr. Crocker—Mr. Reed will tell you how I got the stamps. I did some work for Mr. Reed, he gave me those stamps two weeks ago."

"Mr. Reed," said Mrs. Crocker acidly. She did not turn her head. "I call it mighty funny."

"Mr. Crocker," Grover said, "if you'll just let me have three ones-—"

"You get out of here!" cried Mr. Crocker, and he began rocking forward toward Grover. "Now don't you come in here again, boy! There's something funny about this whole business! I don't like the look of it," said Mr. Crocker. "If you can't pay as other people do, then I don't want your trade."

"Mr. Crocker," Grover said again, and underneath the olive skin his face was gray, "if you'll just let me have those three—"

"You get out of here!" Mr. Crocker cried, rocking down toward the counter's end. "If you don't get out, boy—"

"*I'd* call a policeman, that's what I'd do," Mrs. Crocker said.

Mr. Crocker rocked around the lower end of the counter. He came rocking up to Grover. "You get out," he said.

He took the boy and pushed him with his bony little hands, and Grover was sick and gray down to the hollow pit of his stomach.

"You've got to give me those three ones," he said.

"You get out of here!" shrilled Mr. Crocker. He seized the screen door, pulled it open, and pushed Grover out. "Don't you come back in here," he said, pausing for a moment, and working thinly at the lips. He turned and rocked back in the shop again. The screen door slammed behind him. Grover stood there on the pavement. And light came and went and came again into the Square.

The boy stood there, and a wagon rattled past. There were some people passing by, but Grover did not notice them. He stood there blindly, in the watches of the sun, feeling this was Time, this was the center of the universe, the granite core of changelessness, and feeling, this is Grover, this the Square, this is Now.

But something had gone out of day. He felt the overwhelming, soul-sickening guilt that all the children, all the good men of the earth, have felt since Time began. And even anger had died down, had been drowned out, in this swelling tide of guilt, and "This is the Square" — thought Grover as before— "This is Now. There is my father's shop. And all of it is as it has always been—save I."

And the Square reeled drunkenly around him, light went in blind gray motes before his eyes, the fountain sheeted out to rainbow iridescence and returned to its proud, pulsing plume again. But all the brightness had gone out of day, and "Here is the Square, and here is permanence, and here is Time—and all of it is the same as it has always been, save I."

The scuffed boots of the lost boy moved and stumbled blindly. The numb feet crossed the pavement—reached the cobbled street, reached the plotted central square—the grass plots, and the flower beds, so soon to be packed with red geraniums.

"I want to be alone," thought Grover, "where I cannot go near him. . . . Oh God, I hope he never hears, that no one ever tells him—"

The plume blew out, the iridescent sheet of spray blew over him. He passed through, found the other side and crossed the street, and— "Oh God, if papa ever hears!" thought Grover, as his numb feet started up the steps into his father's shop.

He found and felt the steps—the width and thickness of old lumber twenty feet in length. He saw it all—the iron columns on his father's porch, painted with the dull anomalous black-green that all such columns in this land and weather come to; two angels, fly-specked, and the waiting stones. Beyond and all around, in the stonecutter's shop, cold shapes of white and marble, rounded stone, the languid angel with strong marble hands of love.

He went on down the aisle, the white shapes stood around him. He went on to the back of the workroom. This he knew—the little cast-iron stove in left-hand corner, caked, brown, heat-blistered, and the elbow of the long stack running out across the shop; the high and dirty window looking down across the Market Square toward Niggertown; the rude old shelves, plank-boarded, thick, the wood not smooth but pulpy, like the strong hair of an animal; upon the shelves the chisels of all sizes and a layer of stone dust; an emery wheel with pump tread; and a door that let out on the alleyway, yet the alleyway twelve feet below. Here in the room, two trestles of this coarse spiked wood upon which rested gravestones, and at one, his father at work.

The boy looked, saw the name was Creasman: saw the carved analysis of John, the symmetry of the s,[2] the fine sentiment that was being polished off beneath the name and date: "John Creasman, November 7, 1903."

Gant looked up. He was a man of fifty-three, gaunt-visaged, mustache cropped, immensely long and tall and gaunt. He wore good dark clothes—heavy, massive—save he had no coat. He worked in shirt-sleeves with his vest on, a strong watch chain stretching across his vest, wing collar and black tie, Adam's apple, bony forehead, bony nose, light eyes, gray-green, undeep and cold, and, somehow, lonely-looking, a striped apron going up around his shoulders and starched cuffs. And in one hand a tremendous rounded wooden mallet like a butcher's bole; and in his other hand, a strong cold chisel.

"How are you, son?"

He did not look up as he spoke. He spoke quietly, absently. He worked upon the chisel and the wooden mallet, as a jeweler might work on a watch, except that in the man and in the wooden mallet there was power too.

"What is it, son?" he said.

He moved around the table from the head, started up on "J" once again.

"Papa, I never stole the stamps," said Grover.

Gant put down the mallet, laid the chisel down. He came around the trestle.

"What?" he said.

As Grover winked his tar-black eyes, they brightened, the hot tears shot out. "I never stole the stamps," he said.

"Hey? What is this?" his father said. "What stamps?"

"That Mr. Reed gave me, when the other boy was sick and I worked there for three days.... And Old Man Crocker," Grover said, "he took all the stamps. And I told him Mr. Reed had given them to me. And now he owes me three ones—and Old Man Crocker says he don't believe that they were mine. He says—he says—that I must have taken them somewhere," Grover blurted out.

"The stamps that Reed gave you—hey?" the stonecutter said. "The stamps you had—" He wet his thumb upon his lips, threw back his head and slowly swung his gaze around the ceiling, then turned and strode quickly from his workshop out into the storeroom.

Almost at once he came back again, and as he passed the old gray painted-board partition of his office he cleared his throat and wet his thumb and said, "Now, I tell you—"

Then he turned and strode up toward the front again and cleared his throat and said, "I tell you now—" He wheeled about and started back, and as he came along the aisle between the marshaled rows of gravestones he said beneath his breath, "By God, now—"

He took Grover by the hand and they went out flying. Down the aisle they went by all the gravestones, past the fly-specked angels waiting there, and down the wooden steps and across the Square. The fountain pulsed, the plume blew out in sheeted iridescence, and it swept across them; an old gray horse, with a peaceful look about his torn lips, swucked up the cool mountain water from the trough as Grover and his father went across the Square, but they did not notice it.

They crossed swiftly to the other side in a direct line to the candy shop. Gant was still dressed in his long striped apron, and he was still holding Grover by the hand. He opened the screen door and stepped inside.

"Give him the stamps," Gant said.

Mr. Crocker came rocking forward behind the counter, with the prim and careful look that now was somewhat like a smile. "It was just—" he said.

"Give him the stamps," Gant said, and threw some coins down on the counter.

Mr. Crocker rocked away and got the stamps. He came rocking back. "I just didn't know—" he said.

The stonecutter took the stamps and gave them to the boy. And Mr. Crocker took the coins.

"It was just that—" Mr. Crocker began again, and smiled.

Gant cleared his throat: "You never were a father," he said. "You never knew the feelings of a father, or understood the feelings of a child; and that is why you acted as you did. But a judgment is upon you. God has cursed you. He has afflicted you. He has made you lame and childless as you are—and lame and childless, miserable as you are, you will go to your grave and be forgotten!"

And Crocker's wife kept kneading her bony little hands and said, imploringly, "Oh, no—oh don't say that, please don't say that."

The stonecutter, the breath still hoarse in him, left the store, still holding the boy tightly by the hand. Light came again into the day.

"Well, son," he said, and laid his hand on the boy's back. "Well, son," he said, "now don't you mind."

They walked across the Square, the sheeted spray of iridescent light swept out on them, the horse swizzled at the water-trough, and "Well, son," the stonecutter said.

And the old horse sloped down, ringing with his hoofs upon the cobblestones.

"Well, son," said the stonecutter once again, "be a good boy."

And he trod his own steps then with his great stride and went back again into his shop.

The lost boy stood upon the Square, hard by the porch of his father's shop.

"This is Time," thought Grover. "Here is the Square, here is my father's shop, and here am I."

And light came and went and came again—but now not quite the same as it had done before. The boy saw the pattern of familiar shapes and knew that they were just the same as they had always been. But something had gone out of day, and something had come in again. Out of the vision of those quiet eyes some brightness had gone, and into their vision had come some deeper color. He could not say, he did not know through what transforming shadows life had passed within that quarter hour. He only knew that something had been lost—something forever gained.[3]

Just then a buggy curved out through the Square, and fastened to the rear end was a poster, and it said "St. Louis" and "Excursion" and "The Fair."

Ⅱ THE MOTHER

As we went down through Indiana—you were too young, child, to remember it—but I always think of all of you the way you looked that morning, when we went down through Indiana, going to the Fair. All of the apple trees were coming out, and it was April; it was the beginning of spring in southern Indiana and everything was getting green. Of course we don't have farms at home like those in Indiana. The children had never seen such farms as those, and I reckon, kidlike, they had to take it in.

So all of them kept running up and down the aisle—well, no, except for you and Grover. *You* were too young, Eugene. You were just three, I kept you with me. As for Grover—well, I'm going to tell you about that.

But the rest of them kept running up and down the aisle and from one window to another. They kept calling out and hollering to each other every time they saw something new. They kept trying to look out on all sides, in every way at once, as if they wished they had eyes at the back of their heads. It was the first time any of them had ever been in Indiana, and I reckon that it all seemed strange and new.

And so it seemed they could't get enough. It seemed they never could be still. They kept running up and down and back and forth, hollering and shouting to each other, until— "I'll vow! You children! I never saw the beat of you!" I said. "The way that you keep running up and down and back and forth and never can be quiet for a minute beats all I ever saw," I said.

You see, they were excited about going to St. Louis, and so curious over everything they saw. They couldn't help it, and they wanted to see everything. But— "I'll vow!" I said. "If you children don't sit down and rest you'll be worn to a frazzle before we ever get to see St. Louis and the Fair!"

Except for Grover! He—no, sir! not him. Now, boy, I want to tell you—I've raised the lot of you—and if I do say so, there wasn't a numbskull in the lot. But *Grover*! Well, you've all grown up now, all of you have gone away, and none of you are children any more.... And of course, I hope that, as the fellow says, you have reached the dignity of man's estate. I suppose you have the judgment of grown men.... But *Grover*! *Grover* had it even then!

Oh, even as a child, you know—at a time when I was almost afraid to trust the rest of you out of my sight—I could depend on Grover. He could go anywhere, I could send him anywhere, and I'd always know he'd get back safe, and do exactly what I told him to!

Why, I didn't even have to tell him. You could send that child to market and tell him what you wanted, and he'd come home with *twice* as much as you could get yourself for the same money!

Now you know, I've always been considered a good trader. But *Grover*! —why, it got so finally that I wouldn't even tell him. Your papa said to me: "You'd be better off if you'd just tell him what you want and leave the rest to him. For," your papa says, "damned if I don't believe he's a better trader than you are. He gets more for the money than anyone I ever saw."

Well, I had to admit it, you know. I had to own up then. Grover, even as a child, was a far better trader than I was.... Why, yes, they told it on him all over town, you know. They said all of the market men, all of the farmers, knew him. They'd begin to laugh when they saw him coming—they'd say: "Look out! Here's Grover! Here's one trader you're not going to fool!"

And they were right! *That* child! I'd say, "Grover, suppose you run uptown and see if they've got anything good to *eat* today"—and I'd jus t wink at him, you know, but he'd know what I meant. I wouldn't let on that I *wanted* anything exactly, but I'd say, "Now it just occurs to me that some good fresh stuff may be coming in from the country, so suppose you take this dollar and just see what you can do with it."

Well, sir, that was all that was needed. The minute you told that child that you depended on his judgment, he'd have gone to the ends of the earth for you—and, let me tell you something, he wouldn't *miss*, either!

His eyes would get as black as coals—oh! the way that child would look at you, the intelligence and sense in his expression. He'd say: "Yes, *ma'am*! Now don't you worry, mama. You leave it all to me—and I'll do *good*!" said Grover.

And he'd be off like a streak of lightning and—oh Lord! As your father said to me, "I've been living in this town for almost thirty years," he said— "I've seen it grow up from a crossroads village, and I thought I knew everything there was to know about it—but that child—" your papa says— "he knows places that I never heard of!"... Oh, he'd go right down there to that place below your papa's shop where the draymen and the country people used to park their wagons—or he'd go down there to those old lots on Concord Street where the farmers used to keep their wagons. And, child that he was, he'd go right in among them, sir—*Grover* would! —go right in and barter with them like a grown man!

And he'd come home with things he'd bought that would make your eyes stick out. . . . Here he comes one time with another boy, dragging a great bushel basket full of ripe termaters[4] between them. "Why, Grover!" I says. "How on earth are we ever going to use them? Why they'll go bad on us before we're half way through with them," "Well, mama," he says, "I know—" oh, just as solemn as a judge— "but they were the last the man had," he says, "and he wanted to go home, and so I got them for ten cents," he says. "They were so cheap," said Grover, "I thought it was a shame to let 'em go, and I figgered that what we couldn't eat—why," says Grover, "you could *put up*!" Well, the way he said it—so earnest and so serious—I had to laugh. "But I'll vow!" I said. "If you don't beat all!". . . But that was *Grover*! —the way he was in *those* days! As everyone said, boy that he was, he had the sense and judgment of a grown man. . . . Child, child, I've seen you all grow up, and all of you were bright enough. There were no half-wits in *my* family. But for all-round intelligence, judgment, and general ability, Grover surpassed the whole crowd. I've never seen his equal, and everyone who knew him as a child will say the same.

So that's what I tell them now when they ask me about all of you. I have to tell the truth. I always said that *you* were smart enough, Eugene—but when they come around and brag to me about you, and about how you have got on and have a kind of name—I don't let on, you know. I just sit there and let them talk. I don't brag on you—if *they* want to brag on you, that's *their* business. I never bragged on one of my own children in my life. When father raised us up, we were all brought up to believe that it was not good breeding to brag about your kin. "If the others want to do it," father said, "well, let *them* do it, Don't ever let on by a word or sign that you know what they are talking about. Just let *them* do the talking, and say nothing."

So when they come around and tell me all about the things *you've* done—I don't let on to them, I never say a word. Why yes! —why, here, you know—oh, along about a month or so ago, this feller comes—a well-dressed man, you know—he looked intelligent, a good substantial sort of person. He said he came from New Jersey, or somewhere up in that part of the country, and he began to ask me all sorts of questions—

what you were like when you were a boy, and all such stuff as that.

I just pretended to study it all over and then I said, "Well, yes"— real serious-like, you know— "well, yes—I reckon I ought to know a little something about him. Eugene was my child, just the same as all the others were. I brought him up just the way I brought up all the others. And," I says—oh, just as solemn as you please— "he wasn't a *bad* sort of a boy. Why," I says, "up to the time that he was twelve years old he was just about the same as any other boy—a good, average, normal sort of fellow."

"Oh," he says, "But didn't you notice something? Wasn't there something kind of strange?" he says— "something different from what you noticed in the other children?"

I didn't let on, you know—I just took it all in and looked as solemn as an owl—I just pretended to study it all over, just as serious as you please.

"Why no," I says, real slow-like, after I'd studied it all over. "As I remember it, he was a good, ordinary, normal sort of boy, just like all the others."

"Yes," he says—oh, all excited-like, you know— "But didn't you notice how brilliant he was? Eugene must have been more brilliant than the rest!"

"Well, now," I says, and pretended to study that all over too. "Now let me see.... Yes," I says—I just looked him in the eye, as solemn as you please— "he did pretty well.... Well, yes," I says, "I guess he was a fairly bright sort of a boy. I never had no complaints to make of him on that score. He was bright enough," I says. "The only trouble with him was that he was lazy."

"Lazy!" he says—oh, you should have seen the look upon his face, you know—he jumped like someone had stuck a pin in him. "Lazy!" he says. "Why, you don't mean to tell me—"

"Yes," I says—oh, I never cracked a smile— "I was telling him the same thing myself the last time that I saw him. I told him it was a mighty lucky thing for him that he had the gift of gab. Of course, he went off to college and read a lot of books, and I reckon that's where he got this flow of language they say he has. But as I said to him the last time that I saw him: 'Now look a-here,' I said. 'If you can earn your living doing a light, easy class of work like this you do,' I says, 'you're mighty lucky, because none of the rest of your people,' I says, 'had any such luck as that. They had to work hard for a living,'"

Oh, I told him, you know. I came right out with it. I made no bones about it. And I tell you what—I wish you could have seen his face. It was a study.[5]

"Well," he says, at last, "you've got to admit this, haven't you—he was the brightest boy you had, now wasn't he?"

I just looked at him a moment. I had to tell the truth. I couldn't fool him any longer. "No", I says. "He was a good, bright boy—I got no complaint to make about him on that score—but the brightest boy I had, the one that surpassed all the rest of them in sense, and understanding, and in judgment—the best boy I had—the smartest boy I ever saw—was—well, it wasn't Eugene," I said. "It was another one."

He looked at me a moment, then he said, "Which boy was that?"

Well, I just looked at him, and smiled. I shook my head, you know. I wouldn't tell him. "I never brag about my own," I said. "You'll have to find out for yourself."

But—I'll have to tell *you*—and you know yourself, I brought the whole crowd up, I knew you all. And you can take my work for it—the best one of the lot was—*Grover*!

And when I think of Grover as he was along about that time, I always see him sitting there, so grave and earnest-like, with his nose pressed to the window, as we went down through Indiana in the morning, to the Fair.

All through that morning we were going down along beside the Wabash River—the Wabash River flows through Indiana, it is the river that they wrote the song about—so all that morning we were going down along the river. And I sat with all you children gathered about me as we went down through Indiana, going to St. Louis, to the Fair.

And Grover sat there, so still and earnest-like, looking out the window, and he didn't move. He sat there like a man. He was just eleven and a half years old, but he had more sense, more judgment and more understanding than any child I ever saw.

So here he sat beside this gentleman and looked out the window. I never knew the man—I never asked his name—but I tell you what! He was certainly a finelooking, well-dressed, good, substantial sort of man, and I could see that he had taken a great liking to Grover. And Grover sat there looking out, and then turned to this gentleman, as grave and earnest as a grown-up man, and says, "What kind of crops grow here, sir?" Well, this gentleman threw his head back and just hah-hahed. "Well, I'll see if I can tell you," says this gentleman, and then, you know, he talked to him, they talked together, and Grover took it all in, as solemn as you please, and asked this gentleman every sort of question—what the trees were, what was growing there, how big the farms were—all sorts of questions, which this gentleman would answer, until I said: "Why, I'll vow, Grover! You shouldn't ask so many questions. You'll bother the very life out of this gentleman."

The gentleman threw his head back and laughed right out. "Now you leave that boy alone. He's all right," he said. "He doesn't bother me a bit, and if I know the answers to his questions I will answer him. And if I don't know, why, then, I'll tell him so. But he's *all right*," he said, and put his arm around Grover's shoulders. "You leave him alone. He doesn't bother me a bit."

And I can still remember how he looked that morning, with his black eyes, his black hair, and with the birthmark on his neck—so grave, so serious, so earnest-like—as he sat by the train window and watched thd apple trees, the farms, the barns, the houses, and the orchards, taking it all in, I reckon, because it was strange and new to him.

It was so long ago, but when I think of it, it all comes back, as if it happened yesterday. Now all of you have either died or grown up and gone away, and nothing is the same as it was then. But all of you were there with me that morning and I guess I should remember how the others looked, but somehow I don't. Yet I can still see Grover just the way he was, the way he looked that morning when we went down through Indiana, by the river, to the Fair.

〔注释〕

1. the Singer place："胜家"缝纫厂。"胜家"是美国名牌缝纫机。

2. the carved analysis of John, the symmetry of the S：指名字"John creasman"中"John"的4个字母刻在石上分开的样子，Creasman中的字母"S"的上下对称状。

3. something had been lost—something forever gained：指失去了童稚，孩子成熟起来。

4. termaters＝tomatoes.

5. It was a study：这张脸的表情值得琢磨。

KATHERINE ANNE PORTER

〔作者介绍〕

凯瑟琳·安·波特(Katherine Anne Porter, 1890～1980),美国杰出的小说家,评论界公认的文体家,以写短篇小说著称。波特生于德克萨斯州印第安河市一个声名显赫的天主教家庭,两岁丧母,由祖母抚养成人,后就读于汤姆逊寄宿学校。她16岁时结婚,1910年皈依天主教。第一次世界大战期间,她担任报社记者,后来访问过墨西哥和德国等国,于1937年回美国定居。1922年波特发表第一篇短篇小说,开始写作生涯。她虽未受过高等教育,但被许多大学授予荣誉学位并被邀请去讲学。1958年她继美国著名作家威廉·福克纳之后被聘为弗吉尼亚大学的驻校作家。波特的两次婚姻均以离异告终。她曾坦率地解释道:“他们无法和我一起生活,因为我是作家,不论过去还是现在,写作总是占第一位的。”

波特是个严肃的作家。她一生中虽只发表过27篇中篇和短篇小说、一部长篇小说、一部文学评论集和一部回忆录,但质量俱佳,很受赞赏。她曾先后获得欧·亨利奖、普利策奖、全国图书奖,1976年荣获美国国家文学艺术学院颁发的小说金质奖。在文学评论集《过去的日子》(*The Days Before*)中,波特谈到自己的创作意图时说:“我一向致力于发现和了解人的动机和感情,并将我的心灵所能感受到的人际关系和人的经历加以提炼。…我热切地关注着那些生活在迁徙和灾难中的人们,没有这一个个的人,一切‘广阔的历史运动’便不可能发生。”正是出于对历史的创造者人民的热爱,波特把研究和反映人的思想感情及社会生活作为自己的首要任务。她的一些作品,如相互连接的米兰达的故事,以她熟悉的美国南方为背景,通过米兰达姑娘的遭遇,展现南方家庭的历史和南方社会的风貌。她也写过关于爱尔兰人和墨西哥人的故事,表现人类共同的情感。

波特的作品具有一定的思想深度。她力图表现新旧秩序的冲突、传统与变革的矛盾以及人的理想与现实的矛盾,揭示现代“荒原”中存在的问题——

人无法按照自己的梦想去生活。波特作品的主人公多为女性，她们由于受到男性统治社会的不公正待遇，或隐遁，或抗争。波特唯一的长篇小说《愚人船》(*Ship of Fools*)更是一部深刻的作品。她于1940年开始写作《愚人船》，至1962年小说出版，共花去22年。其间评论界和读者只是断断续续地从杂志上读到一些章节片断。小说问世后，评论界反应强烈，总的说来褒多于贬。该书还被改编成电影，并被译成17种文字。《愚人船》以作者1931年访问德国见到纳粹势力兴起的经历为依据，描写一艘由墨西哥开往德国的客船上形形色色乘客的故事。作品通过众多的人物揭示了20世纪西方社会中人的劣根性，并指出这正是滋生纳粹主义的土壤。由于小说披露了人的缺点，有评论家认为作者有厌恶人类的倾向，然而波特在前言中已明确指出，她本人也是乘客之一。她还强调说，她的小说讲的是西方文明逐日衰落的情况。波特的作品也具有很高的艺术性。她的创作态度十分严谨，对每篇作品都要字斟句酌，反复修改，绝不轻易发表。她的每一篇小说都是融题材、结构、语言和风格于一体的完美的艺术品。波特善于细致地描写和分析人物的内心活动和感情变化，在一些作品中还成功地运用了意识流手法。她从不轻易使用象征手法，但用时则恰到好处。她的文笔简洁优美，表现力强，没有丝毫斧凿的痕迹。由于这些成就，波特被誉为优秀的文体家。

波特的主要作品包括：短篇小说集《开花的犹大树》(*Flowering Judas*, 1930)和《斜塔及其它》(*The Leaning Tower and Other Stories*, 1945)、中篇小说集《灰色骑士灰色马》(*Pale Horse, Pale Rider*, 1939)，长篇小说《愚人船》(*Ship of Fools*, 1962)、文学评论集《过去的日子》(*The Days Before*, 1953)和回忆录《千古奇冤》(*The Never-Ending Wrong*, 1977)。

Flowering Judas

〔**作品介绍**〕

《开花的犹大树》(“Flowering Judas”)是波特的早期作品，收在1930年出版的短篇小说集《开花的犹大树》中。故事以20世纪初民主革命时期的墨西哥为背景，以作者1918至1921年间在墨西哥学习艺术并参与革命运动的经历为基础。

墨西哥的资产阶级民主革命始于1901年，持续到1970年。革命势力推翻波菲里奥·迪亚斯的统治后，制定了宪法，建立起新的社会，从1921年起实行土地、经济、金融、文教等方面的改革。不幸的是，从革命开始直到1928

年始终存在内部分裂的问题，曾发生多起军事叛乱。《开花的犹大树》的故事就发生在20年代。

美国姑娘劳拉是个纯洁、正直、充满幻想的天主教徒。她被卷入墨西哥革命的浪潮之中，自愿帮助革命者做了许多工作，但在思想深处却感到与周围的一切格格不入。她力图抛弃对天主教的信仰，却又找不到坚定的新信仰来代替。她厌恶自私自利、冷酷无情的革命领导人布拉焦尼，痛恨革命队伍中的弊端。当发现自己的理想和现实之间有着不可逾越的鸿沟时，劳拉痛苦地感到生活背叛了她。出于对革命前途和个人前途的恐惧，她采取了自我抑制的态度，拒绝同一切人交往，以保护自己。她对另一位革命者欧亨尼奥同情眷恋，但又未能阻止他吞服自己送去的安眠药自杀。作者通过对劳拉的梦境的描写，揭示出她那被压抑的感情和因自己背叛同志而内疚自责的心情。

故事的另一主要人物布拉焦尼是个脑满肠肥、腐化堕落的机会主义分子。他借革命以营私，背叛妻子，背叛同志，也背叛了革命的宗旨。

作者在不长的篇幅里集中表现不同人物在不同层次上的背叛，主题突出，含蓄凝炼。作者以开花的犹大树作为象征，运用《圣经》中犹大背叛耶稣的典故表现主题，恰到好处，也增加了讽刺意味。这篇作品对主题挖掘深刻，人物性格刻划细致，语言优美，被誉为20世纪以来的美国优秀短篇小说之一。

Flowering Judas

Braggioni sits heaped upon the edge of a straight-backed chair much too small for him, and sings to Laura in a furry, mournful voice. Laura has begun to find reasons for avoiding her own house until the latest possible moment, for Braggioni is there almost every night. No matter how late she is, he will be sitting there with a surly, waiting expression, pulling at his kinky yellow hair, thumbing the strings of his guitar, snarling a tune under his breath.[1] Lupe the Indian maid meets Laura at the door, and says with a flicker of a glance towards the upper room, "He waits."

Laura wishes to lie down, she is tired of her hairpins and the feel of her long tight sleeves, but she says to him, "Have you a new song for me this evening?" If he says yes, she asks him to sing it. If the says no, she remembers his favorite one, and asks him to sing it again. Lupe brings her a cup of chocolate and a plate of rice, and Laura eats at the small table under the lamp, first inviting Braggioni, whose answer is always the same: "I have eaten, and besides, chocolate thickens the voice."

Laura says, "Sing, then," and Braggioni heaves himself into song. He scratches the guitar familiarly as though it were a pet animal, and sings passionately off key, taking the high notes in a prolonged painful squeal. Laura, who haunts the markets listening to the ballad singers, and stops every day to hear the blind boy playing his reed-flute in Sixteenth of September Street,[2] listens to Braggioni with pitiless courtesy, because she dares not smile at his miserable performance. Nobody dares to smile at him. Braggioni is cruel to everyone, with a kind of specialized insolence, but he is so vain of his talents, and so sensitive to slights, it would require a cruelty and vanity greater than his own to lay a finger on the vast cureless wound of his self-esteem. It would require courage, too, for it is dangerous to offend him, and nobody has this courage.

Braggioni loves himself with such tenderness and amplitude and eternal charity that his followers—for he is a leader of men, a skilled revolutionist, and his skin has been punctured in horrible warfare—warm themselves in the reflected glow,[3] and say to each other: "He has a real nobility, a love of humanity raised above mere personal affections." The excess of this self-love has flowed out, inconveniently for her, over Laura, who, with so many others, owes her comfortable situation and her salary to him. When he is in a very good humor, he tells her, "I am tempted to forgive you for being a *gringa*. *Gringita*!"[4] and Laura, burning, imagines herself leaning forward suddenly, and with a sound back-handed slap wiping the suety smile[5] from his face. If he notices her eyes at these moments he gives no sign.

She knows what Braggioni would offer her, and she must resist tenaciously without appearing to resist, and if she could avoid it she would not admit even to herself the slow drift of his intention. During these long evenings which have spoiled a long month for her, she sits in her deep chair with an open book on her knees, resting her eyes on the consoling rigidity of the printed page when the sight and sound of Braggioni singing threaten to identify themselves with all her remembered afflictions and to add their weight to her uneasy premonitions of the future. The gluttonous bulk of Braggioni has become a symbol of her many disillusions, for a revolutionist should be lean, animated by heroic faith, a vessel of abstract virtues. This is nonsense, she knows it now and is ashamed of it. Revolution must have leaders, and leadership is a career for energetic men. She is, her comrades tell her, full of romantic error, for what she defines as cynicism in them is merely "a developed sense of reality." She is almost too willing to say, "I am wrong, I suppose I don't really understand the principles," and afterward she makes a secret truce with herself, determined not to surrender her will to such expedient logic. But she cannot help feeling that she has been betrayed irreparably by the disunion between her way of living and her feeling of what life should be,[6] and at times she is almost contented to rest in this sense of grievance as a private source of consolation. Sometimes she wishes to run away, but she stays. Now she longs to fly out of this room, down the narrow stairs, and into the street where the houses lean together like conspirators under a single mottled lamp, and leave Braggioni singing to himself.

Instead she looks at Braggioni, frankly and clearly, like a good child who understands the rules of behavior. Her knees cling together under sound blue serge, and her round white collar is not purposely nunlike. She wears the uniform of an idea, and has renounced vanities. She was born Roman Catholic, and in spite of her fear of being seen by someone who might make a scandal of it, she slips now and again into some crumbling little church, kneels on the chilly stone, and says a Hail Mary[7] on the gold rosary she bought in Tehuantepec.[8] It is no good and she ends by examining the altar with its tinsel flowers and ragged brocades, and feels tender about the battered doll-shape of some male saint whose white, lace-trimmed drawers hang limply around his ankles below the hieratic dignity of his velvet robe. She has encased herself in a set of principles derived from her early training, leaving no detail of gesture or of personal taste untouched, and for this reason she will not wear lace made on machines. This is her private heresy, for in her special group the machine is sacred, and will be the salvation of the workers. She loves fine lace, and there is a tiny edge of fluted cobweb[9] on this collar, which is one of twenty precisely alike, folded in blue tissue paper in the upper drawer of her clothes chest.

Braggioni catches her glance solidly as if he had been waiting for it, leans forward, balancing his paunch between his spread knees, and sings with tremendous emphasis, weighing his words. He has, the song relates, no father and no mother, nor even a friend to console him; lonely as a wave of the sea he comes and goes, lonely as a wave. His mouth opens round and yearns sideways, his balloon cheeks grow oily with the labor of song. He bulges marvelously in his expensive garments. Over his lavender collar, crushed upon a purple necktie, held by a diamond hoop: over his ammunition belt of tooled leather worked in silver, buckled cruelly around his gasping middle: over the tops of his glossy yellow shoes Braggioni swells with ominous ripeness, his mauve silk hose stretched taut, his ankles bound with the stout leather thongs of his shoes.

When he stretches his eyelids at Laura she notes again that his eyes are the true tawny yellow cat's eyes. He is rich, not in money, he tells her, but in power, and this power brings with it the blameless ownership of things, and the right to indulge his love of small luxuries. "I have a taste for the elegant refinements," he said once, flourishing a yellow silk handkerchief before her nose. "Smell that? It is Jockey Club,[10] imported from New York." Nonetheless he is wounded by life. He will say so presently. "It is true everything turns to dust in the hand, to gall on the tongue." He sighs and his leather belt creaks like a saddle girth. "I am disappointed in everything as it comes. Everything." He shakes his head. "You, poor thing, you will be disappointed too. You are born for it. We are more alike than you realize in some things. Wait and see. Some day you will remember what I have told you, you will know that Braggioni was your friend."

Laura feels a slow chill, a purely physical sense of danger, a warning in her blood that violence, mutilation, a shocking death, wait for her with lessening patience. She has translated this fear into something homely, immediate, and sometimes hesitates before crossing the street. "My personal fate is nothing, except as testimony of a mental attitude," she reminds herself, quoting from some forgotten philosophic primer, and is sensible enough to add, "Anyhow, I shall not be killed by an automobile if I can help it."

"It may be true I am as corrupt, in another way, as Braggioni," she thinks in spite of herself, "as callous, as incomplete," and if this is so, any kind of death seems preferable. Still she sits quietly, she does not run. Where could she go? Uninvited she has promised herself to this place; she can no longer imagine herself as living in another country, and there is no pleasure in remembering her life before she came here.

Precisely what is the nature of this devotion, its true motives, and what are its obligations? Laura cannot say. She spends part of her days in Xochimilco,[11] near by, teaching Indian children to say in English, "The cat is on the mat." When she appears in the classroom they crowd about her with smiles on their wise, innocent, clay-colored faces, crying, "Good morning my ticher!"[12] in immaculate voices, and they make of her desk a fresh garden of flowers every day.

During her leisure she goes to union meetings and listens to busy important voices quarreling over tactics, methods, internal politics. She visits the prisoners of her own political faith in their cells, where they entertain themselves with counting cockroaches, repenting of their indiscretions, composing their memoirs, writing out manifestoes and plans for their comrades who are still walking about free, hands in pockets, sniffing fresh air. Laura brings them food and cigarettes and a little money, and she brings messages disguised in equivocal phrases from the men outside who dare not set foot in the prison for fear of disappearing into the cells kept empty for them. If the prisoners confuse night and day, and complain, "Dear little Laura, time doesn't pass in this infernal hole, and I won't know when it is time to sleep unless I have a reminder," she brings them their favorite narcotics, and says in a tone that does not wound them with pity, "Tonight will really be night for you," and though her Spanish amuses them, they find her comforting, useful. If they lose patience and all faith, and curse the slowness of their friends in coming to their rescue with money and influence, they trust her not to repeat everything, and if she inquires, "Where do you think we can find money, or influence?" they are certain to answer, "Well, there is Braggioni, why doesn't he do something?"

She smuggles letters from headquarters to men hiding from firing squads in back streets in mildewed houses, where they sit in tumbled beds and talk bitterly as if all Mexico were at their heels, when Laura knows positively they might appear at the band concert in the Alameda[13] on Sunday morning, and no one would notice them. But Braggioni says, "Let them sweat a little. The next time they may be careful. It is very restful to have them out of the way for a while." She is not afraid to knock on any door in any street after midnight, and enter in the darkness, and say to one of these men who is really in danger: "They will be looking for you—seriously—tomorrow morning after six. Here is some money from Vincente.[14] Go to Vera Cruz[15] and wait."

She borrows money from the Roumanian agitator to give to his bitter enemy the Polish agitator. The favor of Braggioni is their disputed territory,[16] and Braggioni holds the balance nicely, for he can use them both. The Polish agitator talks love to her over café tables, hoping to exploit what he believes is her secret sentimental preference for him, and he gives her misinformation which he begs her to repeat as the solemn truth to certain persons. The Roumanian is more adroit. He is generous with his money in all good causes, and lies to her with an air of ingenuous candor, as if he were her good friend and confidant. She never repeats anything they may say. Braggioni never asks questions. He has other ways to discover all that he wishes to know about them.

Nobody touches her, but all praise her gray eyes, and the soft, round under lip which promises gayety, yet is always grave, nearly always firmly closed: and they cannot understand why she is in Mexico. She walks back and forth on her errands, with puzzled eyebrows, carrying her little folder of drawings and music and school papers. No dancer dances more beautifully than Laura walks, and she inspires some amusing, unexpected ardors, which cause little gossip, because nothing comes of them. A young captain who had been a soldier in Zapata's[17] army attempted, during a horseback ride near Cuernavaca,[18] to express his desire for her with the noble simplicity befitting a rude folk-hero: but gently, because he was gentle. This gentleness was his defeat, for when he alighted, and removed her foot from the stirrup, and essayed to draw her down into his arms, her horse, ordinarily a tame one, shied fiercely, reared and plunged away. The young hero's horse careered blindly after his stable-mate, and the hero did not return to the hotel until rather late that evening. At breakfast he came to her table in full charro[19] dress, gray buckskin jacket and trousers with strings of silver buttons down the leg, and he was in a humorous, careless mood. "May I sit with you?" and "You are a wonderful rider. I was terrified that you might be thrown and dragged. I should never have forgiven myself. But I cannot admire you enough for your riding!"

"I learned to ride in Arizona," said Laura.

"If you will ride with me again this morning, I promise you a horse that will not shy with you," he said. But Laura remembered that she must return to Mexico City at noon.

Next morning the children made a celebration and spent their playtime writing on the blackboard, "We lov ar ticher,"[20] and with tinted chalks they drew wreaths of flowers around the words. The young hero wrote her a letter: "I am a very foolish, wasteful, impulsive man. I should have first said I love you, and then you would not have run away. But you shall see me again." Laura thought, "I must send him a box of colored crayons," but she was trying to forgive herself for having spurred her horse at the wrong moment.[21]

A brown, shock-haired youth came and stood in her patio one night and sang like a lost soul for two hours, but Laura could think of nothing to do about it. The moonlight spread a wash of gauzy silver over the clear spaces of the garden, and the shadows were cobalt blue. The scarlet blossoms of the Judas tree[22] were dull purple, and the names of the colors repeated themselves automatically in her mind, while she watched not the boy, but his shadow, fallen like a dark garment across the fountain rim, trailing in the water. Lupe came silently and whispered expert counsel in her ear: "If you will throw him one little flower, he will sing another song or two and go away." Laura threw the flower, and he sang a last song and went away with the flower tucked in the band of his hat. Lupe said, "He is one of the organizers of the Typographers Union, and before that he sold corridos[23] in the Merced market,[24] and before that, he came from Guanajuato, where I was born. I would not trust any man, but I trust least those from Guanajuato."[25]

She did not tell Laura that he would be back again the next night and the next, or that he would follow her at a certain fixed distance around the Merced market, through the Zócalo,[26] up Francisco I. Madero Avenue,[27] and so along the Paseo de la Reforma[28] to Chapultepec Park,[29] and into the Philosopher's Footpath,[30] still with that flower withering in his hat, and an indivisible attention in his eyes.

Now Laura is accustomed to him, it means nothing except that he is nineteen years old and is observing a convention with all propriety,[31] as though it were founded on a law of nature, which in the end it might well prove to be. He is beginning to write poems which he prints on a wooden press, and he leaves them stuck like handbills in her door. She is pleasantly disturbed by the abstract, unhurried watchfulness of his black eyes which will in time turn easily towards another object. She tells herself that throwing the flower was a mistake, for she is twenty-two years old and knows better; but she refuses to regret it, and persuades herself that her negation of all external events as they occur is a sign that she is gradually perfecting herself in the stoicism[32] she strives to cultivate against that disaster she fears, though she cannot name it.

She is not at home in the world. Every day she teaches children who remain strangers to her, though she loves their tender round hands and their charming opportunist savagery.[33] She knocks at unfamiliar doors not knowing whether a friend or a stranger shall answer, and even if a known face emerges from the sour gloom of that unknown interior, still it is the face of a stranger. No matter what this stranger says to her, nor what her message to him, the very cells of her flesh reject knowledge and kinship in one monotonous word. No. No. No. She draws her strength from this one holy talismanic word which does not suffer her to be led into evil. Denying everything, she may walk anywhere in safety, she looks at everything without amazement.

No, repeats this firm unchanging voice of her blood; and she looks at Braggioni without amazement. He is a great man, he wishes to impress this simple girl who covers her great round breasts with thick dark cloth, and who hides long, invaluably beautiful legs under a heavy skirt. She is almost thin except for the incomprehensible fullness of her breasts, like a nursing mother's, and Braggioni, who considers himself a judge of women, speculates again on the puzzle of her notorious virginity, and takes the liberty of speech which she permits without a sign of modesty, indeed, without any sort of sign, which is disconcerting.

"You think you are so cold, *gringita*! Wait and see. You will surprise yourself some day! May I be there to advise you!"[34] He stretches his eyelids at her, and his ill-humored cat's eyes waver in a separate glance for the two points of light marking the opposite ends of a smoothly drawn path between the swollen curve of her breasts. He is not put off by that blue serge, nor by her resolutely fixed gaze. There is all the time in the world. His cheeks are bellying with the wind of song. "O girl with the dark eyes," he sings, and reconsiders. "But yours are not dark. I can change all that. O girl with the green eyes, you have stolen my heart away!" then his mind wanders to the song, and Laura feels the weight of his attention being shifted elsewhere. Singing thus, he seems harmless, he is quite harmless, there is nothing to do but sit patiently and say "No," when the moment comes. She draws a full breath, and her mind wanders also, but not far. She dares not wander too far.

Not for nothing has Braggioni taken pains to be a good revolutionist and a professional lover of humanity. He will never die of it. He has the malice, the cleverness, the wickedness, the sharpness of wit, the hardness of heart, stipulated for loving the world profitably. *He will never die of it.* He will live to see himself kicked out from his feeding trough by other hungry world-saviors. [35] Traditionally he must sing in spite of his life which drives him to bloodshed, he tells Laura, for his father was a Tuscany[36] peasant who drifted to Yucatan[37] and married a Maya[38] woman: a woman of race, an aristocrat. They gave him the love and knowledge of music, thus: and under the rip of his thumbnail, the strings of the instrument complain like exposed nerves.

Once he was called Delgadito[39] by all the girls and married women who ran after him; he was so scrawny all his bones showed under his thin cotton clothing, and he could squeeze his emptiness to the very backbone with his two hands. He was a poet and the revolution was only a dream then; too many women loved him and sapped away his youth, and he could never find enough to eat anywhere, anywhere! Now he is a leader of men, crafty men who whisper in his ear, hungry men who wait for hours outside his office for a word with him, emaciated men with wild faces who waylay him at the street gate with a timid, "Comrade, let me tell you. . . " and they blow the foul breath from their empty stomachs in his face.

He is always sympathetic. He gives them handfuls of small coins from his own pocket, he promises them work, there will be demonstrations, they must join the unions and attend the meetings, above all they must be on the watch for spies. They are closer to him than his own brothers, without them he can do nothing—until tomorrow, comrade!

Until tomorrow. "They are stupid, they are lazy, they are treacherous, they would cut my thoat for nothing," he says to Laura. He has good food and abundant drink, he hires an automobile and drives in the Paseo on Sunday morning, and enjoys plenty of sleep in a soft bed beside a wife who dares not disturb him; and he sits pampering his bones in easy billows of fat, singing to Laura, who knows and thinks these things about him. When he was fifteen, he tried to drown himself because he loved a girl, his first love, and she laughed at him. "A thousand women have paid for that," and his tight little mouth turns down at the corners. Now he perfumes his hair with Jockey Club, and confides to Laura: "One woman is really as good as another for me, in the dark. I prefer them all."

His wife organizes unions among the girls in the cigarette factories, and walks in picket lines, and even speaks at meetings in the evenings. But she cannot be brought to acknowledge the benefits of true liberty. "I tell her I must have my freedom, net.[40] She does not understand my point of view." Laura has heard this many times. Braggioni scratches the guitar and meditates. "She is an instinctively virtuous woman, pure gold, no doubt of that. If she were not, I should lock her up, and she knows it."

His wife, who works so hard for the good of the factory girls, employs part of her leisure lying on the floor weeping because there are so many women in the world, and only one husband for her, and she never knows where nor when to look for him. He told her: "Unless you can learn to cry when I am not here, I must go away for good." That day he went away and took a room at the Hotel Madrid.[41]

It is this month of separation for the sake of higher principles that has been spoiled not only for Mrs. Braggioni, whose sense of reality is beyond criticism, but for Laura, who feels herself bogged in a nightmare. Tonight Laura envies Mrs. Braggioni, who is alone, and free to weep as much as she pleases about a concrete wrong. Laura has just come from a visit to the prison, and she is waiting for tomorrow with a bitter anxiety as if tomorrow may not come, but time may be caught immovably in this hour, with herself transfixed, Braggioni singing on forever, and Eugenio's body not yet discovered by the guard.

Braggioni says: "Are you going to sleep?" Almost before she can shake her head, he begins telling her about the May-day disturbances coming on in Morelia,[42] for the Catholics hold a festival in honor of the Blessed Virgin, and the Socialists celebrate their martyrs on that day. "There will be two independent processions, starting from either end of town, and they will march until they meet, and the rest depends..." He asks her to oil and load his pistols. Standing up, he unbuckles his ammunition belt, and spreads it laden across her knees. Laura sits with the shells slipping through the cleaning cloth dipped in oil, and he says again he cannot understand why she works so hard for the revolutionary idea unless she loves some man who is in it. "Are you not in love with someone?" "No," says Laura. "And no one is in love with you?" "No." "Then it is your own fault. No woman need go begging. Why, what is the matter with you? The legless beggar woman in the Alameda has a perfectly faithful lover. Did you know that?"

Laura peers down the pistol barrel and says nothing, but a long, slow faintness rises and subsides in her; Braggioni curves his swollen fingers around the throat of the guitar and softly smothers the music out of it, and when she hears him again he seems to have forgotten her, and is speaking in the hypnotic voice he uses when talking in small rooms to a listening, close-gathered crowd. Some day this world, now seemingly so composed and eternal, to the edges of every sea shall be merely a tangle of gaping trenches, of crashing walls and broken bodies. Everything must be torn from its accustomed place where it has rotted for centuries, hurled skyward and distributed, cast down again clean as rain, without separate identity. Nothing shall survive that the stiffened hands of poverty have created for the rich and no one shall be left alive except the elect spirits[43] destined to procreate a new world cleansed of cruelty and injustice, ruled by benevolent anarchy[44]: "Pistols are good, I love them, cannon are even better, but in the end I pin my faith to good dynamite," he concludes, and strokes the pistol lying in her hands. "Once I dreamed of destroying this city, in case it offered resistance to General Ortíz,[45] but it fell into his hands like an overripe pear."

He is made restless by his own words, rises and stands waiting. Laura holds up the belt to him: "Put that on, and go kill somebody in Morelia, and you will be happier," she says softly. The presence of death in the room makes her bold. "Today, I found Eugenio going into a stupor. He refused to allow me to call the prison doctor. He had taken all the tablets I brought him yesterday. He said he took them because he was bored."

"He is a fool, and his death is his own business," says Braggioni, fastening his belt carefully.

"I told him if he had waited only a little while longer, you would have got him set free," says Laura. "He said he did not want to wait."

"He is a fool and we are rid of him," says Braggioni, reaching for his hat.

He goes away. Laura knows his mood has changed, she will not see him any more for a while. He will send word when he needs her to go on errands into strange streets, to speak to the strange faces that will appear, like clay masks with the power of human speech, to mutter their thanks to Braggioni for his help. Now she is free, and she thinks, I must run while there is time. But she does not go.

Braggioni enters his own house where for a month his wife has spent many hours every night weeping and tangling her hair upon her pillow. She is weeping now, and she weeps more at the sight of him, the cause of all her sorrows. He looks about the room. Nothing is changed, the smells are good and familiar, he is well acquainted with the woman who comes toward him with no reproach except grief on her face. He says to her tenderly: "You are so good, please don't cry any more, you dear good creature." She says, "Are you tired, my angel? Sit here and I will wash your feet." She brings a bowl of water, and kneeling, unlaces his shoes, and when from her knees she raises her sad eyes under her blackened lids, he is sorry for everything, and bursts into tears. "Ah, yes, I am hungry, I am tired, let us eat something together," he says, between sobs. His wife leans her head on his arm and says, "Forgive me!" and this time he is refreshed by the solemn, endless rain of her tears.

Laura takes off her serge dress and puts on a white linen nightgown and goes to bed. She turns her head a little to one side, and lying still, reminds herself that it is time to sleep. Numbers tick in her brain like little clocks,[16] soundless doors close of themselves around her. If you would sleep, you must not remember anything, the children will say tomorrow, good morning, my teacher, the poor prisoners who come every day bringing flowers to their jailor. 1—2—3—4—5—it is monstrous to confuse love with revolution, night with day, life with death—ah, Eugenio!

The tolling of the midnight bell is a signal, but what does it mean? Get up, Laura, and follow me: come out of your sleep, out of your bed, out of this strange house. What are you doing in this house? Without a word, without fear she rose and reached for Eugenio's hand, but he eluded her with a sharp, sly smile and drifted away. This is not all, you shall see—Murderer, he said, follow me, I will show you a new country, but it is far away and we must hurry. No, said Laura, not unless you take my hand, no; and she clung first to the stair rail, and then to the topmost branch of the Judas tree that bent down slowly and set her upon the earth, and then to the rocky ledge of a cliff, and then to the jagged wave of a sea that was not water but a desert of crumbling stone. Where are you taking me, she asked in wonder but without fear. To death, and it is a long way off, and we must hurry, said Eugenio. No, said Laura, not unless you take my hand. Then eat these flowers, poor prisoner, said Eugenio in a voice of pity, take and eat: and from the Judas tree he stripped the warm bleeding flowers, and held them to her lips. She saw that his hand was fleshless, a cluster of small white petrified branches, and his eye sockets were without light, but she ate the flowers greedily for they satisfied both hunger and thirst. Murderer! said Eugenio, and Cannibal! This is my body and my blood. Laura cried No! and at the sound of her own voice, she awoke trembling, and was afraid to sleep again.[47]

〔注释〕

1. under his breath：细声地。

2. Sixteenth of September Street：墨西哥城一街道名。1810 年 9 月 16 日在墨西哥爆发了由乡区神甫米格尔·伊达尔哥（Miguel Hidalgo y Costilla）领导的独立解放战争，反对西班牙殖民统治。该街道以此日期命名。

3. Braggioni loves himself…warm themselves in the reflected glow：布拉焦尼作为革命的领导人，有着强烈的自爱和超凡的魅力，如同白热的光；而他的追随者们则在这白热光的反射光中得到温暖，受到庇护。句中…his skin has been punctured in horrible warfare 指他在可怕的战争里曾中弹受伤。

4. …*gringa*. *Gringita*!：（西班牙语）外国姑娘。外国小姑娘。

5. suety smile＝oily smile.

6. But she cannot help feeling that she has been betrayed irreparably by the disunion between her way of living and her feeling of what life should be…：作者在此处点明故事主题的一个重要方面：劳拉发现她的理想与现实相距甚远，感到生活背叛了她。

7. Hail Mary：天主教徒经常说的"万福玛利亚！"

8. Tehuantepec：特旺特佩克，墨西哥南部一小城。

9. a tiny edge of fluted cobweb：指劳拉的衣领上有一圈薄如蛛网的带褶的花边。

10. Jockey Club：名贵的"赛马俱乐部"牌香水。

11. Xochimilco：索奇米尔科，墨西哥城附近一市镇。

12. ticher＝teacher.

13. Alameda：位于墨西哥城中心的阿拉梅达公园。

14. Vincente：布拉焦尼的名字。

15. Vera Cruz：维拉克鲁斯，墨西哥一城市，濒临墨西哥湾。

16. The favor of Braggioni is their disputed territory：他们两人都想争得布拉焦尼的欢心。

17. Zapata：埃米利亚诺·萨帕塔（Emiliano Zapata，1877?～1919），墨西哥革命领袖。

18. Cuernavaca：奎尔纳瓦卡，墨西哥城以南一城市。

19. charro：墨西哥骑手，墨西哥牛仔。

20. We lov ar ticher：We love our teacher.

21. …she was trying to forgive herself for having spurred her horse at the wrong moment.：这一矛盾心理的描写表现出劳拉实际上渴望得到异性的爱，但是由于她是天主教徒，所以总是压抑自己的情感，现在则为此感到后悔。

22. Judas tree：犹大树，又名紫荆（redbud），生长在北美大陆，早春盛开深红色花朵。传说《圣经》中出卖耶稣的犹大（Judas Iscariot）自缢于这种树上。作者在本文中以犹大树作为背叛的象征。

23. corridos：（西班牙语）民谣歌本。

24. Merced market：墨西哥城中一露天市场。

25. Guanajuato：瓜那华托市，墨西哥瓜纳华托州的首府。

26. Zócalo：墨西哥城宪法广场的俗名。

27. Francisco I. Madero Avenue：墨西哥城一街道名，以墨西哥革命领袖弗朗西斯科·伊·马德罗（1873-1913）的名字命名。马德罗在1911至1913年间曾任墨西哥总统。

28. Paseo de la Reforma：墨西哥城的改革大道。paseo＝avenue.

29. Chapultepec Park：墨西哥城查普尔特佩克公园。

30. Philosopher's Footpath：上述公园中的小径。

31. …he…is observing a convention with all propriety.：他在按照一种风俗行事。

32. Stoicism：斯多葛派哲学，公元前4世纪由芝诺（Zeno of Citium，335-263B. C.）首创于雅典。该学派认为美德是善的最高形式，主张人必须不断地在大自然中生活，人的行为必须与自然规律相协调。人只有抑制自己的情欲和邪念，并以正确的态度履行职责，才能真正获得自由并主宰自己的命运。这一观点也叫作禁欲主义。

33. their charming opportunist savagery：他们在适当时机表现出来的可爱的野蛮行为。

34. May I be there to advise you!：但愿那时我能在场给你出主意！

35. Not for nothing has Braggioni taken pains to be a good revolutionist…by

other hungry world-saviors：注意这段中尖刻的讽刺意味。

36. Tuscany：即托斯卡纳（Toscana），意大利中西部的一个区。

37. Yucatan：尤卡坦州，位于墨西哥东南部。

38. Maya：玛雅族，中美洲印第安人的一族。

39. Delgadito：（西班牙语）瘦子，皮包骨。

40. I tell her I must have my freedom，net.：我告诉她我要不折不扣的自由。

41. Hotel Madrid：墨西哥城一旅馆。

42. Morelia：莫雷利亚，墨西哥城以西一城市。

43. the elect spirits：被选中的人，指革命者。

44. Some day this world，…ruled by benevolent anarchy.：这段写出布拉焦尼本人对革命的理解：革命将毁灭一切，只有少数革命者得以幸存，并以"仁慈的无政府"统治世界。注意作者的嘲讽口气。

45. General Ortíz：即奥尔蒂斯·鲁毕奥（Pascual Ortiz Rubio，1877～1963）将军，20世纪20年代的墨西哥革命领袖，曾在1930至1932年间任墨西哥总统。

46. Numbers tick in her brain like little clocks：这句话以及下文中的数字1—2—3—4—5都指劳拉数着数字，想快点入睡。

47. The tolling of the midnight bell is a signal…she awoke trembling，and was afraid to sleep again.：最后一段完全描写劳拉的噩梦。作者援引《圣经·新约全书》中犹大出卖耶稣的典故。《马太福音》（Matthew）第26章和第27章中记载：犹大为了30个银币向罗马当局出卖了耶稣。耶稣在被捕前与12个弟子一起吃最后的晚餐时，说明他本人将为拯救天下的罪人而献身，并将酒和面包分给大家，说那象征他的血和肉。犹大率领官兵逮捕了耶稣。后来犹大得知耶稣已被定罪，他又良心发现，感到内疚。他把那30个银币仍到神甫和长老面前，后自缢身亡。作者用此典故进一步点明故事的主题——背叛。劳拉显然对欧亨尼奥有一定的好感，她为自己无意中促成他的死而感到内疚和痛苦，觉得自己犹如背叛耶稣的犹大。另一方面，劳拉在欧亨尼奥的要求下如饥似渴地吞吃犹大树的花朵，从而违背了她自我抑制的原则，也背叛了她自己。

RICHARD WRIGHT

〔作者介绍〕

理查德·赖特（Richard Wright，1908～1960），杰出的美国黑人作家，出生在密西西比州纳齐兹镇附近一个生活极度贫困的黑人佃户家里，祖辈都是奴隶。赖特在恐惧和耻辱中度过苦难的童年，在逆境中养成了倔强不屈的性格。因此，在外面时常遭白人的侮辱，在家里也常挨母亲的打骂。在自传体小说《黑孩子》（*Black Boy*）里，他生动地描述了 17 岁以前在南方的生活情景。赖特 5 岁时，父亲弃家出走，体弱多病的母亲带着他和弟弟四处流浪。他和弟弟先是进了孤儿院，后又随母亲投奔外祖母。小赖特饱尝艰难生活的辛酸，受尽种族歧视的凌辱。在白人统治的世界里，广大黑人过着非人的生活。他怀着对不公平世界的恐惧和愤恨苦苦地挣扎着。

赖特没有受过系统的正规教育，但他那饱受压迫和损害的种族意识驱使他如饥似渴地读书。他读过德莱赛（Theodore Dreiser，1871～1945）、菲茨杰拉德、刘易斯和门肯（H. L. Mencken，1880～1956）的许多著作。他曾说过："只有通过读书……我才能支撑着生活下来……我的全部生活经历使我特别容易接受现代小说的现实主义和自然主义，这些作品我百读不厌。"评论家门肯在其《序言集》（*A Book of Prefaces*）里披露美国社会丑恶现象时所表现出的勇气使赖特深受鼓舞，他立志将来当作家，以文学为武器，向不合理的社会宣战。

1927 年，年仅 19 岁的赖特为了摆脱南方白人统治的桎梏，寻求发展自我的机会，来到芝加哥。在那里，他开始接受马克思主义学说，看清了资本主义的现实和本质，认识到资本主义和种族主义是黑人的敌人，这对他的思想和文学创作都产生了积极的影响。1932 年，赖特加入左派组织"约翰·理德俱乐部"（John Reed Club），在《左派前哨》（*Left Front*）、《国际》（*International*）和《工人日报》（*Daily Worker*）等进步刊物上发表文章和诗歌。后来他参加了美国共产党。1937 年，赖特赴纽约任美共机关报《工人日报》（*Daily*

Worker）哈莱姆区编辑。后因种族问题与党内领导人产生分歧，于 1942 年退党。

自 1938 年至 1945 年，赖特先后发表中篇小说集《汤姆叔叔的孩子们》（*Uncle Tom's Children*）、长篇小说《土生子》（*Native Son*）和自传《黑孩子》。这些作品曾轰动美国文坛，受到文学批评界的好评。特别是后两部作品，以空前深刻的笔触和充满激情的描述揭示出生活在白人社会里黑人紧张、恐惧和仇恨的复杂心理，愤怒声讨了种族歧视现象和种族隔离政策。

1947 年，赖特离美赴法定居，直至 1960 年病逝。在巴黎，他与萨特（Jean-Paul Sartre，1905～1980）相交甚厚，并在创作上受其存在主义哲学影响。那时期，他的主要作品有小说《局外人》（*The Outsider*，1953）、《野蛮的假日》（*Savage Holiday*，1954）。这两部作品分别描写了一个叫克罗斯·达尔农的黑人和一个叫厄斯金·福勒的白人为了生存而苦苦挣扎的故事。《黑人的力量》（*Black Power*，1954）描写非洲加纳黑人在英国殖民者统治下的悲惨生活。此外还有其它 10 余部作品。在他去世后出版的短篇小说集《八个男人》（*Eight Men*，1961），收集了他在不同时期写的 8 个短篇小说。赖特后期的作品试图从描写被压迫黑人的痛苦生活与反抗转到描写所有被压迫人民的痛苦与斗争，但多数缺乏早期作品的那种感人的激情和震撼人心的力量。

赖特的整个文学生涯和全部作品表明，他不愧是美国“抗议”文学的开拓者，是继兰斯顿·休斯之后又一个获得广泛承认的黑人作家。《土生子》的出版标志美国黑人文学的成熟。他的作品为后来黑人文学现实主义的发展铺平了道路。赖特以其生动、洗练的艺术手法创造了众多鲜明有力的艺术形象，并以他的文学创作和成就影响了包括拉尔夫·艾里森（Ralph Ellison）和詹姆斯·鲍德温（James Baldwin）在内的一代黑人作家。

Native Son

〔作品介绍〕

1940 年，赖特发表了轰动美国文坛的长篇小说《土生子》（*Native Son*）。小说以 30 年代的芝加哥为背景，描写一个名叫比格·托马斯的黑人青年，因无意中杀死白人小姐玛丽·道尔顿，最后被判处死刑的故事。比格全家 4 口住在黑人区一间老鼠成灾的小屋里，因比格失业而生活无着，家庭终日笼罩在阴沉、紧张的气氛里。在街上，他经常与无业黑人青年厮混，结伙抢劫。白人的种族歧视把他变成社会生活的局外人。他挣扎在穷困、恐惧、耻辱和仇恨之中，不仅憎恨白人社会，也怨恨自己、家庭和其他黑人。经慈善组织介绍，他为一个富有的白人道尔顿先生开车兼烧锅炉。当天夜里，他开车送道尔顿的独生女玛丽小姐回家，玛丽因喝酒过量醉得不醒人事，比格只好将她抱回房间。此时，双目失明的道尔顿太太出现在房间门口，叫着玛丽的名字，问她是否已经回来。比格惊恐万状，一旦被人发现，便会背上半夜闯入白人小姐房间的可怕罪名，后果将不堪设想。于是，为了防止玛丽出声，他用枕头堵住她的嘴。不料因用力过猛，玛丽被憋死。他急中生智，将玛丽的尸体背到锅炉房，塞进炉堂焚尸灭迹。然后，为了制造假象，他又写了一封匿名信，把怀疑的目标引向玛丽的男朋友、共产党员简·厄尔隆，说他绑架了玛丽。当事情真相败露以后，比格畏罪潜逃，继之而来的是一场全城大追捕，最后，警察在一幢楼顶上将比格抓获。在审判过程中，虽然有共产党员律师麦克斯为他辩护，比格终不能逃脱被处以电刑的命运，因为他的命运和其他黑人的命运一样，早已注定要被种族大歧视的社会所吞噬。

美国当代黑人作家拉尔夫·艾里森在论述理查德·赖特的文章《理查德·赖特的布鲁斯》里说，一般来讲，黑人以三种不同的方式面对他们的命运："通过希望和黑人宗教的感情净化的作用，他们能够扮演白人为他们规定的角色，并能永远解决由此而产生的矛盾冲突；他们能够把对于歧视黑人的社会关系的不满埋在心里，同时努力寻求通往中产阶级的路，因此，有意无意地变成压迫他们黑人兄弟的白人的同伙；或者，他们抵制眼前的现实，采取犯罪的态度，与白人展开一场无休止的心理战，这一心理战常常引发为暴力。"在《土生子》问世之前，文学作品中的黑人几乎都是在白人统治的社会里被侮辱、被损害的形象，他们忍受着饥寒交迫的生活和种族社会的歧视与侮辱，他们向往平等、自由和美好的生活，到头来还是逃不脱被压迫、被奴役的结局。《土生子》中的比格·托马斯这一形象的意义在于，他以一个完全崭新的形象出现于现代美国文学史上。当白人社会的残酷统治发展到极点、被奴役的黑人再也无法忍受时，他们就要反抗。比格·托马斯的暴力行为就是一个先兆。他单枪匹马向整个白人社会发动了一场战争。他杀死的虽然只是一个白人小姐，但他的行为却震撼了全芝加哥、全美国，使白人统治者惊慌、害怕、手足无措，瞻望前景，不寒而栗。他为此而感到高兴和自豪，因为他终于发现了自我，一个在白人眼里不是人，而只不过是一个"畜牲"的他，终于找到了自身的价值。此时的比格·托马斯已不再是白人的奴隶，他已经变成了自己的主人、自己的上帝。

比格是美国现代文明的产物，他的行为和结局是美国社会及其歧视黑人的法律造成的，在这个意义上，他是美国本乡本土的土生子。

《土生子》全书分 3 部：《恐惧》、《逃跑》和《命运》。这里选注的是第 1 部《恐惧》的开头部分。

Native Son

BOOK I FEAR

Brrrrrrriiiiiiiiiiiiiiiiiinng![1]

An alarm clock clanged in the dark and silent room. A bed spring creaked. A woman's voice sang out impatiently:

"Bigger, shut that thing off!"

A surly grunt sounded above the tinny ring of metal. Naked feet swished dryly across the planks in the wooden floor and the clang ceased abruptly.

"Turn on the light, Bigger."

"Awright," came a sleepy mumble.

Light flooded the room and revealed a black boy standing in a narrow space between two iron beds, rubbing his eyes with the backs of his hands. From a bed to his right the woman spoke again:

"Buddy, get up from there! I got a big washing on my hands today and I want you-all out of here."

Another black boy rolled from bed and stood up. The woman also rose and stood in her nightgown.

"Turn your heads so I can dress," she said.

The two boys averted their eyes and gazed into a far corner of the room. The woman rushed out of her nightgown and put on a pair of step-ins. She turned to the bed from which she had risen and called:

"Vera! Get up from there!"

"What time is it, Ma?" asked a muffled, adolescent voice from beneath a quilt.

"Get up from there, I say!"

"O.K., Ma."

A brown-skinned girl in a cotton gown got up and stretched her arms above her head and yawned. Sleepily, she sat on a chair and fumbled with her stockings. The two boys kept their faces averted while their mother and sister put on enough clothes to keep them from feeling ashamed; and the mother and sister did the same while the boys dressed. Abruptly, they all paused, holding their clothes in their hands, their attention caught by a light tapping in the thinly plastered walls of the room. They forgot their conspiracy against shame and their eyes strayed apprehensively over the floor.

"There he is again, Bigger!"[2] the woman screamed, and the tiny one-room apartment galvanized into violent action. A chair toppled as the woman, half-dressed and in her stocking feet, scrambled breathlessly upon the bed. Her two sons, barefoot, stood tense and motionless, their eyes searching anxiously under the bed and chairs. The girl ran into a corner, halfstooped and gathered the hem of her slip into both of her hands and held it tightly over her knees.

"Oh! Oh!" she wailed.

"There he goes!"

The woman pointed a shaking finger. Her eyes were round with fascinated horror.

"Where?"

"I don't see 'im!"

"Bigger, he's behind the trunk!" the girl whimpered.

"Vera!" the woman screamed. "Get up here on the bed! Don't let that thing *bite* you!"

Frantically, Vera climbed upon the bed and the woman caught hold of her. With their arms entwined about each other, the black mother and the brown daughter gazed open mouthed at the trunk in the corner.

Bigger looked round the room wildly, then darted to a curtain and swept it aside and grabbed two heavy iron skillets from a wall above a gas stove. He whirled and called softly to his brother, his eyes glued to the trunk.

"Buddy!"

"Yeah?"

"Here; take this skillet."

"O. K."

"Now, get over by the door!"

"O. K."

Buddy crouched by the door and held the iron skillet by its handle, his arm flexed and poised. Save for the quick, deep breathing of the four people, the room was quiet. Bigger crept on tiptoe toward the trunk with the skillet clutched stiffly in his hand, his eyes dancing and watching every inch of the wooden floor in front of him. He paused and, without moving an eye or muscle, called:

"Buddy!"

"Hunh?"

"Put that box in front of the hole so he can't get out!"

"O. K."

Buddy ran to a wooden box and shoved it quickly in front of a gaping hole in the molding and then backed again to the door, holding the skillet ready. Bigger eased to the trunk and peered behind it cautiously. He saw nothing. Carefully, he stuck out his bare foot and pushed the trunk a few inches.

"There he is!" the mother screamed again.

A huge black rat squealed and leaped at Bigger's trouserleg and snagged it in his teeth, hanging on.

"Goddamn!" Bigger whispered fiercely, whirling and kicking out his leg with all the strength of his body. The force of his movement shook the rat loose and it sailed through the air and struck a wall. Instantly, it rolled over and leaped again. Bigger dodged and the rat landed against a table leg. With clenched teeth, Bigger held the skillet; he was afraid to hurl it, fearing that he might miss. The rat squeaked and turned and ran in a narrow circle, looking for a place to hide; it leaped gagin past Bigger and scurried on dry rasping feet to one side of the box and then to the other, searching for the hole. Then it turned and reared upon its hind legs.

"Hit 'im, Bigger!" Buddy shouted.

"Kill 'im!" the woman screamed.

The rat's belly pulsed with fear. Bigger advanced a step and the rat emitted a long thin song of defiance, its black beady eyes glittering, its tiny forefeet pawing the air restlessly. Bigger swung the skillet; it skidded over the floor, missing the rat, and clattered to a stop against a wall.

"Goddamn!"

The rat leaped. Bigger sprang to one side. The rat stopped under a chair and let out a furious screak. Bigger moved slowly backward toward the door.

"Gimme that skillet, Buddy," he asked quietly, not taking his eyes from the rat.

Buddy extended his hand. Bigger caught the skillet and lifted it high in the air. The rat scuttled across the floor and stopped again at the box and searched quickly for the hole; then it reared once more and bared long yellow fangs, piping shrilly, belly quivering.

Bigger aimed and let the skillet fly with a heavy grunt. There was a shattering of wood as the box caved in. The woman screamed and hid her face in her hands. Bigger tiptoed forward and peered.

"I got 'im," he muttered, his clenched teeth bared in a smile. "By God, I got 'im."

He kicked the splintered box out of the way and the flat black body of the rat lay exposed, its two long yellow tusks showing distinctly. Bigger took a shoe and pounded the rat's head, crushing it, cursing hysterically:

"You sonofa*bitch*!"

The woman on the bed sank to her knees and buried her face in the quilts and sobbed:

"Lord, Lord, have mercy...."

"Aw, Mama," Vera whimpered, bending to her. "Don't cry. It's dead now."

The two brothers stood over the dead rat and spoke in tones of awed admiration.

"Gee, but he's a big bastard."

"That sonofabitch could cut your throat."

"He's over a foot long."

"How in hell do they get so big?"

"Eating garbage and anything else they can get."

"Look, Bigger, there's a three-inch rip in your pant-leg."

"Yeah; he was after me, all right."

"Please, Bigger, take 'im out," Vera begged.

"Aw, don't be so scary," Buddy said.

The woman on the bed continued to sob. Bigger took a piece of newspaper and gingerly lifted the rat by its tail and held it out at arm's length.

"Bigger, take 'im out," Vera begged again.

Bigger laughed and approached the bed with the dangling rat, swinging it to and fro like a pendulum, enjoying his sister's fear.

"Bigger!" Vera gasped convulsively; she screamed and swayed and closed her eyes and fell headlong across her mother and rolled limply from the bed to the floor.

"Bigger, for God's sake!" the mother sobbed, rising and bending over Vera. "Don't do that! Throw that rat out!"

He laid the rat down and started to dress.

"Bigger, help me lift Vera to the bed," the mother said.

He paused and turned round.

"What's the matter?" he asked, feigning ignorance.

"Do what I asked you, Will you, boy?"

He went to the bed and helped his mother lift Vera. Vera's eyes were closed. He turned away and finished dressing. He wrapped the rat in a newspaper and went out of the door and down the stairs and put it into a garbage can at the corner of an alley. When he returned to the room his mother was still bent over Vera, placing a wet towel upon her head. She straightened and faced him, her cheeks and eyes wet with tears and her lips tight with anger.

"Boy, sometimes I wonder what makes you act like you do."

"What I do now?" he demanded belligerently.

"Sometimes you act the biggest fool I ever saw."

"What you talking about?"

"You scared your sister with that rat and she *fainted*! Ain't you got no sense at *all*?"

"Aw, I didn't know she was that scary."

"Buddy!" the mother called."

"Yessum."

"Take a newspaper and spread it over that spot."

"Yessum."

Buddy opened out a newspaper and covered the smear of blood on the floor where the rat had been crushed. Bigger went to the window and stood looking out abstractedly into the street. His mother glared at his back.

"Bigger, sometimes I wonder why I birthed you," she said bitterly.

Bigger looked at her and turned away.

"Maybe you oughtn't've. Maybe you ought to left me where I was."

"You shut your sassy mouth!"

"Aw, for chrissakes!" Bigger said, lighting a cigarette.

"Buddy, pick up them skillets and put 'em in the sink," the mother said.

"Yessum."

Bigger walked across the floor and sat on the bed. His mother's eyes followed him.

"We wouldn't have to live in this garbage dump if you had any manhood in you," she said.

"Aw, don't start that again."

"How you feel, Vera?" the mother asked.

Vera raised her head and looked about the room as though expecting to see another rat.

"Oh, Mama!"

"You poor thing!"

"I couldn't help it. Bigger scared me."

"Did you hurt yourself?"

"I bumped my head."

"Here; take it easy. You'll be all right."

"How come Bigger acts that way?" Vera asked, crying again.

"He's just crazy," the mother said. "Just plain dumb black crazy."

"I'll be late for my sewing class at the Y. W. C. A.," Vera said.

"Here; stretch out on the bed. You'll feel better in a little while," the mother said.

She left Vera on the bed and turned a pair of cold eyes upon Bigger.

"Suppose you wake up some morning and find your sister dead? What would you think then?" she asked. "Suppose those rats cut our veins at night when we sleep? Naw! Nothing like that ever bothers you! All you care about is your own pleasure! Even when the relief offers you a job you won't take it till they threaten to cut off your food and starve you! Bigger, honest, you the most no-countest man I ever seen in all my life!"

"You done told me that a thousand times," he said, not looking round.

"Well, I'm telling you agin! And mark my word, some of these days you going to set down and *cry*. Some of these days you going to wish you had made something out of yourself, instead of just a tramp. But it'll be too late then."

"Stop prophesying about me," he said.

"I prophesy much as I please! And if you don't like it, you can get out. We can get along without you. We can live in one room just like we living now, even with you gone," she said.

"Aw, for chrissakes!" he said, his voice filled with nervous irritation.

"You'll regret how you living some day," she went on. "If you don't stop running with that gang of yours and do right you'll end up where you never thought you would. You think I don't know what you boys is doing, but I do. And the gallows is at the end of the road you traveling, boy. Just remember that."[3] She turned and looked at Buddy. "Throw that box outside, Buddy."

"Yessum."

There was silence. Buddy took the box out. The mother went behind the curtain to the gas stove. Vera sat up in bed and swung her feet to the floor.

"Lay back down, Vera," the mother said.

"I feel all right now, Ma. I got to go to my sewing class."

"Well, if you feel like it, set the table," the mother said, going behind the curtain again. "Lord, I get so tired of this I don't know what to do," her voice floated plaintively from behind the curtain. "All I ever do is try to make a home for you children and you don't care."

"Aw, Ma," Vera protested. "Don't say that."

"Vera sometimes I just want to lay down and quit."

"Ma, please don't say that."

"I can't last many more years, living like this."

"I'll be old enough to work soon, Ma."

"I reckon I'll be dead then. I reckon God'll call me home."

Vera went behind the curtain and Bigger heard her trying to comfort his mother. He shut their voices out of his mind. He hated his family because he knew that they were suffering and that he was powerless to help them. He knew that the moment he allowed himself to feel to its fullness how they lived, the shame and misery of their lives, he would be swept out of himself with fear and despair. So he held toward them an attitude of iron reserve; he lived with them, but behind a wall, a curtain. And toward himself he was even more exacting. He knew that the moment he allowed what his life meant[4] to enter fully into his consciousness, he would either kill himself or someone else. So he denied himself and acted tough.

He got up and crushed his cigarette upon the window sill. Vera came into the room and placed knives and forks upon the table.

"Get ready to eat, you-all," the mother called.

He sat at the table. The odor of frying bacon and boiling coffee drifted to him from behind the curtain. His mother's voice floated to him in song.

Life is like a mountain railroad
With an engineer that's brave
We must make the run successful
From the cradle to the grave. . . .

The song irked him and he was glad when she stopped and came into the room with a pot of coffee and a plate of crinkled bacon. Vera brought the bread in and they sat down. His mother closed her eyes and lowered her head and mumbled,

"Lord, we thank Thee for the food You done placed before us for the nourishment of our bodies. Amen." She lifted her eyes and without changing her tone of voice, said, "You going to have to learn to get up earlier than this, Bigger, to hold a job."

He did not answer or look up.

"You want me to pour you some coffee?" Vera asked.

"Yeah."

"You going to take the job,[5] ain't you, Bigger?" his mother asked.

He laid down his fork and stared at her.

"I told you last night I was going to take it. How many times you want to ask me?"

"Well, don't bite her head off," Vera said. "She only asked you a question."

"Pass the bread and stop being smart."

"You know you have to see Mr. Dalton at five-thirty," his mother said.

"You done said that ten times."

"I don't want you to forget, son."

"And you know how you can forget," Vera said.

"Aw, lay off Bigger," Buddy said. "He told you he was going to take the job."

"Don't tell 'em nothing," Bigger said.

"You shut your mouth, Buddy, or get up from this table," the mother said. "I'm not going to take any stinking sass from you. One fool in the family's enougy."

"Lay off, Ma," Buddy said.

"Bigger's setting here like he ain't glad to get a job," she said.

"What you want me to do? Shout?" Bigger asked.

"Oh, Bigger!" his sister said.

"I wish you'd keep your big mouth out of this!" he told his sister.

"If you get that job," his mother said in a low, kind tone of voice, busy slicing a loaf of bread, "I can fix up a nice place for you children. You could be comfortable and not have to live like pigs."

"Bigger ain't decent enough to think of nothing like that," Vera said.

"God, I wish you-all would let me eat," Bigger said.

His mother talked on as though she had not heard him and he stopped listening.

"Ma's talking to you, Bigger," Vera said.

"So *what*?"

"Don't be that way, Bigger!"

"He laid down his fork and his strong black fingers gripped the edge of the table; there was silence save for the tinkling of his brother's fork against a plate. He kept staring at his sister till her eyes fell.

"I wish you'd let me eat," he said again.

As he ate he felt that they were thinking of the job he was to get that evening and it made him angry; he felt that they had tricked him into a cheap surrender.

"I need some carfare," he said.

"Here's all I got," his mother said, pushing a quarter to the side of his plate.

He put the quarter in his pocket and drained his cup of coffee in one long swallow. He got his coat and cap and went to the door.

"You know, Bigger," his mother said, "if you don't take that job the relief'll cut us off. We won't have any food."

"I told you I'd take it!" he shouted and slammed the door.

He went down the steps into the vestibule and stood looking out into the street through the plate glass of the front door. Now and then a street car rattled past over steel tracks. He was sick of his life at home. Day in and day out there was nothing but shouts and bickering. But what could he do? Each time he asked himself that question his mind hit a blank wall and he stopped thinking. Across the street directly in front of him, he saw a truck pull to a stop at the curb and two white men in overalls got out with pails and brushes. Yes, he could take the job at Dalton's and be miserable, or he could refuse it and starve. It maddened him to think that he did not have a wider choice of action. Well, he could not stand here all day like this. What was he to do with himself? He tried to decide if he wanted to buy a ten-cent magazine, or go to a movie, or go to the poolroom and talk with the gang, or just loaf around. With his hands deep in his pockets, another cigarette slanting across his chin, he brooded and watched the men at work across the street. They were pasting a huge colored poster to a signboard. The poster showed a white face.

"That's Buckley!" He spoke softly to himself. "He's running for State's Attorney again." The men were slapping the poster with wet brushes. He looked at the round florid face and wagged his head. "I bet that sonofabitch rakes off a million bucks in graft a year. Boy, if I was in his shoes for just one day I'd *never* have to worry again."

When the men were through they gathered up their pails and brushes and got into the truck and drove off. He looked at the poster: the white face was fleshy but stern; one hand was uplifted and its index finger pointed straight out into the street at each passer-by. The poster showed one of those faces that looked straight at you when you looked at it and all the while you were walking and turning your head to look at it it kept looking unblinkingly back at you until you got so far from it you had to take your eyes away, and then it stopped, like a movie blackout. Above the top of the poster were tall red letters: IF YOU BREAK THE LAW, YOU CAN'T WIN!

He snuffed his cigarette and laughed silently. "You crook," he mumbled, shaking his head. "You let whoever pays *you* off win!" He opened the door and met the morning air. He went along the sidewalk with his head down, fingering the quarter in his pocket. He stopped and searched all of his pockets; in his vest pocket he found a lone copper cent. That made a total of twenty-six cents, fourteen cents of which would have to be saved for carfare to Mr. Dalton's; that is, if he decided to take the job. In order to buy a magazine and go to the movies he would have to have at least twenty cents more. "Goddammit, I'm always broke!" he mumbled.

〔注释〕

1. Brrrrrriiiiiiiiiiiiiiiiiinng!：闹钟声的象征意义在于，比格的每一天都充满了困忧、耻辱与仇恨；今天则是他走向死亡的开始。

2. "There is he is again, Bigger!"这个"he"指老鼠。老鼠的出现一方面说明比格一家人经常被老鼠搅得不安宁；另一方面也有寓意：老鼠之于比格一家尤如比格之于白人社会，老鼠的死寓喻比格的死。

3. "You'll regret…Just remember that."：母亲表面上诅咒儿子，实则在诅咒白人社会。

4. He knew that the moment he allowed what his life meant：意在表明一个有反抗个性的黑人的自身价值，为他后来的暴力行为埋下伏笔。

5. "You going to take the job, aren't you, Bigger?"：指给道尔顿一家开车。

EUDORA WELTY

〔作者介绍〕

尤多拉·韦尔蒂（Eudora Welty，1909～ ），美国小说家，生于密西西比州杰克逊城。父亲经营保险公司，家境宽裕。韦尔蒂自幼受到良好的教育，曾就读于威斯康星大学和哥伦比亚大学。1931年美国经济萧条，她返回故里，从事广告宣传和新闻报道，广泛地接触社会生活，积累了丰富的创作素材。在此期间她开始写作，于1936年发表第一篇短篇小说《旅行推销员之死》（“Death of a Traveling Salesman”），受到名作家罗伯特·佩恩·华伦（Robert Penn Warren，1905～ ）的重视。从那时起，韦尔蒂发表过许多短篇小说和几部中、长篇小说，并先后获得欧·亨利纪念奖、威廉·狄恩·豪威尔斯奖章和普利策奖，1986年获得美国国家文学艺术奖章。

韦尔蒂的父母是北方人，但她长期居住在南方。这一特殊背景使她独具许多南方作家所缺乏创作的优势：既对南方故土感情深厚，又能客观地估价它的历史与现状。韦尔蒂的作品多以南方为背景，乡土气息浓重。她在《小说中的地点》（“Place in Fiction”）一文中指出：地点是小说中已经和即将感受到的事物的汇集点。它具体、确切、可信，能使故事和人物更加真实。韦尔蒂宣称，“出自其发源地，并以极清晰、明确、直接和热情的方式所表达的艺术，最能长久地为人们所理解。”

传统南方社会的家族观念和家庭关系是韦尔蒂作品的重要题材。但她的重点并不在于描述社会的兴衰和家族的沉浮，而在于探索人物的内心世界，表现人与人之间的亲疏关系以及爱情的力量等。她以通俗、明快、抒情的语言塑造出从贵族到农夫的一系列人物形象，向读者表达他们的“内心独白”，展现他们的感情纠葛和悲欢离合。人物的自我探索和对生活意义的追求成为韦尔蒂作品的突出特点。这些作品也反映出作者对待人生的态度是严肃而乐观的。

韦尔蒂孜孜不倦地革新写作技巧，变换叙述方法。她的手法有时古雅，有时怪诞，善寓讽刺于令人解颐的诙谐之中。韦尔蒂擅长摄影，因此她在写作中也常借用摄影的手法，如：从客观的叙事角度生动地展现生活场景；刻意表现光与影及色彩与氛围以烘托人物形象。

韦尔蒂的中、长篇小说相继获得成功，但她的主要成就还是体现在短篇小说的创作上。她的主要作品包括：短篇小说集《绿窗帘》(*A Curtain of Green*, 1941)、《宽网》(*The Wide Net*, 1943)、《金苹果》(*The Golden Apples*, 1949)、《韦尔蒂短篇小说集》(*The Collected Stories of Eudora Welty*, 1980)；中篇小说《庞德的心》(*The Ponder Heart*, 1954)；长篇小说《三角洲的婚礼》(*Delta Wedding*, 1946)、《败局》(*Losing Battles*, 1970)、《乐观者的女儿》(*The Optimist's Daughter*, 1972)、评论和散文集《发掘小说的眼力》(*The Eye of the Story*, 1978) 以及自传《一个作家的开始》(*One Writer's Beginnings*, 1984)。

Death of a Traveling Salesman

〔作品介绍〕

《旅行推销员之死》是作者1936年发表在《文稿》(*Manuscript*) 杂志上的第1篇短篇小说。主人公鲍曼是个为生计所迫而长年奔波的旅行推销员。他旅行时大病未愈便继续赶路，中途因汽车出事来到一个农户家求援。由于疾病缠身，鲍曼变得易动感情，渴望得到爱抚和温暖。他看到善良的农家夫妇情爱甚笃，互相信任，配合默契，正在期待婴儿的降生。对比自己孤苦的处境，鲍曼感慨万端，最后倒在漫漫的夜路上。

鲍曼是现代西方人理智和感情失调的典型。他与世人隔绝，生活没有意义，没有归宿，没有“结果”。而他偶遇的夫妇尽管贫穷，却执著地追求自己的生活方式，憧憬着幸福的未来。他们是内心与外界、理智与感情协调一致的楷模。小说以巧妙的对比手法表达了这一具有强烈现代气息的主题。

作家通过对鲍曼所见所闻所思的细节描写，揭示了人物性格，展现其心理和感情的变化。作品的语言形象生动，不落俗套。

Death of a Traveling Salesman

R. J. Bowman, who for fourteen years had traveled for a shoe company through Mississippi, drove his Ford along a rutted dirt path. It was a long day! The time did not seem to clear the noon hurdle and settle into a soft afternoon.[1] The sun, keeping its strength here even in winter, stayed at the top of the sky, and every time Bowman stuck his head out of the dusty car to stare up the road, it seemed to reach a long arm down and push against the top of his head, right through his hat—like the practical joke of an old drummer,[2] long on the road. It made him feel all the more angry and helpless. He was feverish, and he was not quite sure of the way.

This was his first day back on the road after a long siege of influenza. He had had very high fever, and dreams, and had become weakened and pale, enough to tell the difference in the mirror, and he could not think clearly.... All afternoon, in the midst of his anger, and for no reason, he had thought of his dead grandmother. She had been a comfortable soul.[3] Once more Bowman wished he could fall into the big feather bed that had been in her room.... Then he forgot her again.

This desolate hill country! And he seemed to be going the wrong way—it was as if he were going back, far back. There was not a house in sight.... There was no use wishing he were back in bed, though. By paying the hotel doctor his bill he had proved his recovery. He had not even been sorry when the pretty trained nurse said good-bye. He did not like illness, he distrusted it, as he distrusted the road without signposts. It angered him. He had given the nurse a really expensive bracelet, just because she was packing up her bag and leaving.

But now—what if in fourteen years on the road he had never been ill before and never had an accident? His record was broken, and he had even begun almost to question it.... He had gradually put up at better hotels, in the bigger towns, but weren't they all, eternally, stuffy in summer and drafty in winter? Women? He could only remember little rooms within little rooms, like a nest of Chinese paper boxes, and if he thought of one woman he saw the worn loneliness that the furniture of the room seemed built of. And he himself—he was a man who always wore rather wide-brimmed black hats, and in the wavy hotel mirrors he had looked something like a bullfighter, as he paused for that inevitable instant on the landing, walking downstairs to supper.... He leaned out of the car again, and once more the sun pushed at his head.

Bowman had wanted to reach Beulah[4] by dark, to go to bed and sleep off his fatigue. As he remembered, Beulah was fifty miles away from the last town, on a graveled road. This was only a cow trail. How had he ever come to such a place? One hand wiped the sweat from his face, and he drove on.

He had made the Beulah trip before, but he had never seen this hill or this petering-out path before—or that cloud, he thought shyly, looking up and then down quickly—any more than he had seen this day before. Why did he not admit he was simply lost and had been for miles?... He was not in the habit of asking the way of strangers, and these people never knew where the very roads they lived on went to; but then he had not even been close enough to anyone to call out. People standing in the fields now and then, or on top of the haystacks, had been too far away, looking like leaning sticks or weeds, turning a little at the solitary rattle of his car across their countryside, watching the pale sobered winter dust where it chunked out behind like big squashes down the road. The stares of these distant people had followed him solidly like a wall, impenetrable, behind which they turned back after he had passed.

The cloud floated there to one side like the bolster on his grandmother's bed. It went over a cabin on the edge of a hill, where two bare chinaberry trees clutched at the sky. He drove through a heap of dead oak leaves, his wheels stirring their weightless sides to make a silvery melancholy whistle as the car passed through their bed. No car had been along this way ahead of him. Then he saw that he was on the edge of a ravine that fell away, a red erosion, and that this was indeed the road's end.

He pulled the brake. But it did not hold, though he put all his strength into it. The car, tipped toward the edge, rolled a little. Without doubt, it was going over the bank.

He got out quietly, as though some mischief had been done him and he had his dignity to remember. He lifted his bag and sample case out, set them down, and stood back and watched the car roll over the edge. He heard something—not the crash he was listening for, but a slow, unuproarious crackle. Rather distastefully he went to look over, and he saw that his car had fallen into a tangle of immense grapevines as thick as his arm, which caught it and held it, rocked it like a grotesque child in a dark cradle, and then, as he watched, concerned somehow that he was not still inside it, released it gently to the ground.

He sighed.

Where am I? he wondered with a shock. Why didn't I do something? All his anger seemed to have drifted away from him. There was the house, back on the hill. He took a bag in each hand and with almost childlike willingness went toward it. But his breathing came with difficulty, and he had to stop to rest.

It was a shotgun house,[5] two rooms and an open passage between, perched on the hill. The whole cabin slanted a little under the heavy heaped-up vine, that covered the roof, light and green, as though forgotten from summer. A woman stood in the passage.

He stopped still. Then all of a sudden his heart began to behave strangely. Like a rocket set off, it began to leap and expand into uneven patterns of beats which showered into his brain, and he could not think. But in scattering and falling it made no noise. It shot up with great power, almost elation, and fell gently, like acrobats into nets. It began to pound profoundly, then waited irresponsibly, hitting some sort of inward mockery first at his ribs, then against his eyes, then under his shoulder blades, and against the roof of his mouth when he tried to say, "Good afternoon, madam." But he could not hear his heart—it was as quiet as ashes falling. This was rather comforting; still, it was shocking to Bowman to feel his heart beating at all.

Stock-still his confusion, he dropped his bags, which seemed to drift in slow bulks gracefully through the air and to cushion themselves on the gray prostrate grass near the doorstep.

As for the woman standing there, he saw at once that she was old. Since she could not possibly hear his heart, he ignored the pounding and now looked at her carefully, and yet in his distraction dreamily, with his mouth open.[6]

She had been cleaning the lamp, and held it, half blackened, half clear, in front of her. He saw her with the dark passage behind her. She was a big woman with a weather-beaten but unwrinkled face; her lips were held tightly together, and her eyes looked with a curious dulled brightness into his. He looked at her shoes, which were like bundles. If it were summer she would be barefoot.... Bowman, who automatically judged a woman's age on sight, set her age at fifty. She wore a formless garment of some gray coarse material, rough-dried from a washing, from which her arms appeared pink and unexpectedly round. When she never said a word, and sustained her quiet pose of holding the lamp, he was convinced of the strength in her body.

"Good afternoon, madam," he said.

She stared on, whether at him or at the air around him he could not tell, but after a moment she lowered her eyes to show that she would listen to whatever he had to say.

"I wonder if you would be interested—" He tried once more. "An accident—my car..."

Her voice emerged low and remote, like a sound across a lake. "Sonny[7] he ain't here."

"Sonny?"

"Sonny ain't here now."

Her son—a fellow able to bring my car up, he decided in blurred relief[8]. He pointed down the hill。"My car's in the bottom of the ditch. I'll need help."

"Sonny ain't here, but he'll be here."

She was becoming clearer to him and her voice stronger, and Bowman saw that she was stupid.

He was hardly surprised at the deepening postponement and tedium of his journey. He took a breath, and heard his voice speaking over the silent blows of his heart. "I was sick. I am not strong yet.... May I come in?"

He stooped and laid his big black hat over the handle of his bag. It was a humble motion, almost a bow, that instantly struck him as absurd and betraying[9] of all his weakness. He looked up at the woman, the wind blowing his hair. He might have continued for a long time in this unfamiliar attitude; he had never been a patient man, but when he was sick he had learned to sink submissively into the pillows, to wait for his medicine. He waited on the woman.[10]

Then she, looking at him with blue eyes, turned and held open the door, and after a moment Bowman, as if convined in his action, stood erect and followed her in.

Inside, the darkness of the house touched him like a professional hand, the doctor's. The woman set the half-cleaned lamp on a table in the center of the room and pointed, also like a professional person, a guide, to a chair with a yellow cowhide seat. She herself crouched on the hearth, drawing her knees up under the shapeless dress.

At first he felt hopefully secure. His heart was quieter. The room was enclosed in the gloom of yellow pine boards. He could see the other room, with the foot of an iron bed showing, across the passage. The bed had been made up with a red-and-yellow pieced quilt that looked like a map or a picture, a little like his grandmother's girlhood painting of Rome burning.

He had ached for coolness, but in this room it was cold. He stared at the hearth with dead coals lying on it and iron pots in the corners. The hearth and smoked chimney were of the stone he had seen ribbing the hills, mostly slate. Why is there no fire? he wondered.

And it was so still. The silence of the fields seemed to enter and move familiarly through the house. The wind used the open hall. He felt that he was in a mysterious, quiet, cool danger. It was necessary to do what?... To talk.

"I have a nice line of women's low-priced shoes..." he said.

But the woman answered, "Sonny'll be here. He's strong. Sonny'll move your car."

"Where is he now?"

"Farms for Mr. Redmond."

Mr. Redmond. Mr. Redmond. That was someone he would never have to encounter, and he was glad. Somehow the name did not appeal to him.... In a flare of touchiness and anxiety, Bowman wished to avoid even mention of unknown men and their unknown farms.

"Do you two live here alone?" He was surprised to hear his old voice, chatty, confidential, inflected for selling shoes, asking a question like that—a thing he did not even want to know.

"Yes. We are alone."

He was surprised at the way she answered. She had taken a long time to say that. She had nodded her head in a deep way too. Had she wished to affect him with some sort of premonition? he wondered unhappily. Or was it only that she would not help him, after all, by talking with him? For he was not strong enough to receive the impact of unfamiliar things without a little talk to break their fall. He had lived a month in which nothing had happened except in his head and his body—an almost inaudible life of heartbeats and dreams that came back, a life of fever and privacy, a delicate life which had left him weak to the point of—what? Of begging[11]. The pulse in his palm leapt like a trout in a brook.

He wondered over and over why the woman did not go ahead with cleaning the lamp. What prompted her to stay there across the room, silently bestowing her presence upon him? He saw that with her it was not a time for doing little tasks. Her face was grave; she was feeling how right she was. Perhaps it was only politeness. In docility he held his eyes stiffly wide; they fixed themselves on the woman's clasped hands as though she held the cord they were strung on.

Then, "Sonny's coming," she said.

He himself had not heard anything, but there came a man passing the window and then plunging in at the door, with two hounds beside him. Sonny was a big enough man, with his belt slung low about his hips. He looked at least thirty. He had a hot, red face that was yet full of silence. He wore muddy blue pants and an old military coat stained and patched. World War? Bowman wondered. Great God, it was a Confederate coat[12]. On the back of his light hair he had a wide filthy black hat which seemed to insult Bowman's own. He pushed down the dogs from his chest. He was strong, with dignity and heaviness in his way of moving.... There was the resemblance to his mother.

They stood side by side.... He must account again for his presence here.

"Sonny, this man, he had his car to run off over the prec'pice[13] an'[14] wants to know if you will git[15] it out for him," the woman said after a few minutes.

Bowman could not even state his case.

Sonny's eyes lay upon him.

He knew he should offer explanations and show money—at least appear either penitent or authoritative. But all he could do was to shrug slightly.

Sonny brushed by him going to the window, followed by the eager dogs, and looked out. There was effort even in the way he was looking, as if he could throw his sight out like a rope. Without turning Bowman felt that his own eyes could have seen nothing: it was too far.

"Got me a mule out there an' got me a block an' tackle," said Sonny meaningfully. "I *could* catch me my mule an' git me my ropes, an' before long I'd git your car out the ravine."[16]

He looked completely around the room, as if in meditation, his eyes roving in their own distance. Then he pressed his lips firmly and yet shyly together, and with the dogs ahead of him this time, he lowered his head and strode out. The hard earth sounded, cupping to his powerful way of walking—almost a stagger.

Mischievously, at the suggestion of those sounds, Bowman's heart leapt again. It seemed to walk about inside him.

"Sonny's goin' to do it," the woman said. She said it again, singing it almost, like a song. She was sitting in her place by the hearth.

Without looking out, he heard some shouts and the dogs barking and the pounding of hoofs in short runs on the hill. In a few minutes Sonny passed under the window with a rope, and there was a brown mule with quivering, shining, purple-looking ears. The mule actually looked in the window. Under its eyelashes it turned targetlike eyes into his. Bowman averted his head and saw the woman looking serenely back at the mule, with only satisfaction in her face.

She sang a little more, under her breath. It occurred to him, and it seemed quite marvelous, that she was not really talking to him, but rather following the thing that came about with words that were unconscious and part of her looking.

So he said nothing, and this time when he did not reply he felt a curious and strong emotion, not fear, rise up in him.

This time, when his heart leapt, something—his soul—seemed to leap too, like a little colt invited out of a pen. He stared at the woman while the frantic nimbleness of his feeling made his head sway. He could not move; there was nothing he could do, unless perhaps he might embrace this woman who sat there growing old and shapeless before him.

But he wanted to leap up, to say to her, I have been sick and I found out then, only then, how lonely I am. Is it too late? My heart puts up a struggle inside me, and you may have heard it, protesting a gainst emptiness.... It should be full, he would rush on to tell her, thinking of his heart now as a deep lake, it should be holding love like other hearts. It should be flooded with love. There would be a warm spring day... Come and stand in my heart, whoever you are, and a whole river would cover your feet and rise higher and take your knees in whirlpools, and draw you down to itself, your whole body, your heart too. [17]

But he moved a trembling hand across his eyes, and looked at the placid crouching woman across the room. She was still as a statue. He felt ashamed and exhausted by the thought that he might, in one more moment, have tried by simple words or embraces to communicate some strange thing—something which seemed always to have just escaped him....

Sunlight touched the furthest pot on the hearth. It was late afternoon. This time tomorrow he would be somewhere on a good graveled road, driving his car past things that happened to people, quicker than their happening. Seeing ahead to the next day, he was glad, and knew that this was no time to embrace an old woman. He could feel in his pounding temples the readying of his blood for motion and for hurrying away.

"Sonny's hitched up your car by now," said the woman. "He'll git it out the ravine right shortly."

"Fine!" he cried with his customary enthusiasm.

Yet it seemed a long time that they waited. It began to get dark. Bowman was cramped in his chair. Any man should know enough to get up and walk around while he waited. There was something like guilt in such stillness and silence. [18]

But instead of getting up he listened.... His breathing restrained, his eyes powerless in the growing dark, he listened uneasily for a warming sound, forgetting in wariness what it would be. Before long he heard something—soft, continuous, insinuating.

"What's that noise?" he asked, his voice jumping into the dark. Then wildly he was afraid it would be his heart beating so plainly in the quiet room, and she would tell him so.

"You might hear the stream," she said grudgingly.

Her voice was closer. She was standing by the table. He wondered why she did not light the lamp. She stood there in the dark and did not light it.

Bowman would never speak to her now, for the time was past. I'll sleep in the dark, he thought, in his bewilderment pitying himself.

Heavily she moved on to the window. Her arm, vaguely white, rose straight from her full side and she pointed out into the darkness.

"That white speck's Sonny," she said, talking to herself.

He turned unwillingly and peered over her shoulder; he hesitated to rise and stand beside her. His eyes searched the dusky air. The white speck floated smoothly toward her finger, like a leaf on a river, growing whiter in the dark. It was as if she had shown him someting secret, part of her life, but had offered no explanation. He looked away. He was moved almost to tears, feeling for no reason that she had made a silent declaration equivalent to his own. His hand waited upon his chest.

Then a step shook the house, and Sonny was in the room. Bowman felt how the woman left him there and went to the other man's side.

"I done got your car out[19], mister," said Sonny's voice in the dark. "She's settin'[20] a-waitin[21] in the road, turned to go back where she come from."

"Fine!" said Bowman, projecting his own voice to loudness. "I'm surely much obliged—I could never have done it myself—I was sick····"

"I could do it easy," said Sonny.

Bowman could feel them both waiting in the dark, and he could hear the dogs panting out in the yard, waiting to bark when he should go. He felt strangely helpless and resentful. Now that he could go, he longed to stay. From what was he being deprived? His chest was rudely shaken by the violence of his heart. These people cherished something here that he could not see, they withheld some ancient promise of food and warmth and light.[22] Between them they had a conspiracy. He thought of the way she had moved away from him and gone to Sonny, she had flowed toward him. He was shaking with cold, he was tired, and it was not fair. Humbly and yet angrily he stuck his hand into his pocket.

"Of course I'm going to pay you for everything—"

"We don't take money for such," said Sonny's voice belligerently.

"I want to pay. But do something more... Let me stay—tonight.... " He took another step toward them. If only they could see him, they would know his sincerity, his real need! His voice went on, "I'm not very strong yet, I'm not able to walk far even back to my car, maybe, I don't know—I don't know exactly where I am—"[23]

He stopped. He felt as if he might burst into tears. What would they think of him!

Sonny came over and put his hands on him. Bowman felt them pass (they were professional too) across his chest, over his hips. He could feel Sonny's eyes upon him in the dark.

"You ain't no revenuer[24] come sneakin'[25] here, mister, ain't got no gun?"[26]

To this end of nowhere![27] And yet *he* had come. He made a grave answer. "No."

"You can stay."

"Sonny," said the woman, "you'll have to borrow some fire."

"I'll go git it from Redmond's," said Sonny.

"What?" Bowman strained to hear their words to each other.

"Our fire, it's out, and Sonny's got to borry[28] some, because it's dark an' cold." she said.

"But matches—I have matches—"

"We don't have no need for' em," she said proudly. "Sonny's goin' after his own fire."[29]

"I'm goin' to Redmond's," said Sonny with an air of importance, and he went out.

After they had waited a while, Bowman looked out the window and saw a light moving over the hill. It spread itself out like a little fan. It zigzagged along the field, darting and swift, not like Sonny at all.... Soon enough, Sonny staggered in, holding a burning stick behind him in tongs, fire flowing in his wake, blazing light into the corridors of the room.

"We'll make a fire now," the woman said, taking the brand.

When that was done she lit the lamp. It showed its dark and light. The whole room turned golden-yellow like some sort of flower, and the walls smelled of it and seemed to tremble with the quiet rushing of the fire and the waving of the burning lampwick in its funnel of light.

The woman moved among the iron pots. With the tongs she dropped hot coals on top of the iron lids. They made a set of soft vibrations, like the sound of a bell far away.

She looked up and over at Bowman, but he could not answer. He was trembling....

"Have a drink, mister?" Sonny asked. He had brought a chair from the other room and sat astride it with folded arms across the back. Now we are all visible to one another, Bowman thought, and cried, "Yes sir, you bet, thanks!"

"Come after me and do just what I do," said Sonny.

It was another excursion into the dark.[30] They went through the hall, out to the back of the house, past a shed and a hooded well. They came to a wilderness of thicket.

"Down on your knees," said Sonny.

"What?" Sweat broke out on his forehead.

He understood when Sonny began to crawl through a sort of tunnel that the bushes made over the ground. He followed, startled in spite of himself when a twig or a thorn touched him gently without making a sound, clinging to him and finally letting him go.

Sonny stopped crawling and, crouched on his knees, began to dig with both his hands into the dirt. Bowman shyly struck matches and made a light. In a few minutes Sonny pulled up a jug. He poured out some of the whisky into a bottle from his coat pocket, and buried the jug again. "You never know who's liable to knock at your door," he said, and laughed. "Start back," he said, almost formally. "Ain't no need for us to drink outdoors, like hogs."

At the table by the fire, sitting opposite each other in their chairs, Sonny and Bowman took drinks out of the bottle, passing it across. The dogs slept; one of them was having a dream.

"This is good," said Bowman. "This is what I needed." It was just as though he were drinking the fire off the hearth.

"He makes it," said the woman with quiet pride.

She was pushig the coals off the pots, and the smells of corn bread and coffee circled the room. She set everything on the table before the men, with a bonehandled knife stuck into one of the potatoes, splitting out its golden fiber. Then she stood for a minute looking at them, tall and full above them where they sat. She leaned a little toward them.

"You all can eat now," she said, and suddenly smiled.

Bowman had just happened to be looking at her. He set his cup back on the table in unbelieving protest. A pain pressed at his eyes. He saw that she was not an old woman. She was young, still young. He could think of no number of years for her. She was the same age as Sonny, and she belonged to him. She stood with the deep dark corner of the room behind her, the shifting yellow light scattering over her head and her gray formless dress, trembling over her tall body when it bent over them in its sudden communication[31]. She was young. Her teeth were shining and her eyes glowed. She turned and walked slowly and heavily out of the room, and he heard her sit down on the cot and then lie down. The pattern on the quilt moved.

"She's goin' to have a baby," said Sonny, popping a bite into his mouth.

Bowman could not speak. He was shocked with knowing what was really in this house. A marriage, a fruitful marriage. That simple thing. Anyone could have had that.

Somehow he felt unable to be indignant or protest, although some sort of joke had certainly been played upon him. There was nothing remote or mysterious here—only something private. The only secret was the ancient communication between two people[32]. But the memory of the woman's waiting silently by the cold hearth, of the man's stubborn journey a mile away to get fire, and how they finally brought out their food and drink and filled the room proudly with all they had to show, was suddenly too clear and too enormous within him for response....

"You ain't as hungry as you look," said Sonny.

The woman came out of the bedroom as soon as the men had finished, and ate her supper while her husband stared peacefully into the fire.

Then they put the dogs out, with the food that was left.

"I think I'd better sleep here by the fire, on the floor," said Bowman.

He felt that he had been cheated, and that he could afford now to be generous. Ill though he was, he was not going to ask them for their bed. He was through with asking favors in this house, now that he understood what was there.

"Sure, mister."

But he had not known yet how slowly he understood. They had not meant to give him their bed. After a little interval they both rose and looking at him gravely went into the other room.

He lay stretched by the fire until it grew low and dying. He watched every tongue of blaze lick out and vanish. "There will be special reduced prices on all footwear during the month of January," he found himself repeating quietly, and then he lay with his lips tight shut.

How many noises the night had! He heard the stream running, the fire dying, and he was sure now that he heard his heart beating, too, the sound it made under his ribs. He heard breathing, round and deep, of the man and his wife in the room across the passage. And that was all. But emotion swelled patiently within him, and he wished that the child were his.

He must get back to where he had been before. He stood weakly before the red coals and put on his overcoat. It felt too heavy on his shoulders. As he started out he looked and saw that the woman had never got through with cleaning the lamp[33]. On some impulse he put all the money from his billfold under its fluted glass base, almost ostentatiously.

Ashamed, shrugging a little, and then shivering, he took his bags and went out. The cold air seemed to lift him bodily. The moon was in the sky.

On the slope he began to run, he could not help it. Just as he reached the road, where his car seemed to sit in the moonlight like a boat, his heart began to give off tremendous explosions like a rifle, bang bang bang.

He sank in fright onto the road, his bags falling about him. He felt as if all this had happened before. He covered his heart with both hands to keep anyone from hearing the noise it make.

But nobody heard it.

〔注释〕

1. The time did not seem to clear the noon hurdle and settle into a soft afternoon.：作者采用体育运动中的跳栏暗喻时间尚未越过正午。在本篇中多次出现此类比喻，具有生动的艺术效果。

2. drummer：（美国俚语）旅行推销员，旅行商贩。

3. soul＝person.

4. Beulah：密西西比州一个小镇。

5. shotgun house：房子的两间屋子由露天通道连接，看去仿佛双筒猎枪的两个枪筒。

6. Stock-still in his confusion, …and yet in his distraction dreamily, with his mouth open.：这两段表现鲍曼疾病缠身，精神恍惚，心烦意乱，因而对周围的事物产生幻觉，失去正常的判断能力。

7. Sonny：原为对男孩子的爱称，现为农妇对丈夫的称呼。正是这个称呼使鲍曼（也使读者）误认为他们是母子关系。

8. in blurred relief：既感到宽慰，又感到困惑。

9. betraying：意为 suggestive 或 revealing。

10. He waited on the woman.：他听候那女人吩咐。

11. a delicate life which had left him weak to the point of—what?Of begging.：鲍曼病中的生活使他身心衰弱，到了向人乞求的地步。至于乞求什么，作者故意不作说明，以埋下伏笔。

12. Confederate coat：指美国独立战争时期南部邦联军的军装。

13. prec'pice=precipice.

14. an'=and.

15. git=get.

16. "Got me a mule out there an' got me a block an' tackle,"…"I *could* catch me my mule…."：注意这句中动词的虚拟语态。

17. But he wanted to leap up,... your heart too.：鲍曼的这段内心独白揭示出他突然感到孤独，渴求爱抚的心理状态。这仅是作者运用心理描写手法的一例。

18. There was something like guilt in such stillness and silence.：鲍曼因精疲力竭或心不在焉而行动"失常"，这使他感到疚愧。

19. I done got your car out=I have got your car out.

20. She's settin' =She's sitting. "She"指汽车。

21. a-waitin'=waiting.

22. some ancient promise of food and warmth and light：在《圣经·创世记》("Genesis")中，上帝为人类准备了光亮、食物和温暖等生存的必要条件。这里的"ancient"可追溯到上帝创世的时候。

23. I don't know exactly where I am.：这是双关语，一方面，鲍曼在路途中迷失方向才来到这户农家，所以他不知自己到了什么地方。另一方面，他在思想上与世人隔绝，有失落感，不知自己在生活中处于什么位置。

24. revenuer：税务官，这里指缉私官。1920至1933年间，美国实行《全国禁酒法》。该法律将含酒精超过百分之零点五的饮料定为酒类，并对工业、医药和圣餐用酒的制造和出售严加管制。官方经常进行严格的检查。下文中提到农户自己造酒和把酒埋在野地里的情节均由此而来。

25. sneakin'=sneaking.

26. ain't got no gun? =haven't you got a gun?

27. To this end of nowhere!：意为 To this obscure and remote place!

28. borry=borrow.

29. "Sonny's goin' after his own fire."：男主人拒绝使用鲍曼的火柴，坚持按自己的方式去远处取火。他执著地追求自己的生活方式。这一自助、自立的自由农形象与鲍曼这个不知自己归宿的"现代文明人"形成鲜明的对照。

30. It was another excursion into the dark.：这是双关语。鲍曼一直身处五

里雾中，现在又真地钻进夜幕里。

31. communication=revelation.

32. the ancient communication between two people：这个词组的意义可追溯到《圣经·创世纪》中亚当和夏娃的结合。

33.... the woman had never got through with cleaning the lamp.：故事开始时，鲍曼见到农妇擦拭油灯，但没擦完，灯始终半明半暗。以后作者又多次提到这盏灯。半明半暗的灯是本篇小说中的一个重要象征，它说明农妇对鲍曼来说始终是黑暗中的一个未解之谜，表现鲍曼既不能理解别人又不能理解自己。

TENNESSEE WILLIAMS

〔作者介绍〕

田纳西·威廉斯 (Tennessee Williams, 1911～1983)，美国著名剧作家。他生于密西西比州哥伦布市，12 岁随全家移居圣路易斯城。威廉斯自幼喜爱文学创作，14 岁时曾在一家全国性杂志《时髦人物》(The Smart Set) 举办的散文赛中获头奖，17 岁发表第一篇短篇小说《尼特罗克里斯复仇记》("The Vengeance of Nitrocris")。1929 年他入密苏里大学学习，但在 1932 年因贫穷被迫辍学到一家鞋厂工作，在仓库里度过了 3 年他后来称之为"虽生犹死"的时光，终因精神支撑不住，在祖父家休养 1 年。后来又入学，1938 年在衣阿华大学毕业，获学士学位。

威廉斯在密苏里大学就读时便开始戏剧创作。大学毕业后，他除了干些杂活维持生计以外还坚持写作。1939 年改名"田纳西"，觉得原名"汤姆·威廉斯"太"乏味"。同年他的《美国布鲁士》剧获全国戏剧奖。1940 年他的首部由一家大剧院上演的剧作《天使之战》(*Battle of Angels*)，在波士顿上演失败，只演过一场便停止。两年后，他受雇于好莱坞写角本，也未获成功，几个月后被辞掉，但是其中有一部名为《来访的先生》(*The Gentleman Caller*) 的剧本，后改写成《玻璃动物园》(*The Glass Menagerie*)，成为他在美国剧坛扬名的首部杰作。1945 年《玻璃动物园》演出的成功不仅标志着威廉斯戏剧创作生涯的开端，而且成为美国戏剧发展史上的一个里程碑。

从那以后，威廉斯平均每两年推出一部新作。他的最脍炙人口的作品有《欲望号街车》(*A Streetcar Named Desire*, 1974)、《热铁皮屋顶上的猫》(*Cat on a Hot Tin Roof*, 1955)，这两部剧作皆获普利策奖，被誉为当年最佳剧作，此外，《去年夏天突然来到》(*Suddenly Last Summer*, 1958)、《可爱的青春小鸟》(*Sweet Bird of Youth*, 1959)、《鬣蜥之夜》(*Night of the Iguana*, 1961) 这 3 部剧作都在百老汇剧场取得巨大成功。60 年代似乎是威廉斯创作的"低谷"，他开始担心自己"未老先衰"，但在 70 年代，他的创作力开始恢复。他的其他作品包括《玫瑰刺花》(*The Rose Tatoo*, 1951)、《大路》(Camino Real, 1953)、《琴神下凡》(Orpheus Dessending, 1957)、《一只鹦鹉的精确分析》(*A Perfect Analysis Given by a Parrot*, 1958)、《适应阶段》(*Period of Adjustment*, 1960)、《牛奶车不再在此停留》(*The Milk Train Doesn't Stop Here Anymore*, 1962)、《姑娘》(*The Gnädiges Fräulein*, 1966)、《双人剧》(*The Two Character Play*, 1967)、《世欲王国》(*Kingdom of Earth*, 1968),《在东京旅店酒巴里》(*In the Bar of a Tokyo Hotel*, 1969)、《红鬼炮兵连的信号》(*Red Devil Battery Sign*, 1975)、《小手艺的警告》(*Small Craft Warnings*, 1972)、《维厄·卡雷》(*Vieux Carré*, 1977)及《失恋者的一个愉快的星期天》(*A Lovely Sunday for Creve Coeur*, 1978)等。他有15部作品被改编成电影,其中《小娃娃》(*Baby Doll*)于1951年上映,引起争议;他还写过1部小说、2部诗集、6部散文集和3部短篇小说集。

威廉斯剧作中突出的人物是一个孤独的、脆弱的女人,她的生活毫无安全感,因而时常沉缅于对过去的回忆或对未来的幻想中,而这种幻景又常被一位代表现实的闯入她生活的男人打破,剧情随之步入高潮。此外剧作中常出现的人物有迥异于周围其他人的"局外人"、对可怕的生活看得最透彻的人、身心畸形的人、精神不正常的人、艺术家或伪艺术家、害人者和受害者、外国人或陌生人。他的人物中不乏逃避现实者,他们面对世界的冷漠无情感到惶恐。这些萎缩的男人或女人竭力通过游荡或远走高飞来逃脱生活的折磨、时间的吞噬以及衰萎的命运,但是始终无法成功。威廉斯的写作技巧非常精妙,尤其对人物性格的刻画牵动人心,语言也简炼、生动,富有诗意。他对"疲塌的现实主义戏剧"感到不满,在自己的作品中运用了语言、视觉和听觉上的象征主义手法,尝试了文学和戏剧表演方面的多种表现主义技巧,包括特殊的背景、音乐的烘托、不寻常的声响和灯光效果等,引导观众洞察掩藏在表面现象之后的生活的本来面目。

威廉斯在描写美国生活时擅长"出奇制胜"。他对谋杀、强奸、吸毒、同性恋、酗酒、拜物主义、色情狂等现象的描绘有助于打破禁区,从而促进了美国戏剧的发展,为勒鲁瓦·琼斯及爱德华·阿尔比等后辈剧作家的创作开辟了道路。

The Glass Menagerie

〔作品介绍〕

《玻璃动物园》(*The Glass Menagerie*)1945年在纽约上演,使威廉斯在剧坛上取得首次成功。它获得“纽约戏剧界奖”，被视为当年的最佳剧作。自那时起，评论界逐渐认识到它标志了战后美国新戏剧发展的开端。

《玻璃动物园》的故事情节相当简单：在一处下等中产阶级集居的公寓大楼里，住着一家3口人——阿曼达·温菲尔德夫人以及她的女儿劳拉和儿子汤姆。阿曼达的丈夫已离家出走，女儿自幼跛脚，在家闲居，儿子在一家鞋厂仓库工作，全家生活相当清苦。阿曼达担心女儿成为嫁不出去的老姑娘，也担心儿子吸烟、酗酒，一事无成，最后离家出走。她家境没落前，原是名门闺秀，而今她唯一的慰藉就是，缅怀那一去不复返的美好日子。劳拉因身残而自卑，腼腆到神经质的程度，她中途退学，对职业学习也不适应，孤独、痛苦，整日和她收集的玻璃动物呆在一起。汤姆生性爱冒险，还喜欢作诗，对仓库的工作毫无兴趣，用他母亲的话说，他生活在梦中，自己制造幻象。阿曼达急于给女儿找对象，让汤姆把一位名叫吉姆的同事带回家来热情招待，吉姆讲了许多鼓励劳拉克服自卑、面对生活的话，但他已有对象，这使劳拉和她母亲感到失望。汤姆也终于离家出走。

这3个人生活在只有“永恒黑暗”的“神秘宇宙里，”都以其不同的方式逃避现实。阿曼达是从对美好的过去的回忆中汲取生活勇气的。她一讲起自己充满罗曼蒂克色彩的少女经历就眉飞色舞，一想到现实就悲叹一切皆已成为过去。汤姆心神不定，只能到电影的世界里寻求某种满足，但他对好莱坞式的冒险也感到厌烦。劳拉是威廉斯笔下典型的女主人公，孤独、脆弱，极端内向，竭力躲藏在自己造就的理想世界里，逃避痛苦的现实生活的侵袭。劳拉从她收藏的小玻璃动物的世界里看到了人人友好相处的理想社会秩序。这一家人“逃避精神”的最好象征是挂在墙上的父亲在微笑的照片，他在16年前就离家出走，从而一刀把尘缘剪断。

剧中唯一讲求实际的人是吉姆。他的到来结束了一家3人的幻觉，使他们回到现实中来。他打碎了劳拉的一只玻璃动物——麒麟的角，劳拉的脆弱的世界受到侵扰，但她意识到这可能不是灾祸。吉姆也是威廉斯剧作中的典型人物之一，他是闯入孤独、内向的女主人公的幻想世界的男人，是现实生活的象征。虽然随着吉姆的到来和离去，幻想已破灭，现实已表现出其令人沮丧的真面目，温菲尔德一家因此感到痛苦甚至绝望，但是，在最后一场中，观众看到阿曼达开始克服失落感，恢复勇气，劝慰感情上受到打击的女儿，劳拉也动人地把低垂的头抬起，终于面对母亲露出了笑容，母女怀着信心，挺起身迎向严酷的现实。所以，该剧并不是以绝望告终的。

在这部剧作的创作过程中，威廉斯从自己家庭的经历中汲取了许多素材，他所描写的是他的母亲、姐姐和他本人的生活情况。威廉斯的父亲是推销商，终年在外，他幼时跟母亲住在外祖父家，度过了几年快活的时光。他7岁时，父亲在圣路易斯城一家鞋店当销售部经理，他随母前往，对新生活很不习惯。他性格胆怯，缺少朋友，觉得很痛苦，常去电影院在冒险的情节中寻觅解脱。这一经历对他影响很大,《玻璃动物园》中汤姆这一形象便取自他的这一生活阶段。他后来回忆说，那时他总想爬上银幕，参加活动。这是《玻璃动物园》描绘逼真、情节感人的基本原因之一。

这里选注的是该剧最后两场（第 6 场、第 7 场）。

The Glass Menagerie

SCENE Ⅵ

The light comes up on the fire escape landing. Tom[1] *is leaning against the grill, smoking.*

[*Screen image*: The high school hero.]

TOM: And so the following evening I brought Jim home to dinner. I had known Jim slightly in high school. In high school Jim was a hero. He had tremendous Irish good nature and vitality with the scrubbed and polished look of white chinaware. He seemed to move in a continual spotlight. He was a star in basketball, captain of the debating club, president of the senior class and the glee club and he sang the male lead in the annual light operas. He was always running or bounding, never just walking. He seemed always at the point of defeating the law of gravity. He was shooting with such velocity through his adolescence that you would logically expect him to arrive at nothing short of the White House by the time he was thirty. But Jim apparently ran into more interference after his graduation from Soldan.[2] His speed had definitely slowed. Six years after he left high school he was holding a job that wasn't much better than mine.

[*Screen image*: The Clerk.]

He was the only one at the warehouse with whom I was on friendly terms. I was valuable to him as someone who could remember his former glory, who had seen him win basketball games and the silver cup in debating. He knew of my secret practice of retiring to a cabinet of the washroom to work on poems when business was slack in the warehouse. He called me Shakespeare. And while the other boys in the warehouse regarded me with suspicious hostility, Jim took a humorous attitude toward me. Gradually his attitude affected the others, their hostility wore off and they also began to smile at me as people smile at an oddly fashioned dog who trots across their path at some distance.

I knew that Jim and Laura had known each other at Soldan, and I had heard Laura speak admiringly of his voice. I didn't know if Jim remembered her or not. In high school Laura had been as unobtrusive as Jim had been astonishing. If he did remember Laura, it was not as my sister, for when I asked him to dinner, he grinned and said, "You know, Shakespeare, I never thought of you as having folks!"

He was about to discover that I did....

[*Legend on screen*: "The accent of a coming foot."][3]

[*The light dims out on Tom and comes up in the Wingfield living room—a delicate lemony light. It is about five on a Friday evening of late spring which comes "scattering poems in the sky."*][4]

[*Amanda has worked like a Turk in preparation for the gentleman caller. The results are astonishing. The new floor lamp with its rose silk shade is in place, a colored paper lantern conceals the broken light fixture in the ceiling, new billowing white curtains are at the windows, chintz covers are on the chairs and sofa, a pair of new sofa pillows make their initial appearance. Open boxes and tissue paper are scattered on the floor.*]

[*Laura stands in the middle of the room with lifted arms while Amanda crouches before her, adjusting the hem of a new dress, devout and ritualistic. The dress is colored and designed by memory. The arrangement of Laura's hair is changed; it is softer and more becoming. A fragile, unearthly prettiness has come out in Laura: she is like a piece of translucent glass touched by light, given a momentary radiance, not actual, not lasting.*]

AMANDA [*impatiently*]: Why are you trembling?

LAURA: Mother, you've made me so nervous!

AMANDA: How have I made you nervous?

LAURA: By all this fuss! You make it seem so important!

AMANDA: I don't understand you, Laura. You couldn't be satisfied with just sitting home, and yet whenever I try to arrange something for you, you seem to resist it. [*She gets up.*] Now take a look at yourself. No, wait! Wait just a moment—I have an idea!

LAURA: What is it now?

[*Amanda produces two powder puffs which she wraps in handkerchiefs and stuffs in Laura's bosom.*]

LAURA: Mother, what are you doing?

AMANDA: They call them "Gay Deceivers"!

LAURA: I won't wear them!

AMANDA: You will!

LAURA: Why should I?

AMANDA: Because, to be painfully honest, your chest is flat.

LAURA: You make it seem like we were setting a trap.

AMANDA: All pretty girls are a trap, a pretty trap, and men expect them to be.

[*Legend on screen*: "A pretty trap."]

Now look at yourself, young lady. This is the prettiest you will ever be! [*She stands back to admire Laura.*] I've got to fix myself now! You're going to be surprised by your mother's appearance!

[*Amanda crosses through the portieres, humming gaily. Laura moves slowly to the long mirror and stares solemnly at herself. A wind blows the white curtains inward in a slow, graceful motion and with a faint, sorrowful sighing.*]

AMANDA [*from somewhere behind the portieres*] It isn't dark enough yet.

[*Laura turns slowly before the mirror with a troubled look.*]

[*Legend on screen*: "This is my sister: Celebrate her with strings!" *Music plays.*]

AMANDA: [*laughing, still not visible*]: I'm going to show you something. I'm going to make a spectacular appearance!

LAURA: What is it, Mother?

AMURA: Possess your soul in patience—you will see! Something I've resurrected from that old trunk! Styles haven't changed so terribly much after all.... [*She parts the portieres.*] Now just look at your mother! [*She wears a girlish frock of yellowed voile with a blue silk sash. She carries a bunch of jonquils—the legend of her youth is nearly revived. Now she speaks feverishly*:] This is the dress in which I led the cotillion. Won the cakewalk twice at Sunset Hill, wore one Spring to the Governor's Ball in Jackson! See how I sashayed around the ballroom, Laura? [*She raises her skirt and does a mincing step around the room.*] I wore it on Sundays for my gentlemen callers! I had it on the day I met your father.... I had malaria fever all that Spring. The change of climate from East Tennessee to the Delta—weakened resistance. I had a little temperature all the time—not enough to be serious—just enough to make me restless and giddy! Invitations poured in—parties all over the Delta! "Stay in bed," said Mother, "You have a fever!"—but I just wouldn't. I took quinine but kept on going, going! Evenings, dances! Afternoons, long, long rides! Picnics—lovely! So lovely, that country in May—all lacy with dogwood, literally flooded with jonquils! That was the spring I had the craze for jonquils. Jonquils became an absolute obsession. Mother said, "Honey, there's no more room for jonquils." And still I kept on bringing in more jonquils. Whenever, wherever I saw them, I'd say, "Stop! Stop! I see jonquils!" I made the young men help me gather the jonquils! It was a joke, Amanda and her jonquils. Finally there were no more vases to hold them, every available space was filled with jonquils. No vases to hold them? All right, I'll hold them myself! And then I— [*She stops in front of the picture.*[5] *Music plays.*] met your father! Malaria fever and jonquils and then—this—boy.... [*She switches on the rose-colored lamp.*] I hope they get here before it starts to rain. [*She crosses the room and places the jonquils in a bowl on the table.*] I gave your brother a little extra change so he and Mr. O'Connor could take the service car home.

LAURA [*with an altered look*]: What did you say his name was?

AMANDA: O'Connor.

LAURA: What is his first name?

AMANDA: I don't remember. Oh, yes, I do. It was—Jim!

[*Laura sways slightly and catches hold of a chair.*]

[*Legend on screen*: "Not Jim!"]

LAURA [*faintly*] Not—Jim!

AMANDA: Yes, that was it, it was Jim! I've never known a Jim that wasn't nice!

[*The music becomes ominous.*]

LAURA: Are you sure his name is Jim O'Connor?

AMANDA: Yes. Why?

LAURA: Is he the one that Tom used to know in high school?

AMANDA: He didn't say so. I think he just got to know him at the warehouse.

LAURA: There was a Jim O'Connor we both knew in high school—[*then, with effort*] If that is the one that Tom is bringing to dinner—you'll have to excuse me, I won't come to the table.

AMANDA: What sort of nonsense is this?

LAURA: You asked me once if I'd ever liked a boy. Don't you remember I showed you this boy's picture?

AMANDA: You mean the boy you showed me in the year-book?

LAURA: Yes, that boy.

AMANDA: Laura, Laura, were you in love with that boy?

LAURA: I don't know, Mother. All I know is I couldn't sit at the table if it was him!

AMANDA: It won't be him! It isn't the least bit likely. But whether it is or not, you will come to the table. You will not be excused.

LAURA: I'll have to be, Mother.

AMANDA: I don't intend to humor your silliness, Laura. I've had too much from you and your brother, both! So just sit down and compose yourself till they come. Tom has forgotten his key so you'll have to let them in, when they arrive.

LAURA [*panicky*]: Oh, Mother—*you* answer the door!

AMANDA [*lightly*]: I'll be in the kitchen—busy!

LAURA: Oh, Mother, please answer the door, don't make me do it. !

AMANDA [*crossing into the kitchenette*]: I've got to fix the dressing for the salmon. Fuss, fuss—silliness! —over a gentleman caller!

[*The door swings shut. Laura is left alone.*]

[*Legend on screen*: "Terror!"]

[*She utters a low moan and turns off the lamp—sits stiffly on the edge of the sofa, knotting her fingers together.*]

[*Legend on screen*, "The Opening of a Door!"]

[*Tom and Jim appear on the fire escape steps and climb to the landing. Hearing their approach, Laura rises with a panicky gesture. She retreats to the portieres. The doorbell rings. Laura catches her breath and touches her throat. Low drums sound.*]

AMANDA [*calling*]: Laura, sweetheart! The door!

[*Laura stares at it without moving.*]

JIM: I think we just beat the rain.

TOM: Uh-huh. [*He rings again, nervously. Jim whistles and fishes for a cigarette.*]

AMANDA [*very, very gaily*]: Laura, that is your brother and Mr. O'Connor! Will you let them in, darling?

[*Laura crosses toward the kitchenette door.*]

LAURA [*breathlessly*]: Mother—you go to tho door!

[*Amanda steps out of the kitchenette and stares furiously at Laura. She points imperiously at the door.*]

LAURA: Please, please!

AMANDA [*in a fierce whisper*]: What is the matter with you, you silly thing?

LAURA [*desperately*]: Please, you answer it, *please*!

AMANDA: I told you I wasn't going to humor you, Laura. Why have you chosen this moment to lose your mind?

LAURA: Please, please, please, you go!

AMANDA: You'll have to go to the door because I can't!

LAURA [*despairingly*]: I can't either!

AMANDA: *Why*?

LAURA: I'm *sick*!

AMANDA: I'm sick, too—of your nonsense! Why can't you and your brother be normal people? Fantastic whims and behavior!

[*Tom gives a long ring.*]

Preposterous goings on! Can you give me one reason— [*She calls out lyrically.*] *Coming*! *Just one second*! —why you should be afraid to open a door? Now you answer it, Laura!

LAURA: Oh, oh, oh... [*She returns through the portieres, darts to the Victrola,*[6] *winds it frantically and turns it on.*]

AMANDA: Laura Wingfield, you march right to that door!

LAURA: *Yes—yes, Mother*!

[*A faraway, scratchy rendition of "Dardanella"*[7] *softens the air and gives her strength to move through it. She slips to the door and draws it cautiously open. Tom enters with the caller, Jim O'Connor.*]

TOM: Laura, this is Jim. Jim, this is my sister, Laura.

JIM [*stepping inside*]: I didn't know that Shakespeare had a sister!

LAURA [*retreating, stiff and trembling, from the door*]: How—how do you do?

JIM [*heartily, extending his hand*]: Okay!

[*Laura touches it hesitantly with hers.*]

JIM: Your hand's *cold*, Laura!

LAURA: Yes, well—I've been playing the Victrola....

JIM: Must have been playing classical music on it! You ought to play a little hot swing music to warm you up!

LAURA: Excuse me—I haven't finished playing the Victrola.... [*She turns awkwardly and hurries into the front room. She pauses a second by the Victrola. Then she catches her breath and darts through the portieres like a frightened deer.*]

JIM [*grinning*]: What was the matter?

TOW: Oh—with Laura? Laura is—terribly shy.

JIM: Shy, huh? It's unusual to meet a shy girl nowadays. I don't believe you ever mentioned you had a sister.

TOM: Well, now you know. I have one. Here is the *Post Dispatch*. You want a piece of it?

JIM: Uh-huh.

TOM: What piece? The comics?

JIM: Sports! [*He glances at it.*] Ole Dizzy Dean is on his bad behavior.

TOM [*uninterested*]: Yeah? [*He lights a cigarette and goes over to the fire-escape door.*]

JIM: Where are you going?

TOM: I'm going out on the terrace.

JIM [*going after him*]: You know, Shakespeare—I'm going to sell you a bill of goods!

TOM: What goods?

JIM: A course I'm taking.

TOM: Huh?

JIM: In public speaking! You and me, we're not the warehouse type.

TOM: Thanks—that's good news. But what has public speaking got to do with it?

JIM: It fits you for—executive positions!

TOM: Awww.

JIM: I tell you it's done a helluva lot for me.

[*Image on screen*: Executive at his desk.]

TOM: In what respect?

JIM: In every! Ask yourself what is the difference between you an' me and men in the office down front? Brains? —No! —Ability? —No! Then what? Just one little thing—

TOM: What is that one little thing?

JIM: Primarily it amounts to—social poise! Being able to square up to people and hold your own on any social level!

AMANDA [*from the kitchenette*]: Tom?

TOM: Yes, Mother?

AMANDA: Is that you and Mr. O'Connor?

TOM: Yes, Mother.

AMANDA: Well, you just make yourselves comfortable in there.

TOM: Yes, Mother.

AMANDA: Ask Mr. O'Connor if he would like to wash his hands.

JIM: Aw, no—no—thank you—I took care of that at the warehouse. Tom—

TOM: Yes?

JIM: Mr. Mendoza was speaking to me about you.

TOM: Favorably?

JIM: What do you think?

TOM: Well—

JIM: You're going to be out of a job if you don't wake up.

TOM: I am waking up—

JIM: You show no signs.

TOM: The signs are interior.

[*Image on screen*: The sailing vessel with the Jolly Roger again.]

TOM: I'm planning to change. [*He leans over the fire-escape rail, speaking with quiet exhilaration. The incandescent marquees and signs of the first-run movie houses light his face from across the alley. He looks like a voyager.*] I'm right at the point of committing myself to a future that doesn't include the warehouse and Mr. Mendoza or even a night-school course in public speaking.

JIM: What are you gassing about?

TOM: I'm tired of the movies.

JIM: Movies!

TOM: Yes, movies! Look at them— [*a wave toward the marvels of Grand Avenue*] All of those glamorous people—having adventures—hogging it all, gobbling the whole thing up! You know what happens? People go to the *movies* instead of *moving*! Hollywood characters are supposed to have all the adventures for everybody in America, while everybody in America sits in a dark room and watches them have them! Yes, until there's a war. That's when adventure becomes available to the masses! *Everyone's* dish, not only Gable's![8] Then the people in the dark room come out of the dark room to have some adventures themselves—

goody, goody! It's our turn now, to go to the South Sea Island—to make a safari—to be exotic, far-off! But I'm not patient. I don't want to wait till then. I'm tired of the *movies* and I am *about to move*!

JIM [*incredulously*]: Move?

TOM: Yes.

JIM: When?

TOM: Soon!

JIM: Where? Where?

[*The music seems to answer the question, while Tom thinks it over. He searches in his pockets.*]

TOM: I'm starting to boil inside. I know I seem dreamy, but inside—well, I'm boiling! Whenever I pick up a shoe, I shudder a little thinking how short life is and what I am doing! Whatever that means, I know it doesn't mean shoes—except as something to wear on a traveler's feet! [*He finds what he has been searching for in his pockets and holds out a paper to Jim.*] Look—

JIM: What?

TOM: I'm a member.

JIM [*reading*]: The Union of Merchant Seamen.

TOM: I paid my dues this month, instead of the light bill.[9]

JIM: You will regret it when they turn the lights off.

TOM: I won't be here.

JIM: How about your mother?

TOM: I'm like my father. The bastard son of a bastard! Did you notice how he's grinning in his picture in there? And he's been absent going on sixteen years!

JIM: You're just talking, you drip. How does your mother feel about it?

TOM: Shhh! Here comes Mother! Mother is not acquainted with my plans!

AMANDA [*coming through the portieres*]: Where are you all?

TOM: On the terrace, Mother.

[*They start inside. She advances to them. Tom is distinctly shocked at her appearance. Even Jim blinks a little. He is making his first contact with girlish Southern vivacity and in spite of the night-school course in public speaking is somewhat thrown off the beam by the unexpected outlay of social charm. Certain responses are attempted by Jim but are swept aside by*

Amanda's gay laughter and chatter. Tom is embarrassed but after the first shock Jim reacts very warmly. He grins and chuckles, is altogether won over.]

[*Image on screen*: Amanda as a girl.]

AMANDA [*coyly smiling, shaking her girlish ringlets*]: Well, well, well, so this is Mr. O'Connor. Introductions entirely unnecessary. I've heard so much about you from my boy. I finally said to him, Tom—good gracious! —why don't you bring this paragon to supper? I'd like to meet this nice young man at the warehouse! —instead of just hearing him sing your praises so much! I don't know why my son is so stand-offish—that's not Southern behavior!

Let's sit down and—I think we could stand a little more air in here! Tom, leave the door open. I felt a nice fresh breeze a moment ago. Where has it gone to? Mmm, so warm already! And not quite summer, even. We're going to burn up when summer really gets started. However, we're having—we're having a very light supper. I think light things are better fo' this time of year. The same as light clothes are. Light clothes an' light food are what warm weather calls fo'. You know our blood gets so thick during th' winter—it takes a while fo' us to adjust ou'selves! —when the season changes... It's come so quick this year. I wasn't prepared. All of a sudden—heavens! Already summer! I ran to the trunk an' pulled out this light dress—terribly old! Historical almost! But feels so good—so good an' co-ol, y'know....

TOM: Mother—

AMANDA: Yes, honey?

TOM: How about—supper?

AMANDA: Honey, you go ask Sister if supper is ready! You know that Sister is in full charge of supper! Tell her you hungry boys are waiting for it. [*to Jim*] Have you met Laura?

JIM: She—

AMANDA: Let you in? Oh, good, you've met already! It's rare for a girl as sweet an' pretty as Laura to be domestic! But Laura is, thank heavens, not only pretty but also very domestic. I'm not at all. I never was a bit. I never could make a thing but angel-food cake. Well, in the South we had so many servants. Gone, gone, gone. All vestige of gracious living! Gone completely! I wasn't prepared for what the future brought me. All of my gentlemen callers were sons of planters and so of course I assumed that I would be married to one and raise my family on a large piece of land with plenty of servants. But man proposes—and woman accepts the proposal![10] To vary that old, old saying a little bit—I married no planter! I married a man who worked for the telephone company! That gallantly smiling gentleman over there! [*She points to the picture.*] A telephone man who—fell in love with long-distance! Now he travels and I don't even know where! But what am I going on for about my—tribulations? Tell me yours—I hope you don't have any! Tom?

TOM: [*returning*]: Yes, Mother?

AMANDA: Is supper nearly ready?

TOM: It looks to me like supper is on the table.

AMANDA: Let me look— [*She rises prettily and looks through the portieres.*] Oh, lovely! But where is Sister?

TOM: Laura is not feeling well and she says that she thinks she'd better not come to the table.

AMANDA: What? Nonsense! Laura? Oh, Laura!

LAURA [*from the kitchenette, faintly*]: Yes, Mother.

AMANDA: You really must come to the table. We won't be seated until you come to the table! Come in, Mr. O'Connor. You sit over there, and I'll.... Laura? Laura Wingfield! You're keeping us waiting, honey! We can't say grace until you come to the table!

[*The kitchenette door is pushed weakly open and Laura comes in. She is obviously quite faint, her lips trembling, her eyes wide and staring. She moves unsteadily toward the table.*]

[*Screen legend:* "Terror!"]

[*Outside a summer storm is coming on abruptly. The white curtains billow inward at the windows and there is a sorrowful murmur from the deep blue dusk.*]

[*Laura suddenly stumbles; she catches at a chair with a faint moan.*]

TOM: Laura!

AMANDA: Laura!

[*There is a clap of thunder.*]

[*Screen legend:* "Ah!"]

[*despairingly*] Why, Laura, you are ill, darling! Tom, help your sister into the living room, dear! Sit in the living room, Laura—rest on the sofa. Well! [*to Jim as Tom helps his sister to the sofa in the living room*]Standing over the hot stove made her ill! I told her that it was just too warm this evening, but—

[*Tom comes back to the table.*]

Is Laura all right now?

TOM: Yes.

AMANDA: What *is* that? Rain? A nice cool rain has come up! [*She gives Jim a frightened look.*] I think we may—have grace—now...

[*Tom looks at her stupidly.*] Tom, honey—you say grace!

TOM: Oh... "For these and all thy mercies—"

[*They bow their heads, Amanda stealing a nervous glance at Jim. In the living room Laura, stretched on the sofa, clenches her hand to her lips, to hold back a shuddering sob.*]

God's Holy Name be praised—

[*The scene dims out.*]

SCENE Ⅶ

It is half an hour later. Dinner is just being finished in the dining room, Laura is still huddled upon the sofa, her feet drawn under her, her head resting on a pale blue pillow, her eyes wide and mysteriously watchful. The new floor lamp with its shade of rose-colored silk gives a soft, becoming light to her face, bringing out the fragile, unearthly prettiness which usually escapes attention. From outside there is a steady murmur of rain, but it is slackening and soon stops, the air outside becomes pale and luminous as the moon breaks through the clouds. A moment after the curtain rises, the lights in both rooms flicker and go out.

JIM: Hey, there, Mr. Light Bulb!

[*Amanda laughs nervously.*]

[*Legend on screen:* "Suspension of public service."

AMANDA: Where was Moses when the lights went out? Ha-ha. Do you know the answer to that one, Mr. O'Connor?

JIM: No, Ma'am, what's the answer?

AMANDA: In the dark!

[*Jim laughs appreciatively.*]

Everybody sit still. I'll light the candles. Isn't it lucky we have them on the table? Where's a match? Which of you gentlemen can provide a match?

JIM: Here.

AMANDA: Thank you, Sir.

JIM: Not at all, Ma'am!

AMANDA [*as she lights the candles*]: I guess the fuse has burnt out. Mr. O'Connor, can you tell a burnt-out fuse? I know I can't and Tom is a total loss when it comes to mechanics.

[*They rise from the table and go into the kitchenette, from where their voices are heard.*]

Oh, be careful you don't bump into something. We don't want our gentleman caller to break his neck. Now wouldn't that be a fine howdy-do?

JIM: Ha-ha! Where is the fuse-box?

AMANDA: Right here next to the stove. Can you see anything?

JIM: Just a minute.

AMANDA: Isn't electricity a mysterious thing? Wasn't it Benjamin Franklin who tied a key to a kite? We live in such a mysterious universe, don't we? Some people say that science clears up all the mysteries for us. In my opinion it only creates more! Have you found it yet?

JIM: No, Ma'am. All these fuses look okay to me.

AMANDA: Tom!

TOM: Yes, Mother?

AMANDA: That light bill I gave you several days ago. The one I told you we got the notices about?

[*Legend on screen*: "Ha!"]

TOM: Oh—yeah.

AMANDA: You didn't neglect to pay it by any chance?

TOM: Why, I—

AMANDA: Didn't! I might have known it!

JIM: Shakespeare probably wrote a poem on that light bill, Mrs. Wingfield.

AMANDA: I might have known better than to trust him with it! There's such a high price for negligence in this world!

JIM: Maybe the poem will win a ten-dollar prize.

AMANDA: We'll just have to spend the remainder of the evening in the nineteenth century, before Mr. Edison made the Mazda lamp!

JIM: Candlelight is my favorite kind of light.

AMANDA: That shows you're romantic! But that's no excuse for

TOM. Well, we got through dinner. Very considerate of them to let us get through dinner before they plunged us into everlasting darkness, wasn't it, Mr. O'Connor?

JIM: Ha-ha!

AMANDA: Tom, as a penalty for your carelessness you can help me with the dishes.

JIM: Let me give you a hand.

AMANDA: Indeed you will not!

JIM: I ought to be good for something.

AMANDA: Good for something? [*Her tone is rhapsodic.*] *You*? Why, Mr. O'Connor, nobody, *nobody's* given me this much entertainment in years—as you have!

JIM: Aw, now, Mrs. Wingfield!

AMANDA: I'm not exaggerating, not one bit! But Sister is all by her lonesome. You go keep her company in the parlor! I'll give you this lovely old candelabrum that used to be on the altar at the Church of the Heavenly Rest. It was melted a little out of shape when the church burnt down. Lightning struck it one spring. Gypsy Jones was holding a revival at the time and he intimated that the church was destroyed because the Episcopalians gave card parties.

JIM: Ha-ha.

AMANDA: And how about you coaxing Sister to drink a little wine? I think it would be good for her! Can you carry both at once?

JIM: Sure. I'm Superman!

LAURA: Now, Thomas, get into this apron!

[*Jim comes into the dining room, carrying the candelabrum, its candles lighted, in one hand and a glass of wine in the other. The door of the kitchenette swings closed on Amanda's gay laughter; the flickering light approaches the portieres. Laura sits up nervously as Jim enters. She can hardly speak from the almost intolerable strain of being alone with a stranger.*]

[*Screen legend*: "I don't suppose you remember me at all!"]

[*At first, before Jim's warmth overcomes her paralyzing shyness, Laura's voice is thin and breathless, as though she had just run up a steep flight of stairs. Jim's attitude is gently humorous. While the incident is apparently unimportant, it is to Laura the climax of her secret life.*]

JIM: Hello there, Laura.

LAURA [*faintly*]: Hello.

[*She clears her throat.*]

JIM: How are you feeling now? Better?

LAURA: Yes. Yes, thank you.

JIM: This is for you. A little dandelion wine. [*He extends the glass toward her with extravagant gallantry.*]

LAURA: Thank you.

JIM: Drink it—but don't get drunk!

[*He laughs heartily. Laura takes the glass uncertainly; she laughs shyly.*]
Where shall I set the candles?

LAURA: Oh—oh, anywhere...

JIM: How about here on the floor? Any objections?

LAURA: No.

JIM: I'll spread a newspaper under to catch the drippings. I like to sit on the floor. Mind if I do?

LAURA: Oh, no.

JIM: Give me a pillow?

LAURA: What?

JIM: A pillow!

LAURA: Oh... [*She hands him one quickly.*]

JIM: How about you? Don't you like to sit on the floor?

LAURA: Oh yes.

JIM: Why don't you, then?

LAURA: I—will.

JIM: Take a pillow!

[*Laura does. She sits on the floor on the other side of the candelabrum. Jim crosses his legs and smiles engagingly at her.*] I can't hardly see you sitting way over there.

LAURA: I can—see you.

JIM: I know, but that's not fair, I'm in the limelight.

[*Laura moves her pillow closer.*]
Good! Now I can see you! Comfortable?

LAURA: Yes.

JIM: So am I. Comfortable as a cow! Will you have some gum?

LAURA: No, thank you.

JIM: I think that I will indulge, with your permission. [*He musingly unwraps a stick of gum and holds it up.*]Think of the fortune made by the guy that invented the first piece of chewing gum. Amazing, huh? The Wrigley Building is one of the sights of Chicago—I saw it when I went up to the Century of Progress.[11] Did you take in the Century of Progress?

LAURA: No, I didn't.

JIM: Well, it was quite a wonderful exposition. What impressed me most was the Hall of Science. Give you an idea of what the future will be in America, even more wonderful than the present time is! [*There is a pause. Jim smiles at her.*] Your brother tells me you're shy. Is that right, Laura?

LAURA: I—don't know.

JIM: I judge you to be an old-fashioned type of girl. Well, I think that's a pretty good type to be. Hope you don't think I'm being too personal—do you?

LAURA [*hastily, out of embarrassment*]: I believe I *will* take a piece of gum, if you—don't mind. [*clearing her throat*] Mr. O'Connor, have you—kept up with your singing?

JIM: Singing? Me?

LAURA: Yes. I remember what a beautiful voice you had.

JIM: When did you hear me sing?

[*Laura does not answer, and in the long pause which follows a man's voice is heard singing offstage.*]

VOICE:
O blow, ye winds, heigh-ho,
A-roving I will go!
  I'm off to my love
  With a boxing glove—
Ten thousand miles away!

JIM: You say you've heard me sing?

LAURA: Oh, yes! Yes, very often... I—don't suppose—you remember me—at all?

JIM [*smiling doubtfully*]: You know I have an idea I've seen you before. I had that idea soon as you opened the door. It seemed almost like I was about to remember your name. But the name that I started to call you—wasn't a name! And so I stopped myself before I said it.

LAURA: Wasn't it—Blue Roses?

JIM [*springing up, grinning*]: Blue Roses! My gosh, yes—Blue Roses! That's what I had on my tongue when you opened the door! Isn't it funny what tricks your memory plays? I didn't connect you with high school somehow or other. But that's where it was; it was high school. I didn't even know you were Shakespeare's sister! Gosh, I'm sorry.

LAURA: I didn't expect you to. You—barely knew me!

JIM: But we did have a speaking acquaintance, huh?

LAURA: Yes, we—spoke to each other.

JIM: When did you recognize me?

LAURA: Oh, right away!

JIM: Soon as I came in the door?

LAURA: When I heard your name I thought it was probably you. I knew that Tom used to know you a little in high school. So when you came in the door—well, then I was—sure.

JIM: Why didn't you *say* something, then?

LAURA [*breathlessly*]: I didn't know what to say, I was—too surprised!

JIM: For goodness' sakes! You know, this sure is funny!

LAURA: yes! Yes, isn't it, though...

JIM: Didn't we have a class in something together?

LAURA: Yes, we did.

JIM: What class was that?

LAURA: It was—singing—chorus!

JIM: Aw!

LAURA: I sat across the aisle from you in the Aud.

JIM: Aw.

LAURA: Mondays, Wednesdays, and Fridays.

JIM: Now I remember—you always came in late.

LAURA: Yes, it was so hard for me, getting upstairs. I had that brace on my leg—it clumped so loud!

JIM: I never heard any clumping.

LAURA: [*wincing at the recollection*]: To me it sounded like—thunder!

JIM: Well, well, well, I never even noticed.

LAURA: And everybody was seated before I came in. I had to walk in front of all those people. My seat was in the back row. I had to go clumping all the way up the aisle with everyone watching!

JIM: You shouldn't have been self-conscious.

LAURA: I know, but I was. It was always such a relief when the singing started.

JIM: Aw, yes, I've placed you now! I used to call you Blue Roses. How was it that I got started calling you that?

LAURA: I was out of school a little while with pleurosis. When I came back you asked me what was the matter. I said I had pleurosis—you thought I said *Blue Roses*. That's what you always called me after that!

JIM: I hope you didn't mind.

LAURA: Oh, no—I liked it. You see, I wasn't acquainted with many—people....

JIM: As I remember you sort of stuck by yourself.

LAURA: I—I—never have had much luck at—making friends.

JIM: I don't see why you wouldn't.

LAURA: Well, I—started out badly.

JIM: You mean being—[12]

LAURA: Yes, it sort of—stood between me—

JIM: You shouldn't have let it!

LAURA: I know, but it did, and—

JIM: You were shy with people!

LAURA: I tried not to be but never could—

JIM: Overcome it?

LAURA: No, I—I never could!

JIM: I guess being shy is something you have to work out of kind of gradually.

LAURA: [*sorrowfully*]: Yes—I guess it—

JIM: Takes time!

LAURA: Yes—

JIM: People are not so dreadful when you know them. That's what you have to remember! And everybody has problems, not just you, but practically everybody has got some problems. You think of yourself as having the only problems, as being the only one who is disappointed. But just look around you and you will see lots of people as disappointed as you are. For instance, I hoped when I was going to high school that I would be further along at this time, six years later, than I am now. You remember that wonderful write-up I had in *The Torch*?

LAURA: Yes! [*She rises and crosses to the table.*]

JIM: It said I was bound to succeed in anything I went into!

[*Laura returns with the high school yearbook.*]

Holy Jeez! *The Torch*!

[*He accepts it reverently. They smile across the book with mutual wonder. Laura crouches beside him and they begin to turn the pages. Laura's shyness is dissolving in his warmth.*]

LAURA: Here you are in *The Pirates of Penzance*!

JIM: [*wistfully*]: I sang the baritone lead in that operetta.

LAURA: [*raptly*]: So—*beautifully*!

JIM: [*protesting*]: Aw—

LAURA: Yes, yes—beautifully—beautifully!

JIM: You heard me?

LAURA: All three times!

JIM: No!

LAURA: Yes!

JIM: All three performances?

LAURA: [*looking down*]: Yes.

JIM: Why?

LAURA: I—wanted to ask you to—autograph my program.

[*She takes the program from the back of the yearbook and shows it to him.*]

JIM: Why didn't you ask me to?

LAURA: You were always surrounded by your own friends so much that I never had a chance to.

JIM: You should have just—

LAURA: Well, I—thought you might think I was—

JIM: Thought I might think you was—what?

LAURA: Oh—

JIM: [*with reflective relish*]: I was beleaguered by females in those days.

LAURA: You were terribly popular!

JIM: Yeah—

LAURA: You had such a—friendly way—

JIM: I was spoiled in high school.

LAURA: Everybody—liked you!

JIM: Including you?

LAURA: I—yes, I—did, too— [*She gently closes the book in her lap.*]

JIM: Well, well, well! Give me that program, Laura.

[*She hands it to him. He signs it with a flourish.*]

There you are—better late than never!

LAURA: Oh, I—what a—surprise!

JIM: My signature isn't worth very much right now. But some day—maybe—it will increase in value! Being disappointed is one thing and being discouraged is something else. I am disappointed but I am not discouraged. I'm twenty-three years old. How old are you?

LAURA: I'll be twenty-four in June.

JIM: That's not old age!

LAURA: No, but—

JIM: You finished high school?

LAURA [*with difficulty*]: I didn't go back.

JIM: You mean you dropped out?

LAURA: I made bad grades in my final examinations. [*She rises and replaces the book and the program on the table. Her voice is strained.*] How is—Emily Meisenbach getting along?

JIM: Oh, that kraut-head![13]

LAURA: Why do you call her that?

JIM: That's what she was.

LAURA: You're not still—going with her?

JIM: I never see her.

LAURA: It said in the "Personal" section that you were—engaged!

JIM: I know, but I wasn't impressed by that—propaganda!

LAURA: It wasn't—the truth?

JIM: Only in Emily's optimistic opinion!

LAURA: Oh—

[*Legend*: "What have you done since high school?"]

[*Jim lights a cigarette and leans indolently back on his elbows smiling at Laura with a warmth and charm which lights her inwardly with altar candles.*[14] *She remains by the table, picks up a piece from the glass menagerie collection, and turns it in her hands to cover her tumult.*]

JIM [*after several reflective puffs on his cigarette*]: What have you done since high school?

[*She seems not to hear him.*]

Huh?

[*Laura looks up.*]

I said what have you done since high school, Laura?

LAURA: Nothing much.

JIM: You must have been doing something these six long years.

LAURA: Yes.

JIM: Well, then, such as what?

LAURA: I took a business course at business college—

JIM: How did that work out?

LAURA: Well, not very—well—I had to drop out, it gave me—indigestion—

[*Jim laughs gently.*]

JIM: What are you doing now?

LAURA: I don't do anything—much. Oh, please don't think I sit around doing nothing! My glass collection takes up a good deal of time. Glass is something you have to take good care of.

JIM: What did you say—about glass?

LAURA: Collection I said—I have one— [*She clears her throat and turns away again, acutely shy.*]

JIM [*abruptly*]: You know what I judge to be the trouble with you? Inferiority complex! Know what that is? That's what they call it when someone low-rates himself! I understand it because I had it, too. Although my case was not so aggravated as yours seems to be. I had it until I took up public speaking, developed my voice, and learned that I had an aptitude for science. Before that time I never thought of myself as being outstanding in any way whatsoever! Now I've never made a regular study of it, but I have a friend who says I can analyze people better than doctors that make a profession of it. I don't claim that to be necessarily true, but I can sure guess a person's psychology, Laura! [*He takes out his gum.*] Excuse me, Laura. I always take it out when the flavor is gone. I'll use this scrap of paper to wrap it in. I know how it is to get it stuck on a shoe. [*He wraps the gum in paper and puts it in his pocket.*] Yep—that's what I judge to be your principal trouble. A lack of confidence in yourself as a person. You don't have the proper amount of faith in yourself. I'm basing that fact on a number of your remarks and also on certain observations I've made. For instance that clumping you thought was so awful in high school. You say that you even dreaded to walk into class. You see what you did? You dropped out of school, you gave up an education because of a clump, which as far as I know was practically nonexistent! A little physical defect is what you have. Hardly noticeable even! Magnified thousands of times by imagination! You know what my strong advice to you is? Think of yourself as *superior* in some way!

LAURA: In what way would I think?

JIM: Why, man alive, Laura! Just look about you a little. What do you see? A world full of common people! All of 'em born and all of 'em going to die! Which of them has one-tenth of your good points! Or mine! Or anyone else's, as far as that goes—gosh! Everybody excels in some one thing. Some in many! [*He unconsciously glances at himself in the mirror.*] All you've got to do is discover in *what*! Take me, for instance. [*He adjusts his tie at the mirror.*] My interest happens to lie in electro-dynamics. I'm taking a course in radio engineering at night school. Laura, on top of a fairly responsible job at the warehouse. I'm taking that course and studying public speaking.

LAURA: Ohhhh.

JIM: Because I believe in the future of television! [*turning his back to her.*] I wish to be ready to go up right along with it. Therefore I'm planning to get in on the ground floor. In fact I've already made the right connections and all that remains is for the industry itself to get under way! Full steam— [*His eyes are starry.*] *Knowledge—Zzzzzp! Money—Zzzzzzp! —Power!* That's the cycle democracy is built on!

[*His attitude is convincingly dynamic. Laura stares at him, even her shyness eclipsed in her absolute wonder. He suddenly grins.*]

I guess you think I think a lot of myself!

LAURA: No—o-o-o, I—

JIM: Now how about you? Isn't there something you take more interest in than anything else?

LAURA: Well, I do—as I said—have my—glass collection—

[*A peal of girlish laughter rings from the kitchenette.*]

JIM: I'm not right sure I know what you're talking about. What kind of glass is it?

LAURA: Little articles of it, they're ornaments mostly! Most of them are little animals made out of glass, the tiniest little animals in the world. Mother calls them a glass menagerie! Here's an example of one, if you'd like to see it! This one is one of the oldest. It's nearly thirteen.

[*Music*: "The Glass Menagerie."]

[*He stretches out his hand.*]

Oh, be careful—if you breathe, it breaks!

JIM: I'd better not take it. I'm pretty clumsy with things.

LAURA: Go on, I trust you with him! [*She places the piece in his palm.*] There now—you're holding him gently! Hold him over the light, he loves the light! You see how the light shines through him?

JIM: It sure does shine!

LAURA: I shouldn't be partial, but he is my favorite one.

JIM: What kind of a thing is this one supposed to be?

LAURA: Haven't you noticed the single horn on his forehead?

JIM: A unicorn, huh?

LAURA: Mmmm-hmmm!

JIM: Unicorns—aren't they extinct in the modern world?

LAURA: I know!

JIM: Poor little fellow, he must feel sort of lonesome.

LAURA [*smiling*]: Well, if he does, he doesn't complain about it. He stays on a shelf with some horses that don't have horns and all of them seem to get along nicely together.

JIM: How do you know?

LAURA [*lightly*]: I haven't heard any arguments among them!

JIM [*grinning*]: No arguments, huh? Well, that's a pretty good sign! Where shall I set him?

LAURA: Put him on the table. They all like a change of scenery once in a while!

JIM: Well, well, well, well— [*He places the glass piece on the table, then raises his arms and stretches.*] Look how big my shadow is when I stretch!

LAURA: Oh, oh, yes—it stretches across the ceiling!

JIM [*crossing to the door*]: I think it's stopped raining. [*He opens the fire-escape door and the background music changes to a dance tune.*] Where does the music come from?

LAURA: From the Paradise Dance Hall across the alley.

JIM: How about cutting the rug a little, Miss Wingfield?

LAURA: Oh, I—

JIM: Or is your program filled up? Let me have a look at it. [*He grasps an imaginary card.*] Why, every dance is taken! I'll just have to scratch some out.

[*Waltz music*: "La Golondrina.!]

Ahhh, a waltz! [*He executes some sweeping turns by himself, then holds his arms toward Laura.*]

LAURA [*breathlessly*]: I—can't dance!

JIM: There you go, that inferiority stuff!

LAURA: I've never danced in my life!

JIM: Come on, try!

LAURA: Oh, but I'd step on you!

JIM: I'm not made out of glass.

LAURA: How—how—how do we start?

JIM: Just leave it to me. You hold your arms out a little.

LAURA: Like this?

JIM [*taking her in his arms*]: A little bit higher. Right. Now don't tighten up, that's the main thing about it—relax.

LAURA [*laughing breathlessly*]: It's hard not to.

JIM: Okay.

LAURA: I'm afraid you can't budge me.

JIM: What do you bet I can't? [*He swings her into motion.*]

LAURA: Goodness, yes, you can!

JIM: Let yourself go, now, Laura, just let yourself go.

LAURA: I'm—

JIM: Come on!

LAURA: —trying!

JIM: Not so stiff—easy does it!

LAURA: I know but I'm—

JIM: Loosen th' backbone! There now, that's a lot better.

LAURA: Am I?

JIM: Lots, lots better! [*he moves her about the room in a clumsy waltz.*]

LAURA: Oh, my!

JIM: Ha-ha!

LAURA: Oh, my goodness!

JIM: Ha-ha-ha!

[*They suddenly bump into the table, and the glass piece on it falls to the floor. Jim stops the dance.*]

What did we hit on?

LAURA: Table.

JIM: Did something fall off it? I think—

LAURA: Yes.

JIM: I hope that it wasn't the little glass horse with the horn!

LAURA: Yes. [*She stoops to pick it up.*]

JIM: Aw, aw, aw. Is it broken?

LAURA: Now it is just like all the other horses.

JIM: It's lost its—

LAURA: Horn! It doesn't matter. Maybe it's a blessing in disguise.[15]

JIM: You'll never forgive me. I bet that that was your favorite piece of glass.

LAURA: I don't have favorites much. It's no tragedy, Freckles.[16] Glass breaks so easily. No matter how careful you are. The traffic jars the shelves and things fall off them.

JIM: Still I'm awfully sorry that I was the cause.

LAURA [*smiling*]: I'll just imagine he had an operation. The horn was removed to make him feel less—freakish!

[*They both laugh.*]

Now he will feel more at home with the other horses, the ones that don't have horns....

JIM: Ha-ha, that's very funny! [*Suddenly he is serious.*] I'm glad to see that you have a sense of humor. You know—you're—well—very different! Surprisingly different from anyone else I know! [*His voice becomes soft and hesitant with a genuine feeling.*] Do you mind me telling you that?

[*Laura is abashed beyond speech.*]

I mean it in a nice way—

[*Laura nods shyly, looking away.*]

You make me feel sort of—I don't know how to put it! I'm usually pretty good at expressing things, but—this is something that I don't know how to say!

[*Laura touches her throat and clears it—turns the broken unicorn in her hands. His voice becomes softer.*]

Has anyone ever told you that you were pretty?

[*There is a pause, and the music rises slightly. Laura looks up slowly, with wonder, and shakes her head.*]

Well, you are! In a very different way from anyone else. And all the nicer because of the difference, too.

[*His voice becomes low and husky. Laura turns away, nearly faint with *the novelty of her emotions.*]

I wish that you were my sister. I'd teach you to have some confidence in yourself. The different people are not like other people, but being different is nothing to be ashamed of. Because other people are not such wonderful people. They're one hundred times one thousand.[17] You're one times one! They walk all over the earth. You just stay here. They're common as—weeds, but—you—well, you're—*Blue Roses*!

[*Image on screen*: Blue Roses.]

[*The music changes.*]

LAURA: But blue is wrong for—roses....

JIM: It's right for you! You're—pretty!

LAURA: In what respect am I pretty?

JIM: In all respects—believe me! Your eyes—your hair—are pretty! Your hands are pretty! [*He catches hold of her hand.*] You think I'm making this up because I'm invited to dinner and have to be nice. Oh, I could do that! I could put on an act for you, Laura, and say lots of things without being very sincere. But this time I am. I'm talking to you sincerely. I happened to notice you had this inferiority complex that keeps you from feeling comfortable with people. Somebody needs to build your confidence up and make you proud instead of shy and turning away and—blushing. Somebody—ought to—*kiss* you, Laura!

[*His hand slips slowly up her arm to her shoulder as the music swells tumultuously. He suddenly turns her about and kisses her on the lips. When he releases her, Laura sinks on the sofa with a bright, dazed look. Jim backs away and fishes in his pocket for a cigarette.*]

[*Legend on screen*: "A souvenir."

Stumblejohn![18]

[*He lights the cigarette, avoiding her look. There is a peal of girlish laughter from Amanda in the kitchenette. Laura slowly raises and opens her hand. It still contains the little broken glass animal. She looks at it with a tender, bewildered expression.*]

Stumblejohn! I shouldn't have done that—that was way off the beam. You don't smoke, do you?

[*She looks up, smiling, not hearing the question. He sits beside her rather gingerly. She looks at him speechlessly—waiting. He coughs decorously and moves a little farther aside as he considers the situation and senses her feelings, dimly, with perturbation. He speaks gently.*]

Would you—care for a—mint?

[*She doesn't seem to hear him but her look grows brighter even.*]

Peppermint? Life Saver? My pocket's a regular drugstore—wherever I go....

[*He pops a mint in his mouth. Then he gulps and decides to make a clean breast of it. He speaks slowly and gingerly.*] Laura, you know, if I had a sister like you, I'd do the same thing as Tom. I'd bring out fellows and—introduce her to them. The right type of boys—of a type to—appreciate her. Only—well—he made a mistake about me. Maybe I've got no call to be saying this. That may not have been the idea in having me over. But what if it was? There's nothing wrong about that. The only trouble is that in my ease—I'm not in a situation to—do the right thing. I can't take down your number and say I'll phone. I can't call up next week and—ask for a date. I thought I had better explain the situation in case you—misunderstood it and—I hurt your feelings....

[*There is a pause. Slowly, very slowly, Laura's look changes, her eyes returning slowly from his to the glass figure in her palm. Amanda utters another gay laugh in the kitchenette.*]

LAURA [*faintly*]: You—won't—call again?

JIM: No, Laura, I can't. [*He rises from the sofa.*] As I was just explaining, I've—got strings on me. Laura, I've—been going steady! I go out all the time with a girl named Betty. She's a home-girl like you, and Catholic, and Irish, and in a great many ways we—get along fine. I met her last summer on a moonlight boat trip up the river to Alton, on the *Majestic*. Well—right away from the start it was love!

[*Legend*: Love!]

[*Laura sways slightly forward and grips the arm of the sofa. He fails to notice, now enrapt in his own comfortable being.*]

Being in love has made a new man of me!

[*Leaning stiffty forward, clutching the arm of the sofa, Laura struggles visibly with her storm. But Jim is oblivious; she is a long way off.*]

The power of love is really pretty tremendous! Love is something that—changes the whole world, Laura!

[*The storm abates a little and Laura leans back. He notices her again.*]

It happened that Betty's aunt took sick, she got a wire and had to go to Centralia. So Tom—when he asked me to dinner—I naturally just accepted the invitation, not knowing that you—that he—that I— [*He stops awkwardly.*] Huh—I'm a stumblejohn!

[*He flops back on the sofa. The holy candles on the altar of Laura's face have been snuffed out. There is a look of almost infinite desolation. Jim glances at her uneasily.*]

I wish that you would—say something.

[*She bites her lip which was trembling and then bravely smiles. She opens her hand again on the broken glass figure. Then she gently takes his hand and raises it level with her own. She carefully places the unicorn in the palm of his hand, then pushes his fingers closed upon it.*]

What are you—doing that for? You want me to have him? Laura?

[*She nods.*]

What for?

LAURA: A—souverir....

[*She rises unsteadily and crouches beside the Victrola to wind it up.*]

[*Legend on screen*: "Things have a way of turning out so badly!" *Or image*: "Gentleman caller waving goodbye—gaily."]

[*At this moment Amanda rushes brightly back into the living room. She bears a pitcher of fruit punch in an old-fashioned cut-glass pitcher, and a plate of macaroons. The plate has a gold border and poppies painted on it.*]

AMANDA: Well, well, well! Isn't the air delightful after the shower? I've made you children a little liquid refreshment.

[*She turns gaily to Jim.*] Jim, do you know that song about leminade?

"Lemonade, lemonade
Made in the shade and stirred with a spade—
Good enough for any old maid!"

JIM [*uneasily*]: Ha-ha! No—I never heard it.

AMANDA: Why, Laura! You look so serious!

JIM: We were having a serious conversation.

AMANDA: Good! Now you're better acquainted!

JIM: [*uncertainly*]: Ha-ha! Yes.

AMANDA: You modern young people are much more serious-minded than my generation. I was so gay as a girl!

JIM: You haven't changed, Mrs. Wingfield.

AMANDA: Tonight I'm rejuvenated! The gaiety of the occasion, Mr.

O'Connor! [*She tosses her head with a peal of laughter, spilling some lemonade.*] Oooo! I'm baptizing myself![19]

JIM: Here—let me—

AMANDA: [*setting the pitcher down*]: There now. I discovered we had some maraschino cherries. I dumped them in, juice and all!

JIM: You shouldn't have gone to that trouble, Mrs. Wingfield.

AMANDA: Trouble, trouble? Why, it was loads of fun! Didn't you hear me cutting up in the kitchen? I bet your ears were burning! I told Tom how outdone with him I was for keeping you to himself so long a time! He should have brought you over much, much sooner! Well, now that you've found your way, I want you to be a very frequent caller! Not just occasional but all the time. Oh, we're going to have a lot of gay times together! I see them coming! Mmm, just breathe that air! So fresh, and the moon's so pretty! I'll skip back out—I know where my place is when young folks are having a—serious conversation!

JIM: Oh, don't go out, Mrs. Wingfield. The fact of the matter is I've got to be going.

AMANDA: Going, now? Your're joking! Why, it's only the shank of the evening, Mr. O'Connor!

JIM: Well, you know how it is.

AMANDA: You mean you're a young workingman and have to keep workingmen's hours. We'll let you off early tonight. But only on the condition that next time you stay later. What's the best night for you? Isn't Saturday night the best night for you workingmen?

JIM: I have a couple of time-clocks to punch, Mrs. Wingfield. One at morning, another one at night!

AMANDA: My, but you are ambitious! You work at night, too?

JIM: No, Ma'am, not work but—Betty!

[*He crosses deliberately to pick up his hat. The band at the Paradise Dance Hall goes into a tender waltz.*]

AMANDA: Betty? Betty? Who's—Betty!

[*There is an ominous cracking sound in the sky.*]

JIM: Oh, just a girl. The girl I go steady with!

[*He smiles charmingly. The sky falls.*]

[*Legend*: "The Sky Falls."]

AMANDA [*a long-drawn exhalation*]: Ohhhh…Is it a serious romance, Mr. o'Connor?

JIM: We're going to be married the second Sunday in June.

AMANDA: Ohhhh—how nice! Tom didn't mention that you were engaged to be married.

JIM: The cat's not out of the bag at the warehouse yet. You know how they are. They call you Romeo and stuff like that. [*He stops at the oval mirror to put on his hat. He carefully shapes the brim and the crown to give a discreetly dashing effect.*] It's been a wonderful evening, Mrs. Wingfield. I guess this is what they mean by Southern hospitality.

AMANDA: It really wasn't anyting at all.

JIM: I hope it don't seem like I'm rushing off. But I promised Betty I'd pick her up at the Wabash depot, an' by the time I get my jalopy down there her train'll be in. Some women are pretty upset if you keep 'em waiting.

AMANDA: Yes, I know—the tyranny of women! [*She extends her hand.*] Goodbye, Mr. O'Connor. I wish you luck—and happiness—and success! All three of them, and so does Laura! Don't you, Laura?

LAURA: Yes!

JIM [*taking Laura's hand*]: Goodbye, Laura. I'm certainly going to treasure that souvenir. And don't you forget the good advice I gave you. [*He raises his voice to a cheery shout.*] So long, Shakespeare! Thanks again, ladies. Good night!

[*He grins and ducks jauntily out. Still bravely grimacing, Amanda closes the door on the gentleman caller. Then she turns back to the room with a puzzled expression. She and Laura don't dare to face each other. Laura crouches beside the Victrola to wind it.*]

AMANDA [faintly]: Things have a way of turning out so badly. I don't believe that I would play the Victrola. Well, Well—well! Our gentleman caller was engaged to be married! [*She raises her voice.*] Tom!

TOM [*from the kitchenette*]: Yes, Mother?

AMANDA: Come in here a minute. I want to tell you something awfully funny.

TOM [*entering with a macaroon and a glass of the lemonade*]: Has the gentleman caller gotten away already?

AMANDA: The gentleman caller has made an early departure. What a wonderful joke you played on us!

TOM: How do you mean?

AMANDA: You didn't mention that he was engaged to be married.

TOM: Jim? Engaged?

AMANDA: That's what he just informed us.

TOM: I'll be jiggered! I didn't know about that.

AMANDA: That seems very peculiar.

TOM: What's peculiar about it?

AMANDA: Didn't you call him your best friend down at the warehouse?

TOM: He is, but how did I know?

AMANDA: It seems extremely peculiar that you wouldn't know your best friend was going to be married!

TOM: The warehouse is where I work, not where I know things about people!

AMANDA: You don't know things anywhere! You live in a dream, you manufacture illusions!

[*He crosses to the door.*]

Where are you going?

TOM: I'm going to the movies.

AMANDA: That's right, now that you've had us make such fools of ourselves. The effort, the preparations, all the expense! The new floor lamp, the rug, the clothes for Laura! All for what? To entertain some other girl's fiancé! Go to the movies, go! Don't think about us, a mother deserted, an unmarried sister who's crippled and has no job! Don't let anything interfere with your selfish pleasure! Just go, go, go—to the movies!

TOM: All right, I will! The more you shout about my selfishness to me the quicker I'll go, and I won't go to the movies!

AMANDA: Go, then! Go to the moon—you selfish dreamer!

[*Tom smashes his glass on the floor. He plunges out on the fire escape, slamming the door. Laura screams in fright. The dance-hall music becomes louder. Tom stands on the fire escape, gripping the rail. The moon breaks through the storm clouds, illuminating his face.*]

[Legend on screen: "And so goodbye..."]

[*Tom's closing speech is timed with what is happening inside the house. We see, as though through soundproof glass, that Amanda appears to be making a comforting speech to Laura, who is huddled upon the sofa. Now that we cannot hear the mother's speech, her silliness is gone and she has dignity and tragic beauty. Laura's hair hides her face until, at the end of the speech, she lifts her head to smile at her mother. Amanda's gestures are slow and graceful, almost dancelike, as she comforts her daughter. At the end of her speech she glances a moment at the father's picture—then withdraws through the portieres. At the close of Tom's speech, Laura blows out the candles, ending the play.*]

TOM: I didn't go to the moon, I went much further—for time is the longest distance between two places. Not long after that I was fired for writing a poem on the lid of a shoe-box. I left Saint Louis. I descended the steps of this fire escape for a last time and followed, from then on, in my father's footsteps, attempting to find in motion what was lost in space. I traveled around a great deal. The cities swept about me like dead leaves, leaves that were brightly colored but torn away from the branches. I would have stopped, but I was pursued by something. It always came upon me unawares, taking me altogether by surprise. Perhaps it was a familiar bit of music. Perhaps it was only a piece of transparent glass. Perhaps I am walking along a street at night, in some strange city, before I have found companions. I pass the lighted window of a shop where perfume is sold. The window is filled with pieces of colored glass, tiny transparent bottles in delicate colors, like bits of a shattered rainbow. Then all at once my sister touches my shoulder. I turn around and look into her eyes. Oh, Laura, Laura, I tried to leave you behind me, but I am more faithful than I intended to be! I reach for a cigarette, I cross the street, I run into the movies or a bar, I buy a drink, I speak to the nearest stranger—anything that can blow your candles out!

[*Laura bends over the candles.*]

For nowadays the world is lit by lightning! Blow out your candles, Laura—and so goodbye....

[*She blows the candles out.*]

[注释]

1. Tom：汤姆，本剧的解说者。
2. Soldan：汤姆、吉姆和劳拉读书的中学。
3. "The accent of a coming foot"：有人走来的脚步声，指汤姆一家期待吉姆来访的心情。
4. "scattering poems in the sky"：指富有诗意。
5. the picture：指挂在汤姆家起居室墙上的他父亲的照片。见第一场。
6. the Victrola：劳拉的名牌唱机。

7. Dardanella：电唱机里传出的舞曲声，具有西亚地区风味。

8. Gable：克拉克·盖博（Clark Gable，1901～1960），好莱坞著名演员，主演过65部电影，尤以饰演电影《飘》中的男主角巴特勒（Rhett Butler）出名，有“好莱坞王”之称，是美国粗悍男性的象征。

9. the light bill：电费。

10. But man proposes—and woman accepts the proposal! To vary that old, old saying a little bit：阿曼达所说的古老格言是：“man proposes; God disposes”（“谋事在人，成事在天”）。

11. the Century of Progress：本世纪30年代早期在芝加哥为庆祝该城建城100周年而举行的博览会，旨在鼓舞民心。

12. you mean being—：吉姆省略了“crippled”一字。

13. kraut-head：泡菜脑袋，轻蔑语。

14. candles：这一意象在剧中出现4次，是幻想的象征；剧尾劳拉吹灭蜡烛，是她已面对现实的表现。

15. Maybe it's a blessing in disguise：麒麟（unicorn）似为劳拉的象征，它独自有角，感到孤独；吉姆把它的角碰掉，它就和其他的动物一样了。劳拉似有同感，故曰“（碰掉角）可能会因祸得福。”表明他开始从幻梦中醒来。

16. Freckles：劳拉对吉姆的戏称；吉姆脸上有雀斑。

17. They're one hundred times one thousand：他们成千上万。

18. stumblejohn：冒失鬼。

19. I'm baptizing myself：双关语，“洗礼”有“再生”之内涵。一方面，阿曼达把饮料洒在身上，故出此语。另一方面，综观全剧，她也在经历着一种由期望到失望到正视现实的过程，吉姆走后，她也似乎变成另外一个人，或者说新人。

ARTHUR MILLER

〔作者介绍〕

阿瑟·米勒(Arthur Miller, 1915～　),美国著名剧作家,出生于纽约市一个犹太人家庭,父亲是相当富裕的服装制造商。米勒成长于经济大萧条时期,目睹了父亲的破产,感到现代生活毫无保障。中学毕业后他曾在一个汽车配件库任保管员,后就读于密执安大学并开始写作。1938年大学毕业后,米勒回到纽约从事广播剧创作。1944年他的话剧《鸿运高照的人》(*The Man Who Had All the Luck*)首次在百老汇上演,虽不成功,但引起评论界的注意。1945年他的长篇小说《焦点》(*Focus*)问世,然而他仍决心"把长篇小说的充实性、警世性和复杂性带上舞台"。

米勒的话剧《全是我的儿子》(*All My Sons*)于1947年公演,受到欢迎,获纽约剧评家奖,并使米勒一举成名。该剧的主人公、机器制造商乔·凯勒在二战期间向美国空军出售残次部件,导致21名飞行员机毁人亡,后他又将罪责推给合伙人。当他得知遇难的飞行员中有自己的次子拉里时,受到良心的谴责,终于负疚自杀。米勒通过这个剧探讨了家庭和社会道德的问题。

1949年2月,米勒的话剧《推销员之死》(*Death of a Salesman*)公演,立即引起轰动,连演742场仍盛况不减,赢得了纽约剧评家奖和美国文学最高奖——普利策奖。《推销员之死》的主人公威利·洛曼笃信依靠个人的魅力和不懈的努力便可获得成功,可是他为老板辛劳一生竟在年老时被无理解雇。他走投无路,终于撞车自尽。这是一个普通美国人被"人人都能成功"的梦想所戕害的悲剧,具有深刻的社会意义。此外,米勒在该剧的表现手法上也有所创新。《推销员之死》被公认为米勒最成功的剧作,确立了他在美国戏剧史上的重要地位,并使他饮誉海外。

《炼狱》(*The Crucible*)是米勒的又一部重要剧作,于1953年公演。该剧以1692年在马萨诸塞州的塞勒姆镇发生的驱巫冤案为素材,表现黑暗宗教势力与普通人的良心的斗争,讴歌了人间的浩然正气。当时正值美国反动的麦卡锡主义猖獗时期，这个剧无疑是对非美活动调查委员会审讯共产党人事件的影射和抨击，其影响超越了美国国界。米勒曾因政治思想进步而遭该委员会传讯，但他毫不畏惧，拒绝回答一切问题，后又以古讽今，写成这部意义深远的剧本。

米勒后来的一些剧作，如《堕落之后》(*After the Fall*，1964)、《维希事件》(*Incident at Vichy*，1964)、《代价》(*The Price*，1968) 等，除反映社会生活外还带有内心自省和道德自我完善的色彩，成就不如前期的剧作。但在有些剧中，他对戏剧的表现方法进行了试验性的探讨，例如《创世纪及其它》(*The Creation of the World and Other Business*，1972) 就是喜剧和荒诞剧的尝试。1980年首演的《美国时钟》(*The American Clock*) 则力图展现美国经济大萧条造成的灾难的全貌。

米勒的其它主要剧作包括：《两个星期一的回忆》《*A Memory of Two Mondays*，1955)、《桥头眺望》(*A View from the Bridge*，1955)、《戏剧集》(*Collected Plays*，1957)、《不合时宜的人》(*The Misfits*，1961，电影剧本)、《大主教的天花板》(*The Archbishop's Ceiling*，1977 和《用演奏来延宕时间》(*Playing for Time*，1979，电视剧)。此外，米勒还写过广播剧、短篇小说、报告文学等。

米勒早年曾从挪威著名作家易卜生的剧本中汲取了营养，后来又继承了尤金·奥尼尔开创的美国现代社会剧的传统。在此基础上他探讨戏剧理论，撰写出许多论文，阐发自己独到的见解。例如：在《戏剧集》的引言中，作者阐述了戏剧的功能。他说："我认为观众是这样的人：每一观众都怀有其单独认定的焦虑、希望或当务之急，这使他与人们疏离；从这一点考虑，剧本的功能至少是要向他揭示他自身，这样，他或许能通过揭示出来的他与大家的相互关系而和其他人沟通。仅仅出自这一原因，我就认为戏剧是一项严肃的事业。它使人类或应当使人类更加富有人性，也就是说，使人类不那么孤独。"在《悲剧与普通人》("Tragedy and the Common Man"，1949) 一文中，米勒论述了现代悲剧的特点。他一反古希腊哲学家亚里士多德的悲剧定义，指出："我认为普通人与帝王同样适合于作为最崇高的悲剧的题材。"他还指出："假如悲剧是一个人竭力要求公止地评价自己而产生的后果，那么他因此而遭到的毁灭就揭示出他生活环境中的缺陷或邪恶。这正是悲剧的寓意和教诲之所在。"米勒主张："悲剧的最终结局应加强观众对于人类所持的最光明的见地。"米勒不仅研究戏剧理论，而且革新了戏剧的表现方法。例如：他设计了多功能的舞台，既减少了频繁换景的麻烦，又丰富了戏剧的表现力。他采取了浓缩时间的方法，使过去、现在和将来交织在一起。他还在剧中使用意识流手法，深刻地揭示人物的内心世界。1978年《米勒戏剧论文集》(*The Theatre Essays of Miller*) 出版。他以自己的理论和实践为现代戏剧的发展作出了卓越的贡献。

米勒是和田纳西·威廉斯齐名的战后美国戏剧大师，1965年被选为国际笔会的第1任美国主席，1984年获得华盛顿肯尼迪艺术中心奖。

阿瑟·米勒是中国人民的朋友。1979年米勒夫妇在访华后出版了摄影集《中国见闻》(*Chinese Encounters*). 1983年米勒又亲自来北京执导话剧《推销员之死》，获得极大成功。

Death of a Salesman

〔作品介绍〕

《推销员之死》(*Death of a Salesman*) 发表于1949年，是阿瑟·米勒最成功的剧作，曾获普利策奖和纽约剧评家奖，被公认为二战后美国的重要剧作之一。

此剧通过旅行推销员威利·洛曼一家在一天两夜间的生活场景，展现20世纪三、四十年代美国社会中一个普通人的悲剧。年过六旬的威利像许多美国人一样坚信：人可以靠自己的品格和魅力以及不懈的努力赢得众望，获得成功。然而事与愿违，他为瓦格纳公司辛苦工作了34年，不但没有发财，反因年老体弱、推销不力而遭解雇。他生活拮据，负债累累，精神恍惚，进退维谷。尽管如此，他仍天真地相信，通过自杀的手段可以给儿子留下两万五千美元人寿保险金，这样自己企盼成功的梦想就能在儿子身上得到实现。于是，威利终于撞车自尽。威利·洛曼的悲剧在于他受"美国之梦"的戕害又执迷不悟。他不知道自己的失败既有社会政治经济的原因，又有自身的原因。威利一直生活在自欺欺人的幻梦之中，倒是他那一事无成的长子比夫从父亲的遭遇中悟出一个道理：人必须正视现实，不能继续在谎言、幻想和虚假的价值中生活下去。威利的哥哥本恩是个靠无情竞争取得成功的实业家，与威利形成鲜明的对照。

为了表现威利的心理活动，作者创造性地使用了意识流手法，将威利的回忆和幻想呈现于舞台之上，造成现在与过去、现实与想象交相呼应的局面，深刻地揭示了威利的内心世界。为达此目的，作者还设计了虚实结合的多功能布景，并用音乐烘托人物和主题。这些现实主义与表现主义相结合的处理方法取得了很好的艺术效果。

《推销员之死》是对"美国梦"的有力批判。它以其深刻的哲理性和高度的戏剧性赢得美国人民和各国人民的喜爱，多年来屡演不衰。

此剧由两幕和尾声3部分组成。这里选注的是第2幕的前半部。

Death of a Salesman

ACT Ⅱ

Music is heard, gay and bright. The curtain rises as the music fades away. Willy,[1] *in shirt sleeves, is sitting at the kitchen table, sipping coffee, his hat in his lap. Linda*[2] *is filling his cup when she can.*

WILLY: Wonderful coffee. Meal in itself.
LINDA: Can I make you some eggs?
WILLY: No. Take a breath.
LINDA: You look so rested, dear.
WILLY: I slept like a dead one. First time in months. Imagine, sleeping till ten on a Tuesday morning. Boys[3] left nice and early, heh?
LINDA: They were out of here by eight o'clock.
WILLY: Good work!
LINDA: It was so thrilling to see them leaving together. I can't get over the shaving lotion in this house![4]
WILLY, *smiling*: Mmm—
LINDA: Biff was very changed this morning. His whole attitude seemed to be hopeful. He couldn't wait to get downtown to see Oliver.[5]
WILLY: He's heading for a change. There's no question, there simply are certain men that take longer to get—solidified. How did he dress?
LINDA: His blue suit. He's so handsome in that suit. He could be a—anything in that suit!
Willy gets up from the table. Linda holds his jacket for him.
WILLY: There's no question, no question at all. Gee, on the way home tonight I'd like to buy some seeds.
LINDA, *laughing*: That'd be wonderful. But not enough sun gets back there. Nothing'll grow any more.
WILLY: You wait, kid, before it's all over we're gonna get a little place out in the country, and I'll raise some vegetables, a couple of chickens...
LINDA: You'll do it yet, dear.

Willy walks out of his jacket. Linda follows him.

WILLY: And they'll get married, and come for a weekend. I'd build a little guest house. 'Cause I got so many fine tools, all I'd need would be a little lumber and some peace of mind.

LINDA, *joyfully*: I sewed the lining...

WILLY: I could build two guest houses, so they'd both come. Did he decide how much he's going to ask Oliver for?

LINDA, *getting him into the jacket*: He didn't mention it, but I imagine ten or fifteen thousand. You going to talk to Howard[6] today?

WILLY: Yeah. I'll put it to him straight and simple. He'll just have to take me off the road.[7]

LINDA: And Willy, don't forget to ask for a little advance, because we've got the insurance premium. It's the grace period now.

WILLY: That's a hundred...?

LINDA: A hundred and eight, sixty-eight. Because we're a little short again.

WILLY: Why are we short?

LINDA: Well, you had the motor job on the car...[8]

WILLY: That goddam Studebaker![9]

LINDA: And you got one more payment on the reffigerator...

WILLY: But it just broke again!

LINDA: Well, it's old, dear.

WILLY: I told you we should've bought a well-advertised machine. Charley[10] bought a General Electric[11] and it's twenty years old and it's still good, that son-of-a-bitch.

LINDA: But, Willy—

WILLY: Whoever heard of a Hastings refrigerator?[12] Once in my life I would like to own something outright before it's broken! I'm always in a race with the junkyard! I just finished paying for the car and it's on its last legs.[13] The refrigerator consumes belts like a goddam maniac. They time those things. They time them so when you finally paid for them, they're used up.

LINDA, *buttoning up his jacket as he unbuttons it*: All told, about two hundred dollars would carry us, dear. But that includes the last payment on the mortgage.[14] After this payment, Willy, the house belongs to us.

WILLY: It's twenty-five years!

LINDA: Biff was nine years old when we bought it.

WILLY: Well, that's a great thing. To weather a twenty-five year mortgage is—

LINDA: It's an accomplishment.

WILLY: All the cement, the lumber, the reconstruction I put in this house! There ain't a crack to be found in it any more.

LINDA: Well, it served its purpose.

WILLY: What purpose? Some stranger'll come along, move in, and that's that. If only Biff would take this house, and raise a family... *He starts to go.* Good-by, I'm late.

LINDA, *suddenly remembering*: Oh, I forgot! You're supposed to meet them for dinner.

WILLY: Me?

LINDA: At Frank's Chop House[15] on Forty-eighth[16] near Sixth Avenue.

WILLY: Is that so! How about you?

LINDA: No, just the three of you. They're gonna blow[17] you to a big meal!

WILLY: Don't say! Who thought of that?

LINDA: Biff came to me this morning, Willy, and he said, "Tell Dad, we want to blow him to a big meal. "Be there six o'clock. You and your two boys are going to have dinner.

WILLY: Gee whiz![18] That's really somethin'. I'm gonna knock Howard for a loop,[19] kid. I'll get an advance, and I'll come home with a New York job. Goddammit, now I'm gonna do it!

LINDA: Oh, that's the spirit, Willy!

WILLY: I will never get behind a wheel[20] the rest of my life!

LINDA: It's changing, Willy, I can feel it changing!

WILLY: Beyond a question. G'by,[21] I'm late. *He starts to go again.*

LINDA, *calling after him as she runs to the kitchen table for a handkerchief*: You got your glasses?

WILLY, *feels for them, then comes back in*: Yeah, yeah, got my glasses.

LINDA, *giving him the handkerchief*: And a handkerchief.

WILLY: Yeah, handkerchief.

LINDA: And your saccharine?[22]

WILLY: Yeah, my saccharine.

LINDA: Be careful on the subway stairs.

She kisses him, and a silk stocking is seen hanging from her hand. Willy notices it.

WILLY: Will you stop mending stockings? At least while I'm in the house. It gets me nervous. I can't tell you. Please.

Linda hides the stocking in her hand as she follows Willy across the forestage in front of the house.

LINDA: Remember, Frank's Chop House.

WILLY, *passing the apron*:[23] Maybe beets would grow out there.

LINDA: *laughing*: But you tried so many times.

WILLY: Yeah. Well, don't work hard today. *He disappears around the right corner of the house.*

LINDA: Be caretul!

As Willy vanishes, Linda waves to him. Suddenly the phone rings. She runs across the stage and into the kitchen and lifts it.

LINDA: Hello? Oh, Biff! I'm so glad you called, I just... Yes, sure, I just told him. Yes, he'll be there for dinner at six o'clock, I didn't forget. Listen, I was just dying to tell you. You know that little rubber pipe[24] I told you about? That he connected to the gas heater? I finally decided to go down the cellar this morning and take it away and destroy it. But it's gone! Imagine? He took it away himself, it isn't there! *She listens.* When? Oh, then you took it. Oh—nothing, its just that I'd hoped he'd taken it away himself. Oh, I'm not worried, darling, because this morning he left in such high spirits, it was like the old days! I'm not afraid any more. Did Mr. Oliver see you?... Well, you wait there then. And make a nice impression on him, darling. Just don't perspire too much before you see him. And have a nice time with Dad. He may have big news too!... That's right, a New York job. And be sweet to him tonight, dear. Be loving to him. Because he's only a little boat looking for a harbor. *She is trembling with sorrow and joy.* Oh, that's wonderful, Biff, you'll save his life. Thanks, darling. Just put your arm around him when he comes into the restaurant. Give him a smile. That's the boy... Good-by, dear.... You got your comb?... That's fine. Good-by, Biff dear.

In the middle of her speech, Howard Wagner, thirty-six, wheels on a small typewriter table on which is a wire-recording machine[25] *and proceeds to plug it in. This is on the left forestage. Light slowly fades on Linda as it rises on Howard. Howard is intent on threading the machine and only glances over his shoulder as Willy appears.*

WILLY: Pst! Pst!

HOWARD: Hello, Willy, come in.

WILLY: Like to have a little talk with you, Howard.

HOWARD: Sorry to keep you waiting. I'll be with you in a minute.

WILLY: What's that, Howard?

HOWARD: Didn't you ever see one of these? Wire recorder.

WILLY: Oh. Can we talk a minute?

HOWARD: Records things. Just got delivery yesterday. Been driving me crazy, the most terrific machine I ever saw in my life. I was up all night with it.

WILLY: What do you do with it?

HOWARD: I bought it for dictation, but you can do anything with it. Listen to this. I had it home last night. Listen to what I picked up. The first one is my daughter. Get this. *He flicks the switch and "Roll out the Barrel"*[26] *is heard being whistled.* Listen to that kid whistle.

WILLY: That is lifelike, isn't it?

HOWARD: Seven years old. Get that tone.

WILLY: Ts, ts. Like to ask a little favor if you...

The whistling breaks off, and the voice of Howard's daughter is heard.

HIS DAUGHTER: "Now you, Daddy."

HOWARD: She's crazy for me! *Again the same song is whistled.* That's me! Ha! *He winks.*

WILLY: You're very good!

The whistling breaks off again. The machine runs silent for a moment.

HOWARD: Sh! Get this now, this is my son.

HIS SON: "The capital of Alabama is Montgomery; the capital of Arizona is Phoenix; the capital of Arkansas is Little Rock; the capital of California is Sacramento..." *and on, and on.*

HOWARD, *holding up five fingers*: Five years old, Willy!

WILLY: He'll make an announcer some day!

HIS SON, *continuing*: "The capital..."

HOWARD: Get that—alphabetical order! *The machine breaks off suddenly.* Wait a minute. The maid kicked the plug out.

WILLY: It certainly is a—

HOWARD: Sh, for God's sake!

HIS SON: "It's nine o'clock, Bulova watch time.[27] So I have to go to sleep."

WILLY: That really is—

HOWARD: Wait a minute! The next is my wife.

They wait.

HOWARD'S VOICE: "Go on, say something." *Pause.* "Well, you gonna talk?"

HIS WIFE: "I can't think of anything."

HOWARD'S VOICE: "Well, talk—it's turning."

HIS WIFE, *shyly, beaten*: "Hello." *Silence.* "Oh, Howard, I can't talk into this..."

HOWARD, *snapping the machine off*: That was my wife.

WILLY: That is a wonderful machine. Can we—

HOWARD: I tell you, Willy, I'm gonna take my camera, and my band-saw, and all my hobbies, and out they go. This is the most fascinating relaxation I ever found.

WILLY: I think I'll get one myself.

HOWARD: Sure, they're only a hundred and a half. You can't do without it. Supposing you wanna hear Jack Benny,[28] see? But you can't be at home at that hour. So you tell the maid to turn the radio on when Jack Benny comes on, and this automatically goes on with the radio...

WILLY: And when you come home you...

HOWARD: You can come home twelve o'clock, one o'clock, any time you like, and you get yourself a Coke[29] and sit yourself down, throw the switch, and there's Jack Benny's propram in the middle of the night!

WILLY: I'm definitely going to get one. Because lots of time I'm on the road, and I think to myself, what I must be missing on the radio!

HOWARD: Don't you have a radio in the car?

WILLY: Well, yeah, but who ever thinks of turning it on?

HOWARD: Say, aren't you supposed to be in Boston?

WILLY: That's what I want to talk to you about, Howard. You got a minute? *He draws a chair in from the wing.*

HOWARD: What happened? What're you doing here?

WILLY: Well...

HOWARD: You didn't crack up again, did you?[30]

WILLY: Oh, no. No...

HOWARD: Geez, you had me worried there for a minute. What's the trouble?

WILLY: Well, tell you the truth, Howard. I've come to the decision that I'd rather not travel any more.

HOWARD: Not travel! Well, what'll you do?

WILLY: Remember, Christmas time, when you had the party here? You said you'd try to think of some spot for me here in town.

HOWARD: With us?

WILLY: Well, sure.

HOWARD: Oh, yeah, yeah. I remember. Well, I couldn't think of anything for you, Willy.

WILLY: I tell ya, Howard. The kids are all grown up, y'know. I don't need much any more. If I could take home—well, sixtyfive dollars a week, I could swing it.[31]

HOWARD: Yeah, but Willy, see I—

WILLY: I tell ya why, Howard. Speaking frankly and between the two of us, y'know—I'm just a little tired.

HOWARD: Oh, I could understand that, Willy. But you're a road man, Willy, and we do a road business. We've only got a half-dozen salesmen on the floor here.

WILLY: God knows, Howard, I never asked a favor of any man. But I was with the firm when your father used to carry you in here in his arms.

HOWARD: I know that, Willy, but—

WILLY: Your father came to me the day you were born and asked me what I thought of the name of Howard, may he rest in peace.

HOWARD: I appreciate that, Willy, but there just is no spot here for you. If I had a spot I'd slam you right in, but I just don't have a single solitary spot.

He looks for his lighter. Willy has picked it up and gives it to him. Pause.

WILLY, *with increasing anger*: Howard, all I need to set my table is fifty dollars a week.

HOWARD: But where am I going to put you, kid?

WILLY: Look, it isn't a question of whether I can sell merchandise, is it?

HOWARD: No, but it's a business, kid, and everybody's gotta pull his own weight.[32]

WILLY, *desperately*: Just let me tell you a story, Howard—

HOWARD: 'Cause you gotta admit, business is business.

WILLY, *angrily*: Business is definitely business, but just listen for a minute. You don't understand this. When I was a boy—eighteen, nineteen—I was already on the road. And there was a question in my mind as to whether selling had a future for me. Because in those days I had a yearning to go to Alaska. See, there were three gold strikes in one month in Alaska, and I felt like going out. Just for the ride, you might say.

HOWARD, *barely interested*: Don't say.

WILLY: Oh, yeah, my father lived many years in Alaska. He was an adventurous man. We've got quite a little streak of self-reliance in our family. I thought I'd go out with my older brother and try to locate him, and maybe settle in the North with the old man. And I was almost decided to go, when I met a salesman in the Parker House. [33] His name was Dave Singleman. And he was eighty-four years old, and he'd drummed merchandise in thirty-one states. [34] And old Dave, he'd go up to his room, y'understand, put on his green velvet slippers—I'll never forget—and pick up his phone and call the buyers, and without ever leaving his room, at the age of eighty-four, he made his living. And when I saw that, I realized that selling was the greatest career a man could want. 'Cause what could be more satisfying than to be able to go, at the age of eightyfour, into twenty or thirty different cities, and pick up a phone, and be remembered and loved and helped by so many different people? Do you know? when he died—and by the way he died the death of a salesman, in his green velvet slippers in the smoker of the New York, New Haven and Hartford, going into Boston[35]—when he died, hundreds of salesmen and buyers were at his funeral. Things were sad on a lotta[36] trains for months after that. *He stands up. Howard has not looked at him.* In those days there was personality in it, Howard. There was respect, and comradeship, and gratitude in it. Today, it's all cut and dried, and there's no chance for bringing friendship to bear—or personality. You see what I mean? They don't know me any more.

HOWARD, *moving away, to the right*: That's just the thing, Willy.

WILLY: If I had forty dollars a week—that's all I'd need. Forty dollars, Howard.

HOWARD: Kid, I can't take blood from a stone, [37]I—

WILLY, *desperation is on him now*: Howard, the year Al Smith was nominated, your father came to me and—

HOWARD, *starting to go off*: I've got to see some people, kid.

WILLY, *stopping him*: I'm talking about your father! There were promises made across this desk! You mustn't tell me you've got people to see—I put thirty-four years into this firm, Howard, and now I can't pay my insurance! You can't eat the orange and throw the peel away—a man is not a piece of fruit! *After a pause*: Now pay attention. Your father—in 1928 I had a big year. I averaged a hundred and seventy dollars a week in commissions.[38]

HOWARD, *impatiently*: Now, Willy, you never averaged—

WILLY, *banging his hand on the desk*: I averaged a hundred and seventy dollars a week in the year of 1928! And your father came to me—or rather, I was in the office here—it was right over this desk—and he put his hand on my shoulder—

HOWARD, *getting up*: You'll have to excuse me, Willy, I gotta see some people. Pull yourself together. *Going out*: I'll be back in a little while.

On Howard's exit, the light on his chair grows very bright and strange.

WILLY: Pull myself together! What the hell did I say to him? My God, I was yelling at him! How could I! *Willy breaks off, staring at the light, which occupies the chair, animating it. He approaches this chair, standing across the desk from it.* Frank,[39] Frank, don't you remember what you told me that time? How you put your hand on my shoulder, and Frank... *He leans on the desk and as he speaks the dead man's name he accidentally switches on the recorder, and instantly*

HOWARD'S SON: "... of New York is Albany. The capital of Ohio is Cincinnati, the capital of Rhode Island is..." *The recitation continues.*

WILLY, *leaping away with fright, shouting*: Ha! Howard! Howard! Howard!

HOWARD, *rushing in*: What happened?

WILLY, *pointing at the machine, which continues nasally, childishly, with the capital cities*: Shut it off! Shut it off!

HOWARD, *pulling the plug out*: Look, Willy...

WILLY, *pressing his hands to his eyes*: I gotta get myself some coffee. I'll get some coffee...

Willy starts to walk out. Howard stops him.

HOWARD, *rolling up the cord*: Willy, look...

WILLY: I'll go to Boston.

HOWARD: Willy, you can't go to Boston for us.

WILLY: Why can't I go?

HOWARD: I don't want you to represent us. I've been meaning to tell you for a long time now.

WILLY: Howard, are you firing me?
HOWARD: I think you need a good long rest, Willy.
WILLY: Howard—
HOWARD: And when you feel better, come back, and we'll see if we can work something out.
WILLY: But I gotta earn money, Howard. I'm in no position to—
HOWARD: Where are your sons? Why don't your sons give you a hand?
WILLY: They're working on a very big deal.
HOWARD: This is no time for false pride, Willy. You go to your sons and you tell them that you're tired. You've got two great boys, haven't you?
WILLY: Oh, no question, no question, but in the meantime...
HOWARD: Then that's that, heh?
WILLY: All right, I'll go to Boston tomorrow.
HOWARD: No, no.
WILLY: I can't throw myself on my sons. I'm not a cripple![40]
HOWARD: Look, kid, I'm busy this morninng.
WILLY, *grasping Howard's arm*: Howard, you've got to let me go to Boston!
HOWARD, *hard, keeping himself under control*: I've got a line of people to see this morning. Sit down, take five minutes, and pull yourself together, and then go home, will ya? I need the office, Willy. *He starts to go, turns, remembering the recorder, starts to push off the table holding the recorder.* Oh, yeah. Whenever you can this week, stop by and drop off the samples. You'll feel better, Willy, and then come back and we'll talk. Pull yourself together, kid, there's people outside.
Howard exits, pushing the table off left. Willy stares into space, exhausted. Now the music is heard—Ben's music—first distantly, then closer, closer. As Willy speaks, Ben[41] enters from the right. He carries valise and umbrella.
WILLY: Oh, Ben, how did you do it? What is the answer? Did you wind up the Alaska deal already?
BEN: Doesn't take much time if you know what you're doing. Just a short business trip. Boarding ship in an hour. Wanted to say good-by.
WILLY: Ben, I've got to talk to you.
BEN, *glancing at his watch*: Haven't the time, William.
WILLY, *crossing the apron to Ben*: Ben, nothing's working out. I don't know what to do.

BEN: Now, look here, William. I've bought timberland in Alaska and I need a man to look after things for me.

WILLY: God, timberland! Me and my boys in those grand outdoors!

BEN: You've a new continent at your doorstep, William. Get out of these cities, they're full of talk and time payments[42] and courts of law. Screw on your fists and you can fight for a fortune up there.

WILLY: Yes, yes! Linda, Linda!

Linda enters as of old,[43] *with the wash.*

LINDA: Oh, you're back?

BEN: I haven't much time.

WILLY: No, wait! Linda, he's got a proposition for me in Alaska.

LINDA: But you've got—*To Ben*: He's got a beautiful job here.

WILLY: But in Alaska, kid, I could—

LINDA: You're doing well enough, Willy!

BEN, *to Linda*: Enough for what, my dear?

LINDA, *frightened of Ben and angry at him*: Don't say those things to him! Enough to be happy right here, right now. *To Willy, while Ben laughs*: Why must everybody conquer the world? You're well liked, and the boys love you, and someday—*to Ben*—why, old man Wagner told him just the other day that if he keeps it up he'll be a member of the firm, didn't he, Willy?

WILLY: Sure, sure. I am building something with this firm, Ben, and if a man is building something he must be on the right track, mustn't he?

BEN: What are you building? Lay your hand on it. Where is it?

WILLY, *hesitantly*: That's true, Linda, there's nothing.

LINDA: Why? *To Ben*: There's a man eighty-four years old—

WILLY: That's right, Ben, that's right. When I look at that man I say, what is there to worry about?

BEN: Bah!

WILLY: It's true, Ben. All he has to do is go into any city, pick up the phone, and he's making his living and you know why?

BEN, *picking up his valise*: I've got to go.

WILLY, *holding Ben back*: Look at this boy!

Biff, in his high school sweater, enters carrying suitcase. Happy carries Biff's shoulder guards,[44] *gold helmet, and football pants.*

WILLY: Without a penny to his name, three great universities are begging for him, and from there the sky's the limit, because it's not what you do, Ben. It's who you know and the smile on your face! It's contacts, Ben, contacts! The whole wealth of Alaska passes over the lunch table at the Commodore Hotel, and that's the wonder, the wonder of this country, that a man can end with diamonds here on the basis of being liked! *He turns to Biff.* And that's why when you get out on that field today it's important. Because thousands of people will be rooting for you and loving you. *To Ben, who has again begun to leave*: And Ben! when he walks into a business office his name will sound out like a bell and all the doors will open to him! I've seen it, Ben, I've seen it a thousand times! You can't feel it with your hand like timber, but it's there!

BEN: Good-by, William.

WILLY: Ben, am I right? Don't you think I'm right? I value your advice.

BEN: There's a new continent at your doorstep, William. You could walk out rich. Rich! *He is gone.*

WILLY: We'll do it here, Ben! You hear me? We're gonna do it here!

Young Bernard[45] *rushes in. The gay music of the Boys is heard.*

BERNARD: Oh, gee, I was afraid you left already!

WILLY: Why? What time is it?

BERNARD: It's half-past one!

WILLY: Well, come on, everybody! Ebbets Field[46] next stop! Where's the pennants? *He rushes through the wall-line of the kitchen and out into the living-room.*[47]

LINDA, *to Biff*: Did you pack fresh underwear?

BIFF, *who has been limbering up*: I want to go!

BERNARD: Biff, I'm carrying your helmet, ain't I?

HAPPY: No, I'm carrying the helmet.

BERNARD: Oh, Biff, you promised me.

HAPPY: I'm carrying the helmet.

BERNARD: How am I going to get in the locker room?[48]

LINDA: Let him carry the shoulder guards. *She puts her coat and hat on in the kitchen.*

BERNARD: Can I, Biff? 'Cause I told everybody I'm going to be in the locker room.

HAPPY: In Ebbets Field it's the clubhouse.[49]

BERNARD: I meant the clubhouse. Biff!

HAPPY: Biff!

BIFF, *grandly, after a slight pause*: Let him carry the shoulder guards.
HAPPY, *as he gives Bernard the shoulder guards*: Stay close to us now.
Willy rushes in with the pennants.
WILLY, *handing them out*: Everybody wave when Biff comes out on the field. *Happy and Bernard run off.* You set now, boy?
The music has died away.
BIFF: Ready to go, Pop. Every muscle is ready.
WILLY, *at the edge of the apron*: You realize what this means?
BIFF: That's right, Pop.
WILLY, *feeling Biff's muscles*: You're comin' home this afternoon captain of the All-Scholastic Championship Team of the City of New York.
BIFF: I got it, Pop. And remember, pal, when I take off my helmet, that touchdown[50] is for you.
WILLY: Let's go! *He is starting out, with his arm around Biff, when Charley enters, as of old, in knickers.* I got no room for you, Charley.
CHARLEY: Room? For what?
WILLY: In the car.
CHARLEY: You goin' for a ride? I wanted to shoot some casino. [51]
WILLY, *furiously*: Casino! *Incredulously*: Don't you realize what today is?
LINDA: Oh, he knows, Willy. He's just kidding you.
WILLY: That's nothing to kid about!
CHARLEY: No, Linda, what's goin' on?
LINDA: He's playing in Ebbets Field.
CHARLEY: Baseball in this weather?
WILLY: Don't talk to him. Come on, come on! *He is pushing them out.*
CHARLEY: Wait a minute, didn't you hear the news?
WILLY: What?
CHARLEY: Don't you listen to the radio? Ebbets Field just blew up.
WILLY: You go to hell! *Charley laughs. Pushing them out*: Come on, come on! We're late.
CHARLEY, *as they go*: Knock a homer[52], Biff, knock a homer!
WILLY, *the last to leave, turning to Charley*: I don't think that was funny, Charley. This is the greatest day of his life.
CHARLEY: Willy, when are you going to grow up?
WILLY: Yeah, heh? When this game is over, Charley, you'll be laughing out of the other side of your face. They'll be calling him another Red

Grange.[53] Twenty-five thousand a year.

CHARLEY, *kidding*: Is that so?

WILLY: Yeah, that's so.

CHARLEY: Well, then, I'm sorry, Willy. But tell me something.

WILLY: What?

CHARLEY: Who is Red Grange?

WILLY: Put up your hands. Goddam you, put up your hands!

Charley, chuckling, shakes his head and walks away, around the left corner of the stage. Willy follows him. The music rises to a mocking frenzy.

WILLY: Who the hell do you think you are, better than everybody else? You don't know everything, you big, ignorant, stupid... Put up your hands!

Light rises, on the right side of the forestage, on a small table in the reception room of Charley's office. Traffic sounds are heard. Bernard, now mature, sits whistling to himself. A pair of tennis rackets and an overnight bag are on the floor beside him.

WILLY, *offstage*: What are you walking away for? Don't walk away! If you're going to say something say it to my face! I know you laugh at me behind my back. You'll laugh out of the other side of your goddam face after this game. Touchdown! Touchdown! Eighty thousand people! Touchdown! Right between the goal posts.

Bernard is a quiet, earnest, but self-assured young man. Willy's voice is coming from right upstage now. Bernard lowers his feet off the table and listens. Jenny, his father's secretary, enters.

JENNY, *distressed*: Say, Bernard, will you go out in the hall?

BERNARD: What is that noise? Who is it?

JENNY: Mr. Loman. He just got off the elevator.

BERNARD, *getting up*: Who's he arguing with?

JENNY: Nobody. There's nobody with him. I can't deal with him any more, and your father gets all upset everytime he comes. I've got a lot of typing to do, and your father's waiting to sign it. Will you see him?

WILLY, *entering*: Touchdown! Touch—*He sees Jenny.* Jenny, Jenny, good to see you. How're ya? Workin'? Or still honest?

JENNY: Fine. How've you been feeling?

WILLY: Not much any more, Jenny. Ha, ha! *He is surprised to see the rackets.*

BERNARD: Hello, Uncle Willy.

WILLY, *almost shocked*: Bernard! Well, look who's here! *He comes quickly, guiltily, to Bernard and warmly shakes his hand.*

BERNARD: How are you? Good to see you.

WILLY: What are you doing here?

BERNARD: Oh, just stopped by to see Pop. Get off my feet till my train leaves. I'm going to Washington in a few minutes.

WILLY: Is he in?

BERNARD: Yes, he's in his office with the accountant. Sit down.

WILLY, *sitting down*: What're you going to do in Washington?

BERNARD: Oh, just a case I've got there, Willy.

WILLY: That so? *Indicating the rackets*: You going to play tennis there?

BERNARD: I'm staying with a friend who's got a court.

WILLY: Don't say. His own tennis court. Must be fine people, I bet.

BERNARD: They are, very nice. Dad tells me Biff's in town.

WILLY, *with a big smile*: Yeah, Biff's in. Working on a very big deal, Bernard.

BERNARD: What's Biff doing?

WILLY: Well, he's been doing very big things in the West. But he decided to establish himself here. Very big. We're having dinner. Did I hear your wife had a boy?

BERNARD: That's right. Our second.

WILLY: Two boys! What do you know!

BERNARD: What kind of a deal has Biff got?

WILLY: Well, Bill Oliver—very big sporting-goods man—he wants Biff very badly. Called him in from the West. Long distance, carte blanche,[54] special deliveries. Your friends have their own private tennis court?

BERNARD: You still with the old firm, Willy?

WILLY, *after a pause*: I'm—I'm overjoyed to see how you made the grade,[55] Bernard, overjoyed. It's an encouraging thing to see a young man really—really—Looks very good for Biff—very—*He breaks off, then*: Bernard—*He is so full of emotion, he breaks off again.*

BERNARD: What is it, Willy?

WILLY, *small and alone*: What—what's the secret?

BERNARD: What secret?

WILLY: How—how did you? Why didn't he ever catch on?[56]

BERNARD: I wouldn't know that, Willy.

WILLY, *confidentially, desperately*: You were his friend, his boyhood friend. There's something I don't understand about it. His life ended after that Ebbets Field game. From the age of seventeen nothing good ever happened to him.

BERNARD: He never trained himself for anything.

WILLY: But he did, he did. After high school he took so many correspondence courses. Radio mechanics; television; God knows what, and never made the slightest mark.

BERNARD, *taking off his glasses*: Willy, do you want to talk candidly?

WILLY, *rising, faces Bernard*: I regard you as a very brilliant man, Bernard. I value your advice.

BERNARD: Oh, the hell with the advice, Willy. I couldn't advise you. There's just one thing I've always wanted to ask you. When he was supposed to graduate, and the math teacher flunked him—

WILLY: Oh, that son-of-a-bitch ruined his life.

BERNARD: Yeah, but, Willy, all he had to do was go to summer school and make up that subject.

WILLY: That's right, that's right.

BERNARD: Did you tell him not to go to summer school?

WILLY: Me? I begged him to go. I ordered him to go!

BERNARD: Then why wouldn't he go?

WILLY: Why? Why! Bernard, that question has been trailing me like a ghost for the last fifteen years. He flunked the subject, and laid down and died like a hammer hit him!

BERNARD: Take it easy, kid.

WILLY: Let me talk to you—I got nobody to talk to. Bernard, Bernard, was it my fault? Y'see? It keeps going around in my mind, maybe I did something to him. I got nothing to give him.

BERNARD: Don't take it so hard.

WILLY: Why did he lay down? What is the story there? You were his friend!

BERNARD: Willy, I remember, it was June, and our grades came out. And he'd flunked math.

WILLY: That son-of-a-bitch!

BERNARD: No, it wasn't right then. Biff just got very angry, I remember, and he was ready to enroll in summer school.

WILLY, *surprised*: He was?

BERNARD: He wasn't beaten by it at all. But then, Willy, he disappeared from the block for almost a month. And I got the idea that he'd gone up to New England to see you. Did he have a talk with you then?

Willy stares in silence.

BERNARD: Willy?

WILLY, *with a strong edge of resentment in his voice*: Yeah, he came to Boston. What about it?

BERNARD: Well, just that when he came back—I'll never forget this, it always mystifies me. Because I'd thought so well of Biff, even though he'd always taken advantage of me. I loved him, Willy, y'know? And he came back after that month and took his sneakers—remember those sneakers with "University of Virginia" printed on them? He was so proud of those, wore them every day. And he took them down in the cellar, and burned them up in the furnace. We had a fist fight. It lasted at least half an hour. Just the two of us, punching each other down the cellar, and crying right through it. I've often thought of how strange it was that I knew he'd given up his life. What happened in Boston, Willy?

Willy looks at him as at an intruder.

BERNARD: I just bring it up because you asked me.

WILLY, *angrily*: Nothing. What do you mean, "What happened?" What's that got to do with anything?

BERNARD: Well, don't get sore.

WILLY: What are you trying to do, blame it on me? If a boy lays down is that my fault?

BERNARD: Now, Willy, don't get—

WILLY: Well, don't—don't talk to me that way! What does that mean, "What happened?"

Charley enters. He is in his vest, and he carries a bottle of bourbon.

CHARLEY: Hey, you're going to miss that train. *He waves the bottle.*

BERNARD: Yeah, I'm going. *He takes the bottle.* Thanks, Pop. *He picks up his rackets and bag.* Good-by, Willy, and don't worry about it. You know, "If at first you don't succeed..." [57]

WILLY: Yes, I believe in that.
BERNARD: But sometimes, Willy, it's better for a man just to walk away.
WILLY: Walk away?
BERNARD: That's right.
WILLY: But if you can't walk away?
BERNARD, *after a slight pause*: I guess that's when it's tough. *Extending his hand*: Good-by, Willy.
WILLY, *shaking Bernard's hand*: Good-by, boy.
CHARLEY, *an arm on Bernard's shoulder*: How do you like this kid? Gonna argue a case in front of the Supreme Court.
BERNARE, *protesting*: Pop!
WILLY, *genuinely shocked, pained, and happy*: No! The Supreme Court!
BERNARD: I gotta run. 'By, Dad!
CHARLEY: Knock'em dead, Bernard!
Bernard goes off.
WILLY, *as Charley takes out his wallet*: The Supreme Court! And he didn't even mention it!
CHARLEY, *counting out money on the desk*: He don't have to—he's gonna do it.
WILLY: And you never told him what to do, did you? You never took any interest in him.
CHARLEY: My salvation is that I never took any interest in anything. There's some money—fifty dollars. I got an accountant inside.
WILLY: Charley, look... *With difficulty*: I got my insurance to pay. If you can manage it—I need a hundred and ten dollars.
Charley doesn't reply for a moment; merely stops moving.
WILLY: I'd draw it from my bank but Linda would know, and I...
CHARLEY: Sit down, Willy.
WILLY, *moving toward the chair*: I'm keeping an account of everything, remember. I'll pay every penny back. *He sits.*
CHARLEY: Now listen to me, Willy.
WILLY: I want you to know I appreciate...
CHARLEY, *sitting down on the table*: Willy, what're you doin'? What the hell is goin' on in your head?
WILLY: Why? I'm simply...
CHARLEY: I offered you a job. You can make fifty dollars a week. And I won't send you on the road.

WILLY: I've got a job.

CHARLEY: Without pay? What kind of a job is a job without pay? *He rises.* Now, look, kid, enough is enough. I'm no genius but I know when I'm being insulted.

WILLY: Insulted!

CHARLEY: Why don't you want to work for me?

WILLY: What's the matter with you? I've got a job.

CHARLEY: Then what're you walkin' in here every week for?

WILLY, *getting up*: Well, if you don't want me to walk in here—

CHARLEY: I am offering you a job.

WILLY: I don't want your goddam job!

CHARLEY: When the hell are you going to grow up?

WILLY, *furiously*: You big ignoramus, if you say that to me again I'll rap you one! I don't care how big you are! *He's ready to fight. Pause.*

CHARLEY, *kindly, going to him*: How much do you need, Willy?

WILLY: Charley, I'm strapped. I'm strapped. I don't know what to do. I was just fired.

CHARLEY: Howard fired you?

WILLY: That snotnose. Imagine that? I named him. I named him Howard.

CHARLEY: Willy, when're you gonna realize that them things don't mean anything? You named him Howard, but you can't sell that. The only thing you got in this world is what you can sell. And the funny thing is that you're a salesman, and you don't know that.

WILLY: I've always tried to think otherwise, I guess. I always felt that if a man was impressive, and well liked, that nothing—

CHARLEY: Why must everybody like you? Who liked J. P. Morgan?[58] Was he impressive? In a Turkish bath he'd look like a butcher. But with his pockets on he was very well liked.[59] Now listen, Willy, I know you don't like me, and nobody can say I'm in love with you, but I'll give you a job because—just for the hell of it, put it that way. Now what do you say?

WILLY: I—I just can't work for you, Charley.

CHARLEY: What're you, jealous of me?

WILLY: I can't work for you, that's all, don't ask me why.

CHARLEY, *angered, takes out more bills*: You been jealous of me all your life, you damned fool! Here, pay your insurance. *He puts the money in Willy's hand.*

WILLY: I'm keeping strict accounts.

CHARLEY: I've got some work to do. Take care of yourself. And pay your insurance.

WILLY, *moving to the right*: Funny, y'know? After all the highways, and the trains, and the appointments, and the years, you end up worth more dead than alive. [60]

CHARLEY: Willy, nobody's worth nothin' dead. *After a slight pause*: Did you hear what I said?

Willy stands still, dreaming.

CHARLEY: Willy!

WILLY: Apologize to Bernard for me when you see him. I didn't mean to argue with him. He's a fine boy. They're all fine boys, and they'll end up big—all of them. Someday they'll all play tennis together. Wish me luck, Charley. He saw Bill Oliver today.

CHARLEY: Good luck.

WILLY, *on the verge of tears*: Charley, you're the only friend I got. Isn't that a remarkable thing? *He goes out.*

CHARLEY: Jesus!

Charley stares after him a moment and follows. All light blacks out. Suddenly raucous music is heard, and a red glow rises behind the screen at right. Stanley, a young waiter, appears, carrying a table, followed by Happy, who is carrying two chairs.

STANLEY, *putting the table down*: That's all right, Mr. Loman, I can handle it myself. *He turns and takes the chairs from Happy and places them at the table.*

HAPPY, *glancing around*: Oh, this is better.

STANLEY: Sure, in the front there you're in the middle of all kinds a noise. Whenever you got a party, Mr. Loman, you just tell me and I'll put you back here. Y'know, there's a lotta people they don't like it private, because when they go out they like to see a lotta action around them because they're sick and tired to stay in the house by theirself. [61] But I know you, you ain't from Hackensack. [62] You know what I mean?

HAPPY, *sitting down*: So how's it coming, Stanley?

STANLEY: Ah, it's a dog's life. I only wish during the war they'd a took me in the Army. I coulda[63] been dead by now.

HAPPY: My brother's back, Stanley.

STANLEY: Oh, he come back, heh? From the Far West.

HAPPY: Yeah, big cattle man, my brother, so treat him right. And my father's coming too.

STANLEY: Oh, your father too!

HAPPY: You got a couple of nice lobsters?

STANLEY: Hundred per cent, big.

HAPPY: I want them with the claws.

STANLEY: Don't worry, I don't give you no mice.[64] *Happy laughs.* How about some wine? It'll put a head on the meal.[65]

HAPPY: No. You remember, Stanley, that recipe I brought you from overseas? With the champagne in it?

STANLEY: Oh, yeah, sure. I still got it tacked up yet in the kitchen. But that'll have to cost a buck apiece anyways.

HAPPY: That's all right.

STANLEY: What'd you, hit a number or somethin'?

HAPPY: No, it's a little celebration. My brother is—I think he pulled off a big deal today. I think we're going into business together.

STANLEY: Great! That's the best for you. Because a family business, you know what I mean? —that's the best.

HAPPY: That's what I think.

STANLEY: 'Cause what's the difference? Somebody steals? It's in the family. Know what I mean? *Sotto voce:*[66] Like this bartender here. The boss is goin' crazy what kinda leak he's got in the cash register. You put it in but it don't come out.

HAPPY, *raising his head:* Sh!

STANLEY: What?

HAPPY: You notice I wasn't lookin' right or left, was I?

STANLEY: No.

HAPPY: And my eyes are closed.

STANLEY: So what's the—?

HAPPY: Strudel's comin'.[67]

STANLEY, *catching on, looks around:* Ah, no, there's no—

He breaks off as a furred, lavishly dressed girl enters and sits at the next table. Both follow her with their eyes.

STANLEY: Geez, how'd ya know?

HAPPY: I got radar or something. *Staring directly at her profile*: Oooooooo... Stanley.

STANLEY: I think that's for you, Mr. Loman.

HAPPY: Look at that mouth. Oh, God. And the binoculars.[68]

STANLEY: Geez, you got a life, Mr. Loman.

HAPPY: Wait on her.

STANLEY, *going to the girl's table*: Would you like a menu, ma'am?

GIRL: I'm expecting someone, but I'd like a—

HAPPY: Why don't you bring her—excuse me, miss, do you mind? I sell champagne, and I'd like you to try my brand. Bring her a champagne, Stanley.

GIRL: That's awfully nice of you.

HAPPY: Don't mention it. It's all company money. *He laughs.*

GIRL: That's a charming product to be selling, isn't it?

HAPPY: Oh, gets to be like everything else. Selling is selling, y'know.

GIRL: I suppose.

HAPPY: You don't happen to sell, do you?

GIRL: No, I don't sell.

HAPPY: Would you object to a compliment from a stranger? You ought to be on a magazine cover.

GIRL, *looking at him a little archly*: I have been.

Stanley comes in with a glass of champagne.

HAPPY: What'd I say before, Stanley? You see? She's a cover girl.

STANLEY: Oh, I could see, I could see.

HAPPY, *to the Girl*: What magazine?

GIRL: Oh, a lot of them. *She takes the drink.* Thank you.

HAPPY: You know what they say in France, don't you? "Champagne is the drink of the complexion" —Hya, Biff!

Biff has entered and sits with Happy.

BIFF: Hello, kid. Sorry I'm late.

HAPPY: I just got here. Uh, Miss—?

GIRL: Forsythe.

HAPPY: Miss Forsythe, this is my brother.

BIFF: Is Dad here?

HAPPY: His name is Biff. You might've heard of him. Great football player.

GIRL: Really? What team?

Happy: Are you familiar with football?

Girl: No, I'm afraid I'm not.

Happy: Biff is quarterback with the New York Giants.[69]

Girl: Well, that is nice, isn't it? *She drinks.*

Happy: Good health.

Girl: I'm happy to meet you.

Happy: That's my name. Hap. It's really Harold, but at West Point they called me Happy.

Girl, *now really impressed*: Oh, I see. How do you do? *She turns her profile.*

Biff: Isn't Dad coming?

Happy: You want her?

Biff: Oh, I could never make that.

Happy: I remember the time that idea would never come into your head. Where's the old confidence, Biff?

Biff: I just saw Oliver—

Happy: Wait a minute. I've got to see that old confidence again. Do you want her? She's on call.

Biff: Oh, no. *He turns to look at the Girl.*

Happy: I'm telling you. Watch this. *Turning to the Girl*: Honey? *She turns to him.* Are you busy?

Girl: Well, I am... but I could make a phone call.

Happy: Do that, will you, honey? And see if you can get a friend. We'll be here for a while. Biff is one of the greatest football players in the country.

Girl, *standing up*: Well, I'm certainly happy to meet you.

Happy: Come back soon.

Girl: I'll try.

Happy: Don't try, honey, try hard.

The Girl exits. Stanley follows, shaking his head in bewildered admiration.

Happy: Isn't that a shame now? A beautiful girl like that? That's why I can't get married. There's not a good woman in a thousand. New York is loaded with them, kid!

Biff: Hap, look—

Happy: I told you she was on call!

Biff, *strangely unnerved*: Cut it out, will ya? I want to say something to you.

Happy: Did you see Oliver?

Biff: I saw him all right. Now look, I want to tell Dad a couple of things and I want you to help me.

Happy: What? Is he going to back you?

Biff: Are you crazy? You're out of your goddam head, you know that?

Happy: Why? What happened?

Biff, *breathlessly*: I did a terrible thing today, Hap. It's been the strangest day I ever went through. I'm all numb, I swear.

Happy: You mean he wouldn't see you?

Biff: Well, I waited six hours for him, see? All day. Kept sending my name in. Even tried to date his secretary so she'd get me to him, but no soap.[70]

Happy: Because you're not showin' the old confidence, Biff. He remembered you, didn't he?

Biff, *stopping Happy with a gesture*: Finally, about five o'clock, he comes out. Didn't remember who I was or anything. I felt like such an idiot, Hap.

Happy: Did you tell him my Florida idea?

Biff: He walked away. I saw him for one minute. I got so mad I could've torn the walls down! How the hell did I ever get the idea I was a salesman there? I even believed myself that I'd been a salesman for him! And then he gave me one look and—I realized what a ridiculous lie my whole life has been! We've been talking in a dream for fifteen years. I was a shipping clerk.

Happy: What'd you do?

Biff, *with great tension and wonder*: Well, he left, see. And the secretary went out. I was all alone in the waiting-room. I don't know what came over me, Hap. The next thing I know I'm in his office—paneled walls, everything. I can't explain it. I—Hap, I took his fountain pen.

Happy: Geez, did he catch you?

Biff: I ran out. I ran down all eleven flights. I ran and ran and ran.

Happy: That was an awful dumb—what'd you do that for?

Biff, *agonized*: I don't know, I just—wanted to take somthing, I don't know. You gotta help me, Hap, I'm gonna tell Pop.

Happy: You crazy? What for?

BIFF: Hap, he's got to understand that I'm not the man somebody lends that kind of money to. He thinks I've been spiting him all these years and it's eating him up.

HAPPY: That's just it. You tell him something nice.

BIFF: I can't.

HAPPY: Say you got a lunch date with Oliver tomorrow.

BIFF: So what do I do tomorrow?

HAPPY: You leave the house tomorrow and come back at night and say Oliver is thinking it over. And he thinks it over for a couple of weeks, and gradually it fades away and nobody's the worse.[71]

BIFF: But it'll go on forever!

HAPPY: Dad is never so happy as when he's looking forward to something!

Willy enters.

HAPPY: Hello, scout!

WILLY: Gee, I haven't been here in years!

Stanley has followed Willy in and sets a chair for him. Stanley starts off but Happy stops him.

HAPPY: Stanley!

Stanley stands by, waiting for an order.

BIFF, *going to Willy with guilt, as to an invalid*: Sit down, Pop. You want a drink?

WILLY: Sure, I don't mind.

BIFF: Let's get a load on.[72]

WILLY: You look worried.

BIFF: N-no. *To Stanley*: Scotch all around. Make it doubles.[73]

STANLEY: Doubles, right. *He goes.*

WILLY: You had a couple already, didn't you?

BIFF: Just a couple, yeah.

WILLY: Well, what happened, boy? *Nodding affirmatively, with a smile*: Everything go all right?

BIFF, *takes a breath, then reaches out and grasps Willy's hand*: Pal... *He is smiling bravely, and Willy is smiling too.* I had an experience today.

HAPPY: Terrific, Pop.

WILLY: That so? What happened?

BIFF, *high, slightly alcoholic, above the earth*: I'm going to tell you everything from first to last. It's been a strange day. *Silence. He looks around, composes himself as best he can, but his breath keeps breaking the rhythm of his voice.* I had to wait quite a while for him, and—

WILLY: Oliver?

BIFF: Yeah, Oliver. All day, as a matter of cold fact. And a lot of—instances—facts, Pop, facts about my life came back to me. Who was it, Pop? Who ever said I was a salesman with Oliver?

WILLY: Well, you were.

BIFF: No, Dad, I was a shipping clerk.

WILLY: But you were practically—

BIFF, *with determination*: Dad, I don't know who said it first, but I was never a salesman for Bill Oliver.

WILLY: What're you talking about?

BIFF: Let's hold on to the facts tonight, Pop. We're not going to get anywhere bullin' around.[74] I was a shipping cierk.

WILLY, *angrily*: All right, now listen to me—

BIFF: Why don't you let me finish?

WILLY: I'm not interested in stories about the past or any crap of that kind because the woods are burning, boys, you understand? There's a big blaze going on all around. I was fired today.

BIFF, *shocked*: How could you be?

WILLY: I was fired, and I'm looking for a little good news to tell your mother, because the woman has waited and the woman has suffered. The gist of it is that I haven't got a story left in my head, Biff. So don't give me a lecture about facts and aspects. I am not interested. Now what've you got to say to me?

Stanley enters with three drinks. They wait until he leaves.

WILLY: Did you see Oliver?

BIFF: Jesus, Dad!

WILLY: You mean you didn't go up there?

HAPPY: Sure he went up there.

BIFF: I did. I—saw him. How could they fire you?

WILLY, *on the edge of his chair*: What kind of a welcome did he give you?

BIFF: He won't even let you work on commission?[75]

WILLY: I'm out! *Driving*: So tell me, he gave you a warm welcome?

HAPPY: Sure, Pop, sure!

BIFF, *driven*: Well, it was kind of—

Willy: I was wondering if he'd remember you. *To Happy*: Imagine, man doesn't see him for ten, twelve years and gives him that kind of a welcome!

Happy: Damn right!

Biff, *trying to return to the offensive*: Pop, look—

Willy: You know why he remembered you, don't you? Because you impressed him in those days.

Biff: Let's talk quietly and get this down to the facts, huh?

Willy, *as though Biff had been interrupting*: Well, what happened? It's great news, Biff. Did he take you into his office or'd you talk in the waiting-room?

Biff: Well, he came in, see, and—

Willy, *with a big smile*: What'd he say? Betcha[76] he threw his arm around you.

Biff: Well, he kinda—

Willy: He's a fine man. *To Happy*: Very hard man to see, y'know.

Happy, *agreeing*: Oh, I know.

Willy, *to Biff*: Is that where you had the drinks?

Biff: Yeah, he gave me a couple of—no, no!

Happy, *cutting in*: He told him my Florida idea.

Willy: Don't interrupt. *To Biff*: How'd he react to the Florida idea?

Biff: Dad, will you give me a minute to explain?

Willy: I've been waiting for you to explain since I sat down here! What happened? He took you into his office and what?

Biff: Well—I talked. And—and he listened, see.

Willy: Famous for the way he listens, y'know. What was his answer?

Biff: His answer was—*He breaks off, suddenly angry.* Dad, you're not letting me tell you what I want to tell you!

Willy, *accusing, angered*: You didn't see him, did you?

Biff: I did see him!

Willy: What'd you insult him or something? You insulted him, didn't you?

Biff: Listen, will you let me out of it, will you just let me out of it!

Happy: What the hell!

Willy: Tell me what happened!

Biff, *to Happy*: I can't talk to him!

A single trumpet note jars the ear. The light of green leaves stains the house, which holds the air of night and a dream. Young Bernard enters and knocks on the door of the house.[77]

YOUNG BERNARD, *frantically*: Mrs. Loman, Mrs. Loman!

HAPPY: Tell him what happened!

BIFF, *to Happy*: Shut up and leave me alone!

WILLY: No, no! You had to go and flunk math!

BIFF: What math? What're you talking about?

YOUNG BERNARD: Mrs. Loman, Mrs. Loman!

Linda appears in the house, as of old.

WILLY, *wildly*: Math, math, math!

BIFF: Take it easy, Pop!

YOUNG BERNARD: Mrs. Loman!

WILLY, *furiously*: If you hadn't flunked you'd've been set by now!

BIFF: Now, look, I'm gonna tell you what happened, and you're going to listen to me.

YOUNG BERNARD: Mrs. Loman!

BIFF: I waited six hours—

HAPPY: What the hell are you saying?

BIFF: I kept sending in my name but he woudln't see me. So finally he... *He continues unheard as light fades low on the restaurant.*

YOUNG BERNARD: Biff flunked math!

LINDA: No!

YOUNG BERNARD: Birnbaum[78] flunked him! They won't graduate him!

LINDA: But they have to. He's gotta go to the university. Where is he? Biff! Biff!

YOUNG BERNARD: No, he left. He went to Grand Central.[79]

LINDA: Grand—You mean he went to Boston!

YOUNG BERNARD: Is Uncle Willy in Boston?

LINDA: Oh, maybe Willy can talk to the teacher. Oh, the poor, poor boy!

Light on house area snaps out.

BIFF, *at the table, now audible, holding up a gold fountain pen*: ... so I'm washed up with Oliver,[80] you understand? Are you listening to me?

WILLY, *at a loss*: Yeah, sure. If you hadn't flunked—

BIFF: Flunked what? What're you talking about?

WILLY: Don't blame everything on me! I didn't flunk math—you did! What pen?

HAPPY: That was awful dumb, Biff, a pen like that is worth—
WILLY, *seeing the pen for the first time*: You took Oliver's pen?
BIFF, *weakening*: Dad, I just explained it to you.
WILLY: You stole Bill Oliver's fountain pen!
BIFF: I didn't exactly steal it! That's just what I've been explaining to you!
HAPPY: He had it in his hand and just then Oliver walked in, so he got nervours and stuck it in his pocket!
WILLY: My God, Biff!
BIFF: I never intended to do it, Dad!

〔**注释**〕

1. Willy：威利，即威廉·洛曼（William Loman），本剧主人公，瓦格纳公司的推销员。威利年过六旬，穿着朴素，性格活跃，耽于梦想。Loman 为 low man（下层人）的谐音，暗示主人公的社会地位。

2. Linda：林达，威利的妻子。她生性快活，深爱并崇拜丈夫，因而惯于压抑自己对威利某些行为的不满。

3. Boys：指威利的两个儿子。长子比夫（Biff）34 岁，未婚，身材匀称，形容有些憔悴，显得缺乏自信。他浪迹四方，一事无成，感到困惑迷惘。次子海皮（Happy）32 岁，未婚，身材高大健壮，性感极强。他虽经商，但同样感到迷惘。他表面上是个乐天派，但实际上从不正视自己的失败，因而比他的哥哥更加困惑，更加不知羞耻。

4. I can't get over the shaving lotion in this house!：我到现在还能闻见屋里有刮脸油的味儿。在第一幕中林达曾说：她喜欢看两个儿子一起刮脸，爱闻那刮脸油的味儿。

5. Oliver：即比尔·奥利弗（Bill Oliver），体育用品商。威利和长子比夫多年里一直幻想着比夫是奥利弗的推销员。

6. Howard：即霍华德·瓦格纳（Howard Wagner），36 岁，瓦格纳公司的老板。

7. He'll just have to take me off the road.：他不能再让我东跑西颠了（指外出推销）。

8. Well, you had the motor job on the car...：你修汽车发动机还花了钱呢...。

9. Studebaker：威利的汽车牌号。

10. Charley：查利，威利的邻居。他身材高大，说话缓慢，措词简炼，冷静刻板。他不论说什么，话里总透出怜悯的意味。

11. a General Electric：一台美国通用电气公司生产的发动机。

12. Hastings refrigerator：黑斯廷斯公司生产的电冰箱。

13. it's on its last legs：车已经快磨损了。

14. the mortgage：指以抵押的方式分期付款购买住房。

15。Frank's Chop House：纽约市一饭馆名。

16. Forty-Eighth＝Forty-Eighth Street.

17. blow：（俚语）款待。

18. Gee whiz：与后面出现的 Geez 一样，是表达惊奇或热情的感叹词。

19. I'm gonna knock Howard for a loop：我要给霍华德一个好印象。To knock somebody for a loop 是俚语。

20. get behind a wheel：此处指驾汽车外出推销商品。

21. G'by＝Goodbye.

22. And your saccharine?：Saccharine＝saccharin. 你带糖精了吗？糖尿病和肥胖症患者因不宜食用普通食糖，外出时常自带糖精。

23. the apron＝the apron stage，舞台幕前向乐池（或观众席）突出的半圆形部分。按照作者对本剧布景的描述，舞台上出现的是威利家的内景，而前面半圆形部分则为他家的后院。此外，这个区域也用来表现威利回忆或幻想的场景以及发生在其它地方的现实场景。

24. that little rubber pipe：指林达在自家地下室的电闸盒后面发现的一根小橡皮管，上面装有接口，她还在热水器下面的煤气导管上发现一个新的螺纹接套。她认为这显然是威利安装的，以备自杀之用。

25. wire-recording machine＝wire recorder：钢丝录音机。

26. "Roll out the Barrel"：歌曲名。

27. It's nine o'clock，Bulova watch time.：这是美国 Bulova 钟表公司的广告用语。

28. Jack Benny：杰克·本尼（1894～1974），美国著名喜剧演员。他的广播喜剧节目曾深受美国人民的喜爱。

29. Coke＝Coca Cola：可口可乐饮料。

30. You didn't crack up again，did you?：你不是车又坏了吧？

31. swing it：（俚语）维持下去。

32. everybody's gotta pull his own weight：每个人都得尽力而为。gotta＝got to.

33. Parker House：波士顿一饭店名。

34. he'd drummed merchandise in thirty-one states：他曾到 31 个州去推销商品。To drum merchandise 意为：外出向各零售商推销商品。

35. in the smoker of the New York，New Haven and Hartford，going into Boston：在从纽约经纽黑文和哈特福德到波士顿的火车上的吸烟者车厢里。

36. lotta＝lot of。

37. I can't take blood from a stone：（俗语）我从石头里挤不出血来。

38. commissions：佣金。

39. Frank：即弗兰克·瓦格纳（Frank Wagner），霍华德·瓦格纳的父亲，威利过去的老板。

40. I can't throw myself on my sons, I'm not a cripple!：我不能投靠儿子们过活，我又不是残废人！

41. Ben：本恩，威利已故的哥哥，仅在威利回忆或幻想的场景中出现。下面一段就是威利的回忆，那时他和本恩都较年轻。本恩出场时有特定的音乐（Ben's music）伴随。据作者介绍，本恩在第一幕中出现时60多岁，留着小胡子，手提旅行包和雨伞。他表情冷漠，摆出一副权威的架势，还有些异国风度。他对自己的命运充满信心。

42. time payments：分期付款。

43. Linda enters as of old：林达象往日一样上场。

44. shoulder guards：美式足球（即橄榄球）球员用的护肩。

45. Bernard：伯纳德，威利的邻居查利之子。

46. Ebbets Field：纽约市埃比茨体育场。

47. He rushes through the wall-line of the kitchen and out into the living-room.：本剧的主要布景为威利家的内景。当剧情发生在现在时，演员必须假设房子有墙壁，只从左面的门出入。但当剧情发生在过去或威利的想象中时，假设的墙壁便不复存在，演员可以随意出入。

48. locker room：更衣室，内有带锁的存衣箱。

49. clubhouse：运动员的更衣室或存衣室。

50. touchdown：（美式足球）底线得分。

51. casino：一种纸牌戏。

52. knock a homer：（棒球术语）打本垒球，即击球后连续跑完四个垒得分。

53. Red Grange：即哈罗德·爱德华·格兰奇（Harold Edward Grange，1903～ ），美国足球球星。

54. carte blanche：全权委托。

55. made the grade：成功。

56. Why didn't he ever catch on?：他（指比夫）为什么总出不了名呢？

57. "If at first you don't succeed...”：这是一句俗语，后半句为“try, try and try again.”。

58. J. P. Morgan：即约翰·皮尔庞特·摩根（John Pierpont Morgan，1837～1913），美国金融家和工业组织家，第一次世界大战前20年间世界金融巨头之一。

59. In a Turkish bath he'd look like a butcher. But with his pockets on he was

very well liked.：洗土耳其浴时，他会像个屠夫；可一穿上衣服，口袋里装满钞票，他就受人爱戴了。

60. you end up worth more dead than alive：到头来你死了倒比活着值钱。此处指参加了人寿保险，死后可得到一笔数目可观的保险金，威利想到了死。

61. theirself＝themselves。

62. Hackensack：哈肯萨克，位于美国新泽西州东北部的小城，为纽约市一郊区。

63. coulda＝could have.

64. I don't give you no mice.：我不会给你小个的。

65. How about some wine? It'll put a head on the meal.：要葡萄酒吗？有了它这顿饭才像个样子。

66. Sotto voce：低声地说。

67. Strudel's comin'：Strudel 原意为果馅奶酪卷，此处为妓女的绰号。

68. the binoculars：此处指妓女的一双大眼睛。

69. New York Giants：纽约巨人足球队。

70. no soap：（美国俗语）没有结果，不成功。

71. nobody's the worse：谁也不会受影响。

72. Let's get a load on.：我们喝点酒吧。

73. Scotch all around. Made it doubles.：每人一杯苏格兰威士忌酒。要大杯的（即小杯的双倍）。

74. bullin' around＝bulling around（俚语）瞎聊，不着边际地谈话。

75. work on commission：此处指干推销员工作，但无固定工资，仅取佣金作为报酬。

76. Betcha＝I bet you.

77. Young Bernard enters and knocks on the door of the house.：少年伯纳德的出现说明威利在与两个儿子谈话时又突然回忆起过去的事。作者将意识流手法巧妙地运用到戏剧中，使现在和过去交织在一起。

78. Birnbaum：伯恩鲍姆，比夫的数学老师。

79. Grand Central：纽约中心火车站。

80. I'm washed up with Oliver.：我和奥利弗的事就算完了。

CHARLES OLSON

〔作者介绍〕

查尔斯·奥尔森 (Charles Olson, 1910～1970)，美国当代诗人、评论家。他曾就读于耶鲁大学和哈佛大学，后在哈佛和北卡罗莱纳州的黑山学院 (Black Mountain College) 任教。作为学者，奥尔森在考古、教育、人类学等领域均作过卓有成效的工作。在他担任校长期间，黑山学院达到了其鼎盛期，许多刻意求新的艺术家云集于此。他们的创作活动，尤其是通过《黑山评论》(*Black Mountain Review*) 杂志所提出的抑艾略特之拘谨，扬威廉斯 (William Carlos Williams) 之自由等艺术主张，对本世纪五、六十年代美国诗歌的发展产生了重要影响。1950 年奥尔森发表《投射体诗》("Projective Verse") 一文，它被认为是黑山诗派的宣言书。

所谓"投射体诗"，即是放弃传统诗歌中的形式安排与韵律节奏，把组成全诗的词句象音乐中的音符与绘画中的色块那样自由地散布在书页上，以尽可能直接地体现诗人创作时的具体心境与"气韵"(breath)；诗歌应将作者从自然或社会中获得的"能"(energy) 生动地传达给读者；诗不是对某一具体心境的总结与描述，而是对这一心境的"符号记录"(notation)。上述理论可从下面所选的作品中略见一斑。此外，还须指出，"投射体诗"之所以在许多诗人中产生反响，是因为它为诗人真实地记录自己的片刻感受提供了良好的形式；而这些片刻感受的组合，恰好构成了当代诗人孜孜以求的"心灵成长的画卷。"

奥尔森的主要著作包括《麦克西姆诗集》(*The Maximus Poems*, 1960)，以及研究麦尔维尔《白鲸》的专著《叫我伊斯梅尔》(*Call Me Ishmael*, 1947) 等。

Maximus, to Gloucester, Sunday, July 19

〔作品介绍〕

这是奥尔森花毕生精力创作的长篇组诗《麦克西姆诗集》中的一首。

在这首诗中，故乡 Gloucester 和在那里举行的每年一度的仪式，为诗人探索昔与今、生与死等人生基本问题提供了佳缘，在诗人心中引发起联想与沉思。因而，故乡和仪式颇似中国诗论中的“起兴之物”。了解这一点对理解此诗至关重要，因为奥尔森的意识和联想的活动范围远远超出了某种特定的物质范畴，甚至有些空灵与飘渺。读者从诗中可以窥察出考古学家与人类学家那种探本求源的精神，甚至某些意象都带着很浓的考古勘察味道，这是奥尔森诗歌的重要特色。

Maximus, to Gloucester, Sunday, July 19[1]

and they[2] stopped before that bad sculpture of a fisherman

— "as if one were to talk to a man's house,
knowing not what gods or heroes are" —

not knowing what a fisherman is
instead of going straight to the Bridge
and doing no more than—saying no more than[3]—
in the Charybdises[4] of the
Cut[5] waters the flowers tear off

the wreaths

the flowers
turn
the character of the sea The sea jumps
the fate of the flower The drowned men are undrowned

in the eddies

of the eyes
of the flowers
opening
the sea's eyes[6]

The disaster[7]
is undone
What was received as alien
—the flower
on the water, that a man drowns
that he dies in water as he dies on earth, the impossible[8]
that this gross fact can return to us
in this upset
on a summer day
of a particular tide[9]

that the sensation is ture,[10]
that the transformations of fire are, first of all, sea—
"as gold for wares wares for gold"[11]

Let them be told who stopped first
by a bronze idol[12]

A fisherman is not a successful man
he is not a famous man he is not a man
of power, these are the damned by God

II

whose surface[13] bubbles
with these gimlets[14]
which screw-in like

potholes,[15] caustic
caked earth of painted
pools,[16] Yellowstone

Park[17] of holes
is death the diseased
presence on us, the spilling lesion

of the brilliance[18]
it is to be alive: to walk onto it
as Jim Bridger the first into it,[19]

it is more true a scabious
field than it is a pretty
meadow

When a man's coffin is the sea
the whole of creation shall come to his funeral,[20]

it turns out; the globe
is below, all lapis

and its blue surface golded
by what happened

this afternoon: there are eyes
in this water

the flowers
from the shore,

awakened
the sea[21]

Men are so sure they know very many things,
they don't even know night and day are one

A fisherman works without reference to
that difference.[22] It is possible he also

by lying there when he does lie, jowl

to the sea, has another advantage: it is said,

"You rectify what can be rectified," and when a man's heart cannot see this, the door of his divine intelligence is shut[23]

let you who paraded to the Cut today
to hold memorial services to all fishermen
who have been lost at sea in a year
when for the first time not one life was lost[24]

radar sonar radio telephone good engines
bed-check seaplanes goodness over and under us

no difference
when men come back[25]

〔注释〕

1. Gloucester：马塞诸萨州的一个渔镇，在那里奥尔森度过了他的童年。每年7月19日当地居民都要在一尊海上遇难的渔民雕像下举行仪式，并向海面上抛撒鲜花。

2. they：指前去观光的旅游者。

3. 旅游者们出于对那尊渔民雕像的好奇，在它面前停步，茫然不解其内涵。这是诗人对所见所闻的描述，引号中的两行应是他的自言自语或想象。doing no more than—saying no more than：意为"no more than going straight to the bridge"。

4. charybdises：荷马史诗《奥德赛》所载奥德修斯在特洛伊战争结束后返回希腊途中必在两座悬崖之间航行。崖上住着两个海魔，一个叫Scylla，另一个叫Charydls。天神将Charydls变形为漩涡。此处指的就是漩涡。

5. cut：内港。此句连下行言花圈上的花朵在漩涡中开始脱落。

6. 此节言花朵似乎改变着大海的秉性，随着波涛上下跳动的花朵使大海睁开了眼睛，又赋予被淹死的人以新生（the drowned men are undrowned）。

7. the disaster：指渔民在海上遇难一事；undone：消除；what was received as alien：为"the disaster"的同位语。这3行似乎在说，（在这种仪式中）大海似乎被人的感情所感动，将它过去无情吞噬的人起死回生。

8. 这3行是诗人当时的感觉：水上的花朵；人被淹死；象死在陆地那样死在水中——对诗人来讲，都是不可能的。

9. this gross fact：指渔民被淹死一事。我们在今天这个夏日，在这起伏

(upset) 的波浪中仍会忆起往事。

10. 诗人申辩说，上述感觉都是真实的。倘若我们记住奥尔森所追求的，是将某一时刻的瞬间感觉直接、客观地记录下来，我们便会发现这几行正是诗人意识随意流动的记录，因而不必去追寻各种感觉之间的逻辑关系。

11. 水火互变，恰如钱物可以互变一样。

12. bronze idol：即那尊渔民铜像。

13. whose surface：此句接上句，即 God's surface，亦即地球。

14. gimlet：一种钻子形的工具。

15. potholes：洞、穴。

16. 此节开首至此言地球千疮百孔。

17. Yellow Stone Park：位于怀俄明州西北部的美国最大的天然公园，以喷吐泥浆的火山和温泉著称。另外还有从地孔里喷射出来的沸腾水柱。

18. 这几行言 Yellow Stone Park 喷射出的明亮水柱对我们来说意味着死亡和危害。

19. Jim Bridger (1804～1881)，美国皮毛商人。据说他是第一位到犹他州大盐湖的人。此句一转，指出尽管地球上满目疮痍，但我们还要勇敢地生活下去。

20. 此句言大海无所不包，故死在海里会受到万物的哀悼。

21. 从"the globe"至此，言那天下午进行的仪式及太阳的光辉使碧蓝的海水变得金碧辉煌，从岸上抛撒的鲜花象眼睛一般，将大海唤醒。

22. that difference：指昼夜间的区别。

23. 死去的人失去了神赋的灵性 (his divine intelligence)，因而就不必为世上的痛苦与邪恶而烦恼，让活着的人去"纠正可以纠正的事吧。"

24. 死者可在仪式中重获新生，故说"not one life is lost。"见本诗注(6)。

25. 仪式一结束，人们又回到高度技术化的现实之中，一切如故。诗人的想象活动也至此中断。

ROBERT LOWELL

〔作者介绍〕

洛威尔（Robert Lowell，1917～1977），美国诗人。他出身于波士顿的名门世家，先辈中有许多人是美国政治和文化界的显赫人物。他本人自幼深受家中严格的清教传统的熏陶，但是对于这种家族“遗风”，洛威尔并不以为然，而且经过一系列反抗，终于成为它的叛逆者。1937年，他离开刚刚就读两年的哈佛大学，来到新批评派主帅之一的兰生（John Crowe Ransom，1888～1974）麾下。新批评派所提倡的有关作品结构的“张力”（tension）和“反讽”（irony）等理论对洛威尔的艺术观及创作实践产生了很大影响。1940年他皈依天主教，这对他那世代以清教“长老”而闻名的家庭显然是莫大的讽刺。洛威尔皈依天主教并非由于他的信仰，而是因为天主教的堂皇仪式（rituals）启发了他的艺术形式感。二战期间，洛威尔因反对美国政府所奉行的政策而入狱1年。他积极反对越南战争，多次与其他作家一起加入游行的行列。洛威尔的私人生活并不平坦。他先后3次结婚。1977年，正当他的艺术生涯处于鼎盛之时，他却猝然去世，享年60岁。

战后的美国诗歌，同20年代的现代派诗歌相比，具有两个突出的特点。一是诗人逐渐成为参与社会与政治活动的公民（citizen-poet），诗歌的内容也因而带有强烈的政治色彩；二是诗歌中的个人成份愈来愈浓。过去，由于受到艾略特所提出的“诗不是个性的表现，而是对个性的逃避”这一主张的影响，现代派诗歌有把个性隐蔽在典故和“客观相联物”（objective correlative）中的倾向；当代诗人则开诚布公地将自己的亲身经历，包括个人隐私，写入诗里。上述这两点重要特色，均在洛威尔的诗作中有突出体现。

洛威尔对美国诗歌的主要贡献，在于他为其注入了一种强烈而又深沉的自白成份，大大缩短了诗人与读者之间的距离。他不但反省自己的历史及内心世界，而且袒露他的家庭传统对个人精神及心理所产生的各种微妙影响与扭曲。在他的作品中，诗人与长辈、妻子及后代的复杂关系及本人的精神失常与抑郁情绪均暴露无遗，因此，有人称他为“最真实的历史学家”。洛威尔的创作使“自白体诗”（confessional poetry）在美国诗坛风靡一时，许多诗人都从他的作品中吸取养分。

洛威尔一生著述很多，主要作品有：诗集《异地》（*Land of Unlikeness*, 1944）、《威尔爵爷的城堡》（*Lord Weary's Castle*, 1946）、《卡瓦纳家庭的磨坊》（*The Mill of the Kavanaughs*, 1951），以及《人生写照》（*Life Studies*, 1959），《日复一日》（*Day by Day*, 1977）等。他翻译过法国剧作家拉辛的《菲德拉》（*Phaedre*），并将他改写的麦尔维尔和霍桑的故事收入题为《过去的光荣》（*Old Glory*）的 集子里。无论从作品的数量还是质量上看，洛威尔都堪称美国当代最杰出的诗人之一。

For the Union Dead

〔作品介绍〕

《献给为联邦阵亡的将士》（“For the Union Dead”）是洛威尔的代表作之一。诗里有两个中心意象，一个是被废弃的水族馆，另一个是一尊遭遇同样命运的北方阵亡将士纪念浮雕。诗人对今昔的一些事件，以及曾在这些事件中扮演角色的人物（包括他本人）的心理作了一番追忆与思考。水族馆似乎象征着一种接近自然的生活秩序，纪念浮雕则象征人们的献身精神和理想，巨型推土机的肆无忌惮则标志着现代工业文明对自然和理想的嘲弄与否定。在这一冲突中，诗人的态度既明朗又复杂。他对当今工业文明怀有显而易见的憎恶，但对阵亡将士，则似乎既有同情，也不乏揶揄。这首诗体现出洛威尔的一贯立场：对清教传统的讽刺以及对战争的厌恶。

这首诗同其他当代诗歌一样，读来颇鹘突难解。作者的思想与想象不停地在几个层次与侧面（过去、现在、将来、眼前的各种客观物象及由此而引起的联想）上活动，初读给人以一种云山雾罩之感。只有通过反复阅读和思索，才能体会到诗人的命意所在。

洛威尔的诗以结构严谨，形象复杂而著称。《献给为联邦阵亡的将士》突出地体现了这些特点。

For the Union Dead[1]

“Relinquunt Omnia Servare Rem Publicam.”[2]

The old South Boston Aquarium[3] stands
in a Sahara of snow[4] now. Its broken windows are boarded.
The bronze weathervane cod[5] has lost half its scales.
The airy tanks are dry.

Once my nose crawled like a snail on the glass;
my hand tingled
to burst the bubbles
drifting from the noses of the cowed, compliant fish.[6]

My hand draws back. I often sigh still
for the dark downward and vegetating kingdom
of the fish and reptile.[7] One morning last March,
I pressed against the new barbed and galvanized

fence on the Boston Common. Behind their cage,
yellow dinosaur steamshovels were grunting
as they cropped up tons of mush and grass
to gouge their underworld garage.[8]

Parking spaces luxuriate like civic
sandpiles in the heart of Boston.
A girdle of orange, Puritan pumpkin colored girders
braces the tingling Statehouse,

shaking over the excavations, as it faces Colonel Shaw
and his bell-cheeked Negro infantry
on St. Gaudens' shaking Civil War relief,
propped by a plank splint against the garage's earthquake.

Two months after marching through Boston,
half the regiment was dead;[9]
at the dedication,
William James[10] could almost hear the bronze Negroes breathe.

Their monument sticks like a fishbone

in the city's throat.
Its Colonel[11] is as lean
as a compass-needle.

He has an angry wrenlike vigilance,
a greyhound's gentle tautness;
he seems to wince at pleasure,
and suffocate for privacy.

He is out of bounds now. He rejoices in man's lovely,
peculiar power to choose life and die—
when he leads his black soldiers to death,
he cannot bend his back.

On a thousand small town New England greens,
the old white churches hold their air
of sparse, sincere rebellion; frayed flags
quilt[12] the graveyards of the Grand Army of the Republic.

The stone statues of the abstract Union Soldier[13]
grow slimmer and younger each year—
wasp-waisted, they doze over muskets
and muse through their sideburns. . .

Shaw's father wanted no monument
except the ditch,
where his son's body was thrown
and lost with his "niggers."

The ditch is nearer.
There are no statues for the last war[14] here;
on Boylston Street,[15] a commercial photograph
shows Hiroshima boiling

over a Mosler Safe, the "Rock of Ages"
that survived the blast,[16] Space is nearer.
When I crouch to my television set,

the drained faces[17] of Negro school-children rise like balloons.

Colonel Shaw
is riding on his bubble,[18]
he waits
for the blessèd break.

The Aquarium is gone. Everywhere,
giant finned cars nose forward like fish;[19]
a savage servility
slides by on grease.[20]

〔注释〕

1. the Union Dead：在内战中阵亡的将士。

2. 内战期间，北方将领 Robert Gould Shaw (1837～1863) 曾统率一支黑人兵团，在一次战役中阵亡。雕塑家 Augustus Saint-Gaudens (1846～1897) 于1897年设计了一尊浮雕，以纪念 Shaw 及其他阵亡的将士。这尊浮雕被安放于波士顿公地的马塞诸萨州政府大楼对面。此处所引用的拉丁文便是雕刻于浮雕上的碑文，意为"他们为共和国而舍弃了一切。"洛威尔对碑文略作改动，将原文中的"他"改为"他们"。

3. Aquarium：水族馆。

4. a Sahara of snow：雪覆盖了大地，看上去有如白色的沙漠 (Sahara，即撒哈拉大沙漠)。

5. The bronze weathervane cod：呈鳕鱼形的青铜风向标。此句言南波士顿水族馆年久失修，破烂不堪。

6. 此节为诗人的回忆，言过去他曾将脸贴近盛鱼的玻璃缸，就象蜗牛贴在上面一样，注视着里面鱼群的活动；看到它们吐出的一串串泡沫，很想用手将其戳破。cowed compliant fish：受到恐吓、和顺的鱼。

7. 诗人从追忆中回到现实，言自己依然常为那鱼及爬行动物的世界而叹息。

8. 从上节中间至此，诗 人再度陷于回忆之中。去年3月他曾来到波士顿公园，但它已被电网围起，巨大的掘土机正在那里挖掘，为建造一个地下停车场做准备。yellow dinosaur steamhovels：指大如恐龙的黄色掘土机。

9. 诗人的视象又转向过去。

10. William James：威廉·詹姆斯 (1842～1910)，美国哲学家、心理学家，小说家亨利·詹姆斯之兄。

11. Its colonel：即 Colonel Shaw。

12. guilt：覆盖。

13. Union soldier：无名的联邦英雄。

14. the last war：指第二次世界大战。

15. Boyston street：波士顿的一条街。

16. a Mosler Safe：Mosler 牌的保险箱。此处用来象征西方的物质文明，颇含讽刺意味。the "Rock of Ages"：意"耶稣"或"信仰的永恒力量"；the blast：指美国向日本广岛投掷原子弹一事。此句言物质追求已成为人们信仰的支柱，原子弹也不能将其摧毁。

17. the drained faces：干瘪的脸。

18. riding on his bubble：朝不保夕。水泡的意象与诗的开首相照应，为诗人在下一节中从各种纷至沓来的思绪中回到最初的经验与印象中来，提供了过渡条件；水泡很自然与水族馆联系起来。

19. 地下车库代替了水族馆，各种汽车连成一线，有如巨大的鱼一样向前行驶。

20. a savage servility：指穿行的汽车，同第 2 节末尾的"cowed compliant fish"相对应。

Skunk Hour

〔作品介绍〕

《臭鼬出没的时候》（"Skunk Hour"）是洛威尔的一篇名作。

女诗人伊丽莎白·毕索普（Elizabeth Bishop，1911～1979）曾将一首题为《犰狳》（"Armadillo"）的诗献给洛威尔。毕索普所描写的，是无辜的犰狳在热汽球比赛事故中惨死之事，诗中隐含着对人们只顾娱乐而破坏自然生态的愤愤不平。洛威尔后来写了这首诗作为酬答。

洛威尔这首诗所表现的，是当代社会中的异化现象及其对人的精神的扭曲。诗中出现的四个人物：古怪的老女人、破产的百万富翁、装饰商及诗人本人都性格怪僻，心理变态，在不同程度反映出新英格兰传统在消亡的事实。然而，意味深长的是，在人们处于堕落与病态之时，令人厌恶的臭鼬却大摇大摆地在大街与教堂出没，宛若世界的主人。此诗令人忆起卡夫卡的《变形记》。在作者那表面平静与超脱的笔调之下，无疑深藏着一种面对这一现代悲剧所感到的极度痛苦与悲哀。

《臭鼬出没的时候》是《人生写照》里最后一首诗作。诗中时而出现表露承认自己精神状态不很平常的词句，也表现了诗人对《人生写照》一书中的某些描述表示歉疚；这有些象 T. S. 艾略特的《小老头》（"Gerontion"）中小老头的自言自语。

Skunk Hour

(FOR ELIZABETH BISHOP)

Nautilus Island's[1] hermit
heiress still lives through winter in her Spartan cottage,[2]
her sheep still graze above the sea.
Her son's a bishop. Her farmer
is first selectman in our village;
she's in her dotage.

Thirsting for
the hierarchic privacy
of Queen Victoria's century,
she buys up all
the eyesores facing her shore,[3]
and lets them fall.

The season's ill—
we've lost our summer millionaire,
who seemed to leap from an L. L. Bean
catalogue.[4] His nine-knot yawl[5]
was auctioned off to lobstermen.
A red fox stain covers Blue Hill.[6]

And now our fairy[7]
decorator brightens his shop for fall;
his fishnet's filled with orange cork,
orange, his cobbler's bench and awl;
there is no money in his work,
he'd rather marry.

One dark night,
my Tudor Ford climbed the hill's skull;[8]
I watched for love-cars.[9] Lights turned down,
they lay together, hull to hull,[10]
where the graveyard shelves on the town[11]...
My mind's not right.

A car radio bleats,
"Love, O careless Love..." I hear
my ill-spirit sob in each blood cell,
as if my hand were at its throat...
I myself am hell,[12]
nobody's here—

only skunks, that search
in the moonlight for a bite to eat.
They march on their soles up Main Street:
white stripes, moonstruck eyes' red fire
under the chalk-dry and spar spire
of the Trinitarian Church.[13]

I stand on top
of our back steps and breathe the rich air—
a mother skunk with her column of kittens swills the garbage pail.
She jabs her wedge-head in a cup
of sour cream, drops her ostrich tail,
and will not scare.[14]

〔注释〕

1. Nautilus Island：在缅因州，洛威尔拥有一处消夏别墅。

2. Spartan cottage：斯巴达式的房舍。斯巴达为古希腊时的城邦，以简朴闻名。

3. 指对岸破破烂烂、简朴不堪的小屋。

4. L. L. Bean：一家郊游和体育用品邮购商店。

5. yawl：一种小渔船。

6. 山上的殷红血迹，暗示百万富翁的不幸。

7. fairy：意即"同性恋的"。

8. hill's skull：山顶；用 skull 指山顶，似有渲染全诗总氛围的效果。

9. love-cars：载有幽会情人的汽车。

10. 汽车一辆辆并排躺在那里。

11. where…town：墓地倾向城镇的方向。

12. I…hell：引自弥尔顿所著《失乐园》中魔鬼 Satan 的一句话："which way I fly is Hell，myself am Hell"。

13. 诗人把这些臭鼬安置于人们经常往来之处，以有效地强调关于人及社会生活堕落的主题。

14. …and will not scare：毫无顾忌。

SAUL BELLOW

〔作者介绍〕

索尔·贝洛（Saul Bellow，1915～　），美国当代小说家。他出生于加拿大魁北克省，是犹太移民的后裔，少年时随父母移居芝加哥，后入芝加哥大学和西北大学，攻读社会学和人类学，毕业后，进威斯康星大学的研究生院。二战期间，他在美国商船队服务，以后从事教育和《大不列颠百科全书》的编辑工作。1946年起，在各大学任教，同时坚持文学创作至今。

贝洛的作品主要反映在物质生活十分优越的现代社会中的人际关系，描述人们在精神上的压抑、心理上的挫伤与生活中的孤独感，指出人与人之间的同情和理解的必要性，倡导情感的复甦，爱的回归和人道、人性。他的小说中的主要人物几乎都是犹太人，故事往往以纽约、芝加哥这样的大都市为背景。

他的第1部小说《摇来晃去的人》（*Dangling Man*，1944），用日记体写成。主人公是一个辞去工作、等待入伍的青年。他独自一人在家赋闲，回避现实，思考人生的价值观念。他象一个悬挂在空中的人，摇来晃去地生活。小说记述了他内心的忧郁与苦闷。

《奥吉·玛琪历险记》（*The Adventures of Augie March*，1953）确立了贝洛在美国文学中的地位。奥吉是一个家境贫寒的犹太青年，一个探索自我的人物。小说一开始，主人公便说道：他是一个美国人，住在芝加哥这个阴郁的城市中。他做事一向遵循自己的信条，喜欢无拘无束，按照自己的方式创造记录。奥吉在生活道路上经历了一系列的遭遇，如政治权术，黑市交易，放纵的性行为等等。他在混乱、动荡和变化多端的社会中生活，学习保护自己的本领。

贝洛于1982年发表《院长的十二月》（*The Dean's December*），小说以一位美国知识分子陪同妻子到罗马尼亚探亲的线索贯穿全书，运用对比的方式，描绘芝加哥的现实。贝洛在谈到这部作品时说，它的主题是关于“美国对于实实在在的现实的否认，回避现实的种种手法，也就是我们拒绝面对那些十分明显、可以切身感受到的东西的态度。”

贝洛所最关心的问题是：在当今世界，人类的生活能不能继续下去？其实，这也是世人所共同关注的问题。正因为如此，对这个问题才众说纷纭。有的人不满现实，怀念往日的美好生活；有的人颓唐；有的人绝望。各种各样的思想都在文学作品中得到了反映。贝洛的回答与许多文学家不同，他认为：今天的人类象一个病人，不过这种病不是不治之症，人类只要振作起来，他们的前途就充满了希望。他在《只争朝夕》（*Seize the Day*，1956）中认为，假如人们能够睁开眼睛，看到自己的伟大，以及自己伟大的未来，那么他们就将兴高采烈、其乐融融了。他写道：“请睁开眼睛向你的前方望去，在清明、宁静的高山脚下，是你的永恒的摇篮。”

人与人之间，应该以“善”相待，贝洛认为我们“不可能在真空中得到‘善’，但是在人们相互结伴中，能够得到它。”他的这个观点在1954年发表的《降雨大王汉德森》（*Handerson the Rain King*）中表述得十分具体、明确：“我听见一个声音，它对我说，‘我要！我要！’是我要吗？它应该对我说，‘她要。’‘他要。’‘他们要。’而且，重要的是，只有爱才能创造现实。与爱相对立的东西，它所创造出来的东西只能是同现实相对立的。”贝洛在他的《牺牲者》（*The Victim*，1947）一书中所讲述的阿萨的故事，其中心内容便是关心他人，阿萨关心他的兄弟，兄弟的家属，甚至他自己的对手奥比尔。贝洛在《赫尔索格》（*Herzog*，1964）中写道：“请问海德格尔教授，你所说的‘……掉进了每日发作一次的疟疾病坑之中’是什么意思？是在什么时候掉下去的？我们在掉下去之前，站在什么地方？”显然，他不同意这位德国哲学家所讲的普通人的生活处丁周期性发作的疟疾病状态之中的观点。

这就是贝洛对于他在《作为道德家的作家》（“Writer as Moralist”）一文中所提出的问题的回答。他在那篇文章中问道：“或者我们使生活继续下去，或者不要它继续下去……假如我们确实要它继续下去，……那么生活应该采取什么方式才合乎道理？”对于这个问题作出正面的答复是一个作家在道义上的职责。贝洛的回答是十分明确的。

贝洛的作品相当丰富，除了剧本、短篇小说，以及本文已经提到的作品外，他的长篇小说还有《赛姆勒先生的行星》（*Mr. Samler's Planet*，1970），《洪堡的礼物》（*Humbold's Gift*，1975）以及近作《心碎人亡者更多》（*More Die of Heartbreak*，1987）等。

贝洛是美国当代最受人推崇的小说家之一。他于1976年获普利策奖，同年被授予诺贝尔文学奖，以表彰他在文学作品中表现出来的丰富的思想、尖锐的讽刺、与强烈的同情心。他塑造了现代的非正统的人物形象，这些人物在自己的摇摇欲坠的世界中努力寻找立足点，永远相信生活的价值在于它的尊严，而不在它的成功与否。

Herzog

〔作品介绍〕

《赫尔索格》(*Herzog*)发表于1964年，是贝洛的力作之一，以小说中的主人公命名。赫尔索格是一位人文学科的教授，犹太人，是战后随着美国高等教育事业的迅速发展而成长起来的一名知识分子。他属于西方人通常所说的中产阶级。小说以他在人生旅程中所遭到的严重挫折为线索，发展故事情节，描述心理活动。

赫尔索格在第二次结婚以后，一心打算美满幸福地生活一辈子，专心致志地从事学术研究。不料他那美貌的第二个妻子却与他的一位朋友——一个只有一条腿的电台音乐唱片节目主持人相好，提出了离婚的要求。她不仅占据了他的房子，而且切断了他同子女的接触，把他抛弃在繁华但却寂寞的世界中。赫尔索格在婚变的打击下，精神恍惚，不能自主，时常自言自语，给一些死去的亲戚、朋友、名人甚至国家总统写信。不过从来不投邮寄出。有时，他在纸片上记录片言只语，虽然不成文章，却颇有几分道理。作者通过赫尔索格的人生危机，塑造了一个既可怜又可笑的喜剧形象。他心地善良，忠实厚道，是一个富有教养的天真的傻瓜。“他承认自己不是一个好丈夫——对待第一个妻子戴西，无情无义，却被第二个妻子马德琳诓骗；对于儿女，他是一个宠爱子女但不尽责任的父亲，对于自己的父母，他是一个不知恩德的儿子；对于国家，他是一个无动于衷的公民；对于兄弟姐妹，他感情深厚，但来往稀疏；对于朋友，他是个自我主义者；对于爱情，他懒散；对于权势，他消极被动；他脑子迟钝，对于自己的灵魂，他躲躲闪闪。”

《赫尔索格》阐述作为学者、知识分子的主人公同社会与整个西方文明史的关系，探讨浪漫主义的乐观情绪和决定论的悲观情绪，衡量人在社会生活中承受痛苦的限度。小说在一定程度上反映出当代美国生活的一个侧面。

这里选注的是本书第1章。

Herzog

If I am out of my mind, it's all right with me, thought Moses Herzog.

Some people thought he was cracked and for a time he himself had doubted that he was all there. But now, though he still behaved oddly, he felf confident, cheerful, clairvoyant, and strong. He had fallen under a spell and was writing letters to everyone under the sun. He was so stirred by these letters that from the end of June he moved from place to place with a valise full of papers. He had carried this valise from New York to Martha's Vineyard,[1] but returned from the Vineyard immediately; two days later he flew to Chicago, and from Chicago he went to a village in western Massachusetts. Hidden in the country, he wrote endlessly, fanatically, to the newspapers, to people in public life, to friends and relatives and at last to the dead, his own obscure dead, and finally the famous dead.

It was the peak of summer in the Berkshires.[2] Herzog was alone in the big old house. Normally particular about food, he now ate Silvercup bread[3] from the paper package, beans from the can, and American cheese.[4] Now and then he picked raspberries in the overgrown garden, lifting up the thorny canes with absent-minded caution. As for sleep, he slept on a mattress without sheets—it was his abandoned marriage bed—or in the hammock, covered by his coat. Tall bearded grass and locust and maple seedlings surrounded him in the yard. When he opened his eyes in the night, the stars were near like spiritual bodies. Fires, of course; gases—minerals, heat, atoms, but eloquent at five in the morning to a man lying in a hammock, wrapped in his overcoat.

When some new thought gripped his heart he went to the kitchen, his headquarters, to write it down. The white paint was scaling from the brick walls and Herzog sometimes wiped mouse droppings from the table with his sleeve, calmly wondering why field mice should have such a passion for wax and paraffin. They made holes in paraffin-sealed preserves; they gnawed birthday candles down to the wicks. A rat chewed into a package of bread, leaving the shape of its body in the layers of slices. Herzog ate the other half of the loaf spread with jam. He could share with rats too.

All the while, one corner of his mind remained open to the external world. He heard the crows in the morning. Their harsh call was delicious. He heard the thrushes at dusk. At night there was a barn owl. When he walked in the garden, excited by a mental letter,[5] he saw roses winding about the rain spout; or mulberries—birds gorging in the mulberry tree. The days were hot, the evenings flushed and dusty. He looked keenly at everything but he felf half blind.

His friend, his former friend, Valentine, and his wife, his ex-wife Madeleine, had spread the rumor that his sanity had collapsed. Was it true?

He was taking a turn around the empty house and saw the shadow of his face in a gray, webby window. He looked weirdly tranquil. A radiant line went from mid-forehead over his straight nose and full, silent lips.

Late in spring Herzog had been overcome by the need to explain, to have it out, to justify, to put in perspective, to clarify, to make amends.

At that time he had been giving adult-education lectures in a New York night school. He was clear enough in April but by the end of May he began to ramble. It became apparent to his students that they would never learn much about The Roots of Romanticism but that they would see and hear odd things. One after another, the academic formalities dropped away. Professor Herzog had the unconscious frankness of a man deeply preoccupied. And toward the end of the term there were long pauses in his lectures. He would stop, muttering "Excuse me," reaching inside his coat for his pen. The table creaking, he wrote on scraps of paper with a great pressure of eagerness in his hands; he was absorbed, his eyes darkly circled. His white face showed everything—everything. He was reasoning, arguing, he was suffering, he had thought of a brilliant alternative—he was wide-open, he was narrow; his eyes, his mouth made everything silently clear—longing, bigotry, bitter anger. One could see it all. The class waited three minutes, five minutes, utterly silent.

At first there was no pattern to the notes he made. They were fragments—nonsense syllables, exclamations, twisted proverbs and quotations or, in the Yiddish of his long-dead mother, *Trepverter*—retorts that came too late, when you were already on your way down the stairs.

He wrote, for instance, *Death—die—live again—die again—live.*

No person, no death.

And, *On the knees of your soul? Might as well be useful. Scrub the floor.*

Next, *Answer a fool according to his folly lest he be wise in his own conceit.*[6]

Answer not a fool according to his folly, lest thou be like unto him.

Choose one.

He noted also, *I see by Walter Winchell*[7] *that J. S. Bach*[8] *put on black gloves to compose a requiem mass.*

Herzog scarcely knew what to think of this scrawling. He yielded to the excitement that imspired it and suspected at times that it might be a symptom of disintegration. That did not frighten him. Lying on the sofa of the kitchenette apartment he had rented on 17th Street, he sometimes imagined he was an industry that manufactured personal history, and saw himself from birth to death. He conceded on a piece of paper, *I cannot justify.*

Considering his entire life, he realized that he had mismanaged everything—everything. His life was, as the phrase goes, ruined. But since it had not been much to begin with, there was not much to grieve about. Thinking, on the malodorous sofa, of the centuries, the nineteenth, the sixteenth, the eighteenth, he truned up, from the last, a saying that he liked:

Grief, Sir, is a species of idleness.[9]

He went on taking stock, lying face down on the sofa. Was he a clever man or an idiot? Well, he could not at this time claim to be clever. He might once have had the makings of a clever character, but he had chosen to be dreamy instead, and the sharpies cleaned him out. What more? He was losing his hair. He read the ads of the Thomas Scalp Specialists, with the exaggerated skepticism of a man whose craving to believe was deep, desperate. Scalp experts! So... he was a formerly handsome man. His face revealed what a beating he had taken. But he had asked to be beaten too, and had lent his attackers strength. That brought him to consider his character. What sort of character was it? Well, in the modern vocabulary, it was narcissistic; it was masochistic; it was anachronistic. His clinical picture was depressive—not the severest type; not a manic depressive. There were worse cripples around. If you believed, as everyone nowadays apparently did, that man was the sick animal, then was he even spectacularly sick, exceptionally blind, extraordinarily degraded? No. Was he intelligent? His intellect would have been more effective if he had had an aggressive paranoid character, eager for power. He was jealous but not exceptionally competitive, not a true paranoiac. And what about his learning? —He was obliged to admit, now, that he was not much of a professor, either. Oh, he was earnest, he had a certain large, immature sincerity, but he might never succeed in becoming systematic. He had made a brilliant start in his Ph. D. thesis—*The State of Nature in 17th and 18th Century English and French Political Philosophy*. He had to his credit also several articles and a book, *Romanticism and Christianity*. But the rest of his ambitious projects had dried up, one after another. On the strength of his early successes he had never had difficulty in finding jobs and obtaining research grants. The Narragansett Corporation had paid him fifteen thousand dollars over a number of years to continue his studies in Romanticism. The results lay in the closet, in an old valise—eight hundred pages of chaotic argument which had never found its focus. It was painful to think of it.

On the floor beside him were pieces of paper, and he occasionally leaned down to write.

He now set down, *Not that long disease, my life*, [10] *but that long convalescence, my life. The liberal-bourgeois revision, the illusion of improvement, the poison of hope.*

He thought awhile of Mithridates, [11] whose system learned to thrive on poison. He cheated his assassins, who made the mistake of using small doses, and was pickled, not destroyed.

Tutto fa brodo. [12]

Resuming his self-examination, he admitted that he had been a bad husband—twice. Daisy, his first wife, he had treated miserably. Madeleine, his second, had tried to do *him* in. To his son and his daughter he was a loving but bad father. To his own parents he had been an ungrateful child. To his country, an indifferent citizen. To his brothers and his sister, affectionate but remote. With his friends, an egotist. With love, lazy. With brightness, dull. With power, passive. With his own soul, evasive.

Satisfied with his own severity, positively enjoying the hardness and factual rigor of his judgment, he lay on his sofa, his arms rising behind him, his legs extended without aim.

But how charming we remain, notwithstanding.

Papa, poor man, could charm birds from the trees, crocodiles from mud. Madeleine, too, had great charm, and beauty of person also, and a brilliant mind. Valentine Gersbach, her lover, was a charming man, too, though in a heavier, brutal style. He had a thick chin, flaming copper hair that literally gushed from his head (no Thomas Scalp Specialists for him), and he walked on a wooden leg, gracefully bending and straightening like a gondolier. Herzog himself had no small amount of charm. But his sexual powers had been damaged by Madeleine. And without the ability to attract women, how was he to recover? It was in this respect that he felt most like a convalescent.

The paltriness of these sexual struggles.

With Madeleine, several years ago, Herzog had made a fresh start in life. He had won her away from the Church—when they met, she had just been converted. With twenty thousand dollars inherited from his charming father, to please his new wife, he quit an academic position which was perfectly respectable and bought a big old house in Ludeyville, Massachusetts. In the peaceful Berkshires where he had friends (the Valentine Gersbachs) it should be easy to write his second volume on the social ideas of the Romantics.

Herzog did not leave academic life because he was doing badly. On the contrary, his reputation was good. His thesis had been influential and was translated into French and German. His early book, not much noticed when it was published, was now on many reading lists, and the younger generation of historians accepted it as a model of the new sort of history, "history that interest *us*"—personal, *engagée*[13]—and looks at the past with an intense need for contemporary relevance. As long as Moses was married to Daisy, he had led the perfectly ordinary life of an assistant professor, respected and stable. His first work showed by objective research what Christianity was to Romanticism. In the second he was becoming tougher, more assertive, more ambitious. There was a great deal of ruggedness, actually, in his character. He had a strong will and a talent for polemics, a taste for the philosophy of history. In marrying Madeleine and resigning from the university (because she thought he should), digging in at Ludeyville, he showed a taste and talent also for danger and extremism, for heterodoxy, for ordeals, a fatal attraction to the "City of Destruction." What he planned was a history which really took into account the revolutions and mass convulsions of the twentieth century, accepting, with de Tocqueville,[14] the universal and durable development of the equality of conditions, the progress of democracy.

But he couldn't deceive himself about this work. He was beginning seriously to distrust it. His ambitions received a sharp check. Hegel[15] was giving him a great deal of trouble. Ten years earlier he had been certain he understood his ideas on consensus and civility, but something had gone wrong. He was distressed, impatient, angry. At the same time, he and his wife were behaving very peculiarly. She was dissatisfied. At first, she hadn't wanted him to be an ordinary professor, but she changed her mind after a year in the country. Madeleine considered herself too young, too intelligent, too vital, too sociable to be buried in the remote Berkshires. She decided to finish her graduate studies in Slavonic languages. Herzog wrote to Chicago about jobs. He had to find a position for Valentine Gersbach, too. Valentine was a radio announcer, a disk-jockey[16] in Pittsfield. You couldn't leave people like Valentine and Phoebe stuck in this mournful countryside, alone, Madeleine said. Chicago was chosen because Herzog had grown up there, and was well-connected. So he taught courses in the Downtown College and Gersbach became educational director of an FM station in the Loop.[17] The house near Ludeyville was closed up—twenty thousand dollars' worth of house, with books and English bone china[18] and new appliances abandoned to the spiders, the moles, and the field mice—Papa's hardearned money!

The Herzogs moved to the Midwest. But after about a year of this new Chicago life, Madeleine decided that she and Moses couldn't make it after all—she wanted a divorce. He had to give it, what could he do? And the divorce was painful. He was in love with Madeleine; he couldn't bear to leave his little daughter. But Madeleine refused to be married to him, and people's wishes have to be respected. Slavery is dead.

The strain of the second divorce was too much for Herzog. He felt he was going to picecs—breaking up—and Dr. Edvig, the Chicago psychiatrist who treated both Herzogs,[19] agreed that perhaps it was best for Moses to leave town. He came to an understanding with the dean of the Downtown College that he might come back when he was feeling better, and on money borrowed from his brother Shura he went to Europe. Not everyone threatened with a crackup can manage to go to Europe for relief. Most people have to keep on working; they report daily, they still ride the subway. Or else they drink, they go to the movies and sit there suffering. Herzog ought to have been grateful. Unless you are utterly exploded, there is always something to be grateful for. In fact, he was grateful.

He was not exactly idle in Europe, either. He made a cultural tour for the Narragansett Corporation, lecturing in Copenhagen, Warsaw, Cracow, Berlin, Belgrade, Istanbul, and Jerusalem. But in March when he came to Chicago again his condition was worse than it had been in November. He told his dean that it would probably be better for him to stay in New York. He did not see Madeleine during his visit. His behavior was so strange and to her mind so menacing, that she warned him through Gersbach not to come near the house on Harper Avenue. The police had a picture of him and would arrest him if he was seen in the block.

It was now becoming clear to Herzog, himself incapable of making plans, how well Madeleine had prepared to get rid of him. Six weeks before sending him away, she had had him lease a house near the Midway at two hundred dollars a month. When they moved in, he built shelves, cleared the garden, and repaired the garage door; he put up the storm windows. [20] Only a week before she demanded a divorce, she had his things cleaned and pressed, but on the day he left the house, she flung them all into a carton which she then dumped down the cellar stairs. She needed more closet space. And other things happened, sad, comical, or cruel, depending on one's point of view. Until the very last day, the tone of Herzog's relations with Madeleine was quite serious—that is, ideas, personalities, issues were respected and discussed. When she broke the news to him, for instance, she expressed herself with dignity, in that lovely, masterful style of hers. She had thought it over from every angle, she said, and she had to accept defeat. They could not make the grade together. [21] She was prepared to shoulder some of the blame. Of course, Herzog was not entirely unprepared for this. But he had really thought matters were improving.

All this happened on a bright, keen fall day. He had been in the back yard putting in the storm windows. The first frost had already caught the tomatoes. The grass was dense and soft, with the peculiar beauty it gains when the cold days come and the gossamers lie on it in the morning; the dew is thick and lasting. The tomato vines had blackened and the red globes had burst.

He had seen Madeleine at the back window upstairs, putting June down for her nap, and later he heard the bath being run. Now she was calling from the kitchen door. A gust from the lake made the framed glass tremble in Herzog's arms. He propped it carefully against the porch and took off his canvas gloves but not his beret, as though he sensed that he would immediately go on a trip.

Madeleine hated her father violently, but it was not irrelevant that the old man was a famous impresario—sometimes called the American Stanislavsky.[22] She had prepared the event with a certain theatrical genius of her own. She wore black stockings, high heels, a lavender dress with Indian brocade from Central America. She had on her opal earrings, her bracelets, and she was perfumed; her hair was combed with a new, clean part and her large eyelids shone with a bluish cosmetic. Her eyes were blue but the depth of the color was curiously affected by the variable tinge of the whites. Her nose, which descended in a straight elegant line from her brows, worked slightly when she was peculiarly stirred. To Herzog even this tic was precious. There was a flavor of subjugation in his love for Madeleine. Since she was domineering, and since he loved her, he had to accept the flavor that was given. In this confrontationn in the untidy parlor, two kinds of egotism were present, and Herzog from his sofa in New York now contemplated them—hers in triumph (she had prepared a great moment, she was about to do what she longed most to do, strike a blow) and his egotism in abeyance, all converted into passivity. What he was about to suffer, he deserved; he had sinned long and hard; he had earned it. This was it.

In the window on glass shelves there stood an ornamental collection of small glass bottles, Venetian and Swedish. They came with the house. The sun now caught them. They were pierced with the light. Herzog saw the waves, the threads of color, the spectral intersecting bars, and especially a great blot of flaming white on the center of the wall above Madeleine. She was saying, "We can't live togehter any more."

Her speech continued for several minutes. Her sentences were well formed. This speech had been rehearsed and it seemed also that he had been waiting for the performance to begin.

Theirs was not a marriage that could last. Madeleine had never loved him. She was telling him that. "It's painful to have to say I never loved you. I never will love you, either," she said. "So there's no point in going on."

Herzog said, "I do love you, Madeleine."

Stey by step, Madeleine rose in distinction, in brilliance, in insight. Her color grew very rich, and her brows, and that Byzantine nose of hers, rose, moved; her blue eyes gained by the flush that kept deepening, rising from her chest and her throat. She was in an ecstasy of consciousness. It occurred to Herzog that she had beaten him so badly, her pride was so fully satisfied, that there was an overflow of strength into her intelligence. He realized that he was witnessing one of the very greatest moments of her life.

"You should hold on to that feeling," she said. "I believe it's true. You do love me. But I think you also understand what a humiliation it is to me to admit defeat in this marriage. I've put all I had into it. I'm crushed by this."

Crushed? She had never looked more glorious. There was an element of theater in those looks, but much more of passion.

And Herzog, a solid figure of a man, if pale and suffering, lying on his sofa in the lengthening evening of a New York spring, in the background the trembling energy of the city, a sense and flavor of river water, a stripe of beautifying and dramatic filth contributed by New Jersey to the sunset, Herzog in the coop of his privacy and still strong in the body (his health was really a sort of miracle; he had done his best to be sick) pictured what might have happened if instead of listening so intensely and thoughtfully he had hit Madeleine in the face. What if he had knocked her down, clutched her hair, dragged her screaming and fighting around the room, flogged her until her buttocks bled. What if he had! He should have torn her clothes, ripped off her necklace, brought his fists down on her head. He rejected this mental violence, sighing. He was afraid he was really given in secret to this sort of brutality. But suppose even that he had told *her* to leave the house. After all, it was *his* house. If she couldn't live with him, why didn't she leave? The scandal? There was no need to be driven away by a little scandal. It would have been painful, grotesque, but a scandal was after all a sort of service to the community. Only it had never entered Herzog's mind, in that parlor of flashing bottles, to stand his ground. He still thought perhaps that he could win by the appeal of passivity, of personality, win on the ground of being, after all, Moses—Moses Elkanah Herzog—a good man, and Madeleine's particular benefactor. He had done everything for her—everything!

"Have you discussed this decision with Doctor Edvig?" he said. "What does he think?"

"What difference could his opinion make to me? He can't tell me what to do. He can only help me understand. . . . I went to a lawyer," she said.

"Which lawyer?"

"Well, Sandor Himmelstein. Because he is a buddy of yours. He says you can stay with him until you make your new arrangements."

The conversation was over, and Herzog returned to the storm windows in the shadow and green damp of the back yard—to his obscure system of idiosyncrasies. A person of irregular tendencies, he practiced the art of circling among random facts to swoop down on the essentials. He often expected to take the essentials by surprise, by an amusing stratagem. But nothing of the sort happened as he maneuvered the rattling glass, standing among the frost-scorched drooping tomato vines tied to their stakes with strips of rag. The plant scent was strong. He continued with the windows because he couldn't allow himself to feel crippled. He dreaded the depths of feeling he would eventually have to face, when he could no longer call upon his eccentricities for relief.

If his posture of collapse on the sofa, arms abandoned over his head and legs stretched away, lying with no more style than a chimpanzee, his eyes with greater than normal radiance watched his own work in the garden with detachment, as if he were looking through the front end of a telescope at a tiny clear image.

That suffering joker.

Two points therefore: He knew his scribbling, his letter-writing, was ridiculous. It was involuntary. His eccentricities had him in their power.

There is someone inside me. I am in his grip. When I speak of him I feel him in my head, pounding for order. He will ruin me.

It has been reported, he wrote, that several teams of Russian Cosmonauts have been lost; disintegrated, we must assume. One was heard calling "SOS[23]*—world SOS." Soviet confirmation has been withheld.*

Dear Mama, As to why I haven't visited your grave in so long. . .

Dear Wanda, Dear Zinka, Dear Libbie, Dear Ramona, Dear Sono, I need help in the worst way. I am afraid of falling apart. Dear Edvig, the fact is that madness also has been denied me. I don't know why I should write to you at all. Dear Mr. President, Internal Revenue regulations will turn us into a nation of bookkeepers. The life of every citizen is becoming a business. This, it seems to me, is one of the worst interpretations of the meaning of human life history has ever seen. Man's life is not a business.

And how shall I sign this? thought Moses. Indignant citizen? Indignation is so wearing that one should reserve it for the main injustice.

Dear Daisy, he wrote to his first wife, *I know it's my turn to visit Marco in camp on Parents' Day but this year I'm afraid my presence might disturb him. I have been writing to him, and keeping up with his activities. It is unfortunately true, however, that he blames me for the breakup with Madeleine and feels I have deserted also his little half-sister. He is too young to understand the difference between the two divorces.* Here Herzog asked himself whether it would be appropriate to discuss the matter further with Daisy and, picturing to himself her handsome and angry face as she read his as yet unwritten letter, he decided against this. He continued, *I think it would be best for Marco not to see me. I have been sick—under the doctor's care.* He noted with distaste his own trick of appealing for sympathy. A personality had its own ways. A mind might observe them without approval. Herzog did not care for his own personality, and at the moment there was apparently nothing he could do about its impulses. *Rebuilding my health and strength gradually*—as a person of sound positive principles, modern and liberal, news of his progress (if true) should please her. As the victim of those impulses she must be looking in the paper for his obituary.

The strength of Herzog's constitution worked obstinately against his hypochondria. Early in June, when the general revival of life troubles many people, the new roses, even in shop windows, reminding them of their own failures, of sterility and death, Herzog went to have a medical checkup. He paid a visit to an elderly refugee, Dr. Emmerich, on the West Side, facing Central Park. [24] A frowzy doorman with an odor of old age about him, wearing a cap from a Balkan campaign half a century gone, let him into the crumbling vault of the lobby. Herzog undressed in the examining room—a troubled, dire green; the dark walls seemed swollen with the disease of old buildings in New York. He was not a big man but he was sturdily built, his muscles developed by the hard work he had done in the country. He was vain of his muscles, the breadth and strength of his hands, the smoothness of his skin, but he saw through this too, and he feared being caught in the part of the aging, conceited handsome man. Old fool, he called himself, glancing away from the small mirror, the graying hair, the wrinklse of amusement and bitterness. Through the slats of the blind he looked instead at the brown rocks of the park, speckled with mica, and at the optimistic leaping green of June. It would tire soon, as leaves broadened and New York deposited its soot on the summer. It was, however, especially beautiful now, vivid in all particulars—the twigs, the small darts and subtly swelling shapes of green. Beauty is not a human invention. Dr. Emmerich, stooped but energetic, examined him, sounded his chest and back, flashed the light in his eyes, took his blood, felt his prostate gland, wired him for the electrocardiograph.

"Well, you are a healthy man—not twenty-one, but strong."

Herzog heard this with satisfaction, of course, but still he was faintly unhappy about it. He had been hoping for some definite sickness which would send him to a hospital for a while. He would not have to look after himself. His brothers, who had given up on him, more or less, would rally to him then and his sister Helen might come to take care of him. The family would meet his expenses and pay for Marco and June. That was out, now. Apart from the little infection he had caught in Poland, his health was sound, and even that infection, now cured, had been nonspecific. It might have been due to his mental state, to depression and fatigue, not to Wanda. For one horrible day he had thought it was gonorrhea. He must write to Wanda, he thought as he pulled his shirttails forward, buttoned his sleeves. *Chère Wanda*, he began, *Bonnes nouvelles. T'en seras contente.*[25] It was another of his shady love affairs in French. For what other reason had he ground away at his Frazer and Squair[26] in high school, and read Rousseau and de Maistre[27] in college? His achievements were not only scholarly but sexual. And were those achievements? It was his pride that must be satisfied. His flesh got what was left over.

"Then what is the matter with you?" said Dr. Emmerich. An old man, hair grizzled like his own, face narrow and witty, looked up into his eyes. Herzog believed he understood his message. The doctor was telling him that in this decaying office he examined the truly weak, the desperately sick, stricken women, dying men. Then what did Herzog want with him? "You seem very excited," Emmerich said.

"Yes, that's it. I am excited."

"Do you want Miltown?[28] Snakeroot? Do you have insomnia?"

"Not seriously," said Herzog. "My thoughts are shooting out all over the place."

"Do you want me to recommend a psychiatrist?"

"No, I've had all the psychiatry I can use."

"Then what about a holiday? Take a young lady to the country, the seashore. Do you still have the place in Massachusetts?"

"If I want to reopen it."

"Does your friend still live up there? The radio announcer. What is the name of the big fellow with red hair with the wooden leg?"

"Valentine Gersbach is his name. No, he moved to Chicago when I—when we did."

"He's a very amusing man."

"Yes. Very."

"I heard of your divorce—who told me? I am sorry about it."

Looking for happiness—ought to be prepared for bad results.

Emmerich put on his Ben Franklin eyeglasses and wrote a few words on the file card. "The child is with Madeleine in Chicago, I suppose," said the doctor.

"Yes—"

Herzog tried to get Emmerich to reveal his opinion of Madeleine. She had been his patient, too. But Emmerich would say nothing. Of course not; a doctor must not discuss his patients. Still, an opinion might be construed out of the glances he gave Moses.

"She's a violent, hysterical woman," he told Emmerich. He saw from the old man's lips that he was about to answer; but then Emmerich decided to say nothing, and Moses, who had an odd habit of completing people's sentences for them, made a mental note about his own perplexing personality.

A strange heart. I myself can't account for it.

He now saw that he had come to Emmerich to accuse Madeleine, or simply to talk about her with someone who knew her and could take a realistic view of her.

"But you must have other women," said Emmerich. "Isn't there somebody? Do you have to eat dinner alone tonight?"

〔注释〕

1. Martha's Vineyard：马萨诸塞州东南的一个岛屿，夏季旅游的地方。

2. Berkshires：马萨诸塞州境内的伯克希尔山。

3. Silvercup bread：银杯面包（面包的商标名称）

4. American Cheese：美国蹇达干酪。

5. a mental letter：一封信的腹稿。

6. Answer a fool according to his folly lest he be wise in his own conceit：见《圣经·旧约全书》中的"箴言"第26章，第4、5节。

7. Walter Winchell：沃尔特·温切尔（1897～1972），美国记者，广播员。在本世纪30年代至50年代期间，影响颇大。

8. J. S. Bach：巴赫（1685～1750），德国最著名的作曲家之一，其主要作品有《勃兰登堡协奏曲》。《B小调弥撒曲》等。

9. Grief, Sir, is a species of idleness：见塞缪尔·约翰逊致思雷尔夫人的信，《约翰逊书信集》第1卷。

10. Not that long disease, my life：试比较亚历山大·蒲柏的（Alexander Pope，1688～1744）的"Epistle to Dr. Arbuthnot"中两行诗句"The muse but serv'd to ease some Friend, not wife, /To help me thro' this long disease, my Life."

11. Mithridates：本都（Pontus）王国的国王（公元前120～公元前63），传说他经常服用由72种成份配制的解毒剂，使身体产生一种防毒能力。

12. Tutto fa brodo：（意大利语）一切都是有用的

13. engagee：（法）正在进行的，同当前实际联系起来的。

14. de Tocqueville：托克维尔（1805～1859），法国政治学家、历史学家，主要著作有《美国民主》（*Democracy in America*）、《旧制度与大革命》（*The Old Regime and the Revolution*）。

15. Hegel：黑格尔（1770～1831），德国哲学家，主要著作有《精神现象学》（*Phenomenology of Mind*））、《逻辑学》（*Logic*）、《哲学全书纲要》等。

16. a disk-jocky：电台音乐唱片节目主持人。

17. an FM station in the Loop：（芝加哥）市中心的一家调频电台。

18. English bone china：半透明、白色的英国瓷器（用骨头灰或磷酸钙与瓷土混合烧制而成）。

19. who treated both Herzogs：他为赫尔索格和赫的妻子治病。

20. the storm window：按装在窗户外部的、防御恶劣气候的窗扇。

21. They could not make the grade together：他们在一起，不能够圆满。

22. Stanislavsky：斯坦尼斯拉夫斯基（1863～1938），苏联演员、导演。20世纪影响深远的表演理论革新者。著作有《性格塑造》、《我的艺术生活》、

《演员自我修养》等。

23. “SOS”：国际通用呼救信号。

24. Central Park：纽约市的中心公园。

25. Chere wanda... Bonnes nouvelles. T'en seras contente：亲爱的万达……好消息，你会满意的。

26. Frazer and Sqair：可能指中学使用的法语课本的编者。

27. Rousseau and Maistre：卢梭（1712～1778），欧洲伟大的思想家。著作有《爱弥尔》、《论社会契约》、《忏悔录》等。迈斯特尔（1753～1821），法国论辩作家和外交官，著作有《圣彼得堡之堡之夜》等。

28. Do you want Miltown？密尔通，一种镇静剂的商标名称。

NORMAN MAILER

〔作者介绍〕

诺曼·梅勒 (Norman Mailer，1923～)，美国当代小说家。生于新泽西州朗布兰奇市，在纽约市布鲁克林区长大。16岁时入哈佛大学攻读航空工程学，后对文学创作发生兴趣，决心当一名著名作家，1941年获《故事》(*Story*) 杂志颁发的大学创作奖。1944年梅勒从哈佛获工程学士学位后不久，入伍参加第二次世界大战，做为一支侦察队的来福枪手在菲律宾服役。他参军的一个主要目的是要写一部关于战争的长篇小说。在菲律宾，他每周给妻子写回四五封长信，内容极其丰富，心想纵使他不能活着回来，他的小说也能问世。他的愿望实现了。1948年，他的处女作《裸者与死者》(*The Naked and the Dead*) 出版，立即轰动一时。批评界高兴地看到，一位新的有希望的作家出现了。

但是，人们对梅勒的热情不久便冷却下来。他的第2部小说《北非之岸》(*Barbary Shore*，1951) 并未引起太大的反响。而第3部作品《鹿园》(*The Deer Park*，1955) 在读者和评论界中亦反应平淡。此后，他虽然继续写作，评论界也一直注视着他的创作活动，然而直到1968年他的《夜里的军队》(*The Armies of the Night*) 先后获国家图书奖、普利策奖、波尔克奖时，批评界才出现对他的作品的严肃认真的专论和专著。《夜里的军队》是以描写华盛顿和平示威实况为中心内容的"非虚构小说"，也是自《裸者和死者》发表以来梅勒最受读者欢迎的书。《刽子手之歌》(*The Executioner's Song*，1979) 使他第二次获普利策奖；《古代的黄昏》(*Ancient Evenings*，1983) 是他计划中三部曲的第1部。梅勒其他作品还包括《我自己的广告》 (*Advertisements for Myself*，1959)，《总统文件》(*The Presidential Papers*，1963)，《一场美国梦》(*An American Dream*，1965)，《食人者与基督徒》(*Cannibals and Christians*，1966)，《我们为什么在越南?》(*Why Are We in Viet Nam*，1967)，《迈阿密和芝加哥之围》(*Miami and the Siege of Chicago*，1968)，《月球上的火光》(*Of a Fire on the Moon*，1970)，《性的俘虏》(*The Prisoner of Sex*，1971)，《存在主义的使命》(*Existential Errands*，

1972)，《圣乔治与教父》(*St. George and the Godfather*, 1972)，《玛莉琳》(*Marilyn*, 1973)，及《天才与欲望》(*Genius and Lust*, 1976) 等。梅勒的作品甚丰，已成为某些评论家注意的焦点。

梅勒的创作天才是多方面的。除小说以外，他还创作诗歌、剧本、撰写新闻文章，还制做电影，参加政治活动（曾竞选州长未成功）。他对自己的评论常直言不讳，称自己是“变色龙”。从某种意义上说，梅勒的注意力太分散，写作的文体太杂，说他有时在浪费他的天才和创作力并不过分。他的思想变化极快，他的文风亦如此。虽然他已显露了出众的想像力和充沛的精力，但他并没有一贯地写出能体现他的主导思想和独特风格的文学作品；这说明他尚未完全发现自己。有人为他辩解说，他的多变是文学适应多变的现实需要的体现；然而经过 40 余年的创作，其风格仍未“定形”，无怪乎人们对他的伟大产生怀疑。

梅勒悉心探讨散文文学及创作技巧的各种潜在可能性，对心理学、神学、政治及小说史有深刻了解，他的创作实践和理论扩展了美国文学传统的界限。他的灵感极富个人风格，他的创作态度总的看来是严肃的。他是战后美国文坛出现的重要作家之一。

The Naked and the Dead

〔作品介绍〕

《裸者和死者》(*The Naked and the Dead*) 是梅勒的处女作，一般也被认为是他的最佳作品。

小说描写的是一个由 14 人组成的美国侦察队二战期间在日军占领区内进行活动的故事。这支侦察队是一支 6000 人大部队的小分队，负责侦察位于南太平洋上的阿诺波贝 (Anopopei) 岛，为大部队挺进菲律宾铺平道路。小说的主要人物包括一位密西西比州农民，一位布鲁克林犹太人，一位墨西哥人，一个来自得克萨斯州西部的农场主，一位蒙大拿煤矿的工人，一位来自南波士顿工人阶层的爱尔兰人，一个堪萨斯州的售货员，一个芝加哥的地痞，和一位来自佐治亚州的的享乐主义者。显然，小说作者企图勾划一幅美国社会的缩影图。

美军的卡明斯将军命令他的参谋赫恩中尉率领这支侦察队在阿诺波贝岛登陆，穿过该岛的南部森林。在行动过程中，列兵威尔逊腹部中弹，由 4 个人负责把他抬到安全地带去。由于劳累过度，其中两人终于支撑不住；另外两人竭尽全力把威尔逊抬进森林中，他在那里终于死去。侦察队继续前进，途中步履维艰，充满困难和危险，赫恩中尉和罗斯下士先后牺牲。无情的中士克罗夫特逼着士兵们向安纳卡山上爬，就在他们将到山顶时，一窝黄蜂向他们扑来，他们吓得从山坡滚下来。与此同时，在卡明斯将军不在的情况下，达洛森少校命令一营士兵冲破敌军防线，摧毁敌军一个重要的军火库以及敌军总指挥部。美军取得了战役的胜利，但对卡明斯将军个人来说，这是一次失败，因为他的"精彩的"作战计划未能付诸实现。侦察小队又回到大部队中来。

这部小说颇有自然主义的倾向。它描绘的是一个冷漠无情的世界，人在这里的努力不是徒劳，便是导致无谓的死亡，而上帝对人的命运是毫不关心的。在这种背景下，有3个人通过自己的行动表现出人的境遇的可悲性。卡明斯将军虽然才智出众，但他主要是为了获得个人的尊荣而尽力工作的。克罗夫特中士则着魔似地寻机取得自己梦寐以求的权力。赫恩和他们不同。他不寻求权力；虽然他经常不能如愿以偿，但在生活中他不是弱者，他不向权力低首和认输。

《裸者和死者》的写作方法颇具独到之处。作者在正常叙事中间，巧妙地加入了"合唱"(chorus)及"时间机器"(the time machine)两种穿插或倒述文学。"合唱"都是战士谈话片断的简短记录，全书共出现5段。谈话地点有饭棚、工事地点、厕所、宿营地等，反映了战士的思想和态度。"合唱"一般较短，约占一页左右。"时间机器"是书中主要人物的简历，包括他们的相貌、品格、成长环境、参战前的工作经历等。虽是简历，但以短篇故事的生动文学形式写成，有叙述，有对话，完全没有档案文学的枯燥味道。"时间机器"共有10段，介绍包括卡明斯将军、赫恩中尉及克罗夫特中士在内的10个人物的情况，是对小说故事的重要注释和补充。"合唱"与"时间机器"两种穿插和倒述文字除在内容上起到烘托和注脚的作用外，在语言上也为小说带来一种活泼的气氛，克服了这种洋洋数十万言的作品可能出现的单调和板滞。

《裸者和死者》被认为是描写第二次世界大战的最佳小说之一。

这里选注的是小说第2章的前一部分。

The Naked and the Dead

PART Ⅱ ARGIL AND MOLD

1 IN THE EARLY BRIEFINGS OF HIS STAFF, Major General Edward Cummings, commander of the troops on the island, had described

Anopopei by saying it was shaped like an ocarina. It was a reasonably accurate image. The body of the island, about a hundred and fifty miles long and a third as wide, was formed generally in a streamline with a high spine of mountains along its axis. On a line almost perpendicular to the main body of Anopopei, the mouthpiece, a peninsula, jutted out for twenty miles.

General Cummings's task force had landed on the tip of this peninsula, and in the first few days of the campaign had advanced almost five miles. The initial wave of assault troops had splashed out of their boats, run up the beach, and entrenched themselves at the edge of the jungle. Subsequent waves passed their position and filed through the brush along trails the Japanese had cut previously. There was little resistance the first day or two, for the majority of Japanese had been withdrawn from the beach when the Navy shelling[1] began. The early advances were only briefly delayed by a minor ambush, or a temporary defense position set up along a ravine or across a trail. The troops pawed forward gingerly a few hundred yards at a time, sending out many patrols to examine the ground ahead before each company moved up. There was no front line for several days at least. Little groups of men filtered through the jungle, fought minor skirmishes with still smaller groups, and then moved on again. Cumulatively there was a motion forward, but each individual unitmoved in no particular direction at any given time. They were like a nest of ants wrestling and tugging at a handful of bread crumbs in a field of grass.

On the third day the men captured a Japanese airfield. It was a minor affair, a quarter-mile strip of cleared jungle with a small hangar recessed in the brush and a few buildings already destroyed by the Japanese, but the Pacific communiques[2] included it, and radio announcers mentioned the victory toward the end of their news broadcasts. The airfield had been taken by two platoons who circled the jungle about it, routed the sole machine-gun squad still defending the clearing, and radioed back to Battalion Headquarters. The nightly defense positions of the General's troops had some coherence for the first time. The General established a front line a few hundred yards beyond the airstrip, and listened that evening to the Japanese artillery bombarding the field. By midmorning the next day his troops had moved forward another half mile up the peninsula, and the front had broken again into sluggish separate globules of mercury.

It seemed impossible to maintain any sort of order. Two companies might start in the morning with perfect liaison between their flanks, and by nightfall would be bivouacking a mile apart. The jungle offered far more resistance than the Japanese, and the troops tried to avoid it wherever they could, threading their way along creekbanks, forging trails through the comparatively uncluttered wilderness of natural coconut groves, and moving with pleasure through the occasional clearings of kunai grass. The Japanese in response would shell the clearings at unpredictable hours, so that the troops avoided them finally, and blundered through the uncertain avenues which thinner patches of jungle might provide.

In the first week of the campaign the jungle was easily the General's worst opponent. The division task force had been warned that the forests of Anopopei were formidable, but being told this did not make it easier. Through the densest portions, a man would lose an hour in moving a few hundred feet. In the heart of the forests great trees grew almost a hundred yards high, their lowest limbs sprouting out two hundred feet from the ground. Beneath them, filling the space, grew other trees whose shrubbery hid the giant ones from view. And in the little room left, a choked assortment of vines and ferns, wild banana trees, stunted palms, flowers, brush and shrubs squeezed against each other, raised their burdened leaves to the doubtful light that filtered through, sucking for air and food like snakes at the bottom of a pit. In the deep jungle it was always as dark as the sky before a summer thunderstorm, and no air ever stirred. Everything was damp and rife and hot as though the jungle were an immense collection of oily rags growing hotter and hotter under the dark stifling vaults of a huge warehouse. Heat licked at everything, and the foliage, responding, grew to prodigious sizes. In the depths, in the heat and the moisture, it was never silent. The birds cawed, the small animals and occasional snakes rustled and squealed, and beneath it all was a hush, almost palpable, in which could be heard the rapt absorbed sounds of vegetation growing.

No Army could live or move in it. The men skirted the jungle forests, and moved through second-growth brush, past smaller woods of coconut trees. Even here they could never see for more than fifty or a hundred feet ahead, and the early stages of the operation were conducted by groping movements of tiny groups of men. The peninsula was only a few miles wide at this point, and the General had two thousand men stretched across it, but there was little connection between them. Between one company of a hundred and eighty men and another, there was room for any number of Japanese troops to slip through. Even when the terrain was comparatively clear, the companies would not often try to set up a partial line. After a week of fumbling through the jungle, the military concept of a connected line could see no more than a concept. There were Japanese left everywhere behind the front troops, and all through the jungle, in every part of the area that the General had captured on the peninsula there were subsidiary ambushes and skirmishes, until the mouthpiece of the ocarina seemed covered with burs. There was an intense and continuous confusion.

The General had expected this, had even made his allowances for it. Two-thirds of his force of six thousand men were kept in the rear working on supplies, and threshing the jungle in security patrols. He had known from intelligence reports before the campaign began that the Japanese had at least five thousand men against him, and of these, his men had not come in contact with more than a few hundred. The Japanese commander, General Toyaku, was obviously holding them for a protracted defense. As if in assurance, the scattered air reconnaissance that was granted Cummings occasionally from Army Headquarters, brought back photos which showed a powerful defense line set up by Toyaku on a front which ran from the main mountain range of Anopopei to the sea. When Cummings came to the base of the peninsula he would have to pivot his troops through a ninety-degree arc to the left and face the defense line Toyaku had built.

For this reason, Cummings did not mind the leisureliness of his advance. Once his troops had reached the Toyaku Line it would be essential to keep them well supplied, and for that he would need a road which could keep pace with his men. On the second day after the invasion, the General had reasoned quite correctly that the main battles with the Japanese would occur miles away. He had immediately diverted a thousand men to building a road. They started on an improved trail which the Japanese had used for motor transport from the airfield to the beach, and the division engineers widened it, sodding the top surface with gravel from the beach. But beyond the airfield the trails were rudimentary, and after the first week still another thousand men were assigned to the road.

It took them three days to build each mile, and the front troops drew constantly ahead. By the end of three weeks the division task force had moved fifteen miles up the peninsula and the road reached only halfway to them. Along the rest of the route, supplies were carried up by pack trains, and almost a thousand more men were occupied with that.

The campaign progressed uneventfully from day to day, no longer being mentioned in news broadcasts. The division's casualties were light, and the front had finally achieved some form. The General watched the constant activity of men and trucks out of all the bivouacs in the jungle adjacent to the beach, and contented himself temporarily with cleaning out the Japanese who were left in the rear, with building the road, and with moving his front forward at an easy and calculated rate. He knew that in a week or two, at most a month, the actual campaign would begin.

2

TO THE REPLACEMENTS, EVERYTHING WAS new and they were miserable. They seemed to be wet all the time, and no matter how they set up their pup tents, they would always blow down during the night. They could find no way to anchor their short tent pins in the sand. When the rain started they could discover no alternative to drawing up their feet and hoping their blankets would not become drenched again. In the middle of the night they would be awakened for guard, and would stumble through the moonlight to sit numbly in a wet sandy hole, starting at every sound.

There were three hundred of them and they all felt a little pathetic. Everything was strange. Somehow they had not expected to do labor details in a combat zone, and they were bewildered by the contrast between the activity of the day when trucks and landing craft were constantly in motion and the quiet of evening when everything was so peaceful. Then it was cooler, and out across the water the sunset was usually beautiful. Men would be smoking their last cigarettes before dark or writing letters or attempting to secure their tents with a piece of driftwood. The sounds of battle were muted at night and the distant crackling of small-arms fire, the remote echoes of the artillery seemed detached from them. It was a confusing period, and most of them were pleased when they were assigned to their companies.

But Croft was not. He had been hoping against his better judgment that recon would be given the eight replacements they needed, and to his disgust they had been assigned only four. It was the culmination of a series of frustrations for him since the platoon had landed on Anopopei.

In the beginning, the first annoyance was that they saw no combat. The General had been forced to leave half his division behind to garrison Motome, and as a result he had brought to Anopopei only a fraction of the officers and personnel from Division Headquarters. These men were merged with the bivouac of headquarters company of the 460th Regiment, and the Combined Headquarters was established in a coconut grove on a low sandy bluff overlooking the sea.

Recon had been assigned to set it up. After working on the beach for only two days, they were diverted to the bivouac, and spent the rest of the week in clearing the brush, laying barbed wire around the perimeter, and leveling an earthen floor for the mess tents. After that, their duties had been routine. Each morning Croft had assembled the platoon and reported to work on the beach detail or the road gang. A week went by and then another without any patrols.

Croft fretted. The labor details irked him, and although he had employed the same efficiency with which he managed all the platoon's activities, he was sullen, bored with the unchanging pattern of each day. He was seeking for an outlet to his resentment and the replacements provided it. Before they were assigned, he had noticed them on the beach every day, had watched them fold their pup tents and be counted off for labor details. And like an entrepreneur considering improvements, he had been calculating what kind of patrols he could manage with a full seventeen men.

When he learned that recon had been given only four new men, he was infuriated. It brought them up to thirteen, but since the paper strength of the unit was twenty men this gave him no balm. On Motome, the headquarters squad, consisting of seven men, had been assigned permanently to the regimental intelligence section, and for all practical purposes were out of the platoon. They never went on patrols, they never shared guard or labor details, they took their orders from other noncoms, and by now he no longer knew all of them by name. On Motome the rifleman in the platoon had gone out sometimes with three or four men on a patrol which needed twice as many. And all that time there had been seven additional men in his platoon over whom he had no authority.

To increase his anger he discovered that a fifth man had been assigned to the platoon, but had been diverted already to headquarters squad. After evening chow, he stalked over to the orderly room tent and started an argument with the Headquarters Company Commander, Captain Mantelli.

"Listen, Cap'n, you're gonna give me that other man in headquarters squad."

Mantelli was a light-haired man with glasses, and a highpitched merry laugh. He held his hands before his face in a mock attitude of defense as Croft burst in on him.

"Hold on, Croft," he laughed. "I ain't a goddam Jap. What the hell do you mean busting in here and tearing down this orderly room?"

"Cap'n, I been shorthanded too long, and I ain't gonna take it any more. I'm tired of taking the men out and risking their ass, when there's seven men, seven men goddammit, just sitting around in headquarters, being orderlies and to hell knows what for you officers."

Mantelli giggled. He was smoking a cigar which looked incongruous on his thin face. "Croft, suppose I was to give you those seven men? Who the hell would hand me a piece of toilet paper in the morning?"

Croft gripped the desk and glared down at him. "It's one thing to kid around, Cap'n, but I know my rights and the platoon ought to get that fifth man. All they'll use him for over at Operations 'n' Intelligence is to sharpen pencils."

Mantelli giggled again. "Sharpen pencils. Goddam! Croft, I don't think you got a good opinion of me." The evening air was blowing in from the beach, rustling the pyramidal tent flaps. At the moment there was no one else in the orderly room. "Listen," Mantelli went on, "I know it's a damn shame your platoon's short, but what can I do?"

"You can give me that fifth man. He's assigned to the platoon, and I'm the platoon sergeant. I want him."

Mantelli scraped his feet on the dirt floor of the tent. "What do you think happens over at Operations? Colonel Newton walks in, and by God there's a piece of work ain't done, and he sorta[3] sighs, and says, 'Things are going too slow here,' and damn if I don't hear about it. Croft, wake up, you ain't important, the only thing that counts is to have enough clerks to keep a headquarters going." He rolled his cigar tentatively in his mouth. "Now that we got the General and all his staff right in our bivouac, so you can't spit without hitting a courtmartial, they need even more men out of your platoon. If you don't shut up, I'll put you to cleaning typewriter ribbons."

"Cap'n, I don't care. I'm gettin' that other man if I gotta go see Major Pfeiffer, Colonel Newton, General Cummings, I don't give a damn. The platoon ain't gonna be hanging around the beach forever, and I want all the man I can get."

Mantelli groaned. "Croft, if you had your way, you'd be picking through the replacements as if you were buying horses."

"You're damn right I would, Cap'n."

"Oh, Jesus, you guys never give me a minute's rest." Mantelli leaned back and kicked the desk once or twice with his foot. Out through the tent flaps he could see the beach framed through a clump of coconut trees. Far in the distance an artillery piece fired once.

"You gonna give me that extra man?"

"Yeah... yeah... yeah." Mantelli squinted. On the sand, not a hundred yards away, the replacements were erecting their pup tents. Far off in the harbor a few Liberty ships at anchor were disappearing in the evening haze. "Yeah, I'll give him to you, the poor sonofabitch." Mantelli flipped through a few sheets of paper, ran his finger down a column of names, and underlined one of them with his nail. "His name's Roth, and his MOS is clerk. You'll probably make a hell of a rifleman out of him."

The replacements remained on the beach for another day or two. The evening after Croft had talked to Captain Mantelli, Roth walked forlornly through the replacement bivouac. The man with whom he was bunking, a big good-natured farm boy, was still over at another tent with his friends, and Roth didn't want to join them. He had gone along the previous night and, as it usually happened, he had felt left out of things. His bunkmate and his bunkmate's friends were all young, probably just out of high school, and they laughed a lot at stupid jokes and wrestled with each other and swore. He never knew what to say to them. Roth felt a familiar wistful urge for somebody he could talk to seriously. He realized again there wasn't anyone he knew well among the replacements—all the men with whom he had come overseas had been separated from him at the last replacement depot. Even then, it wasn't as if they had anything special about them. They were all stupid, Roth thought. All they could think about was getting women.

He stared gloomily at the pup tents scattered over the sand. In a day or two he would be sent up to his new platoon, and the thought gave him no joy. A rifleman now! It was such a dirty trick. At least, if they hadn't told him he was going to be a clerk. Roth shrugged. All the Army wanted you for was cannon fodder. They even made riflemen out of men like himself, fathers, with poor health. He was qualified for other things, a college graduate, familiar with office work. But try and explain it to the Army.

He passed a tent where a soldier was pounding some stakes into the sand. Roth paused, and then recognized the man. It was Goldstein, one of the soldiers who had been assigned with him to the reconnaissance platoon. "Hello," Roth said, "you're all occupied, I see."

Goldstein looked up. He was a man of about twenty-seven with very blond hair and friendly serious blue eyes. He stared intently at Roth as if he were nearsighted, his eyes bulging slightly. Then he smiled with a great deal of warmth, cocking his head forward. Because of this and the staring concentration of his eyes he gave an immediate impression of great sincerity. "I'm just fixing my tent," Goldstein said now. "I was thinking and thinking about it today, and I finally decided what the trouble was. The Army never designed tent pins to be used in sand." He smiled enthusiastically. "So I cut some branches off a bush, and I'm making stakes out of them now. I bet it'll hold up in any kind of a wind." Goldstein's speech was always earnest but a little breathless as if he were afraid of being interrupted. Except for the unexpectedly sad lines which ran from his nose to the corners of his mouth, he would have looked like a boy.

"That's quite an idea," Roth said. He couldn't think of anything to add, and he hesitated for a moment, and then sat down on the sand. Goldstein kept working, humming to himself. "What do you think of our assignment?" he asked.

Roth shrugged. "It's what I expected. No good." Roth was a small man with an oddly hunched back and long arms. Everything about him seemed to droop; he had a long dejected nose and pouches under his eyes; his shoulders slumped forward. His hair was clipped very short and it accentuated his large ears. "No, I don't care for our assignment," he repeated a little pompously. Altogether, Roth looked like a frail mournful ape.

"I think we were pretty lucky," Goldstein said mildly. "After all, it isn't as if we're going to see the worst kind of combat. I hear a headquarters company is pretty good, and there'll be a more intelligent type fellow in it."

Roth picked up a handful of sand and let it drop. "What's the use of kidding myself?" he said. "The way I look at it, every step in the Army turns out to be worse than you expected, and this is going to be the worst of all." His voice was deep and sepulchral; he spoke so slowly that Goldstein became a little impatient for him to finish.

"No, no, you're too pessimistic," Goldstein told him. He picked up a helmet and began to use it as a mallet on one of the stakes. "If you'll excuse me for saying so, that's no way to look at it." He pounded several times with the helmet and then whistled sadly. "Very poor steel in these," he said. "Look at the way I dented it just hitting in a stake."

Roth smiled a little contemptuously. Goldstein's animation irritated him. "Aaah, it's all very well to talk," he said, "but you never do get a break in the Army. Look at the ship we came over on. They had us packed in like sardines."

"I suppose they did the best they could," Goldstein suggested.

"The best they could? I don't think so." He paused as if to edit his woes and select the most telling ones. "Did you notice how they treated the officers? They slept in staterooms when we were jammed in the hold like pigs. It's to make them feel superior, a chosen group. That's the same device Hitler uses when he makes the Germans think they're superior." Roth felt as if he were on the edge of something profound.

Goldstein held up his hand. "But that's why *we* can't afford to have such an attitude. *We*'re fighting against that." Then as if his words had rubbed against a bruised part of his mind, he frowned angrily and added, "Aaah, I don't know, they're just a bunch of Anti-Semiten."

"Who, the Germans?"

Goldstein didn't answer right away. "...Yes."

"That's one approach to it," Roth said, a little pontifically. "However, I don't think it's as simple as that." He went on talking.

Goldstein did not listen. Gloom had settled over him. He had been cheerful until a moment ago, and now suddenly he was very upset. As Roth talked, Goldstein would shake his head from time to time or make a clucking sound with his tongue. This had no relation to what Roth said. Goldstein was remembering an episode which had occurred that afternoon. Several soldiers had been talking to a truck driver and he had heard their conversation. The truck driver was a big fellow with a round red face, and he had been telling the replacements which companies were good and which were not. As he meshed his gears and started to pull away he had shouted back, "Just hope you all don't get in F Company, that's where they stick the goddam Jewboys." There had been a roar of laughter, and someone had yelled after him, "If they stick me there, I'm resigning plumb out of the Army." And there had been more laughter. Goldstein flushed with anger recalling it. But more, he felt a hopelessness even in his rage, for he knew it would do him no good. He wished he had said something to the boy who had answered the truck driver, but the boy didn't matter. He was ony trying to be smart, Goldstein thought. It was the truck driver. Goldstein saw again his brutal red face, and despite himself he felt fear. That *grobe jung*,[4] that peasant, he said to himself. He felt an awful depression: that kind of face was behind all the pogroms against the Jews.

He sat down beside Roth and looked off moodily at the ocean. When Roth finished talking, Goldstein nodded his head. "Why are they like that?" he asked.

"Who?"

"The Anti—Semiten. Why don't they ever learn? Why does God permit it?"

Roth sneered. "God is a luxury I don't give myself."

Goldstein struck the palm of his hand with his fist. "No, I just don't understand it. How can God look down on it and permit it? We're supposed to be the chosen people." He snorted. "Chosen! Chosen for *tsoris*!"[5]

"Personally, I'm an agnostic," Roth said.

For a time Goldstein stared at his hands, and then he smiled sadly. The lines deepened about his mouth, and he had a sarcastic indrawn look on his lips. "When the time comes," he said solemnly, "they won't ask you what kind of Jew you are."

"I think you worry too much about those things," Roth said. Why was it, he asked himself, that so many Jews were filled with all kinds of old wives' tales? His parents at least were modern, but Goldstein was like an old grandfather full of mutterings and curses, certain he would die a violent death. "The Jews worry too much about themselves," Roth said. He rubbed his long sad nose. Goldstein was an odd fellow, he told himself; he was enthusiastic about almost everything to the point of being a moron, and yet just start talking about politics or economics or about anything that was current affairs, and like all Jews he would turn the conversation to the same topic.

"If we don't worry," Goldstein said bitterly, "no one else will."

Roth was irritated. Just because he was a Jew too, they always assumed he felt the same way about things. It made him feel a little frustrated. No doubt some of his bad luck had come because he was one; but that was unfair; it wasn't as if he took an interest, it was just an accident of birth. "Well, let's stop talking about it," he said.

They sat watching the final brilliant striations of the sunset. After a time, Goldstein looked at his watch and squinted at the sun, which was almost entirely below the horizon. "It's two minutes later than last night," he told Roth, "I like to keep track of things like that."

"I had a friend once," Roth said, "who used to work at the weather bureau in New York."

"Did he?" Goldstein asked. "You know I always wanted to do work like that, but you need a good education for it. I understand it takes a lot of calculus."

"He did go to college," Roth admitted. He preferred a conversation like this. It was less controversial. "Yes, he went to college," Roth repeated, "but just the same he was more lucky than most of us. I'm a graduate of CCNY[6] but it never did me any good."

"How can you say that?" Goldstein asked. "For years I wanted to be an engineer. Think of what a wonderful thing it is to be able to design anything you want." He sighed a little wistfully and then smiled. "Still I can't complain. I've been pretty lucky."

"You're better off," Roth assured him. "I never found a diploma any help in getting a job." He snorted bitterly. "Do you know I went two years without any job at all. Do you know what that's like?"

"My friend," Goldstein said, "you don't have to tell me. I've always had a job, but some of them are not worth mentioning." He smiled deprecatingly. "What's the use of complaining?" he asked. "Taken all together, we're pretty well off." He held out his hand, palm upward. "We're married and we have kids—you have a child, don't you?"

"Yes," said Roth. He drew out his wallet, and Goldstein peered through the evening light to discern the features of a handsome boy about two years old. "You've got a beautiful baby," he said, "and your wife is very…very pleasant looking." She was a plain woman with a pudgy face.

"I think so," Roth said. He looked at the pictures of Goldstein's wife and child, and returned the compliments automatically. Roth was feeling a gentle warmth as he thought of his son. He was remembering the way his son used to awaken him on Sunday mornings. His wife would put the baby in bed with him, and the child would straddle his stomach and pull feebly at the hairs on Roth's chest, cooing with delight. It gave him a pang of joy to think of it, and then, back of it, a realization that he had never enjoyed his child as much when he had lived with him. He had been annoyed and irritable at having his sleep disturbed, and it filled him with wonder that he could have missed so much happiness when he had been so close to it. It seemed to him now that he was very near a fundamental understanding of himself, and he felt a sense of mystery and discovery as if he had found unseen gulfs and bridges in all the familiar drab terrain of his life. "You know," he said, "life is funny."

Goldstein sighed. "Yes," he answered quietly.

Roth had a flush of warmth for Goldstein. There was something very sympathetic about him, he decided. These thoughts he had were the kind of things you could tell only to a man. A woman had to be concerned with her children, and with all the smaller things. "There are lots of things you can't tell a woman," Roth said.

"I don't think so," Goldstein said eagerly. "I like to discuss things with my wife. We have a wonderful companionship. She understands so much." He paused as if to find a way to phrase his next thoughts.

"I don't know, when I was a kid of about eighteen, nineteen, I used to have a different idea of women. I wanted them, you know, for sex. I remember I used to go to prostitutes, and I would be disgusted, and then after a week or so I would want to go again." He gazed at the water for a moment, and then smiled wisely. "But being married made me understand a lot about women. It's so different from the way you think of it when you're just a kid. It's…I don't know, it isn't so important. Women," he said solemnly, "don't like it the way we do. It doesn't mean as much to them."

Roth was tempted to ask Goldstein some questions about his wife, but he hesitated. He was relieved by what Goldstein had said. The private aches, the selt-doubts he had known when he heard soldiers talking about their affairs with women were a little soothed now. "That's true," he admitted gladly. "Women just aren't interested in it." He felt very close to Goldstein as if they shared a deep knowledge. There was something very nice, very kind, about Goldstein. He would never be cruel to anybody, Roth thought.

But even more, he was certain that Goldstein liked him. "It's very nice, sitting here," Roth said in his deep hollow voice. The tents had a silver color in the moonlight and the beach glistened at the water's edge. Roth was full of many things he found difficult to utter. Goldstein was a kindred soul, a friend. Roth sighed. He supposed a Jew always had to go to a fellow Jew to find understanding.

The thought depressed him. Why should things be that way? He was a college graduate, educated, far above nearly all the men here, and what good did it do him? The only man he could find who was worth talking to sounded a little like an old Jew with a beard.

They sat there without talking for several minutes. The moon had gone behind a cloud, and the beach had become very dark and quiet. A few muted noises of speech and laughter from the other pup tents filtered through the night. Roth realized he would have to return to his tent in a few minutes, and he dreaded the prospect of being awakened for guard. He watched a soldier come walking toward them.

"I guess that's Buddy Wyman," Goldstein said. "He's a nice kid."

"Is he coming to that reconnaissance platoon with us?" Roth asked.

Goldstein nodded. "Yes. When we found out we were both going to the same place we decided to bunk together if they let us."

Roth smiled sourly. He should have known. He moved aside as Wyman crouched to come into the tent, and waited for Goldstein to introduce them. "I think I saw you when they got us all together," Roth said.

"Oh, sure, I remember you," Wyman said pleasantly. He was a tall slim youth with light hair and a bony face. He dropped on one of the blankets and yawned. "Boy, I didn't think I'd be talking that long," he apologized to Goldstein.

"That's all right," Goldstein said. "I got an idea on how to fix the tent, and I think it's going to stay up tonight." Wyman examined it, and noticed the stakes. "Hey, that's swell," he said. "I'm sorry I wasn't here to help you, Joe."

"That's okay," Goldstein said.

Roth felt as if he were no longer wanted. He stood up and stretched his body. "I guess I'll be taking off," he said. He rubbed his hand along his thin forearm.

"Stay around awhile," Goldstein said.

"No, I want to get some sleep before guard." Roth started walking back to his tent. In the darkness, his feet dragged. He was thinking that Goldstein's friendliness did not mean very much. "Just a surface part of his personality. It doesn't go deep."

Roth sighed. As he walked, his feet made soft slushing sounds through the sand.

"Sure, Listen," Polack said, "There's all kinds of ways of beating a game." He extended his long pointed jaw at Steve Minetta and grinned. "They ain't[7] a way you can't figure out to get around something."

Minetta was only twenty, but his hair had receded far enough to give him a high forehead. He had developed a thin mustache which he trimmed carefully. Once he had been told he looked like William Powell,[8] and he combed his hair to increase the resemblance. "Naw, I don't agree with you," he said. "Some raps you can't beat."

"What're you talkin' about?" Polack wanted to know. He twisted about in his blankets, and turned to face Minetta. "Listen," he said, "once in the butcher shop, I'm drawin' a fowl for this old biddy, and I try to get away with one of the two pieces of fat around the belly." He paused dramatically, and Minetta laughed at the grin on Polack's big lewd mobile mouth.

"Yeah, so what?" Minetta asked.

"Well, she's watching me real close, and when I start to wrap up the fowl, she says, 'Where's the other piece of fat?' I look at her and I say, 'You don't want it, lady, it's diseased. It'll ruin the taste of the whole chicken.' She shakes her head and says, 'Never mind, young man, I want it.' So what could I do, I give it to her."

"How'd you beat the game there?" Minetta wanted to know.

"Hah, before I give it to her, I cut open the bile sack on the liver. That chicken must have tasted like shit."

Minetta shrugged. The moon cast enough light into the tent for him to see Polack's face. He was grinning, and Minetta decided Polack was comical with the three teeth missing on the left side of his mouth.

Polack was perhaps twenty-one but his eyes were shrewd and bawdy, and when he laughed his skin was wizened, tough, like the skin of a middle-aged man. Minetta felt a little uncomfortable with him. Secretly he was afraid to match his knowledge against Polack's.

"Stop throwing it," Minetta said. Who did Polack think he was telling the story to?

"No, it's the truth," Polack said in a hurt voice. he always dropped the "h" when he said "think" or "the" or "truth."

"Yeah, it's da troot," Minetta said, mimicking him.

"You havin'a good time?" Polack asked.

"I can't complain," Minetta said. "You talk like something out of a comic book." He yawned. "Anyway, one thing nobody ever beat was the Army."

"I ain't done so bad," Polack said.

"You're doing bad till the day you get out of it," Minetta told him. He clapped his hand against his forehead, and sat up. "The goddam mosquitoes," he said. He rummaged underneath his pillow, a towel wrapped about a soiled shirt, and drew out a small bottle of mosquito lotion. As he rubbed it over his face and hands he grumbled. "What a way for a guy to live." He propped himself on an elbow and lit a cigarette. He remembered he was not supposed to smoke at night, and for a moment debated with himself. "Aaah, fug it," he said aloud. Unconsciously his hand shielded the cigarette, however. He turned toward Polack and said, "Boy, I don't like to live like a pig." He pounded his pillow smooth. "Sleeping on top of your own filthy clothes, wearing dirty clothes to sleep. Nobody lives like that."

Polack shrugged. He was next to the youngest of seven brothers and sisters, and until he went to an orphanage he had always slept with a blanket spread out on the floor near a coal stove in the center of the room. When the fire died down in the middle of the night the first child to become chilled would get up and fill the stove again. "It ain't so bad wearin' dirty clothes," he told Minetta, "it keeps the bugs off ya." He had washed his own clothing since he was five years old.

"Ain't that a hell of a choice?" Minetta asked. "Smell your own stink or get carried away by the bugs." He was thinking of the clothes he used to wear. He was always known as the best dresser on the block, the first kid to pick up the new dance steps, and now he had a shirt which was two sizes too big for him. "Hey, did you hear that joke about Army clothes?" he asked. "It comes in two sizes, too large and too small."

"I heard it," Polack said.

"Aaah." Minetta remembered the way he would spend an hour in the middle of an afternoon dressing himself carefully, and combing his hair several times. It gave him pleasure to do that even when he had no place to go. "You tell me how to get out of the Army, and I'll say you can beat every game."

"There's ways," Polack said.

"Sure, you can go to heaven too, but who does?"

"There's ways," Polack repeated mysteriously again, nodding his head in the darkness. Minetta could just make out his profile, and he decided that he looked like a cartoon of Uncle Sam with his hooked broken nose and his long jaw slanting back to his receded gums.

"Well, what way?" Minetta asked.

"You ain't got the guts for it," Polack said.

"I don't see you getting out," Minetta persisted.

Polack's voice was rasping and humorous. "I like it in the Army," he said.

Minetta was becoming irritated. It was impossible ever to win an argument with Polack. "Aaah, fug you," he said.

"Yeah, fug you too."

They turned away from each other and settled down in their blankets. A mist was blowing in from the ocean, and Minetta shivered a little. He thought of the reconnaissance platoon to which they had been assigned, and wondered with a little quiver of fear if he could take combat. He started to drowse, and thought dreamily of returning to his block wearing his overseas ribbons. It would be a long time, he realized, and the fear of combat came back again. He heard a battery fire a few miles away, and pulled the blanket over his shoulder. It gave him a cozy sensation. "Hey, Polack," he said.

"Wha…at?" Polack was almost asleep.

Minetta forgot what it was he wanted to say, and on an impulse he asked, "You think it'll rain tonight?"

"Cats and dogs."

"Yeah." Minetta's eyes closed.

That same night Croft was discussing the new arrangement of the platoon with Martinez. They were squatting on the blankets inside their pup tent. "That Mantelli's a funny wop," Croft said.

Martinez shrugged. Italians were like Spanish, like Mexicans. He didn't like this kind of conversation. "Five new men," he mumbled thoughtfully. "Goddam big platoon." He smiled in the dark and clapped Croft on the back lightly. It was rare for Martinez to show any affection. After a moment he muttered, "Recon lots of fighting now, huh?"

Croft shook his head. "Damn if I know." He cleared his throat. "Listen, Japbait,[9] they's something I want to talk about to ya. I'm gonna divide us into two squads again, and I been thinkin' I'm gonna keep most of the old men in one squad and set up the other one with you and Toglio."

Martinez fingered his delicate aquiline nose. "The old squad with Brown?"

"Yeah."

"Red, Brown's corporal?" Martinez asked.

Croft snorted. "I wouldn't pick Red on a bet. That boy can't take any orders so how the hell could he give 'em?" He picked up a stick and lashed it against his leggins. "Naw, I thought of Wilson," he said, "but Wilson can't even read a map."

"Gallagher?"

"I would have liked to make Gallagher, but he just blows his top in a tight spot." Croft hesitated. "I tell you, I picked Stanley. Brown's been batting my ear about how good Stanley is. I figured he'd be the best man to work with Brown."

Martinez shrugged. "Your platoon."

Croft broke the stick in two. "I know. Stanley is the biggest goddam brown—nose in the platoon, but at least he wanted the job, which is more than you can say for Red or Wilson. If he ain't any good, I'll bust him, that's all."

Martinez nodded. "Only pick, I guess." He looked at Croft. "You say I have squad with goddam men who are···who are *new*?"

"That's right." Croft slapped Martinez on the shoulder. He was the only man in the platoon whom Croft liked, and he felt an anxious, almost paternal care for Martinez, which was at odds with the rest of his nature. "I'll tell you, Japbait," he said roughly, "you been through more than any other man in the platoon including me. The way I figure it, I'm going to use the squad of old men for most of the patrols because they know what to do. That new squad is going to get the easy ones for quite a while. That's why I want you to have it."

Martinez paled. His face was expressionless but one of his eyes winked nervously several times. "Brown, bad nerves," Martinez said.

"The hell with Brown. Ever since the rubber boats he's been missing all the shit storms. It's his turn. You need a rest, man."

Martinez fingered his belt. "Martinez goddam good scout, okay," he said proudly. "Brown good boy, but his nerves... no fuggin good. I'm with old squad, okay?"

"The new one's gonna have it easier."

Martinez shook his head. "New men, no know me.[10] No fuggin good, don't like it." He tensed himself with the effort to put his feelings into English. "Give order... trouble. Don't listen to me."

Croft nodded. The argument had validity. And yet he knew how frightened Martinez was. Sometimes at night Croft could hear him groaning fom a nightmare. When he put his hand on Martinez's back to awaken him, Martinez would spring up like a bird startled into flight. "You really sure, Japbait?" Croft asked.

"Yes."

Japbait was a good old boy, Croft thought. There were good Mexicans and bad Mexicans, but you couldn't beat a good one. "A good man'll hold on to his job," Croft said to himself. He felt a surprising flush of warmth for Martinez. "You're a good old sonofabitch," he told him.

Martinez lit a cigarette. "Brown scared, Martinez scared, but Martinez better scout," he said softly. His left eye still quivered nervously. And as if his eyelid were transparent, it seemed to reveal his heart beating behind it in anguished sudden ambush.

the time machine:

JULIO MARTINEZ

SHOEING THE MARE

A small slim and very handsome Mexican with neat wavy hair, small sharp features. His body had the poise and grace of a deer. And like a deer his head was never quite still. His brown liquid eyes always seemed nervous and alert as if he were thinking of flight.

LITTLE MEXICAN BOYS also breathe the American fables, also want to be heroes, aviators lovers, financiers.

Julio Martinez, age of eight, walks the festering streets of San Antonio in 1926, stumbles over pebbles, and searches the Texas sky. Yesterday he has seen an airplane arching overhead; today, being young, he hopes to see another.

(When I am big I build fly-planes.)

Short white pants which reach the middle of his thighs. His white open shirt shows slim brown boy-arms, his hair is dark and clustered with ringlets. Cunning little Mex.

Teacher likes me, Momma likes me, big fat Momma with the smell; her arms are great and her breasts are soft; at night in the two little rooms there is the sound of Momma and Poppa, shlup-shlup, shlup-shlup, giggle in your pillow. (When I am big I build fly-planes.)

The Mexican quarter is unpaved, and little wood lean-tos sag in the heat. You can always breathe earth-powder, always smell the kerosene, the cooking grease, always sniff the mangy summer odor of spavined horses drawing carts, barefooted old men sucking at pipes.

Momma shakes him, talks in Spanish. Lazy one, get me a pepper and a pound of pinto beans. He grasps the coin, which is cold against his palm.

Momma, when I am big I fly plane.

You are my good smart boy (the wet pungent smack of her lips, flesh smells), now get what I have sent you for.

There are many things I will do, Momma.

She laughs. You will make money, you will own land, but now you hurry.

Little Mexican boys grow up, have hair creep like minuscule vines across their chins. When you are quiet and shy it is hard to find girls.

Ysidro is your big brother; he is twenty and slick dresser. His shoes are brown and white and his sideburns are two inches long. Julio listens to him.

I screw good stuff. Big girls. Girls with plat'num blonde. Alice Stewart, Peggy Reilly, Mary Hennessey. Protestant girls.

I screw *them* too.

Ysidro laughs. You make love to your hand. Later you will be smart. You will learn to play a woman like a guitar.

Julio makes love when he is fifteen. There is a little girl on the earth-pressed street who wears no bloomers. Ysabel Flores, dirty little girl. All the boys she makes love to.

Julio, you are sweet sweet sweet.

Under the tree behind the empty house in the dark. Julio, like the dogs, okay?

He feels the sweet sick nausea. (Protestant girls like me, I will make much money.) Ysabel, when I am big I buy you many dresses.

Her wet velveted body relaxes. She lies down on her spreadout dress, her premature breasts lolling in the summer heat. Dresses? she asks. What color will they be?

Julio Martinez is big boy now, big financier; he works in a hash-house. Counterman. The foul rich barbecue smell, the garlic molten in the hot dogs on the griddle. Joe and Nemo, Harry and Dick, White Tower. Grease on a sizzling plate and the crumblings, the rancid fat, all to be scraped with the spatula. Martinez wears a white jacket.

Texans can be impatient. Hey, you boy, hurry up that chili.

Yes, sir.

Prostitutes look through him. Lots of relish, boy.

Yes, miss.

The cars flare by the electric light, his feet ache on the concrete floor. (I will make much money.)

But there are no jobs with much money. What can a Mexican boy do in San Antone? He can be counterman in hashhouse; he can be bellhop; he can pick cotton in season; he can start store; but he cannot be a doctor, a lawyer, big merchant, chief.

He can make love.

Rosalita has a big belly; it is almost as big as the belly of her father Pedro Sanchez. You will marry my daughter, Pedro says.

Sí.[11] But there are prettier girls than Rosalita.

It was time you were married anyway.

Sí. (Rosalita will grow fat, and children will run through the house. Shlup-shlup, shlup-shlup, giggle in your pillow. He will dig ditches on the roads.)

You are the first with her in any case.

Sí (It was not his fault. Sheik, Ramses, Golden Trojan. Sometimes it was even two dollars out of the twenty he made in a week.)

I will talk with Señora Martinez.

Sí. If you wish.

The night is dull with woe. Roselita is sweet but there are girls sweeter. He walks along the dirt-impacted streets. They are beginning to pave them now.

Tired? Restless? Knock up a dame? Join The Army.

Martinez is a buck private in 1937. He is still a private in thirty-nine. Nice shy Mex kid with good manners. His equipment is always spotless, and that's sufficient for the cavalry.

There are details. You weed the officers' gardens, you can be houseboy at their parties. You groom a horse after you ride it; if it is a mare you swab out its dock. The stables are hot and fermy. (I will buy you many dresses.) A soldier strikes a horse across the head. That's the only way that dumb four-legged sonofabitch knows. The horse neighs with pain, lashes out with its feet. The soldier strikes it again. Sonofabitch kept tryin' to throw me today. Treat a horse like a nigger and it'll act up right.

Martinez steps out from his stall, is seen for the first time. Hey, Julio, the soldier says, keep your mouth shut.

The instinctive quiver. (Hey, you boy, hurry up that chili.)

The nod, the grin. I do that, Martinez says.

Fort Riley is big and green and the barracks are of red brick. The officers live in pretty little houses with gardens. Martinez is orderly for Lieutenant Bradford.

Julio, will you do a good job on my boots today?

Yes, sir.

The Lieutenant takes a drink. Want one, Martinez?

Thank you, sir.

I want you to do a real good job on the house today.

Yes, sir, I do that.

The Lieutenant winks. Don't do anything I wouldn't do.

No, sir.

The Lieutenant and his wife leave. Ah think yore the best boy we eveh had, Hooley, Mrs. Bradford says.

Thank you, ma'am.

When the draft starts Martinez makes corporal. The first time he drills a squad he is so frightened he can barely sound the commands. (Fugged if I'll take an order from a Mex.) Squad left, left by squads. To the rear, march; to the rear, march. (You men must understand your responsibility. There is nothing more difficult in the world than to be a perfect noncom. Firm and aloof, firm and aloof, those are the key-words.) COL-umn RIGHT. The shoes tamping on the red clay, the sweat drips down. Hut, hup, hip, hor,[12] hut, hup, hip, hor. (I screw white Protestant girls, firm and aloof. I WILL BE GOOD NONCOM.)

Squad halt! PaRADE rest!

Martinez is in the cadre for General Cummings's infantry division, goes overseas as a corporal in recon.

There are discoveries. Aussie girls can be made. The streets of Sydney, the blonde girl with the freckles who holds his hand. I think you're awful cute, Joolio.

You too. The taste of Aussie beer, and the Aussie soldiers hitting him for a buck.

Yank, got a shilling or two?

Yank? Okay, he mumbles.

The blonde prostitutes to whom he makes love. Oh, what a roll you got, Joolie, what a bloody bloody roll. Gi' it to me, again.

I do that. (I screw Mrs. Lieutenant Bradford now. I screw Peggy Reilly and Alice Stewart, I will be hero.)

Martinez looks at a blade of grass. BEE-Yowww, BEE-Yoww. The whip of the bullet is lost crying in the wilderness. He crawls, slithers behind a stump. BEE-Yowwww. The grenade is heavy and dull in his palm. He lofts it into the air, hugs his head in the deep secret embrace. (Momma's arms are great and her breasts are soft.) BAAA-ROWWWWWMM.

Did ya get the sonofabitch?

Where the hell is he?

Martinez inches forward. The Jap lies on his back with his chin jerked toward heaven. The white tripe of his gut makes a flower on the field of red.

I got him.

You're a good old bastard, Martinez.

Martinez makes sergeant. Little Mexican boys also breathe the American fables. If they cannot be aviators or financiers or officers they can still be heroes. No need to stumble over pebbles and search the Texas sky. Any man jack can be a hero.

Only that does not make you white Protestant, firm and aloof.

3....

chorus:

THE CHOW LINE

(The mess tent is on a low bluff overlooking the beach. In front of it is a low serving bench on which are placed four or five pots containing food. The

troops file by in an irregular line, their mess gear opened and extended. Red, Gallagher, Brown and Wilson shuffle past to receive their rations. As they go by they sniff at the main course which has been dumped into a big square pan. It is canned Meat and Vegetable Stew heated slightly. The second cook, a fat red-faced man with a bald spot and a perpetual scowl, slaps a large spoonful in each of their mess plates.)

RED: What the fug is that swill?

COOK: It's owl shit. Wha'd you think it was?

RED: Okay, I just thought it was somethin' I couldn't eat. (Laughter)

COOK: (good naturedly) Move on, move on, before I knock the-crap-out-of-you.

RED: (pointing below his belt) Take a bite of this.

GALLAGHER: That goddam stew again.

COOK: (shouting to the other cooks and KPs on the serving line) Private Gallagher is bitching, men.

KP: Send him to officers' mess.

GALLAGHER: Give me a little more, will ya?

COOK: These portions are scientifically measured by Quartermaster. Move on!

GALLAGHER: You sonofabitch.

COOK: Go beat your meat. (Gallagher moves on.)

BROWN: General Cummings, you're the best damn guy in the outfit.

COOK: You looking for more meat? You won't get it. They ain't no meat.

BROWN: You're the worst guy in the outfit.

COOK: (turning to the serving line) Sergeant Brown is now passing in review.

BROWN: As you were, men. Carry on, pip, pip. (Brown moves by.)

WILSON: Ah swear, don't you ration destroyers know another way to fug up this stew?

COOK: 'When it's smokin', it's cookin'; when it's burnin', it's done.' That's our motto.

WILSON: (chuckling) Ah figgered[13] you all had a system.

COOK：Take a bite on this.

WILSON：You got to wait your turn boy. They's five men in recon is ahead of ya.

COOK：For you，I'll wait. Move on，move on. Who're you to block traffic?

(The soldiers file by.)

〔注释〕

1. the Navy shelling：美军登陆前先用军舰上的炮火轰击小岛。见小说第1章。

2. the Pacific communiques：美国太平洋战事公报。

3. sorta＝sort of.

4. grobe jung：犹太语，意即“粗野的小伙子”。

5. tsoris：可能是希伯莱语，意即“毁灭”。

6. CCNY：Community Colloge of New york.

7，They ain't＝There is not.

8. William Powell：威廉·鲍威尔，美国三、四十年代著名电影演员。

9. Japbait＝bait for Japanese.

10. no know me＝do not know me.

11. si＝yes（西班牙语）。

12. Hut，hup，hip，hor：走步声（拟声字）。

13. Ah figgered＝I figured.

RALPH ELLISON

〔作者介绍〕

拉尔夫·艾里森（Ralph Ellison，1914～），美国当代小说家，生长在美国南方的俄克拉荷马州。中学毕业时，因学习成绩优异，获该州颁发的奖学金，进了黑人教育家布克·T·华盛顿（Booker T. Washington，1856～1915）创办的塔斯克吉学院（Tuskegee Institute）学习音乐。他自幼酷爱音乐，结识了一些当时颇负盛名的布鲁斯（the Blues）歌曲演唱家。他在音乐方面的造诣很深，对他后来的文学创作影响很大。有人说，布鲁斯之于他的小说创作犹如主发条对钟表一样重要。

在塔斯克吉学院学习期间，他不但刻苦学习音乐，还读了很多文学书籍。他说，那时他"不但生活在音乐声中，同时也生活在书的海洋里"。艾略特的《荒原》对他的影响很深，他说，"那真是我文学启蒙的开始，实际上，那是我从一个未来的作曲家到小说家的转折。"他决心把文学当作表现黑人特殊历史的手段，使其变成自己的文学，成为美国文学传统有机体的一部分。

1936 年，艾里森离开塔斯克吉到纽约学习音乐和雕塑，在那里与黑人作家理查德·赖特和兰斯顿·休斯相识。在他们两人的鼓励下，艾里森开始了文学创作活动。最初他只写了一些短篇小说和评论文章，后来这些文章都收在论文集《影子和行动》（*Shadow and Act*，1964）里。

他一边创作一边研读欧美优秀作家的作品。对他影响较深的有俄罗斯作家陀思妥耶夫斯基(Feodor Dostoevski，1821～1881)、爱尔兰作家乔伊斯(James Joyce，1882～1941)、美国作家麦尔维尔、福克纳、海明威和亨利·詹姆斯。在谈到《看不见的人》的创作时，艾里森说，该书前言的节奏直接取法于陀思妥耶夫斯基的《来自地下的笔记》（*Notes from the Underground*）。

1944 年冬，他获得罗森瓦尔德基金会(Rosenwald Foundation)提供的 1500 美元的研究员基金，着手写作长篇小说《看不见的人》（*Invisible Man*），历时 7 载。该书于 1952 年出版时，立即轰动美国文坛，并荣获当年全国图书奖。美国文学评论界对这本书毁誉不一。曾撰文赞扬理查德·赖特的"抗议"小说的白人批评家欧文·豪（Irving Howe，1920～）批评艾里森逃避作为一个黑人受害者的社会责任，而对所谓的"人类自由"的前景过于乐观。艾里森对这类批评的回答是，他是一个作家，而不是某一事业的代言人；他的作品只是一部小说，而不是关于黑人问题的声明。他还说："我是一个人，不仅仅是理查德·赖特的一个黑人继承者。我可以用很多方式表达我的经历，这些方式比'抗议'之类的提法要复杂得多。"由于艾里森的经历与赖特不同，他对种族问题的感受也不同；他采取更复杂的方式、在更广泛的意义上剖析不合理的社会现象，但这并没有冲淡他作为一个黑人作家对种族歧视和种族压迫的抨击。

《看不见的人》发表以后，艾里森相继获得一系列奖励和学术头衔，并应邀到全国很多大学去讲学。

拉尔夫·艾里森不仅是美国当代杰出的小说家，也是学识渊博的学者和思想深邃的文学理论家。1986年，艾里森发表了继《影子与行动》之后的第2本论文集《走向领域》(*Going to the Territory*，1986)，收集他1957至1985年期间发表的部分论文和讲演稿，对种族问题、美国文化和黑人文学等问题都作了极其精辟的论述。

自从他的第1部长篇小说问世以来，将近40年的时间已经过去，人们还在期待着他第2部小说的出版，足见他的影响之大、创作态度之严谨。

Invisible Man

〔**作品介绍**〕

1965年，美国著名评论杂志《每周书评》(*Book Week*)召集200名评论家、作家和编辑，推荐自第二次世界大战以来"最出色的一部作品"。拉尔夫·艾里森的《看不见的人》(*Invisible Man*)被公认为佼佼之作而夺冠。这本书自出版30多年来，一直被视为当代美国文学的一部杰作，受到广大读者的喜爱。

小说描写一个无名无姓的黑人青年，躲在纽约一家白人住宅的地下室里，叙述自己从种族歧视和种族压迫根深蒂固的南方来到工业发达的北方大城市，为了寻求自我反而失去自我的经过，抒发20多年来淤结在心头的郁闷，使自己得到一些慰藉；同时也揭示了存在于资本主义美国的人与人、人与社会以及种族之间的种种不正常关系，因而小说是对不合理社会关系的深刻披露和强烈抗议。

故事开始时，主人公引用了祖父留给父亲的临终遗言："儿啊，我死后，希望你继续战斗。我没有对你说过，我们的生活就是一场战争。我一辈子都是个叛徒。自从重建时期开始，我缴了枪以来，我就成了潜伏在敌国里的密探。你要在险境中周旋。希望你对他们唯唯诺诺，叫他们忘乎所以；对他们笑脸相迎；叫他们丧失警惕；对他们百依百顺，叫他们彻底完蛋。让他们吞食你吧，要撑得他们呕吐，要胀得他们爆裂。"虽然主人公对这遗言的含义并不十分理解，然而这番话对他的影响却很大，成了他从南到北求生存寻"自我"所遵循的原则，也是读者理解这部小说的关键所在。

小说采用追述手法。主人公在中学毕业典礼上发表"进步的秘密在于谦卑"的演说，十分成功，被邀请到当地白人显赫人物的集会上发表同样主题的演说，受到教育董事会的尝识，并得到一张进入州立黑人学院的奖学金证书。后来因带领一个白人校董参观了一些不体面的地方，惹怒了院长，被驱逐出黑人学院。于是他开始了从南方到北方寻求"自我"的旅程。他来到纽约，先在"自由油漆公司"当工人，后来又给该公司的锅炉工当助手。锅炉工存心不良，引爆锅炉，使主人公险些丧命。在医院经过一段治疗以后又来到纽约黑人集中的哈莱姆区。在那里他抗议白人警察强行收回黑人住房的无理行为，发表措词激烈的演讲，被黑人进步组织"兄弟会"看中，被吸收为会员，并代表"兄弟会"在黑人集会上发表演说，宣传"兄弟会"的主张。这时，他事实上已成为"兄弟会"在哈莱姆的代言人。后来他与"兄弟会"的某些领导人在方针上产生分歧，又遭到与"兄弟会"作对的黑人民族主义者的追捕，他只好多次乔装打扮，改头换面，变成一个具有多重身份的人。最后在黑人民族主义者拉斯一伙的追逐下，主人公跳进一个检修口，在一个地下煤库里躲起来。就这样，他始终没有找到自己的社会"身份"，也没有得到社会的承认。因此，他感到痛苦、愤恨。他在地下室里反复思索，终于悟出一个道理。他要向全世界宣告："我是一个看不见的人。"

艾里森在谈到"寻求自我"是美国文字的一个重要主题时说："我们社会的本质是不允许我们知道自己是谁。"小说的主人公也说过，"你时常会怀疑自已是否真的存在。"所以他在地下室里打开1369个灯，把自己的住处照得通明，以证实他不仅是可见的，而且是一个活生生的人。

他在地下蛰伏，"蛰伏是为公开活动作秘密准备，""因为，即使一个看不见的人也可以在社会上扮演一个重要角色"。

由于种族、宗教和地理的原因，在美国种族矛盾显得特别突出。黑人争取平等、要求自由的斗争此起彼伏，从未间断过。进入20世纪以来，这种斗争越演越烈。它在文学上的反映就是20年代的"哈莱姆文艺复兴"运动和40年代以理查德·赖特为首所开创的"抗议小说"的出现。艾里森在其文学创作的初期，在一定程度上受过理查德·赖特的影响，后来他却选择了一个不同的角度来考察种族问题，将其置于多元的社会组成和错综复杂的社会结构中来研究“我们（指黑人）是谁”的问题。艾里森认为，在美国，关键的问题是不断斗争，以使人们认识存在于美国社会中的复杂关系及其历史的演进过程。因此，他决心用象征和比喻的手法将美国人民当中各种范围之内、不同种族和不同阶级之间的复杂关系写进他的作品，用小说的形式将美国的种族历史作为一个有机的整体加以阐明，从而使人们能够在更广阔的背景中来衡量种族问题。因此可以说，《看不见的人》不仅在艺术上是一部杰作，它同样也蕴藏着抗议的呼声。艾里森的创作继承并发扬了美国文学的现实主义优良传统。

这部小说的结构颇具特色，开头是前言部分，在情节发展上前言又是结束语的继续，这样，小说一开始就将结局展现在读者面前，然后读者又随着主人公一起追述故事。小说的写作手法也随着情节的发展而变化，当主人公在南方黑人学院上学时，作者运用自然主义手法；当主人公来到纽约，在黑人与种族主义者的冲突中满怀激愤时，作者运用表现主义手法；当主人公掉进地下室，经过思索对种族问题和人际关系有了领悟时，作者运用超现实主义手法。

这部小说从结构到内容都受到黑人爵士乐特别是布鲁斯音乐的影响。主人公就象布鲁斯乐曲的演唱者，叙述过去的失败、痛苦和忧伤。他在地下室里 听着黑人爵士乐歌星路易·阿姆斯特朗的歌曲：“我造了什么孽/为何我/周身漆黑，如此忧伤?”这首歌意味深长，它就象布鲁斯歌曲里的迭句一样，在小说里重复出现。

此外，运用民间传说和黑人口语也是这部小说的一个突出特点。

Invisible Man

PROLOGUE[1]

I am an invisible man. No, I am not a spook like those who haunted Edgar Allan Poe; nor am I one of your Hollywood-movie ectoplasms. I am a man of substance, of flesh and bone, fiber and liquids—and I might even be said to possess a mind. I am invisible, understand, simply because people refuse to see me. Like the bodiless heads you see sometimes in circus sideshows, it is as though I have been surrounded by mirrors of hard, distorting glass. When they approach me they see only my surroundings, themselves, or figments of their imagination—indeed, everything and anything except me.

Nor is my invisibility exactly a matter of a bio-chemical accident to my epidermis. That invisibility to which I refer occurs because of a peculiar disposition of the eyes of those with whom I come in contact. A matter of the construction of their *inner eyes*, those eyes with which they look through their physical eyes upon reality. I am not complaining, nor am I protesting either. It is sometimes advantageous to be unseen, although it is most often rather wearing on the nerves. Then too, you're constantly being bumped against by those of poor vision. Or again, you often doubt if you really exist. You wonder whether you aren't simply a phantom in other people's minds. Say, a figure in a mightmare which the sleeper tries with all his strength to destroy. It's when you feel like this that, out of resentment, you begin to bump people back. And, let me confess, you feel that way most of the time. You ache with the need to convince yourself that you do exist in the real world, that you're a part of all the sound and anguish, and you strike out with your fists, you curse and you swear to make them recognize you. And, alas, it's seldom successful.

One night I accidentally bumped into a man, and perhaps because of the near darkness he saw me and called me an insulting name. I sprang at him, seized his coat lapels and demanded that he apologize. He was a tall blond man, and as my face came close to his he looked insolently out of his blue eyes and cursed me, his breath hot in my face as he struggled. I pulled his chin down sharp upon the crown of my head, butting him as I had seen the West Indians do, and I felt his flesh tear and the blood gush out and I yelled, "Apologize! Apologize!" But he continued to curse and struggle, and I butted him again and again until he went down heavily, on his knees, profusely bleeding. I kicked him repeatedly, in a frenzy because he still uttered insults though his lips were frothy with blood. Oh yes, I kicked him! And in my outrage I got out my knife and prepared to slit his throat, right there beneath the lamplight in the deserted street, holding him by the collar with one hand, and opening the knife with my teeth—when it occurred to me that the man had not *seen* me, actually; that he, as far as he knew, was in the midst of a walking nightmare! And I stopped the blade, slicing the air as I pushed him away, letting him fall back to the street. I stared at him hard as the lights of a car stabbed through the darkness. He lay there, moaning on the asphalt; a man almost killed by a phantom. It unnerved me. I was both disgusted and ashamed. I was like a drunken man myself, wavering about on weakened legs. Then I was amused. Something in this man's thick head had sprung out and beaten him within an inch of his life. I began to laugh at this crazy discovery. Would he have awakened at the point of death? Would Death himself have freed him for wakeful living? But I didn't linger. I ran away into the dark, laughing so hard I feared I might rupture myself. The next day I saw his picture in the *Daily News*, beneath a caption stating that he had been "mugged." Poor fool, poor blind fool, I thought with sincere compassion, mugged by an invisible man!

Most of the time (although I do not choose as I once did to deny the violence of my days by ignoring it) I am not so overtly violent. I remember that I am invisible and walk softly so as not to awaken the sleeping ones. Sometimes it is best not to awaken them; there are few things in the world as dangerous as sleepwalkers. I learned in time though that it is possible to carry on a fight against them without their realizing it. For instance, I have been carrying on a fight with Monopolated Light & Power[2] for some time now. I use their serice and pay them nothing at all, and they don't know it. Oh, they suspect that power is being drained off, but they don't know where. All they know is that according to the master meter back there in their power station a hell of a lot of free current is disappearing somewhere into the jungle of Harlem. The joke, of course, is that I don't live in Harlem but in a border area. Several years ago (before I discovered the advantage of being invisible) I went through the routine process of buying service and paying their outrageous rates. But no more. I gave up all that, along with my apartment, and my old way of life: That way based upon the fallacious assumption that I, like other men, was visible. Now, aware of my invisivibity, I live rent-free in a building rented strictly to whites, in a section of the basement that was shut off and forgotten during the nineteenth century, which I discovered when I was trying to escape in the night from Pas the Destroyer.[3] But that's getting too far ahead of the story, almost to the end, although the end is in the beginning and lies far ahead.

The point now is that I found a home—or a hole in the ground, as you will. Now don't jump to the conclusion that because I call my home a "hole" it is damp and cold like a grave; there are cold holes and warm holes. Mine is a warm hole. And remember, a bear retires to his hole for the winter and lives until spring; then he comes strolling out like the Easter chick breaking from its shell. I say all this to assure you that it is incorrect to assume that, because I'm invisible and live in a hole, I am dead. I am neither dead nor in a state of suspended animation. Call me Jack-the-Bear, for I am in a state of hibernation.

My hole is warm and full of light. Yes, *full* of light. I doubt if there is a brighter spot in all New York than this hole of mine, and I do not exclude Broadway. Or the Empire State Building on a photographer's dream night. But that is taking advantage of you. Those two spots are among the darkest of our whole civilization—pardon me, our whole *culture* (an important distinction, I've heard) —which might sound like a hoax, or a contradiction, but that (by contradiction, I mean) is how the world moves: Not like an arrow, but a boomerang. (Beware of those who speak of the *spiral* of history; they are preparing a boomerang. Keep a steel helmet handy.) I know; I have been boomeranged across my head so much that I now can see the darkness of lightness. [4] And I love light. Perhaps you'll think it strange that an invisible man should need light, desire light, love light. But maybe it is exactly because I *am* invisible. Light confirms my reality, gives birth to my form. A beautiful girl once told me of a recurring nightmare in which she lay in the center of a large dark room and felt her face expand until it filled the whole room, becoming a formless mass while her eyes ran in bilious jelly up the chimney. And so it is with me. Without light I am not only invisible, but formless as well; and to be unaware of one's form is to live a death. I myself, after existing some twenty years, did not become alive until I discovered my invisibility.

That is why I fight my battle with Monopolated Light & Power. The deeper reason, I mean: It allows me to feel my vital aliveness. I also fight them for taking so much of my money before I learned to protect myself. In my hole in the basement there are exactly 1, 369 lights. I've wired the entire ceiling, every inch of it. And not with fluorescent bulbs, but with the older, more-expensive-to-operate kind, the filament type. An act of sabotage, you know. I've already begun to wire the wall. A junk man I know, a man of vision, has supplied me with wire and sockets. Nothing, storm of flood, must get in the way of our need for light and ever more and brighter light. The truth is the light and light is the truth. When I finish all four walls, then I'll start on the floor. Just how that will go, I don't know. Yet when you have lived invisible as long as I have you develop a certain ingenuity. I'll solve the problem. And maybe I'll invent a gadget to place my coffeepot on the fire while I lie in bed, and even invent a gadget to warm my bed—like the fellow I saw in one of the picture magazines who made himself a gadget to warm his shoes! Though invisible, I am in the great American tradition of tinkers.[5] That makes me kin to Ford,[6] Edison[7] and Franklin.[8] Call me, since I have a theory and a concept, a "thinker-tinker." Yes, I'll warm my shoes; they need it, they're usually full of holes. I'll do that and more.

Now I have one radio-phonograph; I plan to have five. There is a certain acoustical deadness in my hole, and when I have music I want to *feel* its vibration, not only with my ear but with my whole body. I'd like to hear five recordings of Louis Armstrong[9] playing and singing "What Did I Do to Be so Black and Blue"-all at the same time. Sometimes now I Listen to Louis while I have my favorite dessert of vanilla ice cream and sloe gin. I pour the red liquid over the white mound, watching it glisten and the vapor rising as Louis bends that military instrument into a beam of lyrical sound. Perhaps I like Louis Armstrong because he's made poetry out of being invisibile. I think it must be because he's unaware that he is invisible. And my own grasp of invisibility aids me to understand his music. Once when I asked for a cigarette, some jokers gave me a reefer, which I lighted when I got home and sat listening to my phonograph. It was a strange evening. Invisibility, let me explain, gives one a slightly different sense of time. you're never quite on the beat. Sometimes you're ahead and sometimes behind. Instead of the swift and imperceptible flowing of time, you are aware of its nodes, those points where time stands still or from which it leaps ahead. And you slip into the breaks and look around. That's what you hear vaguely in Louis' music.

Once I saw a prizefighter boxing a yokel. The fighter was swift and amazingly scientific. His body was one violent folw of rapid rhythmic action. He hit the yokel a hundred times while the yokel held up his arms in stunned surprise. But suddenly the yokel, rolling about in the gale of boxing gloves, struck one blow and knocked science, speed and footwork as cold as a well-digger's posterior. The smart money hit the canvas. [10] The long shot got the nod. [11] The yokel had simply stepped inside of his opponent's sense of time. So under the spell of the reefer[12] I discovered a new analytical way of listening to music. The unheard sounds came through, and each melodic line existed of itself, stood out clearly from all the rest, said its piece, and waited patiently for the other voices to speak. That night I found myself hearing not only in time, but in space as well. I not only entered the music but descended, like Dante, into its depths. [13] And *beneath the swiftness of the hot tempo there was a slower tempo and a cave and I entered it and looked around and heard an old woman singing a spiritual as full of Weltschmerz as flamenco,* [14] *and beneath that lay a still lower level on which I saw a beautiful girl the color of ivory pleading in a voice like my mother's as she stood before a group of slave owners who bid for her naked body, and below that I found a lower level and a more rapid tempo and I heard someone shout:*

"Brothers and sisters, my text this morning is the 'Blackness of Blackness.'"

And a congregation of voices answered: "That blackness is most black, brother, most black…"

"In the beginning…"

"At the very start," they cried.

"…there was blackness…"

"Preach it…"

"…and the sun…"

"The sun, Lawd…"

"…was bloody red…"

"Red…"

"Now black is…" the preacher shouted.

"Bloody…"

"I said black is…"

"Preach it, brother…"

"…an' black ain't…"

"Red, Lawd, red: He said it's red!"

"Amen, brother…"

"Black will git you…"

"Yes, it will…"

"…an' black won't…"

"Now, it won't!"

"It do..."

"It do, Lawd..."

"...an' it don't."

"Halleluiah..."

"... It'll put you, glory, glory, Oh my Lawd, in the WHALE'S BELLY."[15]

"Preach it, dear brother..."

"...an' make you tempt..."

"Good God a-mighty!"

"Old Aunt Nelly!"

"Black will make you..."

"Black..."

"...or black will un-make you."

"Ain't it the truth, Lawd?"

And at that point a voice of trombone timbre screamed at me, "Git out of here, you fool! Is you ready to commit treason?"

And I tore myself away, hearing the old singer of spirituals moaning, "Go curse your God, boy, and die."

I stopped and questioned her, asked her what was wrong.

"I dearly loved my master, son," she said.

"You should have hated him," I said.

"He gave me several sons," she said, "and because I loved my sons I learned to love their father though I hated him too."

"I too have become acquainted with ambivalence," I said. "That's why I'm here."

"What's that?"

"Nothing, a word that doesn't explain it. Why do you moan?"

"I moan this way 'cause he's dead," she said.

"Then tell me, who is that laughing upstairs?"

"Them's my sons. They glad."

"Yes, I can understand that too," I said.

"I laughs too, but I moans too. He promised to set us free but he never could bring hisself to do it. Still I loved him..."

"Loved him? You mean..."

"Oh yes, but I loved something else even more."

"What more?"

"Freedom."

"Freedom," I said. "Maybe freedom lies in hating."

"Naw, son, it's in loving. I loved him and give him the poison and he withered away like a frost-bit apple. Them boys woulda tore him to pieces with they homemake knives."

"A mistake was made somewhere," I said, "I'm confused." And I wished to say other things, but the laughter upstairs became too loud and moan-like for me and I tried to break out of it, but I couldn't. Just as I was leaving I felt an urgent desire to ask her what freedom was and went back. She sat with her head in her hands, moaning softly; her leather-brown face was filled with sadness.

"Old woman, what is this freedom you love so well?" I asked around a corner of my mind.

She looked surprised, then thoughtful, then baffled. "I done forgot, son. It's all mixed up. First I think it's one thing, then I think it's another. It gits my head to spinning. I guess now it ain't nothing but knowing how to say what I got up in my head. But it's a hard job, son. Too much is done happen to me in too short a time. Hit's like I have a fever. Ever' time I starts to walk my head gits to swirling and I falls down. Or if it ain't that, it's the boys; they gits to laughing and wants to kill up the white folks. They's bitter, that's what they is…"

"But what about freedom?"

"Leave me 'lone, boy; my head aches!"

I left her, feeling dizzy myself. I didn't get far.

Suddenly one of the sons, a big fellow six feet tall, appeared out of nowhere and struck me with his fist.

"What's the matter, man?" I cried.

"You made Ma cry!"

"But how?" I said, dodging a blow.

"Askin' her them questions, that's how. Git outa here and stay, and next time you got questions like that, ask yourself!"

He held me in a grip like cold stone, his fingers fastening upon my windpipe until I thought I would suffocate before he finally allowed me to go. I stumbled about dazed, the music beating hysterically in my ears. It was dark. My head cleared and I wandered down a dark narrow passage, thinking I heard his footsteps hurrying behind me. I was sore, and into my being had come a profound craving for tranquillity, for peace and quiet, a state I felt I could never achieve. For one thing, the trumpet was blaring and the rhythm was too hectic. A tomtom beating like heart-thuds began drowning out the trumpet, filling my ears. I longed for water and I heard it rushing through the cold mains my fingers touched as I felt my way, but I couldn't stop to search because of the footsteps behind me.

"Hey, Ras," I called. "Is it you, Destroyer? Rinehart?"

No answer, only the rhythmic footsteps behind me. Once I tried crossing the road, but a speeding machine struck me, scraping the skin from my leg as it roared past.

Then somehow I came out of it,[16] ascending hastily from this underworld of sound to hear Louis Armstrong innocently asking,

What did I do
To be so black
And blue?

At first I was afraid; this familiar music had demanded action, the kind of which I was incapable, and yet had I lingered there beneath the surface I might have attempted to act. Nevertheless, I know now that few really listen to this music. I sat on the chair's edge in a soaking sweat, as though each of my 1,369 bulbs had everyone become a klieg light in an individual setting for a third degree with Ras and Rinehart in charge. It was exhausting—as though I had held my breath continuously for an hour under the terrifying serenity that comes from days of intense hunger. And yet, it was a strangely satisfying experience for an invisible man to hear the silence of sound. I had discovered unrecognized compulsions of my being—even though I could not answer "yes" to their promptings. I haven't smoked a reefer since, however; not because they're illegal, but because too *see* around corners is enough (that is not unusual when you are invisible). But to hear around them is too much; it inhibits action. And despite Brother Jack and all that sad, lost period of the Brotherhood, I believe in nothing if not in action.

Please, a definition: A hibernation is a covert preparation for a more overt action.

Besides, the drug destroys one's sense of time completely. If that happened, I might forget to dodge some bright morning and some cluck would run me down with an orange and yellow street car, or a bilious bus! Or I might forget to leave my hole when the moment for action presents itself.

Meanwhile I enjoy my life with the compliments of Monopolated Light & Power. Since you never recognize me even when in closest contact with me, and since, no doubt, you'll hardly believe that I exist, it won't matter if you know that I tapped a power line leading into the building and ran it into my hole in the ground. Before that I lived in the darkness into which I was chased, but now I see. I've illuminated the blackness of my invisibility—and vice versa. And so I play the invisible music of my isolation. The last statement doesn't seem just right, does it? But it is; you hear this music simply because music is heard and seldom seen, except by musicians. Could this compulsion to put invisibility down in black and white be thus an urge to make music of invisibility? But I am an orator, a rabble rouser—Am? I *was*, and perhaps shall be again. Who knows? All sickness is not unto death, neither is invisibility.

I can hear you say, "What a horrible, irresponsible bastard!" And you're right. I leap to agree with you. I am one of the most irresponsible beings that ever lived. Irresponsibility is part of my invisibility; any way you face it, it is a denial. But to whom can I be responsible, and why should I be, when you refuse to see me? And wait until I reveal how truly irresponible I am. Responsibility rests upon recognition, and recognition is a form of agreement. Take the man whom I almost killed: Who was responsible for that near murder—I? I don't think so, and I refuse it. I won't buy it. You can't give it to me. *He* bumped *me*, *he* insulted *me*. Shouldn't he, for his own personal safety, have recognized my hysteria, my "danger potential"? He, let us say, was lost in a dream world. But didn't *he* control that dream world—which, alas, is only too real! —and didn't *he* rule me out of it? And if he had yelled for a policeman, wouldn't *I* have been taken for the offending one? Yes, yes, yes! Let me agree with you, I was the irresponsible one; for I should have used my knife to protect the higher interests of society. Some day that kind of foolishness will cause us tragic trouble. All dreamers and sleepwalkers must pay the price, and even the invisible victim is responsible for the fate of all. But I shirked that responsibility; I became too snarled in the incompatible notions that buzzed within my brain. I was a coward ...

But what did I do to be so blue? Bear with me.

〔注释〕

1. Prologue：小说《看不见的人》的结构独具特色，除故事主体之外，开头有一个"前言"，末尾有一个"结束语"。这两部分都是故事接近尾声时，主人公在黑人民族主义者拉斯一伙的追逐下掉进"洞"里以后，回顾以往走过的道路，对"善"与"恶"、"爱"与"恨"、"光明"与"黑暗"、"幻想"与"现实"以及"自由"、"真理"和"社会责任"等问题有所领悟而发的议论，"直到发现自己是个看不见的人，才意识到自己是个活人"。

2. Monopolated Light and Power：电力专利公司。

3. Ras the Destroyer：毁灭者拉斯，小说主要人物之一，纽约市哈莱姆区黑人民族主义者领导人。主人公就是在他的追逐下躲进地下室的。

4. the darkness of lightness：指头部被撞击以后眼冒金花的状态；双关语，意指黑白混淆。

5. the great American tradition of tinkers：指美国历史上有发明创造的工匠们的伟大传统。

6. Ford：亨利·福特（Henry Ford，1863～1947），美国汽车工业大王。

7. Edison：托马斯·艾尔瓦·爱迪生（Thomas Alva Edison，1847～1931），美国发明家。

8. Franklin：本杰明·富兰克林（Bejamin Franklin，1706～1790）美国革命时期杰出政治家、文学家和发明家。

9. Louis Armstrong：路易·阿姆斯特朗（1900～1971），美国著名黑人爵士乐演奏家。

10. The smart money hit the canvas：（俚）自负的家伙倒在地上。

11. The long shot got the nod：（俚）没有希望的人得胜了。

12. under the spell of the reefer：在大麻叶烟卷的迷醉下。

13. 卜文斜体字部分表示主人公的思绪在随着音乐的声音而起伏跌宕。

14. as spiritual…flamenco：一首既忧伤又狂热的黑人圣歌。

15. "…Oh my Lawd，in the WHALE'S BELLY."暗指希伯来先知约拿的故事（详见《圣经·约拿书》）。

16. it：指主人公的思绪。

J. D. SALINGER

〔作者介绍〕

塞林杰（J. D. Salinger，1919～），美国当代小说家，生于纽约市一个犹太中产阶级家庭。他幼时拘谨好静，在学校里成绩中上。13 岁入曼哈顿区一所很好的中学学习，一年后因不及格而离开。少年时期不好交际，喜欢独自做出奇的事情。15 岁入宾夕法尼亚州瓦利福奇军校（Valley Forge Military Academy）学习，在这里他开始感到自己不能适应环境。这所军校是塞林杰后来的代表作《麦田里的守望者》（*The Catcher in the Rye*，1951）中潘西中学的张本，塞林杰也像小说的叙事者霍尔登一样，是那里的击剑队队长。他在军校的一个同学象霍尔登一样被开除，另一个同学象小说中的一个人物一样跳楼自尽。在军校里他担任学校一个刊物的文学编辑，并开始写作小说，曾想进入电影界或为好莱坞写剧本。他 17 岁在军校结业，18 岁入纽约大学华盛顿广场学院，学习几星期后，随父到欧州经商，战前回国。经济萧条时期，他曾在哥伦比亚大学举办的一个短篇小说创作训练班里学习写作，1940 年在《故事》（*Story*）杂志上正式发表处女作《年轻人》（“The Young Folks”），第一次接触到他日后一直刻意描写的主题——受到成人世界捉弄的青少年的情状。1941 年他开始成为著名杂志《柯里尔》（*Collier's*）及《老爷》（*Esguire*）的成功的撰稿人，后《纽约客》（*The New Yorker*）发表了他的短篇小说《麦迪逊街边的小乱子》（“Slight Rebellion off Madison”），在这篇故事首次出现了《麦田里的守望者》的主人公的名字——霍尔登。随后，塞林杰又发表过 20 余篇短篇小说，但在评论家及读者中未能引起注意。1951 年他发表长篇小说《麦田里的守望者》，声名大振，这部小说尤其受到青年学生的青睐。两年后，他的短篇小说集《九篇故事》（*Nine Stories*）问世，小说里的一些主题在他后来的作品中又描写过，一些人物特别是塞林杰想象出的格拉斯家（the Glass Family）的成员们，在他五、六十年代较长篇的故事中又再现过。1961 年，他发表《弗拉尼和佐依》（*Franny and Zooey*），描写格拉斯家最年轻的成员弗拉尼和她哥哥佐依的故事。格拉斯家的故事又构成1963年发表的《木工们，升高顶梁；及西摩介绍》(*Raise High the Roof Beam, Carpenters; and Seymour: An Introduction*) 的内容。这个集子包括两个中篇小说。

近20年来，塞林杰行动古怪，几乎与外界隔绝，很少发表作品，这一方面给他的生活罩上了一层神秘的色彩，同时也使他从文学界逐渐消逝。在多数人的心目中，大概只有他的代表作《麦田里的守望者》令人记忆犹新。

The Catcher in the Rye

〔作品介绍〕

《麦田里的守望者》(*The Catcher in the Rye*)描写的是一个中学生的故事。16岁的霍尔登因学习成绩太差而被学校开除，在家长没有得到学校正式通知以前不敢回家，流荡在纽约街头。在近3天的时间里，历尽艰辛，险些丧命。小说以动人的笔墨勾勒出一个天真无邪的少年堕入颓废荒唐的成人世界中的一幅令人深思的画面。

霍尔登被开除后离校去纽约短住。这座城市的灯红酒绿和奇男怪女使他感到惊悸不已。深夜，他在旅馆里惨遭妓女等的暗算和毒打，神经险些失常。他在酒馆里闷坐独酌，在极端痛苦中以冷水浇头，险些患病丧生。他感到孤苦不堪，于是半夜摸回家去看望心爱的妹妹，同时又时刻担心父母自外归来"要他的命"。而平时对他最好的老师的同性恋行为又使他丧魂失胆，离校不足两天的孩子便已觉得走头无路，视自杀为上策了。他感到凄凉寂寞，害怕患病死去。他厌恶成人世界的堕落，决心隐遁到西部去寻求解脱，后来还是靠着深厚而纯真的兄妹情谊才温暖了他的冰冷的心。他大病一场，在精神病院里叙述了这一段凄惨的经历。

成人世界的颓废和堕落在霍尔登的少年心灵上留下了深刻的创伤。成年人的性反常行为使他感到在他栖身的旅馆里他可能是"里里外外唯一一个正常的龟儿子"。妹妹学习的小学墙壁上出现的脏词秽语令他恶心。他难过地醒悟到，"你就是能活100万年专来涂掉这些东西，世上有那么多，你连一半也干不完，没法干完。"人生使他感到沮丧和厌恶，似乎这个世界上没有任何东西可以让他舒心适意。他对周围一切都不感兴趣，切身体验到生活的空虚和无聊。他认识到，这个世界是业已丧失天真和纯洁的堕落所在，世道不对头，生活不对头，人只要活着就会不可避免地"假里假气"起来，就注定要与世沉浮。

生活在这个世界里，他感到孤独和绝望。在纽约短短的48小时里，他发自肺腑地呼叫："我真他妈的孤单低沉极啦！"这种呼叫多达30余次。在最黑暗的时刻，他前后有5次表达出死的愿望。有一次他还想自尽以结束生活的痛苦。在他东奔西撞的过程中，竟然只有博物馆里埃及木乃伊的坟墓令他感到"美好和平静"。他觉得解脱自己的方法是离开这个可恨的地方，决定搭车去西部，在那里装聋做哑，以便达到"这一辈子再也不和人谈话"的目的。

在他沉沦于纽约的时间里，也有过几次短暂的快活时刻；这些倏忽即逝的时刻多和孩子及他们的天真烂漫相关。他的妹妹菲比仿佛是他阴郁生活中唯 一光明的火花。她淳朴率直，洁白无瑕，使他又看到生活的光明一面，他的幼小心灵又似枯木萌发，出现了生机勃勃的阳春。可是他又痛苦地认识到，成长和变化是不可抗拒的，他和妹妹都必然要长大成人，到那令人窒息的成人世界里去生活。于是他产生了拯救天真的孩子使之免受堕落之苦的念头：他想立在一个又高又深的悬崖峭壁边上，守望着在旁边麦地里做游戏的成千上万的孩子们，他们当中如有人不当心而快要掉到山下去，他就把他拉住。他要做麦地里的拉人的人。这应当说是本书书名《麦田里的守望者》的寓意所在。

《麦田里的守望者》有力地表明，西方青少年在成长中的痛苦和消沉主要是因西方文化本身的颓废性而引起的。青少年的悲观厌世及生活的空虚，是这种文化背景影响的必然产物。如果在美国现当代生活中存在着失望和悲观情绪，那末，这部小说则是对那种情绪的极好写照。

这里选注的是小说第22、23两章。

The Catcher in the Rye

CHAPTER XXII

When I came back, she had the pillow off her head all right[1]—I knews he would—but she still wouldn't look at me, even though she was laying on her back and all. When I came around the side of the bed and sat down again, she turned her carzy face the other way. She was ostracizing[2] the hell out of me. Just like the fencing team at Pencey when I left all the goddam foils on the subway.[3]

"How's old Hazel Weatherfield?"[4] I said. "You write any new stories about her? I got that one you sent me right in my suitcase. It's down at the station. It's very good."

"Daddy'll *kill* you."

Boy, she really gets somethimg on her mind when she gets something on her mind.

"No, he won't. The worst he'll do, he'll give me hell again, and then he'll send me to that goddam military school. That's all he'll do to me. And in the *first* place, I won't even be around. I'll be away. I'll be—I'll probably be in Colorado on this ranch."

"Don't make me laugh. You can't even ride a horse."

"Who can't? Sure I can. Certainly I can. They can teach you in about two minutes," I said. "Stop picking at that." She was picking at that adhesive tape on her arm. "Who gave you that haircut?" I asked her. I just noticed what a stupid haircut somebody gave her. It was way too short.

"None of your business," she said. She can be very snotty sometimes. She can be quite snotty. "I suppose you failed in every single subject again," she said—very snotty. It was sort of funny, too, in a way. She sounds like a goddam schoolteacher sometimes, and she's only a little child.

"No, I didn't," I said. "I passed English." Then, just for the hell of it, I gave her a pinch on the behind.[5] It was sticking way out in the breeze, the way she was laying on her side. She has hardly any behind. I didn't do it hard, but she tried to hit my hand anyway, but she missed.

Then all of a sudden, she said, "Oh, why did you *do* it?" She meant why did I get the ax again. It made me sort of sad, the way she said it.

"Oh, God, Phoebe, don't ask me. I'm sick of everybody asking me that," I said. "A million reasons why. It was one of the worst schools I ever went to. It was full of phonies.[6] And mean guys. You never saw so many mean guys in your life. For instance, if you were having a bull session[7] in somebody's room, and somebody wanted to come in, nobody'd let them in if they were some dopey, pimply guy. Everybody was always locking their door when somebody wanted to come in. And they had this goddam secret fraternity[8] that I was too yellow not to join. There was this one pimply, boring guy, Robert Ackley, that wanted to get in. He kept trying to join, and they wouldn't let him. Just because he was boring and pimply. I don't even feel like talking about it. It was a stinking school. Take my word."

Old Phoebe didn't say anything, but she was listening. I could tell by the back of her neck that she was listening. She always listens when you tell her something. And the funny part is she knows, half the time, what the hell you're talking about. She really does.

I kept talking about old Pencey. I sort of felt like it.

"Even the couple of *nice* teachers on the faculty, they were phonies, too," I said. "There was this one old guy, Mr. Spencer. His wife was always giving you hot chocolate and all that stuff, and they were really pretty nice. But you should've seen him when the headmaster, old Thurmer, came in the history class and sat down in the back of the room. He was always coming in and sitting down in the back of the room for about a half an hour. He was supposed to be incognito or something. After a while, he'd be sitting back there and then he'd start interrupting what old Spencer was saying to crack a lot of corny jokes. Old Spencer'd practically kill himself chuckling and smiling and all, like as if Thurmer was a goddam prince or something."

"Don't swear so much."

"It would've made you puke, I swear it would," I said. "Then, on Veterans' Day. They have this day, Veterans' Day, that all the jerks that graduated from Pencey around 1776[9] come back and walk all over the place, with their wives and children and everybody. You should've seen this one old guy that was about fifty. What he did was, he came in our room and knocked on the door and asked us if we'd mind if he used the bathroom. The bathroom was at the end of the corridor—I don't know why the hell he asked *us*. You know what he said? He said he wanted to see if his initials were still in one of the can doors. What he did, he carved his goddam stupid sad old initials in one of the can doors about ninety years ago, and he wanted to see if they were still there. So my roommate and I walked him down to the bathroom and all, and we had to stand there while he looked for his initials in all the can doors. He kept talking to us the whole time, telling us how when he was at Pencey they were the happiest days of his life, and giving us a lot of advice for the future and all. Boy, did he depress me! I don't mean he was a bad guy—he wasn't. But you don't have to be a bad guy to depress somebody—you can be a *good* guy and do it. All you have to do to depress somebody is give them a lot of phony advice while you're looking for your initials in some can door—that's all you have to do. I don't know. Maybe it wouldn't have been so bad if he hadn't been all out of breath. He was all out of breath from just climbing up the stairs, and the whole time he was looking for his initials he kept breathing hard, with his nostrils all funny and sad, while he kept telling Stradlater and I to get all we could out of Pencey. God, Phoebe! I can't explain. I just didn't like anything that was *hap*pening at Pencey. I can't explain."

Old Phoebe said something then, but I couldn't hear her. She had the side of her mouth right smack on the pillow, and I couldn't hear her.

"What?" I said. "Take your mouth away. I can't hear you with your mouth that way."

"You don't like *any*thing that's happening."[10]

It made me even more depressed when she said that.

"Yes I do. Yes I do. *Sure* I do. Don't say that. Why the hell do you say that?"

"Because you don't. You don't like any schools. You don't like a million things. You *don't.*"

"I do! That's where you're wrong—that's exactly where you're wrong! Why the hell do you have to say that?" I said. Boy, was she depressing me.

"Because you don't," she said. "Name one thing."

"One thing? One thing I like?" I said. "Okay."

The trouble was, I couldn't concentrate too hot. Sometimes it's hard to concentrate.

"One thing I like a lot you mean?" I asked her.

She didn't answer me, though. She was in a cockeyed position way the hell over the other side of the bed. She was about a thousand miles away. "C'mon, answer me," I said. "One thing I like a lot, or one thing I just like?"

"You like a lot."

"All right," I said. But the trouble was, I couldn't concentrate. About all I could think of were those two nuns that went around collecting dough in those beatup old straw baskets. Especially the one with the glasses with those iron rims. And this boy I knew at Elkton Hills. There was this one boy at Elkton Hills, named James Castle,[11] that wouldn't take back something he said about this very conceited boy, Phil Stabile. James Castle called him a very conceited guy, and one of Stabile's lousy friends went and squealed on him to Stabile. So Stabile, with about six other dirty bastards, went down to James Castle's room and went in and locked the goddam door and tried to make him take back what he said, but he wouldn't do it. So they started in on him. I won't even tell you what they did to him—it's too repulsive—but he *still* wouldn't take it back, old James Castle. And you should've seen him. He was a skinny little weak-looking guy, with wrists about as big as pencils. Finally, what he did, instead of taking back what he said, he jumped out the window. I was in the *shower* and all, and even *I* could hear him land outside. But I just thought something fell out the window, a radio or a desk or something, not a *boy* or anything. Then I heard everybody running through the corridor and down the stairs, so I put on my bathrobe and I ran downstairs too, and there was old James Castle laying right on the stone steps and all. He was dead, and his teeth, and blood, were all over the place, and nobody would even go near him. He had on this turtleneck sweater I'd lent him. All they did with the guys that were in the room with him was expel them. They didn't even go to jail.

That was about all I could think of, though. Those two nuns I saw at breakfast and this boy James Castle I knew at Elkton Hills. The funny part is, I hardly even know James Castle, if you want to know the truth. He was one of these very quiet guys. He was in my math class, but he was way over on the other side of the room, and he hardly ever got up to recite or go to the blackboard or anything. Some guys in school hardly ever get up to recite or go to the blackboard. I think the only time I ever even had a conversation with him was that time he asked me if he could borrow this turtleneck sweater I had. I damn near dropped dead when he asked me, I was so surprised and all. I remember I was brushing my teeth, in the can, when he asked me. He said his cousin was coming in to take him for a drive and all. I didn't even know he knew I *had* a turtleneck sweater. All I knew about him was that his name was always right ahead of me at roll call. Cabel, R., Cabel, W., Castle, Caulfield—I can still remember it. If you want to know the truth, I almost didn't *lend* him my sweater. Just because I didn't know him too well.

"What?" I said to old Phoebe. She said something to me, but I didn't hear her.

"You can't even think of one thing."

"Yes, I can. Yes, I can."

"Well, do it, then."

"I like Allie,[12]" I said. "And I like doing what I'm doing right now. Sitting here with you, and talking, and thinking about stuff, and—"

"Allie's *dead*—You always say that! If somebody's dead and everything, and in *Heaven*, then it isn't really—"

"I know he's dead! Don't you think I know that? I can still like him, though, can't I? Just because somebody's dead, you don't just stop liking them, for God's sake—especially if they were about a thousand times nicer than the people you know that're *alive* and all."

Old Phoebe didn't say anything. When she can't think of anything to say, she doesn't say a goddam word.

"Anyway, I like it now," I said. "I mean right now. Sitting here with you and just chewing the fat and horsing—"

"That isn't anything *real*ly!"

"It is so something *real*ly! Certainly it is! Why the hell isn't it? People never think anything is anything *really*. I'm getting goddam sick of it."

"Stop swearing. All right, name something else. Name something you'd like to *be*. Like a scientist. Or a *lawyer* or something."

"I couldn't be a scientist. I'm no good in science."

"Well, a lawyer—like Daddy and all."

"Lawyers are all right, I guess—but it doesn't appeal to me," I said. "I mean they're all right if they go around saving innocent guys' lives all the time, and like that, but you don't *do* that kind of stuff if you're a lawyer. All you do is make a lot of dough and play golf and play bridge and buy cars and drink Martinis and look like a hot-shot. And besides. Even if you *did* go around saving guys' lives and all, how would you know if you did it because you really *wanted* to save guys' lives, or because you did it because what you *real*ly wanted to do was be a terrific lawyer, with everybody slapping you on the back and congratulating you in court when the goddam trial was over, the reporters and everybody, the way it is in the dirty movies? How would you know you weren't being a phony? The trouble is, you *wouldn't*."

I'm not too sure old Phoebe knew what the hell I was talking about. I mean she's only a little child and all. But she was listening, at least. If somebody at least listens, it's not too bad.

"Daddy's going to kill you. He's going to *kill* you," she said.

I wasn't listening, though. I was thinking about something else—something crazy. "You know what I'd like to be?" I said. "You know what I'd like to be? I mean if I had my goddam choice?"

"What? Stop *swearing*."

"You know that song 'If a body catch a body comin' through the rye'? I'd like—"

"It's 'If a body *meet* a body coming through the rye'!"[13] old Phoebe said. "It's a poem. By Robert *Burns*."

"I *know* it's a poem by Robert Burns."

She was right, though. It *is* "If a body meet a body coming through the rye." I didn't know it then, though.

"I thought it was 'If a body catch a body,'" I said. "Anyway, I keep picturing all these little kids playing some game in this big field of rye and all. Thousands of little kids, and nobody's around—nobody big, I mean—except me. And I'm standing on the edge of some crazy cliff. What I have to do, I have to catch everybody if they start to go over the cliff—I mean if they're running and they don't look where they're going I have to come out from somewhere and *catch* them. That's all I'd do all day. I'd just be the catcher in the rye and all. I know it's crazy, but that's the only thing I'd really like to be. I know it's crazy."[14]

Old Phoebe didn't say anything for a long time. Then, when she said something, all she said was, "Daddy's going to kill you."

"I don't give a damn if he does," I said. I got up from the bed then, because what I wanted to do, I wanted to phone up this guy that was my English teacher at Elkton Hills, Mr. Antolini. He lived in New York now. He quit Elkton Hills. He took this job teaching English at N. Y. U.. "I have to make a phone call," I told Phoebe. "I'll be right back. Don't go to sleep." I didn't want her to go to sleep while I was in the living room. I knew she wouldn't but I said it anyway, just to make sure.

While I was walking toward the door, old Phoebe said, "Holden!" and I turned around.

She was sitting way up in bed. She looked so pretty. "I'm taking belching lessons from this girl, Phyllis Margulies," she said. "Listen."

I listened, and I heard *some*thing, but it wasn't much. "Good,"

I said. Then I went out in the living room and called up this teacher I had, Mr. Antolini.

CHAPTER XXIII

I MADE IT very snappy on the phone because I was afraid my parents would barge in on me right in the middle of it. They didn't, though. Mr. Antolini was very nice. He said I could come right over if I wanted to. I think I probably woke he and his wife up, because it took them a helluva long time to answer the phone. The first thing he asked me was if anything was wrong, and I said no. I said I'd flunked out of Pencey, though. I thought I might as well tell him. He said "Good God," when I said that. He had a good sense of humor and all. He told me to come right over if I felt like it.

He was about the best teacher I ever had, Mr. Antolini. He was a pretty young guy, not much older than my brother D. B., and you could kid around with him without losing your respect for him. He was the one that finally picked up that boy that jumped out the window I told you about, James Castle. Old Mr. Antolini felt his pulse and all, and then he took off his coat and put it over James Castle and carried him all the way over to the infirmary. He didn't even give a damn if his coat got all bloody.

When I got back to D. B.'s room, old Phoebe'd truned the radio on. This dance music was coming out. She'd turned it on low, though, so the maid wouldn't hear it. You should've seen her. She was sitting smack in the middle of the bed, outside the covers, with her legs folded like one of those Yogi guys. She was listening to the music. She kills me.

"C'mon," I said. "You feel like dancing?" I taught her how to dance and all when she was a tiny little kid. She's a very good dancer. I mean I just taught her a few things. She learned it mostly by herself. You can't teach somebody how to *really* dance.

"You have shoes on," she said.

"I'll take 'em off. C'mon."

She practically jumped off the bed, and then she waited while I took my shoes off, and then I danced with her for a while. She's really damn good. I don't like people that dance with little kids, because most of the time it looks terrible. I mean if you're out at a restaurant somewhere and you see some old guy take his little kid out on the dance floor. Usually they keep yanking the kid's dress up in the back by mistake, and the kid can't dance worth a damn *any*way, and it looks terrible, but I don't do it out in public with Phoebe or anything. We just horse around in the house. It's different with her anyway, because she can *dance*. She can follow anything you do. I mean if you hold her in close as hell so that it doesn't matter that your legs are so much longer. She stays right with you. You can cross over, or do some corny dips, or even jitterbug a little, and she stays right with you. You can even *tango*, for God's sake.

We danced about four numbers. In between numbers she's funny as hell. She stays right in position. She won't even talk or anything. You both have to stay right in position and wait for the orchestra to start playing again. That kills me. You're not supposed to laught or anything, either.

Anyway, we danced about four numbers, and then I turned off the radio. Old Phoebe jumped back in bed and got under the covers. "I'm improving, aren't I? she asked me.

"And how," I said. I sat down next to her on the bed gagin. I was sort of out of breath. I was smoking so damn much, I had hardly any wind. She wasn't even out of breath.

"Feel my forehead," she said all of a sudden.

"Why?"

"*Feel* it. Just feel it once."

I felt it. I didn't feel anything, though.

"Does it feel very feverish?" she said.

"No. Is it supposed to?"

"Yes—I'm making it. Feel it again."

I felt it again, and I still didn't feel anything, but I said, "I think it's starting to, now." I didn't want her to get a goddam inferiority complex.

She nodded. "I can make it go up to over the thermometer."

"Ther*mom*eter. Who said so?"

"Alice Holmborg showed me how. You cross your legs and hold your breath and think of something very, very hot. A radiator or something. Then your whole forehead gets so hot you can burn somebody's hand."

That killed me. I pulled my hand away from her forehead, like I was in terrific danger. "Thanks for *tell*ing me," I said.

"Oh, I wouldn't've burned *your* hand. I'd've stopped before it got too—*Shhh!*" Then, quick as hell, she sat way the hell up in bed.

She scared hell out of me when she did that. "What's the matter?" I said.

"The front door!" she said in this loud whisper. "It's them!"

I quick jumped up and ran over and turned off the light over the desk. Then I jammed out my cigarette on my shoe and put it in my pocket. Then I fanned hell out of the air, to get the smoke out—I shouldn't even have been smoking, for God's sake. Then I grabbed my shoes and got in the closet and shut the door. Boy, my heart was beating like a bastard.

I heard my mother come in the room.

"Phoebe?" she said. "Now, stop that. I saw the light, young lady."

"Hello!" I heard old Phoebe say. "I couldn't sleep. Did you have a good time?

"Marvelous," my mother said, but you could tell she didn't mean it. She doesn't enjoy herself much when she goes out. "Why are you awake, may I ask? Were you warm enough?"

"I was warm enough, I just couldn't sheep."

"Phoebe, have you been smoking a cigarette in here? Tell me the truth, please, young lady."

"What?" old Phoebe said.

"You heard me."

"I just lit one for one second. I just took *one puff*. Then I threw it out window."

"*Why*, may I ask?"

"I couldn't sleep."

"I don't like that, Phoebe. I don't like that at all," my mother said. "Do you want another blanket?"

"No, thanks. G'night!" old Phoebe said. She was trying to get rid of her, you could tell.

"How was the movie?" my mother said.

"Excellent. Except Alice's mother. She kept leaning over and asking her if she felt grippy during the whole entire movie. We took a taxi home."

"Let me feel your forehead."

"I didn't catch anything. She didn't have anything. It was just her mother."

"Well. Go to sleep now. How was your dinner?"

"Lousy," Phoebe said.

"You heard what your father said about using that word. What was lousy about it? You had a lovely lamb chop. I walked all over Lexington Avenue just to—"

"The lamb chop was all right, but Charlene always *breathes* on me whenever she puts something down. She breathes all over the food and everything. She *breathes* on everything."

"Well. Go to sleep. Give Mother a kiss. Did you say your prayers?"

"I said them in the bathroom. G'night!"

"Good night. Go right to sleep now. I have a splitting headache," my mother said. She gets headaches quite frequently. She really does.

"Take a few aspirins," old Phoebe said. "Holden'll be home on Wednesday, won't he?"

"So far as I know. Get under there, now. Way down."

I heard my mother go out and close the door. I waited a couple of minutes. Then I came out of the closet. I bumped smack into old Phoebe when I did it, because it was so dark and she was out of bed and coming to tell me. "I hurt you?" I said. You had to whisper now, because they were both home. "I gotta get a move on," I said. I found the edge of the bed in the dark and sat down on it and started putting on my shoes. I was pretty nervous. I admit it.

"Don't go *now*," Phoebe whispered. "Wait'll they're asleep!"

"No. Now. Now's the best time," I said. "She'll be in the bathroom and Daddy'll turn on the news or something. Now's the best time." I could hardly tie my shoelaces, I was so damn nervous. Not that they would've *killed* me or anything if they'd caught me home, but it would've been very unpleasant and all. "Where the hell are ya?" I said to old Phoebe. It was so dark I couldn't see her.

"Here." She was standing right next to me. I didn't even see her.

"I got my damn bags at the station," I said. "Listen. You got any dough, Phoeb? I'm practically broke."

"Just my Christmas dough. For presents and all. I haven't done any shopping at *all* yet."

"Oh." I didn't want to take her Christmas dough.

"You want some?" she said.

"I don't want to take your Christmas dough."

"I can lend you *some*," she said. Then I heard her over at D. B.'s desk, opening a million drawers and feeling around with her hand. It was pitch-black, it was so dark in the room. "If you go away, you won't see me in the play," she said. Her voice sounded funny when she said it.

"Yes, I will. I won't go way before that. You think I wanna miss the play?" I said. "What I'll do, I'll probably stay at Mr. Antolini's house till maybe Tuesday night. Then I'll come home. If I get a chance, I'll phone ya."

"Here," old Phoebe said. She was trying to give me the dough, but she couldn't find my hand.

"Were?"

She put the dough in my hand.

"Hey, I don't need all this," I said. "Just give me two bucks, is all. No kidding—Here." I tried to give it back to her, but she wouldn't take it.

"You can take it all. You can pay me back. Bring it to the play."

"How much is it, for God's sake?"

"Eight dollars and eighty-five cents. *Sixty*-five cents. I spent some."

Then, all of a sudden, I started to cry. I couldn't help it. I did it so nobody could hear me, but I did it. It scared hell out of old Phoebe when I started doing it, and she came over and tried to make me stop, but once you get started, you can't just stop on a goddam *dime*. I was still sitting on the edge of the bed when I did it, and she put her old arm around my neck, and I put my arm around her, too but I still couldn't stop for a long time. I thought I was going to choke to death or something. Boy, I scared hell out of poor old Phoebe. The damn window was open and everything, and I could feel her shivering and all, because all she had on was her pajamas. I tried to make her get back in bed, but she wouldn't go. Finally I stopped. But it certainly took me a long, long time. Then I finished buttoning my coat and all. I told her I'd keep in touch with her. She told me I could sleep with her if I wanted to, but I said no, that I'd better beat it, that Mr. Antolini was waiting for me and all. Then I took my hunting hat out of my coat pocket and gave it to her. She likes those kind of crazy hats. She didn't want to take it, but I made her. I'll bet she slept with it on. She really likes those kind of hats. Then I told her again I'd give her a buzz if I got a chance, and then I left.

It was a helluva lot[15] easier getting out of the house than it was getting in, for some reason. For one thing, I didn't give much of a damn any more if they caught me. I really didn't. I figured if they caught me, they caught me. I almost wished they did, in a way.

I walked all the way downstairs, instead of taking the elevator. I went down the back stairs. I nearly broke my neck on about ten million garbage pails, but I got out all right. The elevator boy didn't even see me. He probably *still* thinks I'm up at the Dicksteins.'[16]

〔注释〕

1. When I came back, she had the pillow off her head all right：指霍尔登半夜溜回家中，恰值父母外出，妹妹菲比（Phoebe）听说他已离校，心中非常害怕，每当她害怕时，她就躺在床上，把枕头压在脑袋上。霍尔登又劝阻又拉枕头，她仍不听，后来他到起居室去取烟。见小说第21章。

2. Ostracizing：意"狠骂"、"狠狠地批评"。

3. Just like the fencing team at Pency when I left all the goddam foils on the subway：Pency指潘西中学，小说里讲该校位于宾夕法尼亚州亚格兹城；该校有一支击剑队，霍尔登曾任队长；一次他们去纽约参赛，回来的路上把剑和设备都丢在地铁火车上，队员们都狠狠地埋怨他。见小说第1章。

4. Hazel Weatherfield：菲比写的小故事的主人公。

5. the behind：意"屁股"。

6. phonies："phony"一字的复数，在小说中是霍尔登用得最多的一个字，意"假里假气的"、"假里假气的人"，是他用以表达他对堕落的成人世界的厌恶的最有力的措词。此字由于小说之故曾流行一时。

7. a bull session：闲扯、"神聊"。

8. this goddam secret fraternity：这个该死的秘密的兄弟会。

9. around 1776：夸张说法，指历年毕业的。下文的"ninety years ago"系同类手法。

10. you don't... happening：菲比一语破的，指出霍尔登对生活所持的态度。

11. this one boy at Elkton Hills，named James Castle：Elkton Hills 是霍尔登上过的小学；James Castle 跳楼自尽一事在他的幼小的心灵里留下了不可磨灭的暗影，这是他在流浪纽约时想到死的一个例子。

12. Allie：霍尔登的弟弟。见小说第 5 章。

13. 引自英国诗人罗伯特·彭斯的诗"Coming through the Rye"。

14. 此段是解题（书名），为全书的主旨所在。

15. a helluva lot＝a hell of a lot.

16. the Dicksteins：霍尔登家的邻居，主人公半夜回家时害怕父母查出，便向开电梯的人撒谎说，他要去看望这家邻居，而不说回家看妹妹。

JOHN CHEEVER

〔作者介绍〕

约翰·契弗（John Cheever，1912～1982），美国小说家，生于马萨诸塞州昆西市一个中产阶级家庭。契弗17岁时被塞耶学院开除，后迁居纽约市，开始写作生涯。他在18岁时发表第1篇短篇小说《开除》（"Expelled"）。此后他长期为《纽约客》等杂志撰稿。他的第2部短篇小说集《巨型收音机及其它》（*The Enormous Radio and Other Stories*）于1953年发表，奠定了他在美国短篇小说创作史上的地位。契弗虽写过5部长篇小说，但评论界认为他的主要成就还是在短篇小说方面。他的作品曾多次获奖。

契弗是一位擅长描写社会风尚的小说家。他主要描写美国城郊富裕中产阶级的生活、人际关系、心理状态和道德观念，从而反映出社会生活的某些侧面。契弗小说中的主人公虽然受过教育，拥有钱财，但缺乏明确的生活目的。他们精神空虚，醉心享乐。物质上的成功使他们失去了生活中一切真正重要的东西。在丑恶的社会现实面前，他们进退维谷，沮丧失望。由于为失败感所困扰，他们的精神极端苦闷，以至做出一些不合常理的事情。契弗常把老一代人的价值观念和自信心作为背景，以衬托当代人的迷惘和失意。例如他的长篇小说《韦普肖特纪事》（*The Wapshot Chronicle*，1957）及其续集《韦普肖特丑闻》（*The Wapshot Scandal*，1964）就以幽默的笔调描写了一个历史悠久的新英格兰家庭在当代社会中的衰败和解体。他的作品中也不乏对当代人命运的关注。

契弗善于从日常琐事中探微索隐，并凭借艺术手法对生活和人物进行真实的刻画，从中展示重要的社会内容。他常用讽刺手法针砭社会的丑恶现象，其淋漓尽致常令人忍俊不禁。因此契弗被誉为社会批评家和"美国的契诃夫"。

简洁规范的语言和优美生动的文笔构成了契弗作品的突出特点。

契弗的其它主要作品有：短篇小说集《某些人的生活方式》（*The Way Some*

People Live: *A Book of Stories*, 1943)、《绿荫山窃贼及其它》(*The Housebreaker of Shady Hill and Other Stories*, 1958)、《陆军准将和高尔夫球迷的妻子》(*The Brigadier and the Golf Widow*, 1964)、《苹果的世界》(*The World of Apples*, 1973)和《契弗小说选》(*The Stories of John Cheever*, 1978)还有长篇小说《布莱特公园》(*Bullet Park*, 1969)、《鹰猎者》(*Falconer*, 1977)和《啊，那多么像天堂》(*Oh What a Paradise It Seems*, 1982)。

The Swimmer

〔**作品介绍**〕

《游泳者》("The Swimmer")发表于1964年，收在短篇小说集《陆军准将和高尔夫球迷的妻子》中。

一个仲夏的星期天下午，正在朋友家饮酒欢聚的主人公奈迪·麦瑞尔突然决定取道"水路"回家，即沿着一条特殊的路线步行回家，其间要游泳通过14户人家的游泳池和一个公共游泳池。作者描写奈迪长游途中遇见的人和事物，展现出美国城郊富裕的中产阶级的生活场景，揭示他们醉心享乐、无所事事、金钱至上、俗不可耐的本质。当奈迪来到自家门前时，发现人去楼空，门上的锁已锈痕斑斑。原来奈迪的生活并不幸福愉快。他在经济上已破产，卖掉了房子，失去了原有的社会地位，他的女儿也遭不测。

奈迪开始游泳时正值仲夏时节，他充满年轻人的幻想和活力，所到之处备受欢迎。一场暴风雨过后，初秋降临，他的境遇也急转直下。及至长游结束时已是深秋，奈迪年老力衰，幻梦破灭，众叛亲离。这一描写虽然荒诞，却蕴涵无穷。奈迪的长游象征着人生的旅途，他追求一生，毫无结果，只得以失败告终，因为在金钱至上的美国社会中，失去钱财便失去一切。正是失败的压力和痛苦促使奈迪决定通过游泳来证明自己的力量，显示自己的独创精神。但无情的现实粉碎了他的幻想，使他不得不正视自己的困窘处境，从而陷入更大的痛苦之中。奈迪的朋友哈洛伦夫妇似乎是富裕的中产阶级中正视现实的人物典型，在他们身上寄托了作者的希望。

《游泳者》篇幅不长，故事含蓄，但寓意极其深刻。作品最初给人以现实主义的印象，而后又显示出象征主义的特点。这种现实主义与象征主义手法的巧妙结合，给读者留下了充分想象和回味的余地。作者还运用讽刺手法，并将人物和环境融合在一起，取得了很好的效果。

这篇小说通过主人公的长游把一组关系松散的事件连贯起来，展现社会生活的画面，体现了社会风尚小说的特点，可谓是契弗短篇小说的成功之作。

The Swimmer

It was one of those midsummer Sundays when everyone sits around saying, "I *drank* too much last night." You might have heard it whispered by the parishioners leaving church, heard it from the lips of the priest himself, struggling with his cassock in the *vestiarium*,[1] heard it from the golf links and the tennis courts, heard it from the wildlife preserve where the leader of the Audubon group[2] was suffering from a terrible hangover. "I *drank* too much," said Donald Westerhazy. "We all *drank* too much," said Lucinda Merrill. "It must have been the wine," said Helen Westerhazy. "I *drank* too much of that claret."

This was at the edge of the Westerhazys' pool. The pool, fed by an artesian well with a high iron content, was a pale shade of green. It was a fine day. In the west there was a massive stand of cumulus cloud so like a city seen from a distance—from the bow of an approaching ship—that it might have had a name. Lisbon. Hackensack. The sun was hot. Neddy Merrill[3] sat by the green water, one hand in it, one around a glass of gin. He was a slender man—he seemed to have the especial slenderness of youth—and while he was far from young he had slid down his banister that morning and given the bronze backside of Aphrodite[4] on the hall table a smack, as he jogged toward the smell of coffee in his dining room. He might have been compared to a summer's day, particularly the last hours of one,[5] and while he lacked a tennis racket or a sail bag the impression was definitely one of youth, sport, and clement weather. He had been swimming and now he was breathing deeply, stertorously as if he could gulp into his lungs the components of that moment, the heat of the sun, the intenseness of his pleasure. It all seemed to flow into his chest. His own house stood in Bullet Park,[6] eight miles to the south, where his four beautiful daughters would have had their lunch and might be playing tennis. Then it occurred to him that by taking a dogleg to the southwest[7] he could reach his home by water.

His life was not confining and the delight he took in this observation could not be explained by its suggestion of escape.[8] He seemed to see, with a cartographer's eye, that string of swimming pools, that quasi-subterranean stream[9] that curved across the county. He had made a discovery, a contribution to modern geography; he would name the stream Lucinda after his wife. He was not a practical joker nor was he a fool but he was determinedly original and had a vague and modest idea of himself as a legendary figure.[10] The day was beautiful and it seemed to him that a long swim might enlarge and celebrate its beauty.

He took off a sweater that was hung over his shoulders and dove in. He had an inexplicable contempt for men who did not hurl themselves into pools. He swam a choppy crawl,[11] breathing either with every stroke or every fourth stroke and counting somewhere well in the back of his mind the one-two one-two of a flutter kick.[12] It was not a serviceable stroke for long distances but the domestication of swimming[13] had saddled the sport with some customs and in his part of the world a crawl was customary. To be embraced and sustained by the light green water was less a pleasure, it seemed, than the resumption of a natural condition, and he would have liked to swim without trunks, but this was not possible, considering his project. He hoisted himself up on the far curb—he never used the ladder—and started across the lawn. When Lucinda asked where he was going he said he was going to swim home.

The only maps and charts he had to go by were remembered or imaginary but these were clear enough. First there were the Grahams, the Hammers, the Lears, the Howlands, and the Crosscups. He would cross Ditmar Street to the Bunkers and come, after a short portage, to the Levys, the Welchers, and the public pool in Lancaster. Then there were the Hallorans, the Sachses, the Biswangers, Shirley Adams, the Gilmartins, and the Clydes.[14] The day was lovely, and that he lived in a world so generously supplied with water seemed like a clemency, a beneficence. His heart was high and he ran across the grass. Making his way home by an uncommon route gave him the feeling that he was a pilgrim, and explorer, a man with a destiny,[15] and he knew that he would find friends all along the way; friends would line the banks of the Lucinda River.

He went through a hedge that separated the Westerhazys' land from the Grahams', walked under some flowering apple trees, passed the shed that housed their pump and filter, and came out at the Grahams' pool. "Why, Neddy," Mrs. Graham said, "what a marvelous surprise.

I've been trying to get you on the phone all morning. Here, let me get you a drink." He saw then, like any explorer, that the hospitable customs and traditions of the natives would have to be handled with diplomacy if he was ever going to reach his destination. He did not want to mystify or seem rude to the Grahams nor did he have the time to linger there. He swam the length of their pool and joined them in the sun and was rescued, a few minutes later, by the arrival of two carloads of friends from Connecticut. [16] During the uproarious reunions he was able to slip away. He went down by the front of the Grahams' house, stepped over a thorny hedge, and crossed a vacant lot to the Hammers'. Mrs. Hammer, looking up from her roses, saw him swim by although she wasn't quite sure who it was. The Lears heard him splashing past the open windows of their living room. The Howlands and the Crosscups were away. After leaving the Howlands' he crossed Ditmar Street and started for the Bunkers', where he could hear, even at that distance, the noise of a party.

The water refracted the sound of voices and laughter and seemed to suspend it in midair. The Bunkers' pool was on a rise and he climbed some stairs to a terrace where twenty-five or thirty men and women were drinking. The only person in the water was Rusty Towers, who floated there on a rubber raft. Oh, how bonny and lush were the banks of the Lucinda River! Prosperous men and women gathered by the sapphire-colored waters while caterer's men[17] in white coats passed them cold gin. Overhead a red de Haviland trainer[18] was circling around and around and around in the sky with something like the glee of a child in a swing. Ned felt a passing affection for the scene, a tenderness for the gathering, as if it was something he might touch. In the distance he heard thunder. As soon as Enid Bunker saw him she began to scream: "Oh, look who's here! What a marvelous surprise! When Lucinda said that you couldn't come I thought I'd *die*." She made her way to him through the crowd, and when they had finished kissing she led him to the bar, a progress that was slowed by the fact that he stopped to kiss eight or ten other women and shake the hands of as many men. A smiling bartender he had seen at a hundred parties gave him a gin and tonic[19] and he stood by the bar for a moment, anxious not to get stuck in any conversation that would delay his voyage. When he seemed about to be surrounded he dove in and swam close to the side to avoid colliding with Rusty's raft. At the far end of the pool he bypassed the Tomlinsons with a broad smile and jogged up the garden path. The gravel cut his feet but this was the only unpleasantness. The party was confined to the pool, and as he went toward the house he heard the brilliant, watery sound of voices fade, heard the noise of a radio from the Bunkers' kitchen, where someone was listening to a ball game. Sunday afternoon. He made his way through the parked cars and down the grassy border of their driveway[20] to Alewives Lane. He did not want to be seen on the road in his bathing trunks but there was no traffic and he made the short distance to the Levys' driveway, marked with a PRIVATE PROPERTY sign and a green tube for *The New York Times*.[21] All the doors and windows of the big house were open but there were no signs of life; not even a dog barked. He went around the side of the house to the pool and saw that the Levys had only recently left. Glasses and bottles and dishes of nuts were on a table at the deep end, where there was a bathhouse or gazebo,[22] hung with Japanese lanterns. After swimming the pool he got himself a glass and poured a drink. It was his fourth or fifth drink and he had swum nearly half the length of the Lucinda River. He felt tired, clean, and pleased at that moment to be alone; pleased with everything.

It would storm. The stand of cumulus cloud—that city—had risen and darkened, and while he sat there he heard the percussiveness of thunder again. The de Haviland trainer was still circling overhead and it seemed to Ned that he could almost hear the pilot laugh with pleasure in the afternoon; but when there was another peal of thunder he took off for home. A train whistle blew and he wondered what time it had gotten to be. Four? Five? He thought of the provincial station at that hour, where a waiter, his tuxedo concealed by a raincoat, a dwarf with some flowers wrapped in newspaper, and a woman who had been crying would be waiting for the local.[23] It was suddenly growing dark; it was that moment when the pin-headed birds seem to organize their song into some acute and knowledgeable recognition of the storm's approach. Then there was a fine noise of rushing water from the crown of an oak at his back, as if a spigot there had been turned. Then the noise of fountains came from the crowns of all the tall trees. Why did he love storms, what was the meaning of his excitement when the door sprang open and the rain wind fled rudely up the stairs, why had the simple task of shutting the windows of an old house seemed fitting and urgent, why did the first watery notes of a storm wind have for him the unmistakable sound of good news, cheer, glad tidings? Then there was an explosion, a smell of cordite, and rain lashed the Japanese lanterns that Mrs. Levy had bought in Kyoto[24] the year before last, or was it the year before that?

He stayed in the Levys' gazebo until the storm had passed. The rain had cooled the air and he shivered. The force of the wind had stripped a maple of its red and yellow leaves and scattered them over the grass and the water. Since it was midsummer the tree must be blighted, and yet he felt a peculiar sadness at this sign of autumn. He braced his shoulders, emptied his glass, and started for the Welchers' pool. This meant crossing the Lindleys' riding ring[25] and he was surprised to find it overgrown with grass and all the jumps dismantled. He wondered if the Lindleys had sold their horses or gone away for the summer and put them out to board. [26] He seemed to remember having heard something about the Lindleys and their horses but the memory was unclear. On he went, barefoot through the wet grass, to the Welchers', where he found their pool was dry.

This breach in his chain of water disappointed him absurdly, and he felt like some explorer who seeks a torrential headwater and finds a dead stream. He was disappointed and mystified. It was common enough to go away for the summer but no one ever drained his pool. The Welchers had definitely gone away. The pool furniture was folded, stacked, and covered with a tarpaulin. The bathhouse was locked. All the windows of the house were shut, and when he went around to the driveway in front he saw a FOR SALE sign nailed to a tree. When had he last heard from the Welchers—when, that is, had he and Lucinda last regretted an invitation to dine with them? It seemed only a week or so ago. Was his memory failing or had he so disciplined it in the repression of unpleasant facts that he had damaged his sense of the truth?[27] Then in the distance he heard the sound of a tennis game. This cheered him, cleared away all his apprehensions and let him regard the overcast sky and the cold air with indifference. This was the day that Neddy Merrill swam across the county. That was the day! He started off then for his most difficult portage.

Had you gone for a Sunday afternoon ride that day you might

have seen him, close to naked, standing on the shoulders of Route 424,[28] waiting for a chance to cross. You might have wondered if he was the victim of foul play, had his car broken down, or was he merely a fool. Standing barefoot in the deposits of the highway—beer cans, rags, and blowout patches[29]—exposed to all kinds of ridicule, he seemed pitiful. He had known when he started that this was a part of his journey—it had been on his maps—but confronted with the lines of traffic, worming through the summery light, he found himself unprepared. He was laughed at, jeered at, a beer can was thrown at him, and he had no dignity or humor to bring to the situation. He could have gone back, back to the Westerhazys', where Lucinda would still be sitting in the sun. He had signed nothing, vowed nothing, pledged nothing, not even to himself. Why, believing as he did, that all human obduracy was susceptible to common sense,[30] was he unable to turn back? Why was he determined to complete his journey even if it meant putting his life in danger? At what point had this prank, this joke, this piece of horseplay become serious? He could not go back, he could not even recall with any clearness the green water at the Westerhazys', the sense of inhaling the day's components, the friendly and relaxed voices saying that they had *drunk* too much. In the space of an hour, more or less, he had covered a distance that made his return impossible.

An old man, tooling down the highway at fifteen miles an hour, let him get to the middle of the road, where there was a grass divider.[31] Here he was exposed to the ridicule of the northbound traffic, but after ten or fifteen minutes he was able to cross. From here he had only a short walk to the Recreation Center at the edge of the village of Lancaster, where there were some handball courts and a public pool.

The effect of the water on voices, the illusion of brilliance and suspense, was the same here as it had been at the Bunkers' but the sounds here were louder, harsher, and more shrill, and as soon as he entered the crowded enclosure he was confronted with regimentation.[32] "ALL SWIMMERS MUST TAKE A SHOWER BEFORE USING THE POOL. ALL SWIMMERS MUST USE THE FOOTBATH. ALL SWIMMERS MUST WEAR THEIR IDENTIFICATION DISKS."[33] He took a shower, washed his feet in a cloudy and bitter solution, and made his way to the edge of the water. It stank of chlorine and looked to him like a sink. A pair of lifeguards in a pair of towers blew police whistles at what seemed to be regular intervals and abused the swimmers through a public address system.[34] Neddy remembered the sapphire water at the Bunkers' with longing and thought that he might contaminate himself—damage his own prosperousness and charm—by swimming in this murk, but he reminded himself that he was an explorer, a pilgrim, and that this was merely a stagnant bend in the Lucinda River. He dove, scowling with distaste, into the chlorine and had to swim with his head above water to avoid collisions, but even so he was bumped into, splashed, and jostled. When he got to the shallow end both lifeguards were shouting at him: "Hey, you, you without the identification disk, get outa[35] the water." He did, but they had no way of pursuing him and he went through the reek of suntan oil and chlorine out through the hurricane fence[36] and passed the handball courts. By crossing the road he entered the wooded part of the Halloran estate. The woods were not cleared and the footing was treacherous and difficult until he reached the lawn and the clipped beech hedge that encircled their pool.

The Hallorans were friends, an elderly couple of enormous wealth who seemed to bask in the suspicion that they might be Communists. They were zealous reformers but they were not Communists, and yet when they were accused, as they sometimes were, of subversion, it seemed to gratify and excite them. Their beech hedge was yellow and he guessed this had been blighted like the Levys' maple. He called hullo, hullo, to warn the Hallorans of his approach, to palliate his invasion of their privacy. The Hallorans, for reasons that had never been explained to him, did not wear bathing suits. No explanations were in order,[37] really. Their nakedness was a detail in their uncompromising zeal for reform and he stepped politely out of his trunks before he went through the opening in the hedge.

Mrs. Halloran, a stout woman with white hair and a serene face, was reading the *Times*. Mr. Halloran was taking beech leaves out of the water with a scoop. They seemed not surprised or displeased to see him. Their pool was perhaps the oldest in the country, a fieldstone rectangle, fed by a brook. It had no filter or pump and its waters were the opaque gold of the stream.

"I'm swimming across the county," Ned said.

"Why, I didn't know one could," exclaimed Mrs. Halloran.

"Well, I've made it from the Westerhazys'," Ned said. "That must be about four miles."

He left his trunks at the deep end, walked to the shallow end, and swam this stretch. As he was pulling himself out of the water he heard Mrs. Halloran say, "We've been *terribly* sorry to hear about all your misfortunes, Neddy."[38]

"My misfortunes?" Ned asked. "I don't know what you mean."

"Why, we heard that you'd sold the house and that your poor children..."

"I don't recall having sold the house," Ned said, "and the girls are at home."

"Yes," Mrs. Halloran sighed. "Yes..." Her voice filled the air with an unseasonable melancholy and Ned spoke briskly. "Thank you for the swim."

"Well, have a nice trip," said Mrs. Halloran.

Beyond the hedge he pulled on his trunks and fastened them. They were loose and he wondered if, during the space of an afternoon, he could have lost some weight. He was cold and he was tired and the naked Hallorans and their dark water had depressed him. The swim was too much for his strength but how could he have guessed this, sliding down the banister that morning and sitting in the Westerhazys' sun? His arms were lame. His legs felt rubbery and ached at the joints. The worst of it was the cold in his bones and the feeling that he might never be warm again. Leaves were falling down around him and he smelled wood smoke on the wind. Who would be burning wood at this time of year?

He needed a drink. Whiskey would warm him, pick him up, carry him through the last of his journey, refresh his feeling that it was original and valorous to swim across the county. Channel swimmers took brandy. He needed a stimulant. He crossed the lawn in front of the Hallorans' house and went down a little path to where they had built a house for their only daughter, Helen, and her husband, Eric Sachs. The Sachses' pool was small and he found Helen and her husband there.

"Oh, *Neddy*," Helen said. "Did you lunch at Mother's?"

"Not *really*," Ned said. "I *did* stop to see your parents." This seemed to be explanation enough. "I'm terribly sorry to break in on you like this but I've taken a chill and I wonder if you'd give me a drink."

"Why, I'd *love* to," Helen said, "but there hasn't been anything in this house to drink since Eric's operation. That was three years ago."

Was he losing his memory, had his gift for concealing painful facts let him forget that he had sold his house, that his children were in trouble, and that his friend had been ill? His eyes slipped from Eric's face to his abdomen, where he saw three pale, sutured scars, two of them at least a foot long. Gone was his navel, and what, Neddy thought, would the roving hand, bed-checking one's gifts at 3 A. M. ;make of a belly with no navel, no link to birth, this breach in the succession?[39]

"I'm sure you can get a drink at the Biswangers'," Helen said. "They're having an enormous do. [40] You can hear it from here. Listen!"

She raised her head and from across the road, the lawns, the gardens, the woods, the fields, he heard again the brilliant noise of voices over water. "Well, I'll get wet," he said, still feeling that he had no freedom of choice about his means of travel. He dove into the Sachses' cold water and, gasping, close to drowning, made his way from one end of the pool to the other. "Lucinda and I want *terribly* to see you," he said over his shoulder, his face set toward the Biswangers'. "We're sorry it's been so long and we'll call you *very* soon."

He crossed some fields to the Biswangers' and the sounds of revelry there. They would be honored to give him a drink, they would be happy to give him a drink. The Biswangers invited him and Lucinda for dinner four times a year, six weeks in advance. They were always rebuffed and yet they continued to send out their invitations, unwilling to comprehend the rigid and undemocratic realities of their society. They were the sort of people who discussed the price of things at cocktails, exchanged market tips during dinner, and after dinner told dirty stories to mixed company. [41] They did not belong to Neddy's set—they were not even on Lucinda's Christmas-card list. He went toward their pool with feelings of indifference, charity, and some unease, since it seemed to be getting dark and these were the longest days of the year. The party when he joined it was noisy and large. Grace Biswanger was the kind of hostess who asked the optometrist, the veterinarian, the real-estate dealer, and the dentist. No one was swimming and the twilight, reflected on the water of the pool, had a wintry gleam. There was a bar and he started for this. When Grace Biswanger saw him she came toward him, not affectionately as he had every right to expect, but bellicosely.

"Why, this party has everything," she said loudly, "including a gate crasher."[42]

She could not deal him a social blow[43]—there was no question about this and he did not flinch. "As a gate crasher," he asked politely, "do I rate a drink?"

"Suit yourself," she said. "You don't seem to pay much attention to invitations."

She turned her back on him and joined some guests, and he went to the bar and ordered a whiskey. The bartender served him but he served him rudely. His was a world in which the caterer's men kept the social score, and to be rebuffed by a part-time barkeep meant that he had suffered some loss of social esteem. Or perhaps the man was new and uninformed. Then he heard Grace at his back say: "They went for broke overnight[44]—nothing but income—and he showed up drunk one Sunday and asked us to loan him five thousand dollars...." She was always talking about money. It was worse than eating your peas off a knife.[45] He dove into the pool, swam its length and went away.

The next pool on his list, the last but two, belonged to his old mistress, Shirley Adams. If he had suffered any injuries at the Biswangers' they would be cured here. Love—sexual roughhouse[46] in fact—was the supreme elixir, the pain killer, the brightly colored pill that would put the spring back into his step, the joy of life in his heart. They had had an affair last week, last month, last year. He couldn't remember. It was he who had broken it off, his was the upper hand, and he stepped through the gate of the wall that surrounded her pool with nothing so considered as self-confidence. It seemed in a way to be his pool, as the lover, particularly the illicit lover, enjoys the possessions of his mistress with an authority unknown to holy matrimony. She was there, her hair the color of brass, but her figure, at the edge of the lighted, cerulean water, excited in him no profound memories. It had been, he thought, a lighthearted affair, although she had wept when he broke it off. She seemed confused to see him and he wandered if she was still wounded. Would she, God forbid, weep again?

"What do you want?" she asked.

"I'm swimming across the county."

"Good Christ. Will you ever grow up?"

"What's the matter?"

"If you've come here for money," she said, "I won't give you another cent."

"You could give me a drink."

"I could but I won't. I'm not alone."

"Well, I'm on my way."

He dove in and swam the pool, but when he tried to haul himsef up onto the curb he found that the strength in his arms and shoulders had gone, and he paddled[47] to the ladder and climbed out. Looking over his shoulder he saw, in the lighted bathhorse, a young man. Going out onto the dark lawn he smelled chrysanthemums or marigolds—some stubborn autumnal fragrance—on the night air, strong as gas. Looking overhead he saw that the stars had come out, but why should he seem to see Andromeda, Cepheus, and Cassiopeia?[48] What had become of the constellations of midsummer? He began to cry.

It was probably the first time in his adult life that he had ever cried, certainly the first time in his life that he had ever felt so miserable, cold, tired, and bewildered. He could not understand the rudeness of the caterer's barkeep or the rudeness of a mistress who had come to him on her knees and showered his trousers with tears. He had swum too long, he had been immersed too long, and his nose and his throat were sore from the water. What he needed then was a drink, some company, and some clean, dry clothes, and while he could have cut directly across the road to his home he went on to the Gilmartins' pool. Here, for the first time in his life, he did not dive but went down the steps into the icy water and swam a hobbled sidestroke[49] that he might have learned as a youth. He staggered with fatigue on his way to the Clydes' and paddled the length of their pool, stopping again and again with his hand on the curb to rest. He climbed up the ladder and wondered if he had the strength to get home. He had done what he wanted, he had swum the county, but he was so stupefied with exhaustion that his triumph seemed vague. Stooped, holding on to the gateposts for support, he turned up the driveway of his own house.

The place was dark. Was it so late that they had all gone to bed? Had Lucinda stayed at the Westerhazys' for supper? Had the girls joined her there or gone someplace else? Hadn't they agreed, as they usually did on Sunday, to regret all their invitations and stay at home? He tried the garage doors to see what cars were in but the doors were locked and rust came off the handles onto his hands. Going toward the house, he saw that the force of the thunderstorm had knocked one of the rain gutters loose. It hung down over the front door like an umbrella rib, but it could be fixed in the morning. The house was locked, and he thought that the stupid cook or the stupid maid must have locked the place up until he remembered that it had been some time since they had employed a maid or a cook. He shouted, pounded on the door, tried to force it with his shoulder, and then, looking in at the windows, saw that the place was empty.

〔注释〕

1. vestiarium＝vestry（拉丁语），教堂内存放法衣和祭具的房间。

2. the Audubon group：指奥杜邦学会的会员。奥杜邦学会是美国最大的私立自然资源保护组织，以美国博物学家、艺术家约翰·詹姆斯·奥杜邦的名字命名，其会员遍布全国。该组织的宗旨是向公众宣传保护野生动植物及其它自然资源的重要性，并教育人们合理利用这些资源为人类造福。

3. Neddy Merrill：主人公的姓名。注意 Neddy 是 Ned 的昵称，通常用来称呼儿童。作者使用这个称呼暗示主人公在心理上不甚成熟。

4. Aphrodite：希腊神话中爱和美的女神阿佛洛狄忒，相当于罗马神话中的女神维纳斯。此处指阿佛洛狄忒的青铜雕像。

5. He might have been compared to a summer's day, particularly the last hours of one：在英语文化中，夏日象征青春活力。莎士比亚在他的十四行诗第 18 首中就曾将其好友比做夏日。此处形容主人公奈迪虽人到中年，但仍保持着青春活力。

6. Bullet Park：作者虚构的纽约郊区地名。

7. by taking a dogleg to the southwest：向西南方向拐一个斜角。

8. His life was not confining and the delight he took in this observation could not be explained by its suggestion of escape.：他的生活无拘无束。他从观察中得到乐趣，其原因不能肤浅地解释为寻求解脱。

9. that quasi-subterranean stream：那条想象中的地下河流。

10. He had made a discovery, …and had a vague and modest idea of himself as a legendary figure.：注意这两句话中的讽刺意味。讽刺手法是契奇弗创作的突出特点，阅读时应仔细品味。

11. crawl：爬泳，自由泳。

12. flutter kick：自由泳时双腿轮换打水。

13. the domestication of swimming：指每家都有游泳池，游泳运动已普及到家庭。

14. First there were the Grahams, …and the Clydes.：这 3 句中提到的一系列人名都是奈迪计划在回家时要经过的人家。Portage 原为在连水陆路间搬运船只和货物的路线，注意这里的幽默意味。

15. a man with a destiny：掌握自己命运的人，有崇高目标的人。

16. Connecticut：美国康涅狄格州。

17. caterer's men：Caterer 是包办酒宴和筹办娱乐节目的人。遇有顾客举行酒会或宴会，他们派人上门服务。这里 caterer's men 指招待员。

18. de Haviland trainer：一种小型复翼教练机。

19. gin and tonic：加入滋补强身剂的杜松子酒。

20. driveway：住宅庭院中的汽车道。

21. a green tube for *The New York Times*：《纽约时报》专用的绿色投报筒。

22. gazebo：凉亭。

23. the local：慢车。

24. Kyoto：日本京都市。

25. riding ring：练马场。

26. put them out to board：把马寄养在别人家。

27. Was his memory failing or had he so disciplined it in the repression of unpleasant facts that he had damaged his sense of the truth?：作者借主人公的自问揭示其力图忘却不愉快的事的精神状态。下文中还有类似的心理描写。

28. Route 424：424 号公路。

29. blowout patches：破轮胎片。

30. all human obduracy was susceptible to common sense：人们的执拗易于顺从常理。

31. grass divider：公路中间植草的隔离带。

32. regimentation：此处指规章制度，有贬意。

33. identification disks：游泳者在公共游泳池租更衣箱时领到的标明号码的金属牌。

34. public address system：广播系统。

35. outa＝out of.

36. hurricane fence：防风栅。

37. in order：意为 required by the circumstance。

38. "We've been *terribly* sorry to hear about all your misfortunes, Neddy."：作者直到此时才借哈洛伦太太之口道出奈迪家遭遇不幸。在此之前的叙述曾给人以奈迪幸福愉快的印象。作者运用这一反差衬托奈迪痛苦的心情，也说明他进行长游的原因。

39. Gone was his navel, and what, Neddy thought, would the roving hand, bed-checking one's gifts at 3 A. M., make of a belly with no navel, no link to birth, this breach in the succession?：埃里克失去了肚脐，这使奈迪深思。当一个人凌晨三点醒来在床上抚摸自己天赐的身体时，发现缺少肚脐，也就是说在生命延续的系列中缺少一个与出生相联的环节，那他会作何感想呢？

40. do=party，entertainment，非正式用语。

41. mixed company：指有男有女。

42. gate crasher：不请自来的人，不速之客。

43. She could not deal him a social blow：意为她不能拒他于门外。

44. They went for broke overnight.：他们一夜之间就破了产。

45. eating your peas off a knife：按照西方的习俗，就餐时不用叉子而用刀子送食物入口是不礼貌的行为。

46. sexual roughhouse：两性的乱闹，床上的游戏。

47. paddled：踩水。

48. Andromeda，Cepheus，and Cassiopeia：仙女座、仙王座和仙后座。这些都是当地秋夜天空出现的星座。

49. sidestroke：侧泳。

BERNARD MALAMUD

〔作者介绍〕

伯纳德·马拉默德（Bernard Malamud，1914～1986），美国小说家。他出生于纽约布鲁克林区一个俄国移民家庭，1936年毕业于纽约市立学院，后入哥伦比亚大学学习，1942年获硕士学位。后来他在一所高中教书，1949年至1961年间，在勒俄勒冈州立大学执教，之后又到本宁顿大学及哈佛大学工作。

马拉默德自少年时代起便喜好文学和写作。1952年发表处女作《天生有才能的人》（*The Natural*），以嘲讽然而又富于同情的笔调探索美国棒球"神话"内涵及圣杯传说，并以此为主题叙述主人公罗伊·霍卜斯的短暂荣耀和最后遭遇。做为他的第1部作品，这篇小说写得很成功。1957年，他的《店员》问世。这部作品集中描写犹太人的生活，表现了马拉默德作品的中心主题，即在"只有爱才能照亮"的污秽的世界上赎罪，获得新生。许多评论家认为这是作者的最成功的作品。《魔桶》（*The Magic Barrel*，1958），是一部短篇小说集，获全国图书奖，同样反映出人生内在的悲剧和喜剧。《新生活》（*A New Life*，1963）是马拉默德的畅销书之一，集中描写了纽约一个英语教师在一处"学术荒原"——太平洋西北部一家学院——寻找新生和发现自我的故事；这部书虽然畅销，但未能避免反映美国大学生活的小说的通病，即'自由的"教员单枪匹马和"反动的"学院领导之间进行斗争，以及教员和学生、和其他教员的妻子之间的性关系。1963年他的《白痴第一》（*Idiots First*）问世，其中最优秀的故事和《店员》一样，描绘犹太人生活的世界。小说《基辅怨》（*The Fixer*，1966）描写1914年以前沙俄时代犹太人的痛苦生活；主人公雅可夫·博克这个可怜的犹太装配工由于被诬告出于宗教目的杀害了一个小基督徒，而在监狱中度过了两年半的非人生活，表现出他的坚强和忍耐性。《基辅怨》1967年获全国图书奖及普利策奖。1969年发表的《费尔德曼写照》（*Pictures of Fidelman*）是一部颇具滑稽意味的短篇小说集，系列地描写一位美国犹太艺术家在意大利旅行时的作为。《房客》（*The Tenants*，1971）叙述一个住在破旧的房子里、竭力在充满敌意的世界上寻觅仁慈的中年犹太作家的生活故事。1979年马拉默德发表他的第7部小说《杜宾的生活》(*Dubin's Lives*)，讲的是婚姻与不忠的故事：一位年事渐高的作家，欲逃脱腐朽的世界以求新生，从痛苦的经历中洞察到爱情在人生中的地位。《上帝的恩惠》(*The Grace of God*，1982)是作者虚构的寓言故事，具有浓郁的圣经风格，它描写在一场洪水般的核战争过后，一个幸免厄运的人在猿猴中开创新文明的故事。马拉默德的其他作品还包括《拉姆布兰特的帽子》(*Rembrandt's Hat*，1973)等。

The Assistant

〔作品简介〕

《店员》(*The Assistant*，1957)是马拉默德的主要作品之一，它描写的是典型的犹太人的生活及性格特点。

小说开首部分描述了莫里斯·鲍伯的艰难生活。鲍伯是犹太移民，在纽约布鲁克林区开了一家小杂货店，它的生意受街角处的一家熟食店的影响，正日益肃条。鲍伯为了维持家人—妻子艾达和女儿海伦—的生活，每日在简陋的小铺里度过漫长的空虚的一天，唯一的安慰是午后可上楼小憩片刻。一天晚上要关门时，两个抢劫者进店，因嫌钱少用手枪打伤了他的头。

过了些日子，一个名叫弗兰克·阿尔平的年轻人来到店里帮忙，希望被雇为店员。鲍伯拒不收留，后来当他发现弗兰克冻馁不堪的状况时，同意年轻人进店工作。弗兰克对顾客和气，生意有所改进。鲍伯的妻子和女儿对弗兰克有戒心：艾达极不愿意一个非犹太人闯进他们的生活中；海伦觉得年轻人有隐私。一天，弗兰克在从钱柜里偷钱时被鲍伯发现，迫不得已离去。同时，一家新的更大的店铺开始营业，鲍伯的小店受到破产威胁。鲍伯中煤气住院，弗兰克又返回店中，并说他欠鲍伯的“债”。他除经营小店外，晚上还在一家咖啡店做工，以维持小店的营业。鲍伯回家后，弗兰克终于承认自己是两个劫店者之一，而鲍伯却不吃惊，他说他早已知道。然而，他不能原谅年轻人在店里偷钱，因而又把他辞掉。不久，鲍伯死于肺炎，弗兰克又回店，继续做夜工以支撑小店和鲍伯一家。他的表现愈来愈象鲍伯，仿佛已变成另外一人。后来他行了割礼，逾越节后成为一个犹太人。

小说出色地刻画了一个心地善良、富于同情、忍受生活煎熬的诚实的犹太人鲍伯的形象。他有感染弗兰克改过自新的一种“犹太人气息”。鲍伯是犹太受苦者的典型。受苦是他的生活的主要特点之一；他在为人类赎罪而受苦。这是他善的本性的一部分：倘若他不善良，早已象他的犹太邻居那样在物质生活方面富裕起来了。小说令人信服地表明，鲍伯在营业上虽然失败，但他在精神和道德方面却取得了成功。弗兰克在他影响下浪子回头般的转变便是这种成功的最好的佐证。

《店员》巧妙地运用了犹太人的幽默来渲染鲍伯世界的犹太气息。作者选用了犹太民间素材，并用一种具有双重用途的荒诞性讽刺把它表现出来，收到了乐观和悲观两种情绪、希望和绝望两种心理状态相互作用而达到某种平衡的精妙效果。鲍伯极象犹太民间文学中那种一再跌倒但总是努力站起再试运气的傻瓜式人物，他明知自已命乖运蹇，却又不失信心和希望。《店员》的语言具有浓厚的犹太语味道，诸如倒装的句型、对动词及其补语的处理、修饰语的经常中断和插入等，不一而足。

这里选注的是小说第1章。

The Assistant

CHAPTER I

The early November street was dark though night had ended, but the wind, to the grocer's surprise, already clawed. It flung his apron into his face as he bent for two milk cases at the curb. Morris Bober dragged the heavy boxes to the door, panting. A large brown bag of hard rolls stood in the doorway along with the sour-faced, gray-haired Poilisheh huddled there, who wanted one.

"What's the matter so late?"

"Ten after six," said the grocer.

"Is cold," she complained.

Turning the key in the lock he let her in. Usually he lugged in the milk and lit the gas radiators, but the Polish woman was impatient. Morris poured the bag of rolls into a wire basket on the counter and found an unseeded one for her. Slicing it in halves, he wrapped it in white store paper. She tucked the roll into her cord market bag and left three pennies on the counter. He rang up the sale on an old noisy cash register, smoothed and put away the bag the rolls had come in, finished pulling in the milk, and stored the bottles at the bottom of the refrigerator. He lit the gas radiator at the front of the store and went into the back to light the one there.

He boiled up coffee in a blackened enamel pot and sipped it, chewing on a roll, not tasting what he was eating. After he had cleaned up he waited; he waited for Nick Fuso, the upstairs tenant, a young mechanic who worked in a garage in the neighborhood. Nick came in every morning around seven for twenty cents' worth of ham and a loaf of bread.

But the front door opened and a girl of ten entered, her face pinched and eyes excited. His heart held no welcome for her.

"My mother says," she said quickly, "can you trust her till tomorrow for a pound of butter, loaf of rye bread and a small bottle of cider vinegar?"

He knew the mother. "No more trust."

The girl burst into tears.

Morris gave her a quarter-pound of butter, the bread and vinegar. He found a penciled spot on the worn counter, near the cash register, and wrote a sum under "Drunk Woman." The total now came to $2.03, which he never hoped to see. But Ida would nag if she noticed a new figure, so he reduced the amount to $1.61. His peace—the little he lived with—was worth forty-two cents.

He sat in a chair at the round wooden table in the rear of the store and scanned, with raised brows, yesterday's Jewish paper that he had already thoroughly read. From time to time he looked absently through the square windowless window cut through the wall, to see if anybody had by chance come into the store. Sometimes when he looked up from his newspaper, he was startled to see a customer standing silently at the counter.

Now the store looked like a long dark tunnel.

The grocer sighed and waited. Waiting he thought he did poorly. When times were bad time was bad. It died as he waited, stinking in his nose.

A workman came in for a fifteen-cent can of King Oscar Norwegian sardines.

Morris went back to waiting. In twenty-one years the store had changed little. Twice he had painted all over, once added new shelving. The old-fashioned double windows at the front a carpenter had made into a large single one. Ten years ago the sign hanging outside fell to the ground but he had never replaced it. Once, when business hit a long good spell, he had had the wooden icebox ripped out and a new white refrigerated showcase put in. The showcase stood at the front in line with the old counter and he often leaned against it as he stared out of the window. Otherwise the store was the same. Years ago it was more a delicatessen; now, though he still sold a little delicatessen, it was more a poor grocery.

A half-hour passed. When Nick Fuso failed to appear, Morris got up and stationed himself at the front window, behind a large cardboard display sign the beer people had rigged up in an otherwise empty window. After a while the hall door opened, and Nick came out in a thick, hand-knitted green sweater. He trotted around the corner and soon returned carrying a bag of groceries. Morris was now visible at the window. Nick saw the look on his face but didn't look long. He ran into the house, trying to make it seem it was the wind that was chasing him. The door slammed behind him, a loud door.

The grocer gazed into the street. He wished fleetingly that he could once more be out in the open, as when he was a boy—never in the house, but the sound of the blustery wind frightened him. He thought again of selling the store but who would buy? Ida still hoped to sell. Every day she hoped. The thought caused him grimly to smile, although he did not feel like smiling. It was an impossible idea so he tried to put it out of his mind. Still, there were times when he went into the back, poured himself a spout of coffee and pleasantly thought of selling. Yet if he miraculously did, where would he go, where? He had a moment of uneasiness as he pictured himself without a roof over his head. There he stood in all kinds of weather, drenched in rain, and the snow froze on his head. No, not for an age had he lived a whole day in the open. As a boy, always running in the muddy, rutted streets of the village, or across the fields, or bathing with the other boys in the river; but as a man, in America, he rarely saw the sky. In the early days when he drove a horse and wagon, yes, but not since his first store. In a store you were entombed.

The milkman drove up to the door in his truck and hurried in, a bull, for his empties. He lugged out a caseful and returned with two half-pints of light cream. Then Otto Vogel, the meat provisions man, entered, a bushy-mustached German carrying a smoked liverwurst and string of wieners in his oily meat basket. Morris paid cash for the liverwurst; from a German he wanted no favors. Otto left with the wieners. The bread driver, new on the route, exchanged there fresh loaves for there stale and walked out without a word. Leo, the cake man, glanced hastily at the package cake on top of the refrigerator and callcd, "See you Monday, Morris."

Morris didn't answer.

Let hesitated. "Bad all over, Morris."

"Here is the worst."

"See you Monday."

A young housewife from close by bought sixty-three cents' worth; another came in for forty-one cents'. He had earned his first cash dollar for the day.

Breitbart, the bulb peddler, laid down his two enormous cartons of light bulbs and diffidently entered the back.

"Go in," Morris urged. He boiled up some tea and served it in a thick glass, with a slice of lemon. The peddler eased himself into a chair, derby hat and coat on, and gulped the hot tea, his Adam's apple bobbing.

"So how goes now?" asked the grocer.

"Slow," shrugged Breitbart.

Morris sighed. "How is your boy?"

Breitbart nodded absently, then picked up the Jewish paper and read. After ten minutes he got up, scratched all over, lifted across his thin shoulders the two large cartons tied together with clothesline and left.

Morris watched him go.

The world suffers. *He* felt every schmerz. [1]

At lunchtime Ida came down. She had cleancd the whole house.

Morris was standing before the faded couch, looking out of the rear window at the back yards. He bad been thinking of Ephraim. [2]

His wife saw his wet eyes.

"So stop sometimes, please." Her own grew wet.

He went to the sink, caught cold water in his cupped palms and dipped his face into it.

"The Italyener,"[3] he said, drying himself, "bought this morning across the street."

She was irritated. "Give him for twenty-nine dollars five rooms so he should spit in your face."

"A cold water flat," he reminded her.

"You put in gas radiators."

"Who says he spits? This I didn't say."

"You said something to him not nice?"[4]

"Me?"

"Then why he went across the street?"

"Why? Go ask him," he said angrily.

"How much you took in till now?"

"Dirt."

She turned away.

He absent-mindedly scratched a match and lit a cigarette.

"Stop with the somking," she nagged.

He took a quick drag, clipped the butt with his thumb nail and quickly thrust it under his apron into his pants pocket. The smoke made him cough. He coughed harshly, his face lit like a tomato. Ida held her hands over her ears. Finally he brought up a gob of phlegm and wiped his mouth with his handkerchief, then his eyes.

"Cigarettes," She said bitterly. "Why don't you listen what the doctor tells you?"

"Doctors," he remarked.

Afterward he noticed the dress she was wearing. "What is the picnic?"

Ida said, embarrassed, "I thought to myself maybe will come today the buyer."[5]

She was fifty-one, nine years younnger than he, her thick hair still almost all black. But her face was lined, and her legs hurt when she shood too long on them, although she now wore shoes with arch supports. She had waked that morning resenting the grocer for having dragged her, so many years ago, out of a Jewish neighborhood into this. She missed to this day their old friends and landsleit[6]—lost for parnusseh unrealized.[7] That was bad enough, but on top of their isolation, the endless worry about money embittered her. She shared unwillingly the grocer's fate though she did not show it and her dissatisfaction went no farther than nagging—her guilt that she had talked him into a grocery store when he was in the first year of evening high school, preparing, he had said, for pharmacy. He was, through the years, a hard man to move. In the past she could sometimes resist him, but the weight of his endurance was too much for her now.

"A buyer," Morris grunted, "will come next Purim."

"Don't be so smart. Karp[8] telephoned him."

"Karp," he said in disgust. "Where he telephoned—the cheapskate?"

"Here."

"When?"

"Yesterday. You were sleeping."

"What did he told him?"

"For sale a store—yours, cheap."

"What do you mean cheap?"

"The key is worth now nothing. For the stock and the fixtures that they are worth also nothing, maybe three thousand, maybe less."

"I paid four."

"Twenty-one years ago," she said irritably. "So don't sell, go in auction."

"He wants the house too?"

"Karp don't know. Maybe."

"Big mouth. Imagine a man that they held him up[9] four times in the last three years and he still don't take in a telephone. What he says ain't worth a cent. He promised me he wouldn't put in a grocery around the corner, but what did he put? —a grocery. Why does he bring me buyers? Why didn't he keep out the German[10] around the corner?"

She sighed. "He tries to help you now because he feels sorry for you."

"Who needs his sorrow?" Morris said. "Who needs him?"

"So why *you* didn't have the sense to make out of your grocery a wine and liquor store when came out the licenses?"

"Who had cash for stock?"

"So if you don't have, don't talk."

"A business for drunken bums." [11]

"A business if a business. What Julius Karp takes in next door in a day we don't take in in two weeks."

But Ida saw he was annoyed and changed the subject.

"I told you to oil the floor."

"I forgot."

"I asked you special. By now would be dry."

"I will do later."

"Later the customers will walk in the oil and make everything dirty."

"What customers?" he shouted. "Who customers? Who comes in here?"

"Go," she said quietly. "Go upstairs and sleep. I will oil myself."

But he got out the oil can and mop and oiled the floor until the wood shone darkly. No one had come in.

She had prepared his soup. "Helen left this morning without breakfast."

"She wasn't hungry."

"Something worries her."

He said with sarcasm, "What worries her?" Meaning: the store, his health, that most of her meager wages went to keep up payments on the house; that she had wanted a college education but had got instead a job she disliked. Her father's daughter, no wonder she didn't feel like eating.

"If she will only get married," Ida murmured.

"She will get."

"Soon." She was on the verge of tears.

He grunted.

"I don't understand why she don't see Nat Pearl anymore. All summer they went together like lovers."

"A showoff."

"He'll be someday a rich lawyer."

"I don't like him."

"Louis Karp also likes her. I wish she will give him a chance."

"A stupe," Morris said, "like the father."

"Everybody is a stupe but not Morris Bober."

He was staring out at the back yards.

"Eat already and go to sleep," she said impatiently.

He finished the soup and went upstairs. The going up was easier than coming down. In the bedroom, sighing, he drew down the black window shades. He was half asleep, so pleasant was the anticipation. Sleep was his one true refreshment; it excited him to go to sleep. Morris took off his apron, tie and trousers, and laid them on a chair. Sitting at the edge of the sagging wide bed, he unlaced his misshapen shoes and slid under the cold covers in shirt, long underwear and white socks. He nudged his eye into th pillow and waited to grow warm. He crawled toward sleep. But upstairs Tessie Fuso was running the vacuum cleaner, and though the grocer tried to blot the incident out of his mind, he remembered Nick's visit to the German and on the verge of sleep felt bad.

He recalled the bad times he had lived through, but now times were worse than in the past; now they were impossible. His store was always a marginal one, up today, down tomorrow—as the wind blew. Overnight business could go down enough to hurt; yet as a rule it slowly recovered—sometimes it seemed to take forever—went up, not high enough to be really *up*, only not down. When he had first bought the grocery it was all right for the neighborhood; it had got worse as the neighborhood had. Yet even a year ago, staying open seven days a week, sixteen hours a day, he could still eke out a living. What kind of living? —a living; you lived. Now, though he toiled the same hard hours, he was close to bankruptcy, his patience torn. In the past when bad times came he had somehow lived through them, and when good times returned, they more or less returned to him. But now, since the appearance of H. Schmitz across the street ten months ago, all times were bad.

Last year a broken tailor, a poor man with a sick wife, had locked up his shop and gone away, and from the minute of the store's emptiness Morris had felt a gnawing anxiety. He went with hesitation to Karp, who owned the building, and asked him to please keep out another grocery. In this kind of neighborhood one was more than enough. If another squeezed in they would both starve. Karp answered that the neighborhood was better than Morris gave it credit (for schnapps, thought the grocer), but he promised he would look for another tailor or maybe a shoemaker, to rent to. He said so but the grocer didn't believe him. Yet weeks went by and the store stayed empty. Though Ida pooh-poohed his worries, Morris could not overcome his underlying dread. Then one day, as he daily expected, there appeared a sign in the empty store window, announcing the coming of a new fancy delicatessen and grocery.

Morris ran to Karp. "What did you do to me?"

The liquor dealer said with a one-shouldered shrug, "You saw how long stayed empty the store. Who will pay my taxes? But don't worry," he added, "he'll sell more delicatessen but you'll sell more groceries. Wait, you'll see he'll bring you in customers."

Morris groaned; he knew his fate.

Yet as the days went by, the store still sitting empty—emptier, he found himself thinking maybe the new business would never materialize. Maybe the man had changed his mind. It was possible he had seen how poor the neighborhood was and would not attemtp to open the new place. Morris wanted to ask Karp if he had guessed right but could not bear to humiliate himself further.

Often after he had locked his grocery at night, he would go secretly around the corner and cross the quiet street. The empty store, dark and deserted, was one door to the left of the corner drugstore; and if no one was looking the grocer would peer through its dusty window, trying to see through shadows whether the emptiness had changed. For two months it stayed the same, and every night he went away reprieved. Then one time—after he saw that Karp was, for once, avoiding him—he spied a web of shelves sprouting from the rear wall, and that shattered the hope he had climbed into.

In a few days the shelves stretched many arms along the other walls, and soon the whole tiered and layered place glowed with new paint. Morris told himself to stay away but he could not help coming nightly to inspect, appraise, then guess the damage, in dollars, to himself. Each night as he looked, in his mind he destroyed what had been built, tried to make of it nothing, but the growth was too quick. Every day the place flowered with new fixtures—streamlined counters, the latest refrigerator, fluorescent lights, a fruit stall, a chromium cash register; then from the wholesalers arrived a mountain of cartons and wooden boxes of all sizes, and one night there appeared in the white light a stranger, a gaunt German with a German pompadour, who spent the silent night hours, a dead cigar stuck in his teeth, packing out symmetrical rows of brightly labeled cans, jars, gleaming bottles. Though Morris hated the new store, in a curious way he loved it too, so that sometimes as he entered his own old-fashioned place of business, he could not stand the sight of it; and now he understood why Nick Fuso had that morning run around the corner and crossed the street—to taste the newness of the place and be waited on by Heinrich Schmitz, an energetic German dressed like a doctor, in a white duck jacket. And that was where many of his other customers had gone, and stayed, so that his own poor living was cut in impossible half.

Morris tried hard to sleep but couldn't and grew restless in bed. After another quarter of an hour he decided to dress and go downstairs, but there drifted into his mind, with ease and no sorrow, the form and image of his boy Ephraim, gone so long from him, and he fell deeply and calmly asleep.

Helen Bober squeezed into a subway seat between two women and was on the last page of a chapter when a man dissolved in front of her and another appeared; she knew without looking that Nat Pearl was standing there. She thought she would go on reading, but couldn't, and shut her book.

"Hello, Helen." Nat touched a gloved hand to a new hat. He was cordial but as usual held back something—his future. He carried a fat law book, so she was glad to be protected with a book of her own. But not enough protected, for her hat and coat felt suddenly shabby, a trick of the mind, because on her they would still do.

"*Don Quixote*"?

She nodded.

He seemed respectful, then said in an undertone, "I haven't seen you a long time. Wlihere've you boon keeping yourself?"

She blushed under her clothes.

"Did I offend you in some way or other?"

Both of the women beside her seemed stolidly deaf. One held a rosary in her heavy hand.

"No." The offense was hers against herself.

"So what's the score?" Nat's voice was low, his gray eyes annoyed.

"No score," she murmured.

"How so?"

"You're you, I'm me."

This he considered a minute, then remarked, "I haven't much of a head for oracles."

But she felt she had said enough.

He tried another way. "Betty asks for you."

"Give her my best." She had not meant it but this sounded funny because they all lived on the same block, separated by one house.

Tight-jawed, he opened his book. She returned to hers, hiding her thoughts behind the antics of a madman until memory overthrew him[12] and she found herself ensnared in scenes of summer that she would gladly undo, although she loved the season; but how could you undo what you had done again in the fall, unwillingly willing? Virginity she thought she had parted with without sorrow, yet was surprised by torments of conscience, or was it disappointment at being valued under her expectations? Nat Pearl, handsome, cleft-chinned, gifted, ambitious, had wanted without too much trouble a lay and she, half in love, had obliged and regretted. Not the loving, but that it had taken her so long to realize how little he wanted. Not her, Helen Bober.

Why should he? —magna cum laude, Columbia, now in his second year at law school, she only a high school graduate with a year's evening college credit mostly in lit; he with firstrate prospects, also rich friends he had never bothered to introduce her to; she as poor as her name sounded, with little promise of a better future. She had more than once asked herself if she had meant by her favors to work up a claim on him. Always she denied it. She had wanted, admittedly, satisfaction, but more than that—respect for the giver of what she had to give, had hoped desire would become more than just that. She wanted, simply, a future in love. Enjoyment she had somehow had, felt very moving the freedom of fundamental intimacy with a man. Though she wished for more of the same, she wanted it without aftermath of conscience, or pride, or sense of waste. So she promised herself next time it would go the other way; first mutual love, then loving, harder maybe on the nerves, but easier in memory. Thus she had reasoned, until one night in September, when coming up to see his sister Betty, she had found herself alone in the house with Nat and had done again what she had promised herself she wouldn't. Afterward she fought self-hatred. Since then, to this day, without telling him why, she had avoided Nat Pearl.

Two stations before their stop, Helen shut her book, got up in silence and left the train. On the platform, as the train moved away, she caught a glimpse of Nat standing before her empty seat, calmly reading.

She walked on, lacking, wanting, not wanting, not happy.

Coming up the subway steps, she went into the park by a side entrance, and despite the sharp wind and her threadbare coat, took the long way home. The leafless trees left ber with unearned sadness. She mourned the long age before spring and feared loneliness in winter. Wishing she hadn't come, she left the park, searching the faces of strangers although she couldn't stand their stares. She went quickly along the Parkway, glancing with envy into the lighted depth of private houses that were, for no feason she could give, except experience, not for her. She promised herself she would save every cent possible and register next fall for a full program at NYU, night.

When she reached her block, a row of faded yellow brick houses, two stories squatting on ancient stores, Sam Pearl, stifling a yawn, was reaching into his corner candy store window to put on the lamp. He snapped the string and the dull glow from the fly-specked globe fell upon her. Helen quickened her step. Sam, always sociable, a former cabbie, bulky, wearing bifocals and chewing gum, beamed at her but she pretended not to see. Most of the day he sat hunched over dope sheets spread out on the soda fountain counter, smoking as he chewed gum, making smeary marks with a pencil stub under horses' names. He neglected the store; his wife Goldie was the broad-backed one, yet she did not much complain, because Sam's luck with the nags was exceptional and he had nicely supported Nat in college until the scholarships started rolling in.

Around the corner, through the many-bottled window that blinked in neon "KARP wines and liquors," she glimpsed paunchy Julius Karp, with bushy eyebrows and an ambitious mouth, blowing imaginary dust off a bottle as he slipped a deft fifth of something into a paper bag, while Louis, slightly popeyed son and heir, looking up from clipping to the quick his poor fingernails, smiled amiably upon a sale. The Karps, Pearls and Bobers, representing attached houses and stores, but otherwise detachment, made up the small Jewish segment of this gentile community. They had somehow, her father first, then Karp, later Pearl, drifted together here where no other Jews dwelt, except on the far fringes of the neighborhood. None of them did well and were too poor to move elsewhere until Karp, who with a shoe store that barely made him a living, got the brilliant idea after Prohibition gurgled down the drain and liquor licenses were offered to the public, to borrow cash from a white-bearded rich uncle and put in for one. To everybody's surprise he got the license, though Karp, when asked how, winked a heavy-lidded eye and answered nothing. Within a short time after cheap shoes had become expensive bottles, in spite of the poor neighborhood—or maybe because of it, Helen supposed—he became astonishingly successful and retired his overweight wife from the meager railroad flat above the store to a big house on the Parkway—from which she hardly ever stepped forth—the house complete with two-car garage and Mercury,[13] and at the same time as Karp changed his luck—to hear her father tell it—he became wise without brains.

The grocer, on the other hand, had never altered his fortune, unless degrees of poverty meant alteration, for luck and he were, if not natural enemies, not good friends. He labored long hours, was the soul of honesty—he could not escape his honesty, it was bedrock; to cheat would cause an explosion in him, yet he trusted cheaters—coveted nobody's nothing and always got poorer. The harder he worked—his toil was a form of time devouring time—the less he seemed to have. He was Morris Bober and could be nobody more fortunate. With that name you had no sure sense of property, as if it were in your blood and history not to possess, or if by some miracle to own something, to do so on the verge of loss. At the end you were sixty and had less than at thirty. It was, she thought, surely a talent.

Helen removed her hat as she entered the grocery. "Me," she called, as she had from childhood. It meant that whoever was sitting in the back should sit and not suddenly think he was going to get rich.

Morris awoke, soured by the long afternoon sleep. He dressed, combed his hair with a broken comb and trudged downstairs, a heavy-bodied man with sloping shoulders and bushy gray hair in need of a haircut. He came down with his apron on. Although he felt chilly he poured out a cup of cold coffee, and backed against the radiator, slowly sipped it. Ida sat at the table, reading.

"Why you let me sleep so long?" the grocer complained.

She didn't answer.

"Yesterday or today's paper?"

"Yesterday."

He rinsed the cup and set it on the top of the gas range. In the store he rang up "no sale" and took a nickel out of the drawer Morris lifted the lid of the cash register, struck a match on the underside of the counter, and holding the flame cupped in his palm, peered at the figure of his earnings. Ida had taken in three dollars. Who could afford a paper?

Nevertheless he went for one, doubting the small pleasure he would get from it. What was so worth reading about the world? Through Karp's window, as he passed, he saw Louis waiting on a customer while four others crowded the counter. Der oilem iz a goilem. [14] Morris took the *Forward* from the newstand and dropped a nickel into the cigar box. Sam Pearl, working over a green racing sheet, gave him a wave of his hammy hand. They never bothered to talk. What did he know about race horses? What did the other know of the tragic quality of life? Wisdom flew over his hard head.

The grocer returned to the rear of his store and sat on the couch, letting the diminishing light in the yard fall upon the paper. He read nearsightedly, with eyes stretched wide, but his thoughts would not let him read long. He put down the newspaper.

"So where is your buyer?" he asked Ida.

Looking absently into the store she did not reply.

"You should sell long ago the store," she remarked after a minute.

"When the store was good, who wanted to sell? After came bad times, who wanted to buy?"

"Everything we did too late. The store we didn't sell in time. I said, 'Morris, sell now the store.' You said, 'Wait.' What for? The house we bought too late, so we have still a big mortgage that it's hard to pay every month. 'Don't buy,' I said, 'times are bad.' 'Buy,' you said, 'will get better. We will save rent.'"

He answered nothing. If you had failed to do the right thing, talk was useless.

When Helen entered, she asked if the buyer had come. She had forgotten about him but remembered when she saw her mother's dress.

Opening her purse, she took out her pay check and handed it to her father. The grocer, without a word, slipped it under his apron into his pants pocket.

"Not yet," Ida answered, also embarrassed. "Maybe later."

"Nobody goes in the night to buy a store," Morris said. "The time to go is in the day to see how many customers. If this man comes here he will see with one eye the store is dead, then he will run home."

"Did you eat lunch?" Ida asked Helen.

"Yes."

"What did you eat?"

"I don't save menus, Mama."

"Your supper is ready." Ida lit the flame under the pot on the gas range.

"What makes you think he'll come today?" Helen asked her.

"Karp told me yesterday. He knows a refugee that he looks to buy a grocery. He works in the Bronx, so he will be here late."

Morris shook his head.

"He's a young man," Ida went on, "maybe thirty—thirtytwo. Karp says he saved a little cash. He can make alterations, buy new goods, fix up modern, advertise a little and make here a nice business."

"Karp should live so long," the grocer said.

"Let's eat." Helen sat at the table.

Ida said she would eat later.

"What about you, Papa?"

"I am not hungry." He picked up his paper.

She ate alone. It would be wonderful to sell out and move but the possibility struck her as remote. If you had lived so long in one place, all but two years of your life, you didn't move out overnight.

Afterward she got up to help with the dishes but Ida wouldn't let her. "Go rest," she said.

Helen took her things and went upstairs.

She hated the drab five-room flat; a gray kitchen she used for breakfast so she could quickly get out to work in the morning. The living room was colorless and cramped; for all its overstuffed furniture of twenty years ago it seemed barren because it was lived in so little, her parents being seven days out of seven in the store; even their rare visitors, when invited upstairs, preferred to remain in the back. Sometimes Helen asked a friend up, but she went to other people's houses if she had a choice. Her bedroom was another impossibility, tiny, dark, despite the two by three foot opening in the wall, through which she could see the living room windows; and at night Morris and Ida had to pass through her room to get to theirs, and from their bedroom back to the bathroom. Thev had several times talked of giving her the big room, the only comfortable one in the house, but there was no place else that would hold their double bed. The fifth room was a small icebox off the second floor stairs, in which Ida stored a few odds and ends of clothes and furniture. Such was home. Helen had once in anger remarked that the place was awful to live in, and it had made her feel bad that her father had felt so bad.

She heard Morris's slow footsteps on the stairs. He came aimlessly into the living room and tried to relax in a stiff armchair. He sat with sad eyes, saying nothing, which was how he began when he wanted to say something.

When she and her brother were kids, at least on Jewish holidays Morris would close the store and venture forth to Second Avenue to see a Yiddish play, or take the family visiting; but after Ephraim died he rarely went beyond the corner. Thinking about his life always left her with a sense of the waste of her own.

She looks like a little bird, Morris thought. Why should she be lonely? Look how pretty she looks. Whoever saw such blue eyes?

He reached into his pants pocket and took out a five-dollar bill.

"Take," he said, rising and embarrassedly handing her the money. "You will need for shoes."

"You just gave me five dollars downstairs."

"Here is five more."

"Wednesday was the first of the month, Pa."

"I can't take away from you all your pay."

"You're not taking, I'm giving."

She made him put the five away. He did, with renewed shame. "What did I ever give you? Even your college education I took away."

"It was my own decision not to go, yet maybe I will yet. You can never tell."

"How can you go? You are twenty-three years old."

"Aren't you always saying a person's never too old to go to school?"

"My child," he sighed, "for myself I don't care, for you I want the best but what did I give you?"

"I'll give myself," she smiled. "There's hope."

With this he had to be satisfied. He still conceded her a future.

But before he went down, he said gently, "What's the matter you stay home so much lately? You had a fight with Nat?"

"No." Blushing, she answered, "I don't think we see things in the same way."

He hadn't the heart to ask more.

Going down, he met Ida on the stairs and knew she would cover the same ground.

In the evening there was a flurry of business. Morris's mood quickened and he exchanged pleasantries with the customers. Carl Johnsen, the Swedish painter, whom he hadn't seen in weeks, came in with a wet smile and bought two dollars' worth of beer, cold cuts and sliced Swiss cheese. The grocer was at first worried he would ask to charge—he had never paid what he owed on the books before Morris had stopped giving trust—but the painter had the cash. Mrs. Anderson, an old loyal customer, bought for a dollar. A stranger then came in and left eighty-eight cents. After him two more customers appeared. Morris felt a little surge of hope. Maybe things were picking up. But after half-past eight his hands grew heavy with nothing to do. For years he had been the only one for miles around who stayed open at night and had just about made a living from it, but now Schmitz matched him hour for hour. Morris sneaked a little smoke, then began to cough. Ida pounded on the floor upstairs, so he clipped the butt and put it away. He felt restless and stood at the fromt window, watching the street. He watched a trolley go by. Mr. Lawler, formerly a customer, good for at least a fiver on Friday nights, passed the store. Morris hadn't seen him for months but knew where he was going. Mr Lawler averted his gaze and hurried along. Morris watched him disappear around the corner. He lit a match and again checked the register—nine and a half dollars, not even expenses.

Julius Karp opened the front door and poked his foolish head in.

"Podolsky came?"

"Who Podolsky?"

"The refugee."

Morris said in annoyance, "What refugee?"

With a grunt Karp shut the door behind him. He was short, pompous, a natty dresser in his advanced age. In the past, like Morris, he had toiled long hours in his shoe store, now he stayed all day in silk pajamas until it came time to relieve Louis before supper. Though the little man was insensitive and a blunderer, Morris had got along fairly well with him, but since Karp had rented the tailor shop to another grocer, sometimes they did not speak. Years ago Karp had spent much time in the back of the grocery, complaining of his poverty as if it were a new invention and he its first victim. Since his success with wines and liquors he came in less often, but he still visited Morris more than his welcome entitled him to, usually to run down the grocery and spout unwanted advice. His ticket of admission was his luck, which he gathered wherever he reached, at a loss, Morris thought, to somebody else. Once a drunk had heaved a rock at Karp's window, but it had shattered his. Another time, Sam Pearl gave the liquor dealer a tip on a horse, then forgot to place a bet himself. Karp collected five hundred for his ten-dollar bill. For years the grocer had escaped resenting the man's good luck, but lately he had caught himself wishing on him some small misfortune.

"Podolsky is the one I called up to take a look at your gesheft,"[15] Karp answered.

"Who is this refugee, tell me, an enemy yours?"

Karp stared at him unpleasantly.

"Does a man," Morris insisted, "send a friend he should buy such a store that you yourself took away from it the best business?"

"Podolsky ain't you," the liquor dealer replied. "I told him about this place. I said, 'The neighborhood is improving. You can buy cheap and build up this store. It's run down for years, nobody changed anything there for twenty years.'"

"You should live so long how much I changed—" Morris began but he didn't finish, for Karp was at the window, peering nervously into the dark street.

"You saw that gray car that just passed," the liquor dealer said. "This is the third time I saw it in the last twenty minutes." His eyes were restless.[16]

Morris knew what worried him. "Put in a telephone in your store," he advised, "so you will feel better."

Karp watched the street for another minute and worriedly replied, "Not for a liquor store in this neighborhood. If I had a telephone, every drunken bum would call me to make deliveries, and when you go there they don't have a cent."

He opened the door but shut it in afterthought. "Listen, Morris," he said, lowering his voice, "if they come back again, I will lock my front door and put out my lights. Then I will call you from the back window so you can telephone the police."

"This will cost you five cents," Morris said grimly.

"My credit is class A."

Karp left the grocery, disturbed.

God bless Julius Karp, the grocer thought. Without him I would have my life too easy. God made Karp so a poor grocery man will not forget his life is hard. For Karp, he thought it was miraculously not so hard, but what was there to envy? He would allow the liquor dealer his bottles and gelt just not to be him.[17] Life was bad enough.

At nine-thirty a stranger came in for a box of matches. Fifteen minutes later Morris put out the lights in his window. The street was deserted except for an automobile parked in front of the laundry across the car tracks. Morris peered at it sharply but could see nobody in it. He considered locking up and going to bed, then decided to stay open the last few minutes. Sometimes a person came in at a minute to ten. A dime was a dime.

A noise at the side door which led into the hall frightened him.

"Ida?"

The door opened slowly. Tessie Fuso came in in her housecoat, a homely Italian girl with a big face.

"Are you closed. Mr. Bober?" she asked embarrassedly.

"Come in," said Morris.

"I'm sorry I came through the back way but I was undressed and didn't want to go out in the street."

"Don't worry."

"Please give me twenty cents' ham for Nick's lunch tomorrow."

He understood. She was making amends for Nick's trip around the corner that morning.[18] He cut her an extra slice of ham.

Tessie bough also a quart of milk, package of paper napkins and loaf of bread. When she had gone he lifted the register lid. Ten dollars. He thought he had long ago touched bottom but now knew there was none.

I slaved my whole life for nothing, he thought.

Then he heard Karp calling him from the rear. The grocer went inside worn out.

Raising the window he called harshly, "What's the matter there?"

"Telephone the police," cried Karp. "The car is parked across the street."

"What car?"

"The holdupniks."

"There is nobody in this car, I saw myself."

"For God's sake, I tell you call the police. I will pay for the thelephone."

Morris shut the window. He looked up the phone number and was about to dial the police when the store door opened and he hurried inside.

Two men were standing at the other side of the counter, with handkerchiefs over their faces. One wore a dirty yellow clotted one, the other's was white. The one with the white one began pulling out the store lights. It took the grocer a halfminute to comprehend that he, not Karp, was their victim.

Morris sat at table, the dark light of the dusty bulb falling on his head, gazing dully at the few crumpled bills before him, including Helen's check, and the small pile of silver. The gunman with the dirty handkerchief, fleshy, wearing a fuzzy black hat, waved a pistol at the grocer's head. His pimply brow was thick with sweat; from time to time with furtive eyes he glanced into the darkened store. The other, a taller man in an old cap and torn sneakers, to control his trembling leaned against the sink, cleaning his fingernails with a matchstick. A cracked mirror hung behind him on the wall above the sink and every so often he turned to stare into it.

"I know damn well this ain't everything you took in," said the heavy one to Morris, in a hoarse, unnatural voice. "Where've you got the rest hid?"

Morris, sick to his stomach, couldn't speak.

"Tell the goddamn truth." He aimed the gun at the grocer's mouth.

"Times are bad," Morris muttered.

"You're a Jew liar."

The man at the sink fluttered his hand, catching the other's attention. They met in the center of the room, the other with the cap hunched awkwardly over the one in the fuzzy hat, whispering into his ear.

"No," snapped the heavy one sullenly.

His partner bent lower, whispering earnestly through his handkerchief.

"I say he hid it," the heavy one snarled, "and I'm gonna get it if I have to crack his goddam head."

At the table he whacked the grocer across the face.

Morris moaned.

The one at the sink hastily rinsed a cup and filled it with water. He brought it to the grocer, spilling some on his apron as he raised the cup to his lips.

Morris tried to swallow but managed only a dry sip. His frightened eyes sought the man's but he was looking elsewhere.

"Please," murmured the grocer.

"Hurry up," warned the one with the gun.

The tall one straightened up and gulped down the water. He rinsed the cup and placed it on a cupboard shelf.

He then began to hunt among the cups and dishes there and pulled out the post on the bottom. Next, he went hurriedly through the drawers of an old bureau in the room, and on hands and knees searched under the couch. He ducked into the store, removed the empty cash drawer from the register and thrust his hand into the slot, but came up with nothing.

Returning to kitchen he took the other by the arm and whispered to him urgently.

The heavy one elbowed him aside.

"We better scram out of here.

"Are you gonna go chicken on me?"

"That's all the dough he has, let's beat it."

"Business is bad," Morris muttered.

"Your Jew ass is bad, you understand?"

"Don't hurt me."

"I will give you your last chance. Where have you got it hid?"

"I am a poor man." He spoke through cracked lips.

The one in the dirty handkerchief raised his gun. The other, staring into the mirror, waved frantically, his black eyes bulging, but Morris saw the blow descend and felt sick of himself, of soured expectations, endless frustration, the years gone up in smoke, he could not begin to count how many. He had hoped for much in America and got little. And because of him Helen and Ida had less. He had defrauded them, he and the bloodsucking store.

He fell without a cry. The end fitted the day. It was his luck, others had better.

〔注释〕

1. schmerz：德文，意为"痛苦"。

2. Ephraim：鲍伯死去的儿子。

3. Italyener＝Italian；指上文的 Nick Fuso。

4. You said something to him not nice：鲍伯夫妇一直在商议把小铺卖掉，但鲍伯并不想卖，所以他对买主讲话不客气。

5. the buyer：买主。

6. landsleit：犹太语，意"同乡"。

7. parnusseh：犹太语，意"生计"。

8. Karp：指 Julius Karp，鲍伯的邻居，也是犹太人，最初开鞋店，后来开酒店致富。

9. held him up：抢劫他。

10. the German：指 H. Schmitz，他的店铺对鲍伯威胁很大。

11. A business for drunken bums：指 Julius Karp 开的酒店。

12. hiding her thoughts behind the antics of a madman until memory overthrew him：把她的想法隐藏在一个疯人的古怪行为的后面，直到记忆把他推倒之时。a madman：指海伦在读的《唐·吉诃德》的主人公；memory：指海伦忆起夏天的经历，因而开始走神。

13. Mercury：福特汽车公司生产的一种汽车。

14. Der oilem iz a goilem：这个人是蠢货。这句话引自犹太诗人哈尔波恩(Leivick Halpurn) 1921 年所写剧作《蠢货》(*Der Goilem*)，此剧用犹太语写成，在欧、美上演多年，并拍成德文、法文、犹太语电影。

15. gesheft：铺子。

16. His eyes were restless：Karp 害怕被抢劫。

17. He would…him：只要能和这位卖酒的人不一样，他愿容许他卖酒赚钱。指诚实的鲍伯极不喜欢 Karp 的为人。

18. She was making…morning：指早上 Nick Fuso 到 H. Schmitz 的店里去购物，Tessie Fuso 对此感到内疚，因此以买火腿向鲍伯表示歉意。

JAMES BALDWIN

〔作者介绍〕

詹姆斯·鲍德温（James Baldwin，1924～），美国小说家、散文作家、剧作家。他出生在纽约哈莱姆区，青少年时代的生活颇受其做牧师的父亲的严厉左右，14 岁经历了一种深刻的宗教体验，开始讲道，和父亲相坑衡，对他来说，这是一种具有个人和宗教意义的矛盾。与此同时，他开始写作，中学毕业后继续创作，并在纽约格林威治村受文学训练。1944 年冬，他和理查德·赖特（Richard Wright）会面，赖特鼓励他坚持文学创作；鲍德温日后成为赖特的“土生子”和继承人。

鲍德温 24 岁时离美赴欧，客居欧洲达 9 年之久。此举主要原因是躲避种族歧视，发现自我的价值。在这期间，他的作品开始在美国发表。他的小说《向苍天呼吁》（*Go Tell It on the Mountain*，1953）取材于他少年时的经历，不少评论认为这是他的最佳作品。1955 年他出版了散文集《土生子的札记》（*Notes of a Native Son*），次年他的小说《乔万尼的房间》（*Giovanni's Room*）问世，写的是一个青年白人在法国的同性恋故事。

1957 年鲍德温回国，立即参加了当时的民权斗争。他在这期间出版的论文集《没有人知道我的名子》（*Nobody Knows My Name*，1961）、《土生子札记续》（*More Notes of a Native Son*，1961）及《下一次将是烈火》（*The Fire Next Time*，1963），文笔遒劲，见解深刻，许多人认为他是当代美国主要散文作家之一。他的另一部小说《另一个国家》（*Another Country*，1962）和他的短篇小说集《去见那个人》（*Going to Meet the Man*，1965）都反映出他对美国种族关系的忧虑与关切。他在 1968 年出版的《告诉我火车开走多久了》（*Tell Me How Long the Train's Been Gone*）写的是他的作品一贯描写的题材：种族关系、种族冲突、同性恋。

1971 年，鲍德温发表与著名人类学家玛格丽特·米德（*Margaret Mead*，1901～1978）的谈话集《论种族》（*A Rap on Race*），次年发表见闻与评论集

《街上没有名字》(*No Name in the Street*)，强烈地表达出他对美国和世界的愤怒与失望。1974 年他的激烈的抗议小说《假如比尔街能够讲话》(*If Beale Street Could Talk*)出版。鲍德温虽然曾被人指责缺乏战斗性，但他做为小说家始终以其独特的声音警告美国白人将会发生的“爆炸”，劝说黑人避免因种族仇恨引起的自我毁灭的过激行动。他坚持认为，美国的“复杂命运”将必然使 20 世纪美国黑人与白人的生活联系在一起。他和其他黑人作家一起，通过自己的作品，使美国认识到自己在种族问题上的可耻行为。

鲍德温是一位严肃的艺术家。他所关心的并非只是“黑人问题”；他关心的是人的状况。他希望自己成为一个诚实的人，一个优秀的作家。他在《自传札记》(“An Autobiographical Note”)中曾写道：“我爱美国甚于世界上其他任何国家，正因如此，我坚持永远批评她的权利。我考虑到我身负多种责任，但其最大者莫过于此：继续下去，如海明威所说，做完我的工作。”他的作品力求在内容和技巧上渐臻完善，反映出艺术家的诚实态度。没有人指责他为某种宣传目的进行创作。他的文风也表现出他悉心探索自己独特风格的不懈努力。他的散文笔锋犀利、风格清新，给人的印象尤其深刻；世人认为他将以散文家的身份垂名文学史册。如果说理查德·赖特是一位著名黑人作家的话，那么，鲍德温和艾里森一样，业已从“黑人”的分类中超脱出来，而成为美国当代一位主要作家了。

鲍德温的其他作品还包括剧作《查理先生的布鲁斯》(*Blues for Mister Charlie*，1964) 等。

Go Tell It on the Mountain

〔作品介绍〕

《向苍天呼吁》(*Go Tell It on the Mountain*)描写的是一个男孩子的信仰的形成过程。主人公约翰·格兰姆斯是一个 14 岁的黑人少年。他的继父加布里埃尔·格兰姆斯是狂热的店铺教堂的牧师，在约翰一两岁时和他的母亲伊丽沙白·格兰姆斯结婚。他们婚后又生下一男二女。加布里埃尔不喜欢约翰，这使敏感的约翰感到紧张和难过。约翰虽自幼生活在贫困、污秽的哈莱姆黑人区的环境中，但对未来充满憧憬。他对父辈的生活很厌恶，决心过一种不同的生活。然而他生活环境中歇斯底里般的家教气氛，也深深地感染了他。父母的期望，“火的洗礼圣殿”里圣徒的影响，使他别无选择：他只能通过信仰的转变而成为他父兄当中的一员。这种转变终于在他 14 岁生日之夜举行的教堂仪式中，在他的灵魂经过激烈的震荡之后而完成了。

故事自始至终在黑人饱受煎熬、感到窒息的氛围中发展。小说开首便把读者带入一种令人窒息的环境中：刚满14岁的约翰早晨醒来，开始担心他的生日会在人们的遗忘中度过。母亲似已忘记，她吩咐他打扫庭院，破旧地毯上升腾起的尘土令他作呕。后来母亲终于取出几枚硬币，让他去买自己喜爱的生日礼物或以自己喜爱的方式去过生日。然而当他回到家时，却发现弟弟罗伊被白人孩子刺伤头部，父亲、姑姑、父母在绝望中吵做一团。第1部分把约翰14年生活的环境——贫困和压迫——勾勒得淋漓尽致。第二部分以约翰的父母及姑母在教堂祈祷时对自己痛苦身世进行回忆的方式，把黑人种族的苦难详述出来，给约翰信仰的转变巧妙地埋下伏笔。约翰的姑母弗罗伦斯为追求美好的生活自南部奔向北方，丈夫虽然爱她，但不知未雨绸缪，终于与她在争吵中分手，后死在法国。她年届60仍需拖着疲惫的身躯出去谋生。弗罗伦斯的弟弟加布里埃尔幼时不务正业，给他们的母亲带来极大烦恼。后来他皈依宗教，转变成出色的牧师。他和少年时曾受过白人凌辱的德博拉结婚，但又和另一女人、年轻漂亮的埃斯特私通，生下一子。加布里埃尔对两个女人都未尽到责任，在客观上导致了她们的悲惨结果。唯有弗罗伦斯了解他的罪孽，对他的虔诚和狂热持怀疑、甚至否定的态度。伊丽莎白在18岁时曾和一个富有自尊心的黑人青年理查德相爱，理查德后因不堪坐白人冤狱而自杀，他们的儿子约翰在理查德去世后才出世。这些给伊丽莎白年轻的生命涂上一层暗淡的色调。后来她在弗罗伦斯家和加布里埃尔相遇、结婚、生儿育女。她的心灵深处充满内疚、忧虑和痛苦。当她看到约翰"新生"时，心头升起希望的曙光。第3部分又回到约翰身上，描绘他在"圣徒"们的狂热环境中，内心深处发生激烈的转变，经过幻觉、迷梦等阶段，灵魂终于受到"拯救"，成为祖辈的社会及传统的一员。

《向苍天呼吁》是一部艺术价值很高的作品。小说的3部分相互咬合，丝丝相扣，结构极为严谨：第1部分把故事的脉络勾勒出来，在第2部分中加以充实，第3部分再返回第1部分的结尾处，把前面松散的线索收拢起来，使故事成为一个有机的整体；而故事的发展虽横跨半个世纪的时空，但却集中到主人公14周岁生日这一天来写。小说集中写格兰姆斯一家，然却据此收到了以点带面的艺术效果：作者运用的重要艺术手段，是通过自然援引《旧约全书》的有关情节为故事渲染气氛，《旧约·出埃及记》尤其有力地烘托出黑人的苦难遭遇及其寻求解脱和拯救的强烈愿望，小说的语言极富《圣经》的语言格调。这部作品的另一特色是它的意识流技巧，这在第2、3部分里表现尤其明显。小说的讽刺性显示出作者艺术技巧的娴熟：读者虽沉浸在故事的"狂热"气氛里，但又时刻听到一个不同的声音，即冷眼旁观者的声音。例如在第3部分约翰思想高度兴奋之后，作者却通过弗罗伦斯对加布里埃尔的指责而暗示出，这种信仰转变可能有其虚伪的一面。

这里选注的是小说第1部分。

Go Tell It on the Mountain

I looked down the line,
And I wondered.

EVERYONE had always said that John would be a preacher when he grew up, just like his father. It had been said so often that John, without ever thinking about it, had come to believe it himself. Not until the morning of his fourteenth birthday did he really begin to think about it, and by then it was already too late.

His earliest memories—which were, in a way, his only memories—were of the hurry and brightness of Sunday mornings. They all rose together on that day; his father, who did not have to go to work, and led them in prayer before breakfast; his mother, who dressed up on that day, and looked almost young, with her hair straightened, and on her head the close-fitting white cap that was the uniform of holy women; his younger brother, Roy, who was silent that day because his father was home. Sarah, who wore a red ribbon in her hair that day, and was fondled by her father. And the baby, Ruth, who was dressed in pink and white, and rode in her mother's arms to chruch.

The church was not very far away, four blocks up Lenox Avenue, on a corner not far from the hospital. It was to this hospital that his mother had gone when Roy, and Sarah, and Ruth were born. John did not remember very clearly the first time she had gone, to have Roy; folks said that he had cried and carried on the whole time his mother was away; he remembered only enough to be afraid every time her belly began to swell, knowing that cach time the swelling began it would not end until she was taken from him, to come back with a stranger. Each time this happened she became a little more of a stranger herself. She would soon be going away again, Roy said—he knew much more about such things than John. John had observed his mother closely, seeing no swelling yet, but his father had prayed one morning for the "little voyager soon to be among them," and so John knew that Roy spoke the truth.

Every Sunday morning, then, since John could remember, they had taken to the streets, the Grimes family on their way to church. Sinners along the avenue watched them—men still wearing their Saturday-night clothes, wrinkled and dusty now, muddy-eyed and muddy-faced; and women with harsh voices and tight, bright dresses, cigarettes between their fingers or held tightly in the corners of their mouths. They talked, and laughed, and fought together, and the women fought like the men. John and Roy, passing these men and women, looked at one another briefly, John embarrassed and Roy amused. Roy would be like them when he grew up, if the Lord did not change his heart. These men and women they passed on Sunday mornings had spent the night in bars, or in cat houses, or on the streets, or on rooftops, or under the stairs. They had been dirnking. They had gone from cursing to laughter, to anger, to lust. Once he and Roy had watched a man and woman in the basement of a condemned house. They did it standing up. The woman had wanted fifty cents, and the man had flashed a razor.

John had never watched again; he had been afraid. But Roy had watched them many times, and he told John he had done it with some girls down the block.

And his mother and father, who went to church on Sundays, they did it too, and sometimes John heard them in the bedroom behind him, over the sound of rat's feet, and rat screams, and the music and cursing from the harlot's house downstairs.

Their church was called the *Temple of the Fire Baptized*. It was not the biggest church in Harlem, nor yet the smallest, but John had been brought up to believe it was the holiest and best. His father was head deacon in this church—there were only two, the other a round, black man named Deacon Braithwaite—and he took up the collection, and sometimes he preached. The pastor, Father James, was a genial, well-fed man with a face like a darker moon. It was he who preached on Pentecost Sundays, and led revivals in the summertime, and anointed and healed the sick.

On Sunday mornings and Sunday nights the church was always full; on special Sundays it was full all day. The Grimes family arrived in a body, always a little late, usually in the middle of Sunday school, which began at nine o'clock. This lateness was always their mother's fault—at least in the eyes of their father; she could not seem to get herself and the children ready on time, ever, and sometimes she actually remained behind, not to appear until the morning service. When they all arrived together, they separated upon entering the doors, father and mother going to sit in the Adult Class, which was taught by Sister McCandless, Sarah going to the Infant's Class, John and Roy sitting in the Intermediate, which was taught by Brother Elisha.

When he was young, John had paid no attention in Sunday school, and always forgot the golden text, which earned him the wrath of his father. Around the time of his fourteenth birthday, with all the pressures of church and home uniting to drive him to the altar, he strove to appear more serious and therefore less conspicuous. But he was distracted by his new teacher, Elisha, who was the pastor's nephew and who had but lately arrived from Georgia. He was not much older than John, only seventeen, and he was already saved and was a preacher. John stared at Elisha all during the lesson, admiring the timbre of Elisha's voice, much deeper and manlier than his own, admiring the leanness, and grace, and strength, and darkness of Elisha in his Sunday suit, wondering if he would ever be holy as Elisha was holy. But he did not follow the lesson, and when, sometimes, Elisha paused to ask John a question, John was ashamed and confused, feeling the palms of his hands become wet and his heart pound like a hammer. Elisha would smile and reprimand him gently, and the lesson would go on.

Roy never knew his Sunday school lesson either, but it was different with Roy—no one really expected of Roy what was expected of John. Everyone was always praying that the Lord would change Roy's heart, but it was John who was expected to be good, to be a good example.

When Sunday school service ended there was a short pause before morning service began. In this pause, if it was good weather, the old folks might step ouside a moment to talk among themselves. The sisters would almost always be dressed in white from crown to toe. The small children, on this day, in this place, and oppressed by their elders, tried hard to play without seeming to be disrespectful of God's house. But sometimes, nervous or perverse, they shouted, or threw hymnbooks, or began to cry, putting their parents, men or women of God, under the necessity of proving—by harsh means or tender—who, in a sanctified household, ruled. The older children, like Jonh or Roy, might wander down the avenue, but not too far. Their father never let John and Roy out of his sight, for Roy had often disappeared between Sunday school and morning serivce and had not come back all day.

The Sunday morning serivce began when Brother Elisha sat down at the piano and raised a song. This moment and this music had been with John, so it seemed, since he had first drawn breath. It seemed that there had never been a time when he had not known this moment of waiting while the packed church paused—the sisters in white, heads raised, the brothers in blue, heads back; the white caps of the women seeming to glow in the charged air like crownss the kinky, gleaming heads of the men seeming to be lifted up—and the rustling and the whispering ceased and the children were quiet; perhaps someone coughed, or the sound of a car horn, or a curse from the streets came in; then Elisha hit the keys, beginning at once to sing, and everybody joined him, clapping their hands, and rising, and beating the tambourines.

The song might be: *Down at the cross where my Saviour died!*

Or: *Jesus, I'll never forget how you set me free!*

Or: *Lord, hold my hand while I run this race!*

They sang with all the strength that was in them, and clapped their hands for joy. There had never been a time when John had not sat watching the saints rejoice with terror in his heart, and wonder. Their singing caused him to believe in the presence of the Lord; indeed, it was no longer a question of belief, because they made that presence real. He did not feel it himself, the joy they felt, yet he could not doubt that it was, for them, the very bread of life—could not doubt it, that is, until it was too late to doubt. Something happened to their faces and their voices, the rhythm of their bodies, and to the air they breathed; it was as though wherever they might be became the upper room, and the Holy Ghost were riding on the air. His father's face, always awful, became more awful now; his father's daily anger was transformed into prophetic wrath. His mother, her eyes raised to heaven, hands arched before her, moving, made real for John that patience, that endurance, that long suffering, which he had read of in the Bible and found so hard to imagine.

On Sunday mornings the women all seemed patient, all the men seemed mighty. While John watched, the Power struck someone, a man or woman; they cried out, a long wordless crying, and, arms outstretched like swings, they began the Shout.[1] Someone moved a chair a little to give them room, the rhythm paused, the singing stopped, only the pounding feet and the clapping hands were heard; then another cry, another dancer; then the tambourines began again, and the voices rose again, and the music swept on again, like fire, or flood, or judgment. Then the church seemed to swell with the Power it held, and, like a planet rocking in space, the temple rocked with the Power of God. John watched, watched the faces, and the weightless bodies, and listened to the timeless cries. One day, so everyone said, this Power would possess him; he would sing and cry as they did now, and dance before his King. He watched young Ella Mae Washington, the seventeen-year-old granddaughter of Praying Mother Washington, as she began to dance. And then Elisha danced.

At one moment, head thrown back, eyes closed, sweat standing on his brow, he sat at the piano, singing and playing; and then, like a great, black cat in trouble in the jungle, he stiffened and trembled, and cried out. *Jesus, Jesus, oh Lord Jesus!* He struck on the piano one last, wild note, and threw up his hands, palms upward, stretched wide apart. The tambourines raced to fill the vacuum left by his silent piano, and his cry drew answering cries. Then he was on his feet turning, blind, his face congested, contorted with this rage, and the muscles leaping and swelling in his long, dark neck. It seemed that he could not breathe, that his body could not contain this passion, that he would be, before their eyes, dispersed into the waiting air. His hands, rigid to the very fingertips, moved outward and back against his hips, his sightless eyes looked upward, and he began to dance. Then his hands closed into fists, and his head snapped downward, his sweat loosening the grease that slicked down his hair; and the rhythm of all the others quickened to match Elisha's rhythm; his thighs moved terribly against the cloth of his suit, his heels beat on the floor, and his fists moved beside his body as though he were beating his own drum. And so, for a while, in the center of the dancers, head down, fists beating, on, on, unbearably, until it seemed the walls of the church would fall for very sound; and then, in a moment, with a cry, head up, arms high in the air, sweat pouring from his forehead, and all his body dancing as though it would never stop. Sometimes he did not stop until he fell—until he dropped like some animal felled by a hammer—

moaning, on his face. And then a great moaning filled the church.

There was sin åmong them. One Sunday, when regular service was over, Father James had uncovered sin in the congregation of the righteous. He had uncovered Elisha and Ella Mae. They had been "walking disorderly"; they were in danger of straying from the truth. And as Father James spoke of the sin that he knew they had not committed yet, of the unripe fig plucked too early from the tree—to set the children's teeth on edge—John felt himself grow dizzy in his seat and could not look at Elisha where he stood, beside Ella Mae, before the altar. Elisha hung his head as Father James spoke and the congregation murmured. And Ella Mae was not so beautiful now as she was when she was singing and testifying, but looked like a sullen, ordinary girl. Her full lips were loose and her eyes black—with shame, or rage, or both. Her grandmother, who had raised her, sat watching quietly, with folded hands. She was one of the pillars of the church, a powerful evangelist and very widely known. She said nothing in Ella Mae's defense, for she must have felt, as the congregation felt, that Father James was only exercising his clear and painful duty; he was responsible, after all, for Elisha, as Praying Mother Washington was responsible for Ella Mae. It was not an easy thing, said Father James, to be the pastor of a flock. It might look easy to just sit up there in the pulpit night after night, year in, year out, but let them remember the awful responsibility placed on his shoulders by almighty God—let them remember that God would ask an accounting of him one day for every soul in his flock. Let them remember this when they thought he was hard, let them remember that the World was hard, that the way of holiness was a hard way. There was no room in God's army for the coward heart, no crown awaiting him who put mother, or father, sister, or brother, sweetheart, or friend above God's will. Let the chruch cry amen to this! And they cried: "Amen! Amen!"

The Lord had led him, said Father James, looking down on the boy and girl before him to give them a public warning before it was too late. For he knew them to be sincere young people, dedicated to the service of the Lord—it was only that, since they were young, they did not know the pitfalls Satan laid for the unwary. He knew that sin was not in their minds—not yet; yet sin was in the flesh; and should they continue with their walking out alone together, their secrets and laughter, and touching of hands, they would surely sin a sin beyond all forgiveness. And John wondered what Elisha was thinking—Elisha, who was tall and handsome, who playd basketball, and had been saved at the age of eleven in the improbable fields down south. *Had* he sinned? Had he been tempted? And the girl beside him, whose white robes now seemed the merest, thinnest covering for the nakedness of breasts and inststent thighs—what was her face like when she was alone with Elisha, with no singing, when they were not surrounded by the saints? He was afraid to think of it, yet he could think of nothing else; and the fever of which they stood accused began also to rage in him.

After this Sunday Elisha and Ella Mae no longer met each other each day after school, no lnoger spent Saturday afternoons wandering through Central Park, or lying on the beach. All that was over for them. If they came together again it would be in wedlock. They would have children and raise them in the church.

This was what was meant by a holy life, this was what the way of the cross demanded. It was somehow on that Sunday, a Sunday shortly before his birthday, that John first realized that this was the life awaiting him—realized it consciously, as smoething no longer far off, but imminent, coming closer day by day.

John's birthday fell on a Saturday in March, in 1935. He awoke on this birthday morning with the feeling that there was menace in the air around him—that something irrevocable had occurred in him. He stared at a yellow stain on the ceiling just above his head. Roy was still smothered in the bedclothes, and his breath came and went with a small, whistling sound. There was no other sound anywhere; no one in the house was up. The neighbor's radios were all silent, and his mother hadn't yet risen to fix his father's breakfast. John wondered at his panic, then wondered about the time; and then (while the yellow stain on the ceiling slowly transformed itself into a woman's nakedness) he remembered that it was his fourteenth birthday and that he had sinned.

His first thought, nevertheless, was: "Will anyone remember?" For it had happened, once or twice, tat his birthday had passed entirely unnoticed, and no one had said "Happy Birthday, Johnny," or given him anything—not even his mother.

Roy stirred again and John pushed him away, listening to the silence. On other mornings he awoke hearing his mother singing in the kitchen, hearing his father in the bedroom behind him grunting and muttering prayers to himself as he put on his clothes; hearing, perhaps, the chatter of Sarah and the squalling of Ruth, and the radios, the clatter of pots and pans, and the voices of all the folks near by. This morning not even the cry of a bedspring disturbed the silence, and John seemed, therefore, to be listening to his own unspeaking doom. He could believe, almost, that he had awakened late on that great getting-up morning; that all the saved had been transformed in the twinkling of an eye, and had risen to meet Jesus in the clouds, and that he was left, with his sinful body, to be bound in hell a thousand years.

He had sinned. In spite of the saints, his mother and his father, the warnings he had heard from his earliest beginnings, he had sinned with his hands a sin that was hard to forgive. In the school lavatory, alone, thinking of the boys, older, bigger, braver, who made bets with each other as to whose urine could arch higher, he had watched in himself a transformation of which he would never dare to speak.

And the darkness of John's sin was like the darkness of the church on Saturday evenings; like the silence of the church while he was there alone, sweeping, and running water into the great bucket, and overturning chairs, long before the saints arrived. It was like his thoughts as he moved about the tabernacle in which his life had been spent; the tabernacle that he hated, yet loved and feared. It was like Roy's curses, like the echoes these curses raised in John: he remembered Roy, on some rare Saturday when he had come to help John clean the church, cursing in the house of God, and making obscene gestures before the eyes of Jesus. It was like all this, and it was like the walls that witnessed and the placards on the walls which testified that the wages of sin was death. The darkness of his sin was in the hardheartedness with which he resisted God's power; in the scorn that was often his while he listened to the crying, breaking voices, and watched the black skin glisten while they lifted up their arms and fell on their faces before the Lord. For he had made his decision. He would not be like his father, or his father's father. He would have another life.

For John excelled in school, though not, like Elisha, in mathematics or basketball, and it was said that he had a Great Future. He might become a Great Leader of His People. John was not much interested in his people and still less in leading them anywhere, but the phrase so often repeated rose in his mind lke a great brass gate, opening outward for him on a world where people did not live in the darkness of his father's house, did not pray to Jesus in the darkness of his father's church, where he would eat good food, and wear fine clothes, and go to the movies as often as he wished. In this world John who was, his father said, ugly, who was always the smallest boy in his class, and who had no friends, became immediately beautiful, tall, and popular. People fell all over themselves to meet John Grimes. He was a poet, or a college president, or a movie star; he drank expensive whisky, and he smoked Lucky Strike cigarettes in the green package.

It was not only colored people who praised John, since they could not, John felt, in any case really know; but white people also said it, in fact had said it first and said it still. It was when John was five years old and in the first grade that he was first noticed; and five since he was noticed by an eye altogether alien and impersonal, he began to perceive, in wild uneasiness, his individual existence.

They were learning the alphabet that day, and six children at a time were sent to the blackboard to write the letters they had memorized. Six had finished and were waiting for the teacher's judgment when the back door opened and the school principal, of whom everyone was terrified, entered the room. No one spoke or moved. In the silence the principal's voice said:

"Which child is that?"

She was pointing at the blackboard, at Jonh's letters. The possibility of being distinguished by her notice did not enter John's mind, and so he simply stared at her. Then he realized, by the immobility of the other children and by the way they avoided looking at him, that it was he who was selected for punishment.

"Speak up, John," said the teacher, gently.

On the edge of tears, he mumbled his name and waited. The principal, a woman with white hair and an iron face, looked down at him.

"You're a very bright boy, John Grimes," she said. "Keep up the good work."

Then she walked out of the room.

That moment gave him, from that time on, if not a weapon at least a shield; he apprehended totally, without belief or understanding, that he had in himself a power that other people lacked; that he could use this to save himself, to raise himself; and that, perhaps, with this power he might one day win that love which he so longed for. This was not, in John, a faith subject to death or alteration, nor yet a hope subject to destruction; it was his identity, and part, therefore, of that wickedness for which his father beat him and to which he clung in order to withstand his father. His father's arm, rising and falling, might make him cry, and that voice might cause him to tremble; yet his father could never be entirely the victor, for John cherished something that his father could not reach. It was his hatred and his intelligence that he cherished, the one feeding the other. He lived for the day when his father would be dying and he, John, would curse him on his deathbed. And this was why, though he had been born in the faith and had been surrounded all his life by the saints and by their prayers and their rejoicing, and though the tabernacle in which they worshipped was more completely real to him than the several precarious homes in which he and his family had lived, John's heart was hardened against the Lord. His father was God's minister, the ambassador of the King of Heaven, and John could not bow before the throne of grace without first kneeling to his father. On his refusal to do this had his life depended, and John's secret heart had flourished in its wickedness until the day his sin first overtook him.

In the midst of all his wonderings he fell asleep again, and when he woke up this time and got out of bed his father had gone to the factory, where he would work for half a day. Roy was sitting in the kitchen, quarreling with their mother. The baby, Ruth, sat in her high chair banging on the tray with an oatmeal-covered spoon. This meant that she was in a good mood; she would not spend the day howling, for reasons known only to herself, allowing no one but her mother to touch her. Sarah was quiet, not chattering today, or at any rate not yet, and stood near the stove, arms folded, staring at Roy with the flat black eyes, her father's eyes, that made her look so old.

Their mother, her head tied up in an old rag, sipped black coffee and watched Roy. The pale end-of-winter sunlight filled the room and yellowed all their faces; and John, drugged and morbid and wondering how it was that he had slept again and had been allowed to sleep so long, saw them for a moment like figures on a screen, an effect that the yellow light intensified. The room was narrow and dirty; nothing could alter its dimensions, no labor could ever make it clean. Dirt was in the walls and the floorboards, and triumphed beneath the sink where roaches spawned; was in the fine ridges of the pots and pans, scoured daily, burnt black on the bottom, hanging above the stove; was in the wall against which they hung, and revealed itself where the paint had cracked and leaned outward in stiff squares and fragments, the paper-thin underside webbed with black. Dirt was in every corner, angle, crevice of the monstrous stove, and lived behind it in delirious communion with the corrupted wall. Dirt was in the baseboard that John scrubbed every Saturday, and roughened the cupboard shelves that held the cracked and gleaming dishes. Under this dark weight the walls leaned, under it the ceiling, with a great crack like lightning in its center, sagged. The windows gleamed like beaten gold or silver, but now John saw, in the yellow light, how fine dust veiled their doubtful glory. Dirt crawled in the gray mop hung out of the windows to dry. John thought with shame and horror, yet in angry hardness of heart: *He who is filthy, let him be filthy still.* Then he looked at his mother, seeing, as though she were someone else, the dark, hard lines running downward from her eyes, and the deep, perpetual scowl in her forehead, and the downturned, tightened mouth, and the strong, thin, brown, and bony hands; and the phrase turned against him like a two edged sword, for was it not he, in his false pride and his evil imagination, who was filthy? Through a storm of tears that did not reach his eyes, he stared at the yellow room; and the room shifted, the light of the sun darkened, and his mother's face changed. Her face became the face that he gave her in his dreams, the face that had been hers in a photograph he had seen once, long ago, a photograph taken before he was born. This face was young and proud, uplifted, with a smile that made the wide mouth beautiful and glowed in the enormous eyes. It was the face of a girl who knew that no evil could undo her, and who could laugh, surely, as his mother did not laugh now. Between the two faces there stretched a darkness and a mystery that John feared, and that sometimes caused him to hate her.

Now she saw him and she asked, breaking off her conversation with Roy: "You hungry, little sleepyhead?"

"Well! About time you was getting up," said Sarah.

He moved to the table and sat down, feeling the most bewildering panic to his life, a need to touch things, the table and chairs and the walls of the room, to make certain that the room existed and that he was in the room. He did not look at his mother, who stood up and went to the stove to heat his breakfast. But he asked, in order to say something to her, and to hear his own voice:

"What we got for breakfast?"

He realized, with some shame, that he was hoping she had prepared a special breakfast for him on his birthday.

"What you *think* we got for breakfast?" Roy asked scornfully. "You got a special craving for something?"

John looked at him. Roy was not in a good mood.

"I ain't said nothing to you," he said.

"Oh, I *beg* your pardon," said Roy, in the shrill, little-girl tone he knew John hated.

"What's the *matter* with you today?" John asked, angry, and trying at the same time to lend his voice as husky a pitch as possible.

"Don't you let Roy bother you," said their mother. "He cross as two sticks this morning."

"Yeh," said John, "I reckon." He and Roy watched each other. Then his plate was put before him: hominy grits and a scrap of bacon. He wanted to cry, like a child: "But, Mama, it's my birthday!" He kept his eyes on his plate and began to eat.

"You can *talk* about your Daddy all you want to," said his mother, picking up her battle with Roy, "but *one* thing you can't say—you can't say he ain't always done his best to be a father to you and to see to it that you ain't never gone hungry."

"I been hungry plenty of times," Roy said, proud to be able to score this point against his mother.

"Wasn't *his* fault, then. Wasn't because he wasn't *trying* to feed you. That man shoveled snow in zero weather when he ought've been in bed just to put food in your belly."

"Wasn't just *my* belly," said Roy indignantly. "He got a belly, too, I *know*—it's a *shame* the way that man eats. I sure ain't asked him to shovel no snow for me." But he dropped his eyes, suspecting a flaw in his argument. "I just don't want him beating on me all the time," he said at last. "I ain't no dog."

She sighed, and turned slightly away, looking out of the window.

"Your Daddy beats you," she said, "because he loves you."

Roy laughed. "That ain't he kind of love I understand, old lady. What you reckon he'd do if he didn't love me?"

"He'd let you go right on," she flashed, "right on down to hell where it looks like you is just determined to go anyhow! Right on, Mister Man, till somebody puts a knife in you, or takes you off to jail!"

"Mama," John asked suddenly, "is Daddy a good man?"

He had not known that he was going to ask the question, and he watched in astonishment as her mouth tightened and her eyes grew dark.

"That ain't no kind of question," she said mildly. "You don't know no better men, do you?"

"Looks to me like he's a mighty good man," said Sarah. "He sure is praying all the time."

"You children is young," their nother said, ignoring Sarah and sitting down again at the table, "and you don't know how lucky you is to have a father what worries about you and tries to see to it that you come up right."

"Yeah," said Roy, "We don't know how lucky we *is* to have a father what don't want you to go to movies and don't want you to play in the streets, and don't want you to have no friends, and he don't want this and he don't want that, and he don't want you to do *nothing*. We so *lucky* to have a father who just wants us to go to church and read the Bible and beller[2] like a fool in front of the altar and stay home all nice and quiet, like a little mouse. Boy, we sure is lucky, all right. Don't know what I done to be so lucky."

She laughed. "You going to find out one day," she said, "you mark my words."

"Yeah," said Roy.

"But it'll be too late, then," she said. "It'll be too late when you come to be... sorry." Her voice had changed. For a moment her eyes met John's eyes and John was frightened. He felt that her words, after the strange fashion God sometimes chose to speak to men, were dictated by Heaven and were meant for him. He was fourteen—was it too late? And this uneasiness was reinforced by the impression, which at that moment he realized had been his all along, that his mother was not saying everything she meant. What, he wondered, did she say to Aunt Florence when they talked together? Or to his father? What were her thoughts? Her face would never tell. And yet, looking down at him in a moment that was like a secret, passing sign, her face did tell him. Her thoughts were bitter.

"I don't care," Roy said, rising. "When I have children I ain't going to treat them like this." John watched his mother; she watched Roy. "I'm *sure* this ain't no way to be. Ain't got no right to have a houseful of children if you don't know how to treat them."

"You mighty grown up this morning," his mother said. "You be careful."

"And tell me something else," Roy said, suddenly leaning over his mother, "tell me how come he don't never let me talk to him like I talk to you? He's my father, ain't he? But he don't never listen to me—no, I all the time got to listen to him."

"Your father," she said, watching him, "knows best. You listen to your father, I guarantee you you won't end up in no jail."

Roy sucked his teeth in fury. "I ain't looking to go to no *jail*. You think that's all that's in the world is jails and churches? You ought to know better than that, Ma."

"I know," she said, "there ain't no safety except you walk humble before the Lord. You going to find it out, too, one day. You go on, hardhead. You going to come to grief."

And suddenly Roy grinned. "But you be there, won't you, Ma—when I'm in trouble?"

"You don't know," she said, trying not to smile, "how long the Lord's going to let me stay with you."

Roy turned and did a dance step. "That's all right," he said. "I know the Lord ain't as hard as Daddy. Is he, boy?" he demanded of John, and struck him lightly on the forehead.

"Boy, let me eat my breakfast," John muttered—though his plate had long been empty, and he was pleased that Roy had turned to him.

"That sure is a crazy boy," ventured Sarah, soberly.

"Just listen," cried Roy, "to the little saint! Daddy ain't never going to have no trouble with her—*that* one, she was born holy. I bet the first words she ever said was 'Thank you, Jesus.' Ain't that so, Ma.?"

"You stop this foolishness," she said, laughing, "and go on about your work. Can't nobody play the fool with you all morning."

"Oh, is you got work for me to do this morning? Well, I declare," said Roy, "what you got for me to do?"

"I got the woodwork in the dining-room for you to do. And you going to do it, too, before you set foot out of *this* house."

"Now, why you want to talk like that, Ma? Is I said I wouldn't do it? You know I'm a right good worker when I got a mind. After I do it, can I go?"

"You go ahead and do it, and we'll see. You better do it right."

"I *always* do it right," said Roy. "You won't know your old woodwork when *I* get through."

"John," said his mother, "you sweep the front room for me like a good boy, and dust the furniture. I'm going to clean up in here."

"Yes'm," he said, and rose. She *had* forgotten about his birthday. He swore he would not mention it. He would not think about it any more.

To sweep the front room meant, principally, to sweep the heavy red and green and purple Oriental-style carptet that had once been that room's glory, but was now so faded that it was all one swimming color, and so frayed in places that it tangled with the broom. John hated sweeping this carpet, for dust rose, clogging his nose and sticking to his sweaty skin, and he felt that should he sweep it forever, the clouds of dust would not diminish, the rug would not be clean. It became in his imagination his impossible, lifelong task, his hard trial, like that of a man he had read about somewhere,[3] whose curse it was to push a boulder up a steep hill, only to have the giant who guarede the hill roll the boulder down again—and so on, forever, throughout eternity; he was still out there, that hapless man, somewhere at the other end of the earth, pushing his boulder up the hill. He had John's entire sympathy, for the longest and hardest part of his Saturday mornings was his voyage with the broom across this endless rug; and, coming to the French doors that ended the living-room and stopped the rug, he felt like an indescribably weary traveler who sees his home at last. Yet for each dustpan he so laboriously filled at the doorsill demons added to the rug twenty more; he saw in the expanse behind him the dust that he had raised settling again into the carpet; and he gritted his teeth, already on edge because of the dust that filled his mouth, and nearly wept to think that so much labor brought so little reward.

Nor was this the end of John's labor; for, having put away the broom and the dustpan, he took from the small bucket under the sink the dustrag and the furniture oil and a damp cloth, and returned to the living-room to excavate, as it were, from the dust that threatened to bury them, his family's goods and gear. Thinking bitterly of his birthday, he attacked the mirror with the cloth, watching his face appear as out of a cloud. With a shock he saw that his face had not changed, that the hand of Satan was as yet invisible. His father had always said that his face was the face of Satan—and was there not something—in the lift of the eyebrow, in the way his rough hair formed a V on his brow—that bore witness to his father's words? In the eye there was a light that was not the light of Heaven, and the mouth trembled, lustful and lewd, to drink deep of the wines of Hell. He stared at his face as though it were, as indeed it soon appeared to be, the face of a stranger, a stanger who held secrets that John could never know. And, having thought of it as the face of a stranger, he tried to look at it as a stranger might, and tried to discover what other people saw. But he saw only details: two great eyes, and a broad, low forehead, and the triangle of his nose, and his enormous mouth, and the barely perceptible cleft in his chin, which was, his father said, the mark of the devil's little finger. These details did not help him, for the principle of their unity was undiscoverable, and he could not tell what he most passionately desired to know: whether his face was ugly or not.

And he dropped his eyes to the mantelpiece, lifting one by one the objects that adorned it. The mantelpiece held, in brave confusion, photographs, greeting cards, flowered nottoes, two silver candlesticks that held no candles, and a green metal serpent, poised to stike. Today in his apathy John stared at them, not seeing; he began to dust them with the exaggerated care of the profoundly preoccupied. One of the mottoes was pink and blue, and proclaimed in raised letters, which made the work of dusting harder:

Come in the evening, or come in the morning,
Come when you're looked for, or come without warning,
A thousand welcomes you'll find here before you,
And the oftener you come here, the more we'll adore you.

And the other, in letters of fire against a background of gold, stated:

For God so loved the world, that He gave His only begotten Son, that whosoever should believe in Him should not perish, but have everlasting life. *John iii*, 16[4]

These somewhat unrelated sentiments decorated either side of the mantelpiece, obscured a little by the silver candlesticks. Between these two extremes, the greeting cards, received year after year, on Christmas, or Easter, or birthdays, trumpeted their glad tidings; while the green metal serpent, perpetually malevolent, raised its head proudly in the midst of these trophies, biding the time to strike. Against the mirror, like a procession, the photographs were arranged.

These photographs were the true antiques of the family, which seemed to feel that a photograph should commemorate only the most distant past. The photographs of John and Roy, and of the two girls, which seemed to violate this unspoken law, served only in fact to prove it most iron-hard: they had all been taken in infancy, a time and a condition that the children could not remember. John in his photograph lay naked on a white counterpane, and people laughed and said that it was cunning. But John could never look at it without feeling shame and anger that his nakedness should be here so unkindly revealed. None of the other children was naked; no, Roy lay in his crib in a white gown and grinned toothlessly into the camera, and Sarah, somber at the age of six months, wore a white bonnet, and Ruth was held in her mother's arms. When people looked at these photographs and laughed, their laughter differed from the laughter with which they greeted the naked John. For this reason, when visitors tried to make advances to John he was sullen, and they, feeling that for some reason he disliked them, retaliated by deciding that he was a "funny" child.

Among the other photographs there was one of Aunt Florence, his father's sister, in which her hair, in the old-fashioned way, was worn high and tied with a ribbon; she had been very young when this photograph was taken, and had just come North. Sometimes, when she came to visit, she called the photograph to witness that she had indeed been beautiful in her youth. There was a photograph of his mother, not the one John liked and had seen only once, but one taken immediately after her marriage. And there was a photograph of his father, dressed in black, sitting on a country porth with his hands folded heavily in his lap. The photograph had been taken on a sunny day, and the sunlight brutally exaggerated the planes of his father's face. He stared into the sun, head raised, unbearable, and though it had been taken when he was young, it was not the face of a young man; only something archaic in the dress indicated that this photograph had been taken long ago. At the time this picture was taken, Aunt Florence said, he was already a preacher, and had a wife who was now in Heaven. That he had been a preacher at that time was not astonishing, for it was impossible to imagine that he had ever been anything else; but that he had had a wife in the so distant past who was now dead filled John with a wonder by no means pleasant. If she had lived, John thought, then he would never have been born; his father would never have come North and met his mother. And this shadow woman, dead so many years, whose name he knew had been Deborah, held in the fastness of her tomb, it seemed to John, the key to all those mysteries he so longed to unlock. It was she who had known his father in a life where John was not, and in a country John had never seen. When he was nothing, nowhere, dust, cloud, air, and sun, and falling rain, *not even thought of*, said his mother, *in Heaven with the angels*, said his aunt, she had known his father, and shared his father's house. She had loved his father. She had known his father when lightning flashed and thunder rolled through Heaven, and his father said: "Listen. God is talking." She had known him in the mornings of that far-off country when his father turned on his bed and opened his eyes, and she had looked into those eyes, seeing what they held, and she had not been afraid. She had seen him baptized, *kicking like a mule and howling*, and she had seen him weep when his mother died; *he was a right young man then*, Florence said. Because she had looked into those eyes before they had looked on John, she knew what John would never know—the purity of his father's eyes when John was not reflected in their depths. She could have told him—had he but been able from his hiding-place to ask! —how to make his father love him. But now it was too late. She would not speak before the judgment day. And among those many voices, and stammering with his own, John would care no longer for her testimony.

When he had finished and the room was ready for Sunday, John felt dusty and weary and sat down beside the window in his father's easy chair. A glacial sun filled the streets, and a high wind filled the air with scraps of paper and frosty dust, and banged the hanging signs of stores and storefront churches. It was the end of winter, and the garbage-filled snow that had been banked along the edges of sidewalks was melting now and filling the gutters. Boys were playing stickball in the damp, cold streets; dressd in heavy woolen sweaters and heavy pants, they danced and shouted, and the ball went *crack*! as the stick struck it and sent it speeding through the air. One of them wore a bright-red stocking cap with a great ball of wool hanging down behind that bounced as he jumped, like a bright omen above his head. The cold sun made their faces like copper and brass, and through the closed window John heard their coarse, irreverent voices. And he wanted to be one of them, playing in the streets, unfrightened, moving with such grace and power, but he knew this could not be. Yet, if he could not play their games, he could do something they could not do; he was able, as one of his teachers said, to think. But this brought him little in the way of consolation, for today he was terrified of his thoughts. He wanted to be with these boys in the street, heedless and thoughtless, wearing out his treacherous and bewildering body.

But now it was eleven o'clock, and in two hours his father would be home. And then they might eat, and then his father woud lead them in prayer, and then he would give them a Bible lesson. By and by it would be evening and he would go to clean the church, and remain for tarry service. Suddenly, sitting at the window, and with a violence unprecedented, there arose in John a flood of fury and tears, and he bowed his head, fists clenched against the windowpane, crying, with teeth on edge: "What shall I do? What shall I do?"

Then his mother called him; and he remembered that she was in the kitchen washing clothes and probably had something for him to do. He rose sullenly and walked into the kitchen. She stood over the washtub, her arms wet and soapy to the elbows and sweat standing on her brow. Her apron, improvised from an old sheet, was wet where she had been leaning over the scrubbing board. As he came in, she straightened, drying her hands on the edge of the apron.

"You finish your work, John?" she asked.

He said: "Yes'm," and though how oddly she looked at him; as though she were looking at someone else's child.

"That's a good boy," she said. She smiled a shy, strained smile. "You know you your mother's right—hand man?"

He said nothing, and he did not smile, but watched her, wondering to what task this preamble led.

She turned away, passing one damp hand across her forehead, and went to the cupboard. Her back was to him, and he watched her while she took down a bright, figured vase, filled with flowers only on the most special occasions, and emptied the contents into her palm. He heard the chink of money, which meant that she was going to send him to the store. She put the vase back and turned to face him, her palm loosely folded before her.

"I didn't never ask you," she said, "what you wanted for your birthday. But you take this, son, and go out and get yourself something you think you want."

And she opened his palm and put the money into it, warm and wet from her hand. In the moment that he felt the warm, smooth coins and her hand on his, John stared blindly at her face, so far above him. His heart broke and he wanted to put his head on her belly where the wet spot was, and cry. But he dropped his eyes and looked at his palm, at the small pile of coins.

"It ain't much there," she said.

"That's all right." Then he looked up, and she bent down and kissed him on the forehead.

"You getting to be," she said, putting her hand beneath his chin and holding his face away from her, "a right big boy. You going to be a mighty fine man, you know that? Your mama's counting on you."

And he knew again that she was not saying everything she meant; in a kind of secret language she was telling him today something that he must remember and understand tomorrow. He watched her face, his heart swollen with love for her and with an anguish, not yet his own, that he did not understand and that frightened him.

"Yes, Ma," he said, hoping that she would realize, despite his stammering tongue, the depth of his passion to please her.

"I know," she said, with a smile, releasing him and rising, "there's a whole lot of things you don't understand. But don't you fret. The

Lord'll reveal to you in His own good time everything He wants you to know. You put your faith in the Lord, Johnny, and He'll surely bring you out. Everything works together for good for them that love the Lord."

He had heard her say this before—it was her text, as *Set thine house in order*[5] was his father's—but he knew that today she was saying it to him especially; she was trying to help him because she knew he was in trouble. And this trouble was also her own, which she would never tell to John. And even though he was certain that they could not be speaking of the same things—for then, surely, she would be angry and no longer proud of him—this perception on her part and this avowal of her love for him lent to John's bewilderment a reality that terrified and a dignity that consoled him. Dimly, he felt that he ought to console her, and he listened, astounded, at the words that now fell from his lips:

"Yes, Mama. I'm going to try to love the Lord."

At this there sprang into his mother's face something startling, beautiful, unspeakably sad—as though she were looking far beyond him at a long, dark road, and seeing on that road a traveler in perpetual danger. Was it he, the traveler? or herself? or was she thinking of the cross of Jesus? She turned back to the washtub, still with this strange sadness on her face.

"You better go on now," she said, "before your daddy gets home."

In Central Park the smow had not yet melted on his favorite hill. This hill was in the center of the park, after he had left the circle of the reservoir, where he always found, outside the high wall of crossed wire, ladies, white, in fur coats, walking their great dogs, or old, white gentlemen with canes. At a point that he knew by instinct and by the shape of the buildings surrounding the park, he struck out on a steep path overgrown with trees, and climbed a short distance until he reached the clearing that led to the hill. Before him, then, the slope stretched upward, and above it the brilliant sky, and beyond it, cloudy and far away, he saw the skyline of New York. He did not know why, but there arose in him an exultation and a sense of power, and he ran up the hill like an engine, or a madman, willing to throw himself headlong into the city that glowed before him.

But when he reached the summit he paused; he stood on the crest of the hill, hands clasped beneath his chin, looking down. Then he, John, felt like a giant who might crumble this city with his anger; he felt like a tyrant who might crush this city beneath his heel; he felt like a long-awaited conquerer at whose feet flowers would be strewn, and before whom multitudes cried, Hosanna! He would be, of all, the mightiest, the most beloved, the Lord's anointed; and he would live in this shining city which his ancestors had seen with longing from far away. For it was his; the inhabitants of the city had told him it was his; he had but to run down, crying, and they would take him to their hearts and show him wonders his eyes had never seen.

And still, on the summit of that hill he paused. He remembered the people he had seen in that city, whose eyes held no love for him. And he thought of their feet so swift and brutal, and the dark gray colthes they wore, and how when they passed they did not see him, or, if they saw him, they smirked. And how their lights, unceasing, crashed on and off above him, and how he was a stranger there. Then he remembered his father and his mother, and all the arms stretched out to hold him back, to save him from this city where, they said, his soul would find perdition.

And certainly perdition sucked at the feet of the people who walked there; and cried in the lights, in the gigantic towers; the marks of Satan could be found in the faces of the people who waited at the doors of movie houses; his words were printed on the great movie posters that invited people to sin. It was the roar of the damned that filled Broadway, where motor cars and buses and the hurrying people disputed every inch with death. *Broadway*: the way that led to death *was* broad, and many could be found thereon; but narrow was the way that led to life eternal, and few there were who found it. But he did not long for the narrow way, where all his people walked; where the houses did not rise, piercing, as it seemed, the unchanging clouds, but huddled, flat, ignoble, close to the filthy ground, where the streets and the hallways and the rooms were dark, and where the unconquerable odor was of dust, and sweat, and urine, and homemade gin. In the narrow way, the way of the cross, there awaited him only humiliation forever; there awaited him, one day, a house like his father's house, and a church like his father's, and a job like his father's, where he would grow old and black with hunger and toil. The way of the cross had given him a belly filled with wind and had bent his mother's back; they had never worn fine colthes, but here, where the buildings contested God's power and where the men and women did not fear God, here he might eat and drink to his heart's content and clothe his body with wondrous fabrics, rich to the eye and pleasing to the touch. And then what of his soul, which would one day come to die and stand naked before the judgment bar? What would his conquest of the city profit him on that day? To hurl away, for a moment of ease, the glories of eternity!

These glories were unimaginable—but the city was real. He stood for a moment on the melting snow, distracted, and then began to run down the hill, feeling himself fly as the descent became more rapid, and thinking: "I can climb back up. If it's wrong, I can always climb back up." At the bottom of the hill, where the ground abruptly leveled off onto a gravel path, he nearly knocked down an old white man with a white beard, who was walking very slowly and leaning on his cane. They both stopped, astonished, and looked at one another. John struggled to catch his breath and apologize, but the old man smiled. John smiled back. It was as though he and the old man had between them a great secret; and the old man moved on. The snow glittered in patches all over the park. Ice, under the pale, strong sun, melted slowly on the branches and the trunks of trees.

He came out of the park at Fifth Avenue where, as always, the old-fashioned horse-carriages were lined along the curb, their drivers sitting on the high seats with rugs around their knees, or standing in twos and threes near the horses, stamping their feet and smoking pipes and talking. In summer he had seen people riding in these carriages, looking like people out of books, or out of movies in which everyone wore old-fashioned clothes and rushed at nightfall over frozen roads, hotly pursued by their enemies who wanted to carry them back to death. "*Look back, look back,*" had cried a beautiful woman with long blonde curls, "*and see if we are pursued!*"—and she had come, as John remembered, to a terrible end. Now he stared at the horses, enormous and brown and patient, stamping every now and again a polished hoof, and he thought of what it would be like to have one day a horse of his own. He would call it Rider, and mount it at morning when the grass was wet, and from the horse's back look out over great, sun-filled fields, his own. Behind him stood his house, great and rambling and very new, and in the kitchen his wife, a beautiful woman, made breakfast, and the smoke rose out of the chimney, melting into the morning air. They had children, who called him Papa and for whom at Christmas he bought electric trains. And he had turkeys and cows and chickens and geese, and other horses besides Rider. They had a closet full of whisky and wine; they had cars—but what church did they go to and what would he teach his children when they gathered around him in the evening? He looked straight ahead, down Fifth Avenue, where graceful women in fur coats walked, looking into the windows that held silk dresses, and watches, and rings. What church did they go to? And what were their houses like when in the evening they took off these coats, and these silk dresses, and put their jewelry in a box, and leaned back in soft beds to think for a moment before they slept of the day gone by? Did they read a verse from the Bible every night and fall on their knees to pray? But no, for their thoughts were not of God, and their way was not God's way. They were in the world, and of the world, and their feet laid hold on Hell.

Yet in school some of them had been nice to him, and it was hard to think of them burning in Hell forever, they who were so gracious and beautiful now. Once, one winter when he had been very sick with a heavy cold that would not leave him, one of his teachers had bought him a bottle of cod liver oil, especially prepared with heavy syrup so that it did not taste so bad; this was surely a Christian act. His mother had said that God would bless that woman; and he had got better. They were kind—he was sure that they were kind—and on the day that he would bring himself to their attention they would surely love and honor him. This was not his father's opinion. His father said that all white people were wicked, and that God was going to bring them low. He said that white people were never to be trusted, and that they told nothing but lies, and that not one of them had ever loved a nigger. He, John, was a nigger, and he would find out, as soon as he got a little older, how evil white people could be. John had read about the things white people did to colored people; how, in the South, where his parents came from, white people cheated them of their wages, and burned them, and shot them—and did worse things, said his father, which the tongue could not endure to utter. He had read about colored men being burned in the electric chair for things they had not done; how in riots they were beaten with clubs; how they were tortured in prisons; how they were the last to be hired and the first to be fired. Niggers did not live on these streets where John now walked; it was forbidden; and yet he walked here, and no one raised a hand against him. But did he dare to enter this shop out of which a woman now casually walked, carrying a great round box? Or this apartment before which a white man stood, dressed in a brilliant uniform? John knew he did not dare, not today, and he heard his father's laugh: "*No, nor tomorrow neither!*" For him there was the back door, and the dark stairs, and the kitchen or the basement. This world was not for him. If he refused to believe, and wanted to break his neck trying, then he could try until the sun refused to shine; they would never let him enter. In John's mind then, the people and the avenue underwent a change, and he feared them and knew that one day he could hate them if God did not change his heart.

He left Fifth Avenue and walked west towards the movie houses. Here on 42nd Street it was less elegant but no less strange. He loved this street, not for the people or the shops but for the stone lions that guarded the great main building of the Public Library, a building filled with books and unimaginably vast, and which he had never yet dared to enter. He might, he knew, for he was a member of the branch in Harlem and was entitled to take books from any library in the city. But he had never gone in becausee the building was so big that it must be full of corridors and marble steps, in the maze of which he would be lost and never find the book he wanted. And then everyone, all the white people inside would know that has was not used to great buildings, or to many books, and they would look at him with pity. He would enter on another day, when he had read all the books uptown, an achievement that would, he felt, lend him the poise to enter any building in the world. People, mostly men, leaned over the stone parapets of the raised park that surrounded the library, or walked up and down and bent to drink water from the public drinking-fountains. Silver pigeons lighted briefly on the heads of the lions or the rims of fountains, and strutted along the walks. John loitered in front of Woolworth's,[6] starting at the candy display, trying to decide what candy to buy—and buying none, for the store was crowded and he was certain that the salesgirl would never notice him—and before a vender of artificial flowers and crossed Sixth Avenue where the Automat was, and the parked taxis, and the shops, which he would not look at today, that displayed in their windows dirty postcards and practical jokes. Beyond Sixth Avenue the movie houses began, and now he studied the stills carefully, trying to decide which of all these theaters he should enter. He stopped at last before a gigantic, colored poster that represented a wicked woman, half undressed, leaning in a doorway, apparently quarreling with a blond man who stared wretchedly into the street. The legend above their heads was: "There's a fool like him in every family—and a woman next door to take him over!" He decided to see this, for he felt indentified with the blond young man, the fool of his family, and he wished to know more about his so blatantly unkind fate.

And so he stared at the price above the ticket-seller's window and, showing her his coins, received the piece of paper that was charged with the power to open doors. Having once decided to enter, he did not look back at the street again for fear that one of the saints might be passing and, seeing him, might cry out him name and lay hands on him to drag him back. He walked very quickly across the carpeted lobby, looking at nothing, and pausing only to see his ticket torn, half of it thrown into a silver box and half returned to him. And then the usherette opened the doors of this dark palace and with a flashlight held behind her took him to his heat. Not even then, having pushed past a wilderness of knees and feet to reach his designated seat, did he dare to breathe; nor, out of a last, sick hope for forgiveness, did he look at the screen. He stared at the darkness around him, and at the profiles that gradually emerged from this gloom, which was so like the gloom of Hell. He waited for this darkness to be shattered by the light of the second coming, for the ceiling to crack upward, revealing, for every eye to see, the chariots of fire on which descended a wrathful God and all the host of Heaven. He sank far down in his seat, as though his crouching might make him invisible and deny his presence there. But then he thought: "*Not yet. The day of judgment is not yet*," and voices reached him, the voices no doubt of the hapless man and the evil woman, and he raised his eyes helplessly and watched the screen.

The woman was most evil. She was blonde and pasty white, and she had lived in London, which was in England, quite some time ago, judging from her clothes, and she coughed. She had a terrible disease, tuberculosis, which he had heard about. Someone in his mother's family had died of it. She had a great many boy friends, and she smoked cigarettes and drank. When she met the young man, who was a student and who loved her very much, she was very cruel to him. She laughed at him because he was a cripple. She took his money and she went out with other men, and she lied to the student—who was certainly a fool. He limped about, looking soft and sad, and soon all John's sympathy was given to this violent and unhappy woman. He understood her when she raged and shook her hips and threw back her head in laughter so furious that it seemed the veins of her neck would burst. She walked the cold, foggy streets, a little woman and not pretty, with a lewd, brutal swagger, saying to the whole world: "You can kiss my ass." Nothing tamed or broke her, nothing touched her, neither knidness, or scorn, nor hatred, nor love. She had never thought of prayer. It was unimaginable that she would ever bend her knees and come crawling along a dusty floor to anybody's altar, weeping for forgiveness. Perhaps her sin was so extreme that it could not be forgiven; perhaps her pride was so great that she did not need forgiveness. She had fallen from that high estate which God had intended for men and women, and she made her fall glorious because it was so complete. John could not have found in his heart, had he dared to search it, any wish for her redemption. He wanted to be like her, only more powerful, more thorough, and more cruel; to make those around him, all who hurt him, suffer as she made the student suffer, and laugh in their faces when they asked pity for their pain. *He* would have asked no pity, and his pain was greater than theirs. Go on, girl, he whispered, as the student, facing her implacable ill will, sighed and wept. Go on, girl. One day he would talk like that, he would face them and tell them how much he hated them, how they had made him suffer, how he would pay them back!

Nevertheless, when she came to die, which she did eventually, looking more grotesuque than ever, as she deserved, his thoughts were abruptly arrested, and he was chilled by the expression on her face. She seemed to stare endlessly outward and down, in the face of a wind more piercing than any she had felt on earth, feeling herself propelled with speed into a kingdom where nothing could help her, neither her pride, nor her courage, nor her glorious wickedness. In the place where she was going, it was not these things that mattered but something else, for which she had no name, only a cold intimation, something that she could not alter in any degree, and that she had never thought of. She began to cry, her depraved face breaking into an infant's grimace; and they moved away from her, leaving her dirty in a dirty room, alone to face her maker. The scene faded out and she was gone; and though the movie went on, allowing the student to marry another girl, darker, and very sweet, but by no means so arresting, John thought of this woman and her dreadful end. Again, had the thought not been blasphemous, he would have thought that it was the Lord who had led him into this theater to show him an example of the wages of sin. The movie ended and people stirred around him; the newsreel came on, and while girls in bathing suits paraded before him and boxers growled and fought, and baseball players ran home safe and presidents and kings of countries that were only names to him moved briefly across the flickering square of light John thought of Hell, of his soul's redemption, and struggled to find a compromise between the way that led to life everlasting and the way that ended in the pit. But there was none, for he had been raised in the truth. He could not claim, as African savages might be able to claim, that no one had brought him the gospel. His father and mother and all the saints had taught him from his earliest childhood what was the will of God. Either he arose from this theater, never to return, putting behind him the world and its pleasures, its honors, and its glories, or he remained here with the wicked and partook of their certain punishment. Yes, it was a naarrow[7] way—and John stirred in his seat, not daring to feel it God's injustice that he must make so cruel a choice.

〔注释〕

1. the shout：宗教仪式中的一部分，其间信徒狂歌狂舞。

2. beller＝bellow.

3. a man he had read about：可能指希腊神话中的西昔孚斯(Sisyphus)。据希腊神话，在地府里有一个罪孽深重的人，叫西昔孚斯，他被冥王判处苦役，每日滚动一块沉重的石头上山，一到山顶，巨石就从他手中脱落，一路滚下去。西昔孚斯欲求生路，便要不停地推石上山。

4. John iii，16：《约翰福音》3：16。

5. Set thine house in order：引自《旧约全书·列王记下》第20章第1节。

6. Woolworth's：一商店名。

7. naarrow＝narrow.

FLANNERY O'CONNOR

〔作者介绍〕

弗兰纳里·奥康纳（Flannery O'Connor，1925～1964），美国当代南方作家。她于1945年毕业于佐治亚州女子学院，两年后在衣阿华州立大学获文学创作硕士学位。她在结业以前便已开始发表作品，1952年出版第1部长篇小说《智慧的血》（*Wise Blood*）。奥康纳是一位严谨的作家。除上述作品外，她生前还发表过一部短篇小说集《好人难寻》（*A Good Man Is Hard to Find*，1955）和一部长篇小说《强暴者抱走了它》（*The Violent Bear It Away*，1960）。她因患狼疮医治无效，39岁便离开人世。奥康纳的一些散载作品在她死后被收入名为《发生的一切都会汇合在一起》（*Everything That Rises Must Converge*，1965）的作品集中。《奥康纳全集》（*The Complete Stories*）于1971年出版.

奥康纳的作品充溢着浓郁的南方气息。她善于以细腻的文笔描绘人生中奇异而荒诞的现象。她对描写信奉原教旨主义的乡下人的生活尤感兴趣，她的长篇和短篇小说常常出现迷信宗教的贫穷愚昧的南方人形象。奥康纳在刻画这些通常为苦难者的形象时，既通情达理，又注重探索他们的内心世界。这些痛苦的灵魂成为她的作品的主人公，在一定程度上成为表达她的思想认识的媒介。痛苦和死亡是她的作品的基调和主题。古怪的人物、异常的事件、骇人的暴力，以及这些所表达出的浓重的宗教信念，令人感到奥康纳既是一位哥特式（Gothic）小说作家，又是一位宗教作家。奥康纳写作技巧高妙，词句流利，常以生动的富有喜剧性和戏剧性的细节引人入胜。她冷静地、以不介入的态度描写突发的、意想不到的事情，把人性中觉察不到的东西挖掘出来，作品具有很大的震撼效果和讽刺意义，有较明显的荒诞倾向。

奥康纳以其富于感染力的作品，成为战后美国文坛上的佼佼者之一。

A Good Man Is Hard to Find

〔作品简介〕

《好人难寻》（“A Good Man Is Hard to Find”）是作者写的一篇杰出的短篇小说。它和奥康纳的大多数短篇故事一样，把日常生活的琐碎细节同令人发指的暴行巧妙地结合在一起，从而收到奇妙的艺术效果。作者写作奇妙之处似乎在于：首先安抚和镇定读者的情绪，接着便在不动声色的平淡叙述中突然来个惊人之笔，使读者对这骤变的情节瞠目结舌，不知所措。奥康纳认为，对于一个关心基督教信仰的小说家说来，现代生活充满了令人厌恶的怪诞现象，他的责任是使对这些现象习以为常的读者认识到它们的怪诞面貌。由于读者的认识不同，作家必须采取异常剧烈的手段使他们震惊：“对耳背者你要大喊，对近似失明的，你要画大而惊人的形体。”《好人难寻》对暴力的描写貌似漫不经心，实则透过平淡无奇的描绘，逐渐使恐怖的气氛感染读者，令他们感到作者所探索的乃是人生中诸如信仰之类的根本性问题。当人们读到老祖母和在逃犯对话的末尾部分时，这种感觉尤其强烈。令人啼笑皆非的是，似乎是逃犯对这些问题表现得更为关心、有更深刻的理解：这位精神变态的犯人无情地杀人，目的在于强迫上帝显身。

小说深刻地揭示出美国社会生活中存在的令人毛骨悚然的暴力，发出了“好人难寻”的悲凉的呼声。不论对老祖母一家和客店主，还是对在逃犯说来，“好人难寻”都是无法回避的残酷现实。

A Good Man Is Hard to Find

The grandmother didn't want to go to Florida.[1] She wanted to visit some of her connections in east Tennessee[2] and she was seizing at every chance to change Bailey 's mind. Bailey was the son she lived with, her only boy. He was sitting on the edge of his chair at the table, bent over the orange sports setion of the *Journal*. “Now look here, Bailey,” she said, “see here, read this,” and she stood with one hand on her thin hip and the other rattling the newspaper at his bald head. “Here this fellow that calls himself The Misfit is aloose from the Federal Pen[3] and headed toward Florida and you read here what it says he did to these people. Just you read it. I wouldn't take my children in any direction with a criminal like that aloose in it. I couldn't answer to my conscience if I did."

Bailey didn't look up from his reading so she wheeled around then and faced the children's mother, a young woman in slacks, whose face was as broad and innocent as a cabbage and was tied round with a green head-kerchief that had two points on the top like rabbit's ears. She was sitting on the sofa, feeding the baby his apricots out of a jar. "The children have been to Florida before," the old lady said. "You all ought to take them somewhere else for a change so they would see different parts of the world and be broad.[4] They never have been to east Tennessee."

The children's mother didn't seem to hear her but the eight-year-old boy, John Wesley, a stocky child with glasses, said, "If you don't want to go to Florida, why dontcha stay at home?" He and the little girl, June Star, were reading the funny papers on the floor.

"She wouldn't stay at home to be queen for a day," June Star said without raising her yellow head.

"Yes and what would you do if this fellow, The Misfit, caught you?" the grandmother asked.

"I'd smack his face," John Wesley said.

"She wouldn't stay at home for a million bucks," June Star said. "Afraid she'd miss something. She has to go everywhere we go."

"All right, Miss," the grandmother said. "Just remember that the next time you want me to curl your hair."

June Star said her hair was naturally curly.

The next morning the grandmother was the first one in the car, ready to go. She had her big black valise that looked like the head of a hippoptamus in one corner, and underneath it she was hiding a basket with Pitty Sing, the cat, in it. She didn't intend for the cat to be left alone in the house for three days because he would miss her too much and she was afraid he might brush against one of the gas burners and accidentally asphyxiate himself. Her son, Bailer, didn't like to arrive at a motel with a cat.

She sat in the middle of the back seat with John Wesley and June Star on either side of her. Bailey and the children's mother and the baby sat in the front and they left Atlanta[5] at eight forty-five with the mileage on the car at 55890. The grandmother wrote this down because she thought it would be interesting to say how many miles they had been when they got back. It took them twenty minutes to reach the outskirts of the city.

The old lady settled herself comfortably, removing her white cotton gloves and putting them up with her purse on the shelf in front of the back window. The children's mother still had on slacks and still had her head tied up in a green kerchief, but the grandmother had on a navy blue straw sailor hat with a bunch of white violets on the brim and a navy blue dress with a small white dot in the print. Her collar and cuffs were white organdy trimmed with lace and at her neckline she had pinned a purple spray of cloth violets containing a sachet. In case of an accident, anyone seeing her dead on the highway would know at once that she was a lady.

She said she thought it was going to be a good day for driving, neither too hot nor too cold, and she cautioned Bailey that the speed limit was fifty-five miles an hour and that the patrolmen hid themselves behind billboards and small clumps of trees and sped out after you before you had a chance to slow down. She pointed out interesting details of the scenery: Stone Mountain; the blue granite that in some places came up to both sides of the highway; the brilliant red clay banks slightly streaked with purple; and the various crops that made rows of green lace-work on the ground. The trees were full of silver-white sunlight and the meanest of them sparkled. The children were reading comic magazines and their mother had gone back to sleep.

"Let's go through Georgia[6] fast so we won't have to look at it much," John Wesley said.

"If I were a little boy, said the grandmother, "I wouldn't talk about my native state that way. Tennessee has the mountains and Georgia has the hills."

"Tennessee is just a hillbilly dumping ground," John Wesley said, "and Georgia is a lousy state too."

"You said it," June Star said.

"In my time," said the grandmother, folding her thin veined fingers, "children were more respectful of their native states and their parents and everything else. People did right then. Oh look at the cute little pickaninny!" she said and pointed to a Negro child standing in the door of a shack. "Wouldn't that make a picture, now?" she aked and they all turned and looked at the little Negro out of the back window. He waved.

"He didn't have any britches[7] on," June said.

"He poobably didn't have any,"the grandmother explained. "Little niggers in the country don't have things like we do. If I could paint I'd paint that picture," she said.

The children exchanged comic books.

The grandmother offered to hold the baby and the children's mother passed him over the front seat to her. She set him on her knee and bounced him and told him about the things they were passing. She rolled her eyes and screwed up her mouth and stuck her leathery thin face into his smooth bland one. Occasionally he gave her a faraway smile. They passed a large cotton field with five or six graves fenced in the middle of it, like a small island. "Look at the graveyard!" the grandmother said, pointing it out. "That was the old family burying ground. That belonged to the plantation."

"Where's the plantation?" John Wesley asked.

"Gone With the Wind,"[8] said the grandmother. "Ha. Ha."

When the children finished all the comic books they had brought, they opened the lunch and ate it. The grandmother ate a peanut butter sandwich and an olive and would not let the children throw the box and the paper napkins out the window. When there was nothing else to do they played a game by choosing a cloud and making the other two guess what shape it suggested. John Wesley took one the shape of a cow and June Star guessed a cow and John Wesley said, no, an automobile, and June Star said he didn't play fair, and they began to slap each other over the grandmother.

The grandmother said she would tell them a story if they would keep queit. When she told a story, she rolled her eyes and waved her head and was very dramatic. She said once when she was a maiden lady she had been courted by a Mr. Edgar Atkins Teagarden from Jasper, Georgia. She said he was a very good-looking man and a gentleman and that he brought her a watermelon every Saturday afternoon with his initials cut in it, E. A. T. Well, one Saturday, she said Mr. Teagarden brought the watermelon and there was nobody at home and he left it on the front porch and returned in his buggy to Jasper, but she never got the watermelon, she said because a nigger boy ate it when he saw the initials, E. A. T.! This story tickled John Wesley's funny bone[9] and he giggled and giggled but June Star didn't think it was any good. She said she wouldn't marry a man that just brought her a watermelon on Saturday. The grandmother said she would have done well to marry Mr. Teagarden because he was a gentleman and had bought Coca-Cola stock[10] when it first came out and that he had died only a few years ago, a very wealthy man.

They stopped at The Tower[11] for barbecued sandwiches. The Tower was a part stucco and part wood filling station and dance hall set in a clearing outside of Timothy. [12] A fat man named Red Sammy Butts ran it and there were signs stuck here and there on the building and for miles up and down the highway saying, TRY RED SAMMY'S FAMOUS BARBECUE. NONE LIKE FAMOUS RED SAMMY'S! RED SAM! THE FAT BOY WITH THE HAPPY LAUGH. A VETERAN! SAMMY'S YOUR MAN!

Red Sammy was lying on the bare ground outside The Yower with his head under a truck[13] while a gray monkey about a foot high, chained to a small chinaberry tree, chattered nearby. The monkey sprang back into the tree and got on the highest limb as soon as he saw the children jump out of the car and run toward him.

Inside, The Tower was a long dark room with a counter at one end and tables at the other and dancing space in the middle. They all sat down at a broad table next to the nickelodeon and Red Sam's wife, a tall burnt-brown woman with hair and eyes lighter than her skin, came and took their order. The children's mother put a dime in the machine and played "The Tennessee Waltz," and the grandmother said that tune always made her want to dance. She asked Bailey if he would like to dance but he only glared at her. He didn't have a naturally sunny disposition like she did and trips made him nervous. The grandmother's brown eyes were very bright. She swayed her head from side to side and pretended she was dancing in her chair. June Star said play something she could tap to so the children's mother put in another dime and played a fast number and June Star stepped out onto the dance floor and did her tap routine.

"Ain't she cute?" Red Sam's wife said, leaning over the counter. "Would you like to come be my little girl?"

"No I certainly wouldn't," June Star said. "I wouldn't live in a broken-down place like this for a million bucks!" and she ran back to the table.

"Ain't she cute?" the woman repeated, stretching her mouth politely.

"Aren't you ashamed?" hissed the grandmother.

Red Sam came in and told his wife to quit lounging on the counter and hurry with these people's order. His khaki trousers reached just to his hip bones and his stomach hung over them like a sack of meal swaying under his shirt. He came over and sat down at a table nearby and let out a combination sigh and yodel. "You can't win," he said. "You can't win," and he wiped his sweating red face off with a gray handkerchief. "These days you don't know who to trust," he said. "Ain't that the truth?"

"People are certainly not nice like they used to be," said the grandmother.

"Two fellers come in here last week," Red Sammy said, "driving a Chrysler.[14] It was a old beat-up car but it was a good one and these boys looked all right to me. Said they worked at the mill and you know I let them fellers charge the gas they bough? Now why did I do that?"

"Because you're a good man!" the grandmother said at once.

"Yes'm[15] I suppose so," Red Sam said as if he were struck with the answer.

His wife brougth the orders, carrying the five plates all at once without a tray, two in each hand and one balanced on her arm. "It isn't a soul in this green world[16] of God's that you can trust," she said "And I don't count anybody out of that, not nobody,"[17] she repeated looking at Red Sammy.

"Did you read about that criminal, The Misfit, that's escaped?" asked the grandmother.

"I wouldn't be a bit surprised if he didn't attact[18] this place right here," said the woman. "If he hears about it being here, I wouldn't be none surprised[19] to see him. If he hears it's two cent[20] in the cash register, I wouldn't be a tall[21] supristed if he. . ."

"That'll do," Red Sam said. "Go bring these people their Co'Colas," and the woman went off to get rest of the order.

"A good man is hard to find," Red Sammy said. "Everything is getting terrible. I remember the day you could go off and leave your screen door unlatched. Not no more."

He and the grandmother discussed better times. The old lady said that in her opinion Europe was entirely to blame for the way things were now. She said the way Europe acted you would think we were made of money and Red Sam said it was no use talking about it, she was exactly right. The children ran outside into the white sunlight and looked at the monkey in the lacy chinaberry tree. He was busy catching fleas on himself and biting each one carefully between his teeth as if it were a delicacy.

They drove off again into the hot afternoon. The grandmother took cat naps[22] and woke up every few minutes with her own snoring. Outside of Toombsboro[23] she woke up and recalled an old plantation that she had visited in this neighborhood once when she was a young lady. She said the house had six white columns across the front and that there was an avenue of oaks leading up to it and two little wooden trellis arbors on either side in front where you sat down with you suitor after a stroll in the garden. She recalled exactly which road to turn off to get to it. She knew that Bailey would not be willing to lose any time looking at an old house, but the more she talked about it, the more she wanted to see it once again and find out if the little twin arbors were still standing. "There was a secret panel in this house," she said craftily, not telling the truth but wishing that she were, "and the story went that all the family silver was hidden in it when Sherman[24] came through but it was never found..."

"Hey!" John Wesley said. "Let's go see it! We'll find it! We'll poke all the woodwork and find it! Who lives there? Where do you turn off at? Hey Pop, can't we turn off there?"

"We never have seen a house with a secret panel!" June Star shrieked. "Let's go to the house with the secret panel! Hey, Pop, can't we go see the house with the secret panel!"

"It's not far from here, I know," the grandmother said. "It wouldn't take over twenty minutes."

Bailey was looking straight ahead. His jaw was as rigid as a horseshoe. "No," he said.

The children began to yell and scream that they wanted to see the house with the secret panel. John Wesley kicked the back of the front seat and June Star hung over her mother's shoulder and whined desperately into her ear that they never had any fun even on their vacation, and that they could never do what THEY wanted to do. The baby began to scream and John Wesley kicked the back of the seat so hard that his father could feel the blows in his kidney.

"All right!" he shouted, and drew the car to a stop at the side of the road. "Will you all shut up? Will you all just shut up for one second? If you don't shut up, we won't go anywhere."

"It would be very educational for them," the grandmother murmured.

"All right," Bailey said, "but get this: this is the only time we're going to stop for anything like this. This is the one and only time."

"The dirt road that you have to turn down is about a mile back," the grandmother directed. "I marked it when we passed."

"A dirt road," Bailey groaned.

After they had turned around and were headed toward the dirt road, the grandmother recalled other points about the house, the beautiful glass over the front doorway and the candle-lamp in the hall. John Wesley said that the secret panel was probably in the fireplace.

"You can't go inside this house," Bailey said. "You don't know who lives there."

"While you all talk to the people in front, I'll run around behind and get in a window," John Wesley suggested.

"We'll all stay in the car," his mother said.

They turned onto the dirt road and the car raced roughly along in a swirl of pink dust. The grandmother recalled the times when there were no paved roads and thirty miles was a day's journey. The dirt road was hilly and there were sudden washes[25] in it and sharp curves on dangerous embankments. All at once they would be on a hill, looking down over the blue tops of trees for miles around, then the next minute, they would be in a red depression with the dust-coated trees looking down on them.

"This place had better turn up in a minute," Bailey said, "or I'm going to turn around."

The road looked as if no one had traveled on it in months.

"It's not much farther," the grandmother said and just as she said it, a horrible thought came to her. The thought was so embarrassing that she turned red in the face and her eyes dilated and her feet jumped up, upsetting her valise in the corner. The instant the valise moved, the newspaper top she had over the basket under it rose with a snarl and Pitty Sing, the cat, sprang onto Bailey's shoulder.

The children were thrown to the floor and their mother, clutching the baby, was thrown out the door onto the ground, the old lady was thrown into the front seat. The car turned over once and landed right-side-up in a gulch on the side of the road. Bailey remained in the driver's seat with the cat—gray-striped with a broad white face and an orange nose—clinging to his neck like a caterpillar.

As soon as the children saw they could move their arms and legs, they scrambled out of the car, shouting. "We've had an ACCIDENT!" The grandmother was curled up under the dashboard, hoping she was injured so that Bailey's wrath would not come down on her all at once. The horrible thought she had had before the accident was that the house she had remembered so vivdly was not in Georgia but in Tennessee.

Bailey removed the cat from his neck with both hands and flung it out the window against the side of a pine tree. Then he got out of the car and started looking for the children's mother. She was sitting against the side of the red gutted ditch, holding the screaming baby, but she only had a cut down her face and a broken shoulder. "We've had an ACCIDENT!" the children screamed in a frenzy of delight.

"But nobody's killed," June Star said with disappointment as the grandmother limped out of the car, her hat still pinned to her head but the broken front brim standing up at a jaunty angle and the violet spray hanging off the side. They all sat down in the ditch. excetp the children, to recover from the shock. They were all shhaking.

"Maybe a car will come along," said the children's mother hoarsely.

"I believe I have injured an organ," said the grandmother, pressing her side, but no one answered her. Bailey's teeth were clattering. He had on a yellow sport shirt with bright blue parrots designed in it and his face was as yellow as the shirt. The grandmother decided that she would not mention that the house was in Tennessee.

The road was about ten feet above and they could see only the tops of the trees on the other side of it. Behind the ditch they were sitting in there were more woods, tall and dark and deep. In a few minutes they saw a car some distance away on top of a hill, coming slowly as if the occupants were watching them. The grandmother stood up and waved both arms dramatically to attract their attention. The car continued to come on slowly, disappeared around a bend and appeared again, moving even slower, on top of the hill they had gone over. It was a big black battered hearse-like automobile. There were three men in it.

It came to a stop just over them and for some minutes, the driver looked down with a steady expressionless gaze to where they were sitting, and didn't speak. Then he turned his head and muttered something to the other two and they got out. One was a fat boy in black trousers and a red sweat shirt with a silver stallion embossed on the front of it. He moved around on the right side of them and stood staring, his mouth partly open in a kind of loose grin. The other had on khaki pants and a blue striped coat and a gray hat pulled down very low, hiding most of his face. He came around slowly on the left side. Neither spoke.

The driver got out of the car and stood by the side of it, looking down at them. He was an older man than the other two. His hair was just beginning to gray and he wore silver-rimmed spectacles that gave him a scholarly look. He had a long creased face and didn't have on any shirt or undershirt. He had on blue jeans that were too tight for him and was holding a black hat and a gun. The two boys also had guns.

"We've had an ACCIDENT!" the children screamed.

The grandmother had the peculiar feeling that the bespectacled man was someone she knew. His face was as familiar to her as if she had known him all her life but she could not recall who he was. He moved away from the car and began to come down the embankment, placing his feet carefully so that he wouldn't slip. He had on tan and white shoes and no socks, and his ankles were red and thin. "Good afternoon," he said. "I see you all had you a little spill."

"We turned over twice!" said the grandmother.

"Oncet,"[26] he corrected. "We seen it happen. Try their car and see will it run, Hiram," he said quietly to the boy with the gray hat.

"What you got that gun for?" John Wesley asked. "Whatcha gonna do with that gun?"[27]

"Lady," the man said to the children's mother, "would you mind calling them children to sit down by you? Children make me nervous. I want all you all to sit down right together there where you're at."

"What are you telling us what to do for?" June Star asked.

Behind them the line of woods gaped like a dark open mouth. "Come here," said their mother.

"Look here now," Bailey began suddenly, "we're in a predicament! We're in..."

The grandmother shrieked. She scrambled to her feet and stood staring. "You're The Misfit!" she said. "I recognized you at once."

"Yes'm," the man said, smiling slightly as if he were pleased in spite of himself to be known, "but it would have been better for all of you, lady, if you hadn't of reckernized me."[28]

Bailey turned his head sharply and said something to his mother that shocked even the children. The old lady began to cry and The Misfit reddened.

"Lady," he said, "don't you get upset. Sometimes a man says things he don't mean. I don't reckon he meant to talk to you thataway."[29]

"You wouldn't shoot a lady, would you?" the grandmother said and removed a clean handkerchief from her cuff and began to slap at her eyes with it.

The Misfit pointed the toe of his shoe into the ground and made a little hole and then covered it up again. "I would hate to have to." he said.

"Listen," the grandmother almost screamed, "I know you're a good man. You don't look a bit like you have common blood.[30] I know you must come from nice people!"

"Yes mam,"[31] he said, "finest people in the world." When he smiled he showed a row of strong white teeth. "God never made a finer woman than my mother and my daddy's heart was pure gold," he said. The boy with the red sweat shirt had come around behind them and was standing with his gun at his hip. The Misfit squatted down on the ground. "Watch them children, Bobby Lee," he said. "You know they make me nervous." He looked at the six of them huddled together in front of him and he seemed to be embarrassed as if he couldn't think of anything to say. "Ain't a cloud in the sky," he remarked, looking up at it. "Don't see no sun but don't see no cloud neither."

"Yes, it's a beautiful day," said the grandmother. "Listen," she said, "you shouldn't call yourelf The Misfit because I know you're a good man at heart. I can just look at you and tell."

"Hush!" Bailey yelled. "Hush! Everybody shut up and let me handle this!" He was squatting in the position of a runner about to sprint forward but he didn't move.

"I pre-chate that,[32] lady," The Misfit said and drew a little circle in the ground with the butt of his gun.

"It'll take a half a hour to fix this here car," Hiram called, looking over the raised hood of it.

"Well, first you and Bobby Lee get him and that little boy to step over yonder with you," The Misfit said, pointing to Bailey and John Wesley. "The boys want to ask you something," he said to Bailey. "Would you mind stepping back in them woods there with them?"

"Listen," Bailey began, "we're in a terrible predicament. Nobody realizes what this is," and his voice cracked. His eyes were as blue and intense as the parrots in his shirt and he remained perfectly still.

The grandmother reached up to adjust her hat brim as if she were going to the woods with him but it came off in her hand. She stood staring at it and after a second she let it fall on the ground. Hiram pulled Bailey up by the arm as if he were assisting an old man. John Wesley caught hold of his father's hand and Bobby Lee followed. They went off toward the woods and just as they reached the dark edge, Bailey turned and supporting himself against a gray naked pine trunk, he shouted, "I'll be back in a minute, Mamma, wait on me!"[33]

"Come back this instant!" his mother shrilled but they all disappeared into the woods.

"Bailey Boy!" the grandmother called in a tragic voice but she found she was looking at The Misfit squatting on the ground in front of her. "I just know you're a good man," she said desperately. "You're not a bit common!"

"Nome, I ain't a good man," The Misfit said after a second as if he had considered her statement carefully, "but I ain't the worst in the world neither. My daddy said I was different breed of dog from my brothers and sisters. 'You know,' Daddy said, 'it's some that can live their whole life out without asking about it and it's others has to know why it is, and this boy is one of the latters.[34] He's going to be into everything!'" He put on his black hat and looked up suddenly and then away deep into the woods as if he were embarrassed again. "I'm sorry I don't have on a shirt before you ladies," he said, hunching his shoulders slightly. "We buried our clothes that we had on when we escaped and we're just making do until we can get better. We borrowed these from some folks we met," he explained.

"That's perfectly all right," the grandmother said. "Maybe Bailey has an extra shirt in his suitcase."

"I'll look and see terrectly,"[35]The Misfit said.

"Where are they taking him?" the children's mother screamed.

"Daddy was a card[36] himself," the Misfit said. "You couldn't put anything over on him. [37] He never got in trouble with the Authorities though. Just had the knack of handling them."

"You could be honest too if you'd only try," said the grandmother. "Think how wonderful it would be to settle down and live a comforable life and not have to think about somebody chasing you all the time."

The Misfit kept scratching in the ground with the butt of his gun as if he were thinking about it. "Yes'm, somebody is always after you," he murmured.

The grandmother noticed how thin his shoulder blades were just behind his hat because she was standing up looking down on him. "Do you ever pray?" she asked.

He shook his head. All she saw was the black hat wiggle between his shoulder blades. "Nome," he said.

There was a pistol shot from the woods, followed closely by another. Then silence. The old lady's head jerked around. She could hear the wind move through the tree tops like a long satisfied insuck of breath. "Bailey Boy!" she called.

"I was a gospel singer for a while," The Misfit said. "I been most everything. Been in the arm service, both land and sea, at home and abroad, been twict[38] married, been an undertaker, been with the railroads, plowed Mother Earth, been in a tornado, seen a man burnt alive oncet," and he looked up at the children's mother and the little girl who were sitting close together, their faces white and their eyes glassy; "I even seen a woman flogged," he said.

"Pray, pray," the grandmother began, "pray, pray..."

"I never was a bad boy that I remember of," The Misfit said in an almost dreamy voice, "but somewheres along the line I done[39] something wrong and got sent to the penitentiary. I was buried alive," and he looked up and held her attention to him by a steady stare.

"That's when you should have started to pray," she said. "What did you do to get sent to the penitentiary that first time?"

"Turn to the right, it was a wall," The Misfit said, looking up again at the cludless sky. "Turn to the left, it was a wall. Look up it was a ceiling, look down it was a floor. I forgot what I done, lady. I set[40] there and set there, trying to remember what it was I done and I ain't recalled it to this day. Oncet in a while, I would think it was coming to me, but it never come."

"Maybe they put you in by mistake," the old lady said vaguely.

"Nome," he said. "It wasn't no mistake. They had the papers on me."

"You must have stolen something," she said.

The Misfit sneered slightly. "Nobody had nothing I wanted," he said. "It was a head-doctor at the penitentiary said what I had done was kill my daddy but I know that for a lie. My daddy died in nineteen ought nineteen of the epidemic flu[41] and I never had a thing to do with it. He was buried in the Mount Hopewell Baptist churchyard and you can go there and see for yourself."

"If you would pray," the old lady said, "Jesus would help you."

"That's right," The Misfit said.

"Well then, why don't you pray?" she asked trembling with delight suddenly.

"I don't want no hep," he said. "I'm doing all right by myself."

Bobby Lee and Hiram came ambling back from the woods. Bobby Lee and Hiram came ambling back from the woods. Bobby Lee was dragging a yellow shirt with bright blue parrots in it.

"Throw me that shirt, Bobby Lee," The Misfit said. The shirt came flying at him and landed on his shoulder and he put it on. The grand mother couldn't name what the shirt reminded her of. "No, lady," The Misfit said while he was buttoning it up. "I found out the crime don't matter. You can do one thing or you can do another, kill a man or take a tire off his car, because sooner or later you're going to forget what it was you done and just be punished for it."

The children's mother had begun to make heaving noises as if she couldn't get her breath. "Lady," he asked, "would you and that little girl like to step off yonder with Bobby Lee and Hiram and join your husband?"

"Yes, thank you," the mother said faintly. Her left arm dangled helplessly and she was holding the baby, who had gone to sleep, in the other. "Hep that lady up, Hiram," The Misfit said as she struggled to climb out of the ditch, "and Bobby Lee, you hold onto that little girl's hand."

"I don't want to hold hands with him," June Star said. "He reminds me of a pig."

The fat boy blushed and laughed and caught her by the arm and pulled her off into the woods after Hiram and her mother.

Alone with The Misfit, the grandmother found that she had lost her voice. There was not a cloud in the sky nor any sun. There was nothing around her but woods. She wanted to tell him that he must pray. She opened and closed her mouth several times before anything came out. Finally she found herself saying, "Jesus, Jesus," meaning Jesus will help you, but the way she was saying it, it sounded as if she might be cursing.

"Yes'm," The Misfit said as if he agreed. "Jesus thown[42] everything off balance, It was the same case with Him as with me except He hadn't committed any crime and they could prove I had committed one because they had the papers on me. Of course," he said, "they never shown me any papers. That's why I sign myself now. I said long ago, you get you a signature and sign everything you do and keep a copy of it. Then you'll know what you done and you can hold up the crime to the punishment and see do they match and in the end you'll have something to prove you ain't been treated right. I call myself The Misfit," he said, "because I can't make what all I done wrong fit what all I gone through in punishment."

There was a piercing scream from the woods, followed closely by a pistol report. "Does it seem right to you, lady, that one is punished a heap[43] and another ain't punished at all?"

"Jesus!" the old lady cried. "You've got good blood! I know you wouldn't shoot a lady! I know you come from nice people! Pray! Jesus, you ought not to shoot a lady. I'll give you all the money I've got!"

"Lady," The Misfit said, looking beyond her far into the woods, "there never was a body that give the undertaker a tip."

There were two more pistol reports and the grandmother raised her head like a parched old turkey hen crying for water and called, "Bailey Boy, Bailey Boy!" as if her heart would break.

"Jesus was the only One that ever raised the dead,"[44] The Misfit continued, "and He shouldn't have done it. He thown everything off balance. If He did what He said, then it's nothing for you to do but thow away everything and follow Him, and if He didn't, then it's nothing for you to do but enjoy the few minutes you got left the best way you can—by killing somebody or burning down his house or doing some other meanness to him. No pleasure but meanness," he said and his voice had become almost a snarl.

"Maybe He didn't raise the dead," the old lady mumbled, not knowing what she was saying and feeling so dizzy that she sank down in the ditch with her legs twisted under her.

"I wasn't there so I can't say He didn't," The Misfit said. "I wisht I had of been there,"[45] he said, hitting the ground with his fist. "It ain't right I wasn't there because if I had of been there I would of known. Listen lady," he said in a high voice, "if I had of been there I would of known[46] and I wouldn't be like I am now." His voice seemed about to crack and the grandmother's head cleared for an instant. She saw the man's face twisted close to her own as if he were going to cry and she murmured, "Why you're one of my babies. You're one of my own children!" She reached out and touched him on the shoulder. The Misfit sprang back as if a snake had bitten him and shot her three times through the chest. Then he put his gun down on the ground and took off his glasses and began to clean them.

Hiram and Bobby Lee returned from the woods and stood over the ditch, looking down at the grandmother who half sat and half lay in a puddle of blood with her legs crossed under her like a child's and her face smiling up at the cloudless sky.

Without his glasses, The Misfit's eyes were red-rimmed and pale and defenseless-looking. "Take her off and thow her where you thown the others," he said, picking up the cat that was rubbing itself against his leg.

"She was a talker, wasn't she?" Bobby Lee said, sliding down the ditch with a yodel.

"She would of been a good woman," The Misfit said, "if it had been somebody there to shoot her every minute of her life."

"Some fun!" Bobby Lee said.

"Shut up, Bobby Lee," The Misfit said. "It's no real pleasure in life."

〔注释〕

1. Florida：美国佛罗里达州。

2. Tennessee：美国田纳西州。

3. aloose from the Federal Pen：从联邦监狱中逃出；Pen 为 Penitentiary 的缩写。

4. be broad：开阔眼界。

5. Atanta：亚特兰大，美国佐治亚州的首府。

6. Georgia：美国佐治亚州。

7. britches＝breeches，裤子。

8. Gone with the Wind：双关语。祖母显然在暗指美国女作家玛格丽特·米切尔（Margaret Mitchell）所写的 *Gone with the Wind*（《飘》）。这是一部关于美国南北战争的小说。这里老祖母借用小说的名字表达"一切都随风而去"的意思。

9. tickled John Wesley's funny bone：把约翰·韦斯莱逗笑了。

10. Coca-Cola stock："可口可乐"公司的股票。

11. The Tower：餐馆名。

12. Timothy：佐治亚州一城市名。

13. with his head under a truck：正在卡车底下修车。

14. Chrysler：克里斯勒，一种比较豪华的汽车名。

15. Yes'm＝Yes, madame.

16. It isn't a soul＝There isn't a soul; green world＝good world.

17. not nobody：双重否定，意为"not anybody"。

18. attact＝attack.

19. I wouldn't be none surprised... ＝I wouldn't be surprised at all....

20. it's two cent…＝there are two cents….

21. a tall ＝at all.

22. The grandmother took cat naps：祖母打盹儿。

23. Toombsboro：一镇名。（boro：borough 的缩写。）

24. Sherman：谢尔曼，指（William Tecumsh，1820～1891），美国南北战争中北军将领。

25. washes：洼地。

26. Oncet＝Once（爱尔兰土话发音）。

27. Whatcha gonna do with that gun? ＝What are you going to do with that

gun?

28. if you hadn't of reckernized me=if you hadn't recognized me.

29. thataway=that way.

30. You don't look a bit like you have common blood：你看来一点也不象出身低微的人。

31. mam=madame.

32. I pre-chate that=I appreciate that.

33. wait on me! =wait for me!

34. it's some that can live their whole life out without asking about it and it's others has to know why it is, and this boy is one of the latters：有些人活一辈子也不对生活提出问题，另一些人要知道生活为何如此，这个孩子是属于后者的。

35. terrectly=directly.

36. a card：精明的人。

37. You couldn't put anything over on him：你作弄不了他。

38. twict=twice.

39. done=did.

40. set=sat.

41. nineteen ought nineteen of the epidemic flu：1919年欧洲的大瘟疫。

42. thown=threw.

43. a heap：a lot，做状语用。

44. Jesus was the only One that ever raised the dead：耶稣是唯一能使死人复活的人。

45. I wish I had of been there=I wish I had been there.

46. I would of known=I would have known.

ALLEN GINSBERG

〔作者介绍〕

艾伦·金斯堡（Allen Ginsberg，1926～ ），美国当代诗人。出生在新泽西州，在佩特森市读完中学后于1943年进入哥伦比亚大学学习，后因故曾被开除一段时间，最后于1948年毕业。金斯堡年轻时做过多种工作：在餐馆刷洗碗碟，在商船任炊事员，当过熔焊工，门房等。同时他认真研读了他所喜爱的诗人惠特曼和布莱克的诗作，还通过吸毒来体验精神状态的变化。1948年到1949年间，他曾患幻听，仿佛新耳听见英国诗人布莱克（William Blake，1757～1827）朗诵《啊，葵花》及《病玫瑰》二诗，觉得世界末日即将来临。那时，他的一位吸毒朋友曾在他房间内藏过毒品。为了逃避刑事责任，他以患有精神病为借口，住院8个月进行治疗。50年代他曾为一家杂志写书评，后来当过市场调研员。1954年他旅游墨西哥以后在旧金山定居。两年以后，城市之光书局出版了他的诗集《嚎叫及其他》（*Howl and Other Poems*），立即取得巨大成功，奠定了他在当代美国诗坛的重要地位。他与小说家杰克·凯鲁亚克（Jack Kerouac）、威廉·巴勒斯（William Burroughs）一起成为“垮掉的一代”（the Beat Generation）的代表人物。

金斯堡后来的诗作进一步巩固了他的诗歌艺术成就。《凯地什及其他》（*Kaddish and Other Poems*，1960）、《空镜子》（*Empty Mirror*，1960）、《现实的三明治》（*Reality Sandwiches*，1963）、《行星消息》（*Planet News*，1969）、《美国的衰亡》（*The Fall of America*，1972）及《精神呼吸》（*Mind Breathes*，1977）等诗集，进一步突出了他做为“垮掉的一代”的代表的形象。诚然，金斯堡的诗质量有时优劣不等，某些作品如《凯地什》及《现实的三明治》等，多有诗意欠佳之处；但是他的作品都是他所热情坚持的思想的集中表现，这使他成为年轻一代所崇拜的人物。

金斯堡是50年代普遍感到失望和不满的战后一代的发言人，他的声音成为反叛美国所代表的主流文化的主要声音。他所代表的“垮掉的一代”对抗一切关于性、宗教及美国生活方式的传统价值观，他们感到压抑、疲乏，需要逃避到一种非传统的—群居的—生活方式中去。金斯堡对于他所处时代的美国进行了猛烈的抨击，无情地披露了美国社会对美国最杰出的一些人的疯狂摧残，揭示出美国工业文明所产生的精神痛苦和绝望情绪。他不仅写诗，而且参加社会上的各种运动（如民权运动、反战运动、同性恋解放运动等），进行讲演，在国内外旅行，当众朗诵自己的诗作，在不少人的心目中—不仅在美国人而且在世界其他国家如日本、印度和英国的心目中，他成为争取自由生活、反对专制统治的旗手。随着时间的推移，金斯堡也逐渐为人所接受，成为一种新传统的代表和狂热的宗教追求者。他的作品常有一种神秘主义的幻想成份，其中包含着布莱克的神秘主义、希伯来文化中的幻景和佛教的理想境界。

典型的金斯堡作品有充满个人激情的抒情短诗，也有表达妙悟、寻觅灵感及意识扩张的长段狂想曲。他的幻觉能力，他那邀请读者进行诚恳的、温情的公开交流的能力，在他的诗作和个人生活中表现得极其突出。他的语言是多种成份溶为一炉的产物；他吸收了布莱克、惠特曼、威廉·卡洛斯·威廉斯及哈特·克兰等人的诗歌语言的特长，写出了感情激昂的惠特曼式的长句。他近年来的作品一般较长，具有很强的社会批判性，语言有时散漫无章，这可能是因为，他诗中的某些部分是根据他在旅途中谈话的录音整理成的，这些谈话包含着他在旅途中的思想、所见的意象及对外界所做出的反应。

评论界对金斯堡迄今依然褒贬不一。他的诗语言和内容都不乏污秽之处，讲如同性恋、吸毒及其伴随的精神状态，有时，给人一种颓废的感觉。但多数人似乎比较一致地认为，他的自由体诗及其所表达的激情业已使他成为一位不受拘泥的“美国人行便道歌手”，他将做为“垮掉的一代”的桂冠诗人和代言人载入美国文学史册。

Howl

〔作品介绍〕

《嚎叫》(*Howl*) 1956 年出版以前就已以其激动人心的魅力被人所传诵。它问世后，立即引起人们的普遍注意。由于它思想“偏激”，语言粗野，曾被指控为“淫猥”而受到审判，但是这使它更令世人瞩目，而它由于作家和学者的支持所取得的胜利，更增加了它的知名度和销售量。

初读《嚎叫》，人们会感到它不是诗，而是淫词秽语的堆砌。的确，《嚎叫》有乏淫秽的思想和语言，包括令人尴尬的字句。但是，随着时间的推移，人们逐渐认识到，《嚎叫》是一篇精湛的艺术品，是针对摧毁了战后一代最杰出人物的美国社会而认真写成的一篇流利的诅骂檄文。这首诗由三部分组成。第一部分表现的是一个从地狱经过的金斯堡，堕落、颓废、绝望，诅咒自己命运不佳，口中喷吐着一种旨在惊醒公众的下流语言。读者会突然意识到，“垮掉的一代”的一些怪癖和反常行为，如群居中出现的吸毒、性混乱、同性恋等，其实是这一代人恶梦般经历的必然产物；诗中的嚎叫，只能是发自这些人内心的痛苦的声音。诗的这一部分有力的表达了战后一代，特别是它的知识阶层即它的善于思考的阶层那种受到欺骗和摧残的痛苦感觉。

诗的第 2 部集中抨击美国的机械文明，金斯堡称之为“莫洛克”。这个名字是《圣经》中以儿童为其供品的异教火神的名字。在金斯堡的诗中，现代美国之神的供品已不是儿童，而是民族的精英。莫洛克敲开他们的头颅，吞食他们的大脑和想象力。莫洛克产生孤独、污秽、痛苦，建立魔鬼般的工业，把理想、幻梦、奇迹、启示、妙悟——总之，人的一切敏感的思想，人的一切希望和憧憬，无情地冲刷到河中去。这一部分加强了第一部分的主题，给一幅民族的疯狂和绝望的画面上增添了悲剧的伤感色调。

诗的第 3 总分是诗人献给他的朋友卡尔·索罗门的。关于卡尔·索罗门和这一首诗，美国现代伟大诗人威廉·卡洛斯·威廉斯曾写道：“一切迹象表明，(金斯堡）真地经过了地狱。在路上，他碰到了一个名叫卡尔·索罗门的人，他们一起经历了人世生活的暴戾和污秽，这些本是不可言状的，而只能用他已使用的语言加以形容。”索罗门最终往进精神病 院，他的“纯真而不朽”的灵魂，极有可能会在没有武装看守的精神病院里死去。诗人表示自己和病人在一起，同甘苦共命运。

这首诗明显地借鉴了惠特曼和威廉·卡洛斯·威廉斯的诗风特长。它的散文诗长句显然受惠于惠特曼；它的声调和节奏显然学习了威廉斯。《嚎叫》在结构上略嫌臃肿和散乱，但是它锐不可挡的威力赢得了读者，而成为“垮掉的一代”文学的代表作之一。

Howl *for Carl Solomon*[1]

I

I saw the best minds of my generation destroyed by madness, starving
hysterical naked,
dragging themselves through the negro streets at dawn looking for an

angry fix,
angelheaded hipsters burning for the ancient heavenly connection to the
starry dynamo in the machinery of night,
who poverty and tatters and hollow-eyed and high sat up smoking in the
supernatural darkness of clod-water flats floating across the tops
of cities contemplating jazz,
who bared their brains to Heaven under the El[2] and saw Mohammedan
angels staggering on tenement roofs illuminated,
who passed through universities with radiant cool eyes hallucinating
Arkansas and Blake[3]-light tragedy among the scholars of war,
who were expelled from the academies for crazy & publishing obscene
odes on the windows of the skull,
who cowered in unshaven rooms in underwear, burning their money in
wastebaskets and listening to the Terror through the wall,
who got busted in their pubic beards returning through Laredo[4] with a
belt of marijuana for New York,
who ate fire in paint hotels or drank turpentine in Paradise Alley,
death, or 10 purgatoried their torsos night after night
with dreams, with drugs, with waking nightmares, alcohol and cock and
endless balls,
incomparable blind streets of shuddering cloud and lightning in the mind
leaping toward poles of Canada & Paterson, illuminating all the
motionless world of Time between,
Peyote solidities of halls, backyard green tree cemetery dawns, wine
drunkenness over the rooftops, storefront boroughs of teahead
joyride neon blinking traffic light, sun and moon and tree vibra-
tions in the roaring winter dusks of Brooklyn, ashcan rantings
and kind king light of mind,
who chained themselves to subways for the endless ride from Battery[5] to
holy Bronx on benzedrine until the noise of wheels and children
brought them down shuddering mouth-wracked and battered
bleak of brain all drained of brilliance in the drear light of Zoo,
who sank all night in submarine light of Bickford's[6] floated out and sat
through the stale beer afternoon in desolate Fugazzi's[7], listening
to the crack of doom on the hydrogen jukebox,
who talked continuously seventy hours from park to pad to bar to Belle-
vue[8] to museum to the Brooklyn Bridge,[9]

a lost battalion of platonic conversationalists jumping down the stoops off fire escapes off windowsills off Empire State out of the moon,

yacketayakking[10] screaming vomiting whispering facts and memories and anecdotes and eyeball kicks and shocks of hospitals and jails and wars,

whole intellects disgorged in total recall for seven days and nights with brilliant eyes, meat for the Synagogue cast on the pavement,

who vanished into nowhere Zen New Jersey leaving a trail of ambiguous picture postcards of Atlantic City Hall,

suffering Eastern sweats and Tangerian[11] bone-grindings and migraines of China under junk-withdrawal in Newark[12]'s bleak furnished room,

who wandered around and around at midnight in the railroad yard wondering where to go, and went, leaving no broken hearts,

who lit cigarettes in boxcars boxcars boxcars racketing through snow toward lonesome farms in grandfather night,

who studied Plotinus Poe St. John of the Cross[13] telepathy and bop kaballa because the cosmos instinctively vibrated at their feet it Kansas,

who loned it through the streets of Idaho seeking visionary indian angels who were visionary indian agnels,

who thought they were only mad when Baltimore gleamed in supernatural ecstasy,

who jumped in limousines with the Chinaman of Oklahoma on the impulse of winter midnight streetlight smalltown rain,

who lounged hungry and lonesome through Houston seeking jazz or sex or soup, and followed the brilliant Spaniard to converse about America and Eternity, a hopeless task, and so took ship to Africa,

who disappeared into the volcanoes of Mexico leaving behind nothing but the shadow of dungarees and the lava and ash of poetry scattered in fireplace Chicago,

who reappeared on the West Coast investigating the F. B. I. in beards and shorts with big pacifist eyes sexy in their dark skin passing out incomprehensible leaflets,

who burned cigarette holes in their arms protesting the narcotic tobacco

haze of Capitalism,
who distributed Supercommunist pamphlest in Union Square weeping
and undressing while the sirens of Los Alamos wailed them
down, and wailed down Wall, and the Staten Island[14] ferry also
wailed,
who broke down crying in white gymnasiums naked and trembling be-
fore the machinery of other skeletons,
who bit detectives in the neck and shrieked with delight in policecars for
committing no crime but their own wild cooking pederasty and
intoxication,
who howled on their knees in the subway and were dragged off the roof
waving genitals and manuscripts,
who let themselves be fucked in the ass by saintly motorcyclists, and
screamed with joy,
who blew and were blown by those human seraphim, the sailors, caress-
es of Atlantic and Caribbean love,
who balled in the morning in the evenings in rosegardens and the grass
of public parks and cemeteries scattering their semen freely to
whomever come who may,
who hiccupped endlessly trying to giggle but wound up with a sob be-
hind a partition in a Turkish Bath when the blonde & naked an-
gel came to pierce them with a sword,
who lost their loveboys to the three old shrews of fate the one eyed
shrew of the heterosexual dollar the one eyed shrew that winks
out of the womb and the one eyed shrew that does nothing but
sit on her ass and snip the intellectual golden threads of the
craftsman's loom,
who copulated ecstatic and insatiate with a bottle of beer a sweetheart a
package of cigarettes a candle and fell off the bed, and contin-
ued along the floor and down the hall and ended fainting on the
wall with a vision of ultimate cunt and come eluding the last
gyzym of consciousness,
who sweetened the snatches of a million girls trembling in the sunset,
and were red eyed in the morning but prepared to sweeten the
snatch of the sunrise, flashing buttocks under barns and naked in
the lake,
who went out whoring through Colorado in myriad stolen night-cars, N.

C., secret hero of these poems, cocksman and Adonis of Denver—joy to the memory of his innumerable lays of girls in empty lots & diner backyards, moviehouses' rickety rows, on mountaintops in caves or with gaunt waitresses in familiar roadside lonely petticoat upliftings & especially secret gas-station solipisisms of johnx, & hometown alleys too,

who faded out in vast sordid movies, were shifted in dreams, woke on a sudden Manhattan, and picked themselves up out of basements hungover with heartless Tokay and horrors of Third Avenue iron dreams & stumbled to unemployment offices,

who walked all night with their shoes full of blood on the snowbank docks waiting for a door in the East River to open to a room full of steamheat and opium,

who created great suicidal dramas on the apartment cliff-banks of the Hudson under the wartime blue floodlight of the moon & their heads shall be crowned with laurel in oblivion,

who ate the lamb stew of the imagination or digested the crab at the muddy bottom of the rivers of Bowery,

who wept at the romance of the streets with their pushcarrs full of onions and bad musc,

who sat in boxes breathing in the darkness under the bridge, and rose up to build harpsichords in their lofts,

who coughed on the sixth floor of Harlem crowned with flame under the tubercular sky surrounded by orange crates of theology,

who scribbled all night rocking and rolling over lofty incantations which in the yellow morning were stanzas of gibberish,

who cooked rotten animals lung heart feet tail borsht & tortillas dreaming of the pure vegetable kingdom,

who plunged themselves under meat trucks looking for an egg,

who threw their watches off the roof to cast their ballot for Eternity outside of Time, & alarm clocks fell on their heads every day for the next decade,

who cut their wrists three times successively unsuccessfully, gave up and were forced to open antique stores where they thought they were growing old and cried,

who were burned alive in their innocent flannel suits on Madison Avenue amid blasts of leaden verse & the tanked-up clatter of the iron regiments of fashion & the nitroglycerine shrieks of the fairies of advertising & the mustard gas of sinister intelligent editors, or were run down by the drunken taxicabs of Absolute Reality,

who jumped off the Brooklyn Bridge this actually happened and walked away unknown and forgotten into the ghostly daze of Chinatown soup alleyways & firetrucks, not even one free beer,

who sang out of their windows in despair, fell out of the subway window, jumped in the filthy Passaic,[15] leaped on negroes, cried all over the street, danced on broken wineglasses barefoot smashed phonograph records of nostalgic European 1930's German jazz finished the whiskey and threw up groaning into the bloody toilet, moans in their ears and the blast of colossal steamwhistles,

who barreled down the highways of the past journeying to each other's hotrod-Golgotha jail-solitude watch or Birmingham jazz incarnation,

who drove crosscountry seventytwo hours to find out if I had a vision or you had a vision or he had a vision to find out Eternity,

who journeyed to Denver, who died in Denver, who came back to Denver &waited in vain, who watched over Denver & brooded & loned in Denver and finally went away to find out the Time, & now Denver is lonesome for her heroes,

who fell on their knees in hopeless cathdrals praying for each other's salvation and light and breasts, until the soul illuminated its hair for a second,

who crashed through their minds in jail waiting for impossible criminals with golden heads and the charm of reality in their hearts who sang sweet blues to Alcatraz,[16]

Who retired to Mexico to cultivate a habit, or Rocky Mount[17] to tender Buddh or Tangiers to boys or Southern Pacific to the black locomotive or Harvard to Narcissus to Woodlawn to the daisychain or grave,

who demanded sanity trials accusing the radio of hypnotism & were left with their insanity & their hands & a hung jury,

who threw potato salad at CCNY[18] lecturers on Dadaism and subsequently presented themselves on the granite steps of the madhouse wiht shaven heads and harlequin speech of suicide, de-

manding instantaneous lobotomy,
and who were given instead the concrete void of insulin metrasol electricity hydrotherapy psychotherapy occupational therapy pingpong & amnesia,
who in humorless protest overturned only one symbolic pingpong table, resting briefly in catatonia,
returning years later truly bald except for a wig of blood, and tears and fingers, to the visible madman doom of the wards of the madtowns of the East,
Pilgrim State's Rockland's and Greystone's[19] foetid halls, bickering with the echoes of the soul, rocking and rolling in the midnight solitude-bench dolmenrealms of love, dream of life a nightmare, bodies turned to stone as heavy as the moon,
with mother finally******, and the last fantastic book flung out of the tenement window, and the last door closed at 4 AM and the last telephone slammed at the wall in reply and the last furnished room emptied down to the last piece of mental furniture, a yellow paper rose twisted on a wire hanger in the closet, and even that imaginary, nothing but a hopeful little bit of hallucination—
ah, Carl,[20] while you are not safe I am not safe, and now you're really in the total animal soup of time—
and who therefore ran through the icy streets obsessed with a sudden flash of the alchemy of the use of the ellipse the catalog the meter & the vibrating plane,
who dreamt and made incarnate gaps in Time & Space through images juxtaposed, and trapped the archangel of the soul between 2 visual images and joined the elemental verbs and set the noun and dash of consciousness together jumping with sensation of Pater Omnipotens Aeterna Deus[21]
to recreate the syntax and measure of poor human prose and stand before you speechless and intelligent and shaking with shame, rejected yet confessing out the soul to conform to the rhythm of thought in his naked and endless head,
the madman bum and angel beat in Time, unknown, yet putting down here what might be left to say in time come after death,
and rose reincarnate in the ghostly clothes of jazz in the goldhorn shad-

ow of the band and blew the suffering of America's naked mind for love into an eli eil lamma lamma sabacthani[22] saxophone cry that shivered the cities down to the last radio

with the absolute heart of the poem of life butchered out of their own bodies good to eat a thousand years.

II

What sphinx of cement and aluminum[23] bashed open their skulls and ate up their brains and imagination?

Moloch! Solitude! Filth! Ugliness! Ashcans and unobtainable dollars! Children screaming under the stairways! Boys sobbing in armies! Old men weeping in the parks!

Moloch! Moloch! Nightmare of Moloch! Moloch the loveless! Mental moloch! Moloch the heavy judger of men!

Moloch the imcomprehensible prison! Moloch the crossbone souless jailhouse and Congress of sorrows! Moloch whose buildings are judgement! Moloch the vast stone of war! Moloch the stunned governments!

Moloch whose mind is pure machinery! Moloch whose blood is running money! Moloch whose fingers are ten armies! Moloch whose breast is a cannibal dynamo! Moloch whhose ear is a smoking tomb!

Moloch whose eyes are a thousand blind windows! Moloch whose skyscrapers stand in the long streets like endless Jehovahs! Moloch whose factories dream and croak in the fog! Moloch whose smokestacks and antennae crown the cities!

Moloch whose love is endless oil and stone! Moloch whose soul is electricity and banks! Moloch whose poverty is the specter of genius! Moloch whose fate is a cloud of sexless hydrogen! Moloch whose name is the Mind!

Moloch in whom I sit lonely! Moloch in whom I dream Angels! Crazy in Moloch! Cocksucker in Moloch! Lacklove and manless in Moloch!

Moloch who entered my soul early! Moloch in whom I am a consciousness without a body! Moloch who frightened me out of my natural ecstasy! Moloch whom I abandon! Wake up in Moloch! Light streaming out of the sky!

Moloch! Moloch! Robot apartments! invisible suburbs! skeleton treasuries! blind capitals! demonic industries! spectral nations! invincible madhouses! granite cocks! monstrous bombs!

They broke their backs lifting Moloch to Heaven! Pavements, trees, radios, tons! lifting the city to Heaven which exists and is everywhere about us!

Visions! omens! hallucinations! miracles! ecstasies! gone down the American river!

Dreams! adorations! illuminations! religions! the whole boatload of sensitive bullshit!

Breakthroughs! over the river! flips and crucfixions! gone down the flood! Highs! Epiphanies! Despairs! Ten years'[24] animal screams and suicides! Minds! New loves! Mad generation! down on the rocks of Time!

Real holy laughter in the river! They saw it all! the wild eyes! the holy yells! They bade farewell! They jumped off the roof! to solitude! waving! carrying flowers! Down to the river! into the street!

III

Carl Solomon! I'm with you in Rockland
where you're madder than I am
I'm with you in Rockland
where you must feel very strange
I'm with you in Rockland
where you imitate the shade of my mother
I'm with you in Rockland
where you've murdered your twelve secretaries
I'm with you in Rockland
where you laugh at this invisible humor
I'm with you in Rockland
where we are great writers on the same dreadful typewriter
I'm with you in Rockland
where your condition has become serious and is reported on the radio

I'm with you in Rockland
where the faculties of the skull no longer admit the worms of the senses
I'm with you in Rockland
where you drink the tea of the breasts of the spinsters of Utica[25]
I'm with you in Rockland
where you pun on hte bodies of your nurses the harpies of the Bronx
I'm with you in Rockland
where you scream in a straightjacket that you're losing the game of the actual pingpong of the abyss
I'm with you in Rockland
where you bang on the catatonic piano the soul is innocent and immortal it should never die ungodly in an armed madhouse
I'm with you in Rockland
where fifty more shocks will never return your soul to its body again from its pilgrimage to a cross in the void
I'm with you in Rockland
where you accuse your doctors of insanity and plot the Hebrew socialist revolution against the fascist national Golgotha
I'm with you in Rockland
where you will split the heavens of Long Island and resurrect your living human Jesus from the superhuman tomb
I'm with you in Rockland
where there are twentyfive-thousand mad comrades all together singing the final stanzas of the Internationale
I'm with you in Rockland
where we hug and kiss the United States under our bedsheets the United States that coughs all night and won't let us sleep
I'm with you in Rockland
where we wake up electrified out of the coma by our own souls' airplanes roaring over the roof they've come to drop angelic bombs the hospital illuminates itself imaginary walls collapse O skinny legions run outside O starry-spangled shock of mercy the eternal war is here O victory forget your underwear we're free
I'm with you in Rockland

in my dreams you walk dripping from a sea-journey on the highway across America in tears to the door of my cottage in the Western night

〔注释〕

1. Carl Solomon：纽约市布隆克斯区一位达达主义者（dadaist）、散文诗人。金斯堡在《嚎叫》一书的背面简述自己生平时在最后提到了他。

2. the EL：高架铁道。

3. Blake：布莱克（William Blake，1757～1827），英国神秘主义诗人。

4. Laredo：拉雷多市，位于得克萨斯州南部。

5. Battery：即 Battery Park，亦作 The Battery，位于纽约市曼哈顿岛南端的公园。

6. Bickfrd's：可能是河边一酒馆名。

7. Fugazzi's：一酒馆名。

8. Bellevue：纽约市一医院名。

9. the Brooklyn Bridge：纽约市布鲁克林桥。

10. yacketayak＝yacketyyak.

11. Tangerian：即 Tangerine，丹吉尔的。丹吉尔为摩洛哥国一商埠。诗人在50年代后期曾到过这里。

12. Newark：纽瓦克市，位于新泽西州东北部。

13. Plotinus Poe St. John of the Cross：Plotinus 普鲁提那斯（205～270），罗马哲学家，生于埃及；Poe：坡（Edgar Allan Poe，1809～1849），美国诗人；St. John of the Cross：赤足卡莫尔教派的创始人（1542～1591），以其神秘主义的著作而闻名于世。

14. Union square，Los Alamos，Wall，the Staten Island：皆为纽约市内地区；Wall 即华尔街。

15. the…Passaic：巴塞克河，位于新泽西州西北部。

16. Alcatrag：阿尔卡特拉兹岛，位于加里福尼亚州旧金山湾。

17. Rocky Mount：洛基山市，位于北卡罗莱纳州东北部。

18. CCNY＝City Council of New york.

19. Pilgrim State's Rockland's and Greystone's：3所精神病院名。

20. Carl：即 Carl Solomon.

21. Pater Omnipotens Aeterna Deus：拉丁文，英文为"Mighty God，Everlasting Father"；引自《圣经·以赛亚书》，9:6.

22. eli eli Lamma Lamma sabacthani：为耶稣在十字架上所说，英文为"My God，my God，Why hast thou forsaken me?"

23. Sphinx of cement and aluminum：指美国机械文明。

24. The years'：可能指从第二次世界大战结束到50年代中期诗歌写成这一段时间。

25. utica：尤蒂卡，纽约州东部一城市。

KURT VONNEGUT

〔作者介绍〕

库尔特·冯纳古特（Kurt Vonnegut Jr.，1922～ ）美国当代小说家，生于印第安纳州的印第安那波利斯。1940年中学毕业后就读于康奈尔大学，攻读生物化学。大学三年级时应召服役，被遣赴欧洲作战，次年被德军俘虏，送往德累斯顿城（Dresden）服苦役。德累斯顿是一座不设防的文化城，但在1945年2月13日，盟军飞机对该城狂轰滥炸，将其夷为平地，13.5万人葬身火海。冯纳古特因在一屠宰场的地下冷藏库干活才幸免遇难。这次轰炸和屠杀深深地刻在他的记忆中。在他看来，德累斯顿的烈焰不啻于世界的末日。他于1945年回国，在芝加哥大学研究人类学，同时兼作记者工作，后迁入纽约东部的斯克内克塔迪市（Schenectady），在通用电器公司担任对外联络工作。该地后来成为他的许多小说的背景，即他称之为纽约的伊利翁的地方。他将该地与古代的特洛伊城相联系，以强调当代文化生活的贫乏。

冯纳古特1950年移居科德角（Cape Cod），潜心创作，作品多刊载于科幻小说杂志上，因而公众曾一度把他看作科幻小说家。冯纳古特对此则耿耿于怀。1969年《第五号屠场》（*Slaughterhouse—Five*）出版，确立了他在美国文坛的地位。他的其他作品包括描写未来生活、带有科学幻想色彩的《自动钢琴》（*Player Piano*，1952）、《泰坦的女妖》（*The Sirens of Titan*，1959）、以二战中一位卖身投靠纳粹德国艺术家的遭遇为题材的《夜母》（*Mother Night*，1961），以及《挑绷子》（*Cat's Cradle*，1963）、《上帝保佑你，罗斯沃特先生》（*God Bless You，Mr. Rosewater*，1965）、《胜利者的早餐》（*Breakfast for Champions*，1973）、《滑稽剧》（*Slapstick*，1976）、《囚犯》（*Jailbird*，1979）。此外还有短篇小说和剧作。1972年他当选为国际笔会美国分会副主席和国家文学艺术协会会员。

冯纳古特所处时代的动荡对他的创作有很大影响，如30年代的经济危机，40年代的第二次世界大战，50年代的朝鲜战争和麦卡锡主义的泛滥，60

年代的越南战争和美国社会的广泛骚动。冯纳古特身处当代世界，深感技术文明社会对人的压抑。在这样的社会中，苦难、失望、死亡接踵而至，而人只有逆来顺受。因而他认为这个世界没有目的，没有秩序，没有希望。社会的残酷常使他——以及他小说中的人物——寄情于科学幻想，以期减轻自己的痛苦。

冯纳古特是一位具有人道主义思想、讽刺笔锋极为犀利的作家。《自动钢琴》提出人与机器的关系问题，指出人应当是世界的主人；《泰坦的女妖》说明人要爱自己周围的人；《夜母》通过一个犯下“反人道的罪行”的间谍之口，提出“与其可耻地活着还不如死去”的思想；《挑绷子》针砭宗教和政治对人民的欺骗，预示科学可能对人类造成的威胁；《第五号屠场》则以辛辣的手笔揭示出战争的残酷，以悲凉的笔调强调了死亡的不可避免。冯纳古特是一位富有幽默感的作家。他的幽默独具一格，是60年代“黑色幽默”风格的主要代表之一。他和同代作家赫勒等人一样，从20世纪现代生活悲剧的“黑色”中看到幽默，又用幽默来讽刺“黑色”，以期读者在无可奈何的苦笑之后加深对现实生活悲剧性的认识。

冯纳古特在文体上也独树一帜。他的作品短句较多，情节突兀，叙述秩序常被打乱。这种创作方法也反映了西方当代生活的支离破碎和无目的性。

Slaughterhouse-Five

〔作品介绍〕

本书是冯纳古特人生观和创作方法的代表作，1969年出版，其完整的标题为《第五号屠场或儿童十字军：与死神义不容辞的双人舞》(*Slaughterhouse—Five or the Children's Crusade: A Duty-Dance with Death*)。它是以1945年盟军对德国德累斯顿城的大轰炸为背景，基于作者的亲身经历，揭露战争罪行的一部力作。同时，该书也描写了当代美国社会的庸俗不堪，以及一些心灵敏感的人为了摆脱这种生活所做的努力。书中也充满了作者对许多现代人所面临的问题，特别是死亡问题所做的思考。

该书的主人公比利·皮尔格林同作者一样，参加过第二次世界大战，当过战俘，目击了德累斯顿从城市变为火海和瓦砾。他身体孱弱，心地善良，逆来顺受，在美军队伍和战俘营中是一个令人啼笑皆非的人物。他行军时没有武器，被俘后穿上英国战俘的戏装。但他在二战中的经历，特别是在德累斯顿的经历，始终象梦魇一样困扰着他。战后他在伊利翁过着优裕的生活，结了婚，有了一儿一女。但过去的经历使他郁郁寡欢，精神恍惚。有一件事使他刻骨铭心：德累斯顿城被夷为平地，13.5万人葬身火海；他的伙伴德比因藏起一只在废墟中挖到的茶壶而被就地正法。这是贯穿于全书的线索。比利由于孤独的思考和生活上的刺激，精神开始失常。他在苦思冥想之际曾求助于科幻小说，因而他开始滔滔不绝地讲述他的“时间旅行”，以及被飞碟劫持到特拉法马多星球上的经历。特拉法马多人的生死观给了他极大的启示，使他对死亡漠然置之，总是说一句“就那么回事”来表达他聊以自慰的心情。主人公皮尔格林——正象他的名字(Pilgrim)所代表的那样——是人类寻求超越死亡和战争的代表，作者在书中常把他同耶稣相提并论。

冯纳古特对战争深恶痛绝，反对把战争浪漫化。在本书中，战争意味着恐怖和死亡，没有半点英雄主义色彩。这是本书与其他反战作品的不同之处。同时，冯纳古特还是一位讽刺大师，他对战争以及美国社会的讽刺极为尖刻。“黑色幽默”这一创作技巧在这里得到了绝好的应用。该书的结构也别具一格，迥异于传统的叙述方法。有些情节近乎荒诞，但是，正如作者所说，关于一场屠杀，没有多少理智的东西可言。

本书选注的是该书第5章的一部分。

Slaughterhouse-Five

CHAPTER V

Billy Pilgrim[1] says that the Universe does not look like a lot of bright little dots to the creatures from Tralfamadore.[2] The creatures can see where each star has been and where it is going, so that the heavens are filled with rarefied, lumimous spaghetti. And Tralfamadorians don't see human beings as two-legged creatures, either. They see them as great millepedes— "with babies' legs at one end and old people's legs at the other," says Billy Pilgrim.

Billy asked for something to read on the trip to Tralfamadore. His captors had five million Earthling[3] books on microfilm, but no way to project them in Billy's cabin. They had only one actual book in English, which would be placed in a Tralfamadorian museum. It was *Valley of the Dolls*, by Jacqueline Susann.[4]

Billy read it, thought it was pretty good in spots. The people in it certainly had their ups and downs, ups and downs. But Billy didn't want to read about the same ups and downs over and over again. He asked if there wasn't, please, some other reading matter around.

"Only Tralfamadorian novels, which I'm afraid you couldn't begin to understand," said the speaker on the wall.

"Let me look at one anyway."

So they sent him in several. They were little things. A dozen of them might have had the bulk of *Valley of the Dolls*—with all its ups and downs, ups and downs.

Billy couldn't read Tralfamadorian, of course, but he could at least see how the books were laid out—in brief clumps of symbols separated by stars. Billy commented that the clumps might be telegrams.

"Exactly," said the voice.

"They *are* telegrams?"

"There are no telegrams on Tralfamadore. But you're right: each clump of symbols is a brief, urgent message—describing a situation, a scene. We Tralfamadorians read them all at once, not one after the other. There isn't any particular relationship between all the messages, except that the author has chosen them carefully, so that, when seen all at once, they produce an image of life that is beautiful and surprising and deep. There is no beginning, no middle, no end, no suspense, no moral, no causes, no effects. [5] What we love in our books are the depths of many marvelous moments seen all at one time."

Moments after that, the saucer entered a time warp, and Billy was flung back into his childhood. He was twelve years old, quaking as he stood with his mother and father on Bright Angel Point, at the rim of Grand Canyon. [6] The little human family was staring at the floor of the canyon, one mile straight down.

"Well—" said Billy's father, manfully kicking a pebble into space, "there it *is*." They had come to this famous place by automobile. They had had seven blowouts on the way.

"It was worth the trip," said Billy's mother raptly. "Oh, God—was it ever *worth* it."

Billy hated the canyon. He was sure that he was going to fall in. His mother touched him, and he wet his pants.

There were other tourists looking down into the canyon, too, and a ranger was there to answer questions. A Frenchman who had come all the way from France asked the ranger in broken English if many people committed suicide by jumping in.

"Yes, sir," said the ranger. "About three folks a year." So it goes.[7]

And Billy took a very short trip through time, made a peewee jump of only ten days, so he was still twelve, still touring the West with his family. Now they were down in Carlsbad Caverns,[8] and Billy was praying to God to get him out of there before the ceiling fell in.

A ranger was explaining that the Caverns had been discovered by a cowboy who saw a huge cloud of bats come out of a hole in the ground. And then he said that he was going to turn out all the lights, and that it would probably be the first time in the lives of most people there that they had ever been in darkness that was total.

Out went the lights. Billy didn't even know whether he was still alive or not. And then something ghostly floated in air to his left. It had numbers on it. His father had taken out his pocket watch. The watch had a radium dial.

Billy went from total dark to total light, found himself back in the war, back in the delousing station again. The shower was over. An unseen hand had turned the water off.

When Billy got his clothes back, they weren't any cleaner, but all the little animals that had been living in them were dead. So it goes. And his new overcoat was thawed out and limp now. It was much too small for Billy. It had a fur collar and a lining of crimson silk, and had apparently been made for an impresario about as big as an organ-grinder's monkey. It was full of bullet holes.

Billy Pilgrim dressed himself. He put on the little overcoat, too. It split up the back, and, at the shoulders, the sleeves came entirely free. So the coat became a furcollared vest. It was meant to flare at its owner's waist, but the flaring took place at Billy's armpits. The Germans found him to be one of the most screamingly funny things they had seen in all of World War Two. They laughed and laughed.

And the Germans told everybody else to form in ranks of five, with Billy as their pivot. Then out of doors went the parade, and through gate after gate again. There were more starving Russians with faces like radium dials. The Americans were livelier than before. The jazzing with hot water had cheered them up. And they came to a shed where a corporal with only one arm and one eye wrote the name and serial number of each prisoner in a big, red ledger. Everybody was legally alive now. Before they got their names and numbers in that book, they were missing in action and probably dead.

So it goes.

As the Americans were waiting to move on, an altercation broke out in their rear-most rank. An American had muttered something which a guard did not like. The guard knew English, and he hauled the American out of ranks, knocked him down.

The American was astonished, He stood up shakily, spitting blood. He's had two teeth knocked out. He had meant no harm by what he'd said, evidently, had no idea that the guard would hear and understand.

"Why me?" he asked the guard.

The guard shoved him back into ranks. "Vy[9] you? Vy anybody?" he said.

When Billy Pilgrim's name was inscribed in the ledger of the prison camp, he was given a number, too, and an iron dogtag[10] in which that number was stamped. A slave laborer from Poland had done the stamping. He was dead now. So it goes.

Billy was told to hang the tag around his neck along with his American dogtags, which he did. The tag was like a salt cracker, perforated down its middle so that a strong man could snap it in two with his bare hands. In case Billy died, which he didn't, half of the tag would mark his body and half would mark his grave.

After poor Edgar Derby, the high school teacher, was shot in Dresden later on, a doctor pronounced him dead and snapped his gogtag in two. So it goes.

Properly enrolled and tagged, the Americans were led through gate after gate again. In two days' time now their families would learn from the International Red Cross that they were alive.

Next to Billy was little Paul Lazzaro, who had promised to avenge Roland Weary.[11] Lazzaro wasn't thinking about vengeance. He was thinking about his terrible bellyache. His stomach had shrunk to the size of a walnut. That dry, shriveled pouch was as sore as a boil.

Next to Lazzaro was poor, doomed old Edgar Derby, with his American and German dogs displayed like a necklace, on the outside of his clothes. He had expected to become a captain, a company commander, because of his wisdom and age. Now here he was on the Czechoslovakian border at midnight.

"Halt," said a guard.

The Americans halted. They stood there quietly in the cold. The sheds they were among were outwardly like thousands of other sheds they had passed. There was this difference, though: the sheds had tin chimneys, and out of the chimneys whirled constellations of sparks.

A grard knocked on a door.

The door was flung open from inside. Light leaped out through the door, escaped from prison at 186,000 miles per second. Out marched fifty middle-aged Englishmen. They were singing"Hail,Hail,the Gang's All Here" from the *Pirates of Penzance.*[12]

These lusty, ruddy vocalists were among the first English-speaking prisoners to be taken in the Second World War. Now they were singing to nearly the last. They had not seen a woman or a child for four years or more. They hadn't seen any birds, either. Not even sparrows would come into the camp.

The Englishmen were officers. Each of them had attempted to escape from another prison at least once. Now they were here,dead-center in a sea of dying Russians.

They could tunnel all they pleased. They would inevitably surface within a rectangle of barbed wire,would find themselves greeted listlessly by dying Russians who spoke no English, who had no food or useful information or escape plans of their own. They could scheme all they pleased to hide aboard a vehicle or steal one, but no vehicle ever came into their compound. They could feign illness, if they liked, but that wouldn't earn them a trip anywhere, either. The only hospital in the camp was a six-bed affair in the British compound itself.

The Englishmen were clean and enthusiastic and decent and strong. They sang boomingly well. They had been singing together every night for years.

The Englishmen had also been lifting weights and chinning themselves for years. Their bellies were like washboards. The muscles of their calves and upper arms were like cannonballs. They were all masters of checkers and chess and bridge and cribbage and dominoes and anagrams and charades and Ping-Pong and billiards, as well.

They were among the wealthiest people in Europe, in terms of food. A clerical error early in the war, when food was still getting through to prisoners, had caused the Red Cross to ship them five hundred parcels every month instead of fifty. The Englishmen had hoarded these so cunningly that now, as the war was ending, they had three tons of sugar, one ton of coffee, eleven hundred pounds of chocolate, seven hundred pounds of tobacco, seventeen hundred pounds of tea, two tons of flour, one ton of canned beef, twelve hundred pounds of canned butter, sixteen hundred pounds of canned cheese, eight hundred pounds of powdered milk, and two tons of orange marmalade.

They kept all this in a room without windows. They had ratproofed it by lining it with flattened tin cans.

They were adored by the Germans, who thought they were exactly what Englishmen ought to be. They make war look stylish and reasonable, and fun.[13] So the Germans let them have four sheds, though one shed would have held them all. And, in exchange for coffee or chocolate or tobacco, the Germans gave them paint and lumber and nails and cloth for fixing things up.

The Englishmen had known for twelve hours that American guests were on their way. They had never had guests before, and they went to work like darling elves, sweeping, mopping, cooking, baking—making mattresses of straw and burlap bags, setting tables, putting party favors at each place.

Now they were singing their welcome to their guests in the winter night. Their clothes were aromatic with the feast they had been preparing. They were dressed half for battle, half for tennis or croquet. They were so elated by their own hospitality, and by all the goodies waiting inside, that they did not take a good look at their guests while they sang. And they imagined that they were singing to fellow officers fresh from the fray.

They wrestled the Americans toward the shed door affectionately, filling the night with manly blather and brotherly rodomontades. They called them "Yank," told them "Good show," promised them that "Jerry was on the run," and so on.

Billy Pilgraim wondered dimly who Jerry was.

Now he was indoors, next to an iron cookstove that was glowing cherry red. Dozens of teapots were boiling there. Some of them had whistles. And there was a witches' cauldron full of golden soup. The soup was thick. Primeval bubbles surfaced it with lethargical majesty as Billy Pilgrim stared.

There were long tables set for a banquet. At each place was a bowl made from a can that had once contained powdered milk. A smaller can was a cup. A taller, more slender can was a tumbler. Each tumbler was filled with warm milk.

At each place was a safety razor, a washcloth, a package of razor blades, a chocolate bar, two cigars, a bar of soap, ten cigarettes, a book of matches, a pencil, and a candle.

Only the candles and the soap were of German origin. They had a ghostly, opalescent similarity. The British had no way of knowing it, but the candles and the soap were made from the fat of rendered Jews and Gypsies and fairies and communists, and other enymies of the State.

So it goes.

The banquet hall was illuminated by candlelight. There were heaps of fresh-baked white bread on the tables, gobs of butter, pots of marmalade. There were platters of sliced beef from cans. Soup and scrambled eggs and hot marmalade pie were yet to come.

And, at the far end of the shed, Billy saw pink arches with azure draperies hanging between them, and an enormous clock, and two golden thrones, and a bucket and a mop. It was in this setting that the evening's entertainment would take place, a musical version of *Cinderella*, the most popular story ever told.

Billy Pilgrim was on fire, having stood too close to the glowing stove. The hem of his little coat was burning. It was a quiet, patient sort of fire—like the burning of punk.

Billy wondered if there was a telephone somewhere. He wanted to call his mother, to tell her he was alive and well.

There was silence now, as the Englishmen looked in astonishment at the frowsy creatures they had so lustily waltzed inside. One of the Englishmen saw that Billy was on fire. "You're on fire, lad!" he said, and he got Billy away from the stove and beat out the sparks with his hands.

When Billy made no comment on this, the Englishman asked him, "Can you talk? Can you hear?"

Billy nodded.

The Englishman touched him exploratorily here and there, filled with pity. "My God—what have they done to you, lad? This isn't a man. It's a broken kite."

"Are you really an American?" said the Englishman.

"Yes," said Billy.

"And your rank?"

"Private."

"What became of your boots, lad?"

"I don't remember."

"Is that coat a *joke*?"

"Sir?"

"Where did you get such a thing?"

Billy had to think hard about that. "They gave it to me," he said at last.

"Jerry gave it to you?"

"Who?"

"The Germans gave it to you?"

"Yes."

Billy didn't like the questions. They were fatiguing.

"Ohhhh—Yank, Yank, Yank—" said the Englishman, "that coat was an *insult*."

"Sir?"

"It was a deliberate attempt to humiliate you. You mustn't let Jerry do things like that."

Billy Pilgrim swooned.

Billy came to on a chair facing the stage. He had somehow eaten, and now he was watching *Cinderella*. Some part of him had evidently been enjoying the performance for quite a while. Billy was laughing hard.

The women in the play were really men, of course. The clock had just struck midnight, and Cinderella was lamenting:

"Goodness me, the clock has struck—
Alackday, and fuck my luck."

Billy found the couplet so comical that he not only laughed—he shrieked. He went on shrieking until he was carried out of the shed and into another, where the hospital was. It was a six-bed hospital. There weren't any other patients in there.

Billy was put to bed and tied down, and given a shot of morphine. Another American volunteered to watch over him. This volunteer was Edgar Derby, the high school teacher who would be shot to death in Dresden. So it goes.

Derby sat on a three-legged stool. He was given a book to read. The book was *The Red Badge of Courage*,[14] by Stephen Crane. Derby had read it before. Now he read it again while Billy Pilgrim entered a morphine paradise.

Under morphine, Billy had a dream of giraffes in a garden. The giraffes were following gravel paths, were pausing to munch sugar pears from treetops. Billy was a giraffe, too. He ate a pear. It was a hard one. It fought back against his grinding teeth. It snapped in juicy protest.

The giraffes accepted Billy as one of their own, as a harmless creature as preposterously specialized as themselves. Two approached him from opposite sides, leaned against him. They had long, muscular upper lips which they could shape like the bells of bugles. They kissed him with these. They were female giraffes—cream and lemon yellow. They had horns like doorknobs. The knobs were covered with velvet.

Why?

Night came to the garden of the giraffes, and Billy Pilgrim slept without dreaming for a while, and then he traveled in time. He woke up with his head under a blanket in a ward for nonviolent mental patients in a veterans' hospital near Lake Placid, New York. It was springtime in 1948, three years after the end of the war.

Billy uncovered his head. The windows of the ward were open. Birds were twittering outside. "Poo—tee—weet?" one asked him. The sun was high. There were twenty—nine other patients assigned to the ward, but they were all outdoors now, enjoying the day. They were free to come and go as they pleased, to go home, even, if they liked—and so was Billy Pilgrim. They had come here voluntarily, alarmed by the outside world.

Billy had committed himself in the middle of his final year at the Ilium School of Optometry. Nobody else suspected that he was going crazy. Everybody else thought he looked fine and was acting fine. Now he was in the hospital. The doctors agreed: He *was* going crazy.

They didn't think it had anything to do with the war. They were sure Billy was going to pieces because his father had thrown him into the deep end of the Y. M. C. A. swimming pool when he was a little boy, and had then taken him to the rim of the Grand Canyon.

The man assigned to the bed next to Billy's was a former infantry captain named Eliot Rosewater. Eliot Rosewater was sick and tired of being drunk all the time.

It was Rosewater who introduced Billy to science fiction, and in particular to the writings of Kilgore Trout. Rosewater had a tremendous collection of science-fiction paperbacks under his bed. He had brought them to the hospital in a steamer trunk. Those beloved, frumpish books gave off a smell that permeated the ward—like flannel pajamas that hadn't been changed for a month, or like Irish stew.

Kilgore Trout became Billy's favorite living author, and science fiction became the only sort of tales he could read.

Rosewater was twice as smart as Billy, but he and Billy were dealing with similar crises in similar ways. They had both found life meaningless, partly because of what they had seen in war. Rosewater, for instance, had shot a fourteen-year-old fireman, mistaking him for a

German soldier. So it goes. And Billy had seen the greatest massacre in European history, which was the fire-bombing of Dresden. So it goes.

So they were trying to re-invent themselves and their universe. Science fiction was a big help.[15]

Rosewater said an interesting thing to Billy one time about a book that wasn't science fiction. He said that everything there was to know about life was in *The Brothers Karamazov*, by Feodor Dostoevsky.[16] "But that isn't *enough* any more," said Rosewater.

Another time Billy heard Rosewater say to a psychiatrist, "I think you guys are going to have to come up with a lot of wonderful *new* lies, or people just aren't going to want to go on living."

There was a still life on Billy's bedside table—two pills, an ashtray with three lipstick-stained cigarettes in it, one cigarette still burning, and a glass of water. The water was dead. So it goes. Air was trying to get out of that dead water. Bubbles were clinging to the walls of the glass, too weak to climb out.

The cigarettes belonged to Billy's chain-smoking mother. She had sought the ladies' room, which was off the ward for WACS and WAVES and SPARS and WAFS who had gone bananas. She would be back at any moment now.

Billy covered his head with his blanket again. He always covered his head when his mother came to see him in the mental ward—always got much sicker until she went away. It wasn't that she was ugly, or had bad breath or a bad personality. She was a perfectly nice, standard-issue, brownhaired, white woman with a high-school education.

She upset Billy simply by being his mother. She made him feel embarrassed and ungrateful and weak because she had gone to so much trouble to give him life, and to keep that life going, and Billy didn't really like life at all.

Billy heard Eliot Rosewater come in and lie down. Rosewater's bedsprings talked a lot about that. Rosewater was a big man, but not very powerful. He looked as though he might be made out of nose putty.

And then Billy's mother came back from the ladies' room, sat down on a chair between Billy's and Rosewater's bed. Rosewater greeted her with melodious warmth, asked how she was today. He seemed delighted to hear that she was fine. He was experimenting with being ardently sympathetic with everybody he met. He thought that might make the world a slightly more pleasant place to live in. He called Billy's mother "dear." He was experimenting with calling everybody "dear."

"Some day," she promised Rosewater, "I'm going to come in here, and Billy is going to uncover his head, and do you know what he's going to say?"

"What's he going to say, dear?"

"He's going to say, 'Hello, Mom,' and he's going to smile. He's going to say, 'Gee, it's good to see you, Mom. How have you been?'"

"Today could be the day."

"Every night I pray."

"That's a *good* thing to do."

"People would be surprised if they knew how much in this world was due to prayers."

"You never said a truer word, dear."

"Does your mother come to see you often?"

"My mother is dead," said Rosewater. So it goes.

"I'm sorry."

"At least she had a happy life as long as it lasted."

"That's a consolation, anyway."

"Yes."

"Billy's father is dead, you know," said Billy's mother. So it goes.

"A boy *needs* a father."

And on and on it went that duet between the dumb, praying lady and the big, hollow man who was so full of loving echoes.

"He was at the top of his class when this happened," said Billy's mother.

"Maybe he was *working* too hard," said Rosewater. He held a book he wanted to read, but he was much too polite to read and talk, too, easy as it was to give Billy's mother satisfactory answers. The book was *Maniacs in the Fourth Dimension*, by Kilgore Trout. It was about people whose mental diseases couldn't be treated because the causes of the diseases were all in the fourth dimension, and three-dimensional Earthling doctors couldn't see those causes at all, or even imagine them.

One thing Trout said that Rosewater liked very much was that there really were vampires and werewolves and goblins and angels and so on, but that they were in the fourth dimension. So was William Blake,[17] Rosewater's favorite poet, according to Trout. So were heaven and hell.

"He's engaged to a very rich girl," said Billy's mother.

"That's good," said Rosewater. "Money can be a great comfort sometimes."

"It really *can*."

"Of course it can."

"It isn't much fun if you have to pinch every penny till it screams."

"It's nice to have a little breathing room."

"Her father owns the optometry school where Billy was going. He also owns six offices around our part of the state. He flies his own plane and has a summer place up on Lake George."

"That's a beautiful lake."

Billy fell asleep under his blanket. When he woke up again, he was tied to the bed in the hospital in prison. He opened one eye, saw poor old Edgar Derby reading *The Red Badge of Courage* by candlelight.

Billy closed that one eye, saw in his memory of the future poor old Edgar Derby in front of a firing squad in the ruins of Dresden. There were only four men in that squad. Billy had heard that one man in each firing squad was customarily given a rifle loaded with blank cartridge. Billy didn't think there wonld be a blank cartridge issued in a squad that small, in a war that old.

Now the head Englishman came into the hospital to check on Billy. He was an infantry colonel captured at Dunkirk.[18] It was he who had given Billy morphine. There wasn't a real doctor in the compound, so the doctoring was up to him. "How's the patient?" he asked Derby.

"Dead to the world."

"But not actually dead."

"No."

"How nice—to feel nothing, and still get full credit for being alive."

Derby now came to lugubrious attention.

"No, no—please—as you were. With only two men for each officer, and all the men sick, I think we can do without the usual pageantry between officers and men."

Derby remained standing. "You seem older than the rest," said the colonel.

Derby told him he was forty-five, which was two years older than the colonel. The colonel said that the other Americans had all shaved now, that Billy and Derby were the only two still with beards. And he said, "You know—we've had to imagine the war here, and we have imagined that it was being fought by aging men like ourselves. We had forgotten that wars were fought by babies. When I saw those freshly shaved faces, it was a shock. " 'My God, my God—' I said to myself, 'It's the Children's Crusade.' "[19]

The colonel asked old Derby how he had been captured, and Derby told a tale of being in a clump of trees with about a hundred other frightened soldiers. The battle had been going on for five days. The hundred had been driven into the trees by tanks.

Derby described the incredible artificial weather that Earthlings sometimes create for other Earthlings when they don't want those other Earthlings to inhabit Earth any more. Shells were bursting in the treetops with terrific bangs, he said, showering down knives and needles and razorblades. Little lumps of lead in copper jackets were crisscrossing the woods under the shellbursts, zipping along much faster than sound.

A lot of people were being wounded or killed. So it goes.

Then the shelling stopped, and a hidden German with a loudspeaker told the Americans to put their weapons down and come out of the woods with their hands on the top of thier heads, or the shelling would start again. It wouldn't stop until everybody in there was dead.

So the Americans put their weapons down, and they came out of the woods with their hands on top of their heads, because they wanted to go on living, if they possibly could.

Billy traveled in time back to the veterans' hospital again. The blanket was over his head. It was quiet outside the blanket. "Is my mother gone?" said Billy.

"Yes."

Billy peeked out from under his blanket. His fiancée was out there now, sitting on the visitor's chair. Her name was Valencia Merble. Valencia was the daughter of the owner of the Ilium School of Optometry. She was rich. She was as big as a house because she couldn't stop eating. She was eating now. She was eating a Three Musketeers[20] Candy Bar. She was wearing tri-focal lenses in harlequin frames, and the frames were trimmed with rhinestones. The glitter of the rhinestones was answered by the glitter of the diamond in her engagement ring. The diamond was insured for eighteen hundred dollars. Billy had found that diamond in Germany. It was booty of war.

Billy didn't want to marry ugly Valencia. She was one of the symptoms of his disease. He knew he was going crazy when he heard himself proposing marriage to her, when he begged her to take the diamond ring and be his companion for life.

Billy said, "Hello," to her, and she asked him if he wanted some candy, and he said, "No, thanks."

She asked him how he was, and he said, "Much better, thanks." She said that everybody at the Optometry School was sorry he was sick and hoped he would be well soon, and Billy said, "When you see 'em, tell 'em, 'Hello.'"

She promised she would.

She asked him if there was anything she could bring him from the outside, and he said, "No. I have just about everything I want."

"What about books?" said Valencia.

"I'm right next to one of the biggest private libraries in the world," said Billy, meaning Eliot Rosewater's collection of science fiction.

Rosewater was on the next bed, reading, and Billy drew him into the conversation, asked him what he was reading this time.

So Rosewater told him. It was *The Gospel from Outer Space*, by Kilgore Trout. It was about a visitor from outer space, shaped very much like a Tralfamadorian, by the way. The visitor from outer space made a serious study of Christianity, to learn, if he could, why Christians found it so easy to be cruel. He concluded that at least part of the trouble was slipshod storytelling in the New Testament. He supposed that the intent of the Gospels was to teach people, among other things, to be merciful, ever to the lowest of the low.

But the Gospels actually taught this:

Before you kill somebody, make absolutely sure he isn't well connected. So it goes.

The flaw in the Christ stories, said the visitor from outer space, was that Christ, who didn't look like much, was actually the Son of the Most Powerful Being in the Universe. Readers understood that, so, when they came to the crucifixion, they naturally thought, and Rosewater read out loud again:

Oh, boy—they sure picked the wrong guy to lynch that *time*!

And that thought had a brother: "*There are* right people to *lynch.*" Who? People not well connected. So it goes.

The visitor from outer space made a gift to Earth of a new Gospel. In it, Jesus really *was* a nobody, and a pain in the neck to a lot of people with better connections than he had. He still got to say all the lovely and puzzling things he said in the other Gospels.

So the people amused themselves one day by nailing him to a cross and planting the cross in the ground. There couldn't possibly be any repercussions, the lynchers thought. The reader would have to think that, too, since the new Gospel hammered home again and again what a nobody Jesus was.

And then, just before the nobody died, the heavens opened up, and there was thunder and lightning. The voice of God came crashing down. He told the people that he was adopting the bum as his son, giving him the full powers and privileges of The Son of the Creator of the Universe throughout all eternity. God said this: *From this moment on, He will punish horribly anybody who torments a bum who had no connections*!

Billy's fiancée had finished her Three Musketeers Candy Bar. Now she was eating a Milky Way.

"Forget books," said Rosewater, throwing that particular book under his bed. "The hell with 'em."

"That sounded like an interesting one," said Valencia.

"Jesus—if Kilgore Trout could only *write*!" Rosewater exclaimed. He had a point: Kilgore Trout's unpopularity was deserved. His prose was frightful. Only his ideas were good.

"I don't think Trout has ever been out of the country," Rosewater went on, "My God—he writes about Earthlings all the time, and they're all Americans. Practically nobody on Earth is an American."

"Where does he live?" Valencia asked.

"Nobody knows," Rosewater replied. "I'm the only person who ever heard of him, as far as I can tell. No two books have the same publisher, and every time I write him in care of a publisher, the letter comes back because the publisher has failed."

He changed the subject now, congratulated Valencia on her engagement ring.

"Thank you," she said, and held it out so Rosewater could get a close look. "Billy got that diamond in the war."

"That's the attractive thing about war," said Rosewater. "Absolutely everybody gets a little something."

With regard to the whereabouts of Kilgore Trout: he actually lived in Ilium, Billy's hometown, friendless and despised. Billy would meet him by and by.

"Billy—" said Valencia Merble.

"Hm?"

"You want to talk about our silver pattern?"

"Sure."

"I've got it narrowed down pretty much to either Royal Danish or Rambler Rose."

"Rambler Rose," said Billy.

"It isn't something we should *rush* into," she said, "I mean—whatever we decide on, that's what we're going to have to live with the rest of our lives."

Billy studied the pictures, "Royal Danish," he said at last.

"Colonial Moonlight is nice, too."

"Yes, it is," said Billy Pilgrim.

And Billy traveled in time to the zoo on Tralfamadore. He was forty-four years old, on display under a geodesic dome. He was reclining on the lounge chair which had been his cradle during his trip through space. He was naked. The Tralfamadorians were interested in his body—*all* of it. There were thousands of them outside, holding up their little hands so that their eyes could see him. Billy had been on Tralfamadore for six Earthling months now. He was used to the crowd.

Escape was out of the question. The atmosphere outside the dome was cyanide, and Earth was 446,120,000,000,000miles away.

Billy was displayed there in the zoo in a simulated Earthling habitat. Most of the furnishings had been stolen from the Sears & Roebuck warehouse in Iowa City, Iowa. There was a color television set and a couch that could be converted into a bed. There were end tables with lamps and ashtrays on them by the couch. There was a home bar and two stools. There was a little pool table. There was wall-to-wall carpeting in federal gold, except in the kitchen and bathroom areas and over the iron manhole cover in the center of the floor. There were magazines arranged in a fan on the coffee table in front of the couch.

There was a stereophonic phonograph. The phonograph worked. The television didn't. There was a picture of one cowboy killing another one pasted to the television tube. So it goes.

There were no walls in the dome, no place for Billy to hide. The mint green bathroom fixtures were right out in the open. Billy got off his lounge chair now, went in to the bathroom and took a leak. The crowd went wild.

Billy brushed his teeth on Tralfamadore, put in his partial denture, and went into his kitchen. His bottled-gas range and his refrigerator and his dishwasher were mint green, too. There was a picture painted on the door of the refrigerator. The refrigerator had come that way. It was a picture of a Gay Nineties couple on a bicycle built for two.

Billy looked at that picture now, tried to think something about the couple. Nothing came to him. There didn't seem to be *anything* to think about those two people.

Billy ate a good breakfast from cans. He washed his cup and plate and knife and fork and spoon and saucepan, put them away. Then he did exercises he had learned in the Army—straddle jumps, deep knee bends, sit-ups and pushups. Most Tralfamadorians had no way of knowing Billy's body and face were not beautiful. They supposed that he was a splendid specimen. This had a pleasant effect on Billy, who began to enjoy his body for the first time.

He showered after his exercises and trimmed his toenails. He shaved, and sprayed deodorant under his arms, while a zoo guide on a raised platform outside explained what Billy was doing—and why. The guide was lecturing telepathically, simply standing there, sending out thought waves to the crowd. On the platform with him was the little keyboard instrument with which he would relay questions to Billy from the crowd.

Now the first question came—from the speaker on the television set: "Are you happy here?"

"About as happy as I was on Earth," said Billy Pilgrim, which was true.

There were five sexes on Tralfamadore, each of them performing a step necessary in the creation of a new individual. They looked identical to Billy—because their sex difference were all in the fourth dimension.

One of the biggest moral bombshells handed to Billy by the Tralfamadorians, incidentally, had to do with sex on Earth. They said their flying-saucer crews had identified no fewer than *seven* sexes on Earth, each essential to reproduction. Again: Billy couldn't possibly imagine what five of those seven sexes had to do with the making of a baby, since they were sexually active only in the fourth dimension.

The Tralfamadorians tried to give Billy clues that would help him imagine sex in the invisible dimension. They told him that there could be no Earthling babies without male homosexuals. There *could* be babies without women homosexuals. There couldn't be babies without women over sixty-five years old. There *could* be babies without men over sixty-five. There couldn't be babies without other babies who had lived an hour or less after birth. And so on.

It was gibberish to Billy.

There was a lot that Billy said that was gibberish to the Tralfamadorians, too. They couldn't imagine what time looked like to him. Billy had given up on explaining that. The guide outside had to explain as best he could.

The guide invited the crowd to imagine that they were looking across a desert at a mountain range on a day that was twinkling bright and clear. They could look at a peak or a bird or a cloud, at a stone right in front of them, or even down into a canyon behind them. But among them was this poor Earthling, and his head was encased in a steel sphere which he could never take off. There was only one eyehole through which he could look, and welded to that eyehole were six feet of pipe.

This was only the beginning of Billy's miseries in the metaphor. He was also strapped to a steel lattice which was bolted to a flatcar on rails, and there was no way he could turn his head or touch the pipe. The far end of the pipe rested on a bi-pod which was also bolted to the flatcar. All Billy could see was the little dot at the end of the pipe. He didn't know he was on a flatcar, didn't even know there was anything peculiar about his situation.

The flatcar sometimes crept, sometimes went extremely fast, often stopped—went uphill, downhill, around curves, along straightaways. Whatever poor Billy saw through the pipe, he had no choice but to say to himself, "That's life."

Billy expected the Tralfamadorians to be baffled and alarmed by all the wars and other forms of murder on Earth. He expected them to fear that the Earthling combination of ferocity and spectacular weaponry might eventually destroy part or maybe all of the innocent Universe. Science fiction had led him to expect that.

But the subject of war never came up until Billy brought it up himself. Somebody in the zoo crowd asked him through the lecturer what the most valuable thing he had learned on Tralfamadore was so far, and Billy replied, "How the inhabitants of a whole planet can live in peace! As you know, I am from a planet that had been engaged in senseless slaughter since the beginning of time. I myself have seen the bodies of schoolgirls who were boiled alive in a water tower by my own countrymen, who were proud of fighting pure evil at the time." This was true. Billy saw the boiled bodies in Dresden. "And I have lit my way in a prison at night with candles from the fat of human beings who were butchered by the brothers and fathers of those schoolgirls who were boiled. Earthlings must be the terrors of the Universe! If other planets aren't now in danger from Earth, they soon will be. So tell me the secret so I can take it back to Earth and save us all: How can a planet live at peace?"

Billy felt that he had spoken soaringly. He was baffled when he saw the Tralfamadorians close their little hands on their eyes. He knew from past experience what this meant: He was being stupid.

"Would—would you mind telling me—" he said to the guide, much deflated, "what was so stupid about that?"

"We know how the Universe ends—" said the guide, "and Earth has nothing to do with it, except that *it* gets wiped out, too."

"How—how *does* the Universe end?" said Billy.

"We blow it up, experimenting with new fuels for our flying saucers. A Tralfamadorian test pilot presses a starter button, and the whole Universe disappears." So it goes.

"If you know this," said Billy, "isn't there some way you can prevent it? Can't you keep the pilot from *pressing* the button?"

"He has *always* pressed it, and he always *will*. We *always* let him and we always *will* let him. The moment is *structured* that way."

"So—" said Billy gropingly, "I suppose that the idea of preventing war on Earth is stupid, too."

"Of course."

"But you *do* have a peaceful planet here."

"Today we do. On other days we have wars as horrible as any you've ever seen or read about. There isn't anything we can do about them, so we simply don't look at them. We ignore them. We spend eternity looking at pleasant moments—like today at the zoo. Isn't this a nice moment?"

"Yes."

"That's one thing Earthlings might learn to do, if they tried hard enough: Ignore the awful times, and concentrate on the good ones."

"Um," said Billy Pilgrim.

〔注释〕

1. Pilgrim：小说的主人公，他心灵敏感，为超越战争与死亡夜不甘寝，食不甘味，是人类追求和平的象征。Pilgrim 有"朝圣者"之意。

2. Tralfamadore：作者杜撰的特拉法马多星球。以下是比利被该星球人劫持的经历。

3. Earthling：地球人或地球人的。

4. Jacqueline Susan：苏珊（1921～1974），美国通俗小说家和演员，写过3部畅销书。本文提到的《玩偶的山谷》(*Valley of the Dolls*) 是以年轻明星吸毒为题材的小说。

5. 此处暗示作者对小说的题材、内容、写作方法，自有一番见解，不落俗套。

6. Grand Canyon：大峡谷（由科罗拉多河口至亚利桑纳和内华达边界）。

7. So it goes：就这么回事，这是比利从特拉法马多人那里学来的、在发生死亡时所说的话。参阅原书第2章。

8. Carlsbad Caverns：位于新墨西哥州。

9. Vy＝Why．作者在模仿德语发音。

10. dogtag：指美国士兵用来证明身份的金属牌。

11. Roland Weary：小说中的人物，为美军一名年轻的士兵，他被俘后死去，他的朋友认为是比利害死的。

12. Pirates of Penzance：《彭赞斯的海盗》，吉尔伯特（W. S. Gilbert，1836～1911）和亚瑟·沙利文（Arthur Sullivan，1842～1910）合著。

13. 冯纳古特对这些人深恶痛绝，因为他们把战争浪漫化。

14. 该书所写也是关于战争及其对人的心理影响的。

15. 这两段话说明了科幻小说对比利等人（也包括冯纳古特）的意义。

16. Feodor Dostoevsky：陀思妥耶夫斯基（1821～1881），俄国伟大的作家，本文所提到的《卡拉玛佐夫兄弟》是他的代表作之一。

17. William Blake：威廉·布莱克（1757～1827），英国诗人，他的诗作想象丰富瑰丽，充满象征成分，宗教和玄学色彩较浓。

18. Dunkirk：敦克尔刻，位于法国北部。1940年联军与德军作战遭到惨败后，225,000英军与约112,000法军和比利时军从该地撤往英国。

19. Children's Crusade：儿童十字军东征，原指1213年，3万名天真的儿童在两个骗子的蛊惑下，参加了以期收复圣城耶路撒冷的十字军东征。他们大半在海上遇难，幸存者在非洲被卖为奴。

20. Three Musketeers：三个火枪手，原为法国作家大仲马（Alexander Dumas

père，1802～1870）的一部美化战争和冒险的通俗小说书名。本书中的 Roland Weary 曾把自己和另外两名士兵称作“三个火枪手”。这里指糖棒的商标。

JOSEPH HELLER

〔作者介绍〕

约瑟夫·海勒（Joseph Heller，1923～）美国当代小说家，生于纽约市的布鲁克林区。1941 年毕业于林肯中学，随即参加美国空军，当了一名轰炸手。服役期间执行 60 余次飞行任务。战后就学于加里福尼亚大学，次年转纽约大学。1948 年在哥伦比亚大学获文学硕士，后获富布赖特基金会资助赴英国牛津大学研究英国文学。1952 至 1954 年在宾夕法尼亚大学讲授写作和文学。此后直到 50 年代末，他在纽约为《时代》周刊和《展望》杂志撰写广告。

海勒在学生时期就开始文学创作。1947 年至 1948 年间在《大西洋》和《老爷》等文学杂志上发表《我不再爱你》（“I Don't Love You Anymore”）、《白雪城堡》（“Castle of Snow”）、《来自格林尼治的女孩》（“Girl from Greenwich”）等短篇小说。

1954 年，他着手写作酝酿已久的第 1 部长篇小说《第十八条军规》（*Catch-18*）。次年在《新大陆作品》（*New World Writing*）上刊出该书第 1 章。1958 年海勒与西门——舒斯特公司签订出版合同。根据出版社意见，为了区分美国小说家利昂·尤里斯（Leon Uris，1924～）同期创作的长篇小说《米拉-*18*》（*Mila 18*，1961），海勒将书名改为《第二十二条军规》（*Catch-22*）。

他说：“因为有很多事情重复出现……因此，我觉得两个‘2’倒也与小说的内容十分相宜。”这是战后出现的一部最佳“反抗”文学作品。虽然小说描写的是战时美国空军内部的事情，但作者所讽刺和抨击的却是美国官僚机构的“非人性”倾向以及当权者的腐化现象。小说于 1961 年出版，颇受好评，1970 年被改编成电影后更为畅销。在美国发动侵越战争期间，小说在青年中间广为流传。到 1975 年，共售出 600 多万册。

继《第二十二条军规》之后，海勒于 1974 年完成了第 2 部长篇小说《出了毛病》（*Something Happened*）。小说以主人公罗伯特·斯洛克姆自述的形式揭露美国社会的诸多弊端。斯洛克姆 在一家公司的市场调研部工作，作者通过主人公的口述，揭示了公司里人与人之间、部门与部门之间的勾心斗角和相互倾轧，迫使人们精神崩溃，乃至自杀。作者通过描写家庭婚姻、男女私情以及夫妻之间、父母与子女之间的冲突等，意在阐明这些社会和家庭的矛盾是造成主人公精神苦闷的社会根源。作者着力刻画主人公的心理活动，实则是抨击资本主义制度的腐朽，暗指真正有毛病的是当今的美国社会。

长篇小说《好得不得了》(*Good as Gold*，1979) 讽刺一个憎恶权力却又一心想到首都华盛顿去当国务卿的大学教授，作品影射美国前国务卿基辛格，小说通过对基家庭生活和社会活动各方面的描写，再现了美国社会的腐化状况。

此外，他还写过剧本《我们轰炸纽黑文》(*We Bombed New Haven*，1967)，《第二十二条军规》(*Catch-22*，1971) 和《克莱文杰的考验》(*Clevenger's Trial*，1974) 等。

约瑟夫·海勒是"黑色幽默"文学的杰出代表，美国当代文学的重要作家之一。

Catch-22

〔作品介绍〕

《第二十二条军规》(*Catch-22*)描写的是美国第二十七飞行大队的故事。这个大队在第二次世界大战期间为配合意大利抗击纳粹德国的侵略而驻扎在地中海的某岛上。小说力图通过对空军官兵之间、上下级之间荒诞滑稽的人际关系的描写，展示美军内部的专制和腐败，从而揭示当代美国社会生活中的各种怪诞现象。作者"透过滑稽的表面现象揭露了一个极端自私、残酷无情、草菅人命的世界"(评论家罗伯特·希鲁斯坦 [Robert Brustein] 语)。小说成功地描绘出一幅当今社会人们陷入困境的图景。

小说的主人公、上尉飞行员尤索林时时感到自己的生命在受到威胁，这一威胁不仅来自战争造成的混乱，更来自美国军事和工业体制内部的官僚主义制度。这种制度借"理智"、"爱国"和"正义"的名义牢牢掌握了人的生杀大权。按照空军司令部的规定，飞行员在完成 25 次飞行任务之后便可复员回国；然而，飞行员们却永远不能完成任务，因为上校卡思卡特为了自己晋升将军、中校克恩为了自己晋升上校而不断增加飞行额数，从 25 次增加到 30 次，又从 30 次增加到 35 次、40 次，最后竟增加到 80 次。为了逃避厄运，尤索林常借口有病往进医院，最后不得已冒险逃往瑞典。

《第二十二条军规》所描写的是一个没有理智和希望的世界，在这个世界里，发生过一系列荒诞离奇的事情。活着的人被宣布已经死去，而死了的人在官方的名册上仍然“活”着；一位军官只有不在时才欢迎客人来访；而“学习讨论会”只邀请不肯提问的人来参加，诸如此类。显然，小说所抨击的不仅仅限于基地上的军事官僚机构，而是整个资本主义世界。这个机构和世界的荒诞性集中表现在第二十二条军规上。这条军规虽不成文，也似乎并不存在，可是经过人们随心所欲的解释，它便能置人于无法逃脱的困境和危险之中。

关于“第二十二条军规”的实质，在小说的第5章，尤索林和丹尼卡医生讨论飞行员奥尔因神经有病是否应当停止飞行之后，有一段很好的解释：

> “这里面只有一个圈套，这就是第二十二条军规。这条军规规定，面临真正的、迫在眉睫的危险时，对自身安全表示关注，乃是头脑理性活动的结果。奥尔疯了，可以允许他停止飞行。只要他提出请求就行。可是他一提出请求，他就不再是个疯子，就得再去执行飞行任务。倘若奥尔再去执行飞行任务，那他准是疯了，如果他不肯再去，那他就没有疯，可是即然他没有疯，他就得去执行飞行任务。倘若他去执行飞行任务，他准是疯了，不必再去飞行，可是如果他不想再去，那么他就没有疯，他就非去不可。”（引自《第二十二条军规》中译本，上海译文出版社1981年版）

这就是人们所说的典型的“第二十二条军规局面”。显然，在尤索林看来，在第二十二条军规笼罩下的乃是一个疯狂的世界，为了逃出这个世界，为了保全自己的生命，他时而以肝脏有病为借口躲进医院。他在医院里对人们说：“这是医院里唯一一个精神正常的病房。除我们之外，人们都疯了。这也许是全世界唯一一个精神正常的病房。”当卡思卡特将飞行指标增加到80次时，大部分飞行员都已牺牲或失踪，此时尤索林决定冒险出逃。

作者运用“黑色幽默”的手法在小说里塑造了一群怪诞的人物形象和一系列荒诞的故事情节。

上将佩克姆和德利德尔为争夺空军飞行大队的指挥权而相互倾轧。上校卡思卡特和中校克恩虽口口声声说“为国家而战”，实则是要飞行员们为他们的晋升去送死。他们对战争的胜负并无兴趣，他们参战的目的只有一个——借机获得“将军”的头衔。为了这个目的，他们把飞行指标从25次增加到80次。假如上司还不满意，他们可以把指标增加到“100次，或者甚至200次、300次，或者6000次”。

投机家迈洛是卡思卡特指挥下飞行中队伙食管理员。他一个人经营“M&M联合企业”跨国公司，在只要“有利于M&M联合企业就有利于国家”的口号掩盖下，捞取巨额利润。他身在美军，却与德军勾结，大发战争财，因此飞黄腾达，后来他居然当上了马耳他副总督。

飞行员纳特利在执行轰炸任务中与另一架飞机相撞而死，他的死完全是因为卡思卡特和迈洛合谋所致，而他的妓女朋友不去向他们追究责任，却发疯似地追杀为她通报消息的尤索林。

《第二十二条军规》不论在主题的处理上和艺术形式的安排上都与传统小说不同。“一部反映显然是荒诞和混乱的世界的小说应当用显然是荒诞和混乱的形式来表现”(道格·勾克洛柏语)。《第二十二条军规》在反映当今资本主义社会的“有组织的混乱”和“制度化的疯狂”这一荒诞社会现象时，在结构上作了精心的处理。例如，小说不以故事发展的时间顺序为线索，而是过去发生的事件和现在发生的事件放在同等重要的位置上加以描述。有些情节表面看来好象互不联系，杂乱无章，实际上由于它们在不同的时间层次上再现被扭曲的人物形象，从而突出了小说立意反映荒诞现实的效果。作者的语言也尽力符合表现这一主题的需要。他运用许多语言手段，如“循环式谈话，”问答极其滑稽并出人意料；“套语”的运用，即把俗语中关键字眼换成能产生荒谬效果的字词；谈话语气的突然变化，即由严肃话题到琐细话题的突然跳跃和转换，令人啼笑皆非，等诸如此类的文学修辞手段。这些手法的巧妙结合，使小说的文字呈现一种荒诞状貌，有力地表现了一个疯狂世界缺乏理智和逻辑及其不可逆料的特点。

《第二十二条军规》以其内容和形式的创新而成为美国小说史上的一个里程碑：它开创了美国60年代荒诞小说的先声。

本书共有42章，这里选注的是第40章。

Catch-22

FORTY.[1]

There was, of course, a catch.

"Catch-22?" inquired Yossarian.

"Of course," Colonel Korn answered pleasantly, after he had chased the mighty guard of massive M. P. s out with an insouciant flick of his hand and a slightly contemptuous nod—most relaxed, as always, when he could be most cynical. His rimless square eyeglasses glinted with sly amusement as he gazed at Yossarian. "After all, we can't simply send you home for refusing to fly more missions and keep the rest of the men here, can we? That would hardly be fair to them."

"You're goddam right!" Colonel Cathcart blurted out, lumbering back and forth gracelessly like a winded bull, puffing and pouting angrily. "I'd like to tie him up hand and foot and throw him aboard a plane on every mission. That's what I'd like to do."

Colonel Korn motioned Colonel Cathcart to be silent and smiled at Yossarian. "You know, you really have been making things terribly difficult for Clolnel Cathcart," he observed with flip good humor, as though the fact did not displease him at all. "The men are unhappy and morale is beginning to deteriorate. And it's all your fault."

"It's your fault," Yossarian argued, "for raising the number of missions."

"No, it's your fault for refusing to fly them," Colonel Korn retorted. "The men were perfectly content to fly as many missions as we asked as long as they thought they had no alternative. Now you've given them hope, and they're unhappy. So the blame is all yours."

"Doesn't he know there's a war going on?" Colonel Cath cart, still stamping back and forth, demanded morosely without looking at Yossarian.

"I'm quite sure he does," Colonel Korn answered. "That's probably why he refuses to fly them."

"Doesn't it make any difference to him?"

"Will the knowledge that there's a war going on weaken your decision to refuse to participate in it?" Colonel Korn inquired with sarcastic seriousness, mocking Colonel Cathcart.

"No, sir," Yossarian replied, almost returning Colonel Korn's smile.

"I was afraid of that, "Colonel Korn remarked with an elaborate sigh, locking his fingrs together comfortably on top of his smooth, bald, broad, shiny brown head. "You know, in all fairness, we really haven't treated you too badly, have we? We've fed you and paid you on time. We gave you a medal and even made you a captain."

"I never should have made him a captain," Colonel Cathcart exclaimed bitterly. "I should have given him a courtmartial after he loused up that Ferrara mission and went around twice." [2]

"I told you not to promote him," said Colonel Korn, "but you wouldn't listen to me."

"No you didn't. You told me to promote him, didn't you?"

"I told you not to promote him. But you just wouldn't listen."

"I should have listened."

"You never listen to me," Colonel Korn persisted with relish. "That's the reason we're in this spot."

"All right, gee whiz. Stop rubbing it in, will you?" Colonel Cathcart burrowed his fists down deep inside his pockets and turned away in slouch. "Instead of picking on me, why don't you figure our what we're going to do about him?"

"We're going to send him home, I'm afraid." Colonel Korn was chuckling triumphantly when he turned away from Colonel Cathcart to face Yossarian. "Yossarian, the war is over for you. We're going to send you home. You really don't deserve it, you know, which is one if one of the reasons I don't mind doing it. Skince there's nothing else we can risk doing to you at this time, we've decided to return you to the States. We've worked out this little deal to—"

"What kind of deal?" Yossarian demanded with defiant mistrust.

Colonel Korn tossed his head back and laughed. "Oh, a thoroughly despicable deal, make no mistake about that. It's absolutely revolting. But you'll accept it quickly enough."

"Don't be too sure."

"I haven't the slightest doubt you will, even though it stinks to high heaven. Oh, by the way. You haven't told any of the men you've refused to fly more missions, have you?"

"No, sir," Yossarian answered promptly.

Colonel Korn nodded approvingly. "That's good. I like the way you lie. You'll go far in this world if you ever acquire some decent ambition."

"Doesn't he know there a war going on?" Colonel Cathcart yelled out suddenly, and blew with vigorous disbelief into the open end of his cigarette holder.

"I'm quite sure he does," Colonel Korn replied acidly, "since you brought that identical point to his attention just a moment ago." Colonel Korn frowned wearily for Yossarian's benefit, his eyes twinkling swarthily with sly and daring scorn. Gripping the edge of Colonel Cathcart's desk with both hands, he lifted his flaccid haunches far back on the corner to sit with both short legs dangling freely. His shoes kicked lightly against the yellow oak wood, his sludgebrown socks, garterless, collapsed in sagging circles below ankles that were surprisingly small and white. "You know, Yossarian," he mused affably in a manner of casual reflection that seemed both derisive and sincere, "I really do admire you a bit. You're an intelligent person of great moral character who has taken a very courageous stand. I'm an intelligent person with no moral character at all, so I'm in an ideal position to appreciate it."

"These are very critical times," Colonel Cathcart asserted petulantly from a far corner of the office, paying no attention to Colonel Korn.

"Very critical times indeed," Colonel Korn agreed with a placid nod. "We've just had a change of command above, and we can't afford a situation that might put us in a bad light with either General Scheisskopf of General Peckem. Isn't that what you mean, Colonel?"

Hasn't he got any Patriotism?"[3]

"Won't you fight for your country?" Colonel Korn demanded, emulating Colonel Cathcart's harsh, self-righteous tone. "Won't you give up your life for Colonel Cathcart and me?"

Yossarian tensed with alert astonishment when he heard Colonel Korn's concluding words. "What's that?" he exclaimed. "What have you and Colonel Cathcart got to do with my country? You're not the same."

"How can you separate us?" Colonel Korn inquired with ironical tranquillity.

"That's right," Colonel Cathcart cried emphatically. "You're either for us of against us. There's no two ways about it."

"I'm afraid he's got you," added Colonel Korn. "You're either *for* us or against your country. It's as simple as that."

"Oh, no, Colonel. I don't buy that."

Colonel Korn was unruffled. "Neither do I, frankly, but everyone else will. So there you are."

"You're a disgrace to your uniform!" Colonel Cathcart declared with blustering wrath, whirling to confront Yossarian for the first time. "I'd like to know how you ever got to be a captain, anyway."

"You promoted him," Colonel Korn reminded sweetly, stifling a snicker. "Don't you remember?"

"Well, I never should have done it."

"I told you not to do it," Colonel Korn said. "But you just

wouldn't listen to me."

"Gee whiz, will you stop rubbing it in?" Colonel Cathcart cried. He furrowed his brow and glowered at Colonel Korn through eyes narrow with suspicion, his fists clenched on his hips. "Say, whose side are you on, anyway?"

"Your side, Colonel. What other side could I be on?"

"Then stop picking on me, will you? Get off my back, will you?"

"I'm on your side, Colonel. I'm just loaded with patriotism."

"Well, just make sure you don't forget that." Colonlel Cathcart turned away grudgingly after another moment, incompletely reassured, and began striding the floor again, his hands kneading his long cigarette holder. He jerked a thumb toward Yossarian. "Let's settle with him. I know what I'd like to do with him. I'd like to take him outside and shoot him. That's what I'd like to do with him. That's what General Dreedle would do with him."

"But General Dreedle isn't with us any more," said Colonel Korn, "so we can't take him outside and shoot him." Now that his moment of tension with Colonel Cathcart had passed, Colonel Korn relaxed again and resumed kicking softly against Colonel Cathcart's desk. He returned to Yossarian. "So we're going to send you home instead. It took a bit of thinking, but we finally worked out this horrible little plan for sending you home without causing too much dissatisfaction among the friends you'll leave behind. Doesn't that make you happy?"

"What kind of plan? I'm not sure I'm going to like it."

"I know you're not going to like it." Colonel Korn laughed, locking his hands contentedly on top of his head again. "You're going to loathe it. It really is odious and certainly will offend your conscience. But you'll agree to it quickly enough. You'll agree to it because it will send you home safe and sound in two weeks, and because you have no choice, It's that or a court-martial. That it or leave it."

Yossarian snorted. "Stop bluffing, Colonel. You can't court-martial me for desertion in the face of the enemy. It would make you look bad and you probably coudn't get a conviction."

"But we can court-martial you now for desertion from duty, since you went to Rome without a pass. And we could make it stick. If you think about it a minute, you'll see that you'd leave us no alternative. We can't simply let you keep walking around in open insubordination without punishing you. All the other men would stop flying missions, too. No, you have my word for it. We will court-martial you if you turn our deal down, even though it would raise a lot of questions and be a terrible black eye for Colonel Cathcart."

Colonel Cathcart winced at the words "black eye" and, without any apparent premeditation, hurled his slender onyx-and-ivory cigarette holder down viciously on the wooden surface on his desk. "Jesus Christ!" he shouted unexpectedly. "I hate this goddam cigarteet holder!" The cigarette holder bounced off the desk to the wall, ricocheted across the window sill to the floor and came to a stop almost where he was standing. Colonel Cathcart stared down at it with an irascible scowl. "I wonder if it's really doing me any good."

"It's a feather in your cap with General Peckem, but a black eye for you with General Scheisskopf," Colonel Korn informed him with a mischievous look of innocence.

"Well, which one am I supposed to please?"

"Both."

"How can I please them both? They hate each other. How am I ever going to get a feather in my cap from General Scheisskopf without getting a black eye from General Peckem?"

"March."

"Yeah, march. That's the only way to please him. March. March." Colonel Cathcart grimaced sullenly. "Some generals! They're a disgrace to their uniforms. If people like those two can make general, I don't see how I can miss."

"You're going to go far," Colonel Korn assured him with a flat lack of conviction, and turned back chuckling to Yossarian, his disdainful merriment increasing at the sight of Yossarisn's unyielding expression of antagonism and distrust. "And there you have the crux of the situation. Colonel Cathcart wants to be a general and I want to be a colonel, and that's why we have to send you home."

"Why does he want to be a general?"

"Why? For the same reason that I want to be a colonel. What else have we got to do? Everyone teaches us to aspire to higher things. A general is higher than a colonel, and a colonel is higher than a lieutenant colonel. So we're both aspiring. And you know, Yossarian, it's a lucky thing for you that we are. Your timing on this is absolutely perfect, but

I suppose you took that factor into account in your calculations."

"I haven't been doing any calculating," Yossarian retorted.

"Yes, I really do enjoy the way you lie," Colonel Korn answered. "Won't it make you proud to have your commanding officer promoted to general—to know you served in an outfit that averaged more combat missions per person than any other? Don't you want to earn more unit citations and more oak leaf clusters for your Air Medal? Where's your *'sprit de corps*? Don't you want to contribute further to this great record by flying more combat missions? It's your last chance to answer yes."

"No."

"In that case, you have us over a barrel—" said Colonel Korn without rancor.

"He ought to be ashamed of himself!"

"—and we have to send you home. Just do a few little things for us, and—"

"What sort of things?" Yossarian interrupted with belligerent misgiving.

"Oh, tiny, insignificant things. Really, this is a very generous deal we're making with you. We will issue orders returning you to the States—really, we will—and all you have to do in return is. . ."

"What? What must I do?"

Colonel Korn laughed curtly. "Like us."

Yossarian blinked. "Like you?"

"Like us."

"Like you?"

"That's right," said Colonel Korn, nodding, gratified immeasurably by Yossarian's guileless surprise and bewilderment. "Like us. Join us. Be our pal. Say nice things about us here and back in the States. Become one of the boys. Now, that isn't asking too much, is it?"

"You just want me to like you? Is that all?"

"That's all."

"That's all?"

"Just find it in your heart to like us."

Yossarian wanted to laugh confidently when he saw with amazement that Colonel Korn was telling the truth. "That isn't going to be too easy," he sneered.

"Oh, it will be a lot easier than you think," Colonel Korn taunted in return, undismayed by Yossarian's barb. "You'll be surprised at how easy you'll find it to like us once you begin." Colonel Korn hitched up the waist of his loose, voluminous trousers. The deep black grooves isolating his square chin from his jowls were bent again in a kind of jeering and reprehensible mirth. "You see, Yossarian, we're going to put you on easy street. We're going to promote you to major and even give you another medal. Captain Flume is already working on glowing press releases describing your valor over Ferrara, your deep and abiding loyalty to your outfit and your consummate dedication to duty. Those phrases are all actul quotations, by the way. We're going to glorify you and send you home a hero, recalled by the Pentagon for morale and public-relations purposes. You'll live like a millionaire. Everyone will lionize you. You'll have parades in your honor and make speeches to raise money for war bonds. A whole new world of luxury awaits you once you become our pal. Isn't it lovely?"

Yossarian found himself listening intently to the fascinating elucidation of details. "I'm not sure I want to make speeches."

"Then we'll forget the speeches. The important thing is what you say to people here." Colonel Korn leaned forward earnestly, no longer smiling. "We don't want any of the men in the group to know that we're sending you home as a result of your refusal to fly more missions. And we don't want General Peckem or General Scheisskopf to get wind of any friction between us, either. That's why we're going to become such good pals."

"What will I say to the men who asked me why I refused to fly more missions?"

"Tell them you had been informed in confidence that you were being returned to the States and that you were unwilling to risk your life for another mission or two. Just a minor disagreement between pals, that's all."

"Will they believe it?"

"Of course they'll believe it, once they see what great friends we've become and when they see the press releases and read the flattering things you have to say about me and Colonel Cathcart. Don't worry about the men. They'll be easy enough to discipline and control when you've gone. It's only while you're still here that they may prove troublesome. You know, one good apple can spoil the rest," Colonel Korn concluded with conscious irony. "You know—this would really be wonderful—you might even serve as an inspiration to them to fly more missions."

"Suppose I denounce you when I get back to the States?"

"After you've accepted our medal and promotion and all the fanfare? No one would believe you, the Army wouldn't let you, and why in the world should you want to? You're going to be one of the boys, remember? You'll enjoy a rich, rewarding, luxurious, privileged existence. You'd have to be a fool to throw it all away just for a moral principle, and you're not a fool. Is it a deal?"

"I don't know."

"It's that or a court-martial."

"That's a pretty scummy trick I'd playing on the men in the squadron, isn't it?"

"Odious," Colonel Korn agreed amiably, and waited, watching Yossarian patiently with a glimmer of private delight.

"But what the hell!" Yossarian exclaimed. "If they don't want ot fly more missions, let them stand up and do something about it the way I did. Right?"

"Of course," said Colonel Korn.

"There's no reason I have to risk my life for them, is there?"

"Of course not."

Yossarian arrived at his decision with a swift grin. "It's a deal!" he announced jubilantly.

"Great," said Colonel Korn with somewhat less cordiality than Yossarian had expected, and he slid himself off Colonel Cathcart's desk to stand on the floor. He tugged the folds of cloth of his pants and undershorts free from his crotch and gave Yossarian a limp hand to shake. "Welcome aboard."

"Thanks, Colonel. I—"

"Call me Blackie, John. We're pals now."

"Sure, Blackie. My friends call me Yo-Yo. Blackie, I—"

"His friends call him Yo-Yo," Colonel Korn sang out to Colonel Cathcart. "Why don't you congratulate Yo-Yo on what a sensible move he's making?"

"That's a real sensible move you're making, Yo-Yo," Colonel Cathcart said, pumping Yossarian's hand with clumsy zeal.

"Thank you, Colonel, I—"

"Call him Chuck," said Colonel Korn.

"Sure, call me Chcuk," said Colonel Cathcart with a laugh that was hearty and awkward. "We're all pals now."

"Sure, Chuck."

"Exit smiling," said Colonel Korn, his hands on both their shoulders as the three of them moved to the door.

"Come on over for dinner with us some night, Yo-Yo," Colonel Cathcart invited hospitably. "How about tonight? In the group dining room."

"I'd love to, sir."

"Chuck," Colonel Korn corrected reprovingly.

"I'm sorry, Blackie. Chuck. I can't get used to it."

"That's all right, pal."

"Sure, pal."

"Thanks, pal."

"Don't mention it, pal."

"So long, pal."

Yossarian waved goodbye fondly to his new pals and sauntered out onto the balcony corridor, almost bursting into song the instant he was alone. He was home free: he had pulled it off; his act of rebellion had succeeded; he was safe, and he had nothing to be ashamed of to anyone. He started toward the staircase with a jaunty and exhilarated air. A private in green fatigues saluted him. Yossarian returned the salute happily, staring at the private with curiosity. He looked strangely familiar.[4] When Yossarian returned the salute, the private in green fatigues turned sudenly into Nately's whore and lunged at him murderously with a bone-handled kitchen knife that caught him in hte side below his upraised arm. Yossarian sank to the floor with a shriek, shutting his eyes in overwhelming terror as he saw the girl lift the knife to strike him again. He was already uncouscious when Colonel Korn and Colonel Cathcart dashed out of the office and saved his life by frightening her away.

〔注释〕

1. 这一章通过卡思卡特和克恩设法诱惑尤索林复员回国，深刻揭露第二十二条军规的本质。尤索林拒绝执行飞行任务，在卡思卡特和克恩看来，他的不驯的行为在其他飞行员中间造成极坏影响，成了、他们实现将军梦的一大障碍。因此，他们决定将尤索林送回美国，一旦他离开空军基地，其余的飞行员就不会再给他们制造麻烦；而且将尤索林打扮成荣归故里的英雄还可以鼓舞别的飞行员去执行更多的飞行任务。但尤索林必须答应一个条件，即他必须“从心里喜欢”卡思卡特和克恩他们。“喜欢我们，加入我们一伙，成为我们的朋友。不论在这里，还是回美国，都要说我们的好话。”尤索林若能答应这个条件，他就能回到美国，就能象百万富翁一样享受富贵荣华，原先被指控为怯懦而遭责难的行为也可被当作英雄业绩而受嘉奖。否则，他就要受到军事法庭的审判，被送进监狱。当然，尤索林既不愿无故将自己交给军事法庭，在监狱里度过一生，也不会违心地去“喜欢”他不喜欢的人，更不会替他们去说好话。

为了从长计议，为了逃脱死亡的命运，他权且接受了这个交易，但他并不准备履行他的许诺。最后，他没有回到美国，而是逃往北欧的瑞典，去寻找先他到达那里的奥尔。至于尤索林是否逃跑成功，对小说的主题无关紧要。

2. Ferrara：地名。卡思卡特为了升官，主动应允在24小说内将弗雷拉大桥炸掉。他派尤索林和阿尔菲执行任务。因驾驶员阿尔菲没有弄清轰炸目标，尤索林心中胆怯，未能投弹，只好又一次返回目的地，才把大桥炸毁。这样一个事实在本章里被卡思卡特和克恩随心所欲地作了两种截然不同的解释。

3. Patriotism：“爱国主义”这一字眼出自利欲熏心的卡思卡特和克恩之口使人哭笑不得。他们所说的“爱国主义”和“为国家而战”，实际上是让飞行员为他们送命。“爱国主义”这一命题在小说中多处出现，成为作者讽刺美军中腐败现象的重要手段。在小说的第1章里，尤索林和邓巴都尖锐地指出，美军中“没有爱国主义”。在最后一章，尤索林又直截了当地指出了卡思卡特等的“爱国主义”的真正含义。他说：“不要对我讲为保卫我的国家而战。我一直都在为保卫我的国家而战。现在我要为保卫我自己而作一点斗争。国家不再有危险，而有危险的是我。”他又说：“假如我现在献出我的生命，那不是为了我的国家，那将是为了卡思卡特和克恩。”

正如海明威的《永别了，武器》中的主人公弗雷德里克·亨利是第一次世界大战的受害者一样，《第二十二条军规》中的主人公尤索林是第二次世界大战的受害者。他们对战争有共同的认识和感受。当他们听到决定政策的上层集团喊出“高尚”、“光荣”、“牺牲”、“为国而战”以及“为拯救世界民主而战”的骗人口号时，就感到脸红。最后，两部小说中的主人公一个从意大利前线逃往瑞士，一个从地中海逃往瑞典，而他们的逃遁都是对两次世界大战的抗议。

4. He looked strongly familiar：此人是飞行员纳特利的妓女朋友装扮的。纳特利在一次执行飞行任务时与另一架飞机相撞，机毁人亡。尤索林特地来到罗马把这一不幸的消息通知了纳特利的这位女友，当时她操起一把刀子朝尤索林刺去。尤索林逃出罗马后，她仍穷追不舍。此次就是她化装成穿绿色工作服的士兵，埋伏在外面，伺机刺杀尤索林。在尤索林因伤住院治疗期间，随军牧师塔普曼向他透露，官方报道说，化装的妓女是谋杀卡思卡特和克恩的纳粹刺客，尤索林冒生命危险将刺客赶跑，保护了他们（见第 41 章）。这显然是卡思卡特的用心，为了把尤索林打扮成英雄好送他回国。后来另一个官方报导却说，尤索林因参与向敌人出卖军事情报的黑市活动而被一个女子刺伤（见第 42 章）。

这是利用“第二十二条军规”对同一事实进行任意解释的又一例证。

SYLVIA PLATH

〔作者介绍〕

西尔维亚·普拉斯（Sylvia Plath，1932～1963），美国女诗人。生于波士顿，父亲是波兰移民，母亲是奥地利人。她幼时聪敏过人，但性情古怪。17岁时发表第1首诗及第1篇短篇小说。她入史密斯学院学习，1955年以优秀成绩毕业，获奖学金入剑桥大学学习，1957年取得硕士学位。大学期间，她的精神愈来愈紧张，孤独、恐惧和死亡感经常侵袭她少女的心灵。她觉得自己如生活在钟形坛下的稀薄空气中一样压抑和窒息。感到生活的混乱脱节，感到悲观绝望。内心和外部世界的极不协调曾使她精神失常，在医院进行过短期而集中的治疗。她唯一的一部小说《钟形坛》（*The Bell Jar*，1963）是一部自传体小说，描述了那些年里她的生活情况；其中写到一个女大学生企图自杀后被救起的事。小说是以维多利亚·普卡斯（Victoria Lucas）的笔名发表的。

在剑桥期间，西尔维亚·普拉斯和英国诗人泰德·休斯（Ted Hughes，1930～ ）相遇，1956年结婚，生了两个孩子，除一次回美国短住以外，生前一直住在英国。她的生活是普通的，正常的。然而她内心并不平静，终于在1963年2月11日用煤气自杀。

普拉斯的第一部诗集《巨人》（*The Colossus*）1960年问世，受到评论界好评。这部诗集中的诗多写个人经历和体验，情绪强烈，文字考究，文体表现出年轻女诗人诗才的不凡。在这之后，她开始创作另一种诗歌，后来收入她死后出版的《阿丽尔》（*Ariel*，1965）诗集中。这些诗的创作速度快，作者似在急忙写信一般，而不是如从前一样推敲和雕琢。这些诗集表现出诗人的人生愈来愈混乱的感觉，内容多来自诗人自己的生活，如同诗人在把自己内心的极度痛苦公诸于世，因而成为“自白派”诗歌的上乘之作。诗人写到孤独、暴力、压抑、恐惧和死亡，写到自己的父母，他们的态度和性格，写到自杀。有人称她的诗作是人们一向写过的“最长的自杀曲”。普拉斯 去世后，她的诗作还有几集结集出版，如《没有结集起的诗》(*Uncollecte Poems*，1965)、《渡河》(*Crossing the Water*，1971) 及《冬天的树》(*Winter Trees*，1972) 等。这些作品进一步表明诗人精神的紧张、痛苦和绝望，表达了她通过创作竭力把自己表达清楚的强烈愿望。

普拉斯具有自己独特的文风。她的语言简明、流畅，语法比较规范。但是她的诗并不易读懂。她的意象虽多属明喻，但具有高度的象征意义；诗的叙述形式有时不很合逻辑；她的思想跳跃很快，有时又有狂想和梦幻穿插其中。读者必须跟上诗人头脑的活动节奏和自由联想的模式，才能体味出诗的蕴涵。

Lady Lazarus

〔作品介绍〕

《拉撒路女士》(1963) 是诗人的代表作，可以说是"自白派诗歌"写得最好的一篇。

这首诗是一个自杀成功者的自白。女自杀者年届 30，已自杀过 3 次，最后一次终于成功。在诗中，她叙述了自己自杀的经过，想象到自杀成功后人们的反应，警告人、上帝和魔鬼都注意，她会死而复生，恢复原形，向她的敌人报复。这大概是诗名《拉撒路女士》的内涵所在；据《圣经·约翰福音》(第 11 章)，拉撒路死后 4 天由耶稣起死回生；"女士"则有女权主义的蕴涵，自白者喊出是女人反抗的声音。

这首诗有明显的象征意义。女自杀者把自己视为"废物"—可恨可恶的现代社会的象征；她毁灭了生活在"文明社会"的自我，也便象征性地毁灭了那个令人窒息的社会的一切。

这首诗突出地表现出诗人潜伏在内心深处的自杀冲动，体现出弗洛伊德学说的影响。

Lady Lazarus

I have done it again.
One year in every ten
I manage it[1]——

A sort of walking miracle, my skin
Bright as a Nazi lampshade,[2]
My right foot

A paperweight,
My face a featureless, fine
Jew[3] linen.

Peel off the napkin
O my enemy.[4]
Do I terrify? ——

The nose, the eye pits, the full set of teeth?
The sour breath
Will vanish in a day.

Soon, soon the flesh
The grave cave ate will be
At home on me[5]

And I a smiling woman.
I am only thirty.
And like the cat I have nine times to die.[6]

This is Number Three.[7]
What a trash[8]
to annihilate each decade.

What a million filaments.[9]
The peanut-crunching crowd
Shoves in to see

Them unwrap me hand and foot——
The big strip tease.[10]
Gentleman, ladies,

These are my hands,
My knees.
I may be skin and bone,

Nevertheless, I am the same, identical woman.
The first time it happened I was ten.
It was an accident.

The second time I meant
To last it out and not come back at all.
I rocked shut

As a seashell.
They had to call and call
And pick the worms off me like sticky pearls.

Dying
Is an art, like everything else.
I do it exceptionally well.

I do it so it feels like hell.
I do it so it feels real.
I guess you could say I've a call. [11]

It's easy enough to do it in a cell.
It's easy enough to do it and stay put.
It's the theatrical

Comeback in broad day
To the same place, the same face, the same brute
Amused shout:

"A miracle!"
That knocks me out.
There is a charge[12]

For the eyeing of my scars, there is a charge

For the hearing of my heart——
It really goes.

And there is a charge, a very large charge,
For a word or a touch
Or a bit of blood

Or a piece of my hair or my colthes.
So, so, Herr Doktor.[13]
So, Herr Enemy.

I am your opus,
I am your valuavle,
The pure gold baby

That melts to a shriek.
I turn and burn.
Do not think I underestimate your great concern.

Ash, ash——
You poke and stir.
Flesh, bone, there is nothing there——

A cake of soap,
A wedding ring,
A gold filling.[14]

Herr God, Herr Lucifer,
Beware
Beware.

Out of the ash
I rise with my red hair
And I eat men like air.

〔注释〕

1. it：指自杀。

2. Nazi lampshade：纳粹的灯罩，用人皮制成。

3. Jew：和上一节中的“纳粹”相呼应，表现出自白者的受压抑的心理状态。

4. Peel off the napkin/O my enemy：自白者想象自己死后，遮住面部的“餐巾布”被揭开后的情景；my enemy：泛指“敌人”，可能是“社会”。

5. Soon…on me：意即“我会复活的”。

6. I am…to die：诗人最后一次自杀时年届30岁，当时她已自杀过两次。

7. Number Three：第3次。

8. a trash：“一堆废物”，自喻之语。

9. a million filaments：夸张语，指灯光齐亮。

10. the big strip tease：“大脱衣舞”，指围观者（引伸喻现代人）的观淫癖、性虐待狂。

11. a call：呼唤或神谕。

12. a charge：人群向前凑集状，或骚动状。

13. Herr Doktor：德语，“医生先生”。

14. a gold filling：一只金牙齿。

Daddy

《作品简介》

《爸爸》(1963)是诗人的名作之一。关于这首诗，诗人曾写道：“这是一首有恋父情结的女孩所写的诗，她爸爸去世时，她曾以为他是上帝。但她爸爸又是一个纳粹分子，而她母亲很可能有犹太血统——这一事实使她的境遇极为复杂起来。这两种血统在这个女孩儿身上融为一体，又使之麻痹瘫痪……”。纵观诗人的生平，在诗里那样诋毁自己的父亲是没有理由的。她的父亲奥托·普拉斯是波兰移民，15岁移居美国，以教书为生，1940年去世，并无异常之处。诗人把父亲写成虐待狂式人物，或专横的上帝，或似疯狂的希特勒一般，极可能是把父母做为摧残人性的社会的象征来加以抨击，恰似另一位自白诗人罗伯特·洛威尔以自己的父亲做为传统的象征加以否定一般。从这个角度看，《爸爸》一诗的社会意义是显而易见的。

Daddy

You do not do, you do not do
Any more, black shoe
In which I have lived like a foot
For thirty years,[1] poor and white,
Barely daring to breathe or Achoo.[2]

Daddy, I have had to kill you.
You died before I had time——
Marble-heavy, a bag full of God,
Ghastly statue with one grey toe
Big as a Frisco seal

And a head in the freakish Atlantic
Where it pours bean green over blue
In the waters off beautiful Nauset.[3]
I used to pray to recover you.
Ach, du.[4]

In the German tongue, in the Polish town
Scraped flat by the roller
Of wars, wars, wars.
But the name of the town is common.
My Polack friend

Say there are a dozen or two.
So I never could tell where you
Put your foot, your root,
I never could talk to you.
The tongue stuck in my jaw.

It stuck in a barb wire snare.
Ich, ich, ich, ich,[5]

I could hardly speak.
I thought every German was you.
And the language obscene

An engine, an engine
Chuffiing me off like a Jew.
A jew to Dachau, Auschwitz, Belsen.[6]
I began to talk like a Jew.
I think I may well be a Jew.

The snows of the Tyrol,[7] the clear beer of Vienna
Are not very pure or true.
With my gypsy ancestress and my weird luck
And my Taroc pack[8] and my Taroc pack
I may be a bit of a Jew.

I have always been scared of *you*,
With your Luftwaffe,[9] your gobbledygoo.
And your neat moustache
And your Aryan eye, bright blue.
Panzer[10]-man, panzer-man, O You——

Not God but a swastika
So black no sky could squeak through.
Every woman adores a Fascist,
The boot in the face, the brute
Brute heart of a brute like you.

You stand at the blackboard, daddy,
In the picture I have of you,
A cleft in your chin instead of your foot
But no less a devil for that, no not
Any less the black man who

Bit my pretty red heart in two.
I was ten when they buried you.
At twenty I tried to die

And get back, back, back to you.
I thought even the bones would do.

But they pulled me out of the sack.
And they stuck me together with glue.
And then I knew what to do.
I made a model of you.
A man in black with a Meinkampf[11] look

And a love of the rack and the screw.
And I said I do, I do.
So daddy, I'm finally through.
The black telephone's off at the root,[12]
The voices just can't worm through.

If I've killed one man, I've killed two——
The vampire[13] who said he was you
And drank my blood for a year,
Seven years,[14] if you want to know.
Daddy, you can lie back now.

There's a stake in your fat black heart
And the villagers never liked you.
They are dancing and stamping on you.
They always *knew* it was you.
Daddy, daddy, you bastard, I'm through.[15]

〔注释〕

1. For thirty years：诗写成时，诗人有30岁。
2. Achoo：德文，发惊叹语。
3. Nauset：诺赛特港，位于麻省东南方的科德角半岛上。
4. Ach, du：德文，意“啊，你”。
5. Ich, ich, ich, ich：德文，意即“我，我，我，我”；口吃状。
6. Dachau, Auschwits, Belsen：纳粹在德国和波兰所设集中营名。
7. Tyrol：蒂罗尔地区，阿尔卑斯山以东，主要在奥地利境内，部分地区在1919年后属意大利。
8. Tarot pack：用于算命的纸牌。

9. Luftwaffe：德文，意为“airforce”，第二次世界大战中德国空军名。
10. Panzer：德文，意为“武装的”、“装甲的”。
11. Meinkampf：德文，《我的奋斗》，希特勒的自传和政治宣言。
12. off at the root：（电话）掐断了。
13. vampire：指父亲。
14. seven years：诗人父亲去世时，她刚 7 岁。
15. I'm through：我完了。双关语，意为“我说完了”及“我完蛋了”。

EDWARD ALBEE

〔作者介绍〕

爱德华·阿尔比（Edward Albee，1928～　）美国当代剧作家。生于华盛顿，幼时被一个富有的戏剧之家收为养子。小学时期曾先后被两家私立学校开除，后来在第3所学校表现较好，在诗歌和小说创作上花了不少时间。阿尔比后来毕业于哥伦比亚大学；但他和尤金·奥尼尔一样，是在实践中，在他所从事过的诸如办公室勤杂工、餐馆柜台服务员等工作中，学习到真正的知识的。

从50年代末开始，阿尔比写出了一系列独幕剧，如《动物园的故事》（*The Zoo Story*，1958）、《沙盒》（*The Sandbox*，1959）、《贝西·史密斯之死》（*The Death of Bessie Smith*，1960）、《美国著名剧作家和美国青年剧作家》（*Fam and Yam*，1960）、《美国梦》（*The American Dream*，1961）等；1962年，他的首部长剧《谁害怕弗吉尼亚·沃尔夫?》（*Who's Afraid of Virginia Woolf?*）问世，从而奠定了他在美国剧坛的重要地位。60年代初，文学评论界开始把他和欧洲的荒诞派传统联系起来。阿尔比的这些剧作多是对现代社会及现代人心理问题的精妙的荒诞性分析。《动物园的故事》1959年首次在柏林上演，1962年在美国上演。该剧描写人与人之间的冷漠关系，颇受欢迎。《贝西·史密斯之死》取材于美国一位著名爵士乐歌手的生活，揭示了南部性生活和政治的疯狂性质。《谁害怕弗吉尼亚·沃尔夫?》巧妙地运用了荒诞派戏剧的技巧，出色地描绘了一位历史教授与妻子之间相互伤害而又和解的游戏，显示了现代生活的痛苦和空虚。该剧在百老汇剧场上演，受到观众和评论界的热烈欢迎，获纽约戏剧评论界奖和托尼奖，被誉为1962至1963年的最佳剧作。

《小艾丽丝》（*Tiny Alice*）是一部关于性欲的心理幻想剧，于1964年问世。在这前后，阿尔比还把卡森·麦卡勒斯50年代初出版的小说集《伤心咖啡馆之歌》（*The Ballad of the Sad Cafe*）及詹姆斯·珀迪的首部小说《马尔科姆》（*Malcolm*）分别在1963年和1965年改编成剧作上演，这两部剧都描写了青少年的幻想生活。1966年，阿尔比推出他的《脆弱的平衡》(*A Delicate Balance*)一剧，这部作品综合表现出他在安排剧情时间、描写严重威胁生活的狂欢或伪装以及在决心自毁的家庭里寻找爱等方面的天才。1968年，阿尔比改写了英国剧作家贾尔斯·库珀的《花园中的一切》(*Everything in the Garden*)，几乎改变了原剧所有的词和字，把原来的黑色幽默剧变成他自己的悲喜剧。1968年，他推出《箱子—毛—箱子》(*Box—Mao—Box*)。1971年，阿尔比写成《一切皆已过去》(*All Over*)；1975年完成《海景》(*Sea scape*)和《听》(*Listening*)两部作品，其中《海景》获普利策奖；1976年推出《列数途径》(*Counting the Ways*)；1977年创作《杜布克的女人》(*The Lady from Dubugue*)；1979年改编弗拉基米尔·纳博科夫的小说《罗莉塔》(*Lolita*)。1980年他受到美国文学艺术协会表彰，获金质奖章。阿尔比后来的剧作善发含混、玄奥的议论，因而不如早期的剧作受欢迎；然而他的作品始终表现出他的幽默感以及扣人心弦的对话，始终以感人的笔墨描绘和分析现代人心理和实际生活中的暴力表现，以及现代人的精神空虚症。

阿尔比是第二次世界大战后成长起来的著名剧作家，以奥尼尔和威廉斯的后继者自诩。50年代末期及整个60年代是他创作的高峰期，他的代表作《谁害怕弗吉尼亚·沃尔夫?》业已成为当代美国文学的经典作品。自60年代末以来，他放慢了创作步伐，开始抱怨评论界和公众对他的新作不够注意，但他坚持不断进行创作尝试，不断有新作问世。他在美国戏剧史上的地位是稳固的。

Who's Afraid of Virginia Woolf?

〔作品介绍〕

《谁害怕弗吉尼亚·沃尔夫?》(*Who's Afraid of Virginia Woolf?*)于1962年问世，是阿尔比的代表作，也是50年代和60年代风靡美国的荒诞派戏剧的代表作之一。从一定意义上讲，阿尔比的戏剧似乎只描写了一个问题，即建立在脆弱幻想基础上的人生的荒诞以及人的精神空虚。《谁害怕弗吉尼亚·沃尔夫?》一剧便是最有力的佐证。

乔治和玛莎是一对没有子女的中年夫妇。没有子女使他们感到生活空虚。他们及时行乐，饮酒、游戏，但在内心深处，却蕴存着一种没有勇气正视现实的失落感。他们似已达成默契，即佯装自己已有一个年过20的儿子，只是谁也不许和外人谈起他。在他们的儿子21周岁生日的前一天晚上，他们邀请一对年轻夫妇尼克与哈尼前来和他们一起饮酒作乐，参加他们荒诞而可怕的“游戏”。时间已晚，四个人见面时已近清晨两点。他们不断地饮酒，很快就开始醉了。对他们来说，生活是如此荒诞，夜晚似已替代了白昼，理性已让位于自由想像，下意识已占据统治地位。乔治因玛莎向哈尼透露了关于他们的儿子的事而怀恨在心，不断寻衅和她争吵。哈尼喝得酊酩大醉，躺在卫生间的地板上熟睡过去。一直似乎清醒的尼克后来也终于失去理智，他的内心痛苦使他也行为失常：他竟在厨房和卧室里和女主人“做爱。”原来他本人患阳萎，他妻子骨盆太窄，因而也没有孩子，他们的生活也和他们的中年朋友一样的孤寂与空虚。至清晨四点，四个人开始清醒过来，尼克夫妇突然领会到乔治和玛莎的生活的真相，在凄惨的气氛中告别主人离去。玛莎终于承认自己害怕正视现实，和乔治和解，闭户休息。

在这一剧作中，没有孩子这一事实被作者用来象征生活荒诞和精神空虚。以乔治为例，他是新英格兰一所学院的历史教授，从一开始，他的生活便被蒙上了一层“弑父”的阴影。他和院长的女儿玛莎结婚，有着做院长继承人的前景，可是后来人们发现他的条件不足。战争期间他曾任历史系主任，但显然不成功。所以他的生活是失意、失败和绝望的记录。做为历史教授，他预见到“文化和种族最终将会消失……蚂蚁将接管世界，”因而他在逃避中，在幻想中寻觅慰藉。尼克是生物学家，在乔治看来，他代表现代科学文明对自然生活的威胁。在家里，他制造有一个儿子的幻象，自欺自娱地生活着。但他知道那是幻梦，不是真相，因此内心极其痛苦。同样，玛莎也发自内心呼叫说，“我一直在哭，但只是在内心深处，因而没有人看到。我一直在哭。乔治也一直在哭。我们俩都一直在哭……”尼克和哈尼也感到无比的痛苦和空虚，哈尼曾歇斯底里地尖叫：“我想要一个孩子！”在剧的结尾，幻象破灭以后，剩下的只有绝望和对继续生活下去的畏惧心。

《谁害怕弗吉尼亚·沃尔夫?》在形式和技巧上也是极有特点的作品。“谁害怕弗吉尼亚·沃尔夫”这首已经由作者改词的歌曲自始至终回荡在人们的耳际，起到画龙点睛的作用。这是30年代大萧条时期的一首歌，原词是“谁害怕这只大恶狼?”（“Who's Afraid of the Big Bad Wolf?”）“这只大恶狼”意指贫困，作者出于一种荒诞的幽默感，将词改做“弗吉尼亚·沃尔夫”（英国一女作家名），除沃尔夫与狼在英文里为谐音外，这一改动并无其他意义。在剧中“弗吉尼亚·沃尔夫”（或“这只大恶狼”）象征着生活的真实面目，害怕它就是害怕面对现实。本剧的3个部分，“玩笑和游戏”、“狂欢”及“解除符咒”，代表阿尔比剧作的典型结构模式，即正常的开始，逐步移向感情和心理的崩溃，快速的结尾。作者匠心独具，以悬念紧扣观众的心弦。导致剧中人物激烈争吵和歇斯底里大发作的原因是玛莎向哈尼透露了她的儿子的秘密。乔治扬言要报复一事让人感到迷惑，直到玛莎说出乔治不喜欢这孩子，因为他不肯定那是他的孩子。这引起人们对乔治的性能力的怀疑。乔治受到如此羞辱之后决心报复。他开始的几个游戏项目慢慢地稳步地导向真相的暴露，到最后幻象终于破灭，他们突然发现自己面对着生活的毫无掩饰的真相。观众也慢慢地从迷雾中钻出，恍然大悟，继而 回顾全剧，意味无穷。

这里选注的是第1幕的一部分。

Who's Afraid of Virginia Woolf?

…

NICK

Indeed?

GEORGE

No kids, hunh?

NICK

Not yet.

GEORGE

People do... uh... have kids. That's what I meant about history. You people are going to make them in test tubes, aren't you? You biologists. Babies. Then the rest of us... them as wants to... can screw to their heart's content. What will happen to the tax deduction? Has anyone figured that out yet?

(NICK, *who can think of nothing better to do, laughs mildly*)

But you *are* going to have kids... anyway. In spite of history.

NICK (*Hedging*)

Yes... certainly. We... want to wait... a little... until we're settled.

GEORGE

And this... (*With a handsweep taking in not only the room, the house, but the whole countryside*)... this is your heart's content—Illyria... Penguin Island... Gomorrah.[1]... You think you're going to be happy here in New Carthage,[2] eh?

NICK (*A little defensively*)

I hope we'll stay here.

GEORGE

And every definition has its boundaries, eh? Well, it isn't a bad college, I guess. I mean... it'll do. It isn't M. I. T.... it isn't U. C. L. A.... it isn't the Sorbonne... or Moscow U. either, for that matter.

NICK

I don't mean... forever.

GEORGE

Well, don't you let that get bandied about. The old man wouldn't like it. Martha's father expects loyalty and devotion out of his... staff. I was going to use another word. Martha's father expects his... staff... to cling to the walls of this place, like the ivy... to come here and grow old... to fall in the line of service. One man, a professor of Latin and Elocution, actually fell in the cafeteria line, one lunch. He was buried, as many of us have been, and as many more of us will be, under the shrubbery around the chapel. It is said... and I have no reason to doubt it... that we make excellent fertilizer. But the old man is not going to be buried under the shrubbery... the old man is not going to die. Martha's father has the staying power of one of those Micronesian tortoises. There are rumors... which you must not breathe in front of Martha, for she foams at the mouth... that the old man, her father, is over two hundred years old. There is probably an irony involved in this, but I am not drunk enough to figure out what it is. How many kids you going to have?

NICK

I... I don't know... My wife is....

GEORGE

Slim-hipped. (*Rises*) Have a drink.

NICK

Yes.

GEORGE

MARTHA! (*No answer*) DAMN IT! (*To* NICK) You asked me if I knew women.... Well, one of the things I do *not* know about them is what they talk about while the men are talking. (*Vaguely*) I must find out some time.

MARTHA'S VOICE

WHADD'YA WANT?[3]

GEORGE (*To* NICK)

Isn't that a wonderful sound? What I mean is... what do you think they really *talk* about... or don't you care?

NICK

Themselves, I would imagine.

MARTHA'S VOICE

GEORGE?

GEORGE (*To* NICK)

Do you find women... puzzling?

NICK

Well... yes and no.

GEORGE (*With a knowing nod*)

Unh-hunh. (*Moves toward the hall, almost bumps into* HONEY, *re-entering*) Oh! Well, here's one of you, at least.

(HONEY *moves toward* NICK. GEORGE *goes to the hall*)

HONEY (*To* GEORGE)

She'll be right down. (*To* NICK) You must see this house, dear... this is such a wonderful old house.

NICK

Yes, I....

GEORGE

MARTHA!

MARTHA'S VOICE

FOR CHRIST'S SAKE, HANG ON A MINUTE, WILL YOU?

HONEY (*To* GEORGE)

She'll be right down... she's changing.

GEORGE (*Incredulous*)

She's *what*? She's changing?

HONEY

Yes.

CEORGE

Her clothes?

HONEY

Her dress.

GEORGE (*Suspicious*)

Why?

HONEY

(*With a nervous little laugh*)

Why, I imagine she wants to be... comfortable.

GEORGE

(*With a threatening look toward the hall*)

Oh she does, does she?

HONEY

Well, heavens, I should think....

GEORGE

YOU DON'T KNOW!

NICK (*As* HONEY *starts*)

You feel all right?

HONEY

(*Reassuring, but with the echo of a whine. A long-practiced tone*)

Oh, yes, dear... perfectly fine.

GEORGE

(*Fuming... to himself*)

So she wants to be comfortable, does she? Well, we'll see about that.

HONEY (*To* GEORGE, *brightly*)

I didn't know until just a minute ago that you had a *son*.

GEORGE

(*Wheeling, as if struck from behind*)

WHAT?

HONEY

A son! I hadn't known.

NICK

You to know and me to find out. Well, he must be quite a big....

HONEY

Twenty-one... twenty-one tomorrow... tomorrow's his birthday.

NICK (*A victorious smile*)

Well!

GEORGE (*To* HONEY)

She told you about him?

HONEY (*Flustered*)

Well, *yes*. Well, I mean....

GEORGE (*Nailing it down*)

She told you about him.

HONEY (*A nervous giggle*)

Yes.

GEORGE (*Strangely*)

You say she's changing?

HONEY

Yes....

GEORGE

And she mentioned..?

HONEY

(*Cheerful, but a little puzzled*)

... your son's birthday... yes.

GEORGE

(*More or less to himself*)

O. K. ,Martha. . . O. K.

NICK

You look pale, Honey. Do you want a. . . ?

HONEY

Yes, dear. . . a little more brandy, maybe. Just a drop.

GEORGE

O. K. , Martha.

NICK

May I use the. . . uh . . . bar? [4]

GEORGE

Hm? Oh, yes. . . yes. . . by all means. Drink away. . . you'll need it as the years go on. (*For* MARTHA, *as if she were in the room*) You goddamn destructive. . . .

HONEY (*To cover*)

What time is it, dear?

NICK

Two-thirty.

HONEY

Oh, it's so late. . . we *should* be getting hime.

GEORGE

(*Nastily, but he is so preoccupied he hardly notices his own tone*)

For what? You keeping the babysitter up, or something?

NICK

(*Almost a warning*)

I told you we didn't have children.

GEORGE

Hm? (*Realizing*) Oh, I'm sorry. I wasn't even listening. . . or thinking. . . (*With a flick of his hand*). . . whichever one applies.

NICK (*Softly, to* HONEY)

We'll go in a little while.

GEORGE (*Driving*)

Oh no, now. . . you mustn't. Martha is changing. . . and Martha is not changing for *me*. Martha hasn't changed for *me* in years. If Martha is changing, it means we'll be here for. . . days. You are being accorded an honor, and you must not forget that Martha is the daughter of our beloved boss. She is his. . . right ball, you might say.

NICK

You might not understand this. . . but I wish you wouldn't talk that way in front of my wife.

HONEY

Oh, now. . . .

GEORGE (*Incredulous*)

Really? Well, you're quite right. . . . We'll leave that sort of talk to Martha.

MARTHA (*Entering*)

What sort of talk?

(MARTHA *has changed her clothes, and she looks, now, more comfortable and. . . and this is most important. . . most voluptuous*)

GEORGE

There you are, my pet.

NICK (*Impressed; rising*)

Well, now. . . .

GEORGE

Why, Martha. . . your Sunday chapel dress!

HONEY (*Slightly disapproving*)

Oh, that's most attractive.

MARTHA (*Showing off*)

You like it? Good! (*To* GEORGE) What the hell do you mean screaming up the stairs at me like that?

GEORGE

We got lonely, darling. . . we got lonely for the soft purr of your little voice.

MARTHA

(*Deciding not to rise to it*)

Oh. Well, then, you just trot over to the barie-poo. . .

GEORGE

(*Taking the tone from her*)

. . . and make your little mommy a gweat big dwink.

MARTHA (*Giggles*)

That's right. (*To* NICK) Well, did you two have a nice little talk? You men solve the problems of the world, as usual?

NICK

Well, no, we. . .

GEORGE (*Quickly*)

What we did, actually, if you really want to know, what we did actually is try to figure out what you two were talking about.

(HONEY *giggles*, MARTHA *laughs*)

MARTHA (*To* HONEY)

Aren't they something? Aren't these... (*Cheerfully disdainful*)... *men* the absolute end? (*To* GEORGE) Why didn't you sneak upstairs and listen in?

GEORGE

Oh, I wouldn't have *listened*, Martha.... I would have *peeked*.

(HONEY *giggles*, MARTHA *laughs*)

NICK

(*To* GEORGE, *with false heartiness*)

It's a conspiracy.

GEORGE

And now we'll never know. Shucks!

MARTHA

(*To* NICK, *as* HONEY *beams*)

Hey, you must be quite a boy, getting your Masters[5] when you were... what?... twelve? You hear that, George?

NICK

Twelve-and-a-half, actually. No, nineteen really. (*To* HONEY) Honey, you needn't have mentioned that. It....

HONEY

Ohhhh... I'm *proud* of you....

GEORGE (*Seriously*, *if sully*)

That's very... impressive.

MARTHA (*Aggressively*)

You're damned right!

GEORGE (*Between his teeth*)

I said I was impressed, Martha. I'm beside myself with jealousy. What do you want me to do, throw up? (*To* NICK) That really is very impressive. (*To* HONEY) You should be right proud.

HONEY (*Coy*)

Oh, he's a pretty nice fella.

GEORGE (*To* NICK)

I wouldn't be surprised if you *did* take over the History Department one of these days.

NICK

The Biology Department.

GEORGE

The *Biology* Department... of course. I seem preoccupied with history. Oh! What a remark. (*He strikes a pose, his hand over his heart, his head raised, his voice stentorian*) "I am preoccupied with history."

MARTHA

(*As* HONEY *and* NICK *chuckle*)

Ha, ha, ha, HA!

GEORGE (*With some disgust*)

I think I'll make *myself* a drink.

MARTHA

George is not preoccupied with *history*.... George is preoccupied with the *History Department*. George is preoccupied with the History Department because...

GEORGE

... because he is *not* the History Department, but is only *in* the History Department. We know, Martha... we went all through it while you were upstairs... getting up. There's no need to go through it again.

MARTHA

That's right, baby... keep it clean. (*To the others*) George is bogged down in the History Department. He's an old bog in the History Department, that's what George is. A bog... A fen... A G. D. swamp. Ha, ha, ha, HA! A SWAMP! Hey, swamp! Hey SWAMPY!

GEORGE

(*With a great effort controls himself... then, as if she had said nothing more than "George, dear"...*)

Yes, Martha? Can I get you something?

MARTHA (*Amused at his game*)

Well... uh... sure, you can light my cigarette, if you're of a mind to.

GEORGE

(*Considers, them moves off*)

No... there are limits. I mean, man can put up with only so much without he descends a rung or two on the old evolutionary ladder... (*Now a quick aside to* NICK)... which is up your line... (*Then back to* MARTHA)... sinks, Martha, and it's a funny ladder... you can't reverse yourself... start back up once you're descending.

(MARTHA *blows him an arrogant kiss*)

Now... I'll hold your hand when it's dark and you're afraid of the bogey man, and I'll tote your gin bottles out after midnight, so no one'll see... but I will not light your cigarette. And that, as they say, is that.

(*Brief silence*)

MARTHA (*Under her breath*)

Jesus! (*Then, immediately, to* NICK) Hey, you played football, hunh?

HONEY

(*As* NICK *seems sunk in thought*)

Dear....

NICK

Oh! Oh, yes... I was a ... quarterback... but I was much more... adept... at boxing, really.

MARTHA

(*With great enthusiasm*)

BOXING! You hear that, George?

GEORGE (*Resignedly*)

Yes, Martha.

MARTHA

(*To* NICK, *with peculiar intensity and enthusiasm*)

You musta been pretty good at it... I mean, you don't look like you got hit in the face at all.

HONEY (*Proudly*)

He was intercollegiate state middleweight champion.

NICK (*Embarrassed*)

Honey....

HONEY

Well, you were.

MARTHA

You look like you still got a pretty good body *now*, too... is that right? Have you?

GEORGE (*Intensely*)

Martha... decency forbids....

MARTHA

(*To* GEORGE... *still staring at* NICK, *though*)

SHUT UP! (*Now, back to* NICK) Well, have you? Have you kept your body?

NICK

(*Unselfconscious... almost encouraging her*)

It's still pretty good. I work out.

MARTHA (*With a half-smile*)

Do you!

NICK

Yeah.

HONEY

Oh, yes... he has a very... firm body.

MARTHA

(*Still with that smile... a private communication with* NICK)

Have you! Oh, I think that's very nice.

NICK

(*Narcissistic, but not directly for* MARTHA)

Well, you never know... (*shrugs*)... you know... once you have it....

MARTHA

... you never know when it's going to come in handy.

NICK

I was going to say... why give it up until you have to.

MARTHA

I couldn't agree with you more.

(*They both smile, and there is a rapport of some unformed sort established*)

I couldn't agree with you more.

GEORGE

Martha, your obscenity is more than....

MARTHA

George, here, doesn't cotton much to body talk[6]... do you sweetheart? (*No reply*) George isn't too happy when we get to muscle. You know... flat bellies, pectorals....

GEORGE (*To* HONEY)

Would you like to take a walk around the garden?

HONEY (*Chiding*)

Oh, now....

GEORGE (*Incredulous*)

You're amused? (*Shrugs*) All right.

MARTHA

Paunchy[7] over there isn't too happy when the conversation moves to muscle. How much do you weigh?

NICK

A hundred and fifty-five, a hundred and...

MARTHA

Still at the old middleweight limit, eh? That's pretty good. (*Swings around*) Hey George, tell 'em about the boxing match *we* had.

GEORGE

(*Slamming his drink down, moving toward the hall*)

Christ!

MARTHA

George! Tell 'em about it!

GEORGE

(*With a sick look on his face*)

You tell them, Martha. You're good at it.

(EXITS)

HONEY

Is he... all right?

MARTHA (*Laughs*)

Him? Oh, sure. George and I had this boxing match... Oh, Lord, twenty years ago... a couple of years after we were married.

NICK

A boxing match? The two of you?

HONEY

Really?

MARTHA

Yup[8]... the two of us... really.

HONEY

(*With a little shivery giggle of anticipation*)

I can't imagine it.

MARTHA

Well, like I say, it was twenty years ago, and it wasn't in a ring, or anything like that, you know what I mean. It was wartime and Daddy was on this physical fitness kick... Daddy's always admired physical fitness... says a man is only part brain... he has a body, too, and it's his responsibility to keep both of them up... you know?

NICK

Unh-hunh.

MARTHA

Say the brain can't work unless the body's working, too.

NICK

Well, that's not exactly so....

MARTHA

Well, maybe that *isn't* what he says... something like it. *But*... it was wartime, and Daddy got the idea all the men should learn how to box. . . self-defense. I suppose the idea was if the Germans landed on the coast, or something. the whole faculty'd go out and punch 'em to death. . . . I don't know.

NICK

It was probably more the principle of the thing.

MARTHA

No kidding. Anyway, so Daddy had a couple of us over one Sunday and we went out in the back, and Daddy put on the gloves himself. Daddy's a strong man. . . . Well, *you* know.

NICK

Yes. . . Yes

MARTHA

And he asked George to box with him. Aaaaannnnd . . . George didn't *want* to. . . probably something about not wanting to bloody-up his meal ticket. . . .

NICK

Unh—hunh.

MARTHA

. . . Anyway, George said he didn't want to, and Daddy was saying, "Come on, young man. . . what sort of son-in-law *are* you?". . . and stuff like that.

NICK

Yeah.

MARTHA

So, while this was going on. . . I don't know why I *did* it. . . I got into a pair of gloves myself. . . you know, I didn't lace 'em up, or anything. . . and I snuck up behind George, just kidding, and I yelled "Hey George!" and at the same time I let go sort of a roundhouse right···just kidding, you know?

NICK

Unh—hunh.

MARTHA

. . . and George wheeled around real quick, and he caught it right in the jaw. . . POW! (NICK laughs) I hadn't meant it. . . honestly. Anyway. . . POW! Right in the jaw. . . and he was off balance. . . he must have been- . . . and he stumbled back a few steps, and then CRASH, he landed. . . flat. . . in a huckleberry bush!

(NICK *laughs.* HONEY *goes tsk, tsk, tsk, tsk,*[9] *and shakes her head*)

It was awful, really. It was funny, but it was awful.

(*She thinks; gives a muffled laugh in rueful contemplation of the incident*)

I think it's colored our whole life. Really I do! It's an excuse, anyway.

(GEORGE *enters now, his hands behind his back. No one sees him*)

It's what he uses for being bogged down, anyway... why he hasn't *gone* anywhere.

(CEORGE *advances.* HONEY *sees him*)

MARTHA

And it was an *accident*... a real, goddamn accident!

(GEORGE *takes from behind his back a shortbarreled shotgun, and calmly aims it at the back of* MARTHA'S *head.* HONEY *screams... rises.* NICK *rises, and, simultaneously,* MARTHA *turns her head to face* GEORGE. GEORGE *pulls the trigger*)

GEORGE

POW!!!

(*Pop! From the barrel of the gun blossoms a large red and yellow Chinese parasol.* HONEY *screams again, this time less, and mostly from relief and confusion*)

You're dead! Pow! You're dead!

NICK (*Laughing*)

Good Lord.

(HONEY *is beside herself.* MARTHA *laughs too... almost breaks down, her great laugh booming.* GEORGE *joins in the general laughter and confusion. It dies, eventually*)

HONEY

Oh! My goodness!

MARTHA (*Joyously*)

Where'd you get that, you bastard?

NICK

(*His hand out for the gun*)

Let me see that, will you?

(GEORGE *hands him the gun*)

HONEY

I've never been so frightened in my life! Never!

GEORGE (*A trifle abstracted*)

Oh, I've had it awhile. Did you like that?

MARTHA (*Giggling*)

You bastard.

HONEY (*Wanting attention*)

I've *never* been so frightened... never.

NICK

This is quite a gadget.

GEORGE

(*Leaning over* MARTHA)

You liked that, did you?

MARTHA

Yeah... that was pretty good. (*Softer*) C'mon... give me a kiss.

GEORGE

(*Indicating* NICK *and* HONEY)

Later, sweetie.

(*But* MARTHA *will not be dissuaded. They kiss,* GEORGE *standing, leaning over* MARTHA'S *chair. She takes his hand, places it on her stage-side breast. He breaks away*)

Oh-oh! That's what you're after, is it? What are we going to have... blue games for the guests? Hunh? Hunh?

MARTHA (*Angry-hurt*)

You... prick!

GEORGE (*A Pyrrhic victory*)

Everything in its place, Martha... everything in its own good time.

MARTHA

(*An unspoken epithet*)

You....

GEORGE

(*Over to* NICK, *who still has the gun*)

Here, let me show you... it goes back in, like this.

(*Closes the parasol, reinserts it in the gun*)

NICK

That's damn clever.

GEORGE (*Puts the gun down*)

Drinks now! Drinks for all!

(*Takes* NICK'S *glass without question... goes to* MARTHA)

MARTHA (*Still angry-hurt*)

I'm not finished.

HONEY

(*As* GEORGE *puts out his hand for her glass*)

Oh, I think I need *something*.

(*He takes her glass, moves back to the portable bar*)

NICK

Is that Japanese?

GEORGE

Probably.

HONEY (*To* MARTHA)

I was never so frightened in my life. Weren't you frightened? Just for a second?

MARTHA

(*Smothering her rage at* GEORGE)

I don't remember.

HONEY

Ohhhh, now... I bet you were.

GEORGE

Did you really think I was going to kill you, Martha?

MARTHA (*Dripping contempt*)

You?... Kill me?... That's a laugh.

GEORGE

Well, now, I might... some day.

MARTHA

Fat chance.

NICK

(*As* GEORGE *hands him his drink*)

Where's the john?

GEORGE

Through the hall there... and down to your left.

HONEY

Don't you come back with any guns, or anything, now.

NICK (*Laughs*)

Oh, no.

MARTHA

You don't need any props, do you, baby?

NICK

Unh-unh.

MARTHA (*Suggestive*)

I'll bet not. No fake Jap gun for you, eh?

NICK

(*Smiles at* MARTHA. *Then, to* GEORGE, *indicating a side table near the hall*)

May I leave my drink here?

GEORGE

(*As* NICK EXITS *without waiting for a reply*)

Yeah... sure... why not? We've got half-filled glasses everywhere in the house, wherever Martha forgets she's left them... in the linen closet, on the edge of the bathtub.... I even found one in the freezer, once.

MARTHA

(*Amused in spite of herself*)

You did not!

GEORGE

Yes I did.

MARTHA (*Ibid*)

You did *not*!

GEORGE

(*Giving* HONEY *her brandy*)

Yes I *did* (*To* HONEY) Brandy doesn't give you a hangover?

HONEY

I never mix. And then, I don't drink very much, either.

GEORGE

(*Grimaces behind her back*)

Oh... that's good. Your... your husband was telling me all about the ... chromosomes.

MARTHA (*Ugly*)

The what?

GEORGE

The chromosomes, Martha... the genes, or whatever they are. (*To* HONEY) You've got quite a ... terrifying husband.

HONEY

(*As if she's being joshed*)

Ohhhhhhhhh....

GEORGE

No, really. He's quite terrifying, with his chromosomes, and all.

MARTHA

He's in the Math Department.

GEORGE

No, Martha... he's a biologist.

MARTHA (*Her voice rising*)

He's in the *Math* Department!

HONEY (*Timidly*)

Uh... biology.

MARTHA (*Unconvinced*)

Are *you* sure?

HONEY (*With a little giggle*)

Well, I ought to. (*Then as an afterthought*) Be.

MARTHA (*Grumpy*)

I suppose *so.* I don't know who said he was in the Math Department.

GEORGE

You did, Martha.

MARTHA

(*By way of irritable explanation*)

Well, I can't be expected to remember *everything.* I meet fifteen new teachers and their goddamn wives... present company outlawed, of course... (HONEY *nods, smiles sillily*)... and I'm supposed to remember *everything.* (*Pause*) So? He's a biologist. Good for him. Biology's even better. It's less... abstruse.

GEORGE

Abstract.

MARTHA

ABSTRUSE! In the sense of recondite. (*Sticks her tongue out at* GEORGE) Don't you tell me words. Bilolgy's even better. It's... right at the *meat* of things.

(NICK *re-enters*)

You're right at the meat of things, baby.

NICK

(*Taking his drink from the side table*)

Oh?

HONEY (*With that giggle*)

They thought you were in the Math Department.

NICK

Well, maybe I ought to be.

MARTHA

You stay right where you are... you stay right at the ... *meat* of things.

GEORGE

You're obsessed with that phrase, Martha.... It's ugly.

MARTHA

(*Ignoring* GEORGE... *to* NICK)

You stay right there. (*Laughs*) Hell, you can take over the History Department just as easy from there as anywhere else. God knows, *some*body's going to take over the History Department, *some* day, and it ain't going to be Georgie-boy, there... that's for sure. Are ya, swampy... are ya, hunh?

GEORGE

In my mind, Martha, you are buried in cement, right up to your neck. (MARTAH *giggles*) No... right up to your nose... that's much quieter.

MARTHA (*To* NICK)

Georgie-boy, here, says your're terrifying. Why are you terrifying?

NICK (*With a small smile*)

I didn't know I was.

HONEY (*A little thickly*)

It's because of your chromosomes, dear.

NICK

Oh, the chromosome business....

MARTHA (*To* NICK)

What's all this about chromosomes?

NICK

Well, chromosomes are....

MARTHA

I know what chromosomes are, sweetie, I love 'em.

NICK

Oh.... Well, then.

GEORGE

Martha eats them... for breakfast... she sprinkles them on her cereal. (*To* MARTHA, *now*) It's very simple, Martha, this young man is working on a system whereby chromosomes can be altered... well not all by himself—he probably has one or two co-conspirators—the genetic makeup of a sperm cell changed, reordered... *to* order, actually... for hair and eye color, stature, potency... I imagine... hairiness, features, health... and *mind*. Most important... Mind. All imbalances will be corrected, sifted out... propensity for various diseases will be gone, longevity assured. We will have a race of men... test-tube-bred... incubator-born... superb and sublime.

MARTHA (*Impressed*)

Hunh!

HONEY

How exciting!

GEORGE

But! Everyone will tend to be rather the same.... Alike. Everyone... and I'm sure I'm not wrong here... will tend to look like this young man *here*.

MARTHA

That's not a bad idea.

NICK (*Impatient*)

All right, now....

GEORGE

It will, on the suraface of it, be all rather pretty... quite jolly. But of course there will be a dank side to it, too. A certain amount of regulation will be necessary... uh... for the experiment to succeed. A certain number of sperm tubes will have to be cut.

MARTHA

Hunh!...

GEORGE

Millions upon millions of them... millions of tiny little slicing operations that will leave just the smallest scar, on the underside of the scrotum (MARTHA *laughs*) but which will assure the sterility of the imperfect... the ugly, the stupid... the... unfit.

NICK (*Grimly*)

Now look...!

GEORGE

... with this, we will have, in time, a race of glorious men.

MARTHA

Hunh!

GEORGE

I suspect we will not have much music, much painting, but

we will have a civilization of men, smooth, blond, and right at the middleweight limit.

MARTHA

Awww. . . .

GEORGE

. . . a race of scientists and mathematicians, each dedicated to and working for the greater glory of the supercivilization.

MARTHA

Goody.

GEORGE

There will be a certain. . . loss of liberty, I imagine, as a result of this experiment. . . but diversity will no longer be the goal. Cultures and races will eventually vanish. . . the ants will take over the world.

NICK

Are you finished?

GEORGE (*Ignoring him*)

And I, naturally, am rather opposed to all this. History, which is my field. . . history, of which I am one of the most famous bogs. . . .

MARTHA

Ha, ha, HA!

GEORGE

. . . will lose its glorious variety and unpredictability. I, and with me the. . . the surprise, the multiplexity, the sea-changing rhythm of. . . history, will be eliminated. There will be order and constancy. . . and I am unalterably opposed to it. I will not give up Berlin!

MARTHA

You'll give up Berlin, sweetheart. You going to defend it with your paunch?

HONEY

I don't see what Berlin has to *do* with anything.

GEORGE

There is a saloon in West Berlin where the barstools are five feet high. And the earth. . . the floor. . . is so. . . far. . . below you. I will not give up things like that. No. . . I won't. I will fight you, young man. . . one hand on my scrotum, to be sure. . . but with my free hand I will battle you to the death.

MARTHA (*Mocking, laughing*)

Bravo!

NICK (*To* GEORGE)

That's right. And I am going to be the wave of the future.

MARTHA

You bet you are, baby.

HONEY (*Quite drunk—to* NICK)

I don't see why you want to do all those things, dear. You never told me.

NICK (*Angry*)

Oh for God's sake!--

HONEY (*Shocked*)

OH!

GEORGE

The most profound indication of a social malignancy... no sense of humor. None of the monoliths[10] could take a joke. Read history. I know something about history.

NICK

(*To* GEORGE, *trying to make light of it all*)

You... you don't know much about science, do you?

GEORGE

I know something about history. I know when I'm being threatened.

MARTHA (*Salaciously—to* NICK)

So, everyone's going to look like you, eh?

NICK

Oh, sure. I'm going to be a personal screwing machine!

MARTHA

Isn't that nice.

HONEY

(*Her hands over her ears*)

Dear, you mustn't... you mustn't... you mustn't.

NICK (*Impatiently*)

I'm sorry, Honey.

HONEY

Such language. It's....

NICK

I'm *sorry*. All right?

HONEY (*Pouting*)

Well... all right. (*Suddenly she giggles insanely, subsides. To* GEORGE)... When is your son? (*Giggles again*)

GEORGE

What?

NICK (*Distastefully*)

Something about your son.

GEORGE

SON!

HONEY

When is... where is your son... coming home? (*Giggles*)

GEORGE

Ohhhh. (*Too formal*) Martha? When is our son coming home?

MARTHA

Never mind.

GEORGE

No, no... I want to know... you brought it out into the open. When is he coming home, Martha?

MARTHA

I said never mind. I'm sorry I brought it up.

GEORGE

Him up... not it. You brought *him* up. Well, more or less. When's the little bugger going to appear, hunh? I mean isn't tomorrow meant to be his birthday, or something?

MARTHA

I don't want to talk about it!

GEORGE (*Falsely innocent*)

But Martha....

MARTHA

I DON'T WANT TO TALK ABOUT IT!

GEORGE

I'll bet you don't. (*To* HONEY *and* NICK) Martha does not want to talk about it... him. Martha is sorry she brought it up... him.

HONEY (*Idiotically*)

When's the little bugger coming home? (*Giggles*)

GEORGE

Yes, Martha... since you had the bad taste to bring the matter up in the first place... when *is* the little bugger coming home?

NICK

Honey, do you think you...?

MARTHA

George talks disparagingly about the little bugger because... well, because he has problems.

GEORGE

The little bugger has problems? What problems has the little bugger got?

MARTHA

Not the little bugger... stop calling him that! You! You've got problems.

GEORGE (*Feigned disdain*)

I've never heard of anything more ridiculous in my life.

HONEY

Neither have I!

NICK

Honey....

MARTHA

George's biggest problem about the little... ha, ha, ha, HA!... about our son, about our great big son, is that deep down in the private-most pit of his gut, he's not completely sure it's his own kid.

GEORGE (*Deeply serious*)

My God, you're a wicked woman.

MARTHA

And I've told you a million times, baby... I wouldn't conceive with anyone but you... you know that, baby.

GEORGE

A deeply wicked person.

HONEY (*Deep in drunken grief*)

My, my, my, my. Oh, my.

NICK

I'm not sure that is a subject for....

GEORGE

Martha's lying. I want you to know that, right now. Martha's lying. (MARTHA *laughs*) There are very few things in this world that I *am* sure of... national boundaries, the level of the ocean, political allegiances, practical morality... none of these would I stake my stick on any more... but the one thing in this whole sinking world that I am sure of is my partnership; my chromosomological partnership in the... creation of our... blond-eyed, blue-haired... son.

HONEY

Oh, I'm so glad!

MARTHA

That was a very pretty speech, George.

GEORGE

Thank you, Martha.

MARTHA

You rose to the occasion... good. Real good.

HONEY

Well... real well.

NICK

Honey....

GEORGE

Martha knows... she knows better.

MARTHA (*Proudly*)

I know better. I been to college like everybody else.

GEORGE

Martha been to college. Martha been to a convent when she were a little twig of a thing, too.

MARTHA

And I was an atheist. (*Uncertainly*) I still am.

GEORGE

Not an atheist, Martha... a pagan. (*To* HONEY *and* NICK) Martha is the only true pagan on the eastern seaboard. (MARTHA *laughs*)

HONEY

Oh, that's nice. Isn't that nice, dear?

NICK (*Humoring her*)

Yes... wonderful.

GEORGE

And Martha paints blue circles around her things.

NICK

You do?

MARTHA

(*Defensively, for the joke's sake*)

Sometimes. (*Beckoning*) You wanna see?

GEORGE (*Admonishing*)

Tut, tut, tut.

MARTHA

Tut, tut yourself... you old floozie!

HONEY

He's not a floozie... he can't be a floozie... you're a floozie.

(*Giggles*)

MARTHA

(*Shaking a finger at* HONEY)

Now you watch yourself!

HONEY (*Cheerfully*)

All right. I'd like a nipper of brandy, please.

NICK

Honey, I think you've had enough, now....

GEORGE

Nonsense! Everybody's ready, I think. (*Takes glasses, etc.*)

HONEY (*Echoing* GEORGE)

Nonsense.

NICK (*Shrugging*)

O. K.

〔注释〕

1. Illyria... Penguin Island... Gomorrah："伊里利亚……企鹅岛……歌摩拉"，泛指性自由的地方。
2. New Carthage：指乔治和尼克任教的新迦太基学院。
3. WHADD'YA WANT＝what do you want.
4. the bar：乔治家里摆酒的柜台。
5. Masters：硕士学位。
6. body talk：具有性感的双关语。
7. Paunchy：指大肚子的乔治。
8. yup＝yes，口语。
9. Honey goes tsk, tsk, tsk, tsk：哈尼发出啧啧之声。
10. monolith：指没有分歧和区别的个人。

JOHN BARTH

〔作者介绍〕

约翰·巴思（John Barth，1930～ ）美国当代小说家，生于美国马里兰州坎布里奇。青年时没有表现出什么创作才华，但对家乡的历史、地理极感兴趣，这对他以后的创作有很大影响，他的小说常以家乡为背景。他中学毕业后入纽约市一家音乐学校，后就读于巴尔的摩市约翰斯·霍普金斯大学，1951年以优异成绩毕业于该校文理学院，获文学学士学位，1952年获文学创作硕士学位，并开始攻读美学博士学位，但由于经济原因未能完成学业，而开始他的漫长的教学生涯。从1953至1973年他先后在宾夕法尼亚州立大学和纽约州立大学任讲师、副教授和教授，1973年在约翰斯·霍普金斯大学任英语及文学创作教授至今。

巴思属于二战后成长起来的新一代作家。这些作家和他们的先驱者不同，成长在学术气氛较浓的环境中，而且，一面执教，一面写作。这种生活方式对他们的创作影响极大，这是我们研究这些作家时应予以充分注意的。

巴思认为，小说这门艺术在本世纪五、六十年代面临一种困境：小说形式已被上一世纪和本世纪的大师们发展得尽善尽美，无以复加了。因而，他认为，当代作家应当另辟蹊径，反对在以前作家创作的基础上惨淡经营。他说，“我景仰福楼拜和托尔斯泰，海明威和福克纳。但他们对其他作家不再有吸引力。……我们生在20世纪后三分之一；我们不能写19世纪的书。小说随着乔伊斯和卡夫卡已告结束。”因而巴思一反当代作家信奉弗洛伊德和劳伦斯（D. H. Lawrence，1885～1930）的常态，转向西方小说起源时代的创作大师塞万提斯（Cervantes，1547～1616）、费尔丁（Henry Fielding，1707～1754）、斯特恩（Laurence Sterne，1713～1768）乃至东方阿拉伯的《天方夜谭》（*The Arabian Nights*）中，去寻求创作灵感。在这方面，他在大学的经历使他获益不浅：他在业余时间曾在图书馆工作，如饥似渴地阅读印度文学和阿拉伯文学中的故事集，极其欣赏这些文学作品中把诸多故事连贯在一起的叙述模式。同时，贝克特（Samuel Becket，1906～）和阿根廷作家勃吉斯（Jorge Luis Borges，1899～）的创作手法对他影响也极大，关于后者他曾著长文予以评介。当然也应指出，他的尝试在客观上具有一种肢解和破坏传统小说形式的后果。

在思想上，巴思与当代其他作家如冯纳古特等接近，认为世界荒诞，没有意义和目的可言，因而批评家把他归入荒诞派作家一类。他的作品情节离奇，夸张成分较多，玄学成分也很强。他的第1部小说《流动的歌剧》(*The Floating Opera*，1956)，叙述一个不负责任的单身汉托德·安得鲁斯（Todd Andrews）的经历。Todd 可能源于德语 Tot，死亡之意。书里写托德的精神危机、自杀的企图，以及他对生活的最后态度：既然生无意义，死亦无意义，因而不妨苟且活着。他拟写3部这样的虚无主义的书，《路的尽头》(*The End of the Road*，1958）为第2部。以上两部书依然保留着传统小说的模式。但在第3部《烟草代理商》(*The Sot-Weed Factor*，1960）中，作者采用了令人震惊的全新的创作手法：它在形式上虽然模仿18世纪作家菲尔丁的作品《汤姆·琼斯》(*Tom Jones*)，内容上却并非表现秩序和协调思想；它是用18世纪小说的外壳包装的20世纪的荒诞现实以及这种现实的毫无意义和不可预测性。这部小说充分表现了巴思作为一名荒诞派作家的立场。该书标志着巴思与传统小说技巧的分裂。《牧羊童子贾尔斯》(*Giles Goat-Boy*，1966）在标新立异方面更是登峰造极。该书受勃吉斯的影响极大。作者称该书是一位老师的自述，储存在计算机中，后来由这位教师的儿子记录下来，并由一个尚未成名的作家J. B.（指 John Barth）整理。在该书中，作者表达了他的宗教思想，广泛运用了象征手法：大学象征着宇宙，教师（*Grand Tutor*）象征着救世主，东西校园分别象征着苏联和美国，校园的骚乱象征着世界大战。小说中的人物常影射当代人物，如爱因斯坦、肯尼迪等。这是一部畅销书，销量达5万册，是他前3部书销售量总和的4倍。此外，他还著有《迷失在娱乐场中》(*Lost in the Funhouse: Fiction of Print, Tape, Live Voice*，1968)、《妄想》(*Chimera*，1972）和《书信集》(*Letters*，1976)。《妄想》由3部中篇小说组成，最后一部是对书信体小说的新尝试。

关于巴思的小说，人们众说纷纭，褒贬不一，但他是当代一位富有特色的作家，这是读者和批评家都承认的。

The End of the Road

〔作品介绍〕

《路的尽头》(*The End of the Road*）出版于1958年，当时除在批评界受到一些注意外，未被广大读者重视；但在作者其他作品成功后，此书却一版再版。有的批评家认为该书是巴思艺术性最强的作品。

在作者第一部小说《流动的歌剧》结尾部分，主人公托德想知道“在没有绝对价值的情况下，非绝对价值是否不如绝对价值，是否能据以生存。”巴思接着写道：“但这是另一个研究课题，是另一篇小说的主题。”

《路的尽头》就是这“另一篇小说”，是巴思构想的以不负责任、虚无主义的单身汉为主人公的三部曲的第2部。这部小说的主人公为杰克·霍纳(Jake Horner 或 Jacob Horner)。作者自己曾说，Horner 有两层含义：(1) Jake Horner 影射民谣中的 Little Jack Horner，他总是坐在角落里冥思苦想，把一切都解释为合法；(2) Horner 指与有夫之妇私通的人。

小说的情节是这样的：主人公霍纳在生活所呈现的诸多选择面前无所适从，不知所措，因而全身麻痹。在火车站上，一位心理病理学庸医把他带到自己的康复农场。之后，他听从医生的劝告，去当一名语法教师。这期间，他结识了乔·摩根和他的妻子伦尼。摩根正在写作历史学博士论文，是当地童子军领队。他是一个相对主义者，认为事物没有内在价值，在生活中只能找相对价值。杰克是个虚无主义者，世上一切对他都有相同的吸引力。摩根外出3天，霍纳就与伦尼私通了。乔获悉此事后，采取了一系列完全“理智”的步骤，包括让伦尼继续同霍纳交往。后来小说成了乔和杰克所代表的思想的辩论。显然，作者对乔所代表的思想是持反对态度的。杰克为了承担责任，安排自己的医生给伦尼打胎。在堕胎过程中，伦尼窒息而死。乔被迫离开那所学校，而杰克又回到了那位庸医的农场。

在该书中，巴思描写的人物带有极浓的漫画色彩。他极力强调人物性格中某一突出的方面。情节虽貌似荒诞滑稽，但体味起来却使人感到压抑与忧郁。

这里选注的是该书第1章和第10章的一部分。

The End of the Road

CHAPTER I

In a Sense, I Am Jacob Horner

IN A SENSE, I AM JACOB HORNER.[1]

It was on the advice of the Doctor[2] that I entered the teaching profession; for a time I was a teacher of grammar at the Wicomico State Teachers College, in Maryland.[3]

The Doctor had brought me to a certain point in my original schedule of therapies (this was in June 1953), and then, once when I drove down from Baltimore for my quarterly checkup at the Remobilization Farm, which at that time was near Wicomico, he said to me, "Jacob Horner, you mustn't sit idle any longer. You will have to begin work."

"I'm not idle all the time," said I. "I take different jobs."

We were seated in the Progress and Advice Room of the farmhouse: there is one exactly like it in the present establishment, in Pennsylvania. It is a medium-size room, about as large as an apartment living room, only high-ceilinged. The walls are flat white, the windows are covered by white venetian blinds, usually closed, and a globed ceiling fixture provides the light. In this room there are two straight-backed white wooden chairs, exactly alike, facing each other in the center of the floor, and no other furniture. The chairs are very close together—so close that the advisee almost touches knees with the adviser.

It is impossible to be at ease in the Progress and Advice Room. The Doctor sits facing you, his legs slightly spread, his hands on his knees, and leans a little toward you. You would not slouch down, because to do so would thrust your knees virtually against his. Neither would you be inclined to cross your legs in either the masculine or the feminine manner: the masculine manner, with your left ankle resting on your right knee, would cause your left shoe to rub against the Doctor's left trouser leg, up by his knee, and possibly dirty his white trousers; the feminine manner, with your left knee crooked over your right knee, would thrust the toe of your shoe against the same trouser leg, lower down on his shin. To sit sideways, of course, would be unthinkable, and spreading your knees in the manner of the Doctor makes you acutely conscious of aping his position, as if you hadn't a personality of your own. Your position, then (which has the appearance of choice, because you are not ordered to sit thus, but which is chosen only in a very limited sense, since there are no alternatives), is as follows: you sit rather rigidly in your white chair, your back and thighs describing the same right angle described by the structure of the chair, and keep your legs together, your thighs and lower legs describing another right angle.

The placing of your arms is a separate problem, interesting in its own right and, in a way, even more complicated, but of lesser importance, since no matter where you put them they will not normally come

"You'll have to begin work at a more meaningful job now. A career, you know. A calling. A lifework."

"Yes, sir."

"You are thirty."

"Yes, sir."

"And you have taken an undergraduate degree somewhere. In history? Literature? Economics?"

"Arts and sciences."

"That's everything!"

"No major, sir."

"Arts and sciences! What under heaven that's interesting isn't either an art or a science? Did you study philosophy?"

"Yes."

"Psychology?"

"Yes."

"Political science?"

"Yes."

"Wait a minute. Zoology?"

"Yes."

"Ah, and philology? Romance philology? And cultural anthropology?"

"Later, sir, in the graduate school. You remember, I——"

"*Argh!*" the Doctor said, as if hawking to spit upon the graduate school. "Did you study lock-picking in the graduate school? Fornication? Sailmaking? Cross-examination?"

"No, sir."

"Aren't these arts and sciences?"

"My master's degree was to be in English, sir."

"Damn you! English *what*? Navigation? Colonial policy? Common law?"

"English literature, sir. But I didn't finish. I passed the oral examinations, but I never got my thesis done."

"Jacob Horner, you are a fool."

My legs remained directly in front of me, as before, but I moved my hands from behind my head (which position suggests a rather too casual attitude for many sorts of situations anyway) to a combination position, my left hand grasping my left coat lapel, my right lying palm up, fingers loosely curled, near the mid-point of my right thigh.

After a while the Doctor said, "What reason do you think you have for not applying for a job at the little teachers college here in Wicomico?"

Instantly a host of arguments against applying for a job at the Wicomico State Teachers College presented themselves for my use, and as instantly a corresponding number of refutations lined up opposite them, one for one, so that the question of my application was held static like the rope marker in a tug-o'-war where the opposing teams are perfectly matched.[5] This again is in a sense the story of my life, nor does it really matter if it is not just the same story as that of a few paragraphs ago: as I began to learn not long after this interview, when the schedule of therapies reached Mythotherapy, the same life lends itself to any number of stories—parallel, concentric, mutually habitant, or what you will.

Well.

"No reason, sir," I said.

"Then it's settled. Apply at once for the fall term. And what will you teach? Iconography? Automotive mechanics?"

"English literature, I guess."

"No. There must be a rigid discipline, or else it will be merely an occupation, not an occupational therapy. There must be a body of laws. You mean you can't teach plane geometry?"

"Oh, I suppose——" I made a suppositive gesture, which consisted of a slight outward motion of my lapel-grasping left hand, extending simultaneously the fore and index fingers but not releasing my lapel—the hand motion accompanied by quickly arched (and as quickly released) eyebrows, momentarily pursed lips, and an on-the-one-hand/on-the-other-hand rocking of the head.

"Nonsense. Of course you can't. Tell them you will teach grammar. English grammar."

"But you know, Doctor," I ventured, "there is descriptive as well as prescriptive grammar. I mean, you mentioned a fixed body of rules."

"You will teach prescriptive grammar."

"Yes, sir."

"No description at all. No optional situations. Teach the rules. Teach the truth about grammar."

The advising was at an end. The Doctor stood up quickly (I jerked my legs out of his way) and left the room, and after I had paid Mrs. Dickey, the receptionist-nurse, I returned to Baltimore. That night I composed a letter to the president of the Wicomico State Teachers College, requesting an interview and indicating my desire to join the staff as an instructor in the prescriptive grammar of the English language. There is an art that my diffuse education had schooled me in, perforce: the art of composing a telling letter of application. I was asked to appear for an interview in July.

CHAPTER X

....

During this month,[1] I had of course seen Joe any number of times at school, even though our social relationship had ended. If it had been possible I'd have avoided him altogether, not because I felt any less warmth, admiration, or respect for him—on the contrary, I felt more of all these things, and sympathy besides—but because the sight of him invariably filled me with sudden embarrassment and shame, no matter what feelings I had at other times. To feel, as Joe did, no regret for anything one has done in the past requires at least a strong sense of one's personal unity, and such a sense is one of the things I've always lacked.[2] Indeed, the conflict between individual points of view that Joe admitted lay close to the heart of his subjectivism I should carry even further, for subjectivism implies a self, and where one feels a plurality of selves, one is subject to the same conflict on an intensely intramural level, each of one's several selves claiming the same irrefutable validity for its special point of view that, in Joe's system, individuals and institutions may claim. In other words, judging from my clearest picture of myself, the individual is not individual after all, any more than the atom is really atomistic: he can be divided further, and subjectivism doesn't really become intelligible until one finally locates the subject.[3] I shall say that, if this did not seem to me to be the case. I should assent wholeheartedly to the Morgan ethics.[4] As it is, if I say that sometimes I assent to it anyway and sometimes not, I can't really feel that this represents any more of an inconsistency than can be found in the statement "Some people agree with Morgan and some don't." In the same way, when upon confronting Joe in the hallways, in the cafeteria, or in my office I felt terribly ashamed of the trouble I'd caused him—when in my mind I not only regretted but actually repudiated my adultery—what I really felt was that *I* would not do what that Jacob Horner had done; I felt no identity with that stupid fellow. But as a point of honor (in which some Horner or other believed) I would not claim this pluralism, for fear Joe would interpret it as a defense.

Only once in September did we have what might be called a conversation. It was very near the end of the month, when, happening to see me alone in my office, he came in to talk for a few minutes. As always, he looked fresh, bright, clean, and sharp.

"Mr. MacMahon's complaining that his horses are getting too fat," he said. "How come you quit your riding lessons?" [5]

I blushed. "I thought the course was finished, I guess."

"You want to pick them up again? It's right much trouble for him to take time to exercise them as much as they need."

"No, I guess not. I've kind of lost interest, and I don't think Rennie would enjoy it very mnch."

"Don't you? Why shouldn't she?"

I should say there was no malice evident in his voice, but I couldn't help thinking I was being embarrassed purposely.

"You know why not, Joe. Why do you even suggest it?" I was suddenly indignant on Rennie's behalf. "I feel uncomfortable as hell criticizing you, but I don't see why you're so determined to make her feel worse than she does already."

He jabbed his spectacles back on his nose.

"Don't worry about Rennie."

"You mean it's a little late for me to start being thoughtful. I agree. But unless you're out to punish her I don't know why you make her come up to my room and all." [6]

"I'm not out to punish anybody, Jake; you know that. I'm just out to try to understand her."

"Well, don't you understand that she's pretty much shot these days? I'm surprised she's held up this long."

"She's pretty strong," Joe smiled. "You probably don't realize that in a way Rennie and I have been happier in the last few weeks than we've been for a long time."

"How come?"

"For one thing, since this started I've shelved the dissertation for a while, so we've had more time together than usual. We've talked to each other about ourselves more than we ever did before, necessarily, and all that."

I was appalled. "You can't say she's been happy."

"Not in the way you probably mean, I guess. We certainly haven't been *carefree*; but you can be pretty much happy without being carefree. The point is we've been dealing with each other pretty intensely and objectively—exploring each other as deep as we can. That part of it's been fine. And we've been outdoors a lot, because we didn't want to ruin our health over it. We've probably felt a lot closer to each other than ever, whether we've solved anything or not."

"Do you think you have?"

"Well, we've certainly *learned* some things. For one thing we've found all kinds of ties that we weren't aware of before, so that we probably wouldn't break up even if the thing doesn't straighten itself out. I doubt if I respect her as much as before—how could I? At least not for the same things. But she's been awfully good in this. Pretty damned strong most of the time, and I appreciate that. What do you think of my friend Rennie these days?" [7]

"Me?" I hadn't been especially thinking about what I thought of her, at least since her revelation of two nights earlier. Now I had to think about it quickly. "Oh, I don't know," I stalled.

"You must have had a strange picture of us both before. I'd like to know what you think of her now. Are you disgusted with her for not knowing how she feels?"

I leaned back in my chair and regarded the red pencil with which I'd been correcting grammar exercises.

"As a matter of fact," I said, "I might be in love with her."

"Is that right?" he asked quickly, bright with interest.

"I wouldn't be surprised. It was right a couple of days ago, anyhow. I don't feel it very strongly now, but I don't feel that I'm not, either."

"That's great!" Joe laughed; what he meant, I believe, was *That's interesting*. "Is that what you felt when you went to bed with her the first time? You could have said so."

"No. I didn't feel that way then."

"Does Rennie know about this?"

"No."

"How does she feel about you?"

"Not long ago she despised me. A week or so ago she said she didn't give a damn."

"Does she love you?" he asked, smiling.

Now I've said all along that Joe was without guile, but it's almost impossible really to believe that a man is without guile. It is perhaps a great injustice that I couldn't entirely trust that open smile and clear forehead of Joe's but I confess I did not.

"I'm pretty sure she despises me," I said.

Joe sighed. He was sitting in the swivel chair next to mine, and now he put his feet on the desk in front of him and clasped his hands behind his head.

"Did you ever consider that maybe I'm to blame for all of this? A lot of things could be explained neatly if you just said that for some perverse reason or other I engineered the whole affair. Just a possibility, along with the rest. What do you think?"

"Perversity? I don't know, Joe. If I see anything perverse it's your sending Rennie up to my place now."

He laughed. "I guess you could call all my encouragements of you two perverse now that we know what happened, but if any of it was really perverse it was unconsciously so. But you can't really believe it's perversity that makes me insist on her going up to your place. That business really is a matter of testing her. She's got to decide once and for all what she really feels about you and me and herself, and you know as well as I do that if it weren't for those trips to your place she'd repress that first business as fast as she could."

"Don't you think you're just keeping the wounds open?"

"I guess so. In fact, that's exactly what I'm doing. But in this case we've got to keep the wound open until we know just what kind of wound it is and how deep it goes."

"It seems to me that the important thing about wounds is healing them, no matter how."

"You're getting carried away with the analogy," Joe smiled. "This isn't a physical wound. If you ignore it, it might seem to go away, but in a relationship between two people wounds like this aren't healed by ignoring them—they keep coming back again if you do that." He dropped the subject. "So you love Rennie?"

"I don't know. I've felt that way once or twice."

"Would you marry her if she weren't married to me?"

"I don't know. Honestly."

"How would you take it if it turned out that the best answer to this thing was some kind of a permanent sexual relationship between you and her? I mean a triangle without conflicts or secrecy or jealousy."

"I don't think that's an answer. I'm the kind of guy who could probably live with that sort of thing, but I don't believe either Rennie or you could." As a matter of fact, I was interested to notice that at the very mention of marriage and permanent sexual attachments I began to grow tired of the idea of Rennie. Happy human perversity! There was little of the husband in me.

"I don't either. What's the answer, Jake? You tell me."

I shook my head.

"Shall I shoot you both?" he grinned. "I already own a Colt forty-five[8] and about a dozen bullets. When Rennie and I first got going on this thing, the time I was out of school for three days or so, I dug the old Colt out of the basement and loaded it and put it on the shelf in the living-room closet, in case either of us wanted to use it on ourselves or anybody else."

That statement thrilled me. Perhaps it was Joe Morgan, after all, that I loved. He stood up and clapped me amiably on the shoulder.

"No answers, huh?"

I shook my head. "Damned if I know what to say, Joe."

"Well," he said, stretching and walking out the door, "it's still there in the closet. Maybe we'll use it yet."

The Colt .45 used as a sidearm by the United States military is a big, heavy, murderous-looking pistol. Its recoil raises the shooter's arm, and the fat lead slug that it fires strikes with an impact great enough to knock a man off his feet. The image of this weapon completely dominated my imagination for the next three or four days after Joe had mentioned it: I thought of it, as Joe and Rennie must have thought of it, waiting huge in their living-room closet all through the days and nights during which they had dissected and examined every detail of the adultery—waiting for somebody to reach a conclusion.[9] Little wonder that Rennie's nights were sleepless! So were mine, once that machine had been introduced so casually into the problem. Even in my room it made itself terrifically present as the concrete embodiment of an alternative: the fact of its existence put the game in a different ball park, as it were; flavored all my reflections on the subject with an immediacy which I'm sure the Morgans had felt from the first, but which my isolation, if nothing else, had kept me from feeling.

I dreamed about that pistol, and daydreamed about it. In my imagination I kept seeing it as in a photographic close-up, lying hard and flat in the darkness on the closet shelf, while through the door came the indistinct voices of Joe and Rennie talking through days and nights. Talking, talking, talking. I heard only the tones of their voices—Rennie's calm, desperate, and hysterical by turns; Joe's always quiet and reasonable, hour after hour, until its quiet reasonableness became nightmarish and insane. I'm sure nothing has ever filled my head like the image of that gun. It took on aspects as various as the aspects of Laocoön's[10] smile, but infinitely more compelling and, of course, final. It was its finality that gave the idea of the Colt its persistence. It was with me all the time.

So it was like the realization of a nightmare when, shortly afterwards, I was confronted with the weapon itself in my room, which it had already tenanted in spirit, and that's why I paled and went weak, for I have no abstract fear of pistols. Rennie came in at eight o'clock, after telephoning an hour earlier to say she wanted to see me, and to my surprise Joe came with her, and with Joe came the Colt, in a paper bag. Rennie, I thought, had been crying—her cheeks were white and her eyes swollen—but Joe seemed cheerful enough. The first thing he did after acknowledging my greeting was take the pistol out of the bag and lay it carefully on a little ashtray stand, which he placed in center of the room.

"There she is, Jacob," he laughed. "Everything we have is yours."

I admired the gun without touching it, laughed shortly along with Joe at the poor humor of his gesture, and, as I said before, paled. It was a formidable piece of machinery, as large in fact as it had been in my imagination and no less final-looking. Joe watched my face.

"How about a beer?" I asked. The more I resolved not to show my alarm—alarm was the last thing I wanted to suggest was called for—the more plainly I could see it in my voice and manner.

"All right. Rennie? Want one?"

"No thanks," Rennie said, in a voice something like mine.

She sat in the overstuffed chair by the front window, and Joe on the edge of my monstrous bed, so that when I opened the beer bottles and took the only remaining seat, my rocking chair, we formed most embarrassingly a perfect equilateral triangle, with the gun in the center. Joe observed this at the same instant I did, and though I can't vouch for his grin, my own was not jovial.

"Well, what's up?" I asked him.

Joe pushed his spectacles back on his nose and crossed his legs.

"Rennie's pregnant," he said calmly.

When a man has been sleeping with a woman, no matter under what circumstance, this news always comes like the kick of a horse. The pistol loomed more conspicuous than ever, and it took me several seconds to collect my wits enough to realize that I had nothing to be concerned about.

"Congratulations!"

Joe kept smiling, not cordially, and Rennie fixed her eyes on the rug. Nobody spoke for a while.

"What's wrong?" I asked, not knowing for certain what to be afraid of.

"Well, we're not sure who to congratulate, I guess," Joe said.

"Why not?" My face burned. "You're not afraid *I'm* the father, are you?"

"I'm not particularly afraid of anything," Joe said. "But you might be the father."

"You don't have to worry about that, Joe; believe me." I looked a little wonderingly at Rennie, who I thought should have known better than to complicate things unnecessarily.

"You mean because you used contraceptives every time. I know that. I even know how many times you had to use them and what brand you use, Jacob."

"What the hell's the trouble, then?"

"The trouble is that I used them every time too—same brand, as a matter of fact."

I was stunned. There was the pistol.

"So," Joe went on, "if, as my friend Rennie tells me, this triangle was never a rectangle, and if her obstetrician isn't lying when he says rubbers are about eighty per cent efficient, the congratulations should be pretty much mutual. In fact, other things being equal, there's about one chance in four that you actually are the father."

Neither Joe's voice nor his forehead indicated how he felt about this possibility.

"How sure are you that you're pregnant?" I asked Rennie. To my chagrin my voice was unsteady.

"I'm—I'm pretty late," Rennie said, clearing her throat two or three times. "And I've been vomiting a lot for the last two days."

"Well, you know, you thought you were pregnant once before."

She shook her head. "That was wishful thinking." She had to wait a second before she said anything else. "I wanted to be pregnant that time."

"There's not much doubt," Joe said. "No use to hope along those lines. The obstetricians never commit themselves for a month or so, but Rennie knows her symptoms."

I sighed uncertainly; Joe still gave no hint of his feelings. "Boy, that complicates things, doesn't it?"

"Well, does it or not? How would you say it complicates things?"

"I guess that depends on how you all feel."

"Why is that? Look, Horner, you ought to decide what your point of view is going to be. Rennie's the same distance from me as she is from you."

"We should have allowed for the possibility, I guess," I suggested carefully.

"Aren't you actually saying that I should have allowed for the possibility when I sent Rennie up here? I allowed for all possibilities. That doesn't necessarily mean I like the idea of her being pregnant with your kid. I don't like that possibility a single God-damned bit, if you want to know, and I didn't really look for it to happen. But I did allow for the possibility right from the time I first heard you'd laid her. If you all didn't, you're stupid."

"It's a possibility I'd never allow for at the time." I smiled ruefully. "A bachelor would lead a lonely life if he did."

"Which heaven forbid."

I shrugged. I wasn't sure to what extent I was justified in being annoyed by his manner; the thing was too complicated. There was silence for a while. Joe chewed his thumbnail idly. Rennie still stared at the rug, and I tried to keep the gun out of my eyes and thoughts.

"What do you suggest, Joe?"

"Don't say that, now," he protested. "It's not all my baby. What do *you* suggest?"

"Well, I can't say anything until I know whether you want to keep the child or put it up for adoption or what. You know I'd pay for the obstetrician and the hospital and all, and the kid's support, if you decide to keep it, or help all I can with an adoption. If I could raise the child myself I'd do it."

"But you can't vomit for Rennie or split up the labor pains with her."

"No, I can't do that."

"You're oversimplifying even when you say *if I decide to keep the kid*. That makes it my responsibility. You say you're willing to take on the expense, but that doesn't mean a thing and you know it. Making it a practical problem, like a money problem, is too easy. I'd be a lot happier if you'd take on your share of responsibility. You don't have to take any shit off of me. That's too easy too."

"How do I go about taking on responsibility?" I asked. "I'm willing."

"Then for Christ's sake take a position and stick to it so we'll know who we're dealing with! Don't throw everything in my lap. What the hell do *you* think I should do? Tell Rennie what you want her to do and what you want me to do, and we'll tell you the same thing. Then we can work on the problem, for God's sake!"

"I don't have opinions, Joe," I said flatly. Of course the trouble was that I had, as usual, too many opinions. I was on everybody's side.

Joe jumped from the bed, snatched up the pistol, and aimed it at my face.

"If I told you I was going to pull this trigger, would you have any opinions about that?"

I was sick. "Go ahead and pull it."

"Horseshit; you'd never have to face up to anything then." He put the pistol back on the smoking stand. Rennie had watched the scene with tears in her eyes, but she wasn't weeping for either of us.

"What do *you* want to do?" Joe said roughly to her, and when she whipped her head I saw his eyes water also, although his expression didn't change. There was no alliance against me.

"I don't care about anything," Rennie said. "Do whatever you want to."

"I'll be damned!" Joe shouted, with tears on his cheeks. "I'm not going to do your thinking or his either. Think for yourself, or I don't want anything to do with you! I mean it!"

"I don't want the baby," Rennie said to him.

"You want to put it up for adoption?"

She shook her head. "That wouldn't work. If I carried it for nine months I'd love it, and I want to love it. I don't want to carry it for nine months."

"All right, there's the pistol. Shoot yourself."

Rennie looked at him sadly. "I will if you want me to, Joe."

"God *damn* what I want!"

"Did you mean you want an abortion, Rennie?" I asked.

Rennie nodded. "I want to get rid of this baby. I don't want to carry this baby."

"Where in hell are you going to find an abortionist around here?" Joe asked disgustedly. "This isn't New York."

"I don't know," Rennie said. "But I'm not going to carry this baby. I don't want it."

"Are you going to go to Dr. Walsh like last time and let him insult you?" Joe demanded. "He'd throw you out! I don't believe there's an abortionist in this county."

"I don't know," Rennie said. "I'm going to get an abortion or shoot myself, Joe. I've decided."

"Well, that sounds brave, Rennie, but think clearly about it: you don't know any abortionists around here, do you?"

"No."

"And you don't know any in Baltimore or Washington or anywhere else. And you don't know anybody who's ever had an abortion, do you?"

"No."

"Well, you say you're going to get an abortion or shoot yourself. Suppose you started tomorrow: what are you going to do to find an abortionist?"

"I don't know!" Rennie cried.

"Damn it, if there was ever a time when we've got to think straight, this is it, but you're not thinking straight. You're setting up alternatives that aren't actually open to you."

Rennie gave a little cry and rushed to the smoking stand, but because I had seen as clearly as Joe that that was what she was being driven to I was ready when she made her move. I dived headlong from my rocker for the gun. I fell short (physical coordination was not my forte), but my fingers closed on the edge of the stand and I pulled stand, gun, and all down on top of me. Rennie, in her rush, struck my head with her shoe, a stunning blow, and fell to her knees. She scrabbled for the pistol, which had landed on my left shoulder blade and slid down beside my armpit. By rolling over on it I kept it from her long enough for me to get my own hands on it, and then fended her off until I was able to get to my feet again. She made no attempt to take it from me, but went back to her chair and buried her face in her hands. Very much shaken, I left the smoking stand where it lay and kept the gun.

"You people are insane!" I said.

Joe hadn't moved, although he too was obviously shaken.

"Explain why, Horner," he demanded, with considerable emotion.

"The hell I will," I said. "Do you want her to blow her damned head off?"

"I want her to think for herself," Joe said. "Since you stopped her, you must have some other opinion. Or is it that you just don't want your room messed up? Would you rather we go home and do our shooting?"

"For Christ's sake, Joe, do you love your wife or not?"

"You're begging the question. Do *you* love her? Is that why you stopped her?"

"I don't love anybody right now. I think you're both insane."

"Stop saying things you can't explain. Would you rather force her to have a baby she doesn't want?"

"I don't give a damn what you all do, but I'm going to hold on to this pistol."

"You're talking nonsense," Joe said angrily. "You refuse to think. You're still talking about *us all*, and you know that's a distortion. You say you don't give a damn what Rennie does, but you take away her ability to choose. You're doing all you can to confuse everything."

"What the hell do you want?" I shouted.

"I want you to forget about everything except what's to the point and what's beside the point!" Joe said fiercely. "People act when they're ready whether they've thought clearly or not, and if there's one thing I'd kill you for, Horner, it's for screwing up the issues so that we have to act before we've thought, or taking something as important as this out of the realm of choice. Don't think I'm just talking: I'd kill you for it."

"What's beside the point, then?"

"Your oversimplifying is beside the point, for one thing: asking me *as the husband* what my position is; referring to Rennie and me together as if this were a conspiracy against you; blocking her actions; talking about perversity and insanity."

"Damn it, Joe, if I hadn't jumped she'd be *dead* right now! Would you be satisfied with that?"

"We're not playing games, Jake! Forget all the movies you ever saw and all the novels you ever read. Forget everything except this problem. Everything else obscures and confuses it. Stop looking at me as if I'm a monster!" he shouted, losing his temper. "If you ever knew a guy who's thought straight about these things it's me, God damn it! If you're interested, I'll tell you that you and I would probably be dead by this time too, if Rennie had shot herself; but I wouldn't have stopped her. Nobody else you ever met ever loved a female human being, Horner: they just love pictures in their heads. If I didn't love Rennie do you think I could have sat here when she went for the gun? In the name of Christ, Horner, *open your eyes*! Just this one time open your God-damned eyes and try to understand somebody!"

"Do you want me to put this pistol back on the table?"

"*Stop asking me what I want!*"

I was lost.

"Here," I said, handing Joe the Colt. "If you're so set on acting by your ideas, you put it back."

Joe took the gun and unhesitatingly offered it to Rennie.

"Here," he said gently, gripping the back of her chair for support. "Do you want it?"

Rennie shook her head without looking at him.

"Maybe she'd like to have you do it for her," I said, as acidly as possible, but I was so moved I was dizzy.

Joe glanced at me. "Do you want me to shoot you, Rennie?" he asked sarcastically. She shook her head again. Joe picked up the smoking stand, replaced the pistol on it, and went to his seat on the bed.

"So, Jake, you've decided we'll have the baby. Do you have any more opinions?"

I couldn't speak. Like Rennie, I shook my head. It is a demoralizing thing to deal with a man who will see, face up to, and unhesitatingly act upon the extremest limits of his ideas.

"Apparently you don't," Joe said contemptuously. He rose and began putting on his topcoat. "Do you want to come home now?" he asked Rennie.

Rennie rose and put on her coat. At the last minute Joe slipped the Colt into his pocket. He was extremely upset.

"Look, Joe," I called out as they left. "If Rennie *could* find an abortionist, what would you say?"

"What do you mean? What difference would it make what I said?"

"I mean how would you feel about the idea of her going through with an abortion?"

"I don't like it," Joe said flatly. "If it was a really competent abortion done in a good hospital by a good obstetrician it wouldn't matter, but it couldn't possibly be that. Rennie's in perfect health, and the only abortion she could get even in the city would be a half-ass job by some half-ass doctor who could mess her up for the rest of her life." He turned to go.

"I'll see if I can find somebody to do it," I said, "and if I can find somebody decent I'll pay for it."

"Horseshit," Joe said.

〔注释〕

Chapter Ⅰ

1. In a sense, I am Jacob Horner：表明霍纳对自己本质的迷惘。

2. the Doctor：给霍纳治疗的庸医。

3. Maryland：作者的家乡。作者的许多作品都以该州为背景。

4. I shift…inferior：表明霍纳对呈现在他面前的选择不知所措。参见下文详细的解释。

5. Instantly…perfectly matched：此句描写霍纳在思想上生活上充满矛盾。他毫无主见，听凭环境的摆布，在矛盾的平衡中力图生存。

Chapter Ⅹ

1. During this month：指乔回家、伦尼告知她自己与霍纳的奸情后。

2. such a sense is one of the things I've always lacked：乔·摩根与霍纳是相对立的两极。乔总是把一切都诉诸理智。

3. subjectivism doesn't really become intelligible until one finally locates the subject：指主人公对主体的困惑。

4. I should assent wholeheartedly to the Morgan ethics：在霍纳结识乔后，小说逐渐成了两人所代表的思想的论战。

5. riding lessons：霍纳是通过学骑马和伦尼结识的。

6. Why you make her come up to my room and all：乔发现伦尼与霍纳私通后依然叫伦尼去霍纳处，以便对她进行一次更加严峻的考验。

7. What do you think of my friend Rennie these days：乔的理智有时竟令人难以忍受。

8. Colt forty-five：柯尔特公司出产的左轮枪。

9. The image…conclusion：此句是对乔的极好的写照。

10. Laocoön：拉奥孔，希腊神话中的特洛伊祭司，因泄露天机，与两个儿子一道被天神所派的巨蟒缠死。拉奥孔之死是雕塑家喜爱的主题，霍纳的房间里就有一尊拉奥孔的雕像。

JOHN UPDIKE

〔作者介绍〕

约翰·厄普代克（John Updike，1932～ ）美国当代诗人和小说家，生于宾夕法尼亚州西灵顿（Sillington），父亲是一位中学教师。他中学毕业后就读于哈佛大学，于1954年以优异成绩毕业。之后他赴英国，在牛津的罗斯金美术学院修业一年。自1955年起供职于《纽约客》杂志社，并常为该杂志撰稿，包括喜剧色彩很浓的诗歌、几部长篇小说和短篇小说。1957年他辞去在《纽约客》杂志社的工作，潜心从事创作。

他的早期作品颇受《纽约客》杂志的影响。该杂志一向以对各阶层人的风俗、举止的体悟与描写而著称于世。但厄普代克并未被这种传统所左右。他专事创作后的作品无论在内容上还是在风格上都超越了《纽约客》杂志的范畴。他的作品很多，包括《贫民收容所的集市》（*Poorhouse Fair*，1957）、《兔子，跑》（*Rabbit, Run*，1960）、《半人半马怪》（*Centaur*，1963）、《农场》（*Of the Farm*，1965）、《大妻们》（*Couples*，1968）、《兔子回来了》（*Rabbit Redux*，1971）、《全是星期天的一个月》（*A Month of Sundays*，1975）、《兔子阔了》（*Rabbit Is Rich*，1981）、《比奇回来了》（*Bech Is Back*，1982）、《伊斯特威克的女巫》（*The Witches of Eastwick*，1984）。此外还有文学评论集《惠特曼的自我与艺术》（*Ego and Art in Walt Whitman*，1980）、《霍桑的信条》（*Hawthorne's Creed*，1981）和《拥抱海岸，文论集》（*Hugging the Shore: Essays and Criticism*，1983）等。他的作品常以纽约市和新英格兰郊区中产阶级白人的生活为题材。

厄普代克深感当代社会支离破碎，道德沦丧，人欲横流。但他拒绝接受这一现实。他对美国社会生活的令人窒息的极端物质主义深恶痛绝，并努力在这种无意义的社会生活中发掘出一定的意义来。他对道德问题十分关注。他曾在《跟我结婚吧》（*Marry Me*，1976）中写道，我们处在“旧道德的黄昏中；旧道德的残余只能折磨我们，却不能给我们一点力量”。同时，厄普代克追求宗教对人的启迪作用。

厄普代克的早期作品的素材多源于回忆。在这些作品中，他不止一次地描述自己少年时代的生活经历。一般说来，在诸如《鸽子的羽毛及其他》(*Pigeon Feathers and Other Stories*, 1962)、《半人半马怪》以及《贫民收容院集市》等作品中，厄普代克常巧妙地通过几个人物来表达他的思想，例如一个喜好读书和绘画、害怕变得"女里女气"、最终离家远走的独生子；一个和蔼可亲但怏怏不乐的父亲，在当地中学任教，有点脱离现实，但却是一位好教徒、好公民；一位受过高等教育、不屑于做家务、望子成龙的母亲；一位不如意的外公，以及一位颇有神秘色调的德国血统的外祖母。这些人物使厄普代克得以顺利地表达他的主人公的人生观及其对成年人和老年人的见解。厄普代克善于描写人与人之间的关系，并展示他们的内心活动。

厄普代克后来的作品颇重性描写，尤其在对性爱反常状态的描写方面，他的笔墨浓重得有时令人尴尬不堪。无节制的偷情、不忠、离异、家庭破裂，以及精细的心态分析，构成了《农场》、《音乐学校》(*The Music School*, 1966)、《夫妻们》及《半人半马怪》等作品的基本内容。厄普代克和当代美国著名作家一样，他的关于性生活的描写常是富有寓意的：他常赋予这些描写以某种宗教色调。

厄普代克是一位文体家。他长于观察客观世界，观察人际关系、家庭关系的状貌，体验人的各种感觉，并以细腻、典雅的文笔进行精细的描绘，给人一种缜密、具体的感觉。一般说来他注重写人写事，而对景物，多是几笔勾勒。厄普代克独具一格的文体业已引起人们的注意。

Rabbit, Run

〔作品介绍〕

《兔子，跑》(*Rabbit, Run*)是厄普代克"兔子"三部曲的第1部，是颇能代表他的创作天才的作品。该书的出版奠定了他在美国文坛的地位。

该书描写了一个心态极其紊乱的年轻人的变态行为，情节是这样的：主人公哈里·安斯特洛姆，外号"兔子"，在中学曾是学校篮球队的明星，为学校赢得过几次冠军。但他步入社会以后，生活使他失望、窒息。他的工作是在商店里向顾客介绍某种厨房用具的使用方法。他的妻子珍尼斯反应迟钝，情趣低俗。一日哈里下班回家，发现妻子正在看庸俗电视节目。珍尼斯让他接儿子回家，顺便给她买一包烟。哈里突然觉得这种生活无法忍受，离家出走，与妓女鲁丝同居。两个月后，珍尼斯生产，哈里又回到她的身边。由于产后的珍尼斯不能满足他的欲望，哈里再次出走。珍尼斯由于精神压力，在给刚出生的女儿洗澡时不慎将其溺死。哈里又回到家里，与珍尼斯和解。但在女儿的葬礼上，哈里当着众人推卸自己的责任，引起大家的非议，于是在葬礼进行过程中再次出走，去找鲁丝。这时他发现鲁丝怀孕了。鲁丝要他或者同珍尼斯离婚，或者不要再纠缠她。哈里这时仿佛陷在一张大网里，为逃避选择，他又“跑”了。

作者在该书的扉页引用了法国思想家帕斯卡尔（Blaise Pascal，1623～1662）《思想录》（*Pensées*）中的一句话作为该书的格言：“神恩的运动；内心的顽固；外界的环境”。这是这本书的3个不同侧面。有的批评家强调哈里灵魂中的“神恩的运动”，把他看成是唐·吉诃德式的圣徒；有人强调他“内心的顽固”，强调他的自私、不成熟、不负责任；也有人强调“外界的环境”，强调作者对美国令人窒息的社会生活的描绘。其实，这3个方面贯穿于该书的首尾。在某种程度上说，这3个方面也代表了厄普代克在艺术表现方面的追求。

同作者的其他作品一样，《兔子，跑》也以家庭生活危机为题材，其中也掺杂着很多关于性生活的描写和暗示。但在这里，性生活常有世俗的或宗教的象征意义。该书的象征意义很强。哈里的“跑”正象征着他心中的疑虑。作者对环境的描写也极具象征意蕴，以致有人把该书同班扬的《天路历程》相比拟。作者不满于现代生活，这在他充满讽刺意味的描写中可以清楚地看得出来。同时，厄普代克的说教，特别是关于基督教救赎作用的说教，也是很明显的。

值得注意的是，“兔子”同美国文学经典作品里的文学形象哈克（Huck Finn），霍尔顿（Holdon Caulfield）、奥基·马奇（Augie March）一样，属于逃遁型主人公。但他的性格特征是很突出的。

这里选注的是该书结尾部分。

Rabbit, Run

The funeral parlor was once a home but now is furnished the way no home ever was. Unworn carpets of a very pale green deaden their footsteps. Little silver halftubes on the walls shield a weak glow. The colors of the curtains and walls are atonal half-colors, colors no one would live with, salmon and aqua and a violet like the violet that kills germs on toilet seats in gas stations. They are ushered into a little pink side room. Harry[1] can see into the main room; on a few rows of anditorium chairs about six people sit, five of them women. The only one he knows is Peggy Gring. Her little boy wriggling beside her makes seven. It was meant to be at first nobody but the families, but the Springers[2] then asked a few close friends. His parents are not here. Invisible hands bonelessly trail up and down the keys of an electric organ. [3] The unnatural coloring of the interior comes to a violent head in the hothouse flowers arranged around a little white coffin. The coffin, with handles of painted gold, rests on a platform draped with a deep purple curtain; he thinks the curtain might draw apart and reveal, like a magician's trick, the living baby underneath. Janice[4] looks in and yields a whimper and an undertaker's man, blond and young with an unnaturally red face, conjures a bottle of spirits of ammonia out of his side pocket. Her mother holds it under her nose and Janice suppresses a face of disgust; her eyebrows stretch up, showing the bumps her eyeballs make under the thin membrane. [5] Harry takes her arm and turns her so she can't see into the next room.

The side room has a window through which they can look at the street, where children and cars are running. "Hope the minister hasn't forgotten," the young red-faced man says, and to his own embarrassment chuckles. He can't help being at his ease here. His face seems lightly rouged.

"Does that happen often?" Mr. Springer asks. He is standing behind his wife, and his face tips forward with curiosity, a birdy black gash beneath his pale mustache. Mrs. Springer has sat down on a chair and is pressing her palms against her face through the veil. The purple berries quiver on their stem of wire.

"About twice a year," is the answer.

A familiar old Plymouth slows against the curb outside. Rabbit's mother gets out and looks up and down the sidewalk angrily. His heart leaps and trips his tongue: "Here come my parents." They all come to attention. Mrs. Springer gets up and Harry places himself between her and Janice. Standing in formation with the Springers like this, he can at least show his mother that he's reformed, that he's accepted and been accepted. The undertaker's man goes out to bring them in; Harry can see them standing on the bright sidewalk, arguing which door to go into, Mim[6] a little to one side. Dressed in a church sort of dress and with no make-up, she reminds him of the little sister he once had. The sight of his parents makes him wonder why he was afraid of them.

His mother comes through the door first; her eyes sweep the line of them and she steps toward him with reaching curved arms. "Hassy, what have they done to you?" She asks this out loud and wraps him in a hug as if she would carry him back to the sky from which they have fallen.

This quick it opens, and seals shut again. In a boyish reflex of embarrassment he pushes her away and stands to his full height. As if unaware of what she has said, his mother turns and embraces Janice. Pop, murmuring, shakes Springer's hand. Mim comes and touches Harry on the shoulder and then squats and whispers to Nelson,[7] these two the youngest. All under him Harry feels these humans knit together. His wife and mother cling together. His mother began the embrace automatically but has breathed a great life of grief into it. Her face creases in pain; Janice, rumpled and smothered, yet responds; her weak black arms try to encircle the great frame yearning against her. Mrs. Angstrom yields up two words to her. The others are puzzled; only Harry from his tall cool height understands. His mother had been propelled by the instinct that makes us embrace those we wound, and then she had felt this girl in her arms as a member with her of an ancient abused slave race, and then she had realized that, having restored her son to herself, she too must be deserted.

He had felt in himself these stages of grief unfold in her as her arms tightened. Now she releases Janice, and speaks, sadly and properly, to the Springers. They have let her first outcry pass as madness. They of course have done nothing to Harry, what has been done he has done to them. His liberation is unseen by them. They become remote beside him. The words his mother spoke to Janice, "My daughter," recede. Mim rises from squatting; his father takes Nelson into his arms. Their motions softly jostle him.

And meanwhile his heart completes its turn and turns again, a wider turn in a thinning medium to which the outer world bears a decreasing relevance.

Eccles has arrived by some other entrance and from a far doorway beckons them. The seven of them file with Nelson into the room where the flowers wait, and take their seats on the front row. Black Eccles[8] reads before the white casket. It annoys Rabbit that Eccles should stand between him and his daughter. It occurs to him, what no one has mentioned, the child was never baptized. Eccles reads. "I am the resurrection and the life, saith the Lord: he that believeth in me, though he were dead, yet shall he live: and whosoever liveth and believeth in me, shall never die."[9]

The angular words walk in Harry's head like clumsy blackbirds; he feels their possibility. Eccles doesn't; his face is humorless and taut. His voice is false. All these people are false: except his dead daughter, the white box with gold trim.

"He shall feed his flock like a shepherd: he shall gather the lambs with his arms, and carry them in his bosom."

Shepherd, lamb, arms: Harry's eyes fill with tears. It is as if at first the tears are everywhere about him, a sea, and that at last the saltwater gets into his eyes. His daughter is dead; June[10] gone from him; his heart swims in grief, that had skimmed over it before, dives deeper and deeper into the limitless volume of loss. Never hear her cry again, never see her marbled skin again, never cup her faint weight in his arms again and watch the blue of her eyes wander in search of the source of his voice. Never, the word never stops, there is never a gap in its thickness.

They go to the cemetery. He and his father and Janice's father and the undertaker's man carry the white box to the hearse. There is weight to it but the weight is all wood. They get into their cars and drive through the streets uphill. The town hushes around them; a woman comes out on her porch with a basket of wash and waits there, a small boy stops himself in the middle of throwing a ball to watch them pass. They pass between two granite pillars linked by an arch of wrought iron. The cemetery is beautiful at four o'clock. Its nurtured green nap slopes down somewhat parallel to the rays of the sun. Tombstones cast long slate shadows. Up a crunching blue gravel lane the procession moves in second gear, its destination a meek green canopy smelling of earth and ferns. The cars stop; they get out. Beyond them at a distance stands a crescent sweep of black woods; the cemetery is high on the hill, between the town and the forest. Below their feet chimneys smoke. A man on a power lawnmower rides between the worn teeth of tombstones near the far hedge. Swallows in a wide ball dip and toss themselves above a stone cottage, a crypt. The white coffin is artfully rolled on casters from the hearse's deep body onto crimson straps that hold it above the small nearly square-mouthed but deep-dug grave. The small creaks and breaths of effort scratch on a pane of silence. Silence. A cough. The flowers have followed them; here they are, densely banked within the tent. Behind Harry's feet a neat mound of dirt topped with squares of sod waits to be replaced and meanwhile breathes a deep word of earth. The undertaking men look pleased, their job near done, and fold their pink hands in front of their flies. Silence.

"The Lord is my shepherd; therefore can I lack nothing."

Eccles' voice is fragile outdoors. The distant buzz of the power mower halts respectfully. Rabbit's chest vibrates with excitement and strength; he is sure his girl has ascended to Heaven. This feeling fills Eccles' recited words like a living body a skin. "O God, whose most dear Son did take little children into his arms and bless them; Give us Grace, we beseech thee, to entrust the soul of this child to thy never-failing care and love, and bring us all to the heavenly kingdom; through the same thy Son, Jesus Christ, our Lord. Amen."

"Amen," Mrs. Springer whispers.

Yes. That is how it is. He feels them all, the heads as still around him as tombstones, he feels them all one, all one with the grass, with the hothouse flowers, all, the undertaker's men, the unseen caretaker who has halted his mower, all gathered into one here to give his unbaptized baby force to leap to Heaven.

An electric switch is turned, the straps begin to lower the casket into the grave and stop. Eccles makes a cross of sand on the lid. Stray grains roll one by one down the curved lid into the hole. A pink hand throws crumpled petals. "Deal graciously, we pray thee, with all those who mourn, that, casting every care on thee. . ." The straps whine again. Janice at his side staggers. He holds her arm and even through the cloth it feels hot. A small breath of wind makes the canopy fill and luff. The smell of flowers rises toward them. ". . . and the Holy Ghost, bless you and keep you, now and forevermore. Amen."

Eccles closes his book. Harry's father and Janice's standing side by side, look up and blink. The undertaker's men begin to be busy with their equipment, retrieving the straps from the hole. Mourners move into the sunshine. *Casting every care on thee*. . . The sky greets him. A strange strength sinks down into him. It is as if he has been crawling in a cave and now at last beyond the dark recession of crowding rocks he has seen a patch of light; he turns, and Janice's face, dumb with grief, blocks the light. "Don't look at *me*," he says. "I didn't kill her."

This comes out of his mouth clearly, in tune with the simplicity he feels now in everything. Heads talking softly snap around at a voice so sudden and cruel.

They misunderstand. He just wants this straight. He explains to the heads, "You all keep acting as if *I* did it. I wasn't anywhere near. *She's* the one." He turns to her, and her face, slack as if slapped, seems hopelessly removed from him. "Hey it's O. K.," he tells her. "You didn't mean to." He tries to take her hand but she snatches it back like from a trap and looks toward her parents, who step toward her.

His face burns. His embarrassment is savage. Forgiveness had been big in his heart and now it's hate. He hates his wife's face. She doesn't *see*. She had a chance to join him in truth, just the simplest factual truth, and she turned away. He sees that among the heads even his own mother's is horrified, blank with shock, a wall against him; she asks him what have they done to him and then she does it too. A suffocating sense of injustice blinds him. He turns and runs.

Uphill exultantly. He dodges among gravestones. Dandelions grow bright as butter among the graves. Behind him his name is called in Eccles' voice: "Harry! Harry!" He feels Eccles chasing him but does not turn to look. He cuts diagonally through the stones across the grass toward the woods. The distance to the dark crescent of trees is greater than it seemed from beside the grave. The romping of his body turns heavy; the slope of land grows steeper. Yet there is a softness in the burial ground that sustains his flight, a gentle settled bumpiness that buoys him up with its reminiscence of the dodging spurting runs down a crowded court. He arrives between the arms of the woods and aims for the center of the crescent. Once inside, he is less sheltered than he expected; turning, he can see through the leaves back down the graveyard to where, beside the small green tent, the human beings he had left cluster. Eccles is halfway between them and him. He has stopped running. His black chest heaves. His wide-set eyes concentrate into the woods. The others, thick stalks in dark clothes, jiggle: maneuvering, planning, testing each other's strengths, holding each other up. Their pale faces flash mute signals toward the woods and turn away, in disgust or despair, and then flash again full in the declining sun, fascinated. Only Eccles' gaze is steady. He may be gathering energy to renew the chase.

Rabbit crouches and runs raggedly. His hands and face are

scratched from plowing through the bushes and saplings that rim the woods. Deeper inside there is more space. The pine trees smother all other growth. Their brown needles muffle the rough earth with a slippery blanket; sunshine falls in narrow slots on this dead floor. It is dim but hot in here, like an attic; the unseen afternoon sun bakes the dark shingles of green above his head. Dead lower branches thrust at the level of his eyes. His hands and face feel hot where they were scratched. He turns to see if he has left the people behind. No one is following. Far off, down at the end of the aisle of pines he is in, a green glows which is perhaps the green of the cemetery; but it seems as far off as the patches of sky that flicker through the treetops. In turning he loses some sense of direction. But the tree trunks are at first in neat rows that carry him along between them, and he walks always against the slope of the land. If he walks far enough uphill he will in time reach the scenic drive that runs along the ridge. Only by going downhill can he be returned to the others.

The trees cease to march in rows and grow together more thickly. These are older trees. The darkness under them is denser and the ground is steeper. Rocks jut up through the blanket of needles, scabby with lichen; collapsed trunks hold intricate claws across the path. At places where a hole has been opened up in a roof of evergreen, berrying bushes and yellow grasses grow in a hasty sweet-smelling tumble, and midges swarm. These patches, some of them broad enough to catch a bit of the sun slanting down the mountainside, make the surrounding darkness darker, and in pausing in them Rabbit becomes conscious, by its cessation, of a whisper that fills the brown tunnels all around him. The surrounding trees are too tall for him to see any sign, even a remote cleared landscape, of civilization. Islanded in light he becomes frightened. He is conspicuous; the bears and nameless menaces that whisper through the forest can see him clearly. Rather than hang vulnerable in these wells of visibility he rushes toward the menaces across the rocks and rotting trunks and slithering needles. Insects follow him out of the sun; his sweat is a strong perfume. His chest binds and his shins hurt from jarring uphill into pits and flat rocks that the needles conceal. He takes off his binding blue coat and carries it in a twisted bundle. He struggles against his impulse to keep turning his head, to see what is behind him; there is never anything, just the hushed, deathly life of the woods, but his fear fills the winding space between the tree trunks with agile threats, that just dodge out of the corner of his eye each time he whips his head around. He must hold his head rigid. He's terrorizing himself. As a kid he often went up through the woods. But maybe as a kid he walked under a protection that has now been lifted; he can't believe the woods were this dark then. They too have grown. Such an unnatural darkness, clogged with spiderfine twigs that finger his face incessantly, a darkness in defiance of the broad daylight whose sky leaps in jagged patches from treetop to treetop above him like a silent monkey.

The small of his back aches from crouching. He begins to doubt his method. As a kid he never entered from the cemetery. Perhaps walking against the steepest slope is stupid, carrying him along below the ridge of the mountain when a few yards to his left the road is running. He bears to his left, trying to keep himself in a straight path; the whisper of woods seems to swell louder and his heart lifts with hope: he was right, he is near a road. He hurries on, scrambling ruthlessly, expecting the road to appear with every step, its white posts and speeding metal to gleam. The slope of the ground dies unnoticed under his feet. He stops, stunned, on the edge of a precipitate hollow whose near bank is strewn with the hairy bodies of dead trees locked against trunks that have managed to cling erect to the steep soil and that cast into the hollow a shadow as deep as the last stage of twilight. Something rectangular troubles this gloom; it dawns on him that on the floor of the hollow lie the cellarhole and the crumbled sandstone walls of a forgotten house. To his shrill annoyance at having lost his way and headed himself downhill again is added a clangorous horror, as if this ruined evidence of a human intrusion into a world of blind life tolls bells that ring to the edges of the universe. The thought that this place was once self-conscious, that its land was tramped and cleared and known, blackens the air with ghosts that climb the ferny bank toward him like children clambering up from a grave. Perhaps there were children, fat girls in calico fetching water from a spring, scarring the trees with marks of play, growing old on boards stretched above the cellarhole, dying with a last look out the window at the bank where Harry stands. He feels more conspicuous and vulnerable than in the little clearings of sunshine; he obscurely feels lit by a great spark, the spark whereby the blind tumble of matter recognized itself, a spark struck in the collision of two opposed realms, an encounter a terrible God willed. His stomach slides; his ears seem suddenly open to the sound of a voice. He scrambles back uphill, thrashing noisily in the deepening darkness to drown out the voice that wants to cry out to him from a source that flits from tree to tree in the shadows. In the treacherous light the slope of land is like some fleeing, twisting creature.

The light widens enough for him to spy off to his right a nest of old tin cans and bottles sunken into the needles. He is safe. He strikes the road. He jacks his long legs over the guard fence and straightens up. Gold spots are switching on and off in the corners of his eyes. The asphalt scrapes under his shoes and he seems entered, with the wonderful resonant hollowness of exhaustion, on a new life. Chilly air strokes his shoulder blades; somewhere in there he split old man Springer's shirt right down the back. He has come out of the woods about a half-mile below the Pinnacle Hotel. As he swings along, jauntily hanging his blue coat over his shoulder on the hook of one finger, Janice and Eccles and his mother and his sins seem a thousand miles behind. He decides to call Eccles, like you'd send somebody a postcard. Eccles had liked him and put a lot of trust in him and deserves at least a phone call. Rabbit rehearses what he'll say. *It's O. K.*, he'll tell him, *I'm on the way. I mean, I think there are several ways; don't worry. Thanks for everything.* What he wants to get across is that Eccles shouldn't be discouraged.

On the top of the mountain it is still broad day. Up in the sea of sky a lake of fragmented mackerel clouds drifts in one piece like a school of fish. There are only a couple cars parked around the hotel, jalopies, '52 Pontiacs and '51 Mercs like Springer Motors sells to these blotchy kids that come in with a stripper in their wallets and a hundred dollars in the bank. Inside the cafeteria a few of them are playing a pinball machine called BOUNCING BETSY. They look at him and make wise faces and one of the boys even calls, "Did she rip your shirt?" But, it's strange, they don't really know anything about him except he looks mussed. You do things and do things and nobody really has a clue. The clock says twenty of six. He goes to the pay phone on the butterscotch wall and looks up Eccles' number in the book.

His wife answers dryly, "Hello?" Rabbit shuts his eyes and her freckles dance in the red of his lids.

"Hi. Could I speak to Reverend Eccles please?"

"Who is this?" Her voice has gotten up on a hard little high horse;

she knows who.

"Hey, this is Harry Angstrom. Is Jack there?"

The receiver at the other end of the line is replaced. That bitch. Poor Eccles probably sitting there his heart bleeding to hear the word from me and she going back and telling him wrong number,[11] that poor bastard being married to that bitch. He hangs up himself, hears the dime rattle down, and feels simplified by this failure. He goes out across the parking lot.

He seems to leave behind him in the cafeteria all the poison she must be dripping into the poor tired guy's ears. He imagines her telling Eccles about how he slapped her fanny and thinks he hears Eccles laughing and himself smiles. He'll remember Eccles as laughing; there was that in him that held you off, that you couldn't reach, the nasal business, but through the laughter you could get to him. Sort of sneaking in behind him, past the depressing damp gripping clinging front. What made it depressing was that he wasn't sure, but couldn't tell you,[12] and worried his eyebrows instead, and spoke every word in a different voice. All in all, a relief to be loose from him.

From the edge of the parking lot, Brewer[13] is spread out like a carpet, its flowerpot red going dusty. Some lights are already turned on. The great neon sunflower at the center of the city looks small as a daisy. Now the low clouds are pink but up above, high in the dome, tails of cirrus still hang pale and pure. As he starts down the steps he wonders, *Would she have*? Lucy.[14] Are ministers' wives frigid?

He goes down the mountainside on the flight of log stairs and through the park, where some people are still playing tennis, and down Weiser Street. He puts his coat back on and walks up Summer. His heart is murmuring in suspense but it is in the center of his chest. That lopsided kink about Becky[15] is gone, he has put her in Heaven, he felt her go. If Janice had felt it he would have stayed. Or would he? The outer door is open and an old lady in a Polish sort of kerchief is coming mumbling out of F. X. Pelligrini's door. He rings Ruth's[16] bell.

The buzzer answers and he quickly snaps open the inner door and starts up the steps. Ruth comes to the banister and looks down and says, "Go away."

"Huh? How'd you know it was me?"

"Go back to your wife."

"I can't. I just left her."

She laughs; he has climbed to the step next to the top one, and their faces are on a level. "You're always leaving her," she says.

"No, this time it's different. It's really bad."

"You're bad all around. You're bad with me, too."

"Why?" He has come up the last step and stands there a yard away from her, excited and helpless. He thought when he saw her, instinct would tell him what to do but in a way it's all new, though it's only been a few weeks. She is changed, graver in her motions and thicker in the waist. The blue of her eyes is no longer blank.

She looks at him with a contempt that is totally new. "*Why*?" she repeats in an incredulous hard voice.

"Let me guess," he says. "You're pregnant."

Surprise softens the hardness a moment.

"That's great," he says, and takes advantage of her softness to push her ahead of him into the room. Just from the touches of pushing he remembers what Ruth feels like in his arms. "Great," he repeats, closing the door. He tries to embrace her and she fights him successfully and backs away behind a chair. She had meant that fight; his neck is scraped.

"Go away," she says. "Go *away*."

"Don't you need me?"

"*Need* you," she cries, and he squints in pain at the straining note of hysteria; he feels she has imagined this encounter so often she is determined to say everything, which will be too much. He sits down in an easy chair. His legs ache. She says, "I needed you that night you walked out. Remember how much I needed you? Remember what you made me do?" [17]

"She was in the hospital," he says. "I had to go."

"God, you're cute. God, you're so holy. You had to go. You had to stay, too, didn't you? You know, I was stupid enough to think you'd at least call."

"I wanted to but I was trying to start clean. I didn't know you were pregnant."

"You didn't, why not? Anybody else would have. I was sick enough."

"When, with me?"

"God, yes. Why don't you look outside your own pretty skin once in a while?"

"Well why didn't you tell me?"

"Why should I? What would that have done? You're no help. You're nothing. You know why I didn't? You'll laugh, but I didn't because I thought you'd leave me if you knew. You wouldn't ever let me do anything to prevent it but I figured once it happened you'd leave me. You left me anyway so there you are. Why don't you get out? Please get out. I begged you to get out the first time. The damn first time I begged you. Why are you *here*?"

"I want to be here. It's right. Look. I'm happy you're pregnant."

"It's too late to be happy."

"Why? Why is it too late?" He's frightened, remembering how she wasn't here when he came before. She's here now, she had been away then. Women went away to have it done, he knew. There was a place in Philadelphia.

"How can you sit there?" she asks him. "I can't understand it, how you can sit there; you just killed your baby and there you sit."

"Who told you that?"

"Your ministerial friend.[18] Your fellow saint. He called about a half-hour ago."

"God. He's still trying."

"I said you weren't here. I said you'd never be here."

"I didn't kill the poor kid. Janice did. I got mad at her one night and came looking for you and she got drunk and drowned the poor kid in the bathtub. Don't make me talk about it. Where *were* you, anyway?"

She looks at him with dull wonder and says softly, "Boy, you really have the touch of death, don't you?"

"Hey; have you done something?"

"Hold still. Just sit there. I see you very clear all of a sudden. You're Mr. Death himself. You're not just nothing, You're worse than nothing. You're not a rat, you don't stink, you're not enough to stink."

"Look, I didn't do anything. I was coming to see you when it happened."

"No, you don't do anything. You just wander around with the kiss of death. Get out. Honest to God, Rabbit, just looking at you makes me sick." Her sincerity in saying this leaves her so limp that for support she grips the top slat of the back of a straight chair—one of the chairs they used to sit in to eat—and leans forward over it, openmouthed and staring.

He, who always took a pride in dressing neatly, who had always been led to think he was all right to look at, blushes to feel this sincerity. The sensation he had counted on, of being by nature her master, of getting on top of her, hasn't come. He looks at his fingernails, with their big cuticle moons. His hands and legs are suffused with a paralyzing sensation of reality; his child is really dead, his day is really done, this woman is really sickened by him. Realizing this much makes him anxious to have all of it, to go as far in this direction as he can. He asks her flat, "Did you get an abortion?"

She smirks and says hoarsely, "What do *you* think?"

He closes his eyes and while the gritty grained fur of the chair arms rushes up against his fingertips prays, *God, dear God, no, not another, you have one, let this one go.* A dirty knife turns in his intricate inner darkness. When he opens his eyes he sees, from the tentative hovering way she is standing there, trying to bring off a hard swagger in her stance, that she means to torment him. His voice goes sharp with hope: "Have you?"

A crumbling film comes over her face. "No," she says, "*no*. I should but I keep not doing it. I don't want to do it."

Up he gets and his arms go around her, without squeezing, like a magic ring, and though she stiffens at his touch and twists her head sideways on her muscled white throat, he has regained that feeling, of being on top. "Oh," he says, "good. That's so good."

"It was too ugly," she says. "Margaret had it all rigged up but I kept—thinking about—"

"Yes," he says. "Yes. You're so good. I'm so glad," and tries to nuzzle the side of her face. His nose touches wet. "You have it," he coaxes. "Have it." She is still a moment, staring at her thoughts, and then jerks out of his arms and says, "Don't touch me!" Her face flares; her body is bent forward like a threatened animal's. As if his touch *is* death.

"I love you," he says.

"That meant nothing from you. Have it, have it, you say: how?

Will you marry me?"

"I'd love to."

"You'd love to, you'd love to do anything. What about your wife? What about the boy you already have?"

"I don't know."

"Will you divorce her? No. You love being married to her too. You love being married to everybody. Why can't you make up your mind what you want to *do*?"

"Can't I? I don't know."

"How would you support me? How many wives can you support? Your jobs are a joke. You aren't worth hiring. Maybe once you could play basketball but you can't do *any*thing now. What the hell do you think the world is?"

"Please have the baby," he says. "You got to have it."

"Why? Why do you *care*?"

"I don't know. I don't know any of these answers. All I know is what feels right. You feel right to me. Sometimes Janice used to. Sometimes nothing does."

"Who cares? That's the thing. Who cares *what* you feel?"

"I don't know," he says again.

She groans—from her face he feared she would spit—and turns and looks at the wall that is all in bumps from being painted over peeling previous coats so often.[19]

He says, "I'm hungry. Why don't I go out to the delicatessen and get us something. Then we can think."

She turns, steadier. "I've *been* thinking," she says. "You know where I was when you came here the other day? I was with my parents. You know I have parents. They're pretty poor parents but that's what they are. They live in West Brewer. They know. I mean they know some things. They know I'm pregnant. *Pregnant*'s a nice word, it happens to everybody, you don't have to think too much what you must do to get that way. Now I'd like to marry you. I would. I mean whatever I said but if we're married it'll be all right. Now you work it out. You divorce that wife you feel so sorry for about once a month, you divorce her or forget me. If you can't work it out, I'm dead to you; I'm dead to you and this baby of yours is dead too. Now; get out if you want to." Saying all this unsteadies her and makes her cry, but she pretends she's not. She grips the back of the chair, the sides of her nose shining, and looks at him to say something. The way she is fighting for control of herself repels him; he doesn't like people who manage things. He likes things to happen of themselves.

He has nervously felt her watching him for some sign of resolution inspired by her speech. In fact he has hardly listened; it is too complicated and, compared to the vision of a sandwich, unreal. He stands up, he hopes with soldierly effect, and says, "That's fair. I'll work it out. What do you want at the store?" A sandwich and a glass of milk, and then undressing her, getting her out of that cotton dress harried into wrinkles and seeing that thickened waist calm in its pale cool skin. He loves women when they're first pregnant; a kind of dawn comes over their bodies. If he can just once more bury himself in her he knows he'll come up with his nerves all combed.

"I don't want anything," she says.

"Oh you got to eat," he says.

"I've eaten," she says.

He tries to kiss her but she says "No" and does not look inviting, fat and flushed and her many-colored hair straggled and damp.

"I'll be right back," he says.

As he goes down the stairs worries come as quick as the click of his footsteps. Janice, money, Eccles' phone call, the look on his mother's face all clatter together in sharp dark waves; guilt and responsibility slide together like two substantial shadows inside his chest. The mere engineering of it—the conversations, the phone calls, the lawyers, the finances seems to complicate, physically, in front of his mouth, so he is conscious of the effort of breathing, and every action, just reaching for the doorknob, feels like a precarious extension of a long mechanical sequence insecurely linked to his heart. The doorknob's solidity answers his touch, and turns nicely.

Outside in the air his fears condense. Globes of ether, pure nervousness, slide down his legs. The sense of outside space scoops at his chest. Standing on the step he tries to sort his worries, tries to analyze the machinery behind him in the house, put his finger on what makes it so loud. Two thoughts comfort him, let a little light through the dense pack of impossible alternatives. Ruth has parents, and she will let his baby live; two thoughts that are perhaps the same thought, the vertical order of parenthood, a kind of thin tube upright in time in which our solitude is somewhat diluted. Ruth and Janice both have parents; with this thought he dissolves both of them. Nelson remains; here is a hardness he must carry with him. On this small fulcrum he tries to balance the rest, weighing opposites against each other; Janice and Ruth, Eccles and his mother, the right way and the good way, the way to the delicatessen—gaudy with stacked fruit lit by a naked bulb—and the other way, down Summer Street to where the city ends. He tries to picture how it will end, with an empty baseball field, a dark factory, and then over a brook into a dirt road, he doesn't know. He pictures a huge vacant field of cinders and his heart goes hollow.

Afraid, really afraid, he remembers what once consoled him by seeming to make a hole where he looked through into underlying brightness, and lifts his eyes to the church window. It is, because of church poverty or the late summer nights or just carelessness, unlit, a dark circle in a stone facade.

There is light, though, in the streetlights; muffled by trees their mingling cones retreat to the unseen end of Summer Street. Nearby, to his left, directly under one, the rough asphalt looks like dimpled snow. He decides to walk around the block, to clear his head and pick his path. Funny, how what makes you move is so simple and the field you must move in is so crowded. His legs take strength from the distinction, scissor along evenly. Goodness lies inside, there is nothing outside, those things he was trying to balance have no weight. He feels his inside as very real suddenly, a pure blank space in the middle of a dense net. *I don't know*, he kept telling Ruth; he doesn't know, what to do, where to go, what will happen, the thought that he doesn't know seems to make him infinitely small and impossible to capture. Its smallness fills him like a vastness. It's like when they heard you were great and put two men on you and no matter which way you turned you bumped into one of them and the only thing to do was pass. So you passed and the ball belonged to the others and your hands were empty and the men on you looked foolish because in effect there was nobody there.

Rabbit comes to the curb but instead of going to his right and around the block he steps down, with as big a feeling as if this little side street is a wide river, and crosses. He wants to travel to the next patch of snow. Although this block of brick three-stories is just like the one he left, something in it makes him happy; the steps and window sills seem to twitch and shift in the corner of his eye, alive. This illusion trips him. His hands lift of their own and he feels the wind on his ears even before, his heels hitting heavily on the pavement at first but with an effortless gathering out of a kind of sweet panic growing lighter and quicker and quieter, he runs. Ah: runs. Runs.

〔注释〕

1. Harry：哈里，本书的主人公，绰号为 Rabbit，姓 Angstrom。有的批评家指出 Angtrom 本意为一百亿分之一米，暗指主人公在当代社会微不足道。也有人认为，Angstrom 系由德文 Angst 与 Strom 复合而成，意"忧恐之河"。

2. the Springers：哈里的妻子原姓 Springer。她的父亲经营旧汽车生意，家境比哈里强。

3. 这里的描写很具有厄普代克的特色。

4. Janice：哈里的妻子，有些愚钝。有人认为这一词暗指 January Ice。

5. 珍尼斯是因醉酒无意使女儿溺死的。

6. Mim：即 Miriam，哈里的妹妹。

7. Nelson：哈里的儿子。

8. Black Eccles：指穿黑衣服的 Eccles。他是一位牧师，在本书中起着很大的作用。有人认为他的名字 Eccles 暗指"ecclesiastic"。

9. 出自《新约·约翰福音》第 11 章第 24～25 节。

10. June：哈里给女儿取的名字。

11. 告诉他来的是错电话。

12. but couldn't tell you＝but couldn't tell you that he wasn't sure.

13. Brewer：哈里居住的城市。

14. Lucy：Eccles 的妻子。

15. Becky：指哈里的女儿（Rebecca June Angstrom）。

16. Ruth：鲁丝，哈里曾与之同居的妓女。

17. 指在哈里妻子生产的夜晚，哈里离开鲁斯。

18. 指 Eccles.

19. 指墙因墙皮脱落而显得高低不平。

KEN KESEY

〔作者介绍〕

肯·凯西（Ken Kesey，1935～ ）美国当代小说家。在美国颇有知名度，60年代一度成为青年人崇拜的偶象。他生于科罗拉多州的拉洪塔（La Junta），毕业于俄勒冈大学。在大学修业期间，他积极参与创作、戏剧和体育活动，曾参加奥运会摔跤预赛。大学毕业后一度想当电影演员，写过一部名叫《秋末》（*End of Autumn*）的关于大学体育运动的小说，但未发表。1958年师从当代名师马尔科姆·考利（Malcolm Cowley）等人在斯坦福大学研习创作。1960年夏开始创作《飞越杜鹃巢》（*One Flew over the Cuckoo's Nest*，1962）。当时，他正自愿接受政府的毒品实验，开始吸用L. S. D. 等迷幻药品，这使他有了吸毒的经验。小说里的印第安人叙事者的形象据说就是在迷幻药物的作用下出现在他的脑际的。以后他又在一家精神病院里做助手。为了写好这部书，他曾设法亲身体验电击疗法的效应。

1961年完成《飞越杜鹃巢》后，凯西开始创作第2部小说《异想天开》（*Sometimes a Great Notion*，1964）。当时，他在加州拉洪达（La Honda）购置了地产，并与"垮掉的一代"（Beat Generation）作家和诗人如金斯堡（Allen Ginsberg）等过从甚密。他们藐视权威，为寻求神秘经验和刺激而酗酒、吸毒，着奇装异服，生活放荡。凯西可以说是这些人的领袖。1964年第2部小说脱稿后，凯西买了一辆大轿车，与同伴乘坐该车从西部来到东部，轰动一时。有评论家认为轿车及此次旅行本身即可被视为凯西第3部小说，因为在写完第2部小说之后，凯西便开始讨论小说已经过时，形式上也不自然，他已开始探索新的艺术形式。

凯西的生活愈来愈古怪离奇。他不懈地探求新的生活经验。他模仿连环画里"诚实的美国人"（"The honest American"）形象，使自己显现为一种"神人"，颇有一种宗教领袖的气度。他依靠吸毒以麻醉自己，并进入一种恍恍惚惚的精神境界，甚至觉得自己就是万能的上帝。阅读一下他的《越过边界》(*Over the Border*) 一剧便可知端倪。一些青年人对凯西很崇拜。在这期间，凯西曾公开免费散发毒品。1965 年他因携带大麻而被捕；翌年为了逃避可能为 5 年的徒刑，他逃往墨西哥。他说：“假如社会要我当罪犯，那我会做一名很好的罪犯。人们需要有人这样做。人们总是需要罪犯的。”凯西认为，罪犯比艺术家更能测定生活的限度。他在墨西哥停留几个月后秘密回国，不久被逮捕，1967 年 6 月开始服刑，至 11 月获释后一直住在俄勒岗州。

自 1968 至 1973 年，凯西深居简出。1973 年出版文集《门前小市》(*Garage Sale*)，凯西在这本书里表示，他又开始认真进行写作了。《门前小市》由米勒 (Arthur Miller) 作序，内有金斯堡的文章。这本书再次使他拥有众多读者。书内最重要的一篇应推《越过边界》，它占全书篇幅一半以上，描述凯西逃亡墨西哥的经历。《门前小市》的其他部分谈到凯西作为小说家的过去与未来，其结尾部分表明他对 60 年代中期个人行为和态度的反思，暗示作者在艺术和自我认识方面已达到新的成熟阶段。1973 年后，凯西的知名度又有增高，作品也增多了，其中包括文集《寻找秘密的金字塔》(*The Search for the Secret Pyramid*)，小说《惠蒂埃老太太的七次祈祷》(*Seven Prayers by Grandma Whittier*)，《飞越杜鹃巢》的电影剧本，文集《鬼盒》(*The Demon Box*)，以及同朋友联合出版的小刊物《在大洋里唾吐》(*Spit in the Ocean*) 等。

凯西的作品多为描写“心理上的罪犯”(“psychic outlaw”) 之作，主人公多为“垮掉的一代”里的人物。在许多情况下，他的作品自传成份极浓，比如多次出现在他的作品中的戴夫林·狄包利 (Devlin Deboree) 这个人物就是醒目的例子。这说明凯西自身的强有力的人格深刻地影响着他的艺术。凯西的作品是当代反主流文化的重要组成部份。

One Flew over the Cuckoo's Nest

〔**作品介绍**〕

《飞越杜鹃巢》所描写的是在 所精神病院里发生的事。护士拉其德将病房管理得井井有条，大家都称她为“大个儿护士”。她同各方面都有联系，俨然是精神病院的主人，就连主治医师都要受她摆布。有一天，麦克墨菲被送进这所医院，他正因犯殴打他人罪而在一处农场服劳役，但由于不堪忍受艰苦的劳动而开始装疯。从他来到病房的第一天起，就不失时机地向“大个儿护士”的权威挑战。“大个儿护士”的病房纪律严明，有一批身强力壮的侍者随时准备镇压哪怕是最微弱的反抗。病人早已放弃斗争，对她俯首贴耳、唯命是从。麦克墨菲来后不久便看清了“大个儿护士”的面目和伎俩，他对病友的无条件顺从感到惊讶，于是开展了一场反权威反控制的斗争，开始出于玩耍，后渐趋严肃认真。他纵容病友赌博，把酒和女人带进病房，病人开始活跃起来，病院开始有了欢声笑语。有的患者在麦克墨菲的影响下，竟克服了自己懦弱的习性。后来，双方矛盾激化，麦克墨菲在忍无可忍的情况下殴打了“大个儿护士”。他被捉住，头部被动手术。这使他丧失了思维能力，成为一个瘫痪的人。鉴于这种情况，他的病友、本书的叙述者布朗顿先生——一位印第安人部落首领的后裔，为了结束他的痛苦，使其窒息而死，尔后自己逃出精神病院。他已在麦克墨菲的帮助下克服了自己的心理障碍。麦克墨菲虽然死了，但是他未被打败。他的精神依然充溢在病房里。显然，他已战胜“大个儿护士”，搞垮了她所代表的专制权威。

正象凯西屡次指出的那样，本书中的精神病院代表着整个美国社会。自然、个体、情感与高度机械化的伪善社会的对立和斗争构成本书的主题。书中“大个儿护士”及其一伙所象征的乃是压抑个体和自然情感的邪恶力量。凯西在该书中所提出的问题是尖锐的。对该书描绘的许多事件凯西都有亲身体验。在麦克墨菲这个人物身上存在着不少作者本人生活的痕迹。

本书的书名具有丰富的象征意义。“飞越杜鹃巢”出自一支民间儿歌。“杜鹃”一词在本书书名里已非“杜鹃鸟”之意，而是体现出它的俚语含义——“疯人”。因此，“杜鹃巢”代表的应是精神病院。根据小说的内容判断，“飞越杜鹃巢”的是一只雁，一只带领雁群飞行的雁，因而应是麦克墨菲的象征。“飞越杜鹃巢”是麦克墨菲带领病友为寻求尊严和自由而反抗的标志，取做书名，极为得体。《飞越杜鹃巢》的叙事结构亦独具匠心。小说叙述者布朗顿的作用极为关键。他和主人公关系密切，对他的言行怀着既钦羡又不敢苟同的复杂感情。在小说故事展开的过程里，他从主人公生与死的事迹中不断汲取经验和教训，逐步变得老成干练，最后把自己的潜力和朋友的长处集于一身，从而避免了朋友的遭遇，满怀信心地正视生活。主人公和布朗顿的性格发展可用两条相互交叉的斜线加以表示：随着麦克墨菲力量的减弱，布朗顿的性格渐臻成熟；全书以前者的威力转移到后者身上这一过程的完成而告结束。这种结构可使作家同时享有第一人称和第三人称两种叙事角度的优势：主人公的性格被描绘得饱满酣畅，给人一种栩栩如生的立体感。

这里选注的是该书第1部结尾部分。

One Flew over the Cuckoo's Nest

I[1] know how they work it, the fog machine. We had a whole platoon used to operate fog machines around airfields overseas. Whenever intelligence figured there might be a bombing attack, or if the generals had something secret they wanted to pull—out of sight, hid so good[2] that even the spies on the base couldn't see what went on—they fogged the field.

It's a simple rig: you got[3] an ordinary compressor sucks water out of one tank and a special oil out of another tank, and compresses them together, and from the black stem at the end of the machine blooms a white cloud of fog that can cover a whole airfield in ninety seconds. The first thing I saw when I landed in Europe was the fog those machines make.[4] There were some interceptors close after our transport, and soon as it hit ground the fog crew started up the machines. We could look out the transport's round, scratched windows and watch jeeps draw the machines up close to the plane and watch the the fog boil out till it rolled across the field and stuck against the windows like wet cotton.

You found your way off the plane by following a little referees' horn the lieutenant kept blowing, sounded like a goose honking. Soon as you were out of the hatch you couldn't see no more than maybe three feet in any direction. You felt like[5] you were out on that airfield all by yourself. You were safe from the enemy, but you were awfully alone. Sounds died and dissolved after a few yards, and you couldn't hear any of the rest of your crew, nothing but that little horn squeaking and honking out of a soft furry whiteness so thick that your body just faded into white below the belt; other than that brown shirt and brass buckle, you couldn't see nothing but white, like from the waist down you were being dissolved by the fog too.

And then some guy wandering as lost as you would all of a sudden be right before your eyes, his face bigger and clearer than you ever saw a man's face before in your life. Your eyes were working so hard to see in that fog that when something did come in sight every detail was ten times as clear as usual, so clear both of you had to look away. When a man showed up you didn't want to look at his face and he didn't want to look at yours, because it's painful to see somebody so clear that it's like looking inside him, but then neither did you want to look away and lose him completely. You had a choice: you could either strain and look at things that appeared in front of you in the fog, painful as it might be, or you could relax and lose yourself.

When they first used that fog machine on the ward, one they

bought from Army Surplus[6] and hid in the vents in the new place before we moved in, I kept looking at anything that appeared out of the fog as long and hard as I could, to keep track of it, just like I used to do when they fogged the airfields in Europe. Nobody'd be blowing a horn to show the way, there was no rope to hold to, so fixing my eyes on something was the only way I kept from getting lost. Sometimes I got lost in it anyway, got in too deep, trying to hide, and every time I did, it seemed like I always turned up at that same place, at that same metal door with the row of rivets like eyes and no number, just like[7] the room behind the door drew me to it, no matter how hard I tried to stay away, just like the current generated by the fiends in that room was conducted in a beam along the fog and pulled me back along it like a robot. I'd wander for days in the fog, scared I'd never see another thing, then there'd be that door, opening to show me the mattress padding on the other side to stop out the sounds, the men standing in a line like zombies among shiny copper wires and tubes pulsing light, and the bright scrape of arcing electricity. I'd take my place in the line and wait my turn at the table. The table shaped[8] like a cross, with shadows of a thousand murdered men printed on it, silhouette wrists and ankles running under leather straps sweated green with use, a silhouette neck and head running up to a silver band goes across the forehead. And a technician at the controls beside the table looking up from his dials and down the line and pointing at me with a rubber glove. "Wait, I *know* that big bastard there—better rabbit-punch him or call for some more help or something. He's an awful case for thrashing around."

So I used to try not to get in too deep, for fear I'd get lost and turn up at the Shock Shop[9] door. I looked hard at anything that came into sight and hung on like a man in a blizzard hangs on a fence rail. But they kept making the fog thicker and thicker, and it seemed to me that, no matter how hard I tried, two or three times a month I found myself with that door opening in front of me to the acid smell of sparks and ozone. In spite of all I could do, it was getting tough to keep from getting lost.

Then I discovered something: I don't have to end up at that door if I stay still when the fog comes over me and just keep quiet. The trouble was I'd been finding that door my own self because I got scared of being lost so long and went to hollering so they could track me. In a way,

I was hollering for them to track me; I had figured that anything was better'n being lost for good, even the Shock Shop. Now, I don't know. Being lost isn't so bad.

All this morning I been[10] waiting for them to fog us in again. The last few days they been doing it more and more. It's my idea they're doing it on account of McMurphy. They haven't got him fixed with controls yet, and they're trying to catch him off guard. They can see he's due to be a problem; a half a dozen times already he's roused Cheswick and Harding and some of the others to where it looked like they might actually stand up to one of the black boys—but always, just the time it looked like the patient might be helped, the fog would start, like it's starting now.

I heard the compressor start pumping in the grill a few minutes back, just as the guys went to moving tables out of the day room for the therapeutic meeting, and already the mist is oozing across the floor so thick my pants legs are wet. I'm cleaning the windows in the door of the glass station, and I hear the Big Nurse[11] pick up the phone and call the doctor to tell him we're just about ready for the meeting, and tell him perhaps he'd best keep an hour free this afternoon for a Staff meeting. "The reason being," she tells him, "I think it is past time to have a discussion of the subject of Patient Randle McMurphy and whether he should be on this ward or not." She listens a minute, and tells him, "I don't think it's wise to let him go on upsetting the patients the way he has the last few days."

That's why she's fogging the ward for the meeting. She don't usually do that. But now she's going to do something with McMurphy today, probably ship him to Disturbed.[12] I put down my window rag and go to my chair at the end of the line of Chronics, barely able to see the guys getting into their chairs and the doctor coming through the door wiping his glasses like he thinks the blurred look comes from his steamed lenses instead of the fog.

It's rolling in thicker than I ever seen it before.

I can hear them out there, trying to go on with the meeting, talking some nonsense about Billy Bibbit's stutter and how it came about. The words come to me like through water, it's so thick. In fact it's so much like water if floats me right up out of my chair and I don't know which end is up for a while. Floating makes me a little sick to the stomach at first. I can't see a thing. I never had it so thick it floated me like this.

The words get dim and loud, off and on, as I float around, but as loud as they get, loud enough sometimes I know I'm right next to the guy that's talking, I still can't see a thing.

I recognize Billy's voice, stuttering worse than ever because he's nervous. "... fuh-fuh-flunked out of college be-be-cause I quit ROTC. I c-c-couldn't take it. Wh-wh-wh-whenever the officer in charge of class would call roll, call 'Bibbit,' I couldn't answer. You were s-s-supposed to say heh-heh-heh..." He's choking on the word, like it's a bone in his throat. I hear him swallow and start again. "You were supposed to say, 'Here sir,' and I never c-c-could get it out."

His voice gets dim; then the Big Nurse's voice comes cutting from the left. "Can you recall, Billy, when you first had speech trouble? When did you first stutter, do you remember?"

I can't tell is he laughing[13] or what. "Fir-first stutter? First stutter? The first word I said I st-stut-tered: m-m-m-m-mam-ma."

Then the talking fades out altogether; I never knew that to happen before. Maybe Billy's hid himself in the fog too. Maybe all the guys finally and forever crowded back into the fog.

A chair and me[14] float past each other. It's the first thing I've seen. It comes sifting out of the fog off to my right, and for a few seconds it's right beside my face, just out of my reach. I been accustomed of late to just let things alone when they appear in the fog, sit still and not try to hang on. But this time I'm scared, the way I used to be scared. I try with all I got to pull myself over to the chair and get hold of it, but there's nothing to brace against and all I can do is thrash the air, all I can do is watch the chair come clear, clearer than ever before to where I can even make out the fingerprint where a worker touched the varnish before it was dry, looming out for a few seconds, them fading on off again. I never seen it where things floated around this way. I never seen it this thick before, thick to where I can't get down to the floor and get on my feet if I wanted to and walk around. That's why I'm so scared; I feel I'm going to float off someplace for good this time.

I see a Chronic float into sight a little below me. It's old Colonel Matterson, reading from the wrinkled scripture of that long yellow hand. I look close at him because I figure it's the last time I'll ever see him. His face is enormous, almost more than I can bear. Every hair and wrinkle of him is big, as though I was looking at him with one of those microscopes. I see him so clear I see his whole life. The face is sixty years of southwest Army camps, rutted by iron-rimmed caisson wheels, worn to the bone by thousands of feet on two-day marches.

He holds out that long hand and brings it up in front of his eyes and squints into it, brings up his other hand and underlines the words with a finger wooden and varnished the color of a gunstock by nicotine. His voice is deep and slow and patient, and I see the words come out dark and heavy over his brittle lips when he reads.

"No... The flag is... Ah-mer-ica. America is... the plum. The peach. The wah-ter-mel-on. America is... the gumdrop. The pumpkin seed. America is... tell-ah-vision."

It's true. It's all wrote down on that yellow hand. I can read it along with him myself.

"Now... The cross is... Mex-i-co." He looks up to see if I'm paying attention, and when he sees I am he smiles at me and goes on. "Mexico is... the wal-nut. The hazelnut. The ay-corn. Mexico is... the rain-bow. The rain-bow is... wooden. Mexico is... woo-den."

I can see what he's driving at. He's been saying this sort of thing for the whole six years he's been here, but I never paid him any mind, figured he was no more than a talking statue, a thing made out of bone and arthritis, rambling on and on with these goofy definitions of his that didn't make a lick of sense. Now, at last, I see what he's saying. I'm trying to hold him for one last look to remember him, and that's what makes me look hard enough to understand. He pauses and peers up at me again to make sure I'm getting it, and I want to yell out to him Yes, I see; Mexico *is* like a walnut; it's brown and hard and you feel it with your eye and it *feels* like the walnut! You're making sense, old man, a sense of your own. You're not crazy the way they think. Yes... I see...

But the fog's clogged my throat to where I can't make a sound. As he sifts away I see him bend back over that hand.

"Now... The green sheep is... Can-a-da. Canada is... the fir tree. The wheat field. The cal-en-dar..."

I strain to see him drifting away. I strain so hard my eyes ache and I have to close them, and when I open them again the colonel is gone. I'm floating by myself again, more lost than ever.

This is the time, I tell myself. I'm going for good.

There's old Pete, face like a searchlight. He's fifty yards off to my left, but I can see him plain as though there wasn't any fog at all. Or maybe he's up right close and real small, I can't be sure. He tells me once about how tired he is, and just his saying it makes me his whole life on the railroad, see him working to figure out how to read a watch, breaking a sweat while he tries to get the right button in the right hole of his railroad overalls, doing his absolute damnedest to keep up with a job that comes so easy to the others they can sit back in a chair padded with cardboard and read mystery stories and girlie books. Not that he ever really figured to keep up—he knew from the start he couldn't do that—but he had to try to keep up, just to keep them in sight. So for forty years he was able to live, if not right in the world of men, at least on the edge of it.

I can see all that, and be hurt by it, the way I was hurt by seeing things in Army, in the war. The way I was hurt by seeing what happened to Papa and the tribe. I thought I'd got over seeing those things and fretting over them. There's no sense in it. There's nothing to be done.

"I'm tired," is what he says.

"I know you're tired, Pete, but I can't do you no good fretting about it. You know I can't."

Pete floats on the way of the old colonel.

Here comes Billy Bibbit, the way Pete come by. There're all filing by for a last look. I know Bill can't be more'n a few feet away, but he's so tiny he looks like he's a mile off. His face is out to me like the face of a begger, needing so much more'n anybody can give. His mouth works like a little doll's mouth.

"And even when I pr-proposed, I flubbd it. I said 'Huhhoney, will you muh-muh-muh-muh-muh[15]...' till the girl broke out l-laughing."

Nurse's voice, I can't see where it comes from: "Your mother has spoken to me about this girl, Billy. Apparently she was quite a bit beneath you. What would you speculate it was about her that frightened you so, Billy?"

"I was in luh-love with her."

I can't do nothing for you either, Billy. You know that. None of us can. You got to understand that as soon as a man goes to help somebody, he leaves himself wide open. He has to be cagey, Billy, you should know that as well as anyone. What could I do? I can't fix your stuttering. I can't wipe the razor-blade scars off your wrists or the cigarette burns off the back of your hands. I can't give you a new mother. And as far as the nurse riding you like this, rubbing your nose in your weakness till what little dignity you got left is gone and you shrink up to nothing from humiliation, I can't do anything about that, either. At Anzio,[16] I saw a buddy of mine tied to a tree fifty yards from me, screaming for water, his face blistered in the sun. They wanted me to try to go out and help him. They'd of cut me in half[17] from the farmhouse over there.

Put your face away, Billy.

They kept filing past.

It's like each face was a sign like one of those "I'm Blind"signs the dago accordion players in Portland hung around their necks, only these signs say "I'm tired" or "I'm scared" or "I'dying of a bum liver" or "I'm all bound up with machinery and people *pushing* me alla time."[18] I can read all the signs, it don't make any difference how little the print gets. Sone of the faces are looking around at one another and could read the other fellow's if they would, but what's the sense? The faces blow past in the fog like confetti.

I'm further off than I've ever been. This is what it's like to be dead. I guess this is what it's like to be a Vegetable; you lose yourself in the fog. You don't move. They feed your body till it finally stops eating; then they burn it. It's not so bad. There's no pain. I don't feel much of anything other than a touch of chill I figure will pass in time.

I see my commanding officer pinning notices on the bulletin board, what we're to wear today. I see the US Department of Interior bearing down on our little tribe with a gravel-crushing machine.

I see Papa come loping out of a draw[19] and slow up to try and take aim at a big six-point buck springing off through the cedars. Shot after shot puffs out of the barrel, knocking dust all around the buck. I come out of the draw behind Papa and bring the buck down with my second shot just as it starts climbing the rimrock. I grin at Papa.

I never knew you to miss a shot like that before, Papa.

Eye's gone, boy. Can't hold a bead. Sights on my gun just now was shakin' like a dog shittin' peach pits.

Papa, I'm telling you: that cactus moon of Sid's is gonna make you old before your time.

A man drinks that cactus moon of Sid's[20] *boy, he's already old before his time. Let's go gut*[21] *that animal out before the flies blow him.*

That's not even happening now. You see? There's nothing you can do about a happening out of the past like that.

Look there, my man...

I hear whispers, black boys.

Look there, that old fool Broom, slipped off to sleep.

Tha's right, Chief Broom, tha's right. You sleep an' keep outa trouble Yasss.

I'm not cold any more. I think I've about made it. I'm off to where the cold can't reach me. I can stay off here for good. I'm not scared any more. They can't reach me. Just the words reach me, and those're fading.

Well... in as much as Billy has decided to walk out on the discussion, does anyone else have a problem to bring before the group?

As a matter of fact, ma'am, there does happen to be something...

That's that McMurphy. He's far away. He's still trying to pull people out of the fog. Why don't he leave me be?

"... remember that vote we had a day or so back—about the TV time? Well, today's Friday and I thought I might just bring it up again, just to see if anybody else has picked up a little guts."

"Mr. McMurphy, the purpose of this meeting is therapy, group therapy, and I'm not certain these petty grievances—"

"Yeah, yeah, the hell with that, we've heard it before. Me and some of the rest of the guys decided—"

"One moment, McMurphy, let me pose a question to the group: do any of you feel that Mr. McMurphy is perhaps imposing his personal desires on some of you too much? I've been thinking you might be happier if he were moved to a different ward."

Nobody says anything for a minute. Then someone says, "Let him vote, why dontcha?[22] Why ya want to ship him to Disturbed just for bringing up a vote? What's so wrong with changing time?"

"Why, Mr. Scanlon, as I recall, you refused to eat for three days until we allowed you to turn the set on at six instead of six-thirty."

"A man needs to see the world news, don't he? God, they coulda bombed Washington ant it'd been a week before we'd of heard."

"Yes? And how do you feel about relinquishing your world news to watch a bunch of men play baseball?"

"We can't have both, huh? No, I suppose not. Well, what the dickens—I don't guess they'll bomb us this week."

"Let's let him have the vote, Miss Ratched."

"Very well. But I think this is ample evidence of how much he is upsetting some of you patients. What is it you are proposing, Mr. McMuphy?"

"I'm proposing a revote on watching the TV in the afternoon."

"You're certain one more vote will satisfy you? We have more important things—"

"It'll satisfy me. I just'd kind of like to see which of these birds has any guts and which doesn't."

"It's that kind of talk, Doctor Spivey, that makes me wonder if the patients wouldn't be more content if Mr. McMurphy were moved."

"Let him call the vote, why dontcha?"

"Certainly, Mr. Cheswick. A vote is now before the group. Will a show of hands be adequate, Mr. McMurphy, or are you going to insist on a secret ballot?"

"I want to see the hands. I want to see the hands that don't go up, too."

"Everyone in favor of changing the television time to the afternoon, raise his hand."

The first hand that comes up, I can tell, is McMurphy's, because of the bandage where that control panel cut into him when he tried to lift it.[23] And then off down the slope I see them, other hands coming up out of the fog. It's like... that big red hand of McMurphy's is reaching into the fog and dropping down and dragging the men up their hands, dragging them blinking into the open. First one, then another, then the next. Right on down the line of Acutes, dragging them out of the fog till there they stand, all twenty of them, raising not just for watching TV, but against the Big Nurse, against her trying to send McMurphy to Disturbed, against the way she's talked and acted and beat them down for years.

Nobody says anything. I can feel how stunned everybody is, the patients as well as the staff. The nurse can't figure what happened; yesterday, before he tried lifting that panel, there wasn't but four or five men might of voted. But when she talks she don't let it show in her voice how surprised she is.

"I count only twenty, Mr. McMurphy."

"Twenty? Well, why not? Twenty is all of us there— "His voice hangs as he realizes what she means. "Now hold on just a goddamned minute, lady—"

"I'm afraid the vote is defeated."

"Hold on just one goddamned *minute*!"

"There are forty patients[24] on the ward, Mr. McMurphy. Forty patients, and only twenty voted. You must have a majority to change the ward policy. I'm afraid the vote is closed."

The hands are coming down across the room. The guys know they're whipped, are trying to slip back into the safety of the fog. McMurphy is on his feet.

"Well, I'll be a sonofabitch. You mean to tell me taht's how you're gonna pull it? Count the votes of those old birds over there too?"

"Didn't you explain the voting procedure to him Doctor?"

"I'm afraid—a majority *is* called for, McMurphy. She's right, she's right."

"A majority, Mr. McMurphy; it's in the ward constitution."

"And I suppose the way to change the damned constitution is with a majority vote. Sure. Of all the chicken-shit[25] things I've ever seen, this by God takes the *cake*!"

"I'm sorry, Mr. McMurphy, but you'll find it written in the policy if you'd care for me to—"

"So this's how you work this democratic bullshit—hell's bells!"

"You seem upset, Mr. McMurphy. Doesn't he seem upset, Doctor? I want you to note this."

"Don't give me that noise, lady. When a guy's getting screwed he's got a right to holler. And we've been damn well screwed."

"Perhaps, Doctor, in view of the patient's condition, we should bring this meeting to a close early today—"

"Wait! Wait a minute, let me talk to some of those old guys."

"The vote is closed, Mr. McMurphy."

"Let me talk to 'em."

He's coming across the day room at us. He gets bigger and bigger, and he's burning red in face. He reaches into the fog and tries to drag Ruckly to the surface because Ruckly's the youngest.

"What about you, buddy? You want to watch the World Series? Baseball? Baseball games? Just raise that hand up there—"

"Fffffffuck da wife."

"All right, forget it. You, partner, how about you? What was your name—Ellis? What do you say, Ellis, to watching a ball game on TV? Just raise your hand...."

Ellis's hands are nailed to the wall, can't be counted as a vote.

"I said the voting is closed, Mr. McMurphy. You're just making a spectacle of yourself."

He don't pay attention to her. He comes on down the line of Chronics. "C'mon,[26] c'mon, just one vote from you birds, just raise a hand. Show her you can still do it."

"I'm tired," says Pete and wags his head.

"The night is... the Pacific Ocean." The Colonel is reading off his hand, can't be bothered with voting.

"*One* of you guys, for cryin' out loud! This is where you get the edge, don't you see that? We have to do this—or we're *whipped*! Don't a one of you clucks know what I'm talking about enough to give us a hand? You, Gabriel? George? No? You, Chief, what about you?.

He's standing over me in the mist. Why won't he leave me be?

"Chief, you're our last bet."

The Big Nurse is folding her papers; the other nurses are standing up around her. She finally gets to her feet.

"The meeting is adjourned, then," I hear her say. "And I'd like to see the staff down in the staff room in about an hour. So, if there is nothing el—"

It's too last to stop it now. McMurphy did something to it that first day, put some kind of hex on it with his hand so it won't act like I order it. There's no sense in it, any fool can see; I wouldn't do it on my own. Just by the way the nurse is staring at me with her mouth empty of words I can see I'm in for trouble, but I can't stop it. McMurphy's got hidden wires hooked to it, lifting it slow just to get me out of the fog and into the open where I'm fair game. He's doing it, wires..

No. That's not the truth. I lifted it myself.

McMurphy whoops and drags me standing, pounding my back.

"Twenty-one! The Chief's vote makes it twenty-one! And by God if that ain't a majority I'll eat my hat!"

"Yippee," Cheswick yells. The other Acutes are coming across toward me.

"The meeting was closed," she says. Her smile is still there, but the back of her neck as she walks out of the day room and into the Nurses' Station, is red and swelling like she'll blow apart any second.

But she don't blow up, not right off, not until about an hour later. Behind the glass her smile is twisted and queer, like we've never seen before. She just sits. I can see her shoulders rise and fall as she breathes.

McMurphy looks up at the clock and he says it's time for the game. He's over by the drinking fountain with some of the other Acutes, down on his knees scouring off the baseboard. I'm sweeping out the broom closet for the tenth time that day. Scanlon and Harding, they got the buffer going up and down the hall, polishing the new wax into shining figure eights. McMurpyh says again the he guesses it must be game time and he stands up, leaves the scouring rag where it lies. Nobody else stops work. McMurphy walks past the window where she's glaring out at him and grins at her like he knows he's got her whipped now. When he tips his head back and winks at her she gives that little sideways jerk of her head.

Everybody keeps on at what he's doing, but they all watch out of the corners of their eyes while he drags his armchair out to in front of the TV set, then switches on the set and sits down. A picture swirls onto the screen of a parrot out on the baseball field singing razorblade songs. McMurphy gets up and turns up the sound to drown out the music coming down from the speaker in the ceiling, and he drags another chair in front of him and sits down and crosses his feet on the chair and leans back and lights a cigarette. He scratches his belly and yawns.

"Hoo-*weee*! Man, all I need me now is a can of beer and a red-hot."

We can see the nurse's face get red and her mouth work as she stares at him. She looks around for a second and sees everybody watching what she's going to do—even the black boys and the little nurses sneaking looks at her, and the residents beginning to drift in for the staff meeting, they're watching. Her mouth clamps shut. She looks back at

McMurpyh and waits till the razor-blade song is finished; then she gets up and goes to the steel door where the controls are, and she flips a switch and the TV picture swirls back into the gray. Nothing is left on the screen but a little eye of light beading right down on McMurphy sitting there.

That eye don't faze him a bit. To tell the truth, he don't even let on he knows the picture is turned off; he puts his cigarette between his teeth and pushes his cap forward in his red hair he has to lean back to see out from under the brim.

And sits that way, with his hands crossed behind his head and his feet stuck out in a chair, a smoking cigarette sticking out from under his hatbrim—watching the TV screen.

The nurse stands this as long as she can; then she comes to the door of the Nurses' Station and calls across to him he'd better help the men with the housework. He ignores her.

"I said, Mr. McMurphy, that you are supposed to be working during these hours."Her voice has a tight whine like an electric saw ripping through pine. "Mr. McMurphy, I'm *warning* you!"

Everybody's stopped what he was doing. She looks around her, then takes a step out of the Nurses' Station toward McMurphy.

"You're committed, you realize. You are... under the *jurisdiction* of me... the staff."She's holding up a fist, all those red-orange fingernails burning into her palm. "Under jurisdiction and *control*—"

Harding shuts off the buffer, and leaves it in the hall, and goes pulls him a chair up alongside McMurphy and sits down and lights him a cigarette too.

"Mr. Harding! You return to your scheduled duties!"

I think how her voice sounds like it hit a nail, and this strikes me so funny I almost laugh.

"Mr. Har-*ding*!"

Then Cheswick goes and gets him a chair, and then Billy Bibbit goes, and then Scanlon and then Fredrickson and Sefelt, and then we all put down our mops and brooms and scouring rags and we all go pull us chairs up.

"You *men*—Stop this. *Stop*!"

And we're all sitting there lined up front of that blankedout TV set, watching the gray screen just like we could see the baseball game clear as day, and she's ranting and screaming behind us.

If somebody'd of come in and took a look, men watching a blank TV, a fifty-year-old woman hollering and squealing at the back of their heads about discpline and order and recriminations, they'd of thought the whole bunch was crazy as loons.

〔注释〕

1. "I"：指小说叙事者布朗顿。他是一个印第安部落酋长的后裔，第二次世界大战中曾在美军服役。战争的刺激，特别是美国政府对印第安人种族灭绝行为的刺激，使他精神失常，他在紧张时总想起战场上的烟雾。他害怕与人接触，多年来装聋作哑，一言不发，被认为是无法救药的病人。护士要他搞卫生，他便得以在病房内和护士值班室内进进出出，偷听各种人的谈话，因而知道精神病院所发生的一切。他在叙述时常用军事术语与印第安人生活有关的语言，这使他的叙述栩栩如生，别具一格。

2. good＝well。本文出现一些不合规范的用法，请参阅本书上册马克·吐温篇关于非规范英语的说明。对此以下一般不另加注（除难解者外）。

3. got＝get.

4. make＝made.

5. like＝as if.

6. Army Surplus：军队剩余物质处理部。

7. like＝as.

8. shaped＝was shaped.

9. Shock Shop：指脑部电击治疗室。

10. been＝have been.

11. Big Nurse："大个儿护士"，大家对主管护士的称呼。她实际是病房的主宰，主治医生也要对她俯首听命。在本书中，她是极权、统治的恶的化身。

12. ship him to Disturbed：关他的禁闭。

13. is he laughing＝whether he is laughing.

14. me＝I.

15. 比里想说："Honey, will you marry me?"

16. Anzio：意大利海港。1944年英美海陆军在此登陆，与德军激战。约4个月后，盟军开始进军罗马。这场战争对布朗顿的心灵刺激很大。

17. They'd of cut me in half＝they'd have cut me in half.

18. alla time＝all the time.

19. draw：冲沟。

20. cactus moon of Sid's ：指 alchoholic drinks.

21. gut＝get.

22. Why dontcha? =Why don't you?

23. 麦克墨菲为鼓励患者，曾试图举起一个钢筋水泥的控制盘，他的双手也因此负伤。

24. 大个儿护士把久病不治的病人也算在内了。

25. chicken-shit：骗人的。

26. C'mon=Come on.

JOYCE CAROL OATES

〔作者介绍〕

乔伊斯·卡罗尔·欧茨（Joyce Carol Oates，1938～ ），美国当代小说家，生于纽约州的乡村。童年时期阅读《阿丽斯漫游奇境记》（*Alice in Wonderland*），颇受影响。高中时对梭罗的《华尔腾》（*Walden*）和陀思托耶夫斯基的作品很感兴趣。欧茨17岁入锡拉丘兹大学，接触到福克纳、卡夫卡（Franz Kafka）、弗洛伊德（Sigmund Freud）、尼采（F. W. Nietzsche）、麦尔维尔以及托马斯·曼（Thomas Mann）等人的作品。她如饥似渴地阅读文学、哲学及心理学方面的书籍。大学期间，她的短篇小说《在过去的世界里》（“*In the Old World*）获《小姐》（*Mademoiselle*）杂志举办的大学生小说一等奖。欧茨1960年获学士学位，1961年在威斯康星大学获硕士学位。正当她在赖斯大学读博士学位时，偶然发现她的一篇短篇小说被选载在一本《美国最佳短篇小说集》里；这使她下决心停学，悉力进行文学创作。1962年，她移居底特律市教英语，这个城市就成为她的许多作品的故事背景。1967年，欧茨到加拿大安大略市温莎大学任教，讲授文学与心理学、现代世界文学及文学创作。后来她到美国普林斯敦大学任驻校作家。

欧茨堪称美国现当代文学中最多产的作家之一。自1963年发表首部作品以来，她已出版短篇小说集、长篇小说、诗集、戏剧及散文30余部，其中诸如《他们》（*them*，1969）、《奇境》（*Wonderland*，1970）及《随你拿我怎么办》（*Do With Me What You Will*，1973）等作品均为脍炙人品之作。欧茨曾多次获奖，如欧·亨利奖、理查德—希尔达·罗森托尔基金奖、全国最佳小说奖（奖予小说《他们》）等。1978年她被选为美国文艺协会成员。

欧茨是坚持现实主义传统的社会小说家。她描写现代社会生活中普通人的恐惧和不安。出现在她作品中的人物形象有工人、女学生、商人、教师和牧师等，这些人活动在中产阶级环境中，表面平淡无奇，内心世界却极为复杂。他们受到社会的、命运的、以及自身心理上的种种折磨，生活中充满暴力、谋杀、自杀、强奸、纵火等事件。这是一个充满恐怖和荒唐的“哥特式”世界，有的颇具华盛顿·欧文、埃德加·爱伦·坡、弗兰纳里·奥康纳及福克纳作品的韵味和气氛。欧茨认为她的作品是现代生活的真实写照。她的暗淡笔调使她获得“美国文学的可怕女人”之称。文学批评界在相当长时间内没有把她视为严肃的作家。这种状况近年来已开始改变，欧茨的文学地位也日益提高。

them

〔**作品介绍**〕

《他们》(*them*) 是欧茨的代表作之一。它描述的是一家城市贫民 1937 至 1967 年间的生活悲剧，一场个人与历史、社会及环境相抗衡的斗争，一个未能实现的梦。书中主要人物有 3 个，即母亲洛蕾塔·博茨福德和她的一对儿女——朱尔斯和莫琳，主要情节由 3 个人充满暴力和死亡（或濒临死亡）的生活故事穿插交织而成。洛蕾塔年轻时同一位青年相爱，但她哥哥把她的情人杀死，后畏罪逃走。洛蕾塔迫于无奈和一名警察结婚。二次大战爆发后，她丈夫应征入伍，她带了孩子曾去乡间小住，后来回城企图以卖淫为生，曾被警方拘留。战后全家团圆，但是她的丈夫酗酒成性，经常打骂她。在一次事故中丈夫丧生，洛蕾塔带着孩子再嫁。

莫琳虽然天性柔顺，但是极不喜欢寄居继父家。她梦想离家出走，后来做暗娼以积钱，被发现后遭继父毒打，险些丧命，接着她过了一年神志不清的生活。恢复健康以后，莫琳入夜校学习，和一位有妇之夫相恋，导致后者的家庭破裂，后两人结婚。朱尔斯认识了一位黑社会人物，做了他的司机，因而得以和这位黑社会人物的侄女纳丁相遇，二人一见钟情，这位漂亮的小姐同意和他私奔到美国南部。在南方，天气炎热，身无分文，朱尔斯只好去偷盗，后来他染疾昏迷，纳丁趁机甩了他逃回家去，不久嫁给一位富有的律师。朱尔斯侥幸未死，回到北方，又和纳丁相遇，二人密约到一家旅馆，发生关系后，绝望的纳丁开枪企图和情人同归于尽。朱尔斯再次幸存下来，然而他的头脑和心灵都已一片空虚。在这期间他曾和一个女人同居，奸污过一名少女，并做了她的拉皮条的人。后来城里发生种族骚乱，朱尔斯如大梦初醒，抄起枪支参加骚动，杀死一名追捕他的警察。暴乱后他和一位激进分子一起到加利福尼亚州去谋生。

《他们》是一部骇人听闻的悲剧性作品。它所描绘的是一个混乱和绝望的世界。城市贫民的凄惨经历，谋杀、遗弃、卖淫、战争与死亡等，一幕一幕地展现在读者面前，令人感到窒息和恐惧，感到美国现当代社会生活存在着严重的感情与心理危机。作者以近似自然主义的笔调把这种危机感传达出来，充分表现出她对同代人的思想及社会状况的深切关注。

这里选注的是小说的第2部第9章。

them

CHAPTER Ⅸ

March 11, 1966

Dear Miss Oates,[1]

Thank you for answering my letter. I was sorry I had written it and wished I could take it back, but now I'm glad, it's just as well. I wish I could write down my thoughts not in a mess like most of my life but in some order—I want to explain something. I want to get it clear. Yes, it was in 1964 that I took your course at the University of Detroit. Did you remember that or did you look my name up in a class book? It would mean so much to me to think that you remembered me, but I don't expect that, why should you remember me when I can almost not remember myself? I went to the library last Thursday after work and looked through newspapers again. You can't see what has happened day by day, reading the newspapers, you must look at them for a whole year. Then everything comes rushing at you. You see how the year was a waste. Faster and faster the headlines come, one day has nothing to do with the next, suddenly someone has been killed or a nation is on the front page, the photographs change of people lying in the streets, the names change, everything goes up and down jiggling the eye. In the library I started sweating, so afraid. How can I live my life if the world is like this? The world can't be lived, no one can live it right. It is out of control, crazy. I felt this right in the library though everyone was sitting quiet at tables. I looked around. Those people would like to throw the books out the windows, break the lamps and chairs, hit one another over the head with anything they could grab. But they are quiet, sitting and reading. I don't want to sound crazy to you. I am only saying what

I believe. The library is very clean and modern, I love that kind of place, there is nothing behind it or not much—not much history. I love people walking quietly and very polite. At my house nobody was quiet or polite.

I want to tell you about my family, how we lived. I want to tell you about myself. Now it is March 1966 and I can't believe that date. It is like living in the future—not real. It is so many years later, after what happened to me, but I am still alive, and I am about to begin a new life, start over again with a new life. My heart is frozen so afraid at the thought of going out to begin again, I want to talk to someone. I want to send you a message.

What will happen after today? I am sitting here in my room in Detroit, writing this down for you to read. It is ten at night. I am alone, I live alone. My life is quiet. When I was your student in that night class I had a day job as a secretary, full time, now I have a better job and I am taking a course at Highland Park Junior College two evenings a week. It is supposed to be a much easier school than the University of Detroit. But I want to continue my college career. I want to learn whatever I can, maybe it will help me not to be afraid. Asleep or awake I am afraid, and how can you live that way, always afraid? I am afraid of men out on the street if I see them or don't see them, I am afraid of cars hitting me, of people laughing at me, I am afraid of losing my purse, of throwing up in a store, of screaming out loud in the library and being kicked out and never allowed back. I keep sitting here thinking of the time. Fifteen minutes after ten on March 11, 1966, and I know that should be a sacred time because it will never come again, but I don't feel anything for it. I am numb. What will happen in the future? I am afraid. I am afraid not just of my own future but of all the world. When I read the newspapers I feel that I am losing myself, my own self Maureen Wendall, and becoming like the world itself, not knowing what will happen the next day and never ready for it. Maybe I am writing to you not because you are like me—I sound a little crazy! —but because you are the exact opposite, you are never surprised, you foretell everything, and inside all the mess of the newspapers you live your own life in peace, prepared.

The students in our class, some of them, thought you were a little strange. They think most professors are strange. That was in 1964, January and February, the second semester. They thought you were very intelligent but cold. You were happy about the books we read, you were happy reading passages out loud to us, we could tell that the happiness in the room for you was in the book and not in us. I don't know if I even liked you at first. Sometimes I like women a lot and other times I hate them. You were not much older than me so maybe I was jealous. I always wanted my teachers to be older than me, in fact I would like everybody to be older than me so that I can follow their example. Now I am getting old myself, I am twenty-six years old! —which seems a terrible age to be alone, not to have a career, not to be like everyone else with a definite life. But I have gone through so much that instead of being twenty-six I should really be forty or fifty. Inside my body and face I am an old woman, not even a woman or a man but just an old person; maybe I am writing to you to get rid of all this to make myself young again, to feel the way I should feel at the age of twenty-six about to fall in love.

There is a man I want to marry—I want to fall in love.

We were curious about you, your marriage. You were so calm and intelligent and your sense of humor kept us afraid. How could you be in love and married? That's what I wondered. You reminded me something of my brother Jules. [2] Jules could have been intelligent like you—I mean, he could have been educated except for the way things turned out. I have told Jules about you. My brother Jules is the most important person in my life but what can you do with people who mean a lot to you? Love them? How do you love them, exactly what does that mean? Is it sitting and thinking about them, wanting to protect them? In that case to keep Jules safe he would have to be dead and buried. I want to marry a man and fall in love and be protected by him. I am ready to fall in love. But my heart is hard and my body hard, frozen.

Probably you don't remember me. The course I took with you was "Introduction to Literature." I always loved reading books but in that classroom, in the Commerce and Finance Building, everything seemed cold and strange, a threat. The other students were a threat. It was a night class, that made it worse. At night everything is exaggerated. We could tell you resented teaching a night class. I sat in the third row and I had long hair then, long dark hair, but now I have short hair and I noticed from a photograph of you in the paper that you also have short hair now, short dark hair. That was all three years ago. Did you ever look at me and think about me? Did you think *That girl is something like me*?

One night you read something from *Madame Bovary*,[3] which was our assignment, about the woman going for a walk in a field with her dog. You seemed to think that was important. Out in the field she looks around, she sees—I don't know what. I don't remember. Then she feels a cold wind starting to blow, and she goes back home. You read that passage to us and pointed out something about it, and I could tell you were thinking *That woman is something like me*, like you yourself, a stranger to us, and I sat there hearing myself think, *This is not important*, *none of this is real.* I felt weak and dizzy, thinking of it. Those days I liked to fast, to make up for the days I ate so much, so I got dizzy sometimes at night. I ate crackers in the morning and some bread after work and a banana or orange or something, that was all. I liked to feel my stomach ache with hunger, knowing that I was hungry and not filled up, not fat any more. I used to get dizzy in your class a lot. Why did you think that book about Madame Bovary was so important? All those books? Why did you tell us they were more important than life? They are not more important than my life.

I loved books when I was a different person, before I went crazy. I was crazy for thirteen months.[4] Nobody put me away, they let me stay at home. I lay in bed crazy. I could hear things but I wasn't listening. I was not Maureen Wendall but a certain mass of flesh, lying on a bed. All of my life I could have lain there, but I came back, I woke up. I don't know why I woke up. It happened.

Now I am writing this in a library, not my room. It is dark out. Tomorrow night I will see the man I plan to marry, the man I want, but tonight I am a young woman in a library in Detroit, a small library, alone, sitting alone at a table, writing a letter to a woman named Joyce Carol Oates, a former teacher of mine. There are only three other people here tonight because it is snowing hard out. Almost a blizzard. There is a woman with an overcoat on, still buttoned, with a fake-fur collar that is matted and ugly, a coat that looks like a man's coat; and a man who is maybe seventy, bent over the *Detroit News*, with a very empty face, reading the paper very slowly; and another man, around fifty, I don't want to look at him much because his nose is running and he doesn't have a handkerchief, he wipes it on his fingers. Then there is the librarian, with her white-rimmed glasses. I come in here all the time but she pretends not to know me. She works at her desk. We are all in here and outside it is snowing hard and we should feel close together but we don't. We don't talk or look at each other.

This letter is a crazy idea but I don't care. I don't care what you think. Maybe you get lots of crazy letters. I have given up on what people think, I can't change them. All around me there are shelves with books on them and none of those books are worth anything, I know that now, not the books by Jane Austen I used to love or the book about Madame Bovary you liked so much. Those things didn't happen and won't happen. None of them ever happened. In my life something happened and I have to keep thinking about it, over and over. For a while I was very sick. It was my mind that was sick, it gave up, it got cloudy and slow, it drew back from people talking. You always talked too fast in class, that was a bad thing about you. We would sit trying to make sense of it, your words, and faster and faster you would talk, getting away from us. Did you hate us, that you talked so fast? You left us behind. I wanted to come up to you after class and ask, "Why do you want to leave us behind?" but I had no nerve for that.

When I got well my uncle took me out for walks. He brought me back from where I was, crazy. He woke me up, my uncle. I haven't seen him for years now but never mind, it is Uncle Brock of 1957 I remember, and my mother of 1957 I remember, otherwise everything will be a jumble. My face was a mess. He brought me back by talking to me. He had a sad, serious face, a mess himself, a failure of a man, with no nerve. Ma made hints that he had done something once, something bad, and had to leave town.[5] I don't know. But he brought me back from where I was. I love him no matter what a wreck he is in his own life or no matter that he doen't even have a life himself.

Why do I keep remembering a lady walking in a field in France, somewhere in the country, walking a dog and shivering in the wind? I don't want to remember that when I've forgotten so much else. You read it to us, you read it with a certain serious look and serious sound to your voice that almost made me shiver, it meant so much to you, and you never talked like that to us; that was because you believed the book was more important than your students were. Isn't that true? You hung onto your books and we students, came and went, night students and day students, in and out, and you quit that school and went somewhere else, but you took your books along with you and they all had your name written in them, I bet, and they were more important to you than any of us. That's all right. I didn't know the other students, I didn't have time for them. My life was a flurry. I wanted to succeed in school and find a place, make my way along, get married, but my life was a flurry and I was too nervous to do well. One year I was crazy in bed and a few years later I was in college, in your class, sitting there in the third row staring at you, afraid of you and of school. One year I lay in bed in silence and a few years later I was writing papers for you, trying to write. You failed me. You flunked me out of school.

I don't blame anybody. I never blame anybody. I am like a piece of wood being carried along in the water, drifting along, meeting things and passing by, not judging, not calling anybody names. The man across at the next table sniffs that loud fast sniff that certain men do, in public places, so that you want to scream at them, *Get a handkerchief, you filthy pig! but I think, No, he's just a man, don't pay any attention.* My father was like that. Clearing his sinuses in the morning, in the bathroom next to the room Berry and I shared. Let them. They do such things, they do other things with you, hurt you, breathe their private breaths into your face, and then they die, it's all right. I don't blame them. I don't blame you.

My other English teacher at that school, Mr. Kovack, was very hard when he corrected my papers and I thought he had to be pretending, making things hard when nobody gave a damn, when outside on Livernois brakes were always squealing and the air stank and the Negroes were standing out on the street corners all day long, thinking what to do, making plans. Fires and shootings. Burn Detroit down. But he handed my papers back marked D and F, and in red ink he explained all my mistakes. You gave me F, for the only paper I handed in, but you didn't bother explaining what was wrong. *Lack of coherence and development*, you wrote at the bottom of the paper. You wrote in blue ink, Mr. Kovack in red. Your handwriting was, it still is probably, large and dreamy with circular letters and long crossed t's slanting straight up and down and very clear, but what did you say? I couldn't understand your meaning. You knew what you meant but I didn't. You are not a woman who would lie paralyzed for thirteen months because a man tried to kill you, you are not a woman who would give herself to men for money or for anything, not even love, you don't spend your nights like this in a library writing a letter to a stranger.

I don't ask to turn into you but to see myself like this, living in a house out of the city, a ranch house or a colonial house, with a fence around the back, a woman working in the kitchen, wearing slacks maybe, a baby in his crib in the baby's room, thin white gauzy curtains, a bedroom for my husband and me, a window in the living-room looking out onto the lawn and the street and the house across the street. Every cell in my body aches for this! My eyes ache for it, the balls of my eyes in their sockets, hungry and aching for this, my God how I want that house and that man, whoever he is.

I am thinking of the months I went back to high school, to night school, making up for what I had missed. It was then I began to dream about my future. I went through school, I made up for the months I was crazy. I did it. But how do you fall in love? I heard Ma say to a friend of hers that there was nothing in life but men, nothing but love. "Jesus, when you come right down to it, what else is there?" she said in her flat, amused voice, as if she'd gone through everything and had to admit this truth. But how do you fall in love? I am thinking of Ma throwing things around the kitchen, drunk, crying, her face twisted ugly and the words ugly coming out of her mouth, when some man let her down—they were always letting her down, poor Ma, and she was kind of a pretty woman. Why did she open herself up to that pain? Again and again she opened herself up.

I am going to fall in love. Tomorrow night I'll see the man I have picked out to love. He is already married; he has three children. I want him. I want him to marry me. I am going to make this happen and begin my life. We will have a bedroom together, we will have children, he will leave his own children behind. I am telling you these things even though you are a married woman and would not want any other woman to take your husband from you. But you are a married woman, I think, who would not mind taking someone else's husband, so long as it happened well enough, beautifully enough like a story. Once in a while, though, I don't believe my life will change. I don't believe he will marry me or even think of me. I don't believe something so strange could happen. And I fall into a sad state and can't get out of it. I lean forward and my head droops between my shoulders, my bones seem to turn helpless, I think *Why didn't I die? Why didn't he kill me?* For thirteen months I was an animal. Ma uses other words, she says I was "going through a phase," but I remember it all, I know. Never did I think anything in those months, but pictures floated through my mind, like a nightmare. Even when I was awake I was asleep. Even now, sitting in this library with time ahead of me, so much dangerous time, I feel in my arms and legs a strange soft sensation which is like a memory itself. I can't get such memories out of my body. I felt no love for those men but I put my arms around them. They entered my body in its most secret place, those strangers, and the space between us was only a slick surface of skin and sweat. Is it different with love? What is it like to give yourself with love? Or do you lie there and feel terror to know that, love or not, a husband or a stranger, it is all the same and no words can change it? I was never in love. They did not love me. They embraced me again and again; in my mind I will alway see a man embracing a girl who is me. I can see a man's hands upon her body but the bodies are strangers. I can't get rid of this memory. My body is like the body of an animal, or one of those things that are just one cell, very tiny, that keep everything in them of all their history and are always the same age, I mean in any century, at the time when Christ was alive or right now those things are always the same things, the memory is hard in them and it has nothing to do with their brains. I remember. I will live very long and remember.

So I came back. I woke up. I finished high school, I moved out of my mother's place, I worked as a typist and got a room near a bus stop, I enrolled at the University of Detroit for one course in Fall, 1963, Composition, Mr. Kovack gave me a D. I enrolled for another course, yours. I came to class, I listened to you, I lay awake nights thinking of how I must not fail, how I must get a C in this course, how I must take hold of myself become like other people. But I did fail anyway, you failed me. You gave me an F.

You failed me.

That year at the University of Detroit was strange for me. During the day I worked. Three other typists, myself, a secretary. Downtown. I took the bus both ways. I hated it. I sat by myself. I was afraid but I kept on. I didn't look for another job. I didn't go anywhere except to work and to school. I didn't dare go to the movies. I was afraid of those first few minutes when you can't see well in a theater. At night, from seven until eight-thirty, two nights a week, I took a course at college. I tried to look like other girls. By then I had lost weight, my face had cleared up. I washed my face twice a day. I put cold cream on it, I did everything to it, and the face you saw, if you bothered to see it, was a nice face again. I bought shoes and clothes like the other girls. I put my hair up in rollers. I washed it all the time. I was a pretty girl. Now, at twenty-six, I think I am prettier. I deserve to fall in love and be married. In those days I didn't dare to think about anything so distant, it was enough just to get through a day without breaking down. I never thought of marriage. I was afraid of men. What I envied in you was your easy way with men, the way you talked to them, like friends, other teachers I saw you with in the hall, friends with men? I didn't think that a woman could be friends with any man. One day before class I saw you walking to the building with a man, a professor like yourself, a tall handsome man with gray hair, very well dressed, the two of you talking, smiling, like it was no accomplishment, and the two of you not seeing me, and another time I saw you, in a black Volkswagen, your husband driving you to school, coming up the driveway, your husband.

Everything in me aches for a husband. A house.

I carried this ache in me all my life, not knowing what it was. Everybody is flawed with it, a crack running through them. In you it is filled in for a while. You feel no pain. I know you feel no pain right now. I don't envy you or want to be like you, I only want to escape the doom of being *Maureen Wendall* all of my life. I dream of a world where you can go in and out of bodies, changing your soul, everything changing and not fixed forever, becoming men and women, daughters, children again, even old people, feeling how it is to be them and then not hating them, out on the street. I don't want to hate. There are too many strangers. I am writing this to a stranger, writing in a library about to close. You, the stranger, my ex-teacher who failled me, are reading this as fast as you can, you're impatient with it. You don't want people to make claims on you. I know. I don't blame you or judge anybody. You said, "Literature gives form to life,"[6] I remember you saying that very clearly. What is form? Why is it better than the way life happens, by itself? I hate all that, all those lies, so many words in all those books.

What I like to read in this library is newspapers. I want to know. The old man is reading a newspaper, so is the man with the runny nose. Like me they want to find out what's going on, what is real. They don't have time in their lives for made-up things. But I remember you saying that about form. *Form.* I don't know what that word means. Maybe my brother Jules would know. I don't know. I myself am a certain form, a shape, sitting here with my head emptied out and afraid, that is all.

In the hospital, after her husband beat me up, a doctor was trying to take blood out of me. I was conscious. He had a big needle and was poking in my arm for a vein. He couldn't find it. He took the needle out and put it in again, poking for a vein, and he squeezed my wrist to make the vein swell so he could get inside it, but still that didn't work, so he tried my other arm, holding my arm out now because I was crying. I keep thinking of that, the needle going in and trying to find my vein, the doctor, a man, poking in my arm for a vein and not finding it. I would have made the vein big and soft for him if I could, but how can you do that? Finally he got the blood. He said, "She's got to have a Wasserman," to someone, not talking to me. I would make myself open and ready for love but how can you do that, how can you change yourself?

It is almost closing time in the library.

There is no end to this.

What form is there to the way things happen? I wanted to run up to you after class and ask that question, cry it out at you. Your words were wrong! You were wrong! One day the secretary at work ran in our office. She said to us, "My God, the President was shot! the President was shot!" Mandy, the girl next to me, jumped up and knocked some papers off her desk. They all began asking questions. The radio was on in the next room. Our boss came in, he was very upset. I straightened up the papers and while I was bent over my mind ran along as fast as a train, thinking, *There is something happening here I should understand.* In the restroom Mandy was crying and I didn't want to look at her, those tears, her shoulders that were shaking. I said to her, "But people die every day. Right here in Detroit they get shot like that." Some terrible invisible thing was passing close by me. What was it? Why couldn't I understand? Out on the street people were strange, all upset. I wanted to run up to them, grab their arms, I wanted to shout, "But why? Why? Why is everything stopped? Why now? What has happened? What is it?"

When I got to school that night everybody was talking about it. Some girls were crying. A boy made a joke about Mrs. Kennedy's pink wool suit, something about strawberry jam. The girls drew back from him, making faces. I sat alone by myself, alone, silent. But people die every day, I thought. Who was John Kennedy that he couldn't die? A bullet entered his skull in a certain way and what was inside that skull was ruined. It will happen to us someday. It has already happened to some of us, and it is happening right now in Detroit. A girl said, very excited, "Did you hear about some professor in Finance? I think it was Finance。 He came into class and said, 'Thank God somebody had the guts to do it!' That's what he said, right to the class." The girls exclaimed over this, shaking their heads. One of the boys laughed. I touched my face to see how my skin felt, hoping no one would look at me, hoping they wouldn't find out my secret.

A few minutes to nine. The librarian switches the lights off and on, to warn us. Time to get up get going. Put on your overshoes. It will be very cold outside. The man with the runny nose looks up, surprised. Is he afraid? Nowhere to go? He has a pale, pouchy, freckled face and a rumpled shirt. Better not look at him. The clock hand jumps another minute, the old man folds up his newspaper with care, returns it to the shelf. So much for that day. His hands are fastidious. He lingers there, arranging other newspapers into piles. By the radiator the woman sighs a sigh I cna hear across the room, pushes a magazine away from her as if pushing a plate away, stares at the table top. And I, I am sitting with my heart beating steady and slow, writing all this down out of hate, because it seems to me now that it's you I hate, my ex-teacher, a woman, but that's crazy because I din't know you and I didn't do any work for you, maybe I could have passed the course and maybe not, how was it your fault?

But yes. I hate you and no one else, not even those men, not even Furlong. [7] I hate you and that is the only certain thing in me. Not love for the man I want to marry but hate for you. Hate for you, with your books and words and your knowing so much that never happened, in a perfect form, you being driven to school by your husband, and now there are even photographs of you in the paper sometimes, you with your knowledge while I've lived a lifetime already and turned myself inside out and got nothing out if it, not a thing. I don't know anything now, anything more than I knew before. Those men taught me nothing. I don't even hate them. I lived my life but there is no form to it. No shape. All the people who lie alone at night squirm with hatred they can't get straight, into a shape, all the women who give themselves to men without knowing who those men are, all of us walk fast with hate like pain in our bowels, terrified, and what do you know about it? You write books. What do you know?

The woman by the radiator gets to her feet. She is heavy, she seems pained when she stands: thick cream-colored fatmarbled old legs, poor legs, veins cracking and rising to the surface, a woman of middle-age. Oh, we women know things you don't know, you teachers, you readers and writers of books, we are the ones who wait around libraries when it's time to leave, or sit drinking coffee alone in the kitchen; we make crazy plans for marriage but have no man, we dream of stealing men, we are the ones who look slowly around when we get off a bus and can't even find what we are looking for, can't quite remember how we got there, we are always wondering what will come next, what terrible thing will come next. We are the ones who leaf through magazines with colored pictures and spend long leavy hours sunk in our bodies, thinking, remembering, dreaming, waiting for something to come to us and give a shape to so much pain.

〔注释〕

1. 这是莫琳写给大学教师欧茨的一封信。

2. Jules：朱尔斯，小说的男主人公。

3. *Madame Bovary*：《包法利夫人》，法国小说家福楼拜（Gustave Flaubert，1821～80）的代表作，发表于1857年。

4. I was crazy for thirteen months：指莫琳卖淫被发现遭继父毒打而昏迷一事。详见小说第1部第15、16两章及第2部第1章。

5. Ma hints…town：指Brock多年前杀死其妹Loretta的情人Bernie Malin一事。详见小说第1部第1、2两章。

6. Literature gives form to life：文学赋予生活以形式。西方现代文学评论认为，现代生活杂乱无章、没有意义，文学的作用之一在于给予生活的秩序、形式和意义。

7. Furlong：莫琳的继父.

TONI MORRISON

〔作者介绍〕

托尼·莫瑞森（Toni Morrison，1931～ ），美国当代杰出的黑人女作家，是继兰斯顿·休斯、理查德·赖特和拉尔夫·埃里森之后美国黑人文学的重要继承人。托尼·莫瑞森原名科洛·安东尼·沃福德（Chloe Anthony Wofford），出生在俄亥俄州北部罗伦城一个种族仇恨很深的黑人家庭里。祖父约翰·所罗门·威利斯是美国内战时期的奴隶，他始终不信任白人，认为白人基本上是一个堕落的种族。父亲是一个体力劳动者，为了养家，不得不同时兼做3种工作，这种情况长达17年之久。中学毕业后，莫瑞森进了专为黑人开办的霍华德大学（在首都华盛顿），她学习成绩优异，并成为该校戏剧活动积极分子。1953年进康乃尔大学研究生院，攻读文学，1955年获硕士学位。她曾先后在南得克萨斯大学和霍华德大学任教，直至1964年。在华盛顿期间，她与牙买加藉建筑设计师哈罗德·莫瑞森结婚。60年代初，莫瑞森开始写作。1962年，她在霍华德大学参加一个由教师组成的创作小组。他们每月活动一次，规定每人必须朗读一篇自己的作品。莫瑞森写了一个短篇小说，颇得好评。后来她就以此故事为基础完成了她的第1部长篇小说《最蓝的眼睛》(*The Bluest Eye*，1970)。这是关于一个黑人小女孩佩克拉的故事。她渴望象童星秀兰·邓波儿一样，有一双象征骄傲与尊严的蓝色大眼睛。她每天夜里祈祷，后来，她的梦想神奇般地实现了，她高兴得要飞起来。但是这双眼睛并没有给她带来幸福，她被自己的亲生父亲奸污后，陷进更加痛苦的深渊。

莫瑞森的第2部部长篇小说《秀拉》(*Sula*，1973) 塑造了一个具有反抗性格的黑人妇女秀拉的形象，在美国文学界引起很大反响，曾被提名参加1975年全国图书奖评选。

1977年《所罗门之歌》(*Song of Solomon*) 的问世，牢固地确立了莫瑞森在当代美国文学中的地位。

《柏油孩子》(*Tar Baby*) 于1981年问世，这部小说用象征手法描写了种族问题。

莫瑞森的第五部长篇小说《爱女》(*Beloved*, 1987) 是她文学创作生涯中新的里程碑，在文学界和读者中引起强烈反响，获1988年普利策文学奖。约翰·伦那德在《洛杉矶时报》上撰文说："《爱女》是托尼·莫瑞森的最好的一部小说，成就辉煌，在今后10年内它将成为最引人入胜的一部书。"

托尼·莫瑞森在创作上一直在探索自己的艺术道路和风格。她不满足于一般作家所遵循的社会现实主义的创作方法，常把黑人的神话和民间传说融进作品当中，运用象征手法揭示、剖析存在于美国社会的种族问题。她塑造了一系列在逆境中苦苦抗争的黑人妇女形象。她熟练地运用黑人语言和对话，阅读她的作品时读者好象置身于浓郁的黑人文化传统和风俗之中。莫瑞森的创作道路代表了美国黑人文学发展的新方向。

Song of Solomon

〔作品介绍〕

《所罗门之歌》(*Song of Solomon*, 1977) 是托尼·莫瑞森的第三部长篇小说，美国文学界和读者对这部作品给予很高评价，它是继理查德·赖特的《土生子》和拉尔夫·埃里森的《看不见的人》之后又一部优秀黑人小说，于1978年被评为美国文学艺术协会和全国图书奖。这部小说的出版标志着莫瑞森的文学创作已经走向成熟。

小说以30年代密执安州某小镇上的一个黑人家庭为线索，展示自美国内战至本世纪60年代近100年间黑人的历史，它一方面描写了生活在白人世界里的黑人的悲惨境遇，更主要的是揭示了黑人社会内部错综复杂的矛盾现象，其中包括以经济地位为标志的两极分化；作为社会问题而反映在家庭内部的夫妻关系、兄妹关系和两代人之间的隔阂；在种族制度下的黑人对自己的文明历史的怀念和对自由的渴望与追求。

美国内战结束以后，黑奴麦肯·代德获得自由，与印第安女子辛厄成婚，生下一男一女，即小麦肯·代德和帕立特。麦肯·代德被白人庄园主打死，他辛苦经营16年的土地也被抢去。麦肯死后，小麦肯和帕立特因为在山洞里发现一袋金子而发生争执，从此兄妹结下仇恨，各奔东西。小麦肯来到密执安，在大湖边一个小镇上落脚，与当地唯一的黑人医生的独生女儿鲁思结婚，生下二女一男，男孩名叫奶娃，即本书的主人公。小麦肯经营房产业，是一个自私、贪婪、对穷苦黑人毫无怜悯之心的人。他相信"金钱才是自由……是世界上唯一真正的自由"。他教育儿子去"占有财产，再让财产去占有别的财产，然后你才能占有自己，也才能占有别人。"！不论就他的经济地位或他的处世哲学来来看，他已经成为黑人中的剥削阶级。

在家庭关系上，他阴鸷多疑，无端怀疑妻子和她父亲乱伦。当鲁思的父亲病重时，他把药品扔掉，使其不得医治而死。

帕立特和小麦肯分手后，四处流浪20余载，受尽侮辱，最后也来到小麦肯居住的地方。母女三人以卖酒为生，自己养活自己。20多年来，帕立特完全被社会抛弃，过着孤独的生活。她没有婚姻与家庭生活，没有友谊，没有宗教信仰。人们歧视她，当众羞辱她，但是当她认清自己在这个世界上的处境以及将来的处境时，她就不再一切全凭想当然，她决定从头做起。首先，她剪了短发，往后就不必为头发费心思了。然后，她开始考虑自己应该如何生活，考虑什么对她最有价值。"我什么时候幸福？什么时候忧伤？二者之间有什么区别？为了活下去我需要明白些什么？世界上什么才是真实的？"通过多年来对这些问题的思索，她产生了一个信念：既然死不能使她感到害怕，再没有什么可怕的。再有，她对不幸的人们，特别是对苦难的黑人所持的同情心，使她成为一个具有完整的人格和刚毅性格的黑人妇女的典型。

小麦肯仍然把帕立特视为蛇一般的坏人，因为他认定她独吞了他们20多年前在南方的山洞里共同发现的金子。当他得知金子不在她手里时，他便叫奶娃一人去南方的山洞里寻找。结果金子没有找到，他们却经过多方查访，找到了自己祖先的踪迹。原来黑人民歌中传唱的会飞的所罗门就是奶娃的曾祖父，所罗门的小儿子杰克就是他的祖父，即前面提到的麦肯·代德。当他把这个新发现告诉帕立特以后，他们一起来到南方，重新埋葬了杰克的尸骨。此时跟踪而来的吉它——奶娃的朋友——向奶娃开枪射击，误将帕立特打死，奶娃一跃而起，腾空向吉它飞去。至于奶娃是去和吉它撕杀还是拥抱，是谁死谁活，这似乎并不重要，重要的是如小说结尾所说的那句话，"假如你依附于大气，你就能驾御它"。这时的奶娃已经从祖先和广大黑人群众那里获取了新的知识和智慧，思想感情发生了深刻的变化，因而变成一个会飞的人，即自由的人。

作为牵动小说发展的中心人物，奶娃的性格经历了一个比较复杂的发展过程，在书中描写的人物里，有两个人对他的成长起了重要作用——吉它和帕立特。

奶娃生在富有的房产主家庭里，在父亲的影响下，他自私、保守，对黑人的疾苦熟视无睹。吉它出身贫苦，对穷苦人黑人富有同情心。在种族问题上他表现激进。他加入黑人复仇组织"七日社"，对白人采取"以其人之道还制其人之身"的手段。当他说他这样做不是出于对白人的恨，而是出于对黑人的爱时，奶娃并不理解，这是存在于他们之间的根本分岐。当奶娃来到南方，在宾州的丹维尔和弗吉尼亚的萨里马尔接触了众多黑人男女老幼之后，他发现那里的人民虽然贫穷落后，但他们仍然按照黑人传统的方式生活，保持黑人的风俗习惯。老人们讲述着动人的传说，天真的儿童唱着美丽的民谣，歌颂他自己的祖先。他为自己有这样的祖先、黑人有这样丰富的历史和文化而感到骄傲和自豪。只有这时，他才开始对所说的“爱”有了认识。

另一个对他影响较大的人物是帕立特，她的坎坷经历使他不但懂得正视现实，也使他学会思考过去；帕立特教育他不要躲避责任，而是要对自己的行为负责；不是对人无动于衷，而是要尊重别人、爱别人。伊利莎白·舒尔兹教授在谈及奶娃的成长时说“只有牺牲生命才能发现生命；只有丢弃财产、恐惧和虚荣才能找到自我并获得自由与爱的能力”。

小说的布局与结构错综复杂，但情节前后照应，脉落清晰，反映了作者娴熟的写作技巧。书中多运用神话和民间传说以及形象的手法，歌颂黑人悠久的历史与文化，深刻地鞭笞种族主义的罪恶。从前的黑人作家多以现实主义和自然主义的手法描写黑人在白人统治的社会中的际遇，其作品唤起的是忧伤、愤懑和仇恨。《所罗门之歌》所唤起的是黑人对自己种族的骄傲与自豪以及他们对自由与幸福这些美好理想的憧憬和追求。

本书共分 2 部 15 章，这里选注的是第 12 章。

Song of Solomon

CHAPTER XII

At four o'clock he knocked on the door of the only house back of the ridge with a brick front. Fresh and shining in the army fatigues Sweet[1] had washed and pressed, he had tramped along feeling ready for anything. But he didn't think Guitar would jump him in the daytime on a winding path (which they called a road) that cut through hilly land that was nevertheless tilled and had a smattering of houses and people. If he did confront him (with anything other than a gun) Milkman was sure he could take him, but it would be best to get back before nightfall. He didn't know what was on Guitar's mind, but he knew it had something to do with the gold. If he knows I'm here and where I have been and what I did in each place, then he must know that I'm trying to get it, doing just what I said I would do. Why would he try to kill me before I got it or even found out what happened to it?[2] Most of it was a total mystery to him, but the part that was clear was enough to keep him alert and jittery all the way.

The Byrd[3] house sat on a neat lawn separated by a white picket fence from the field grass on either side of the property. A child's swing dangled from a cedar tree; four little steps painted blue led up to the porch, and from the window, between fluttering curtains, came the smell of gingerbread baking.

A woman who looked to be about his mother's age answered the door.

"Miss Byrd?" Milkman asked her.

"Yes?"

"How are you? My name is, uh, Macon, and I'm visiting here for a few days. I'm from Michigan and I think some of my people lived here a long time ago. I was hoping you'd be able to help me."

"Help you what?" She sounded arch and Milkman had the distinct impression that this lady did not like the color of his skin.

"Find them. I mean find out about them. We're all split up, my family, and some folks in town thought you might know some of them."

"Who's that, Susan?" Another woman's voice came from behind her.

"Somebody to see *me*, Grace."

"Well, why don't you ask him in? Don't make him state his business on the steps."

Miss Byrd sighed. "Please come in, Mr. Macon."

Milkman followed her into a pleasant living room full up with sunshine. "Excuse me," She said. "I didn't mean to be rude. Please have a seat." She motioned to a gray velvet wing—back chair. A woman in a two-piece print dress came into the room, clutching a paper napkin in her hand and chewing on something.

"Who'd you say?" She addressed her question to Miss Byrd, but ran inquisitive eyes over Milkman.

Miss Byrd held out a hand. "This is a friend of mine—Miss Long. Grace Long—Mr. . . ."

"How do you do?" Grace held out her hand to him.

"Fine, thank you."

"Mr. Macon, is it?"

"Yes."

"Susan, perhaps Mr. Macon would like some refreshment." Miss Long smiled and sat on the sofa facing the gray chair.

"Well, he just stepped foot in the door, Grace. Give me time." Miss Byrd turned to Milkman. "Would you like a cup of coffee on some tea?"

"Sure. Thanks."

"Which one?"

"Coffee's all right."

"You've got butter cookies, Susan. Give him some of those butter cookies."

Miss Byrd gave her friend a tired frown. "I'll just be a minute," she said to Milkman, and left the room.

"Yes, well. Did I hear you say you were visiting in these parts? We don't see too many visitors." Grace crossed her ankles. Like Susan Byrd, she wore black laced shoes and cotton stockings. As she made herself comfortable, she inched her dress up a little.

"Yes, visiting."

"You in the service?"

"Ma'am? Oh, no. I was hunting last night. Some friends lent me these." He smoothed the seam Sweet had made in the fatigues.

"Hunting? Oh, Lord, don't tell me you're one of them. I can't stand those hunting people. They make me sick, always prowling round other people's property. Day and night they're shooting up the world. I tell my students—I'm a schoolteacher, you know, I teach over at the normal school. Have you seen it yet?"

"No, not yet."

"Well, there's nothing to see, really. Just a school, like any other. But you're welcome to stop by. We'd be pleased to have you. Where you from again?"

"Michigan."

"I thought so. Susan!" She turned around. "He's from up North." Then back to Milkman: "Where are you staying?"

"Well, nowhere yet. I just met a few people in town and..."

Susan Byrd came in with a tray of coffee cups and a plate of wide pale cookies.

"He's from Michigan," said Grace.

"I heard him. How do you take your coffee?"

"Black."

"Black? No cream or sugar at all?" asked Grace. "Wish I could do that; maybe I could get back into a twelve. But it's never going to happen now." She pressed one hand on her hip and smiled at Mikman.

"What did you want to see me about?" Susan Byrd placed a mild but clear stress on the word "me."

"I'm trying to locate anybody who might have known my grandmother. Her name was Sing."

Grace clapped her hands to her mouth and gave a little squeal. "Relatives! You all are relatives!" Milkman put his cup down. "Well, I'll be!" Grace's eyes were lit and dancing.

"You've come to the right place," said Susan, "but I doubt if I can help you any."

"What are you talking about, Susan? Your mother was named Sing, wasn't she?"

"No, she wasn't, Grace, and if you let me finish a sentence you might learn something you don't know too."

"I thought you said—"

"My mother's name was Mary. *M-a-r-y*, Mary."

"Well, excuse *me*."

Susan turned to Milkman. "My father, Crowell Byrd, had a sister named Sing."[4]

"That must be her! My grandmother! Sing. Did she marry a man named—"

"I knew there was somebody in your family named Sing!"

"She didn't marry anybody that I know of." Susan interrupted them both.

"Oh, this is really something. A stranger walks right into your house and he's your own... what? Cousin? I hate to say it, but this is a small world. Isn't it? You have got to visit my class, Mr. Macon."

Milkman joined Susan Byrd in ignoring Grace Long. "Where did she live?" he asked her.

"The last time my father saw her, she was on a wagon headed for Massachusetts to a private school up there. A Quaker school."

"Your people Quakers? You never told me that. See, Mr. Macon, what your friends hide from you? I bet she'd hide you too."

"And she never married?" Milkman couldn't take the time to acknowledge Grace's attentions.

"Not anybody we heard of. After she went to that Quaker school they lost track of her. I believe they tried to locate her, mostly because my grandmother—her name was Heddy—she was so torn up about it. I always believed the same thing my father believed: that she didn't want to be found after she left that school."

"You know darn well she didn't," said Grace. "She probably started passing[5] like the rest of 'em, that's what." She leaned toward Milkman. "There used to be a lot of that. A lot of it. Not so much nowadays, but there used to be a lot of 'em did it—if they could." She shot a glance at Susan. "Like your cousins, Susan. They're passing now. Lilah, John. I know John is, and he knows I know he is."

"Everybody knows that, Grace."

"Mr. Macon doesn't know it. I saw John on the street in Mayville—"

"Mr. Macon doesn't need to know it. He's not even interested."

"How do you know he's not?"

"Because he said the woman he's looking for was his grandmother, and if she's his grandmother she'd be too dark to..." Susan Byrd hesitated. "Well, too dark to pass. Wouldn't she?" She flushed a little.

Milkman ignored the question. "And you say she lived in Massachusetts, right?"

"Yes. Boston."

"I see." It looked like a dead end, so he decided to follow another line. "Did you ever know or hear of a woman around here named Pilate?"

"Pilate. No. Never. Have you, Grace?"

Grace shook her head. "No, and I've been here most of my life."

"I've been here *all* of mine," said Susan. "Both my parents were born here and so was I. Never been farther away than St. Phillips County. I have people in South Carolina, but I've never even been to visit them."

"That's because they're passing too. Just like John. You couldn't visit them if you wanted to." Grace leaned over the plate of cookies and selected one.

"They're not the only family I have left." Susan was indignant.

"I hope not. It's a sad thing, Mr. Macon, when you're left without any people to claim you. I keep up with my family. I'm not married, you know, not yet anyway, but my family is *very* close." She gave him a meaningful look. Milkman turned his wrist and looked down to see what time it was.

"Oh, look at that." Grace pointed to his hand. "What a good-looking watch. May I see it?" Milkman stood up to hand it to her and remained standing. "Look, Susan, it doesn't have a single number on it. Just dots. Now, how can anybody figure out what time it is from those dots?"

Susan rose too. "You ever been down here before, Mr. Macon?"

"No. This is my first visit."

"Well, I hope it won't be your last. How long will you be here?"

"Oh, I think I'll get on back tonight or tomorrow at the latest." He looked out the window. The sun was dropping.

"That soon?" asked Grace. "Why don't you give him something to take with him, Susan? Would you like to take some butter cookies with you, Mr. Macon?"

"No, thank you."

"You'll be happy to have them later." The woman was wearing him down. He smiled, though, and said, "If you like."

"I'll fix a little package for you. Okay, Susan?" She fled from the room.

Susan managed a small smile. "Wish you could stay and visit with us awhile." Her words were as mechanical as her smile.

"So do I," he said, "but, well, maybe I'll be back."

"That'd be nice. Sorry I couldn't be of any help to you."

"You have been."

"Have I?"

"Oh, sure. You have to know what's wrong before you can find what's right."

She smiled a genuine smile then. "It's important to you, is it, to find your people?"

Milkman thought about it. "No. Not really. I was just passing through, and it was just—just an idea. It's not important."

Grace returned with a little parcel wrapped in white paper napkins. "Here you are," she said. "You'll appreciate this later on."

"Thank you. Thank you both."

"Nice meeting you."

"And you."

He left the house feeling tired and off center. I'll spend one more night here and then leave, he thought. The car should be fixed by now. There's nothing here to know, no gold or any traces of it. Pilate lived in Virginia, but not in this part of the state. Nobody at all has heard of her. And the Sing that lived here went to Boston, not Danville, Pennsylvania, and passed for white. His grandmother would have been "too dark to pass." She had actually blushed. As though she'd discovered something shameful about him. He was both angry and amused and wondered what Omar and Sweet and Vernell[6] thought of Miss Susan Byrd.

He was curious about these people. He didn't feel close to them, but he did feel connected, as though there was some cord or pulse or information they shared.[7] Back home he had never felt that way, as though he belonged to anyplace or anybody. He'd always considered himself the outsider in his family, only vaguely involved with his friends, and except for Guitar, there was no one whose opinion of himself he cared about. Once, long ago, he had cared what Pilate and Hagar thought of him, but having conquered Hagar[8] and having disregarded Pilate enough to steal from her,[9] all that was gone. But there was something he felt now—here in Shalimar, and earlier in Danville—that reminded him of how he used to feel in Pilate's house. Sitting in Susan Byrd's living room, lying with Sweet, eating with those men at Vernell's table, he didn't have to get over, to turn on, or up, or even out.

And there was something more. It wasn't true what he'd said to Susan Byrd: that it wasn't important to find his people. Ever since Danville, his interest in his own people, not just the ones he met, had been growing. Macon Dead, also known as Jake somebody. Sing. Who were they, and what were they like? The man who sat for five nights on a fence with a gun, waiting.[10] Who named his baby girl Pilate, who tore a farm out of a wilderness. The man who ate pecans on a wagon going North. Did he have brothers or sisters whom he left behind? Who was his mother, his father? And his wife. Was she the Boston Sing? If so, what was she doing on a wagon? Why would she go off to a northern private school on a wagon? Not a carriage or a train, but a wagon—full of ex-slaves. Maybe she never got to Boston. Maybe she didn't pass. She could have changed her mind about school and run off with the boy she ate pecans with. And whoever she was, why did she want her husband to keep that awful name? To wipe out the past? What past? Slavery? She was never a slave. *His* slave past? And why didn't his own father, and Pilate, know any of their own relatives? Wasn't there any family to notify when the father died? Macon didn't ever try to get to Virginia. Pilate headed straight for it.

Milkman opened the parcel Grace had fixed for him and took out a cookie. A little piece of paper fluttered to the ground. He picked it up and read: "Grace Long 40 Route 2 three houses down from the Normal School." He smiled. That's why it took her so long to wrap up four cookies. He bit into one of them and sauntered along, crumpling the napkins and Grace's invitation into a wad. The questions about his family still knocked around in his head like billiard balls. If his grandfather, this Jake, was born in the same place his wife was, in Shalimar, why did he tell the Yankee he was born in Macon, thereby providing him with the raw material for the misnaming? And if he and his wife were born in the same place, why did Pilate and his father and Circe all say they "met" on that wagon? And why did the ghost tell Pilate to sing? Milkman chuckled to himself. That wasn't what he was telling her at all; maybe the ghost was just repeating his wife's name, Sing, and Pilate didn't know it because she never knew her mother's name. After she died Macon Dead wouldn't let anybody say it aloud. That was funny. He wouldn't speak it after she died, and after he died that's all he ever said—her name.

Jesus! Here he was walking around in the middle of the twentieth century trying to explain what a ghost had done. But why not? he thought. One fact was certain: Pilate did not have a navel. [11] Since that was true, anything could be, and why not ghosts as well?

He was near the road leading to the town now, and it was getting dark. He lifted his wrist to look at his watch and remembered that Grace had not given it back to him. "Damn," he murmured aloud. "I'm losing everything." He stood still, trying to make up his mind whether to go back for it now or later. If he went now, he'd be forced to return in deep darkness. Totally defenseless before a hit from Guitar. But it would be a real bother to have to come all the way back here—where no car could make it—tomorrow when he was going to leave. But Guitar might be—

"I can't let him direct and determine what I do, where I go or when. If I do that now I'll do it all my life and he'll run me off the earth."

He didn't know what to do, but decided finally that a watch was not worth worrying about. All it could do was tell him the time of day and he really wasn't interested. Wiping cookie crumbs from his mustache, he turned into the main road, and there, outlined in cobalt blue, stood Guitar. Leaned, rather, against a persimmon tree. Milkman stopped, surprised at the calm, steady beat of his heart—the complete absence of fear. But then Guitar was cleaning his fingernails with a harmless match stick. Any weapon he had would have to be hidden in his denim jacket or pants.

They looked at each other for a minute. No, less. Just long enough for the heart of each man to adjust its throb to the downbeat of the other. Guitar spoke first.

"My man."

Milkman ignored the greeting. "Why, Guitar? Just tell me why."

"You took the gold."

"What gold? There wasn't any gold."

"You took the gold."

"The cave was empty, man. I got down on my stomach and looked in that pit. I put my hands—"

"You took the gold."

"You're crazy, Guitar."

"Angry. Never crazy."

"There wasn't any gold!" Milkman tried hard not to shout.

"I saw you, motherfucker."

"Saw me what?"

"Take the gold."

"Where?"

"In Danville."

"You saw me with gold in Danville?"

"I saw you with gold in Danville."

"You've got to be kidding. What was I doing with it?"

"Shipping it."

"Shipping it?"

"Yeah. Why the game, man? You just greedy, like your old man? Or what?" Guitar's eyes rested on the last butter cookie in Milkman's hand. He frowned and began to breathe through his lips.

"Guitar, I didn't ship no gold. There wasn't any gold to ship. You couldn't have seen me."

"I saw you, baby. I was in the station."

"What fuckin station?"

"The freight station in Danville."

Milkman remembered then, going to look for Reverend Cooper, looking all over for him. Then going into the station house to see if he'd gone, and there helping a man lift a huge crate onto the weighing platform. He started to laugh. "Oh, shit. Guitar, that wasn't no gold. I was just helping that man lift a crate. He asked me to help him. Help him lift a big old crate. I did and then I split."

Guitar looked at the cookie again, then back into Milkman's eyes. Nothing changed in his face. Milkman knew it sounded lame. It was the truth, but it sounded like a lie. A weak lie too. He also knew that in all his life, Guitar had never seen Milkman give anybody a hand, especially a stranger; he also knew that they'd even discussed it, starting with Milkman's not coming to his mother's rescue in a dream he had. Guitar had accused him of selfishness and indifference; told him he wasn't serious, and didn't have any fellow feeling—none whatsoever. Now he was standing there saying that he willingly, spontaneously, had helpd an old white man lift a huge, heavy crate. But it was true. It was true. And he'd prove it.

"Guitar, why am I here? If I was shipping gold back home, why am I here dressed like this? Would I be roaming around in the country like a fool with a crate of gold off somewhere? Would I? What the fuck would I do that for and then come here?"

"Maybe you shipped the gold *here*, you jive—ass."

"What the fuck are you talking about?"

"I looked! I saw it! You hear me? I drove down there, followed you there, because I had a funny feeling that you were pulling a fast one. I wasn't sure, but I felt it. If I was wrong, I'd help you get it. But I wasn't wrong. I got into Danville that afternoon. I drove right past the freight depot and there you were in your little beige suit. I parked and followed you into the station. When I got there I saw you shipping it. Giving it to the man. I waited until you left, and I went back in and asked the cracker if my friend" —he slurred the word— "had shipped a crate to Michigan. The man said no. Just one crate on the load, he said. Just one crate. And when I asked him where it was going, all he could remember was Virginia." Guitar smiled. "The bus you caught wasn't headed for Michigan. It was headed for Virginia. And here you are."

Milkman felt whipped. There was nothing to do but let it play.

"Was my name on the crate?"

"I didn't look."

"Would I send a crate of gold to Virginia—*gold*, man."

"You might. You did."

"Is that why you tried to kill me?"

"Yes."

"Because I ripped you off?"

"Because you ripped *us* off! You are fuckin with our work!"

"You're wrong. Dead wrong."

"The 'dead' part is you."

Milkman looked down at the cookie in his hand. It looked foolish and he started to throw it away, but changed his mind. "So my Day has come?"

"Your Day has come, but on *my* schedule.[12] And believe it: I will run you as long as there is ground. Your name is Macon, but you ain't dead yet."[13]

"Tell me something. When you saw me in the station, with the crate, why did you back off and hide? Why didn't you just walk up to me? It could have been settled there."

"I told you. I had this funny funny feeling."

"That I was going to cut you out?"

"Cut *us* out. Yes."

"And you believe I did?"

"Yes."

"Back there in the woods you were angry."

"Yes."

"Now you're going to wait till the gold comes."

"Yes."

"And I pick it up."

"You won't be able to pick it up."

"Do me a favor. When it gets here. Check it first to see if there's gold in it."

"First?"

"Or last. But before you haul it all the way back home."

"Don't worry yourself about it."

"One more thing. Why the message? Why'd you warn me with a message at the store?"

"You're my friend. It's the least I could do for a friend."

"My man. I want to thank you."

"You're welcome, baby."

Milkman slipped into Sweet's bed and slept the night in her perfect arms. It was a warm dreamy sleep all about flying, about sailing high over the earth. But not with arms stretched out like airplane wings, nor shot forward like Superman in a horizontal dive, but floating, cruising, in the relaxed position of a man lying on a couch reading a newspaper. Part of his flight was over the dark sea, but it didn't frighten him because he knew he could not fall. He was alone in the sky, but somebody was applauding him, watching him and applauding. He couldn't see who it was.

When he awoke the next morning and set about seeing to the repair of his car, he couldn't shake the dream, and didn't really want to. In Solomon's store he found Omar and Solomon shaking sacks of okra into peck baskets and he still felt the sense of lightness and power that flying had given him.

"Got a belt for your car," said Omar, "Ain't new, but it ought to fit."

"Hey, that's good. Thanks, Omar."

"You leavin us right away?"

"Yeah, I have to get on back."

"You see that Byrd woman all right?"

"Yeah, I saw her."

"She help you any?" Omar wiped the okra fuzz from his hands onto his trousers.

"No. Not much."

"Well, King Walker say he be down this morning and put the belt on. You probably ought to get a good check up on that car once you get on the road."

"I plan to."

"Sweet give you any breakfast?" asked Solomon.

"She tried, but I wanted to get over here early to see about the car."

"What about a cup a coffee; there's a full pot in back."

"No, thanks. I think I'll walk around a little till he comes."

It was six-thirty in the morning and the town was bustling as though it were high noon. Life and business began early in the South so the coolest part of the day could be taken advantage of. People had already eaten, women had already washed clothes and were spreading them on bushes, and in a few days, when the school in the next town opened, children at this hour would already be walking, running over the roads and fields to class. Now they were sauntering about, doing chores, teasing cats, throwing bread to stray chickens, and some of them were playing their endless round games. Milkman could hear them singing and wandered off toward them and the huge cedar that reared up over their heads. Again their sweet voices reminded him of the gap in his own childhood, as he leaned against the cedar to watch them. The boy in the middle of the circle (it seemed always to be a boy) spun around with his eyes closed and his arm stretched out, pointing. Round and round he went until the song ended with a shout and he stopped, his finger pointing at a child Milkman could not see. Then they all dropped to their knees and he was surprised to hear them begin another song at this point, one he had heard off and on all his life. That old blues song Pilate sang all the time: "O Sugarman don't leave me here,"[14] except the children sang, "Solomon don't leave me here."

Milkman smiled, remembering Pilate. Hundreds of miles away, he was homesick for her, for her house, for the very people he had been hell-bent to leave. His mother's quiet, crooked, apologetic smile. Her hopeless helplessness in the kitchen. The best years of her life, from age twenty to forty, had been celibate, and aside from the consummation that began his own life, the rest of her life had been the same. He hadn't thought much of it when she'd told him, but now it seemed to him that such sexual deprivation would affect her, hurt her in precisely the way it would affect and hurt him. If it were possible for somebody to force him to live that way, to tell him, "You may walk and live among women, you may even lust after them, but you will not make love for the next twenty years," how would he feel? What would he do? Would he continue as he was? And suppose he were married and his wife refused him for fifteen years. His mother had been able to live through that by a long nursing of her son,[15] some occasional visits to a graveyard. What might she have been like had her husband loved her?

And his father. An old man[16] now, who acquired things and used people to acquire more things. As the son of Macon Dead the first, he paid homage to his own father's life and death by loving what that father had loved: property, good solid property, the bountifulness of life. He loved these things to excess. Owning, building, acquiring—that was his life, his future, his present, and all the history he knew. That he distorted life, bent it, for the sake of gain, was a measure of his loss at his father's death.

As Milkman watched the children, he began to feel uncomfortable. Hating his parents, his sisters, seemed silly now. And the skin of shame that he had rinsed away in the bathwater after having stolen from Pilate returned.[17] But now it was as thick and as tight as a caul. How could he have broken into that house—the only one he knew that achieved comfort without one article of comfort in it. No soft worn-down chair, not a cushion or a pillow. No light switch, no water running free and clear after a turn of a tap handle. No napkins, no tablecloth. No fluted plates or flowered cups, no circle of blue flame burning in a stove eye. But peace was there, energy, singing, and now his own remembrances.

His mind turned to Hagar and how he had treated her at the end. Why did he never sit her down and talk to her? Honestly. And what ugly thing was it he said to her the last time she tried to kill him?[18] And God, how hollow her eyes had looked. He was never frightened of her; he never actually believed that she would succeed in killing him, or that she really wanted to. Her weapons, the complete lack of cunning or intelligence even of conviction, in her attacks were enough to drain away any fear. Oh, she could have accidentally hurt him, but he could have stopped her in any number of ways. But he hadn't wanted to. He had used her—her love, her craziness—and most of all he had used her skulking, bitter vengeance. It made him a star, a celebrity in the Blood Bank,[19] it told men and other women that he was one bad dude, that he had the power to drive a woman out of her mind, to destroy her, and not because she hated him, or because he had done some unforgivable thing to her, but because he had fucked her and she was driven wild by the absence of his magnificent joint. His hog's gut, Lena[20] had called it. Even the last time, he used her. Used her imminent arrival and feeble attempt at murder as an exercise of his will against hers—an ultimatum to the universe. "Die, Hagar, die." Either this bitch dies or I do. And she stood there like a puppet strung up by a puppet master who had gone off to some other hobby.

O Solomon don't leave me here.

The children were starting the round again. Milkman rubbed the back of his neck. Suddenly he was tired, although the morning was still new. He pushed himself away from the cedar and sank to his haunches.

Jay the only son of Solomon
Come booba yalle, come. . .

Everybody in this town is named Solomon, he thought wearily. Solomon's General Store, Luther Solomon (no relation), Solomon's Leap, and now the children were singing "*Solomon* don't leave me" instead of "*Sugarman.*" Even the name of the town sounded like Solomon: Shalimar, which Mr. Solomon and everybody else pronounced *Shalleemone.*

Milkman's scalp began to tingle. Jay the only son of Solomon? Was that *Jake* the only son of Solomon? Jake. He strained to hear the children. That was one of the people he was looking for. A man named Jake who lived in Shalimar, as did his wife, Sing.

He sat up and waited for the children to begin the verse again. "Come booba yalle, come booba tambee," it sounded like, and didn't make sense. But another line— "Black lady fell down on the ground" —was clear enough. There was another string of nonsense words, then "Threw her body all around." Now the child in the center began whirling, spinning to lyrics sung in a different, faster tempo: "Solomon 'n' Reiner Belali Shalut. . ."

Solomon again, and Reiner? Ryna? Why did the second name sound so familiar? Solomon and Ryna. The woods. The hunt. Solomon's Leap and Ryna's Gulch, places they went to or passed by that night they shot the bobcat. [21] The gulch was where he heard that noise that sounded like a woman crying, which Calvin said came from Ryna's Gulch, that there was an echo there that folks said was "a woman name Ryna" crying. You could hear her when the wind was right.

But what was the rest: Belali... Shalut... Yaruba? If Solomon and Ryna were names of people, the others might be also. The verse ended in another clear line. "Twenty-one children, the last one *Jake!*" And it was at the shout of *Jake* (who was also, apparently, "the only son of Solomon") that the twirling boy stopped. Now Milkman understood that if the child's finger pointed at nobody, missed, they started up again. But if it pointed directly to another child, that was when they fell to their knees and sang Pilate's song. [22]

Milkman took out his wallet and pulled from it his airplane ticket stub, but he had no pencil to write with, and his pen was in his suit. He would just have to listen and memorize it. He closed his eyes and concentrated while the children, inexhaustible in their willingness to repeat a rhythmic, rhyming action game, performed the round over and over again. And Milkman memorized all of what they sang.

Jake the only son of Solomon
Come booba yalle, come booba tambee
Whirled about and touched the sun
Come konka yalle, come konka tambee

Left that baby in a white man's house
Come booba yalle, come booba tambee
Heddy took him to a red man's house
Come konka yalle, come konka tambee
Black lady fell down on the ground
Come booba yalle, come booba tambee
Threw her body all around
Come konka yalle, come konka tambee

Solomon and Ryna Belali Shalut
Yaruba Medina Muhammet too.

Nestor Kalina Saraka cake.
Twenty-one children, the last one Jake!

O Solomon don't leave me here
Cotton balls to choke me
O Solomon don't leave me here
Buckra's arms to yoke me

Solomon done fly, Solomon done gone
Solomon cut across the sky, Solomon gone home. [23]

He almost shouted when he heard "Heddy took him to a red man's house." Heddy was Susan Byrd's grandmother on her father's side, and therefore Sing's mother too. And "red man's house" must be a reference to the Byrds as Indians. Of course! Sing was an Indian or part Indian and her name was Sing Byrd or, more likely, Sing Bird. No—Singing Bird! That must have been her name originally—Singing Bird. And her brother, Crowell Byrd, was probably Crow Bird, or just Crow. They had mixed their Indian names with American-sounding names. Milkman had four people now that he could recognize in the song: Solomon, Jake, Ryna and Heddy, and a veiled reference to Heddy's Indianness. All of which seemed to put Jake and Sing together in Shalimar, just as Circe[24] had said they were. He couldn't be mistaken. These children were singing a story about his own people! He hummed and chuckled as he did his best to put it all together.

Jake's father was Solomon. Did Jake whirl about and touch the sun? Did Jake leave a baby in a white man's house? No. If the "Solomon don't leave me" line was right, Solomon was the one who left, who "flew away" —meaning died or ran off—not Jake. Maybe it was the baby, or Jake himself, who was begging him to stay. But who was the "black lady" who fell down on the ground? Why did she throw her body all around? It sounded like she was having a fit. Was it because somebody took her baby first to a white man's house, then to an Indian's house? Ryna? Was Ryna the black lady still crying in the gulch? Was Ryna Solomon's daughter? Maybe she had an illegitimate child, and her father—No. It's Solomon she is crying for, not a baby. "Solomon don't leave me." He must have been her lover.

Milkman was getting confused, but he was as excited as a child confronted with boxes and boxes of presents under the skirt of a Christmas tree. Somewhere in the pile was a gift for him.

Yet there were many many missing pieces. Susan Byrd, he thought—she would have to know more than she had told him. Besides, he had to get his watch back.

He ran back to Solomon's store and caught a glimpse of himself in the plate-glass window. He was grinning. His eyes were shining. He was as eager and happy as he had ever been in his life.

〔注释〕

1. Sweet：奶娃在萨里马尔寻访自己祖先时遇到的一个黑人妇女，奶娃曾住在她家，她热情地接待过他（见本书第 11 章）。

2. Why would he…what happned to it?：吉它和奶娃表面上是朋友，实际上，因为他们来自不同的社会阶层，吉它已经把奶娃看作敌人；吉它加入激进的黑人复仇组织“七日社”(Seven Days) 以后，他们在“爱”与“恨”的问题上有过激烈的争论，存在着很大的分歧；奶娃甩开吉它一个人到南方去取以为仍然藏在那里的金子，表现出他是一个自私贪婪的人，因此，吉它决定杀死他。当奶娃和萨里马尔村的猎人们一起在森林里打猎时，吉它已经向他开了冷枪。

3. Byrd：即 Susan Byrd，印第安妇女，她和奶娃是亲戚，是辛厄·伯德的哥哥克罗韦尔的女儿。

4. 辛厄·伯德和克罗韦尔·伯德都是印第安老妇人海地的孩子，即收养杰克（奶娃的祖父）的海地。

5. passing：指黑人或有黑人血统的人把自己当作白人。

6. Omar and Vernell：是奶娃在萨里马尔遇到的两个黑人村民。

7. He didn't feel close to them…they shared：指奶娃回到自己的祖先曾经生活过的地方以后思想感情的变化，过去是孤傲冷漠，现在开始有了人与人之间的感情，这是奶娃性格成长过程中的一个重要变化。

8. Hagar：帕立特的女儿，奶娃的情人。

9. and having disregarded Pilate enough to steal from her：奶娃和吉它曾在帕立特的酒店时发现一个绿色袋子，里面装着很硬的东西，小麦肯说那就是帕立特从南方猎人山洞里带回来的金子，叫他们两个去偷，结果那是一袋人的尸骨。当时帕立特并不知道那是她亲生父亲的尸骨。

10. The man who…waiting：此人即奶娃的祖父老麦肯，他为了保护自己的土地不被白人庄园主巴特勒抢去，持枪守护了 5 个夜晚。

11. Pilate did not have a navel：帕立特没有肚脐，她因此倍受歧视和侮辱。

12. Your Day has come, but on my schedule：吉它在“七日社”里分工专司在星期日对人进行报复，此句的意思是：你的死期已到，我将在星期日干掉你。

13. Your name is Macon, but you ain't dead yet：奶娃的全名也是 Macon Dead，吉它在这里暗示他要杀死奶娃。

14. “O Sugarman don't leave me here,”：帕立特在家里和女儿经常一起唱的一首布鲁斯歌曲，歌词是：

O Sugarman don't leave me here
Cotton balls to choke me
O Sugarman don't leave me here
Buchra's to yoke me....

Sugarman done fly away
Sugarman done gone
Sugarman cut across the sky
Sugarman gone home.

其大意和萨里马尔黑人儿童唱的歌一致。这里的 Sugarman 就是 Solomon，但帕立特并不知道她唱的 Sugarman 就是自己的祖父。

15. by a long nursing of her son：奶娃直到 4 岁还偎在母亲的怀里吃奶，所以人们叫他奶娃。

16. An old man：时值 1963 年，麦肯 72 岁。

17. And the skin of shame…as tight as a caul. 指奶娃曾从帕立特家中偷出一个绿色的袋子，小麦肯以为那里面装着金子，当奶娃发现那是一袋尸骨时，他感到羞耻。现在他来到祖先生活的地方，来到祖藉的黑人中间，发现他们虽然象帕立特一样贫穷落后，但他们都生活在和平的气氛中。特别是当他看到天真无邪的黑人孩子们唱着儿歌时，他的思想感情便产生了变化，想到他过去的所作所为，他更加感到羞耻。

18. And what ugly thing…she tried to kill him? 奶娃与哈格尔是表兄妹，因为社会地位和家庭环境的原因，哈格尔渴望爱情，她真心爱奶娃，想把他据为已有。但她发现，奶娃并不爱她，只是在利用她。绝望之余，便产生了复仇心理，几次设法杀害奶娃。未成，她便自杀身死。

19. It made him a star, a celebrity in the Blood Bank：这里的 Blood Bank 是关于男性的比喻，请参看下面课文的“it told men and other women that he was one bad dude, that he had the power to drive a woman out of her mind, to destroy her, and not because…but because he had fucked her and she was driven wild by the absence of his magni ficent joint。”

20. Lena：奶娃的姐姐。

21. Solomon again…they shot the bobcat.：奶娃和萨里马尔的黑人在森林中打猎时，听见大风呼啸，发出“Ryna”的声音。Ryna和Reina声音相近，实际上是一个人，就是所罗门的妻子。作者借风声制造悲壮的气氛。Solomon's Leap和Ryna's Gulch都是从所罗门和妻子的名字命名的地名。

22. Pilate's song：见注14。

23. 歌词大意是，老黑奴所罗门有21个孩子，杰克是最小的一个。所罗门飞上天，将杰克丢弃在一个白人家的门前，所罗门的妻子悲痛欲绝（Black lady fell down on the ground…Threw her body all around），杰克被印第安老妇人海地抱回家扶养成人。

美国内战以后，杰克获得自由。但他在登记时，被喝得醉醺醺的白人在登记表的姓名一栏里胡乱写成Macon Dead，从那以后，他就被人称作麦肯·代德。后来麦肯与海地的女儿辛厄成婚，他们就是奶娃的祖父祖母。

24. Circe：白人庄园主巴特勒家的女仆，老麦肯被杀后，她帮助了小麦肯和帕立特。